Critical Acclaim for the Novels of Julian Fellowes

"Julian Fellowes is the Noël Coward of our day."

—Lady Antonia Fraser

Snobs

"Like a visit of an English country estate: breezy, beautiful, and charming."   —*The New York Times Book Review*

"[Fellowes's] ability to mix trivial if amusing tidbits and sudden emotional drama gives Snobs real oomph. Fellowes is a writer whose next novel you'll await with excitement."   —*USA Today*

"Fellowes has a high time skewering the foibles of the landed British gentry—their penchant for silly nicknames like Sausage, their stinginess with alcohol, their stodgy food. But in fact, this easy humor detracts from his more serious achievement, which is to lay bare the machinations of a modern, mercenary marriage without turning his characters into monsters."   —*Entertainment Weekly*

"All this would be satire if it weren't so much like a diary, and though those who know about such things generally don't tell, Fellowes, a more genial Evelyn Waugh, seems to hide a notebook in his dinner jacket."   —*People* (four stars)

"Julian Fellowes knows a thing or two about British society and those who dare to infiltrate it. . . . A delightful first novel."   —*Vogue*

"It's not only the rich who are different, it's the British upper classes too. This complicated truth, all the more palatable if delivered amusingly, has been successfully tackled by such insiders as P. G. Wodehouse, Evelyn Waugh, and Nancy Mitford, and is now resurrected by Julian Fellowes."   —*The Miami Herald*

"Fellowes, whose screenplays for *Gosford Park* and *Vanity Fair* show he knows a thing or two about the British caste system, has great fun with this tale of pretension, passion, and prejudice."
—*Town & Country*

"A stinging comedy of manners . . . *Snobs* lays bare the envy and resentment that still bubble between England's upper and middle classes."
—*W*

"A guilty pleasure of a novel [that] seems authentic down to the wallpaper and the Wellingtons. Hilarious . . . sharp, entertaining, and unforgiving."
—Anna Quindlen, author of *Every Last One*

Past Imperfect

"Mr. Fellowes romps through bedroom and ballroom, not to mention down memory lane. A disastrous dinner party referred to throughout the novel—think shattered crockery and illusions—is not described in full until near the end. Even after all that build-up, it proves worth the wait."
—*The Wall Street Journal*

"Forty years ago, London was a swirl of fancy balls, tea parties, and menacing matrons on the hunt for suitable matches to pair with debutantes. That world is so alien now, it could have been an inauspicious subject for novelist Julian Fellowes's new book, *Past Imperfect*, but he's pulled it off."
—Molly Guinness, *The Daily Beast*

"Fellowes exercises his considerable talent for observing the nuances of custom and class distinction . . . Deservedly compared to Tom Wolfe."
—*Publishers Weekly*

"An acerbic, detailed, witty, sometimes poignant, and always entertaining social comedy."
—*The Boston Globe*

JULIAN FELLOWES

SOCIETY RULES

TWO NOVELS

Snobs

&

Past Imperfect

St. Martin's Griffin 🐾 New York

SOCIETY RULES: SNOBS. Copyright © 2004 by Julian Fellowes. PAST IMPERFECT. Copyright © 2009 by Julian Fellowes. All rights reserved. Printed in the United States of America. For information, address St. Martin's Press, 175 Fifth Avenue, New York, N.Y. 10010.

www.stmartins.com

The Library of Congress Cataloging-in-Publication Data is available upon request.

ISBN 978-1-250-11961-2 (trade paperback)

Our books may be purchased in bulk for promotional, educational, or business use. Please contact your local bookseller or the Macmillan Corporate and Premium Sales Department at 1-800-221-7945, extension 5442, or by e-mail at MacmillanSpecialMarkets@macmillan.com.

Snobs and *Past Imperfect* first published in Great Britain by Weidenfeld & Nicolson, a division of The Orion Publishing Group Ltd

First Edition: July 2016

10 9 8 7 6 5 4 3 2 1

Snobs

To darling Emma and Peregrine, of course,
but also to dearest Micky
without whom this book
would not have been possible

PART ONE

~

Impetuoso-Fiero

ONE

~

I do not know exactly how Edith Lavery came first to be taken up by Isabel Easton. Probably they had a friend in common or sat on some committee together, or perhaps they just went to the same hairdresser. But I can remember that from quite early on, for some reason, Isabel decided that Edith was rather a feather in her cap, someone that little bit special to be fed to her country neighbours in rationed morsels. History was of course to prove her right, although there was no tremendously compelling evidence for this when I first met her. Edith was certainly very pretty then but not as she would be later when she had, as designers say, found her style. She was a type, albeit a superior example of it: the English blonde with large eyes and nice manners.

I had known Isabel Easton since we were children together in Hampshire and we enjoyed one of those pleasant, undemanding friendships that are based entirely on longevity. We had very little in common but we knew few other people who could remember us on our ponies at the age of nine and there was a certain comfort in our occasional encounters. I had gone into the theatre after leaving university and Isabel had married a stockbroker and moved to Sussex so our worlds scarcely crossed, but it was fun for Isabel to have an actor to stay occasionally who had been seen on television (though never, as it happens, by any of her friends) and for me, it was pleasant enough to spend the odd weekend with my old playmate.

I was in Sussex the first time that Edith came down and I can testify to Isabel's enthusiasm for her new friend, later queried by her less generous acquaintance. It was quite genuine: 'Things are going to happen for her. She's got something.' Isabel was fond of using phrases that seemed to imply an inside knowledge of the workings of the world. Some might have said that when Edith climbed out of the car half an hour later, she didn't appear to have got very much beyond her

3

appearance and a rather beguiling, relaxed charm, but I was inclined to agree with our hostess. Looking back, there was a hint of what was to come in the mouth, one of those cut-glass mouths, with the clearly defined, almost chiselled lips that one associates with the film actresses of the forties. And then there was her skin. To the English, skin is, as a rule, the compliment of last resort, to be employed when there is nothing else to praise. Good skin is frequently dwelt on when talking of the plainer members of the Royal Family. Be that as it may, Edith Lavery had the loveliest complexion I have ever seen: cool, clear, pastel colours under layers of flawless wax. I have all my life had a weakness for good-looking people and in retrospect, I think I became Edith's ally in that first moment of admiring her face. At all events, Isabel was destined to become a self-fulfilling prophet for it was she who took Edith to Broughton.

Broughton Hall, indeed the very House of Broughton, was a wounding seam that marbled every aspect of the Eastons' Sussex life. As first Barons and then Earls Broughton and lately, since 1879, Marquesses of Uckfield, the Broughtons had held mighty sway over this particular section of East Sussex for a great deal longer than most potentates of the Home Counties. Until little more than a century ago their neighbours and vassals had mainly consisted of lowly farmers eking a living out of the flat and boggy marshland at the base of the downs but the roads and the railways and the invention of the Saturday-to-Monday had brought the *haute bourgeoisie* flooding to the area in search of *ton*, and, like Byron, the Broughtons awoke to find themselves famous. Before long, the local mark of whether one was 'in' or 'out' was largely based on whether or not one was on their visiting list. In fairness I must say that the family did not seek its celebrity, not at first anyway, but as the major representatives of the *anciens riches* in an upwardly mobile area their power was forced upon them.

They had been lucky in other ways. Two marriages, one to a banker's daughter and the other to the heiress of a large section of San Francisco had steered the family craft through the turbulent seas of the agricultural depression and the Great War. Unlike many such dynasties, they had retained some if not all of their London holdings, and various tricks with property in the sixties had brought them to the comparatively safe shores of Mrs Thatcher's Britain. After that, when the socialists did start to regroup they turned out, happily for the upper classes generally, to have been reborn as *New* Labour and so would prove much more accommodating than their rapacious political forebears. All in all, the Broughtons were the very acme of the 'surviving' English family. They had reached the 1990s with their prestige and, more significantly, their estates practically intact.

Not that any of this was a problem for the Eastons. Far from resenting the family's privileges they positively worshipped them. No, the difficulty was that despite living two miles from Broughton Hall itself, despite Isabel's telling her girlfriends over lunch in Walton Street what luck it was having the house 'practically next door', still, after three and a half years, they had never set foot in it, nor succeeded in meeting one single member of the family.

Of course, David Easton was not the first upper-middle-class Englishman to discover that it is easier to demonstrate a spurious aristocratic background in London than in the country. The problem was that after years of lunches at Brooks's, Saturdays at race-meetings and evenings at Annabel's, mouthing his prejudices against the modern, *mobile* society, he had entirely lost touch with the fact that he was a product of it. It was as if he had forgotten his father had been the managing director of a minor furniture factory in the Midlands and it was with some difficulty that his parents had put him through Ardingly. By the time I met him I think he would have been genuinely surprised not to have found his name in Debrett's. I remember once reading an article in which Roddy Llewellyn was quoted as complaining that he had not been to Eton (as his elder brother had) because it was at Eton that one picked up one's lifelong friends. David happened to be passing my chair. 'Quite right,' he said. 'That's exactly how I feel.' I looked across the room to catch Isabel's eye but I saw at once in her sympathetic nod that she did not want to be in my conspiracy but rather in her husband's.

To an outsider it seems a vital ingredient of many marriages that each partner should support the illusions of the other. Protected, as he had been, by a combination of Isabel's kindness and most London hostesses' indifference to anything beyond their guests' ability to talk and eat the food, it was now bitter indeed to sit at smart dinner tables and be asked about Charles Broughton's trip to Italy or how Caroline's new husband was shaping up and to have to murmur that he didn't really know them. 'But how extraordinary,' would come the answer. 'I thought you were neighbours.' And even in this admission there was a certain dishonesty, for it was not that David did not *really* know them. He did not know them at all.

Once at a cocktail party in Eaton Square he had ventured an opinion about the family only to hear his companion ask, 'But isn't that Charles over there? You must introduce me and we'll see if he remembers where we met.' And David had had to say he felt sick (which was more or less true) and go home and miss the dinner they had all been going on to. Lately he had taken to assuming a slightly dismissive air when they were mentioned. He would stand, loudly silent, on the edge of the discussion as if he, David Easton, preferred *not* to know the Broughtons. As if he had tried them and discovered they were not quite to his taste. Nothing could have been further from the truth. In fairness to David I would say that these frustrated social ambitions were probably as secret from his conscious mind as they were supposed to be from the rest of us. Or so it seemed to me as I watched him zip up his Barbour and whistle for the dogs.

Fittingly perhaps, it was Edith who suggested the visit. Isabel asked us at breakfast on Saturday if there was anything we'd like to do and Edith wondered whether there was a local 'stately' and what about that? She looked across at me.

'I wouldn't mind,' I said.

I saw Isabel glance at David deep in his *Telegraph* at the other end of the table. I knew and understood the Broughton situation and Isabel knew I knew, though, being English, we had naturally never discussed it. As it happens, I had met Charles Broughton, the rather lumpish son and heir, a couple of times in London at those hybrid evenings where Show Business and Society congregate but, like the crossing of two rivers, seldom mingle. These encounters I had kept from Isabel for fear of salting the wound.

'David?' she said.

He turned the pages of his newspaper with a large and insouciant gesture.

'You go if you want to. I've got to drive into Lewes. Sutton's lost the petrol cap of the lawn-mower again. He must eat them.'

'I could do that on Monday.'

'No, no. I want to get some cartridges anyway.' He looked up. 'Honestly, you go.'

6

There was reproach in his eyes, which Isabel dealt with by pulling a slight face as if her hand was being forced. The truth was they had an unspoken agreement not to visit the house as 'members of the public'. At first David had avoided it because he had expected to know the family quite soon and he did not want to run the risk of meeting them from the wrong side of the cordon. As the months and then years of disappointment had unfolded, not visiting the house had become a kind of principle, as if he did not want to give the Broughtons the satisfaction of seeing him pay good money to see what should, by rights, have been his for nothing. But Isabel was more pragmatic than her husband, as women generally are, and she had grown accustomed to the idea that their position in the 'County' was going to be deferred for a while. Now she was simply curious to see the place that had become a symbol of their lack of social muscle. She did not therefore require much persuading. The three of us packed into her battered Renault and set off.

I asked Edith if she knew Sussex at all.

'Not really. I had a friend in Chichester for a while.'

'The fashionable end.'

'Is it? I didn't know counties had fashionable ends. It sounds rather American. Like good and bad tables in the same restaurant.'

'Do you know America?'

'I spent a few months in Los Angeles after I left school.'

'Why?'

Edith laughed. 'Why not? Why does one go anywhere at seventeen?'

'I don't know why one goes to Los Angeles. Unless it's to become a film star.'

'Maybe I wanted to be a film star.' She smiled at me with what I have since come to recognise as a habitual expression of slight sadness, and I saw that her eyes were not blue as I had at first thought, but a sort of misty grey.

We turned through a pair of monumental stone piers, topped with lead stags' heads, antlers and all, and started down the wide gravel drive. Isabel stopped the car. 'Isn't it marvellous!' she said. The vast mass of Broughton Hall sprawled before us. Edith smiled enthusiastically and we drove on. She did not think the house marvellous, no more did I, although it was in its way impressive. At any rate, it was very large. It seemed to have been designed by an eighteenth-century forerunner of

7

Albert Speer. The main block, a huge granite cube, was connected to two smaller cubes with stocky and cumbersome colonnades. Unfortunately a nineteenth-century Broughton had stripped the windows of their mullions and replaced them with plate glass so now they gaped, vacant and sightless, across the park. At the four corners of the house squat cupolas had been erected like watch-towers in a concentration camp. All in all, it did not so much complete the view as block it.

The car crunched comfortably to a halt. 'Shall we do the house first or the garden?' Isabel, like a 1960s Soviet military inspector in the heart of NATO, was determined to miss nothing.

Edith shrugged. 'Is there a lot to see inside?'

'Oh, I think so,' said Isabel firmly, striding towards the door marked 'Enter'. It crouched in the embrace of the ponderous horseshoe flight of steps leading up to the *piano nobile*. The rusticated granite swallowed her and we meekly followed.

One of Edith's favourite stories would always be that she first saw Broughton as a paying guest, barred by a red rope from the intimate life of the house. 'Not,' as she would remark with her funny half-laugh, 'that the place has ever had much intimate life.' There are houses with such a sense of the personalities that built them, an all-pervading smell of the lives lived there, that the visitor feels himself a cross between a burglar and a ghost, spying on a private place with hidden secrets. Broughton was not such a house. It had been designed down to the last fender and finial with one single aim: to impress strangers. Consequently its role at the end of the twentieth century had hardly changed at all. The only difference being that now the strangers bought tickets instead of tipping the housekeeper.

For the modern visitor, however, the splendours of the state rooms were deferred, and the cold, dank room by which we entered (later we would know it as the Under Hall) was as welcoming as a deserted stadium. Hard-looking footmen's chairs stood around the walls, conjuring up a vision of endless hours of boredom spent sitting on them, and a long, black table filled the centre of the discoloured stone floor. Apart from four dirty views of Venice, a long way after Canaletto, there were no pictures. Like all the rooms at Broughton, the hall was perfectly enormous, making the three of us feel like the Borrowers.

'Well, they don't believe in the soft sell,' said Edith.

From the Under Hall, clutching our guide-books, we climbed the Great Staircase with its carved oak flights clambering up around a burly and rather depressing bronze of a dying slave. At the top, after crossing the wide landing, we came first to the Marble Hall, a vast, double-storeyed space with a balustraded gallery round all four sides at second-floor level. Had we entered by the exterior horseshoe stair this would have been our (intentionally flattening) introduction to the house. From this we progressed to the Saloon, another huge room, this time with heavy mahogany mouldings picked out in gold and walls hung with crimson flock wallpaper.

'Chicken tikka for me,' said Edith.

I laughed. She was quite right. It looked exactly like a gigantic Indian restaurant.

Isabel opened the guide-book and began to read in a geography-mistress voice: 'The Saloon is hung with its original paper, one of the chief glories of Broughton's interior. The gilt side-tables were made for this room by William Kent in seventeen-thirty-nine. The maritime theme of the carved pier glasses was inspired by the appointment of the third earl to the embassy in Portugal in seventeen thirty-seven. The Earl, himself, is commemorated in this, his favourite room in the full-length portrait by Jarvis, which hangs, together with its companion of his countess by Hudson, on either side of the Italian fireplace.'

Edith and I stared at the pictures. The one of Lady Broughton made a little stab at gaiety by posing the heavy-featured young woman on a bank of flowers, a summer hat trailing from her large hand.

'There's a woman at my gym exactly like that,' said Edith. 'She's always trying to sell me Conservative raffle tickets.'

Isabel droned on. 'The cabinet in the centre of the south wall is by Boulle and was a gift from Marie-Josèphe de Saxe, Dauphine of France, to the bride of the fifth earl on the occasion of her marriage. Between the windows . . .'

I drifted away to these same, tall windows and looked down into the park. It was one of those hot, sulky days in late August when the trees seem overburdened with leaf and the green upon green of the countryside is stuffy and airless. As I stood there, a man came round the corner of the house. He was wearing tweeds and corduroys despite the weather and one of those tiresome brown felt derbies that Englishmen in the country imagine to be dashing. He looked up and I saw it was

9

Charles Broughton. He barely glanced at me and looked away, but then he stopped and looked up again. I supposed that he had recognised me and I raised my hand in greeting, which he acknowledged with some slight gesture of his own and went on about his business.

'Who was that?' Edith was standing behind me. She had also abandoned Isabel to her orisons.

'Charles Broughton.'

'A son of the house?'

'The only son of the house, I think.'

'Will he ask us in for tea?'

'I shouldn't think so. I've met him precisely twice.'

Charles did not ask us in for tea and I'm sure he wouldn't have given me another thought if we hadn't run into him on our way back to the car. He was talking to one of the many gardeners who were drifting about the place and happened to finish just as we started back across the forecourt.

'Hello,' he nodded quite amiably. 'What are you doing here?' He had clearly forgotten my name and probably where we had met but he was pleasant enough and stood waiting to be introduced to the others.

Isabel, taken short by this sudden and unexpected propulsion into the Land Where Dreams Come True, fumbled for something to say that would fasten like a fascinating burr inside Charles's brain and result in a close friendship springing up more or less immediately. No inspiration came.

'He's staying with us. We're two miles away,' she said baldly.

'Really? Do you get down often?'

'We're here all the time.'

'Ah,' said Charles. He turned to Edith. 'Are you local, too?'

She smiled. 'Don't worry, I'm quite safe. I live in London.'

He laughed and his fleshy, hearty features looked momentarily quite attractive. He took off his hat and revealed that fair, Rupert Brooke hair, crinkly curls at the nape of the neck, that is so characteristic of the English aristocrat. 'I hope you liked the house.'

Edith smiled and said nothing, leaving Isabel to reel off her silly gleanings from the guide-book.

I stepped in with the pardon. 'We ought to be off. David will be wondering what's happened to us.'

We all smiled and nodded and touched hands, and a few minutes later we were back on the road.

'You never said you knew Charles Broughton,' said Isabel in a flat tone.

'I don't.'

'Well, you never said you'd met him.'

'Didn't I?'

Although, naturally, I knew I hadn't. Isabel drove the rest of the way in silence. Edith turned from the front passenger seat and made a that's-torn-it expression with her mouth. It was clear I had failed and Isabel was noticeably cool to me for the rest of the weekend.

TWO

~

Edith Lavery was the daughter of a successful chartered accountant, himself the grandson of a Jewish immigrant who had arrived in England in 1905 to escape the pogroms of the late, and to Edith's father, unlamented Tsar Nicholas II. I do not think I ever knew the family's original name, Levy, perhaps, or Levin. At any rate, the Edwardian portraitist, Sir John Lavery, was the inspiration for the change, which seemed, and almost certainly was, a good idea at the time. When asked if they were connected to the painter, the Laverys would answer, 'Vaguely, I think,' thus linking themselves with the British establishment without making any disputable claims. It is quite customary for the English, when asked if they have met so-and-so, to say, 'Yes, but they wouldn't remember me,' or 'Well, I've met them but I don't know them,' when they have not met them.

This is because of a subconscious urge on their part to create the comforting illusion that England, or rather the England of the upper-middle and upper classes, is criss-crossed with a million invisible silken threads that weave them together into a brilliant community of rank and grace and exclude everybody else. There is little dishonesty in it for as a rule they understand each other. To an Englishman or woman of a certain background the answer, 'Well, I've met them but they wouldn't remember me' means 'I have not met them.'

Mrs Lavery, Edith's mother, considered herself a bird of quite different feather to her spouse, fond as she was of him. Her own father had been an Indian army colonel but the salient detail was that *his* mother had been the great-niece of a banking baronet. Although kindly in many ways, Mrs Lavery was passionately snobbish to a degree verging on insanity and so her frail connection to this, the very lowest hereditary rank filled her with the warming sense of belonging to that inner circle of rank and privilege where her poor husband must ever be a stranger. Mr Lavery did not, for this reason, resent his wife. Not in the least. On the contrary he was proud of her. She was, after all, a tall, good-looking woman who knew how to dress and if anything he was rather entertained by the idea that the phrase *'noblesse oblige'* (one of Mrs Lavery's favourites) could have the slightest application to his household.

They lived in a large flat in Elm Park Gardens, which was almost at the wrong end of Chelsea and not quite to Mrs Lavery's taste. Still, it was not exactly Fulham nor, worse, Battersea, names that had only recently begun to appear on Mrs Lavery's mental map. She still felt the thrill of the new, like an intrepid explorer pushing ever further from civilization, whenever she was invited for dinner by one of her friends' married children. She listened perkily as they discussed what a good investment the 'toast rack' was or how the children loved Tooting after that poky flat in Marloes Road. It was all Greek to Mrs Lavery. So far as she was concerned she was in Hell until she got back over the river, her own personal Styx, that forever divided the Underworld from Real Life.

The Laverys were not rich but nor were they poor and, having only one child, there was never any need to stint. Edith was sent off to a fashionable nursery school and then Benenden ('No, *not* because of the Princess Royal. We simply looked around and we thought it the *most* inspiring place'.) Mr Lavery would have liked the girl's education to have been continued at university but when Edith's exam results were not good enough, certainly not for anywhere they were interested in sending her, Mrs Lavery was not disappointed. Her great ambition had always been to bring her daughter out.

Stella Lavery had not been a debutante herself. This was something of which she was deeply ashamed. She would seek to conceal it under a lot of laughing references to the fun she'd had as a girl and, if pushed for specifics, she might sigh that her father had taken rather a tumble in the thirties (thereby connecting herself with the Wall Street Crash and echoes of Scott Fitzgerald and Gatsby). Alternatively, fudging her dates, she would blame it on the war. The truth, as Mrs Lavery was forced to admit to herself in the dark night of the soul, was that in the less socially free-wheeling world of the 1950s, there had been clearer demarcation lines between precisely who was in Society and who was not. Stella Lavery's family was not. She envied those of her friends who had met as debutantes with a deep and secret envy that gnawed at her entrails. She even hated them for including her in their reminiscences about Henrietta Tiarks or Miranda Smiley as if they believed that she, Stella Lavery, had 'come out' when they knew, and she knew they knew, she had not. For these reasons she had been determined from the outset that no such gaps would shadow the life of her beloved Edith. (The name Edith incidentally was chosen for its fragrant overtones of a slower, better England and perhaps, half-consciously, to suggest that it was a family name handed down from some Edwardian beauty. It was not.) At all events, the girl was to be propelled into the charmed circle from the first. Since by the nineties Presentation at Court (which might have posed a problem) was a thing of the distant past, all Mrs Lavery had to do was to convince her husband and her daughter that it would be time and money well spent.

They did not need much persuasion. Edith had no concrete plans for how she was to pass her adult life and to delay the decision-making process with a year-long round of parties seemed a pretty good idea. As for Mr Lavery, he enjoyed the vision of his wife and his daughter in the *beau monde* and was perfectly happy to pay for it. Mrs Lavery's carefully tended connections were enough to get Edith onto Peter Townend's list for the opening tea-parties and the girl's own looks won her a place as a model at the Berkeley Dress Show. After that it was plain sailing. Mrs Lavery went to the mothers' lunches and packed her daughter's dresses for balls in the country and on the whole had a wonderful time. Edith quite enjoyed it, too.

The only reservation for Mrs Lavery was that when the Season was over, when the last, winter Charity Balls had finished and the *Tatler* cuttings had been pasted into a scrap-book along with the invitations, nothing much seemed to have changed. Edith had obviously been entertained by the daughters of several peers – including one duke, which was particularly thrilling – indeed, all of these girls had attended Edith's own cocktail party at Claridge's (one of Mrs Lavery's happiest evenings), but the friends who stayed on after the dances had ceased were very like the girls she had brought home from school, the daughters of prosperous, upper-middle-class businessmen. Exactly what Edith was herself in fact. This did not seem right to Mrs Lavery. She had for so long attributed her own failure to reach the dizzying upper echelons of London Society (a group she rather archly labelled 'the Court') to her lack of a proper launch that she had expected great things from her daughter. Perhaps her enthusiasm blinded her to a simple truth: the fact that the Season had opened its arms to her daughter meant it was no longer in the 1980s the exclusive institution it had been in Mrs Lavery's youth.

Edith was aware of her mother's disappointment but while she was certainly not immune, as we would find out, to the charms of rank and fortune, she did not quite see how she was expected to prosecute these intimacies with the daughters of the Great Houses. To start with they all seemed to have known each other from birth and anyway she couldn't help feeling it would be difficult to cater for their pleasures in a flat in Elm Park Gardens. In the end she remained on nodding terms with most of the girls in her year but returned to a very similar groove to the one she had occupied on leaving school.

I learned all this quite soon after first meeting Edith at the Eastons' because it so transpired that she took a job answering the telephone in an estate agent's in Milner Street, just round the corner from where I had a basement flat. I started bumping into her in Peter Jones, or having a sandwich in one of the local pubs, or buying a five-thirty pint of milk in Partridges and gradually, almost without noticing it, we became quite friendly. One day I saw her coming out of the General Trading Company at about one o'clock and I invited her for some lunch.

'Have you seen Isabel lately?' I asked, as we squeezed into a banquette in one of those little Italian places where the waiters shout.

'I had dinner with them both last week.'

'All well?'

It was, or well enough. They were engaged in some school drama about their child. Isabel had discovered dyslexia. I pitied the headmaster.

'She asked after you. I said I'd seen you,' said Edith.

I remarked that I didn't think Isabel had as yet forgiven me for failing to tell her I knew Charles Broughton, and Edith laughed. It was then that I heard about her mother. I asked if she'd told Mrs Lavery about our time at Broughton. It so happened that Charles was rather on my mind as that morning I'd seen one of those idiotic magazine articles about eligible bachelors and Charles had led the pack. I blush to say I was rather impressed with the list of his assets.

'Not likely. I wouldn't want to give her any ideas.'

'She must be very susceptible.'

'She certainly is. She'd have me up the aisle before you could say knife.'

'And you don't want to get married?'

Edith looked at me as if I were mad. 'Of course I want to get married.'

'You don't see yourself as a career girl? I thought all women want careers now.' I do not know why I slid into this kind of pompous anti-feminism since it does not in the least reflect my views.

'Well, I don't want to spend the rest of my life answering the telephone in an estate agent's office if that's what you mean.'

I was duly reprimanded. 'That's not quite what I had in mind,' I said.

Edith looked at me indulgently as if it were necessary to take me through my three times table. 'I'm twenty-seven. I have no qualifications and, what is worse, no particular talent. I also have tastes that require, at the very least, eighty thousand a year. When my father dies he will leave what money he has to my mother and I don't anticipate either of them quitting the scene much before 2030. What do you suggest I should do?'

I do not know why but I felt rather muted by this Anita Loos-style practicality emanating from the little rose before me, with her Alice band and her neat, navy blue suit.

'So you intend to marry a rich man?' I asked.

Edith looked at me quizzically. Perhaps she felt she had given away too much, perhaps she was trying to ascertain if I was judging her and if so, whether or not she was coming out ahead. She should have been reassured by what she saw in my eyes for it has always seemed to me that if one can face up early on to what one really wants in life, then there is every chance of avoiding the seemingly inevitable modern disease of mid-life crisis.

'Not necessarily,' she answered, with a trace of defensiveness in her voice. 'It's just that I cannot imagine I would be very happy married to a poor one.'

'I do see that,' I said.

Edith and I did not meet for some time after this luncheon. I was cast in one of those unwatchable American mini-series and I left for Paris and, of all places, Warsaw for some months. The job involved the supremely depressing experience of celebrating Christmas and New

Year in a foreign hotel where they give you cheese for breakfast and all the bread is stale, and when I returned to London in May, I certainly did not feel I had very much advanced my art. On the other hand, I was at least a bit better off than when I left. Quite soon after I arrived home I received a card from Isabel asking me to join their party for the second day of Ascot. She must have forgiven me in my absence. I thought I would have to refuse as I had done nothing about applying for my voucher to the Enclosure but it turned out that my mother (who with such gestures would betray a defiant denial of the work and the life I have chosen) had applied for me. Today, in these more graceless times, it would not be possible for her to apply for someone else, even her own child, but then it was. She had in fact undertaken this annual responsibility in my youth and she proved reluctant to give it up. 'You'll be so sorry if you have to miss something fun,' she would say whenever I objected that I had no plans to attend the meeting. And this time my mother was proved right. I accepted Isabel's offer with the half-smile that the prospect of a day at Ascot always brings to my lips.

Like many famous institutions, the image and the reality of the Royal Enclosure at Ascot bear little or no relation to each other. The very name 'Royal Enclosure' (to say nothing of the glutinous coverage in the lowbrow press) conjures up visions of princes and duchesses, famous beauties and Rand millionaires strolling on manicured lawns in *haute couture*. Of this picture, I can, I suppose, testify to the quality of the lawns. The vast majority of visitors to the Enclosure appear to be middle-aged businessmen from the more expensive suburbs of London. They are accompanied by wives wearing inappropriate outfits, generally in chiffon. What, however, makes this disparity between dream and truth unusual and amusing is the wilfully blind support of the fantasy by the participants themselves. Even those members of Society, or rather those members of the upper-middle and upper classes, who do actually go to the meeting, take a touching delight in dressing and behaving as if they were at the smart and exclusive event the papers talk about. Their women wear just as inappropriate but more becoming fitted suits and swan about greeting each other as if they were at some gathering in the Ranelagh Gardens in 1770. For a day or two every year these working people allow themselves the luxury of pretending that they are part of some vanished leisure class, that the world they mourn and admire and pretend they would have belonged to if it still existed (which as a rule they would not) is alive and well and living near Windsor. Their pretensions are naked and vulnerable and for that reason, to me at least, rather charming. I am always happy to spend one day at Ascot.

David collected me in his Volvo estate and I climbed in to find Edith, whom I had expected, and another couple, the Rattrays. Simon Rattray seemed to work for Strutt and Parker and talked a lot about shooting. His wife, Venetia, talked a little about her children and even less about anything else. We nosed our way down the M4 and through Windsor Great Park until we finally reached the course and David's slightly obscure car park. It was a perennial source of irritation to him that he could not get into Number One and he always vented his annoyance on Isabel as she was pointing out the signs. I never minded; it had become part of Ascot for me (like my father shouting at the tree-lights every Christmas – one of my few really vivid childhood memories), I had after all been with them several times.

Before too long the car was safely on its numbered place and the lunch was unpacked. It was clear that Edith had had no hand in it as it was Isabel and Venetia who assumed control, fussing and clucking and slicing and mixing until the feast was spread in all its glory before our eyes. The men and Edith watched from the safety of the folding chairs, clutching plastic glasses of champagne. As usual, there was a certain poignancy in all this preparation, given the brevity allotted to the food's consumption. We had hardly drawn up our seats to the wobbly table when Isabel, as predictable as David's worry over the car park, looked at her watch. 'We mustn't be long. It's twenty-five to two now.' David nodded and helped himself to strawberries. Nobody needed an explanation. Part of this day, Mass-like in its ritual, was getting to the steps in the Enclosure in time to see the arrival of the Royal house-party from Windsor. And getting there early enough to secure a good vantage point. Edith looked at me and rolled her eyes, but we both obediently gulped down our coffee, pinned on our badges and headed for the course.

We passed the stewards at the entrance, busily dividing the wheat from the tares. Two unfortunates had just been stopped, though whether it was because they didn't have the right badge or were wrongly dressed I do not know. Edith squeezed my arm with one of her secret smiles. I looked down. 'Something funny?'

She shook her head. 'No.'

'Well then.'

'I have a soft spot for getting in where others are held back.'

I laughed. 'You may feel that. Many do. But it is rather low to admit it.'

'Oh dear. Then I'm afraid I'm very low. I must just hope it doesn't hold me back.'

'I don't think it will,' I said.

What was interesting about this exchange was its honesty. Edith looked the perfect archetype of the Sloane Ranger girl she was, but I was beginning to understand that she had a disconcerting awareness of the realities of her life and situation when such girls generally make a show of pretended ignorance of these things. It was not that her sentiments marked her apart. The English, of all classes as it happens, are addicted to exclusivity. Leave three Englishmen in a room and they will invent a rule that prevents a fourth joining them. What made Edith different is that most people, and certainly all toffs, put on a great show of not being aware if it. Any suggestion that there is pleasure in being a guest where the public has to buy tickets, of being allowed through a gate, of being ushered into a room, where the people are turned away, will be met by the aristocrat (or would-be aristocrat) with blank looks and studied lack of comprehension. The practised matron will probably suggest with a slight movement of the eyebrows that the very idea denotes a lack of breeding. The dishonesty in all this is of course breathtaking but, as always with these people, the discipline in their unwavering rules commands a certain respect.

We must have dawdled, as the others were all at the steps, which were fast filling up, and waved to us to join them. A distant roar announced that the carriages were on the way and the footmen or stewards or whatever they are rushed forward to open the gates from the course. Edith nudged me and nodded towards Isabel as the first coach carrying Her Majesty and some dusky premier of an oil-rich state swept through the entrance. Like the other men I took my hat off with a perfectly genuine enthusiasm but I could not ignore the look on Isabel's face. It was the glazed, ecstatic expression of a rabbit before a cobra. She was hypnotised, enraptured. To be included in the Ascot house-party, Isabel, like Pervaneh in *Hassan*, would have faced the Procession of Protracted Death. Or at least she would have considered it. It only goes to show, I suppose, that for all the educated classes' contempt of mass star-worship, they themselves are just as susceptible to fantasy when it is presented in a palatable form.

Actually, the procession that year was a bit disappointing. The Prince of Wales, Isabel's paradigm of perfection, was not there and nor were any of the other princes. The only junior Royal was Zara Phillips, brightly attired in revealing beachwear. Edith had been murmuring irreverent criticisms in my ear, much to the annoyance of Isabel and a woman with blue hair standing next to her, so, rather than continue to spoil their fun, we turned to go when I heard a voice right behind me: 'Hello, how are you?' I looked round and found myself face to face with Charles Broughton. This time there was no awkwardness over names, the best part of the Enclosure being that everyone has to wear a badge with their name written on it. There you will find no fumbling of introductions or pretending that people have already met. Just a cursory glance at the lapel or bosom of the unknown one and all is well. Would that such labelling was compulsory at all social gatherings. Charles's badge proclaimed 'The Earl Broughton' in the distinctive, round handwriting of the well-bred girls of the Ascot Office.

'Hello,' I said. 'You remember Edith Lavery?' I had employed the correct English usage for presenting a person whom one is fairly certain will have been forgotten, but in this instance I was wrong.

'Certainly I do. You're the safe one who lives in London.'

'Well, I hope I'm not as safe as all that.' Edith smiled and, either on her own initiative or on Charles's invitation, took his arm.

The Eastons and the Rattrays were bearing down on us and I could almost see the whites of their eyes when I suggested a visit to the paddock. It seems hard and probably reveals a deep insecurity in me but I felt embarrassed for poor old Isabel in her eagerness, and David's ambition looked nearly malevolent in its intensity. Mercifully, Charles, who was after all quite a polite fellow, nodded a greeting to Isabel that dismissed her but showed at least that he was aware they had been introduced. David, seething, hung back and the three of us headed off towards the paddock where the horses were being paraded before the first race.

Predictably Charles turned out to know quite a lot about horses and before long he was happily engaged in informed chatter on fetlocks and form, none of which interested me in the least, but I was kept amused by observing Edith gazing up at him with fascinated, flattering attention. It is a technique that such women seem to acquire at birth. She was wearing a neat linen suit of a pale bluish colour, I think the correct term is eau-de-nil, with a little pill-box hat tipped forward over her forehead. It made her look frivolous but, in contrast to the Weybridge matrons in their organza frills, unsentimental and chic. It was an outfit that added a dash of wit and humour to her face, which, I was by this stage aware, was extremely beguiling. As she studied her card and made notes against the names with Charles's pencil, I watched him watching her and it was perhaps then that I first became aware of a real possibility that he was attracted to her. Not that this was very surprising. She had all the right attributes. She was pretty and witty and, as she had said herself, safe. She was not of his set, of course, but she lived and spoke like his own people. It is a popular fiction that there is a great difference in manner and manners between the upper-middle and upper classes. The truth is, on a day-to-day level they are in most things identical. Of course the aristocracy's circle of acquaintance is much smaller and so there is invariably with them the sense of the membership of a club. This can result in a tendency to display their social security by means of an off-handed rudeness, which doesn't bother them and upsets almost everybody else. But these things apart (and rudeness is very easily learned) there is little to tell between them in social style. No, Edith Lavery was clearly Charles's kind of girl.

We watched a race or two but I could sense that Edith, in the nicest possible way, was trying to shake me off and so when Charles inevitably suggested tea in White's, I excused myself and went off in search of the others. Edith threw me a grateful look and the pair of them walked away arm in arm.

I found Isabel and David in one of the champagne bars behind the grandstand, drinking warm Pimm's. The caterers had run out of ice. 'Where's Edith?'

'She's gone off to White's with Charles.'

David looked sulky. Poor David. He never did manage to be taken into White's at Ascot, neither in their old tent nor, so far as I am aware, in their new, more space-age accommodation. He would have given an arm to be a member. 'Jolly good,' he said through gritted teeth. 'I wouldn't have minded some tea.'

'I think they were going to meet up with the rest of Charles's party.'

'I'm sure they were.'

Isabel in contrast said nothing but kept sipping at the tepid liquid with its four bits of floating cucumber.

'I said we'd meet up at the car after the second last race.'

'Fine,' David said grimly, and we lapsed into silence. Isabel, to her credit, still looked more interested than irritated as she stared into her unappetising drink.

Edith was already leaning against the locked car when we got there and I could see at once that the day had been a success.

'Where's Charles?' I said.

She nodded towards the grandstand. 'He's gone to find the people he's staying with tonight. He's coming tomorrow and Friday.'

'Good luck to him.'

'Haven't you enjoyed yourself?'

'Oh yes,' I said. 'But not half as much as you.'

She laughed and said nothing, and at that moment David arrived to unlock the vehicle. He did not mention Charles and he was noticeably grumpy with Edith, so it was not as a general announcement but in a whisper that she informed me that Charles had asked her out for dinner the following Tuesday. It was of course more than she could do to keep it to herself.

THREE

~

Edith sat at her dressing table, bathed and sweet-smelling, and prepared to paint on her social face. She hadn't told her mother exactly whom she was dining with and now she pondered why she had not. It would certainly have given Stella a great deal of pleasure. It was probably a fear of this very pleasure that kept her daughter silent. And anyway, at this stage, Edith had not made up her mind whether or not she thought there was any what the magazines call 'future' in it.

Edith Lavery was not in the least promiscuous but, at this point, she was certainly not a virgin. She had, in her time, had several boyfriends. None was serious until she was about twenty-three but then there had been a stockbroker, five years older than her and very good-looking, whom she had made up her mind to accept when he proposed. They went out for about a year, stayed in a lot of house-parties, enjoyed quite a few of the same things, and generally were happy or at least as happy as anyone else. His name was Philip, his mother was fairly grand, there was a little money – enough to start them off in Clapham – and in fact it all seemed fine, so no one was more surprised than Edith when he explained one evening, in halting tones, that he had met someone else and it was all over. For a moment Edith had difficulty making sense of this. Partly because he chose to tell her in San Lorenzo in Beauchamp Place, where the customers on the two neighbouring tables were listening to every word, and partly because she couldn't imagine in all modesty what this 'someone else' could have that she, Edith, didn't. She and Philip liked each other, they were a good-looking pair, they both enjoyed country weekends, they both skied. Where was the difficulty?

At any rate, Philip left and three months later she was invited to his wedding. She went, being very gracious and looking (as she was determined to do) ravishing. The bride was plainer than her, naturally, and rather ordinary really but as Edith watched her gazing up at Philip

23

as if he were God on earth, she had an uncomfortable inkling that this had something to do with what had gone wrong.

After that there had been various walk-outs but not much more. One, an estate agent named George, had lasted about six months but this was only because he was the first competent lover she had experienced and the pleasures he unlocked in her made her wilfully blind to his shortcomings until one day, at Henley (which he had taken her to imagining, rather touchingly, that it was a smart event), while they were lunching in some members' tent, she had looked across the table at him, laughing his loud and gummy laugh, and realised that he really was too frightful. After that it was simply a matter of time.

Her parents had been quite sorry about Philip whom they liked, not in the least sorry about George and, on the whole, without an opinion on the various others who had briefly penetrated Elm Park Gardens, but Edith had begun to notice that the veiled hints and half-joking, half-worried remarks from her mother had been getting more frequent since her twenty-seventh birthday. And for the first time she had started to feel a very far-away, distant echo of panic. Just supposing, for the sake of argument, that no one did ask her to marry them, what would she do?

What *on earth* was she going to do?

But then, she thought as she pulled out the heated rollers and picked up her Mason Pearson brush, everything could change so quickly. Being a woman wasn't like being a man. Men were either born with money or they spent years beavering away at careers to make themselves rich while women . . . women can be poor one day and rich, or at least married to a rich man, the next. It might not be fashionable to admit it but even in this day and age, a woman's life can be utterly transformed by means of the right ring.

It is easy to get the impression from these ruminations that Edith was harshly, even exclusively, mercenary at this time in her life but that would be unjust. And it would have surprised her. If asked whether she was materialistic she would have answered she was practical, if snobbish she would have said she was worldly. After all, she read novels, she went to the cinema, she knew about happiness, she believed in love. But she saw her future career as primarily social (how could she not?) and if it was to be social then how could she have a career worthy of the name without money and position? Of course, by the 1990s, these were supposed to be outmoded ambitions but Edith did not have it in her to rush off and found a keep-fit empire or publish a new magazine. As for any of the professions, she had missed her chance of those ten years before when she left school. And it was no longer unfashionable to want to be affluent. The brown rice and dirndl-skirted generation of her childhood had given way to a brasher, post-Thatcherite world and weren't her dreams, in a way, in tune with that development?

Still, if she was ambitious and reluctantly committed to the idea that it would be a man who would open the golden pathway to fulfilment, it would not be true to say that Edith was fundamentally a snob. Certainly not compared to her mother. She said herself that she liked to be on the inside looking out rather than the other way round, but she was more interested in achievement (or power, to use its less fragrant name) than rank. She wanted to be at the centre of things. She wanted a winner, not a coronet. Within limits. She was not looking for a successful costermonger but she was not really looking for an earl either. Which probably explains why she got one.

She stared at her reflection in the glass. She was wearing a short black dress in wild silk. What her mother would have called 'a little black number', the eternal stand-by of the London Lady. It was well-cut, quite expensive and, apart from a French paste bracelet, she wore no ornament. She looked pretty and snappy with that slight tang of severity a certain kind of Englishman finds intriguing. She was satisfied. Edith was not vain but she was glad, not to say relieved, that she had not been saddled with a plain face. The doorbell rang.

She had entertained the idea that she might simply tell Charles to wait downstairs but then he might think she was concealing something far more compromising than a rather routine father and a snobbish mother so she decided to ask him up but to introduce him in the American way, Christian names only. A modern habit that as a rule she particularly disliked as it withheld the only part of a name that might carry any information. Her mother defeated her as soon as she had taken the field. 'Charles what?' she said, while Kenneth was making them all a drink.

'Broughton.' Charles smiled. Edith saw the penny drop with a silent *boing* but not for nothing had her mother been a life-long admirer of Elizabeth I. The mask remained smiling but immobile.

'And how do you know Edith?'

'We met in Sussex at my parents' house.'

'When I was staying with Isabel and David.'

'Oh, so you know the Eastons?'

Charles nodded, for which Edith was grateful. He was not prepared to say, 'No, I do not know them and we were not introduced at a private party. I met your daughter when she had bought a ticket to see where I live.' This was about the size of it but it would have got the evening off to an odd start. Nevertheless, having escaped this manhole, Edith brought the chat to a fairly rapid conclusion rather than chance her arm a second time. So, far from being nervous, she was actually quite relieved when they settled themselves into the gleaming Porsche that awaited them below.

'I thought we'd go to Annabel's.'

'Now?' She was surprised and spoke before she had edited.

'Is that all right? We don't have to.' Charles looked faintly hurt and she felt mean at dashing what he might have supposed to be a bit of a treat. The thought that he had actually planned an evening for her was rather gratifying.

'Lovely.' She smiled warmly into his open, pleasant, slightly dim face. 'It's just that I've always gone on late. I don't think I've ever had dinner there.'

'I rather like it.'

He drove off and they lapsed into silence until the car pulled up outside the famous basement entrance in Berkeley Square. Charles got out and handed the keys to a doorman. Edith had always been to Annabel's with young men who parked their cars around the square and walked to the club. There was a cosy feeling in the knowledge that she was out with someone who had no need to cut corners. They made their way down the steps and in through the door at the bottom. Charles signed in with a lot of 'good evenin', m'lord' going on all round.

There was practically no one in the bar and seemingly even fewer in the restaurant. The empty dance-floor looked dark and maudlin with its black mirrors reflecting nothing. Charles seemed puzzled at first and then embarrassed. 'You're right. It is too early. I don't think it really picks up until about ten. Do you want to go somewhere else?'

'Not at all,' she said with a brisk smile as she settled into the banquette. 'Now, tell me what to eat.'

She had not yet decided what she thought about Charles but one thing she was quite sure of. This evening was going to be a *great* success if it killed her. The menu provided a few minutes of welcome chat. Charles knew about food and drink, and he was happy to take command, although in fact she had only asked for his help in order to re-establish herself as the helpless underdog like the good, nubile girl she was. The last thing she wanted was for him to start apologising. Experience had taught her that much. But in the event he chose well and the dinner was a good one.

Charles Broughton was not exactly handsome. His nose was too large for that and his lips too thin. But in the candlelight he was not unattractive. He was very what Nanny would call 'distinguished'. He looked so like an English gentleman that he could have come from Central Casting and Edith felt herself being quite drawn to him physically. Much more than she had imagined she would be. She was mildly surprised to realise that she was looking forward to his asking her to dance.

'Do you spend a lot of time in London?' she said.

He shook his head. 'Good Lord no. Little as possible.'

'So you're generally in Sussex?'

'Most of the time. We've got a place in Norfolk as well. I have to get up there from time to time.'

'Funny. I'd thought of you as rather social.'

'Me? You must be joking.' He laughed out loud. 'Why was that?'

'I don't know.' She did know although she was not prepared to say that she had read about him in various social columns. Since he and she had run into each other at Ascot, it all seemed to add up to a rather fun-filled image. It was a mistaken impression that lingered for some time before it was firmly put right.

The truth was that, like most of the human race, Charles went to parties if he was asked and had nothing else to do but he did not have many friends – certainly not many that he had made in the last few years – and he saw himself exclusively as a countryman, helping his father to run the estates and the houses that God had seen fit to entrust to their care. He did not question nor resist his position but neither did he exploit it. If he had ever thought about the issues of inheritance or rank he would only have said that he felt very lucky. He would not have said this aloud, however.

Contrary to Edith's belief, he had not taken her to Annabel's as part of any romantic strategy. The truth was that, without admitting it to himself, he liked to take girls to places where he was known. It put a spin on the dinner that anonymity lacked. It was his turn to speak.

'Have you lived a lot in the country?'

'Not much, really.' Edith realised this was an odd answer even as she said it for she had never, for half an hour, actually 'lived' in the country. Unless one counted boarding school, which of course one couldn't. Still, she liked the country. She'd stayed a lot in the country. She'd walked behind the guns. She'd ridden. It wasn't a total lie. She qualified it: 'My father's business. You know.'

Charles nodded. 'I suppose he has to move about quite a bit.'

Edith shrugged. 'Quite a bit.'

Actually, Kenneth Lavery had had to move about from the London Underground to the same office in the city for the last thirty-two years. He had once had to go New York and once to Rotterdam. That was it. This slight re-shading of the truth was never corrected. Charles was forever thereafter under the impression that Edith's father had been some sort of international whizz-kid, jetting between Hong Kong and Zurich. In creating this false picture, however, Edith had read Charles correctly. There is something much less petit bourgeois about a businessman with permanent jet lag than a stationery drudge buying a ticket for the Piccadilly Line northbound, and Charles did like things just so.

Time had passed and the club was filling.

'Charlie!' Edith looked up to see a pretty brunette in a sharply tailored, sequinned cocktail dress bearing down on them. She was accompanied by, or rather trailing, a whale. He wore a suit that must have taken a bale of worsted and a large spotted tie. When they had made it to the table, Edith noticed the rivulets of sweat that trickled continuously from behind his ears over the fat, red neck.

'Jane. Henry.' Charles stood up and gestured at Edith. 'Do you know Edith Lavery? Henry and Jane Cumnor.' Jane took Edith's hand in a swift and lifeless hold then turned back to Charles as she sat down and poured herself a glass of their wine.

'I'm parched. How are you? What happened to you at Ascot?'

'Nothing happened. I was there.'

'I thought we were all having lunch on Thursday. With the Weatherbys? We hunted and hunted for you before we gave up.

Camilla was bitterly disappointed.' She gave a half-smirk to Edith, ostensibly inviting her to join the joke. In fact, of course, consciously excluding her from it.

'Well, she shouldn't have been. I told her and Anne that I had to have lunch with my parents that day.'

'Needless to say they'd completely forgotten. Anyway, doesn't matter now. By the way, tell me: are you going to Eric and Caroline in August? They swore you were but it seemed so unlike you.'

'Why?'

Jane shrugged with a lazy, sinuous movement of the shoulder. 'I don't know. I thought you hated the heat.'

'I haven't made up my mind. Are you going?'

'We don't know, do we, darling?' She reached across to her puffing husband and kneaded his doughy hand. 'We're so behind with everything at Royton. We've hardly been home since Henry got political. I've a ghastly feeling we might be stuck there all summer.' She again broadened her smile to include Edith.

Edith smiled back. She was quite used to this curious need on the part of the upper-classes to demonstrate that they all know each other and do the same things with the same people. This was perhaps an unusually manic example of the palisade mentality but, looking at Lord Cumnor, aka Henry the Green Engine, it was not difficult to see that Jane had made some severe sacrifices to achieve whatever position she was in command of. It would be hard for her to set it aside, even for a moment, as a thing of little importance.

'Are you very political?' Edith said to Henry, who seemed to be recovering from the effort it had taken him to cross the floor.

'Yes,' he said, and turned back to the others.

Edith had been inclined to feel rather sorry for him but she saw in a moment that he perceived no need to feel sorry for himself. He was quite happy being who he was. Just as he was quite happy to demonstrate that he knew Charles and did not know Edith. Charles, however, was not prepared to have the Cumnors be rude to the girl he had invited for dinner and he consciously and obviously turned the conversation back to her.

'Henry's frightfully serious since he took his seat. What was your latest cause? Organic veg for prisoners?'

'Ha, ha,' said Henry.

Jane came to her husband's aid. 'Don't be beastly. He's done a lot of work for the national diet, haven't you, darling?'

'Which didn't include going on it, I gather,' said Charles.

'You laugh now but they'll come after you when your father snuffs it. You'll see,' said Jane.

'No they won't. Labour will win next time and they'll have the hereditaries out before you can say Jack Robinson.'

'Don't be so pessimistic.' Jane did not want to hear that the world she had pinned all her hopes on was threatened with extinction. 'Anyway, it'd be years before they came up with a formula for the Lords that works better and they won't do anything in a hurry.'

Charles stood up and asked Edith to dance.

She raised her eyes in a half-query as they shambled around the floor, by now crammed with Iranian bankers and their mistresses.

He smiled. 'Henry's all right.'

'Is he a great friend?'

'He's a sort of cousin. I've known him all my life. God, he's fat at the moment, isn't he? He looks like a balloon.'

'How long have they been married?'

He shook his head. 'Four, five years, I suppose.'

'Do they have any children?'

He made a wry shape with his mouth. 'Two girls. Poor old Henry. Setchell's got him drinking port and eating cheese and Christ knows what.'

'Why?'

'To get a boy, of course. To get the bloody boy.'

'What happens if they don't have one?'

Charles frowned. 'There are no brothers. I think some bloke in South Africa gets the title although I'm not sure if he or the girls get the swag. Anyway, they're both quite young. They'll bash on for a while longer, I should think.'

'It could get rather expensive.'

'It certainly could. You never know how long to keep going. Look at the Clanwilliams. Six girls before they called it a day and it's worse nowadays.'

'Why?'

'Why do you think? Even the girls have to go to decent schools.'

They danced in silence for a while with Charles occasionally nodding to various acquaintances on the floor. Edith gratefully recognised two girls from her deb season and flashed brilliant smiles at them. Taking in the identity of her partner, they waved back, allowing her to feel less invisible. By the time they returned to the table, she was beginning to feel that she was really having quite a jolly time.

Henry and Jane had not moved and as they approached, Jane jumped up and seized Charles's hand. 'It's time you danced with me. Henry hates dancing. Come on.' She led Charles back to the floor, leaving Edith alone with her porcine husband.

He smiled vaguely. 'She always says that. I don't really hate dancing at all. Would you like to give it a go?'

Edith shook her head. 'Not unless you're dying to, if you don't mind. I'm exhausted.' The thought of being pressed into that pillow of blubber made her shudder.

He nodded philosophically. Being turned down was obviously not a new experience. 'Do you know Charlie well?'

'No. We just met in the country and then again at Ascot and here I am.'

'Where in the country? Who with?' He perked up a bit at the chance of some more Name Exchange.

'With the Eastons. In Sussex. David and Isabel. Do you know them?' She knew very well he would not. She was right.

'I've known Charlie all my life.'

Edith fished idly in her brain for an answer. 'I don't think I've known anybody all my life. Except my parents,' she added with a laugh.

Henry did not laugh back. 'Oh,' he said.

She tried again. 'Who are Eric and Caroline?'

'Caroline's his sister. I've known her all my life too.' He nodded gently to himself, pleased with these long associations. 'Eric's this chap she's just married.'

'I gather you haven't known him all your life.'

'Never saw him before the wedding.'

'Is he nice?'

'I really couldn't tell you.' Obviously Caroline was guilty of some hideous impropriety in Henry's eyes. Some horrible miscegenation had taken place in this coupling of strangers. Edith felt that she herself was hovering at the borders of a solecism by even talking about the interloper.

'Where is Royton?'

This time Henry's face registered surprise rather than distaste. For her not to know where Royton was must surely indicate that she was an eccentric. 'Norfolk.'

'Is it lovely?' Edith was beginning to feel as if she was turning over huge clods of ploughed earth in her effort to keep Henry entertained.

He shrugged and looked round for the bottle to help himself to another glass. 'People seem to think so.'

Edith opened her mouth to try again and then shut it. Not for the last time she was struck by the tyranny of the socially inept. Endless effort is harnessed to a sluggish and boring conversation simply to preserve these dullards from a sense of their inadequacy. The irony being that they are quite impervious to their own shortcomings. If Henry had even noticed things were at all heavy going he would unhesitatingly have blamed it on Edith and the fact that she didn't know anyone interesting. Before the silence had become oppressive Charles and Jane returned and the remainder of the time was spent gossiping about more people that Edith had never met.

'What a lovely evening,' she said, as the car stopped outside her parents' flat. Charles made no attempt to park it so he clearly knew the night would contain no sexual epilogue.

'I'm glad you enjoyed it. I'm sorry we got rather lumbered.'

'Don't be. I liked them,' she lied.

'Did you?' He seemed a bit anxious. 'I'm glad.'

'Henry was telling me about Royton.'

He nodded, back on home territory. 'Yes, they're next door to me up there. That's really why I know them.'

'I thought they were cousins.'

'Well, they are. From a marriage in about eighteen thirty. But I know them because they live next door.'

'It sounds lovely.'

'It is. I'm not sure how good old Henry is at managing it but it is charming. Anyway, there's pots of money so I suppose it doesn't matter too much.' It was easy to see that Charles thought he was *terrifically* good at managing Broughton.

They stared at each other for a moment. Edith realised that she rather wanted him to kiss her. Partly because she wanted to be sure she'd been a success, and partly because she just wanted to kiss him. He leaned forward awkwardly and pressed his mouth against hers. His lips were hard and firmly shut. He sat back. Ah, she thought. More Philip than George. Oh well. What she said was, 'Good night and thank you again. I have so enjoyed it.'

'Good,' he said, and he got out of the car and escorted her across the road to the front door, but he made no attempt to kiss her again as he said good night, nor was there any mention of the next time they would meet. It would be fair to say that, up to that moment, she had not been aware of wanting much more from the evening than the reassurance that Charles found her attractive, liked her company and wanted to see more of her. But now that the ending was proving rather flat, she was filled with a feeling of disappointment, with the sense of a chance lost. This had been a great opportunity and she had blown it without fully understanding why. On the whole, it was with a sense of failure that she crept quietly into her room, trying not to wake the mother who was lying staring at the ceiling two doors down.

She need not have been downcast. She did not know Charles and had misinterpreted his reticence. Because he was generally seen as a prize, she thought he must share this image of himself but this was not so. He felt that it was he, not Edith, on whom the responsibility for the evening lay. He was shy (not rude-shy, really shy) and so, while he could not quite express it, he was very pleased that she had appeared to have enjoyed being with him. In fact, as Charles pushed the key into the lock of his parents' flat in Cadogan Square, it was with a warm sense of an evening well spent. He liked Edith very much. More than he could remember liking any girl. With the respect for hypocrisy that is the due of a hypocritical society, he admired her all the more for pretending to like the Cumnors when it was plain that they, or at least Jane, had been bestial to her all evening. He pushed the door open and stepped inside.

The Uckfields' London flat occupied the ground and first floors of one of those tall, Edwardian Dutch, red brick houses that surround the exclusive, if not exactly bewitching square. It was a pleasant enough place, furnished with that delicately balanced mixture of the comfortable and the grand that his mother had learned from John Fowler and proceeded to make her own. The pictures, from the B-list of the family's collection, were carefully chosen to suggest hereditary importance without overpowering the spaces. The hangings, the ornaments, the very tables and chairs proclaimed the rank of the family but in a modest way. 'This is where we visit,' the artefacts seemed to say, 'but it is not who we are.' Just as no member of the family, not even Caroline, who lived there solidly for four years before her marriage, would ever refer to the place as 'home'. Home was Broughton. 'I'll be in the flat next week', 'I'm going up to the flat', 'Why don't we meet at the flat?' were all very well, but 'I must get home', even at the end of a long London dinner, could only ever mean that the Broughton in question was driving down to Sussex that night. These people may own a house in Chester Square and rent a small cottage in Derbyshire, but you may be pretty sure that 'home' is the one with the grass growing round it. And if no such hide-away exists, then they will make it plain that it is essential to their well-being to escape the smoke and pavements and fly to their rural friends as often as they can, thereby suggesting that while they may spend their lives walking on tarmac or behind a city desk, they will always be country people at heart. It is rare to find an aristocrat who is happier in London – at least, it is rare to find one who admits it.

Charles had his own flat, a jumble of modest rooms on a third floor in Eaton Place but he didn't usually bother with it. Cadogan Square was nicer and more comfortable, and he could pick up any post there and bring it down without a fuss. But perhaps because Broughton was after all the product of many generations' taste, he was always aware of the imprint of his mother whenever he visited her London base. The family's real London headquarters, Broughton House, had been in St James's Square, but it had taken a direct hit in the Blitz and so they were spared the agonising decision of most of their relations as to whether or not it was sensible to abandon the town house at the end of the war. Charles's grandparents had acquired a rather dank flat in Albert Hall Mansions, which his mother had rejected out of hand and it was she who selected and therefore entirely created this apartment as an appropriate setting for the charity work and the entertaining that demanded her presence in the capital from time to time.

As he sat down with a late-night glass of whisky, Charles thought about his mother. He looked at the prettily framed sketch of the seven-year-old Lady Harriet Trevane (as Lady Uckfield was born). It was by Annigoni and was placed on a small *régence* table near the drawing-room chimneypiece. Even as a girl, with a hair-ribbon drooping down among her charcoaled curls, he could detect the familiar, unflinching, cat-like stare. He might as well face facts. His mother would not like Edith. That he knew. If Edith had been presented to his mother as the wife of a friend she might have liked her – if she had taken the smallest notice of her – but Edith would not be welcomed as Charles's girlfriend. Still less, should such a thing ever come to pass, would she be encouraged as Lady Uckfield's ultimate successor, as the one to whom his mother must entrust the house, the position, the very county she had worked so hard on and for so long.

This is not to say that Charles was without sympathy for his mama. On the contrary, he loved her very much and he felt he was right to do so. He saw beyond her public image of studied perfection and he liked what he found there. It pleased Lady Uckfield always to give the impression that everything in life had been handed to her on a plate. This was no truer for her than it is for the rest of the human race but she preferred to be on the receiving end of envy rather than pity and all her life had chosen, in the words of the song, to pack up her troubles in her old kit bag and smile. As a rule, this was not too onerous a choice, since she found her own problems as dull as she found everybody else's, but Charles respected this philosophy and he liked her for it. He did not perhaps fully appreciate the extent to which, in her concerted assumption of the 'brave face', she was only being loyal to the tenets of her kind.

The upper classes are not, as a whole, a complaining lot. As a group they would generally rather not 'go on about it'. A brisk walk and a stiff drink are their chosen methods of recovery whether struck in the heart or the wallet. Much has been written in the tabloid press about their coldness but it is not lack of feeling that marks them apart, rather it is lack of expression of feeling. Naturally they do not see this as a failing in themselves and nor do they admire public emotion in others. They are genuinely bewildered by working-class grief, those bereaved mothers being dragged sobbing and supported into church, those soldiers' widows photographed weeping over 'his last letter'. The very word 'counsellor' sends a shudder of disgust down any truly well-bred spine. What they do not appreciate, of course, is that these tragedies, national and domestic, the war casualties, the random killings, the pile-ups on the M3, offer most ordinary bereaved what is probably their only chance of fleeting celebrity. For once in their lives they can appease that very human craving for some prominence, some public recognition of their plight. The upper classes do not understand this hunger because they do not share it. They are born prominent.

The one arena of his mother's struggles that Charles really knew about was Lady Uckfield's war with his grandmother, the dowager marchioness, who had not been an easy mother-in-law. She was the tall, bony, long-nosed daughter of a duke and so not at all impressed with the pretty little brunette her son had brought home with him. Old Lady Uckfield had been Queen Mary to her daughter-in-law's Lady Elizabeth Bowes-Lyon and the relationship was never warm. Even after her husband's demise and well into Charles's conscious years, the dowager's behaviour continued unchecked and she was still attempting to countermand orders with the housekeeper, instruct the gardeners directly and cancel groceries with a view to replacing them with more 'suitable' items to the day of her largely unlamented death.

That these attempts were not successful, that her power was broken was a direct result of the one real fight between them, the thought of which always made Charles smile. Soon after her dethronement as chatelaine of Broughton, his grandmother had interfered with a new re-hang of the pictures in the saloon while Lady Uckfield was in London. On her return, Lady Uckfield's discovery that her scheme had been abandoned made her so angry that, for the only time in recorded history, she, in modern parlance, lost it. This resulted in a fully fledged screaming match, surely unique in the history of the room in question – at least since the more rollicking days of the eighteenth century. To the enraptured delight of the listening servants, Lady Uckfield denounced her mother-in-law as an ill-mannered, ill-bred, interfering old bitch. 'Ill-bred?' shrieked the dowager, selecting from the list of insults the only one to pierce her carapace. '*Ill-bred!*' and she stalked from the house, determined never to darken its doors again. His mother had told Charles many times that she regretted the incident and it was certainly a relief to her that old Lady Uckfield, having made her point, did eventually return to Broughton for the customary festivals but, even so, the battle had achieved its purpose. Thenceforth the young Marchioness was in charge, and the house, the estate and the village were under no illusions about it.

For these and many other reasons, simple and complicated, Charles admired his mother and the disciplines she lived by. He even admired the way she lived with her husband's stupidity without ever referring to the fact or showing her exasperation. He knew that he, himself, while not quite as slow as his father, was not quick. His mother had guided him well without making him too conscious of his shortcomings but he was aware of them all the same. Because of all this, he would have loved to please her when it came to his choice of a mate. He would have been delighted to arrive at some Scottish stalking party, at some London ball, and find exactly the woman his mother wanted for him. It should have been easy. There must surely have been some peer's daughter, from the old, familiar world Lady Uckfield knew and trusted, who was smart and sharp (for his mother was not a fan of the dowdy, county lady with her wispy hair and her charity shop skirts), and this girl would have made him laugh and he would have felt proud of her and safe, and her arrival would have transformed things.

But, try as he might to find her, somehow she had never turned up. There were nice young women who had done their best but . . . never quite *the* one. This was probably because Charles had a central, guiding belief. Like himself, it was simple but it was strong. Namely, that if he could only marry for love, if he could just find the partner who would stimulate him in mind (for he did value the albeit limited activities of his mind) and body, then the life that was mapped out for him would be a good and rewarding one. If, however, he married suitably but misguidedly, then there could be no redemption possible. He did not believe in divorce (not at least for the head of the Broughtons) and therefore, once unhappily married, he would remain so to the grave. He was, in short, much more than he knew, a thoroughly moral, straightforward fellow. Which made it all the more disturbing to him that here was a real possibility of his being drawn to a woman who, while not being ludicrously unsuitable, while not being a pop queen or a drug-running trapeze artist, was nevertheless not what his mother was hoping for.

It was therefore with a hint of melancholy in his heart that, a couple of days later, Charles telephoned Edith and asked her out again.

FOUR

~

To my amusement, it was not long before the fact that Edith and Charles were going about together had begun to attract attention. Gossip columns without a story for the day picked up on it and those tiresome articles in *Tatler* or *Harpers* about what up-to-the-minute people eat at weekends or wear in Paris or do for Christmas started to include Edith as Charles's paramour. The fascination with celebrities was in full swing at that time and since, by definition, there are never enough genuine celebrities to supply the market – even in a much less greedy era than the 1990s – journalists are forced to drag out their tired 'It Girls' and ex-television presenters to fill the gaps. It was ironically Edith's very ordinariness that played into this. Someone saw her as a latter-day Cinderella, the working girl suddenly transported into Dreamland, and wrote an article in one of the Sundays entitled 'The Lavery Discovery', featuring several large and highly coloured photographs. After that, she caught on. At first she was annoyed at being continually described as climbing the social ladder but, gradually, as the original reason for the press interest faded beneath a welter of fashion articles and award ceremonies and invitations onto afternoon television. Edith came to enjoy the attention. The seductive element in being pursued by newshounds is that inevitably one starts to feel that if so many people are interested in one's life, one's life must *ergo* be interesting and Edith wanted to believe this quite as much as anyone else. Of course, inevitably I suppose, it was not long before she began to lose touch with the fact that she was becoming famous for being famous and nothing more. I was at a charity lunch once when she was invited to give some tabloid award and I remember her saying afterwards how *ghastly* the other presenters were, all sports commentators and fashion gurus, and why on earth had they been invited? I pointed out that even a lowly sports commentator has earned his or her own celebrity in a

38

way Edith had not. She smiled but I could see she rather resented me for saying it. She had started at a perilously early stage to believe her own publicity.

These photo-shoots and column inches meant that, slightly mysteriously, she had begun to dress better or more expensively than before. I'm not quite sure how she managed this as I don't think Charles was forking out at that point. Probably she did one of those deals where designers lend you clothes to wear for the night if there's a likelihood of your getting into the papers. Or perhaps Mrs Lavery was stumping up. If she'd had the money, she wouldn't have minded a bit.

I saw much less of Edith during this time. At this distance, I'm not sure if she was still working in Milner Street but I would think she probably was as she was never one for counting her chickens. However, she was obviously less at a loss as to what to do for lunch. But one day the following March, months after she had started seeing Charles, I spotted her in the corner of the Australian having a tuna sandwich and, after buying myself a drink, I walked over to her table. 'Hello,' I said. 'Shall I join you or are you meditating?'

She looked up with a surprised smile. 'Sit. You're just the person I need.' She was distracted and serious and generally rather unlike the cool blonde I was used to.

'What's up, Doc?'

'Are you, by any chance, going to the Eastons' next weekend?'

'No. Should I be?'

'It would be frightfully convenient if you were.'

'Well, I'm not doing anything else. I suppose I could telephone and invite myself. Why?'

'Charles's mother is giving a dinner party at Broughton on Saturday and I want some of my own people at it. I suppose Isabel and David would come?'

'Are you kidding?'

'That's just it. I want you there to calm them down. Charles likes you.'

'Charles doesn't know me.'

'Well, at least he's met you.' I knew what was worrying her. She was tired of being invisible. Of being entirely surrounded by people who automatically assumed that if she were worth knowing they would

39

already know her. She wanted a friend of hers there whom she didn't have to introduce to Charles.

'I'll come if Isabel can put me up.'

She nodded gratefully. 'I'd ask you to stay at Broughton if I could.'

'Isabel would never forgive me. Have you had them over before?'

'No.' I looked surprised and she shrugged. 'I've only ever been down for the night and usually for something specific and you know what they're like . . .' I knew. I only had to think of the glint in David's eye at Ascot to know only too well.

'So how's it all going? I keep reading about you in the papers.'

She blushed. Isn't it silly?'

'And I saw you on *This Morning with Richard and Judy*.'

'Christ. Your life must be in serious trouble.'

'I had tonsillitis but anyway I rather like Judy,' I said. 'She always looks harassed and real. I thought you were quite good.'

'Did you?' She seemed astonished. 'I thought I was a total idiot. I don't mind the photographs but whenever I open my mouth, I sound like a complete half-wit. I'm sure they only got me because Tara Palmer-Tomkinson chucked.'

'Did she?'

'I don't know. I'm making it up.'

'Perhaps the answer is not to do any talking.'

'That's what Charles says, but it wouldn't make the smallest difference. They quote you anyway.' This is of course quite true.

'You and Charles make a fetching team. Your mother must be thrilled.'

Edith rolled her eyes. 'She's beside herself. She's afraid she'll find Bobby in the shower and it'll all have been a dream.'

'And will she?'

Edith's face hardened into a worldly mask that seemed more suited to an opera box in the *belle époque* than the Australian at lunchtime. 'No, I don't think so.'

I raised my eyebrows. 'Are congratulations in order?'

'Not yet,' she said firmly, 'but promise me you'll be there on Saturday. Eight o'clock. Black tie.'

'All right. But you must tell Isabel. Do you want me to write to Lady Uckfield?'

'No, no, I'll do all that. Just be there.'

When I telephoned Isabel that evening Edith had already spoken to her and the matter was swiftly arranged. And so, a few days later, I found myself joining the others in the Eastons' drawing room for a drink before we set off. David was being gauche and grumpy to conceal his palpitating excitement at finally being received within the citadel. Isabel was less excited and consequently less afraid of its showing.

'Well, do we think the dinner's in aid of anything?' she said with a giggle as I entered.

'I don't know,' I said. 'Do we?'

David pushed a glass into my hand. His whiskies were always warm, which was rather tiresome. He had read somewhere that gentlemen don't have ice. 'Isabel thinks they're going to announce their engagement.'

The thought had obviously crossed my mind, which would explain why Edith felt she had to have a few people on her own team but nursery training has made me beware of the obvious. 'Wouldn't her parents have been asked?'

'Perhaps they have been.' That was a thought. The image of Stella Lavery walking up to her room to find her bags unpacked and her evening dress laid out warmed my heart. Everyone deserves a few moments when life is Quite Perfect.

'Well, we'll know soon enough,' I said.

Isabel looked at the clock. 'Shouldn't we be off?'

'Not yet. There's plenty of time.' David could afford to mumble his prey now that he was sure of it. 'What about another drink?'

But Isabel won and we set off for our first but (as we were all secretly thinking) probably not our last private visit to Broughton Hall.

The house looked no less forbidding than it had before but the fact that this fortress had been breached made its very chill gratifying. We stood outside the same door and rang the bell.

'I wonder if this is the right entrance,' said Isabel, but before we could ponder further, the door was opened by a butler and we were being escorted upstairs into the Red Saloon. I think I was surprised that the family appeared to use those rooms generally on public show. I had expected to be ushered into some other, sloaney sitting room on the first floor where the portraits and the Louis Quinze furniture would be interlarded with squashy sofas and chintz – that being the usual form on such occasions. I was to learn that I was quite right and the fact that we were having drinks in the Red Saloon and dinner in the State Dining Room should have given the game away at once. At all events, when I walked in and saw Mrs Lavery standing by the fireplace next to the burly figure of Lord Uckfield I knew. Edith had brought it off and we were there to witness her triumph.

Lady Uckfield stepped forward. She was a small, fine-boned, attractive woman who must have been extremely pretty in her youth but at first sight she seemed quite unimposing, even cosy. This always stands out in my mind as the most mistaken in a lifetime of incorrect first impressions. When she spoke her voice was light and bell-like with that tremendously far-back enunciation that one associates with wartime newsreels. 'How terribly sweet you all are to be here,' she sparkled, smiling gaily. 'I know you've come down from London.' She directed this to me. The point being to show us that she had done her homework and she knew precisely who we were.

'How very kind you are to ask us.' I know this game and its responses.

'Not at all. We're *delighted* to see you here.' Lady Uckfield spoke with a kind of intimate urgency, which punctuated everything she said, as if she were sharing a permanent private joke that only you (or whomever she was talking to) would understand. I think of her now as the most socially expert individual I have ever known at all well. She combined a watchmaker's eye for detail with a madam's knowledge of the world. She was also utterly confident. I knew she had been born the prettiest daughter of a rich earl and I supposed then, young as I was, that her confidence was nothing to be wondered at, but I know now that such things do not always follow and I later learned that, like all of us, she had had her share of troubles. Maybe these had made her strong, maybe she was born strong anyway; whatever the reason, by the time I met her she was a complete and invulnerable perfectionist. Every evening I have ever participated in at her invitation has been constructed as carefully as a Cellini salt-cellar. From the species of potato to the arrangement of the cushions nothing was left to chance or others' judgement.

Of course, as soon as she said, 'How lovely it is to welcome some friends of our darling Edith,' I could see that she didn't like her future daughter-in-law. Having said that, 'didn't like' is probably not quite accurate. It was amazing to her that her son should be marrying someone she didn't know or even know of. It was fantastic to her that this girl's friends should not be the children of her friends. *Au fond*, it was extraordinary that Edith had got into the house at all. How had it happened? From thoughts like these, unfortunately for Edith, Lady Uckfield had deduced that Charles had been 'caught' and while she later (much later) qualified this impression, she never really changed it. As a matter of fact I'm not at all sure it wasn't true.

Isabel and I drifted over towards the fireplace. 'Hello, Mrs Lavery,' I said, and Edith's mother turned towards us, revealing in an instant that fatal, diffident graciousness that marks the successful social climber. Their manner invariably conveys to their true equals that the ladder has been pulled up and will never, ever be lowered again. The eager, snobbish Mrs Lavery we had known had gone and been replaced by the Snow Queen. It was as if we were in *Invasion of the Body Snatchers* and we were talking to a pod. Almost reluctantly, sounding every bit as vague about our identities as Lord Uckfield, she introduced us to our host.

He shook our hands in a hearty, blank way. 'Jolly good,' he said. 'Did you have a lot of trouble getting here?'

'We've only come from Ringmer,' said Isabel. 'My husband and I live there.'

'Really?' said Lord Uckfield. 'Was there a lot of traffic on the road? All those bloody people trying to escape the city if there's a glimmer of sun in the forecast. Was it difficult getting out?'

Isabel was about to embark on another long explanation of how she had not come from London, which I spared her. 'I came on the train,' I said.

'Very sensible.' He smiled his expansive, florid smile and nodded us away.

The Marquess of Uckfield was a dull and stupid man but there was, on the whole, no harm in him. He had been spoiled all his life and surrounded by the kind of toadies that such people find comfort in, garnered from the distant strands of their own families as well as on the highways and byways, and so he had no conception of how dull and stupid he really was. His uneducated banalities were greeted as if they had come from Solomon and his unfunny, old jokes were rewarded with gales of breathless laughter. If it is the experience of life that shapes us, is it to be wondered at that men like Lord Uckfield are so signally unshaped? People would speak, even out of his hearing, of his wisdom and judgement when he certainly had neither. The reason for this was that if they could convince themselves they truly believed him to possess these qualities, then they would not have to admit to themselves that they were toadies, which is a powerful motive among the fashionable. And if their outer acquaintance ever expressed doubt as to his Lordship's mental prowess, they could always answer, 'Ah, you wouldn't think that if you really knew him,' thereby giving themselves one mark for being on intimate terms with yet another Great House and a second mark for being a genuine person. He was not ungenerous, just lazy with the fundamental laziness that marks most friendships of the privileged with a dead hand. He had long since decided that pursuing relations with any but sycophants and those members of his own class necessary for his self-image was far too like hard work and he had abandoned the effort, but the decision had been a subconscious one and he still thought of himself as a kind man. In truth, he would always be kind to Edith. He was not in the least admirable but nor was he a snob and anyway, apart from anything else, he was just glad she was so pretty.

I could see the butler in the door catching Lady Uckfield's eye. She nodded, cast her professional glance about the room and walked over to me. 'We're having dinner in a minute,' she said. 'I wonder if you'd like to take in Lady Tenby?' She indicated a stout party of sixty-plus wedged in a chair by the fire. I nodded and muttered and Lady Uckfield continued her rounds. We had been almost the last-comers and I suppose everyone else already had their orders. I walked towards my partner, thinking I might be needed to haul her into an upright position. She looked up and extended a fat, jewelled hand.

'Are you taking me in?' she said. I nodded. 'Googie's so brilliant at organising things. She should have run a hotel chain. Help me up.'

I have always been uncomfortable with the *jejune* pseudo-informality implicit in the upper-class passion for nicknames. Everyone is 'Toffee' or 'Bobo' or 'Snook'. They themselves think the names imply a kind of playfulness, an eternal childhood, fragrant with memories of Nanny and pyjamas warming by the nursery fire, but they are really a simple reaffirmation of insularity, a reminder of shared history that excludes more recent arrivals, yet another way of publicly displaying their intimacy with each other. Certainly the nicknames form an effective fence. A newcomer is often in the position of knowing someone too well to continue to call them Lady So-and-So but not nearly well enough to call them 'Sausage', while to use their actual Christian name is a sure sign within their circle that one doesn't really know them at all. And so the new arrival is forced back from the normal development of friendly intimacy that is customary among acquaintances in other classes.

Dinner had been announced and my partner had lumbered to her feet and was now leaning heavily against me. I could see that for her at least this arm-in-arm procession was more than a self-conscious replay of an Edwardian custom: it was a very necessary service. A few couples ahead of us I could see Lady Uckfield chattering gaily into the face of a shell-shocked Kenneth Lavery. They reminded me of the front benches going through into the Lords to hear the Queen's speech, when the Tory ministers always seem to be filmed frenetically gabbling away to their glum and serious Socialist opposite numbers. Behind them Edith was with Lord Uckfield. She was wearing a black velvet dress, cut low at the neck with long tight sleeves and no jewellery of any sort. The effect was beautiful and *triste* like Juliet in mourning. I suppose she felt it would be tasteless to look too merry.

Lady Tenby followed my glance. 'Very good-looking. No question about that. But who on earth is she?'

I smiled down at her. 'She's a great friend of mine,' I said.

'Oops,' said Lady Tenby, and we continued in silence.

I later learned that the Countess of Tenby was the widowed mother of four daughters and, as Lady Uckfield's second cousin, had always rather hoped to get Charles for one of them. It was not an unreasonable ambition. They were nice girls and quite pleasant of face. Any one of them would probably have made him happy. In the end only the eldest, Lady Daphne, married at all 'well' in their mother's opinion (and he was a younger son), two married routine Hoorays and the youngest and best-looking went to California to live with the founder of a rather sinister sect. The point being that Lady Tenby was not a nasty or an unreasonable woman. She had put in many years work on her daughters for what were to be meagre dividends and now, this evening, she had been invited to witness the triumph of an interloper, a stranger who had stolen into their camp under cover of darkness and made off with the fattest sheep of all. Of course she would smile and congratulate and kiss but then she would go home and say how marvellous Googie and Tigger had been, how nobody would have known they were disappointed, how the girl was, after all, *very* pretty and seemed *fond* of Charles. And forever Edith would be marked as a lucky outsider.

Dinner was delicious, which was a surprise. I had been expecting the usual country house fare dispensed by my parents' generation, more redolent of a girls' prep school than the kitchens of the Ivy but I was not then used to Lady Uckfield's command of detail. I had Lady Tenby on my left and I spent the first course in one of those are-you-an-actor-what-might-I-have-seen-you-in conversations, which are so disheartening, but when the plates were taken away and I was allowed to turn to my companion on my right, I found myself talking to a rather hard-faced but intriguing woman of about my own age who introduced herself as Charles's sister, Caroline.

'So you're an old friend of Edith?' she said.

'I don't know how "old". I've known her about a year and a half.'

'Longer than we have,' she said with a crisp little laugh.

'And do you think you're going to like her?' I asked.

'I don't know,' said Caroline, looking down the table to where Edith was flirting gently with her future father-in-law. 'As a matter of fact I think I might. But is she going to like Charles? That's the question.'

This was of course the question. I followed my neighbour's gaze to where Charles was sitting, his heavy, good-natured face frowning over what was in all probability a rather small intellectual problem being posed by his neighbour. I wondered if Edith had faced up to how thick he really was. Or, for that matter, to how bleak the country can be. Caroline was reading my mind. 'It's frightfully dreary down here, you know. I suppose Edith's ready for all that? Flower shows all summer, freezing pipes all winter. Does she hunt?'

'She rides so she probably could hunt.'

'I don't suppose it matters much. With the antis about to kill it off at any moment.'

'Perhaps she's an anti and doesn't approve. You never know these days.'

'Oh, I doubt Edith is anti-blood sport,' said Caroline carefully. 'She looks quite carnivorous to me.'

46

'What about you? Do you hunt?'

'Heavens no. I hate the country. I don't even go to Hyde Park if I can avoid it.'

'What does your husband do? Or is it common to ask?'

'It is. But I'll answer anyway. Mainly advertising but he also organises charity events.'

I have often thought how simple it must have been to live a hundred years ago when every man one knew was in the army, the navy, the Church, or owned land. These extraordinary jobs one hears about every day, that one never even knew existed, have an unsettling effect on me. Headhunting or working in futures, credit management or people skills, as explanations they all sound as if one were concealing one's true activity. Perhaps a lot of them are. I couldn't think of an appropriate response. 'Does he favour any particular cause?' I said.

'So how do you know Edith?' said Caroline, who was obviously as uninterested in her husband's activities as I was. I explained about the Eastons. 'I wondered what they were doing here. It's funny we haven't met before if they're so near.' I was glad David was too far down the table to hear this. After that we turned to more general topics and I soon learned that Lady Caroline Chase was one of those children of the purple who manage to reject their upbringing in their way of living, their philosophy, their chosen partner and their choice of address and yet take their snobbery with them absolutely intact into their new life. I liked her but she was in her way quite as dismissive as her mother only without, perhaps, Lady Uckfield's armour of moral certainty. To Lady Uckfield her social position was an article of faith; to Caroline it was simply a matter of fact.

The meal progressed with some sort of apple snow for pudding, then the cheese and just when I was expecting our hostess to gather up the women with her and leave us to leaden political discussion and port, I was pleased to see that an unused glass in the nest before me was being filled with champagne. This then was the moment.

Lord Uckfield stood. 'I suppose we all know why we're here tonight.' I suppose we all did, although one or two people looked a bit surprised. Kenneth Lavery, himself, seated next to Lady Uckfield, seemed to be full of wonder as well he might. 'It's to welcome a very charming newcomer into our family.' I looked at Mrs Lavery, glazed with delight on Lord Uckfield's right. Precedence had been set aside for

47

this one night. I do not think I ever saw her seated so advantageously again. 'Shall we raise our glasses? Edith and Charles.' We all stood with a lot of chair scraping and a certain amount of panting from Lady Tenby.

'Edith and Charles!' We drank and sat, while poor Charles, scarlet in the face, attempted some sort of answer in an unnaturally base voice.

'I haven't anything to say, really. Except that I think myself a very lucky man.'

'Hear, hear!' The table was alive with muttered gallantries. I was watching Edith as she gazed at Charles with a kind of fresh-faced, open adoration that reminded me of Elizabeth Taylor in *National Velvet*. When she's given the horse. I don't know if this was a lesson she had learned from her ex-suitor's bride four years previously or if she was simply assuming the most suitable expression to quell criticism or if, for that moment at any rate, she simply adored him. It was probably a mixture of all three. I turned my head and I saw that Lady Uckfield was watching me, a tender, perfectly constructed smile on her pretty cat-face. I looked back at her and she raised her eyebrows slightly before standing and bringing the table once more to its feet. I'm not quite sure what she meant to express by this quizzical look.

Probably Caroline spoke for them all (she certainly spoke for me) when she muttered in a low voice: 'Well, she's done it. I only hope she knows what she's getting into.'

FIVE

~

I have not often participated in anything that could remotely be described as a Great Society Event. At any rate, not in an event that garnered much public curiosity. But by then Edith had achieved her status as a minor tabloid heroine and when she did succeed in landing her fish, the journalists who had set her up were only too anxious to reap their rewards. They'd established her as a story and she had not disappointed them. There were consequently offers from *Hello!* and *OK!* – much to Lady Uckfield's hilarity – for exclusive coverage and even though they were of course turned down the level of interest remained high. I do not think Mrs Lavery understood at first why the magazines were not to be allowed their way. I suspect she might have rather liked the idea of Edith and Charles on one of those red-outlined covers surrounded by the noble offspring of Charles's relations but when she had half suggested this to Lady Uckfield, she had been flattened to hear her companion turn to Edith and say, 'Your mother has got a *wicked* sense of humour. She had me quite taken in for a moment.' Naturally, Mrs Lavery then laughed like billyo at the thought that Lady Uckfield might have believed her! And she never mentioned it again. At any rate, for all sorts of reasons, I was curious as well as flattered to be asked to be an usher at what was shaping up to be the Wedding of the Year – or so the newspapers told me.

I received the invitation from Charles, who had written to me in his rather charming, round hand wondering if I would do this for him. It is always hard for an actor to commit in advance to anything social – not least because it is a kind of unwritten law of the theatre that if you accord the slightest importance to anything other than work then you have no talent. I suppose I would have chucked if I had been offered the title role in *Ben Hur* but I was pretty determined to play my part in the Apotheosis of Edith.

Isabel telephoned me the same morning: 'I gather you're an usher,' she said. 'David isn't.' I answered, as I knew I must, that this seemed a bit hard. 'Well, I must say I think it really is. He's in a sulk, which is a great bore and I don't see that there's anything I can do about it.' I said there was absolutely nothing she could do about it and after all, I was the only one of Edith's friends that Charles had even met before the whole thing began. 'I know that and I've said it, but you know David.'

'What about you?'

'What do you mean?'

'Are you going to play any part in it all? I thought Alice might be one of the bridesmaids or something.' Alice was the Eastons' eldest child. She was as plain as a pikestaff but quite amiable withal.

'No.' Isabel's voice was sodden with disappointment. 'Edith tried but apparently there were covens of prior claims and so she's settled for just having tinies. Much nicer really,' she muttered drearily. I could tell she had not finished. 'I was wondering about Charles's night out.'

'What about it?'

'Is he having one?'

'I don't know. I suppose so.'

'But you haven't been asked?'

'No. Should I have been?'

'Well, it's just that David was wondering if he, or both of you, shouldn't do something about organising one ... ' Her voice trailed away.

'Come off it. We hardly know him. What are you thinking of?'

'I dare say you're right.' I wondered if David was in the room with her. 'You might let us know if you are asked.'

David's background anxiety was becoming uncomfortable. He had obviously started on a lifetime's career of dropping Charles's name and he could not face the obloquy of being publicly excluded from his circle of intimates.

'All right,' I said, 'but I'm sure I won't be.'

As it happened, a month later, ten days before the wedding, I was asked. Presumably because of a dropout. A party of twelve was being flown to Paris in a week's time, three days before the Great Event, to dine and stay overnight at the Ritz. I was sent the ticket by bike and all I had to do was to be ready for collection from the flat at the appointed hour. The flight was to take off from the City airport. Instead of telephoning Isabel, I spoke to Edith. 'I've been asked to Charles's shindig.'

'I know. Completely his idea. I think it'll be fun, don't you? I love the Paris Ritz.'

'I suppose David isn't going?'

'No. The thing is Henry Cumnor and Charles's uncle Peter are organising and paying for the whole thing and so he can't have everyone.'

'Fains I tell David.'

'I've told Isabel.' Edith paused. 'As a matter of fact, I do think they're being tiresome. I am fond of Isabel but they want to be such "best friends" all the time. I feel like a heroine out of Angela Brazil. After all, I don't know David well and Charles has hardly met him.'

'My dear,' I said sagely. 'This is only the beginning.'

At three o' clock the following Saturday a capped and uniformed chauffeur rang my basement bell and seized my waiting suitcase to carry it up to the car. I had treated myself to a new one in honour of the elevated company I was about to keep so it was especially irritating when he caught it on the corner of the cellar steps and wrenched one of the handles off. As a result, despite my reckless extravagance, I felt shabby for the entire trip. *Sic transit gloria mundi*, or, I suppose, *sic transit gloria transit.*

Henry Cumnor was already in the car, his corpulence spilling itself across the back seat in vast folds of Turnbull and Asser-shirted flesh, leaving the barest ledge of vacant leather beside him. As I climbed in, I felt like Carrie Fisher squeezing up against Jabba the Hutt. I knew Henry vaguely, as it so happened that we had attended the same school although in different years, and this afforded me a faint protection against his exclusivity, but only faint. At any rate, I knew what to expect as Edith had made quite a funny story out of her 'first date' with Charles.

There was another passenger in the front seat who was cursorily introduced as Tommy Wainwright and whom I recognised as a rising Member of Parliament – if any Tory could be said to be rising at that time. So far as I could remember from those profiles beloved of the Sunday colour sections he was the younger son of a Home Counties peer and was consequently a slightly surprising inclusion in the group on whom Mrs Thatcher had smiled – she not being much in favour of the aristocracy. He was tall, almost lanky, with an amiable, round face and thinning hair that made him look like a kind of trainee old buffer, although, as I would learn, this was not at all the case. He turned, smiled and shook my hand, which placed him three–nil in the courtesy stakes against Henry and we set off.

The talk on the way to the airport was political and I was amused at the contrast between my two companions. Tommy gave his reasons for why the Conservatives had gone so completely down the plug. These were on the whole reasonable and seemed worthy of discussion but Cumnor countered them with a bundle of ridiculous assertions, all smug, all out of date and all apparently received unchewed from his late father (rather like his wardrobe). Feeling that I ought to contribute, I observed that it did not seem to me that the party had been very imaginative in their relationship with the arts.

Cumnor angled his bulk towards me. 'My dear fellow, how many people constitute what you call "the Arts"? We're talking thousands, not hundreds of thousands, not millions. Do you know how many members there are in the TGWU? The plain truth is, whether you like it or not, your "arts" don't matter.' He sat back, having won his point to his own satisfaction.

'Forty million people turn on their televisions every night to find out what they think,' said Tommy. 'What could matter more than that?'

The issue was not important to any of us but I could see that Henry was irritated at Tommy for taking my side, showing that he shared the usual fantasy of the less intelligent members of his class that on every given topic, from port to euthanasia, there is a 'sound' way of thinking and one has only to voice this view to carry the field. Since they are generally only addressing like-minded people, the field is as a rule easy to carry. Tommy Wainwright, in not playing this game, risked creating the impression in Henry's sluggish brain that in some way, ever since Tommy had gone into serious politics, he was 'not quite a gentleman' – the stock response to original thought.

Having arrived at the airport and gone through the procedures, we were shown to a smallish departure gate where we were hailed by the remaining nine of the party. These included Lord Peter Broughton, Lord Uckfield's much younger half-brother, and Caroline's husband, Eric Chase, whom I had met briefly at the engagement dinner. Chase was an unlikely addition to the Broughton clan, being the very definition of a 'Yuppie'. That is to say he was a sleek and belligerent 'executive', whose conversation consisted largely of capitalistic platitudes and references to his membership of Brooks's. His most distinctive feature was an almost pathological rudeness, which made him simultaneously less pathetic and more objectionable although, oddly, he was attractive to women. I cannot imagine why but with the opposite sex (in marked contrast to his own) he undeniably had a good deal of success. I suppose he was handsome in a smooth, over-fed way and his satisfaction with his outward form (as well as, presumably, his dazzling marriage) was demonstrated in a constantly changing wardrobe of over-cut worsteds and tweeds. I later learned that his father had been a manager with British Rail. He made an odd pair with Caroline for politically and philosophically they were streets apart. The plain truth was that he had made a right-wing gesture in marrying her while she had made a left-wing one by marrying him. All this was concealed from them, however, because they seldom talked much when they were alone. It is quite possible in this way for couples often not to discover that they are in profound disagreement over the very fundamentals of life until ten or even twenty years have passed.

Charles strode up with a glass of champagne and a warm smile. For Edith's sake or perhaps for my own he was clearly determined not to let me feel left out of this group who (with the exception of Chase) had all played together in those long-ago nurseries and who he was fearful might be rude to an actor of whom they had never heard. I was touched by his efforts but he needn't have worried. I was not always an actor. I had not only been at school with Cumnor, but I recognised a prep school playmate, a friend from my debbing days and an acquaintance from Cambridge among the others. I also knew that Lord Peter had been engaged at one time to a cousin of my sister-in-law so I did not anticipate much trouble. Such is the world that still exists in a country of sixty million people a century after the Socialists first came to power.

As a further mark of distinction Charles took the seat next to me on the little aeroplane that had been chartered for the event. A raffish steward brought us some more champagne with a tiny bit of caviar squidged onto a slightly tough blini and we settled back.

'This is all very nice,' I said.

'I'm glad you could come.'

'So am I.'

'You were the one who introduced us.'

I laughed. 'In years to come we'll know whether I have earned praise or blame.'

Charles wasn't in joking mood. 'Oh praise. I'd say praise.' He paused. 'Edith thinks you're frightfully intelligent, you know.'

'That's very gratifying.'

He looked down into his drink. 'Of course, she's so bright. You must find that.'

I can't say that I had ever given the matter much thought. Certainly Edith was no Gertrude Stein. Her idea of intellectuality was reading the latest John Mortimer. Still, she was quite funny and in my experience funny people are seldom stupid. 'I'm always pleased to see her, which is probably the same thing,' I said.

He smiled a trifle wryly. 'Well, here's hoping she's always pleased to see me.' I murmured some reassuring nonsense but he was not content to leave it there. He drew in a breath. 'I hope I'm worthy of her,' he said. I suppressed my urge to smile at being trapped in this bit of Frederick Lonsdale dialogue. These were pedestrian sentiments to begin a stag night but they were none the less heartfelt for that. Charles was typical of his kind in that he had no modes of original expression and was almost invariably forced back into cinematic clichés when trying to describe love or hate or anything else not covered by the Jockey Club rules. I said I was sure he would be as worthy as anything and it was Edith who was the lucky one and that he was paying her a great honour, etcetera. I'm usually equal to this sort of thing but I hadn't quite hit the mark this time. He interrupted my encouraging flow. 'It's just that I hope I'm clever enough for her. I don't want her to get bored with me.' He laughed and raised his eyebrows slightly to pass this off as a sort of joke, but I could see he meant it – just as I could see he had a point. Edith was no Einstein but it had already occurred to me that there might come a time when attending race-meetings with a bunch of well-dressed people mouthing received opinions just might not do it for her. I didn't see, however, that there was any useful comment that could be made since I could hardly praise him for his perspicacity.

'Charles,' I said, 'if there's one thing that makes me uncomfortable it's modesty and we'll have no more of it tonight.'

He laughed and the moment was passed.

I love Paris. There are certain cities where you can only have a good time with the help of the residents and there are others where a good time is available to all. Such is Paris, which is just as well given the amount of help one generally gets from the residents. My mother, a poor linguist herself, had been extremely anxious that her children should not suffer as she had suffered, nodding and smiling at French diplomats' wives in a kind of frozen tableau of international goodwill. Consequently, in our early teens we all had one or more school holidays ruined by being sent off to families in the depths of France where, as she had made a ruthless point of checking, we would find no English spoken. As a result of these draconian cruelties we all speak tolerable French, which of course enhances the pleasure of visiting their beautiful capital city.

I had not previously stayed at the Paris Ritz, although I had been there once to a very grand reception, which formed part of a series celebrating a marriage between two spectacularly Faubourg families. It is a great hotel in the sense that it belongs more to that lost era of great hotels, where veiled beauties stood about waiting for their maids to check twenty pieces of luggage before embarking for the Riviera, than to our own eat-and-run epoch. A red, white and gilt palace, sumptuous and yet pretty – quite unlike the modern, Park Lane equivalents got up, as they are, like enormous Maida Vale hairdressing salons. I was thoroughly glad to be there, particularly since I wasn't paying, and even the contemptuous looks the hotel employees cast at my torn and broken luggage could not quench my enthusiasm.

We gathered in the bar, slicked up in our black ties, with that faintly desperate air of the English embarking on a 'good time', and started to tuck into the champagne. Tommy Wainwright came over to me and I asked him if he knew what the plan was for the evening.

He shrugged. 'I imagine we'll have dinner here and then push on to somewhere embarrassing on the Left Bank. Isn't that the form?'

'I expect so. Have you known Charles a long time?'

'We were at Eton together. Then I went out with Caroline for a bit when we were about twenty so we sort of re-met. What about you?'

'I hardly know him. I feel rather a fraud being here. It's just that I introduced him to Edith so I suppose I'm representing her. Just to check that no one tries to put him off the whole idea.'

Wainwright smiled. 'So you're a friend of Edith. How interesting.

We've scarcely met. I must say she's a real beauty. But then she'd have to be to carry off the prize.'

'I imagine there were quite a few noses out of joint when they made the announcement.'

He laughed. 'There certainly were. I think they were all so irritated because none of them knew her. Or none of the ones I know seemed to. Like an outsider winning the Derby. At one point she was starting to sound like a cross between Eliza Doolittle and Rebecca.' I could just imagine and said so. He smiled. 'From the little I know of her, I'm sure she'll do very well.' He nodded over towards the groom. 'He's really smitten, you know. Charming. I like to see it.'

It was a particularly warm evening and the manager had decided to have the tables of the dining room carried out into the little courtyard that lies alongside it. The mellow stone, carefully carved for the seeing eye of César Ritz, and the modest fountain splashing coolly in the darkening night, induced that spirit of contentment, resting on a combination of luxury and beauty, which one would be foolish, whatever one's philosophy, always to resist. God knows it is rare enough. Euro-smart couples sat about, the women in their brilliant jewellery, one with a white poodle, idly barking its unhungry bark. To me it seemed agreeable to watch the rich taking their less controversial pleasures. Unfortunately nothing is perfect and I was seated next to Eric Chase, who proceeded to hijack as much of the arrangement as he could.

'Bring us another bottle,' he said brusquely to the waiter as he sat down. 'And try to get the temperature right this time.' He turned to me. 'We met at my in-laws' house, didn't we?' I nodded. 'You came with those frightful friends of Edith.' I nodded again, since I was certainly not prepared to wreck the evening for the sake of Isabel and David. But like all bullies he was not to be pacified. 'Where on earth did she meet them?'

'I don't really know. I met them because I've known Isabel since we were children.'

'Poor you. Some of this?' Without waiting for an answer he slopped some wine into my glass. 'Well, I'm afraid little Edith'll have to shape up a bit if she wants to bring it off.'

'What do you mean?'

'If she wants to get away with it. As Lady Broughton.' He started to sing, 'There'll be some changes made.'

'Oh, I don't know,' I said. 'Did you find it very difficult to get away with marrying Caroline?' Of course, in a way, this was a mistake and Chase turned to his other neighbour having registered me as an enemy, but I was satisfied to have maintained Edith's honour. Like many aggressive *parvenus* who have climbed the greasy pole, he was under the illusion that the reason people did not point out his social failings was because they were no longer visible. As rude as he was, he could not credit anyone else with politeness. That was his armour. I did not mind crossing him as I had disliked him a good deal on sight and anyway I was not entirely joking when I said I thought I was there as Edith's champion.

The next stage of the evening was quite as embarrassing as anyone could wish. We were transported to Chez Michou in Montmartre, a pocket-handkerchief of a club, where assorted female impersonators mimed to the records of various stars. This was the idea of Lord Peter, who turned out to be, as I think I already vaguely knew, an amiable drunkard with a reputation for being 'quite a card'. Actually we were all pretty drunk by this time, having been at it more or less non-stop since we arrived at the airport in London. Doubtless this helped us enjoy the show, which contained few surprises: Garland, Streisand, a rather compelling Monroe, and an absolutely unlike Rita Hayworth miming to 'Long Ago and Far Away', which Rita herself only mimed to anyway. Drink or no drink, I was beginning to feel the siren call of my bed and I caught Tommy's eye as he made a let's-get-out-of-here gesture towards the door when the compère – or *commère* should it be? – jumped up onto the stage. 'Now, I'd like to introduce our special act for this evening, with our best wishes and congratulations. Ladies and Gentlemen, Miss Edith Lavery!'

I nearly jumped out of my seat as the young man who had given us Monroe reappeared as Edith. An over-made-up Edith with a kind of flashiness she didn't possess, but otherwise astonishingly accurate. Even down to her dress, which could easily have been one of her own. I looked at Charles. He was stunned as were we all. Peter, of course, was grinning like a clown. On the stage the boy/Edith started to sing a song from *Guys and Dolls*. 'Ask me how do I feel, Little me with my quiet upbringing . . .' She wiggled her way across the stage to where Charles sat, still motionless. 'Well, sir, all I can say is if I were a bell I'd be ringing...' At about this moment I realised that this was, in some undefined and complicated way, a terrible insult to Edith. The others started to snicker, as the blonde on the stage frisked and shouted her silly lyrics about striking it lucky. Charles was silent. The performer beckoned him up onto the stage and clearly this was part of what had been pre-arranged but he shook his head and kept his seat, with no change in his expression. The boy/girl looked, puzzled, over to where Peter was sitting with a laughing Eric and a couple of the others. The act was grinding to a halt. In another moment, Peter jumped up onto the stage as her partner and the dance went on. Towards the end, Peter was given a cardboard jewel-box to present to her, which he did, going down on one knee. 'Edith' opened it and started to deck herself out in the glittering gewgaws within. I was reminded of Gillray's cartoon attacks on the actress, Elizabeth Farren, who succeeded in marrying the Earl of Derby in the 1790s. At the bottom of the box was a little coronet, a pantomime walk-down affair, bright with coloured glass. At the last note of the song 'Edith' took it up and planted it on her head.

In fairness to Peter Broughton I'm sure he hadn't quite hoisted in how fantastically offensive the cumulative effect of all this would be to Charles. Certainly the last thing he wanted was for the evening to end as it did. Peter was not one of the cleverest, poor soul, and I remember I thought then that Chase or one of the others must have embellished his original idea of simply having someone impersonate Edith, which, in itself, if 'she' had just sung a love song, could have been quite amusing. As it was, and without I think Peter's really knowing, she was lampooned as a greedy, social-climbing adventuress in front of her bridegroom. Chase and some of the others were applauding loudly. They were sitting behind Charles and so could not see the expression on his face, though for the life of me I can't imagine how they thought he was going to find it funny. But Chase was one of those who insults you and then says, 'Can't you take a joke?' and I suppose he had done this so often he had begun to think these insults really were jokes and that Charles, or anyone who couldn't take them, was simply being dull.

Charles stood up. 'I'm rather tired. I think I'm going back to the hotel,' he said.

Tommy and I volunteered to join him and that was that. We strode off, leaving the others to nurse the failure of Peter's prank.

'Shall we get a taxi?' said Tommy. It was late and the night was perceptibly cooler than it had been but Charles shook his head.

'Is it all right if we walk for a bit? I want some air.' We strode along in silence until he spoke again. 'That was rather unpleasant, wasn't it?'

'Well,' Tommy was placatory, 'I'm sure they didn't mean it to be. I dare say the girl, or boy or whatever she was, misunderstood the brief.'

'It was Peter's fault.'

'Well . . .'

Charles stopped walking for a minute and stood, looking mutely about him. 'Do you know what really depressed me about that?' We both had some pretty good ideas but naturally said nothing. 'It was because I suddenly realised how absolutely bloody stupid most of the people I know really are. These are supposed to be twelve of my best friends, for God's sake!' He chuckled bitterly. 'I'm embarrassed for them and I'm embarrassed for myself.'

In the end we walked home right across Paris. The others must all have gone to bed by the time we fell through the door in the Place Vendôme. We parted and went to our rooms and I suppose, all in all, the evening must be rated as a flop – particularly considering the planning and the cost – but in some odd and undefined way I found myself feeling rather encouraged by Charles's outburst. My assessment of his brain was not revised but I do not think I had appreciated before that night how thoroughly decent he was. It is not a fashionable quality these days but it seemed to me that Edith's happiness was in safer hands than I had realised.

SIX

~

When she opened her eyes she knew at once that this was the last morning in her life when she would awake as Edith Lavery. Henceforth, that girl would have gone away and whatever might happen in the future she would not be coming back. Edith attempted to question herself as to what exactly she was feeling. Just as when you are forced into a decision it is often the mouthing of one choice that makes you realise you really want the other, so she wondered if her stomach would tell her that she was making a ghastly mistake simply because this was the day when the whole thing became irrevocable. But her stomach did not wish to play the part of a goat's entrails at Delphi and declined to give an opinion. She felt neither elated nor depressed – simply that there was a lot to do. There was a faint knock on her door and her mother came in carrying a cup of tea.

It is no exaggeration to say that Stella Lavery was so happy on this morning she really felt she might burst, that her heart might stop, exhausted by pumping the feverish blood of satisfied ambition. It is not true to say she would have gladly sacrificed her daughter to a rich marquess's heir if she had thoroughly disliked him, simply that unless he had attacked her with a knife it was not physically possible that she *could* dislike him. Actually, I don't think she had given Charles *qua* Charles much thought. He was pleasant, well-mannered, not bad-looking. That, to coin a phrase, was all she knew and all she needed to know. That, and the fact that after tomorrow her daughter would be the Countess Broughton.

It had been a source of the faintest irritation to Stella that her daughter's title was not to be Countess *of* Broughton, which she thought more romantic, and it seemed to her tiresome of the first Broughton to receive the earldom not to have asked for the 'of.' After all, the Cholmondeleys had done so and so had the Balfours when they were presented with their titles. True there was a village called Cholmondeley and somewhere in Scotland called Balfour but was there not a place called Broughton? Surely there must be one somewhere? Still, allowing the fact that 'you can't have everything' she had grown used to the form and now gained a good deal of pleasure correcting her friends. After all, the blessed 'of' would come, with the marquessate, all in good time.

'Good morning, darling.' She whispered the words, gently conveying, as she thought, great tenderness. This was a moment when she knew it behoved her to feel some nostalgia and regret at losing the child of her heart. The fact remained, however, that, notwithstanding the very real and deep joy Edith had given her mother over the years, this morning Mrs Lavery was as happy as a sandboy. Not only was she gaining a son, as the saying goes, but, as she saw it, a whole new position in the firmament. Gates as rusty as the ones at Ham, locked after the departure of the last Stuart king, were everywhere springing open before her. Or so it seemed. Stella Lavery was not a complete fool. She did realise that it was up to her to make a success of this opportunity, that if some of the people she was going to meet, most particularly Lady Uckfield, could be induced to like her, could actually want her friendship, then she could turn herself into Edith's asset rather than being (as she very secretly and reluctantly suspected) her liability. She also knew enough to go slowly. Never must there be the slightest scent about her of a beast of prey in pursuit of its quarry. Softly, quietly, mutual interests must be unearthed, books must be lent, dressmakers must be suggested. In her mind, on this dizzy morning, were shining images, holographs of elegant pleasure, showing her tucking into a light lunch with Lady Uckfield before they rushed off together to their shared milliner, pulling on their gloves as they waved for a taxi . . .

''Morning, Mummy.' Edith was by this time used to the dreamreverie in which her mother seemed to exist. She did not grudge her the pleasure this marriage brought, although she hoped it had not been a contributory factor, pushing her into the torrent that Edith felt whirling her towards the coronet. 'Is it raining?'

'No, it's heavenly. Now, there's no need to rush. It's just after half past eight. The hairdresser will be here at ten, then we've got two hours before we have to be at St Margaret's. I'll make some breakfast while you have a bath and if I were you I'd just get into your undies and stick on a dressing gown. Then you can stay in that until everything's ready.'

'I'm not madly hungry.'

'Well, you must have something. Or you'll feel sick.'

Edith nodded and started to get up, sipping her tea as she did so. It was one of those moments when she was acutely aware of every movement of her body, even of the muscles in her face. Each word seemed to come from some other source than her own brain. She felt drugged, but in a bright, unsleepy way. No, not drugged, dazed – or even hypnotised. Am I hypnotised? she thought. Have I been mesmerised by all those unquestioned values I have sucked down since I was three? Have I lost myself in other people's ambitions? But then she thought of Charles, who was a nice man who loved her and of whom, by this time, she really was very fond, and of course, she thought of Broughton and of Feltham, the family's other estate in Norfolk, and most of all she thought of the flat in which she was now standing and the job in the estate agent's in Milner Street and the opportunities the one life offered and the exhausted, negligible opportunities of the other, and so thinking she threw back her head and strode towards the bathroom. Her father was just coming out. He smiled a rather wistful smile.

'Everything all right, Princess?' he said and she knew, even as he spoke, that he would probably have to stop calling her Princess, that it sounded suburban, and she made a resolution there and then that she would not let him stop calling her Princess. It was a resolution she broke almost at once.

'Fine. How about you?'

'Fine.'

The wedding was going to cost Kenneth Lavery a great deal of money. Although less than it might have done, as Lady Uckfield had been given permission for the reception to be held in St James's Palace. Nevertheless, and even because of this, the Laverys had both been determined that they would carry the entire bill for the rest. They had even eschewed the modern, rather charmless custom of expecting the bridesmaids' parents to pay for their dresses. Edith was, after all, their only daughter and they did not want there to be any suspicion that she came from a family which could not afford to pay its way. Mrs Lavery, living as she was a plot from a Barbara Cartland novel, had even wondered if they were not expected to make some sort of dowry settlement on Edith but although her husband had touched on this with Lord Uckfield it had not been taken up. Probably because the Uckfields did not want to embroil themselves in any corresponding legal entitlement. After all, as Lady Uckfield had pointed out before turning out the light, nowadays one could never be sure these things were *for ever*. Edith was grateful to her parents for ensuring she entered Broughton with her head held high, although again she was conscious of yet another of the million threads that pinned her, like Gulliver, to the ground.

She lay back in the bath and tried to conjure up her favourite mental image of herself presiding over charity boards, raising money for the disabled, curtseying to various Royalties before escorting them to her box on gala nights, visiting the sick in the village – she stopped. Do people still visit the sick in the village? She realised she had unconsciously clad herself in a crinoline in her daydreams. And she thought of Lady Uckfield and of what a model daughter-in-law she was going to be, how the day would come when they would all bless the hour that Edith came into their lives.

*   *   *

I arrived at St Margaret's at about twenty past ten to be handed my white carnation, stripped of course of the fern that the florist had so painstakingly arranged with it, and my list for the front pews. It was the expected combination of duchesses and nannies, with places marked for the tenants and staff at Broughton and, behind them, the tenants and staff at Feltham. From the Reigning Family we were to get the Princess Royal and the Kents, all of them, but not the Prince of Wales (a bit of a disappointment for Lady Uckfield, a tragedy for Mrs Lavery) as he was on a goodwill junket somewhere in the South Seas. Nor were we to welcome the Queen. I don't know why as I believe Her Majesty and Lady Uckfield got on well. Needless to say, I was not deputed to usher any of them, this honour going to Lord Peter Broughton, who nodded to me as I came in. I had not seen him since leaving Chez Michou as we had been given a choice of return flights and, having no City deadline to meet, I was still in bed when most of the party had set off. I had written to thank him and Henry but I had obviously said nothing of the debacle.

'I got your letter. You shouldn't have bothered.' The English always say you shouldn't have bothered to thank them when, of all races on earth, they are the most unforgiving when one does not. I smiled in reply. He pulled a face. 'God, I had a head the next day! I was in a meeting by eleven. I do not think I gave it my best.'

I couldn't remember what he did. Something financial, I assumed, although I have noticed of late that the brain standard of the City has been rising in inverse ratio to the fall of its social status. I wonder where this is going to leave people like Peter Broughton. 'You were very kind to lay it all on,' I said.

He nodded in turn, slightly awkwardly. 'I'm afraid Charles was a bit shirty.' I shrugged. 'The thing is, it seemed the most frightfully funny idea, d'you see? Henry and I went over with photographs and things and we'd even borrowed one of Edith's frocks ... She thought it'd be terrifically funny too, d'you see? She was a great sport about it, she even told Charles not to be silly ...' He tailed off rather lamely. Good for Edith, I thought, to come out of that ghastliness ahead. I hardly needed to point out that had she seen the act she would have been less sanguine. We could be sure that Charles had not told her exactly what he had found so offensive.

'I expect the boy doing it misunderstood his brief,' I said, borrowing Tommy Wainwright's line.

Lord Peter nodded furiously. 'That's it, exactly. I think the song was wrong, that was the trouble. That and Eric's idea of the jewel-box. I can see that wasn't too clever.'

I nodded, unsurprised at Eric's complicity. It was interesting, though predictable I suppose, that Edith's first enemy in the Broughton household should be someone of considerably lower rank than herself, who had made an infinitely greater leap in catching at his bride. 'I should forget about it,' I said. 'I'm sure Charles has.' I was actually sure that Charles had not, although I was pretty certain he would never refer to the incident again.

Of course, Edith made a lovely bride and the collection of familiar Royal and Society faces on the Broughton side of the aisle put a glamorous spin into the whole business, which I, for one, thoroughly enjoyed. Even the sermon seemed quite interesting. The Lavery side of the church was inevitably rather over-shadowed but Edith had managed to attract one or two of her new, media-friendly friends and her mother, desperate to keep face, had written to her third cousin, the present baronet, introducing herself and enclosing an invitation to the wedding. Consequently, this very ordinary solicitor who lived in an old vicarage near Swindon (the family's modest pile had gone two generations before), suddenly found himself in the front pew of a London wedding, staring at what seemed to be half the Royal Family a few feet away. Actually, because of St Margaret's custom of keeping an empty pew for the Speaker on the right-hand side of the aisle, this necessitated a kind of half-backwards squint but he soon got the hang of it. At any rate, he was delighted to be there and so was his ugly wife, although she, understanding these things better than her husband, retained an air of having done the Laverys a favour in agreeing to come. Which was, of course, quite true.

We had all been given special stickers to park on the gravel at the edge of the Mall so it was easier than usual to get to the reception. I had never got past the tables in the lower gallery of the Palace where, in those days, you could collect your badge for Ascot, so I was curious, as we stood in a long, slowly-moving, drinkless queue, to see what the state rooms had in store. We shuffled up the great staircase, past a suitably dissolute full-length of Charles II, through a small ante-room, sumptuously lined with dark tapestry, where we were at last given a glass of the inevitable champagne, and then into the first of the three huge, red, white and gold apartments. In the receiving line it was not Mrs Lavery, whom I had met many times, but Lady Uckfield who greeted me by name and to my surprise offered me a cheek to kiss.

'I saw you beavering away in church,' she said, using her habitual tone of sharing a naughty secret that only I would understand. 'What a happy day.'

'We've been jolly lucky with the weather.'

'I think we're jolly lucky all round.' With that she dismissed me by angling me towards her husband, who, needless to say, hadn't a clue who I was, and having shaken his hand, I wandered off into the throng. It was clear that Lady Uckfield was making an effort to be agreeable to me but it wasn't all that obvious as to why. Probably she wanted to make sure that the only friend of Edith's that Charles liked at all would be her ally. She meant to subvert any attempts of Edith's to set up a 'rival court' right from the start. This would ensure that if anyone had to do any adjusting it would be Edith, not her. I would not hazard a guess as to how conscious this was but I am fairly sure it was so. Just as I am sure that she was successful and that we all played our parts. From the start I was very taken by Lady Uckfield's ability to combine the kittenish with the autocratic and I do not think that where she was concerned I was ever a very useful friend for Edith.

I had hardly spoken to the bride in the line and I didn't really expect to get much of a chance to talk to her as I murmured and nodded my way through various chattering and kissing groups. David and Isabel were there of course, but I could see that they had not come to St James's Palace in order to spend their time talking to me so I let them get on with it and wandered into another huge, scarlet and gilded chamber, at right angles to the first. Large, full-length portraits, mostly of Stuarts, hung on chains against the stretched damask. I stopped beneath one, which, from the half-shut eyes and luscious *décolletage* I had taken for Nell Gwyn (who may not have been a Stuart but certainly served under them) so I was surprised to see from the plaque on the frame that the melting beauty was Mary of Modena, Queen of James VII and II.

Edith's voice behind me made me jump. 'What do you think of the show so far?'

'There's nothing like starting at the top,' I said.

'It seems rather fitting that my wedding should be celebrated in a Royal palace, traditional seat of the arranged marriage.'

I looked up at the heaving, painted bosom of the queen. 'I shouldn't think this one was very hard to arrange.'

Edith laughed. We were almost alone in the room for a minute and I had time to marvel at her beauty, now reaching the years of its zenith. She had chosen a dress in the style of the 1870s, with wide flounces and a bustle behind. It was of ivory silk with a tiny self-patterned sprig of flowers. What I assume was someone's mother's lace fell from her thick blonde hair, held there by a light, dazzling tiara, fashioned for a young girl, like a glistening diamond-studded cobweb, not one of those heavy metal plates made for dowagers to sport at the opera, which always look as if they belong in a Marx Brothers comedy. I imagine it was part of the Broughton trove.

'You'll come and visit us?' she said.

'If I'm asked.'

We stared at each other for a moment. 'We're going to Rome for a week, then on to Caroline and Eric in Mallorca.'

'That sounds nice.'

'Yes, it does, doesn't it? I'm not supposed to know but I do. I like Rome. I don't really know Mallorca. I gather Caroline takes a villa every year there so obviously they enjoy it.' She laughed again rather mirthlessly.

There didn't seem to be anything more to say as I wasn't prepared to comment on her melancholy outburst. The last thing I believe in is the deathbed confession. In this case she'd made her bed and was already lying on it. All that was left was to shut her eyes. Anyway, I can't say I was worried. Presumably, many brides, or grooms too for that matter, have a slight what-have-I-done? feeling at the reception.

I kissed her. 'Good luck,' I said. 'Telephone me when you get back.'

'I'm not going yet.'

'No, but I won't have another chance to talk to you.'

And so it proved. Charles came to fetch her to parade her past yet more of his unknown relations and I was left alone again. I wandered into the throne room, which opened out of the end of the first room we had entered. More red, more gilt, this time as a background for a splendid canopied and embroidered throne, and more paintings in chains, these ones Hanoverians. I was admiring the chimneypiece when a fat, red-faced man in his sixties nodded to me. We talked for a while about a painting of George IV by Lawrence that hung in the room, whether it was the original or a copy and so on, when he suddenly leaned towards me conspiratorially. 'Tell me,' he whispered hoarsely, 'are you a friend of the girl or are you one of us?'

I must confess I was momentarily stumped for words.

'Both, I hope,' said Lady Uckfield, approaching at a brisk pace.

I nodded to her for getting me off the hook and she introduced me to my companion, who turned out to be called Sir William Fartley, which nearly made me laugh out loud. He sauntered away as Lady Uckfield took my arm and strolled us both across to the windows.

'I hope you'll come down and see us again soon,' she said. 'I know Charles would like it.'

This was to tell me that Charles was prepared to have me as a friend and also to let me know that they, the family, saw no threat in my friendship with Edith. I thanked her and said I should be delighted. 'I don't suppose you shoot?'

'As a matter of fact I do.'

She was quite surprised. 'Do you? I thought theatre people never shot. I thought they were always terrific antis.'

I shrugged. 'Better death on the wing than in an abattoir is my feeling.'

'What a relief! I was thinking we were going to have to scratch around for some writers and talkers to amuse you. I know Edith thinks you're terribly bright.'

'That's nice.'

'But if you shoot you won't mind normal people.'

'Like Sir William Fartley. Can't wait.'

She laughed and pulled a face. 'Silly old fool but he only lives three miles away so there's nothing I can do.'

I commented inwardly that he was further away than the Eastons, that there were probably two or three hundred people a similar distance from Broughton who would cry out for an invitation and would never receive one but naturally I said nothing.

Lady Uckfield patted my hand. 'Seriously. You must come. I'll see to it.'

'I'd love to, but only if you promise not to ask any writers or talkers. I don't want to lose face in front of Edith.'

She smiled her conspiratorial smile and was gone about her duties.

It was all over quite soon after that. The lucky pair went off to change and we followed them out as a shining barouche landau carried them away. This rather mawkish detail had been specially arranged by Edith's father with the mistaken idea that it would lend glamour to the occasion. At any rate, when we all turned back we found that the Palace had been locked against us. The authorities had decreed that the day was over and there was nothing more to do but go home.

SEVEN

～

To Edith, as much as to anyone else who knew it, one of the oddest aspects of her marriage, at least in the context of the 1990s, was that she had never slept with Charles before their wedding night. It sounds quite remarkable but the fact remains that it was so. At first she had resisted his advances as she knew that he was definitely the type who did not respect in the morning the easy conquest of the night before and several dates had to have taken place before it was sufficiently established that she was a 'nice girl'. This went on for two or three months but when she had decided that it was just about safe to yield she found to her puzzlement that Charles seemed to have accepted the pattern of their relationship and that he did not apparently want more. He would kiss her, of course, and embrace her but without the deadly urgency that she had come to expect in these moments. Once when they were lying on the sofa in her parents' flat (Kenneth and Stella were in Brighton for the weekend) she had casually allowed her hand to slide across the front of his trousers but although she could feel a perfectly satisfactory erection beneath the fabric the gesture made him jump so sharply that she did not repeat it. And after he had asked her to marry him there didn't seem much point. After all, she wanted him whether or not they 'suited' between the sheets but, if they did not, might he be put off? So when, a few weeks before the wedding, he had suggested that they 'get away together' for a weekend she had murmured that she thought it better to wait, now it was so near, and not 'spoil it'. Charles had accepted this because although, being a man of his generation he had acquired a certain amount of sexual experience, deep in his subconscious he still believed that bride-material should enter the wedding-chamber chaste. Of course, Edith was not chaste in this sense but she decided that, if questioned, she would refer to 'an incident' when she had been very young which she didn't want to talk about. In actual fact she never had to as Charles seemed to be satisfied with the fact that this was *their* first time together and sensibly refused to enter into a competition with her past.

He had booked a room in the Hyde Park Hotel in Knightsbridge. The world knows that this establishment now forms part of the Mandarin chain and so, technically, the old name is defunct but the upper classes are slow to alter accepted nomenclature. To them it will be the Hyde Park Hotel at least until their children are in late middle age. The plan was to spend the wedding night there and then fly to Rome at noon the following day. Accordingly the barouche swept them up St James's, down Piccadilly past the Ritz, over Hyde Park Corner, and turned round in front of the Bowater House entrance to the park to deposit them on the steps of the hotel. As they bowled along, passers-by, tourists and Anglo-Saxons alike, turned to smile and even wave. Probably the connection between carriages and Royal occasions is fixed in the public Pavlovian consciousness. So that she might be undisappointing and because the brilliance of her new state filled her brain with a cloud of sparkling lights, Edith waved tentatively back. Charles, on the other hand, looked straight ahead as if somehow his candidacy for officer material was in question. She understood why. Charles was saddled with that most tedious of all English aristocratic affectations, the need to create the illusion that you are completely unaware of any of your privileges. That cool insouciance, so chic in theory so crashingly boring in practice, was to ruin many occasions in the future for the pair as Edith suspected, looking at the frozen profile beside her. But this time at least the drive did not last long, certainly not long enough for Edith. Barely fifteen minutes after they had left the reception they were in the foyer of the hotel. It was still only about half past five and Edith wasn't absolutely clear what happened next.

She thought of suggesting that they stay downstairs and have some tea but since this would betray a total lack of urgency to be alone with Charles (that she was afraid she was feeling) she rejected the idea. They were shown into the Bridal Suite, which they had not requested but was theirs anyway – the difference in price being compliments of the management, following the age-old principle 'To them that hath shall be given' – and there they found their luggage as well as flowers and fruit and more of the bottomless supply of champagne. Then the door shut and they were alone. Married. They stared at each other in silence.

Edith felt a slight tremor of panic as the reality of seeing this man more or less every day for the remainder of her life hit her. What on earth were they going to talk about?

Charles pointed at the bottle. 'Shall I open this?' he said.

'Honestly I don't think I could. I'm swimming in it already.' She paused. 'I think I'll have a bath.'

She started to undress as casually as she could with Charles lying on the bed watching her but at the last moment her nerve failed and, still with her bra and pants on, she snatched her dressing gown out of her suitcase and dashed into the bathroom.

When she came out, half an hour later, Charles was still lying on the bed, reading a newspaper. He had taken off his coat, waistcoat and tie as well as his shoes and socks, and something about the slightly studied relaxation of his pose told Edith that her hour had come. She strolled over to the bed and lay down next to him, naked beneath the gown, and pretended to read the paper over his shoulder.

'Happy?' he said, without raising his eyes.

'Mmm,' she replied, wondering how long it was going to take him to get to it. Now that the moment was here, she was suddenly rather anxious. She felt the need to reassure herself about the physical attraction between them. This, after all, was the side of their relationship that had nothing to do with ambition or even shared interest. It was the sexual conjunction that, at this point at least, she was determined was going to be the only one she would know for the rest of her natural life.

After what seemed an eternity, Charles folded the paper and turned to her. With a deadly earnestness and in absolute silence (which lasted throughout), he started to kiss her as he inexpertly unfastened her dressing gown. She responded as well as she could, trying not to lead. This time when she touched his penis, although he still started like a frightened colt, he didn't actually pull away. And so they lay there, fondling each other through their garments until Charles deemed a suitable period had passed and then he sat up, still in absolute silence, and removed his shirt, trousers and underpants. Edith shrugged off the gown and waited. Charles had quite a good figure, in that he was muscled and covered without being fat, but he had one of those English bodies, white, faintly freckled skin, with a little ginger pubic hair around his groin and none on his chest. His beaky nose and crinkly, public-school hair looked somehow odd on top of an undressed body, as if he had been born in a double-breasted suit and being nude was too raw to be natural. In truth, he seemed more skinned than naked.

Still without a word he turned back to her, the same furious intensity in his face, and, avoiding direct eye contact, he started to kiss her while he planted his right hand against her vagina. Once it was in place, he began to massage her with a kind of dry pumping action, which reminded her of someone blowing up a lilo. She groaned a bit by way of encouragement. He didn't seem to need more as suddenly he heaved himself over between her legs, fumbled himself into her, thrust away a few times – no more than six at the outside – and then, with a terrific gasp to tell her that it was *now* (which she countered with some cries and pants of her own), he collapsed on top of her. The whole business, from the moment he folded the paper, had taken perhaps eight minutes. Ah, thought Edith.

'Thank you, darling.' One of Charles's more irritating habits was always to thank Edith after sex, as if she had just brought him a cup of tea. Of course, at this point, she did not know it was habitual.

She thought of responding, 'Oh, but thank *you*,' then decided it was too like people waving at each other through a hotel door so she settled for simply saying, 'Darling...' in a sort of misty way and kissing him on the neck. He had rolled off her by now and she was feeling a bit chilly lying there but moving seemed the wrong thing as this was all constituting a 'very important moment' for Charles and she had no intention of spoiling it. She did not allow herself any review of the love-making – if that was what they had just been through. It was, after all, early days, and she was beginning to suspect that Charles, for all his *savoir faire* with waiters, was not very confident when it came to the more private areas. At least he seemed to feel that something momentous had taken place, even if her body had never left the station, so the episode surely rated as a success rather than a failure. That said, she did catch herself briefly hoping that things would improve with practice.

They dined in the hotel, more to avoid being spotted and congratulated by any of their friends (who never dine in hotels except with Americans who are staying there) than for any particular enthusiasm for the *cuisine de la maison* and then went to bed around eleven. They had a repeat performance of the afternoon's activity and then rolled over to sleep. Edith stared at the ceiling, contemplating the oddness of life. Here she was with this man, whom she hardly knew when she really thought about it, asleep, naked, beside her. She pondered that central truth, which must have struck many brides from Marie Antoinette to Wallis Simpson, that whatever the political, social or financial advantages of a great marriage, there comes a moment when everyone leaves the room and you are left alone with a stranger who has the legal right to copulate with you. She was not at all sure that she had fully negotiated this simple fact until then.

The thought had not left her when she awoke – the first time for a good long while that she had awakened next to anyone – and she was rather relieved when Charles made it clear, slightly sheepishly, that he was not a 'morning man'. Things eased when they began to discuss the wedding, the various near-dramas, which guests they disliked, who was unhappily married, who was going broke. Of course, thought Edith, this is what we're going to talk about, the things we've done together, and the longer we're married, the more shared experiences we'll have to discuss. She was just comforting herself with these ruminations when Charles lapsed into silence. Not for the last time, he had run dry. There was a knock at the door. A waiter came in wheeling a trolley of breakfast.

'Good morning, my lord,' he said to Charles and then, as he approached the bed with a tray, 'Good morning, my lady.'

Oh well, thought Edith, things could be worse.

Given the fact that their first hours together had not been an overwhelming thrill, it was perhaps a little surprising that the trip to Rome, by contrast, went very well. They stayed at the Hotel de la Ville, quite near the top of the Spanish Steps, and just down from the Villa Medici. Rome is a very beautiful city anyway and this was of course Edith's first experience of being milady'd and contessa'd everywhere she went, which was amusing (though she knew enough not to show it) and a solid reminder of why she was in this spot. The food was delicious and there was plenty to see and consequently to talk about and so as they sat in the Piazza Navona eating under the stars or strolled down the fountain-decked walks of the Villa d'Este out at Tivoli, Edith began to feel that she had after all made a good choice and that the rich and rewarding life of her imaginings really did lie ahead.

During their stay Charles started to talk about Broughton and

Feltham in an affectionate, detailed way that was new to her. Perhaps he had thought that before she had actually, so to speak, *become* a Broughton she would not be interested. He loved his homes and his cares and since this was all fitting in along the lines of her pre-nuptial fantasies, she loved him for it. She was able to respond to his enthusiasm with an unfeigned enthusiasm of her own. To her delight, she discovered that he was a bit rusty on the history of the family itself. Here was her task! She saw herself lovingly cataloguing the furniture and pictures, entertaining ancient aunts and writing up memoirs of long, hot Edwardian summers at Broughton, bringing down and cleaning forgotten pictures in the attics of some particularly amusing ancestor. She was interested in both history and gossip – what could be better qualifications? It is true that the sex did not improve dramatically and the format never varied but once Charles was less nervous with her it did at least take a bit longer. Altogether, as they boarded the aeroplane for Madrid, the first leg of their journey to Mallorca, Edith and Charles were able to stare into each other's eyes in a deliberate imitation of two people who were as 'happy as newly-weds'.

EIGHT

~

At Palma, where they surged out of the ticket hall surrounded by what looked and sounded like the entire supporters' club of Wolverhampton Wanderers, they were hailed by a wrinkled cockney with a face like beaten leather and red nylon shorts. He was, he explained, Eric's 'driver' and had come to take them to the villa. Charles was slightly put out at not being met in person – Edith would learn that like many apparently easy-going grandees his insecurity manifested itself if he ever felt that he was being treated like an 'ordinary person' despite his often saying that this was exactly what he wanted. She, herself, was simply glad to be out of the airport and in a car and gradually her relief transmitted itself to him. In the end he forgave the Chases for staying at home: the drive consisted of two and a half hours of dry scrub and shanties as they crossed the centre of the island. Edith had never visited Mallorca before and had not known what to expect. But she realised on looking out of the car window that the images in her mind had consisted of various combinations of Monte Carlo and Blackpool, not the scratch farming and dust of the plains of Salamanca. As they approached Caloratjada, however, the huge concrete hotels of her imaginings began to materialise together with the crowds – mainly respectable but with the hovering hint of kiss-me-quick hats – and all the sights and smells of the Beach Holiday made their familiar and comforting appearance.

The villa itself was a large, white, modern affair constructed around a kind of hill/courtyard, with vast tiled terraces looking out across the bay. There was a private jetty, which was apparently more for swimming than for tethering boats, and meant that there was no need for the villa's inhabitants to use the crowded, sandy beach that launched the tourist swimmers into the sea from a point a few hundred yards to the left of their position. Across the water, the smart houses of the

Mallorcin could be glimpsed through their modest curtaining of trees and beyond there was the wide, blue ocean. Edith and Charles stood admiring the view, as a pin-figure far below them on the jetty waved and started to run up the steps. A few minutes later Caroline appeared. They were kissed and congratulated and, in turn, they admired the villa.

'Isn't it fabulous? It belongs to some client of Eric's so we've got a frightfully good rate. It's far cheaper than the one we had last year and it's twice the size. Needless to say, we're being used as an absolute boarding-house all summer long.'

Charles frowned slightly. 'I thought it was just going to be us this week.'

'I know. So did I. But then Peter rang because this was the only week he could do. And Jane and Henry suddenly said they could come after all. And then one of Eric's business people appeared with his wife.' Caroline momentarily wrinkled her nose. 'Apparently Eric had asked them and forgotten all about it. Wasn't it frightful? Anyway, they're here now and they seem to have forgiven us.'

'You mean they're all here now? This week?'

'This minute. They're coming up to change for dinner even as we speak. Has anyone shown you your room? You've got the best one so you mustn't grumble.'

Charles threw himself on the bed in what Edith could only describe as a 'pet'. 'Christ! I don't know why we didn't just go to Trafalgar Square and set up a tent.'

Edith lay down next to him. 'Oh, darling, it doesn't matter. I'm sure everyone just does what they want anyway. We'll be able to push off by ourselves.' Actually she was feeling rather guilty as when Caroline was speaking she, Edith, suddenly realised that she was rather relieved to discover it wasn't just going to be the four of them after all. From what she knew of him she didn't like Eric much, Caroline she found rather intimidating and she had to admit that she was feeling just the teeniest bit talked-out with Charles. 'It'll be much easier later when we've done more together,' she said to herself but it was with a faintly sinking feeling that she realised she could already predict what his opinion would be on more or less any given topic. As a sort of private game with herself, she had begun to introduce odd items into the conversation, like psycho synthesis or the Dalai Lama, in the hope of catching herself out and being surprised by something he said. So far she hadn't dropped a point.

They met the rest of the party when they assembled that evening on the top terrace. Edith had been nervous of Caroline during the courting months for the simple reason that Caroline was a good deal more intelligent than Charles, and Edith was half afraid that she would try to put him, if not off her, at least on his guard. This may well have been true but Caroline, snobbish and egocentric as she was, was not essentially bad-hearted. Now that Edith was her sister-in-law she was determined to get on with her and she was equally determined that Charles, of whom she was extremely, if rather parentally, fond, should have a happy stay. All this Edith saw in the genuine smiles and the slightly touching arrangements of festive nibbles and champagne on ice as they walked across the sitting room and out through the glass doors to join the others. All the women wore expensive cocktail, rather than evening, frocks and all the men were in open-necked shirts. They looked oddly mismatched, like a bad hand in Happy Families. Jane Cumnor was the most over-dressed in strapless black moiré, but she held no threat any more for Edith who was quite content in off-the-shoulder cotton. Since they had last met properly she had breached Jane's citadel and Edith was anyway the prettier woman. Their relationship had subtly altered overnight, a fact of which Jane was quite as aware as Edith. She sidled over to plant a lipsticky kiss on the cheek of the bride. Henry lumbered across and pushed his face against hers. In his brightly coloured summer clothes he resembled a nineteenth-century bathing-machine. Edith wondered if his shirt might suddenly open to reveal a timorous swimmer in stripes. Caroline raised her glass: 'Welcome to the family.'

'Yes,' said Eric, who was standing behind the others nearer the edge of the terrace. 'Well done, Edith.'

The others noticed but ignored his tone and raised their glasses to the name, making the salutation sound more normal. Edith smiled and she and Charles drank their thanks and everyone sat down.

The moonlit sea glittered behind their heads as they sprawled and chattered on their cushioned wicker, champagne in their hands, the women in their *couture* dresses, diamonds twinkling in their ears. As she lay there, curled up against the squashy Liberty prints, more spectator than participant, Edith found herself warmed by the enveloping luxury of privilege. All the years of her growing up she had wanted not just to avoid being a have-not but to be an emphatic *have* and now, at last, just at the moment when she had begun to face the possibility of failure, here she was, living her dream. This gaggle of lords and millionaires was a sample of her set from now on, this exotic setting the first of many. Just as a driver can see distant mountains across a desert far before him and then realise that he is up in those very mountains without being aware of their coming nearer, so Edith pondered with wonder her progress from the respectable *haut bourgeois* life of Elm Park Gardens and Milner Street to this cross between an American soap-opera and a novel by Laclos.

The first evening passed uneventfully enough. Edith knew everyone there except for a lacklustre blonde who seemed to have come with Peter and Eric's friends, the Watsons. Of these the husband, Bob, was dull and rather common but the wife, Annette, though also common, was pretty and funny and Edith warmed to her. She had been a model and an actress in the early eighties before her marriage and was full of hilarious anecdotes about various Roman epics and Spanish westerns she had appeared in. She babbled away through dinner, which was served in the loggia/dining room that opened onto the courtyard, and saved Edith from the Name Exchange, which she knew was all she could expect from the others.

Charles was more non-committal about their fellow guests. 'Well, she's got plenty to say for herself, I'll give her that,' was his only comment as he turned the light out.

'I like her. She's funny.'

'Don't speak too soon.' In some mysterious way she felt reprimanded, although his tone had not been angry, and it was with a vague feeling of apprehension, like a child who expects a beating the next day, that Edith lay back on the pillow. Nor was her thought-train interrupted before sleep set in as it was the first night, since their marriage, that they did not make love.

The next morning Edith woke late and found herself alone. With a delicious, almost tangible sense of well-being she rang for breakfast as she had been bidden to do and settled back into her habitual review of the life that lay ahead. The maid arrived with her tray and told her that the others had already eaten and were down on the jetty so as soon as she was ready she put on a bathing suit, took up a towel and set off down the steep paved stairs that were cut into the rock below the villa. She could see the Chases, the Cumnors and Charles, but there was no sign of the rest of the party. On the jetty itself she waved a hello to everyone, spread out her towel and lay down, letting the soft, woolly warmth of the southern sun wash over her body. Charles threw himself down next to her, spraying her with drops of sea and gave her a salty kiss. 'Good morning, darling.' She smiled and kissed him back.

'What shall we do today? Just lie here and drink up the sun?'

Caroline answered her. 'We thought we might go into Calaratjada for lunch and then the Franks have asked us for tea. You're all included.'

'Who are the Franks?'

'They're this rather extraordinary family who are fearfully rich and they have a collection of sculpture that apparently must not be missed.'

'Why are they so rich and how do you know them?'

'To the first, God knows. Something to do with Franco so we'd better not ask, and to the second, we don't, but Mummy's godmother to one of their nephews in Rome and she let them know we were going to be here.'

Edith lay back and closed her eyes. This great network, this web that reached far beyond national boundaries, that crossed seas and mountain ranges, need not threaten her any more because now she was part of it. And soon, in Vienna or Dublin or Rome, people would be saying, 'I saw Edith Broughton when I was in London. She says they might be in New York in September . . .' and this would be greeted by some member of the Inner Circle saying, 'Edith? How is she?' or better still, 'I'm so mad about Edith. Aren't you?' and thus would be excluded all those other people in all those rooms in Vienna or Dublin or Rome who did *not* know Edith Broughton; and they would feel the poorer and the more middle-class for it, which would have been the intention of the name-droppers who would then go away satisfied that they had once again asserted their caste. In all this Edith would play her part by being the kind of person it is hard to meet unless you are in her set. And just for a moment on this particular morning, with the sun caressing her eyelids and the children shouting on the distant beach, Edith pondered the ultimate purpose of this endless raising and lowering of barriers.

There was a terrific thud near her and she opened her eyes to see the awe-inspiring sight of Henry Cumnor stretching out to sunbathe. If anything he looked even larger without his clothes, like a seaside postcard captioned 'Where's my little willy?'

'What about the others? We can't all go to these wretched people, can we?' He spoke undirected, straight up into the air, so that he should not have the inconvenience of moving more than his lips.

Caroline shrugged. 'I don't see why not. I said there were lots of us.' She had that curiously English upper-class belief that whatever the occasion, however much people have put themselves out, even when, as now, total strangers extend their hospitality as a duty, still she, Lady Caroline Chase, was doing them a favour. It is impossible for such people to conceive that they have not necessarily honoured a house by entering it. Consequently, because of this sense of having blessed her hosts by her presence, Caroline made no effort whatsoever with anyone outside her own crowd and despite being an intelligent woman could be a crushingly boring guest. Something of which neither she nor the many others of her kind who are just like her have any suspicion. 'We'll ask them when they come down,' she said.

'How long are they staying?' said Jane, propping herself up on her elbows and reaching for the oil.

'Who? Peter or the others?'

'Oh, not darling Peter. "Bob" and "Annette".' Jane spoke their names in inverted commas, distancing herself from them to make it clear to her listeners that she did not consider them as ordinary members of the house-party but rather as strange specimens of an alien culture. This was carefully judged.

'Tuesday or Wednesday, I think.' Caroline looked over to Eric who nodded and wrinkled his nose. He was quite clear about which team he wished to be on.

'Crikey,' said Henry. 'Who's in the listening chair this evening?' They all laughed.

Edith felt an irresistible urge to tear up her membership of the Club. 'Is this Annette you're talking about?' she said in a tone of feigned disbelief. 'How funny you are. I really like her.'

Henry was unfazed. 'Well, you can sit next to her at dinner. I hope you're ready to discuss her film career *ad nauseam*.'

Edith smiled. 'Why? What would you rather talk about? The people you all know in Shropshire?' She lay back with her smile still intact and her eyes closed, relishing the awkward silence like a naughty schoolgirl.

'I'm not often *in* Shropshire, actually.' Henry rolled away from her, bloated and breathless, like a beached whale far from the water.

'I'm going for a swim,' said Charles.

They lunched late on paella with too much squid in it in an open-air restaurant overlooking the harbour with its bobbing flotilla of yachts and then set off in two cars for the Franks's house, which lay outside the town on the edge of the sea and appeared to be entirely surrounded, on the land-locked frontier at any rate, by a high stone wall, topped with broken glass. The gates were not gates but rather iron doors, which swung open automatically when they identified themselves and then clanged shut, only just missing the rear fender of the second vehicle. 'Well, they're obviously not expecting two cars,' said Annette with a laugh.

Undaunted, Caroline, who was driving the first car with Edith, Annette and Henry, ploughed on through the enormous, empty pleasure gardens. Tantalising glimpses through the trees of Henry Moores and Giacomettis flashed past until rounding a huge clump of rhododendra they came to a fork in the road. One led apparently up to a nineteenth-century castle that was perched on the highest point of the estate, which Edith had assumed was their destination, while the other, incredibly, pointed the way to another house, as large as the first only modern, which had been built at the water's edge. It was too low, with its balconies thrusting out barely higher than the waves, to be seen from the road.

'Which one do we go to?' said Edith.

'The bottom one. Mrs Frank likes to be near the sea.'

'What happens up on the hill?'

Caroline looked suitably vague. 'I think it's mainly for the grandchildren.'

'Blimey O'Reilly,' said Annette and Edith noted with interest that no one else would acknowledge the strangeness, the orgiastic luxury that they were witnessing. She was beginning to understand it is a point of honour in that world that one must never be overawed by any display of wealth, no matter how fabulous. To register that riches on any scale are not routine, even mundane, is to risk being 'middle-class' – a sector of society to which many of them spend most of their lives proving to no one in particular that they do not belong. There are exceptions to this rule. It is possible to exclaim, 'How simply lovely!' but it is done in such a way as to show generosity rather than awe on the part of the speaker. Better yet, 'My dear, how *grand*!' This in a tone to show that the decoration, menu, whatever, is excessive and verging perilously close to vulgar. Lady Uckfield was particularly adept at crushing with smiling enthusiasm. These are hard skills for the novice though and Edith did well not to attempt them.

A white-coated footman took the party through the gleaming marble rooms out on to the terrace where Mrs Frank, a sun-beaten, robust figure, reclined in a brightly coloured cotton sarong, chunky bracelets bouncing and rattling against her sinewy, masculine arms. She waved them all over towards her.

Caroline took charge. 'How do you do?' she said lazily. 'I'm Caroline Chase.'

She started to indicate the other members of the party, deliberately pausing a fraction of a second before the three non-Broughton guests, Bob, Annette and Peter's girl, as if to demonstrate to Mrs Frank that they were not in the first circle and she need not therefore bother with them. Mrs Frank took the signal and welcomed the outsiders with a perceptibly cooler smiling nod than the one she reserved for the principals.

'You must be the bride,' she said, rising and taking Edith by the arm to lead them back into the house. Edith smelled the strong musk of her scent and watched the leathery creases move around the thin, scarlet-greased mouth. 'How are you enjoying Mallorca?'

'We only arrived last night. It seems lovely so far.' She smiled back into the glassy, bored eyes of her grinning hostess.

'You must let us entertain you while you're here. Tell me, how is darling Googie?'

'She's fine. She and Tigger are in Scotland.' As the words came out, Edith realised that this was the first time she had spoken these ludicrous nicknames out loud. Before her marriage she had privately determined to address her in-laws as Harriet and John, but already the unspoken urgings of intimacy, of club-membership, which rippled through Mrs Frank, had made her break her vow because the truth was that whatever she might say to her friends, she did not want to be the 'foreign' daughter-in-law. She did not want people to sympathise with Lady

Uckfield that Charles had not done better. She wanted her mother-in-law to be congratulated on her, Edith's, brilliance, on her taste, on her charm, on her entertaining. And so Edith learned the first lesson of why England has had no revolutions, of what has emasculated so many careers from Edward IV's queen to Ramsay MacDonald. Namely that the way to deal with a troublesome outsider is to let him in, to make him a convert with a convert's zeal and in no time he will be *plus Catholique que le Pape*. Learning this lesson did not reduce Edith's resentment of the forces that taught it to her but she had another heady moment of realising she was now a member of the Gang. It made her feel powerful. She turned and smiled at Charles.

A tour of the sculptures had been planned and the party set off. As they came out of the front door they were approached by a young, rather stringy woman, a reduced, ferret-sized version of Mrs Frank. She had obviously just been playing tennis and carried a slightly oversized racket in front of her, covering her face, half shield half fan. Their hostess introduced her as her niece, Tina. Unlike her aunt the girl was painfully shy. She fell into step with them as she was quite clearly commanded to do but mutely, only muttering miserable, whispered answers if she was directly addressed.

They passed a swimming pool, cut into a small cliff above the sea, and Edith heard Annette asking about the terracotta vases that surrounded it, apparently continually filling it with faintly steaming water.

'They are Roman,' said Tina almost inaudibly. 'My uncle had them brought up from a wreck off the coast near here.'

'And now they're plumbed in?'

'What is "plumbed in" excuse me?'

Charles cut off Annette rather irritably. 'She means that now they're used to feed the pool.'

'Yes. With sea water.'

'Sea water? *Warmed* sea water?'

Tina nodded. 'It's much better for you, no? We have another pool with clear water but I think this is good, no?'

Annette was silent for a while. She was clearly beginning to agree with the others – that she was out of her depth. The group had stopped on a terrace dripping with bougainvillea where a large male torso by Rodin stood on a marble plinth. They murmured and admired. Mrs Frank turned to Caroline and started to enquire about various mutual friends. She appeared to resent the fact that she had not been asked to Charles's wedding, as many of her queries ended by an assumption that 'they must have been at the reception', and time and again Caroline was forced to admit that they had been. The names rippled out as they climbed from terrace to terrace, against the deep azure blue of the Mediterranean sky. Had they seen the Esterhazys? the Polignacs? the Devonshires? the Metternichs? the Frescobaldis? Names torn from history books, names that Edith knew from studies of Philip II of Spain, or the Risorgimento, or the French Revolution, or the Congress of Vienna. And yet here they were, stripped of any real significance. They had simply become court cards, rich court cards, in the game of Name Exchange. These were high stakes indeed and Edith noticed with some amusement that Jane Cumnor and Eric had dropped back with Tina, no doubt anxious to avoid the left-out feeling that it pleased them to inflict on others. Caroline and Charles were unfazed. It was clear that whatever the extent of the Frank millions they could match name for name and top them too. And so the afternoon passed in a litany of duchesses intoned against a background of art enshrined by money. An hour and three quarters after setting out they were back at the modern palace-by-the-sea.

On the terrace a tea had been set out 'English-style', that is to say 'American-hotel-style' and three white-coated footmen waited to serve it. Mrs Frank led them to their chairs. Peter's girl, Bob and Annette were thoroughly squashed by this time and secretly longing to regain the villa and turn this flattening experience into a funny story. Eric brought up the rear, red-faced with his exertions and clearly irritated that his social ignorance had excluded him from the conversation that had revolved around his wife for most of the afternoon. He dumped down onto a *chaise* next to Edith and seized a proffered cup.

Mrs Frank turned her attention back to the bride. 'Tell me, was Hilary Weston at the wedding? Someone said she was stuck in Canada.'

Eric looked up with a snort. 'No good asking Edith, is it, old girl? You'll have to wait until she's done a bit more training.'

Edith ignored him. By some merciful providence it so happened that she had spoken to Mrs Weston for quite a time at the reception. She thanked her patron saint as she spoke chattily across Eric making no reference to him. 'No, she was there. Galen was in Florida and couldn't get back. I suppose that's what they were thinking of.'

Mrs Frank nodded, casting a slightly strange look at Eric. 'She does so much! I feel like a sloth when I think of her.' She moved on. Edith had passed.

Eric lay back and looked at her: 'Well done. Ten out of ten.'

She stared back at him, holding every inch of gained ground. 'Do you know Hilary?'

'I know her as well as you do,' said Eric, and stood up to join Caroline at the other end of the terrace. This interchange was oddly refreshing to Edith because it established beyond any doubt that Eric was her enemy in the family circle. There was no pretence necessary any longer and, best of all, in their first round, Edith had won.

She was singing in the shower when Charles came in to change for dinner later that evening. He smiled. 'You seem very happy. Did you enjoy yourself today? What a collection! What a place!' Even in these circles amazement is not forbidden in private between consenting adults and Charles clearly felt he had been unimpressed for long enough.

'I'll say. And yes, I am happy.' She turned off the tap and kissed him, standing there wet and naked.

The next few minutes, indeed the rest of the evening, were as agreeable as any she had known with Charles and it was with a sense of victory and well-being that she climbed into bed that night.

Charles turned to her. 'I gather the Franks want to give us a dinner before we go.'

She pulled a slight face. 'Oh dear. I suppose we have to?'

'Come on, darling,' said Charles. 'It's good of them and they're not that bad.'

'The old girl's not that bad but the niece is a nightmare.'

He laughed. 'I thought she was rather sweet. We must be kind.'

Edith propped herself up on her elbows beside him. 'Why is it that when someone like Annette is talkative and funny you all cold-shoulder her and wrinkle your noses behind her back and yet with Tina Frank, who must be the most boring and inconsequential young woman I have ever met, you make excuses and pretend that she's a dear?'

'I don't know what you mean.'

'Yes, you do, Charles.' She felt oddly confident, almost breezy. For the first time since her marriage she began to sense that she really was Lady Broughton. She had managed things well and according to the ancient tradition she was 'entitled to her own opinions'. She continued,

85

smilingly severe. 'You know very well. And I'll tell you the answer. Annette does not know the people we know and Tina does and Tina has a hundred million besides. I don't know, darling, doesn't it ever make you wonder? Just a bit?' Edith was feeling her oats. She smiled at her husband quizzically, shaking her head slightly, imagining how charming her hair must look, rippling against her neck.

Charles stared at her. 'Who are all these people that you and Tina Frank know?' he said sourly and turned out the light.

PART TWO

~

Forte-Piano

NINE

~

I did not see a great deal of Edith in the months after she had returned
from her honeymoon although they were in London from time to time.
She did not apparently care for her mother-in-law's lair in Cadogan
Square but they used Charles's little flat in Eaton Place and occasionally
they would come up for a party or a show. I ran into them at a couple
of dinners and I was asked for a drink with a few others in their tiny
second-floor sitting room one day in October but there wasn't much of
an opportunity for talk. Edith looked happy enough and had already
begun to acquire that patina of the privileged, the faint, touch-me-not
aura of *luxe* that marks such people apart from us mortals, and I was
amused to trace the beginnings of an *hauteur* starting to obliterate the
lucky girl from Fulham.

I didn't see them at all in the build-up to Christmas and I was just
beginning to feel myself drifting out of their circle when I received a
letter tucked into a card, not from Edith but from Charles, asking me
for a day's shooting in January. It was to be a Friday so I was asked for
dinner and the night on the Thursday and, since nothing further was
specified, I was presumably intended to vanish after the shoot to make
way for the arrival of Saturday's guests. The lateness of the invitation
meant that someone had chucked, but it was no less attractive for that
and I knew (for once) that I was going to be free on the date in
question. I had already been booked to be villain-of-the-week in one of
those endless boy-and-girl-detective series, which was due to start five
days after the date proposed so I wrote back accepting and received,
almost by return, directions by road or rail. These told me which train
to be on if that was how I would be travelling or alternatively to arrive
at the house at about six o'clock.

I enjoy shooting. This I know is as difficult for one's kind-hearted
London theatrical friends to understand as it is easy for the country-

89

bred fraternity but I do not propose to launch into a defence of blood sports since I have never encountered anyone of either opinion who could be swayed. While I must say that there does not seem much logic in people gaily eating battery-processed food and objecting to conservation-conscious game-keepers, still I accept that there is not necessarily a logical basis for all or even any of one's feelings. At all events, at that time in my life, most of my sport had been of the country shoot variety and so it was with a sense of pleasurable anticipation that I set off for what promised to be a real, Edwardian *Grand Battu*.

I knew the way well enough, as I had often been down for weekends with the Eastons, but getting out of London to the South can be a nightmare and so I was in the habit of leaving time for hold-ups. On this occasion, I had not allowed for the fact that I was making the journey on Thursday instead of Friday and so, after a comparatively free run, I arrived at Broughton not much after half past five. The butler who went by the unlikely name of Jago told me that Lady Uckfield and Lady Broughton were in the yellow drawing room finishing a committee meeting of some sort.

Having no desire to join in – the committees one is forced to attend are bad enough – I settled into a surprisingly comfortable velvet-and-gilt William Kent armchair in the Marble Hall. I didn't have very long to wait before the door opened to release some of the members, muttering fawning farewells to Edith who was in the process of showing them out. She broke away.

'Hello,' she said. 'I didn't know you were here.'

'I'm rather early so I thought I'd wait instead of coming in to spoil your fun.'

She sagged her shoulders with a comic sigh. 'Some fun!' she said. 'Come and have a cup of stewed tea.' Ignoring the nods and smiles of the departing ones, she led the way back into the room. They did not object to this treatment. Far from it. The net result of her cutting them in order to greet me was simply to make them include me in their deferential smiles as they sidled towards the staircase. I imagine they thought that I too had been touched by the golden wand.

The remaining members of the committee, the usual collection of provincial intellectuals, tightly permed councillors and farmers mad with boredom, were in the final stages of leaving. Some of them had that dilatory manner of collecting their things together, which betrays a resolve to 'catch' somebody before they go. The prey that most of the lingerers were after was, of course, Lady Uckfield, who was ensconced in a pretty, buttoned chair by the chimneypiece, surrounded by admirers. A few of the aspirants, disconcerted by the competition, made do with five minutes of Edith and left. I approached my hostess, who rose to greet me with a kiss, which was a kind of signal to the entourage that the audience was over.

'Goodbye, Lady Uckfield,' said a black councillor in a baggy artist's smock, 'and thank you.'

'No, thank *you*.' Lady Uckfield spoke with her usual intimate urgency. 'I gather you're doing the most *marvellous* things down in Cramney. I hear it's simply *buzzing*. I can't *wait* to come and see for myself.'

Her companion beamed, shedding his Socialism on the spot. 'We will be most glad to see you there.' He retreated, wreathed in smiles.

'Where's Cramney?' I said.

Lady Uckfield shrugged. 'Some ghastly little place in Kent. Do you want some tea?'

By the time I made it to my room, my things had been unpacked and my evening shirt, tie, socks and cummerbund lay waiting for me. There was, however, no sign of my clean underpants. I hunted around through various drawers and was just in the process of searching under the bed when I heard a voice behind me. 'What *can* you be looking for?' I turned and saw Tommy Wainwright standing in the doorway that connected my room, aka the Garden Room, with its larger neighbour, the Rose Velvet Room, where Tommy was billeted. Actually, despite these impressive titles, the chambers themselves were rather small, having been squeezed into a sort of mezzanine floor at one side of the house. They had been created by the architect as part of an arrangement to provide a score of secondary bedrooms while only messing up one end facade of the house. Consequently, despite the fragrant names, these chambers overlooked the stable yard, had eight-foot ceilings, and faced north.

We hunted around for my missing undergarment for a bit, then gave up, abandoning it to its fate. Presumably, to this day, a rather old pair of pants is still wedged at the back of some drawer in the Garden Room of Broughton Hall. Tommy retreated to his chamber and returned with a small bottle of Scotch and two tooth glasses. 'Essential equipment for hotels and house-parties,' he said, and poured us both a slug.

'Are they mean with the booze?' I asked. I have often been surprised at the fantastic discomfort and deprivation the grand English are prepared to put their friends (and total strangers) through, particularly in my youth. I've been shown into bathrooms that could just about manage a cold squirt of brown water, bedrooms with doors that don't shut, blankets like tissue, and pillows like rocks. I have driven an hour cross-country to lunch with some grand relations of my father, who gave me one sausage, two small potatoes and twenty-eight peas. Once, during a house-party for a ball in Hampshire, I was so cold that I ended up piling all my clothes, with two threadbare towels, onto the bed and then holding all this together with a worn square of Turkish carpet – the only bit of floor-covering in the room. When my hostess woke me the next day, she made no comment on the fact that I was sleeping in a sort of webbing sarcophagus and clearly could not have been less interested in whether I had ever shut my eyes. When one thinks of the Edwardians who revelled in luxury it seems odd that their grandchildren should be so impervious to it. Recently I have detected that the comfort demanded by new money is effecting a slow improvement in the houses of the *anciens riches* but, heavens, what a time it's taken.

Tommy shook his head in answer to my question. 'No, no. They're not mean at all. Not a bit of it. Lord U chucks it down everyone's throat. It's just too complicated to try and get a dressing drink.'

We sat and gossiped for a bit and I asked if Tommy had seen a lot of the Broughtons.

He shook his head. 'Not really. They're always down here. I must say, I'm quite surprised that Edith is content to coddle the village and give away prizes without taking a breather but the fact is they're hardly in London at all.'

I too found this slightly unlikely. Particularly as the young couple were still living in the big house with Charles's parents. There had been plans to renovate one of the farm houses when they were first married and I asked Tommy if he knew how it was coming along.

'I'm not sure they're going on with that,' he said. 'I gather they've gone off the idea.'

'Really?'

'I know. It's funny, isn't it? She wants to stay here and her in-laws are delighted so Brook Farm will probably be finished quickly and let.'

'Do they have a flat in the house, then?'

'Not as such. Some sort of upstairs sitting room for Edith and Charles has his study, of course. But that's it. Rather like one of those American soap-operas, when they're all worth a hundred million and they still cram together in one house with a big staircase.'

I shook my head. 'I suppose Charles likes the set-up here but it seems rather tiresome for a bride.'

Just as Charles, like all his breed, was not immune to the sense of getting 'special' treatment wherever he went – in fact, as Edith had already observed, he resented its being withheld from him – so I could understand that, after a lifetime of pretending he was unaware of the extraordinary baroque surroundings of his life, it would be hard actually to give them up.

The English upper-classes have a deep, subconscious need to read their difference in the artefacts about them. Nothing is more depressing (or less convincing) to them than the attempt to claim some rank or position, some family background, some genealogical distinction, without the requisite acquaintance and props. They would not dream of decorating a bed sitting room in Putney without the odd watercolour of a grandmother in a crinoline, two or three decent antiques and preferably a relic of a privileged childhood. These things are a kind of sign language that tell the visitor where in the class system the owner places him or herself. But, above all things, the real marker for them, the absolute litmus test, is whether or not a family has retained its house and its estates. Or a respectable proportion of them. You may overhear a nobleman explaining to some American visitor that money is not important in England, that people can stay in Society without a bean, that land is 'more of a liability, these days', but in his heart, he does not believe any of these things. He knows that the family that has lost everything but its coronet, those duchesses in small houses near Cheyne Walk, those viscounts with little flats in Ebury Street, lined as they may be with portraits and pictures of the old place ('It's some sort of farmers' training college, nowadays'), these people are all *déclassé* to their own kind. It goes without saying that this consciousness of the need for the materialisation of rank is as unspoken as the Masonic ritual.

Of course, the Broughton position was an unusually solid one. Few were the families in the 1990s that held their sway and the day would dawn when Charles would enter Broughton Hall as its owner. Still, listening to Tommy, I suspected he might have dreaded the possibility that people, awe-struck as they shook his hand in the Marble Hall, could make the mistake, on finding him at home in a chintz-decorated farmhouse sitting room, of thinking that he was an Ordinary Person. In this, however, I was wrong.

Tommy shook his head. 'No, Charles wouldn't mind. Not now he's used to the idea.' He paused for thought and then decided against it. 'Oh, well. I must get changed.'

We assembled for dinner in the drawing room that the family generally used, a pretty apartment on the garden front, much less cumbrous than the adjacent Red Saloon where we had gathered for the engagement dinner. There were a few vaguely familiar faces besides Tommy. Peter Broughton was there, though apparently without his dreary blonde. Old Lady Tenby's eldest daughter, Daphne, now married to the rather dim second son of a Midlands earl, was talking to Caroline Chase in the corner. They looked up and smiled carefully across the room. Filled with trepidation, I looked around for Eric and saw him scoffing whisky as he lectured some poor old boy on the present state of the City. The listener stood looking into Eric's red face with all the pleasure of a rabbit caught in the headlights of an oncoming car.

'What would you like to drink?' Lady Uckfield stood by my elbow and sent Jago off to fetch a glass of Scotch and water. She followed my glance. 'Heavens! Eric seems to be making very large small talk.'

I smiled. 'Who is the lucky recipient of his confidences?'

'Poor dear Henri de Montalambert.'

For some reason or other, I knew that the Duc de Montalambert was a relation of the Broughtons by marriage. His was not a particularly smart dukedom by French standards (they, having so many more than we do, can afford to grade them) since it had only been given by Louis XVIII in 1820, but a marriage in the 1890s to the heiress of a Cincinnati steel king, had placed the family up there alongside the Trémouilles and the Uzès. Lady Uckfield had referred to him in the manner in which one speaks of an old family friend, but since she always disguised her

94

true feelings about anyone, even from herself, I was, as usual, unable to gauge the true degree of intimacy. 'He looks a bit dazed,' I said.

She nodded with a suppressed giggle. 'I can't imagine what he's making of it all. He hardly speaks a word of English. Never mind. Eric won't notice.' She accepted my laugh as tribute and then rebuked me for it. 'Now, you're not to make me unkind.'

'How long is Monsieur de Montalambert staying?'

Lady Uckfield pulled a face. 'All three days. What are we to do? I'm still at *où est la plume de ma tante*, and Tigger can hardly manage *encore*. Henri married a cousin of ours thirty years ago and I doubt if we've exchanged as many words since.'

'Is there an English-speaking duchesse, then?'

'There was. But since she was deaf and is dead, she cannot help us now. I don't suppose you speak French?'

'I do a bit,' I said with a sinking heart. In my mind's eye, I could see the re-shuffling of place cards and the endless, sticky translated conversation that lay ahead.

She caught my look. 'Cheer up, you'll have Edith between you.' She darted one of her flirtatious, birdlike glances at me. 'How do you find our bride?'

'She's looking very well,' I said. 'In fact, I've never seen her prettier.'

'Yes, she does look well.' Lady Uckfield hesitated for a fraction of a second. 'I only hope she finds it amusing down here. She's been the most marvellous success, you know. The trouble is they all love her so much that it's frightfully hard not to rope her into sharing all the wretched duties. I'm afraid I've been rather selfish in unloading the cares of state.'

'Knowing Edith, I bet she enjoys all that. It's a step up on answering a telephone in Milner Street.'

Lady Uckfield smiled. 'Well, as long as it is.'

'She seems to have given up London so you must be doing something right.'

'Yes,' she said briskly. 'If they're happy, that's the main thing, isn't it?'

She drifted away to greet some new arrivals. It struck me that I had missed some nuance in the coiled recesses of Lady Uckfield's perfectly ordered mind.

The dinner, as predicted, was rather leaden. I had Daphne Boling-broke, Lady Tenby's coolly pleasant daughter, on my right, so I was all right for the first course but behind me I could hear Edith struggling gamely with M. de Montalambert on her other side and, in truth, I found it quite hard to concentrate on my own conversation. The trouble was that Edith's French and her neighbour's English were more or less on a par. That is, terrible but not so non-existent as to preclude all effort. It would have been simpler if neither had commanded a word of the other's language but they had, alas, just enough vocabulary to be utterly confusing. Edith kept maundering on about bits of Paris being so '*bon*' and London being '*épouvantable*' with M. de Montalambert alternately looking completely blank or, worse, when he thought he had understood her observation, answering with a swirling torrent of French of which Edith could barely catch more than the first word or two.

The courses changed and I turned to rescue Edith from her travails but M. de Montalambert declined to obey the English regulations and refused to give her up. Instead, grasping at the slight improvement in communication that my moderate French offered him, he launched into a passionate denunciation of the French government, which had reference, in some mystifying way that was quite lost on me, to Louis XVIII's minister, the Duc Decazes.

'What are we talking about?' said Edith softly under the apparently unstoppable Gallic flow.

'God knows. The French Restoration, I think.'

'Crikey.'

In truth, we were both completely worn out by this time and longing for a reprieve but the Duc resolutely ignored Lady Uckfield on his left and she, needless to say, could not have been more delighted to set aside the conventions this once.

The Duc paused and smiled. I sensed a change of topic. Perversely, having discovered that my French was better than Edith's, he decided it was time to demonstrate his grasp of English. 'You like sex?' he said pleasantly. 'You find you come often?'

At exactly this moment Edith was drinking some of her water and so of course did a massive nose trick. Seizing her napkin, she tried vainly to pass it off as a fit of coughing. To my right I could feel Daphne shaking with silent laughter. A desperate schoolroom hysteria was enveloping the table.

'I think,' said Lady Uckfield, who sensed the whiff of civic unrest, 'that Henri is asking if you are familiar with Sussex.' She spoke firmly, like a schoolmistress with a rowdy troop of children, but inevitably her statement gave rise to another terrible wave of giggles among us all. Edith was literally red in the face and almost weeping in her attempts to control her mirth.

At this point Charles looked up. He had naturally missed everything. 'Darling,' he said, 'do you know what I've done with my other gun sleeve? Richard wants to borrow it tomorrow and I cannot think where it is.'

His words achieved what his mother's had failed to do. They fell like a heavy fire-blanket on the burgeoning hilarity and effectively stifled it. There was a flat pause before Edith spoke. 'You lent it to Billy Westbrook,' she said. And as she turned back to her tiresome neighbour, she caught my eye. It was at that moment, hearing Edith's patient answer and sensing her weariness, that I began to realise her bargain had perhaps not been an easy one.

I was up early the next day, but when I arrived in the dining room, most of the house-party was already there, munching away at the splendid, *fin de siècle* breakfast that was spread out in silver chafing dishes along the sideboard. I helped myself to various cholesterol-rich preparations and took my plate over to an empty chair next to Tommy.

'Do we draw numbers, or do they just tell us where to stand?' I asked.

'Numbers. Charles has got a frightfully swanky silver thing with numbered spills in it. We do it when we assemble in the hall. The great thing is not to draw the place next to Eric.'

I could think of any number of reasons to follow this advice but from Tommy's expression, I gathered that simple self-preservation was the main one. As it happened, I was only one away from Chase, with the hapless M. de Montalambert between us. I could see his face fall when he pulled his number, although it might have been simply because he dreaded another Pound-versus-Euro lecture. I had Peter Broughton on my right. There were eight guns in all and of these four had loaders, so what with wives, dogs etcetera, we made quite a party as we stepped out to be stowed into the team of Range Rovers that waited on the gravel.

Edith, I noticed, was not among us. The reason for this I discovered after the third drive when she appeared with thermoses of delicious *bouillon* laced with vodka (or plain for the virtuous). 'Can I come and stand by you, or will I put you off?' she asked.

'Come, by all means. I can't be put off. I miss alone or accompanied. Won't Charles mind?'

'No. He's much happier with George. He says I talk too much.'

They were driving a high wood, quite a way from the house and the guns were placed in a semi-circle around the base. I had originally drawn the number two, so now, on the fourth drive of the morning, I was in position eight and at the end of the line. Edith and I pottered across the field to the numbered stick that beckoned me, and there we waited.

'Do you really enjoy this?' she said, moving over and leaning against the post-and-rail fence.

'Certainly I do. I wouldn't be here if I didn't.'

'I thought you might have accepted to study me in my splendour.'

'You're right. I might have done. But, as it happens, I do enjoy it. It was kind of you to get Charles to ask me.'

'Oh, it wasn't my idea.' She paused. 'I mean, of course, I'm perfectly thrilled you accepted, but it was Googie who proposed you.' She had long ceased to notice that she used her in-laws' tiresome nicknames.

'Then it was kind of her.'

'Googie is seldom kind for no reason.'

'Well, I can't imagine what her reason could be.' The whistle sounded so I loaded my gun and stared at the tops of the trees. If anything, my turning away from Edith seemed to relax her.

'She's worried about me. She thinks I'm bored and you'll cheer me up. She imagines that you're a good influence.'

'I can't think why.'

'She thinks you'll remind me how lucky I am.'

'And aren't you?' Edith made a wry face and stretched along the fence. 'Oh dear,' I said. 'Don't tell me you're bored already.'

'Yes.'

I sighed slightly. I cannot pretend the idea of Edith's discovering that kind hearts mean more than coronets and simple faith than Norman blood was exactly surprising. I suppose I'd thought it was bound to happen sooner or later but even bearing the previous evening in mind, this really did seem unreasonably early. Like most of her friends, I hoped that by the time she had made the time-honoured discovery that you can only sleep in one bed or eat one meal at a time she would have children to give her a genuine and unfeigned interest in her new life. And after all, whatever one might say of Charles, he did have a kind heart and, I would have thought, a pretty simple faith. I could feel an admonishing spirit rising in me as I spoke.

'What exactly are you bored with? Charles? Or the life? Or just the country? What?'

She didn't answer and my attention was taken by an extremely high bird heading my way. I vainly lifted my gun and blasted away. The pheasant flew merrily on.

'I must say,' I continued, becoming slightly more conciliatory, 'it seems a bit rough to be starting your married life under the same roof as your parents-in-law – capacious as that roof may be.'

'It isn't that. They offered us Brook Farm.'

'Why didn't you take it?'

Edith shrugged. 'I don't know. It seemed rather – poky.'

Of course, it was suddenly quite clear that the real problem was she was bored to sobs with her husband. Her life was just about acceptable in the magnificent surroundings of Broughton Hall where there were people to talk to and where there was always the heady wine of envy in others' eyes to drink but to be alone with Charles in a farmhouse . . . That was out of the question.

'If you're so bored, why don't you spend more time in London? We never see you there, now.'

Edith stared at her green Wellington boots. 'I don't know. The flat's tiny and Charles hates it so. And it's always such a bloody production.'

'Couldn't you sneak up on your own?'

Edith stared at me. 'No, I don't think so. I don't think I should, do you?'

I stared back for a moment. 'No,' I said.

So that was it. She had barely been married eight months and already her husband bored her to death. On top of that she was afraid of starting up a life in London because she knew that, without a shadow of a doubt, it would engulf her entirely and at once. She was at least sufficiently honourable about the Faustian pact she had made to wish to keep it.

I smiled. 'Well, to quote Nanny: you *would* do it,' I said. She nodded rather grimly. 'Whom do you see down here? Not much of Isabel, I'll be bound.'

She pulled a face. 'No. Not too much, I'm afraid. I've been made to feel that I've failed David. He keeps dropping hints about shooting for one thing and I simply haven't dared tell them you were coming today.'

'Won't Charles have him?'

'Oh, it's not that. I mean he would if I asked him but, you know, it's just a different crowd whether they like it or not. And David can be a bit ... ' she paused, 'naff.'

Poor David! That it should come to this! All those years of Ascot and Brooks's and drinks at the Turf! And the end of it was that Edith was embarrassed by him. Harsh world. I was not completely complicit, although of course I knew what she meant.

'You'll have to tell him I was here. I'm not having Isabel finding out and thinking we're in league against her.' Edith nodded. 'What about this "different crowd"? Are they fun?'

She sighed, idly scratching a bit of dried mud from her Barbour. 'Terrific. I know almost everything there is to know about estate planning. I could list the parts of a horse in my sleep. And what I haven't learned about running a charity is, believe me, not worth knowing.'

'You must get about a bit, though. Isn't that quite interesting?'

'Oh, it is! Did you know that in Italy the bowl of water in front of your place is to dip your fruit in, not your fingers? Or that in America you must never discuss acreage? Or that in Spain it is the crudest social solecism to use a knife when eating an egg however it may be cooked?' She paused for breath.

'I didn't know about the egg,' I said. She was silent for a while and I had another go at a bird passing overhead. 'There must be some of them you like.'

'I suppose so.'

'What about the family? Do they know how bored you are?'

'Googie, yes. Not darling old Tigger, of course. He's much too dense to notice anything that doesn't hit him over the head. Caroline, I think.'

'And Charles?'

Edith looked up at the woods above us for a moment. 'The thing is, he finds it all so riveting that he is quite sure that, as I get into it, I will too. He sees it as a "period of adjustment".'

'That sounds very sensible to me.' Of course, as I said these words, I realised I was failing her by taking Charles's part. But I couldn't, for the life of me, think of any other line to take. The simple fact remained that she had married a man who was, through no fault of his own, much duller than she was, for the purpose of her own social advancement. That was the deal she had made. No amount of fretting was going to make Charles witty and dynamic, and I already doubted that Edith was prepared to rejoin the mortals on the tier from which she had so lately risen. She had that common twenty-first-century desire, namely to have her cake and her half penny too. 'Surely there must be a lot to do? Didn't you have great schemes of combing the attics and re-writing the guide book?'

'There really isn't anything in the attics except for a lot of Victorian furniture. Googie rescued all the good stuff years ago. And the librarian got rather ratty when I suggested putting a bit more about the family into the book.' She yawned. 'Anyway, Tigger and Charles were so completely uninterested. They think it's rather common to know too much. It was a bit disheartening in the end.'

'Then you'll have to find something else to take up. I can't believe you're short of offers from the local charities.' Even as I spoke I knew I was sounding more and more like a German governess but the truth was I felt like one, watching this spoiled beauty pouting against the fence.

She sighed drearily. 'So I suppose you're saying I've just got to tough it out?'

'Well, haven't you?'

She caught my eye as the whistle blew. The drive was over and we headed back to the Range Rovers. There we were distracted by a certain amount of fuss and suppressed rage, which appeared to have been caused by Eric Chase firing more or less directly at M. de Montalambert's nose. Eric was, of course, wildly indignant at the very suggestion, while the other side was muttering a collection of extraordinary French phrases, some of which were quite unfamiliar to me. I was appealed to as an independent witness but, needless to say, chatting to Edith, I had missed the whole thing.

Caroline listened to my protestations and nodded her approval. 'Quite right,' she said, blandly. 'I should stay out of it if I were you.' I wasn't absolutely sure as to what she was referring.

After tea, I was just getting into my car at that slightly awkward moment when one lot of guests leaves and the next contingent draws up, when Charles followed me out across the gravel and came up to the driving window. I wound it down, wondering what I'd forgotten as I'd already done all my goodbyes, tips and signing. 'I meant to tell you,' he said, 'we've had an offer from a film company. My father's a bit blank. It's your neck of the woods. What do you think we ought to do?'

'They want to make a film at Broughton?'

'I don't know if it's a real film or one of those television things, but yes. What are they like? Is it safe?'

As a general rule, speaking as an actor, I wouldn't let a film unit within a mile of my house, under any circumstances, but it is nevertheless true that they are fairly reliable when they are dealing with anything that might qualify as 'historic'. Of course, whether or not it is worth it rather depends, like everything else in life, on what one is getting out of it. The best I could do was give Charles the name of an agency who might know the form for negotiating with film companies and suggest that he did what they told him.

He thanked me and nodded. 'We must stipulate you as part of the contract,' he said with a smile, as I drove away.

Oddly enough, and in sharp contrast to most of my Show Business acquaintance in similar circumstances, Charles kept his word. The film in question was one of those made-for-television pieces, which gather together as many fashionable actors as are short of money at the time, and run for three interminable hours on Sunday nights.

It was supposed to be the story of the Gunning sisters, an obscure pair of Irish beauties who arrived in London in 1750, took it by storm and married respectively the Earl of Coventry and the Duke of Hamilton. As it happened, the Hamilton marriage was unhappy – a situation rectified by the early death of the Duke – but the widowed Duchess went on, with some panache, to marry her long-term admirer, Colonel John Campbell, himself the heir to the dukedom of Argyll.

This was clearly the stuff of which pseudo-historical mini-series are made. Broughton was to double as both Hamilton Palace (demolished in the twenties) and Inverary (which I suppose was too far from London. Either that or the present Duke of Argyll didn't relish the prospect). In addition, various interiors would be employed for the vanished splendours of Georgian London.

It was to be directed by an Englishman named Christopher Twist, who had enjoyed some success with a couple of zany pieces at the end of the sixties when that style was in vogue and who was still eking out a living on the scraps of his earlier reputation. I knew the casting director, who had been kind to me in the past and I assumed it was due to her that I had been summoned for the quite reasonable part of Walter Creevey (a gossip of the period who had been written up as the double Duchess's confidant, although I don't believe there was much factual evidence of their friendship) but as soon as I had sat down Twist gave the game away. 'I gather you're a close friend of the Earl of Broughton,' he said.

I suppose anyone who lives in Hollywood may be forgiven for falling into American ways as, unlike many other peoples of the globe, Los Angelinos do not appreciate any code but their own. I was nevertheless slightly irritated, not by the misnaming of Charles's title, nor by the clumsiness of referring to his rank in full, but by that most intrusive phrase, 'close friend'. In my experience, anyone who says they are a 'close friend' of some celebrity has generally a slight acquaintance at best. Just as 'sources close to the Royal Couple' in a newspaper means gossip from the outermost circle of Royal hangers-on. 'I know him,' I said.

Twist wasn't put off. 'Well, he thinks very highly of you,' he continued. He had that odd, mid-Atlantic manner of speech that reminds one of a television chat show where every trivial remark is supposed (a) to denote a caring soul and (b) to bring all reasonable conjecture on the subject to an end.

'That's nice,' I said.

'So,' he lay back in his chair, stretching his legs and revealing a pair of cowboy boots covered in frightful Red Indian patterns, 'tell me a little about yourself.'

It is hard for anyone who is not an actor to comprehend fully the level of depression into which one is plunged by this question, when the credits of one's feeble career must be dragged out and displayed like the tawdry contents of a salesman's battered suitcase. I shall consequently pass over it and say that I was given the job. This was not because of the 'little about myself' that I had told but because Twist did not want to start on the wrong side of Lady Uckfield, who had apparently, I later learned, been most resolute in my cause.

As soon as my agent had confirmed that I was hired for the full eight weeks of the movie – which would involve six weeks in or around Broughton – I telephoned Edith.

'But how perfectly thrilling! Of course you'll stay with us.'

It is always nice to be asked but I had already resolved that I would not stay at Broughton itself. I could foresee a certain amount of awkwardness being generated by my being friendly with the family as it was. Had I stayed with them, in a short time I would have separated myself from the actual 'making' of the film entirely.

'You are kind. I don't think you could stand me for six weeks.'

'Don't be silly. Of course we could.'

'I shan't be so unreasonable as to put you to the test.'

Edith understood this kind of talk well enough to know that she had been turned down and the invitation was not repeated. I told her that I would be at the unit hotel, a converted country house just outside Uckfield, but that we would obviously be seeing a lot of each other. I must confess that after my little taster at the shooting party, I felt a slightly ghoulish curiosity to see her and Charles on their home ground. Perhaps at the back of my mind was a faint glimmering of *Schadenfreude* – that terrible pleasure we feel at our friends' ill-fortune – although I hope not. But I had witnessed Edith's accession to Dreamland and I'm afraid there is always a kind of pleasurable self-justification in others' disappointment in the world's blessings. It is the consolation prize of failure.

Two or three weeks passed. I went for my fittings at Bermans and Wig Creations, occasionally bumping into others in the cast. The Gunnings themselves were to be played by a couple of American blondes on 'hiatus' from a Hollywood cop series. The product was consequently doomed from the start so far as any artistic standards were concerned. I do not wish to sound snobbish here. There are many roles that should unquestionably be filled by American blondes. I only mean to imply that the casting of Louanne Peters and Jane Darnell meant that the producers had entirely abandoned the idea of trying for any kind of truthful representation of eighteenth-century London in favour of viewing figures. One cannot blame them, I suppose, or at least one would not if only they would ever admit what they have done. As it is, the rest of the cast has to sit in endless restaurants on location hearing how hard they've tried to get the right candlesticks or mob-caps when they know as well as you do that the central characters do not and will not bear the slightest semblance of reality. Actors laugh together as they 'take the money and run' but it is disheartening all the same. At any rate I was glad to learn that the sisters' mother, Mrs Gunning, was to be played by an actress called Bella Stevens with whom I had once shared a cottage in Northampton during early rep days after leaving drama school, and it was pleasant to renew a friendship that we had made no effort to maintain during the interim.

A strange and perhaps unique feature of theatrical lives is the depth of involvement one forms with people when working together, only to return home and literally never bother to pick up the telephone to contact them again. Weeks of tearful intimacies, to say nothing of sexual liaisons, are lightly discarded without a backward glance. It is inevitable in that the nature of the work generates intimacy and the number of jobs makes the support of all such relationships impossible. But it is strange nevertheless to contemplate how many people are walking the streets of London who know a great deal more about you than anyone in your immediate family.

Conversely, nothing is more agreeable than the renewal of such a friendship after several years' interlude, as there is no need for the preamble to intimacy. It is already in place. One may immediately pick it up, like a piece of unfinished tapestry, where one left off ten years before. So it was with Bella. She was a ferociously strong personality, with a dark, almost satanic face, a cross between Joan Crawford and the *commedia dell'arte*, but this went along with a kind heart, a witty if promiscuous tongue and a genius for cookery. The repertory company we had worked in – she as leading lady, me as assistant stage manager – had been unusually chaotic even by the standards of the time, run as it was by an amiable, alcoholic cynic who slept through most rehearsals and all performances, and we consequently had a good many shared horror stories to laugh about.

Soon after I had arrived in my hotel room, while I was still reeling from the obligatory brown and orange colour scheme, the telephone rang. It was Bella. I agreed to meet her in the bar in an hour. She was sitting at a table with a companion she introduced to me as Simon Russell, an actor of whom I had more or less heard, who had landed the good part (if any parts in these epics may be defined in such terms) of Colonel John Campbell, faithful lover of our principal heroine and eventually, in the last five minutes of the film, Duke of Argyll.

Physical beauty is a subject that many skirt around and almost everyone attempts to down-play thereby demonstrating some sound moral stance, but it remains one of the glories of human existence. Of course, there are many people who are attractive without being beautiful just as there are beauties who bore, and the danger of beauty in the very young is that it can make the business of life seem deceptively easy. All this I am fully aware of. I know too, however, that of the four great gifts that the fairies may or may not bring to the christening – Brains, Birth, Beauty and Money – it is Beauty that makes locked doors spring open at a touch. Whether it is for a job interview, a place at a dining table, a brilliant promotion or a lift on the motorway, everyone, regardless of their sex or their sexual proclivity, would always rather deal with a good-looking face. And no one is more aware of this than the Beauties themselves. They have a power they simultaneously respect and take for granted. Despite the moralists who tut about its transience, it is generally a power that is never completely lost. One can usually trace in the wrinkled lines of a nonagenarian, stooped and leaning on a stick, the style and confidence that turned heads in a ballroom in 1929.

Simon Russell was without question the most beautiful man I have ever seen. I do not call him handsome for the word implies some kind of masculine confining of the concept of beauty, a rugged state of alluring imperfection. Russell's face had none of this. It was quite simply perfect. Thick waving blond locks fell forward, half shading large, startlingly blue eyes. A chiselled, statue's nose (I have always disliked my nose, and so am rather nose-conscious), and a modelled, girlish mouth framing even, if marginally sharp, teeth completed the picture. Nor did the perfection end there. Instead of the weedy build that one associates with the Blond Toff school of actors, Russell was possessed of an athlete's body, muscular and trim. He was in short a magnificent specimen. Sometimes it seems the Gods grow bored with marring their handiwork and allow someone through without a hitch and Russell was such a one. If he had a fault, and really one had to search for it, I suppose his legs were a little too short for his size. I later learned that this tiny detail, this fleck of dust against the rainbow, caused him hours of mental anguish daily, revealing the paranoia and ingratitude of the human race.

The three of us, having decided to avoid both the director and the hotel dining room, found ourselves some time later ensconced in the booth table of a curious restaurant in Uckfield decorated with, of all odd choices, a Wild West motif. It was a pleasant evening and a heartening start to the job. Simon was good company, one of the lovely things about the lucky being that they are so easy to be with. He was married with three children, a boy and two girls, about whom we heard (and would continue to hear) a great deal, and he talked of himself and his triumphs in that relaxed unselfconscious way that only the deeply egocentric can manage. Still, he was funny and pleasant and charming, and he toned well with Bella's more frenetic volubility. He was also patently a colossal flirt. No interchange with another mortal, from our waitress to a man we stopped to ask for directions, escaped the beam of his arc lamp smile. Everyone, no matter how mean or meagre, had to be roped to his chariot. I enjoyed watching him at work enormously.

'I don't think I can manage six weeks in the room I've got,' said Bella. 'I thought there must have been some mistake. It's the size of a drawer and the lavatory is in a sort of wardrobe.' She waved her hand for another bottle.

It is a truism that the collective noun for actors is 'a grumble'. They are never happier than when they can have a really good whinge about the conditions under which they're working, sleeping, changing. There is the old joke about the actor who, after five years of unemployment, at the point of suicide, is given a starring film role opposite Julia Roberts and when asked if it's really true replies: 'Yes. And the best thing is, I've got tomorrow off.' Nevertheless, even I, who care little about such things, felt daunted by the prospect of six weeks of orange and brown wallpaper and it was at this moment that the idea of the three of us sharing a cottage took shape. It was a risk, of course, and we resolved to make it a week-by-week arrangement, but it would be a great saving on expenses and generally a considerable improvement on our present situation. 'The only thing is,' said Bella, 'I've been asking around. Practically everything near here is part of the Broughton estate and I gather they're not keen on short-term rentals. They have an absolute embargo on holiday lets.'

'Couldn't the film people pull some string?' Simon smiled the gentle smile of one for whom an inconvenient status quo can always be overcome. 'They must be making quite a lot out of us. Who's the location manager? Someone must be on good terms with them. At least at this stage.'

Since we were starting on the film the next day and it was bound to be revealed quite early on that I knew the family, I cut in. 'I know them,' I said. 'I don't know if there's anything to let, but I can certainly ask.'

Bella was pleased and unsurprised at this turn of events. She had known my double life of old and, being unsnobbish, did not feel any attitude to it was called for. I could see, however, from the headlight-glare of Simon's eyes as he turned to me with a chariot-roping smile, that I had risen quantifiably in his estimation.

The next morning I'd barely arrived on the set, a ballroom scene in the Red Saloon where Charles and Edith had received us at the engagement dinner, when my cover, if I had one, was blown. Most of the principals had assembled in their not-very-accurate costumes when Lady Uckfield came in. 'Ah, Marchioness,' said Twist with what I suppose he thought a courtly bow. Not a glimmer of a wince could I trace in her even, smiling features as, portentously, like the local mayor in a Midlands manufactory, he started to introduce her to the cast. Spying me, she broke away, kissed me on both cheeks and led me over to the window. For most of the unit, in that one second, I was a marked man and it took me several weeks of production to regain the slightest credibility as an actor.

'Edith tells me you won't come and stay with us.'

'You are kind but honestly not. I think I'd get muddled about which team I was on.'

She laughed and answered, with a cursory glance round the room, 'I do hope not.' I smiled. 'So where are you going to stay? You can't seriously mean to stick it out in the local pub?'

I thought of those sad brochures on my hotel dressing-table welcoming me to the 'country house splendours of Notley Park', and shook my head. 'I don't think so.'

'Thank goodness for that.'

'As a matter of fact, three of us were wondering if there was anywhere on the estate we might be able to hire. What do you think? It doesn't have to be sumptuous. So long as there are three bedrooms and hot water.'

'Which three?'

I nodded towards Bella, laced into burgundy velvet, who was talking to Simon. He was in pale blue silk, with lace at his throat and wrists, and a wig, which, unlike those of most of the extras, did not look as if it had been removed from a body in the Thames but rather framed his face with even more of the abundant, fair curls he boasted in life. He caught our glance, looked over to us and smiled.

Lady Uckfield smiled carefully back. 'Heavens, what a beauty.'

'He's our love interest.'

'I can well believe it.' She turned back to me. 'I'm sure we can fix up something. You could probably have Brook Farm if you don't mind pretty minimal furnishing. I'll ask Charles to sort it out. Come to dinner tonight and bring the other two. For vetting,' she added crisply, as she moved off. 'About eight and don't change.'

'You're sure this is all right?' said Bella for the twelfth time, as we crunched to a halt outside the front entrance.

'I'm sure.'

She wriggled out of the car. 'God, I've brought nothing but dungarees and sweaters.' Actually she looked quite saucy in a black outfit with big earrings, like a French singer in some politically subversive *bôite*.

Simon was considerably cooler as we approached the great horseshoe stair. He was one of those actors, who come if not in battalions at least not singly, who play aristocrats so often on television that they end by believing in themselves as one. He had worn almost every uniform, gone over the top in almost every conflict, ridden to hounds and danced till he dropped in epic serial after epic serial, and now in some way he believed that he was indeed the sort of person who gets his shoes from Lobb's and his hats from Lock's, that somehow he would be a member of White's if they only knew about him, that he was, in short, a member of the *gratin*. He would lounge around Fulham sitting rooms making disparaging remarks about junior members of the Royal Family with the air of one who would rather not tell all he knows. Not that there was much difference between him and David Easton down the road. It was just that he had been less in the country and so was still unaware that it is a harder act to bring off out of London.

Of course, what neither Simon nor David ever really grasped was that the key to these people is their familiarity with one another. Most of them are unable to receive anyone as 'one of their own' who is not either known to them from early youth or at the very least known to one of their circle. They cannot accept that they would not have come across, at least at one remove, anyone who was entitled to be included in their set. The best that all those grinning racing-drivers and cockney actors can hope for as they glow in the pews at Royal weddings is the position of unofficial court jester, a service that may be dispensed with at any time. Simon was insufficiently familiar with the great world to understand this and so he maintained throughout the evening a kind of swagger, which was presumably supposed to demonstrate to the company that he was always dining in large stately homes all over the country. Needless to say, they were neither deceived nor interested.

There were only the four of them at home when we were ushered by Jago into the family drawing room and when we walked in they were all silent and reading. I thought, although I could not be sure, that I detected a rather torpid atmosphere. Lady Uckfield came over to greet us. Receiving Bella's gushings, she led her instantly to her husband with whom, she could see straight away, Bella was going to be a great hit. When she turned back to us, Simon had already forged over to Charles to ask him about the possibilities of Brook Farm and I watched as Charles almost jumped at the ferocity of this full frontal attack, but he recovered his ground. In fact, he was nodding with an amiable half-smile after a while so I assumed that all would be well. Edith, I noticed, after acknowledging me, had not risen and had returned to her book. I watched Simon eyeing her but she would not be included and after he had tried throwing a few remarks sideways, he gave up for the moment and returned to dazzling her husband.

Lady Uckfield brought me some whisky and water, my evening drink, without being asked, which was flattering. Her glance followed mine. 'Charles seems to think Brook Farm will be fine if you're really serious. He'll have Mr Roberts go over it in the morning. We must have it ready for next month at the latest anyway so it'll be good to have a spurt at it. You could move in the day after tomorrow if you don't mind a bit of work going on around you all. I hope this means we'll be seeing a lot of you.'

'Much too much, I have no doubt.' I hesitated for a moment. 'Wasn't Brook Farm being done up for Charles and Edith?'

Lady Uckfield nodded. 'Yes. But they've changed their minds.' She caught my eye. 'Too lovely for Tigger and me,' she said firmly.

I nodded. 'Lovely,' I said.

Poor Charles had rather a dry time of it at dinner. Bella was having a great success with Lord Uckfield, telling him raucous and unsuitable stories to his obvious delight, and he was not inclined to include anyone else in their exchanges, while Simon was giving the same treatment – though more decorously – to Lady Uckfield at the other end. Edith certainly seemed to have very little to say to her husband though, as it happens, she didn't appear to have much to say to anybody. I saw her watching Simon as he sprayed her mother-in-law with wit and charm.

He had of course met his match in Lady Uckfield who was not to be caught in such a frail net as his but I must say this for him: he clearly knew he was outranked, something that in all the time I knew him he was seldom conscious of.

'Your actor friend seems very confident,' said Edith.

'Why are you so grumpy this evening? What's the matter with you?'

'Nothing. I'm not grumpy. Although I am rather miffed that you turned us down for these two. Do you really think you'll enjoy sharing with them?' She was speaking half under her breath as if to excite curiosity while remaining audible. I found it rather tiresome.

'I don't see why not.'

She looked at Simon again, sharply. 'Googie's taken a great shine to him, I must say. She announced at tea that she'd let Brook Farm to the handsomest man she'd ever seen. I was rather surprised.'

'Were you?' I said.

We were both looking across at Russell as he laughed and flirted with our hostess. The candlelight reflected in his hair, which he constantly tossed back, like a restless stallion. His eyes, darker than by day, shone like two sharply-cut sapphires. I looked back at Edith. She was beautiful too, of course, as a general rule by far the most beautiful at this table but this evening I was aware of how much of her animation had gone. I remembered her twinkling away at Lord Uckfield when her engagement was announced but her flickering secret smile had been replaced by something grander and more resolute. It was not a becoming alteration.

'He is handsome, I suppose,' she said dismissively. 'But actors are such girls about their looks. I can't take a man seriously who worries about eye-drops and mascara.'

I turned to her. 'Who's asking you to take him seriously?' I said.

Edith returned to her plate.

ELEVEN

~

The Countess Broughton lay brooding in her bath, occasionally wriggling her body to disperse the hot water trickling from the tap that she operated expertly with her toes. Soon Mary would be bringing up her breakfast and would be surprised to find her in the bathroom. She was breaking the routine that had already somehow contrived to become established in her cabined life. Even Charles had looked startled when she had rolled out of bed and started to run the water. 'Are you having your bath, now?' he said, watching her like a puzzled puppy. Hardly daring to question her actions, and yet, as ever, fearful of change.

'Yes. Why shouldn't I?'

'No reason. No reason.' Charles was not a fighter. 'You normally have it after your breakfast, that's all.'

'I know. And this morning I'm having it before my breakfast. All right?'

'Yes. Yes. Of course.' He raised his voice, as she moved into the bathroom and started to clean her teeth. 'I'm going up to Brook Farm with Roberts. Do you want to come?'

'Not really.'

'We can look over what has to be done. I don't think much, if they only want it for a few weeks. It seems an odd idea to me. Wouldn't they be better off in a hotel?'

'Well, obviously they don't think so.'

'No. No, I suppose they don't. Well then. Did you like the other two?'

'I hardly spoke to them. Your parents didn't give me much of a look in.'

Charles laughed. 'I must say that Bella gave the Guv'nor a pretty good evening. I can see him wandering up to Brook Farm to see if she wants a cup of sugar. Russell looks a bit of a smoothy to me.'

'Googie seemed very taken with him.'

But Charles had said all he wanted to say. Leaving his wife to her novel arrangements, he pushed off into his dressing room.

Whatever he may have sounded like, he didn't object in the least to letting the farmhouse. Far from it. It gave him an excuse to gee up its completion and now that Edith had gone off the idea of living there he was anxious to hurry up and get the place rented and dealt with. Its empty, pretty rooms, which they had discussed together in such detail just after their marriage, were a reproach to him, a bewildering reminder of his failure to – what? To understand? But what was it he was supposed to be understanding? One minute, they seemed to be having such fun 'setting up home'. He would puzzle obediently over little squares of wallpaper and swatches of fabric (although he couldn't have cared less which she chose) and they would refer coyly to one of the bedrooms possibly being 'useful' later on, as they planned a better bathroom for it than the room might reasonably have expected. Then the next moment it all seemed somehow ... Charles was aware of his wife's dissatisfaction. He was sufficiently anxious as to her well-being not to wish to ignore any signs of her unhappiness but he couldn't see where it had come from. What had changed? Certainly, he was completely stumped when it came to progressing the situation. He offered to spend more time in London but, no, that was not the answer. He invited her to take more of a role in running the house shop and the visitors' centre but, no, she thought she'd be treading on his mother's toes. In the end, he had hoped that doing up Brook Farm and perhaps generating a social life down in Sussex that was separate from his parents' might do the trick but one day Edith had suddenly decided that she didn't want to leave the main house after all and then he had really come to a full stop. 'I just can't quite see us sitting there staring at each other, can you?' she said lightly. These words struck a low and sombre note in Charles's heart because of course this was exactly what he had envisaged. The two of them, possibly eating at the kitchen table or with trays on their laps in the little library, watching television, chatting over the day's dramas ...

Charles's real difficulty, as he would freely admit (to himself, at least) was that he just couldn't see what was wrong with their life. He couldn't grasp what was wrong with seeing the same people and having the same conversations and doing the same things month after month, year after year. His annual round had always been circumscribed by the usual demands: shooting until the end of January, hunting on until March, a bit of time in London, then perhaps a trip away, fishing somewhere and up to Scotland for some stalking. What could be the matter with that? Well, obviously something was the matter with it, but he couldn't see it. And quite what he was supposed to do next to please this wife whom he loved but who bit his head off at the slightest provocation was a serious conundrum to him. A conundrum he was unlikely to solve that morning, he thought, as he put on his tweed jacket and started downstairs for breakfast with his father in the dining room.

Meanwhile, Edith lay back silently in the warm water, listening to his footsteps clattering on the polished wood of the great staircase. She knew she was a worry to Charles, but in some odd and undefined way, she thought he deserved a bit of worry. And this morning, more than usual, she was disturbed and yet she hardly knew why. It was as if some kind of creeping rot had infiltrated itself behind the grand structure of her life and could only be detected by the faintest, acrid smell in the most sensitive of nostrils. There was a knock at the bedroom door and Mary came in with the tray. 'Milady?'

'I'm in here, Mary. Just leave it.'

'Are you all right, Milady?' Mary's voice, hovering discreetly near the open bathroom door, was tinged with worry occasioned, presumably, by this fractional alteration of routine.

'I'm fine, Mary. Thank you. Just leave the tray. I'll be straight out.'

'Very good, Milady.'

Edith listened to the maid bustling about in the bedroom until the door closed and she heard the footsteps retreating along the corridor.

How ordinary her life seemed to her. Today it seemed to be drenched in a kind of grey ordinariness that suffused the atmosphere of these stuffy, chintz-filled rooms and hovered like a mist above the waters of the bath. And yet, how recently these details – these Miladys, these echoing footsteps on polished floors, these male breakfasts far below, sparkling with silver dishes, these lace-covered trays glistening with exquisite china – how sweet to the senses these touches had been. In those early days at Broughton how much pleasure had she derived simply from the monograms on her linen, from the damask-covered bergères in her room, from the Derby figures on her desk, from the telephone with its buttons for 'stables' and 'kitchen', from the footman, Robert, blushing with nervousness when he came to collect her emptied luggage, from the swans on the lake, from the very trees in the park.

She was a princess in fairyland. And how quickly she had learned the tricks of graciousness, of being showily unaware of her setting, of making people ill at ease with her studied relaxation. She delighted in the Eastons' discomfort in their triumph, as they found themselves at the Broughton table (at last!) surrounded by people all of whom knew each other and none of whom knew them. She had quite consciously imitated some of the tricks of the late Princess of Wales in the way she perfected her warm and delightful manner for the village, that combination of undisappointing celebrity and studied informality that was guaranteed to win all hearts. She would glow and gush as she was escorted round the new playgroup facilities or as she gave away prizes at the flower show, winning new friends, disarming old critics. What fun it was to catch the children shyly glancing at her and to disarm them with a sudden, winning smile and then to follow it up with a sunbeam directed at the mothers. But then again it was so easy . . .

With a low groan, she pulled herself out of the water, shut off the tap, pulled out the plug and sloped through into her bedroom to pick at her breakfast. Mary had tidied her bed and lit the fire – the *dernier cri* of luxury, particularly in September – and her tray, as pretty as ever, had been left on the table in the middle of the room. Nestling among the charming flowered china were her letters, appeals, thank-yous, invitations to boring parties in the country, which they would be going to, and amusing parties in London, which they would not. She flicked through them idly as she bit into a piece of toast, mid-brown with its crusts carefully removed. Mary had tidied her clothes, a tweed skirt, a cotton shirt, a jersey with a rabbit motif. She would wear these things, with some pearls and some not very sensible shoes, as a costume for the endless part that she found herself playing. She thought of her day: some errands, the librarian, Mr Cook, to luncheon ('luncheon' – she even thought in the language of her role), a committee meeting in the village to discuss the summer show, a cousin of Googie's for tea. It was a dreary prospect.

But although she had already decided that resuming a London life would not be sensible for her, Edith had not at this point fully articulated her objections to it. She would murmur that it was a 'bad idea' without specifics. She explained these feelings to herself with observations on how 'left out' Charles would feel with her friends. After all, his London acquaintance was tremendously similar to the people they spent their time with in Sussex. And anyway it was true, or sort of true, when she told people how much he hated London and that (at this stage at least) she too had 'come to the end of it'. Still, she was aware that she was talking about being in London with Charles. There was already a potentially fatal sense that it might be more amusing, and therefore more dangerous, to be in the capital on her own. Even so, it was only occasionally, and then in a very faint voice, that she actually admitted to herself she was ready to take a lover.

Edith prided herself on having become, more or less instantly, a Great Lady, on obeying all the rules of her new life as one born to it. Of course, by this time, she had pretty well lost touch with the fact that she was *not* born to it. She had succumbed to her mother's self-image, and now imagined, in some mysterious way, that she had grown up in the Gentry and simply married into the Nobility. This was completely untrue but as an argument it had the supreme merit of allowing her to feel less grateful to Charles than she had formerly felt obliged.

Inevitably, part of her newly acquired rank was the morality it brought with it. She had proudly discarded the last traces of middle-class fastidiousness and assumed, without a struggle, the cold, hard-headed values that were the other facet of the Great World whose cause she had espoused. She had rapidly become one of those flawlessly-dressed women who lunch together and say things like: 'Why did he make such a fuss? The two boys were definitely his', or 'Stupid woman, it would have blown over in a year or two', or 'Oh, she doesn't mind a bit. Her lover's just moved here from Paris', and they lower their voices conspiratorially, half hoping to be overheard, as they bite into a leaf of radicchio. She had acquired the pretended horror of publicity and the genuine horror of scandal that are the hallmarks of Charles's class. And yet there was something truly felt even in these stock attitudes. Edith did not admire scandal. Above all, she did not admire people who had 'brought it off', and then 'made a mess of it'. She had brought it off and she had every intention of dying in the saddle.

And yet . . . and yet . . . with all these thoughts floating through her brain, she took another bite of toast and decided that perhaps she would, after all, go down with Charles to see Brook Farm.

*   *   *

She did not need to tell me later that she had gone on the tour of inspection, as I was watching from one of the windows on the Garden Front when they set off. It was our second day in the house and we were having one of those bitty, unsatisfactory mornings of being filmed coming out of doors and walking up and down corridors. All very useful to get the feel of a costume, of course, or to make friends with the cameraman, but not exactly demanding. Bella was sitting next to me on the window seat, laced into a brown travelling outfit this time, busily engaged in rolling a rather meagre cigarette, this habit being the last obvious trace of her earlier, sixties bohemianism. Simon was with us but not in costume as he was not called that day. He was simply one of those actors who cannot stay away from the set, who would rather be called for a one-minute pick-up shot and spend the day waiting in make-up, than actually take some time off.

'Where are they going?' said Bella, as we watched the pair of them strike off across the park.

'Charles said he'd look over the farmhouse for us, and see if anything needed doing.'

'How long before we can move in, do you think?'

I shrugged. 'Straight away, I gather. If we don't mind roughing it a bit.'

'God knows I'd sleep on a mountain side rather than spend another night in that hotel,' said Bella with a wry laugh as she held a flame to her apparently non-inflammable, little smoke.

Simon took another look at the departing figures below. 'I think I might go up there with them. I can tell him if he's fussing unnecessarily. After all, we want to get in tonight if we can.' He nodded and walked off down the corridor. Bella and I watched him go in silence. She spoke first.

'Off he goes. To break more hearts.'

'Don't you like him?'

She bent down to concentrate harder on her dingy little fag. 'What's not to like? I just get a bit worn out with all that charm.'

'I shouldn't think Charles would notice it,' I said.

118

'Maybe not. But she will. And judging by last night I'm not sure she'll like it much. I hope he doesn't bugger things up before we've even moved in.'

He didn't. Or not enough to prevent us taking up residence that night. We had broken for lunch and were sitting at a rickety caterers' table on the gravel in front of the house, making the best of our cardboard lunch, when Simon returned in triumph, dancing and punching the air as he spoke. 'We're in!'

'When?'

'Today.'

'What about the hotel?'

'All done. I've given them notice for the three of us and told them we'll be back to pack and pay as quickly as we can. They're making so much money out of the film they didn't complain too much.' He beamed. 'Edith and Charles have asked us back for supper tonight so we don't have to worry about any shopping.'

'But how very generous of Edith and Charles.' Bella let the unaccustomed names linger on her tongue with a conspiratorial half-smile at me. I could see that Simon was destined to give her a great deal of amusement.

It was of course rather a bore to have to return to Broughton for the second evening running and make more polite conversation with 'Tigger' and 'Googie'. Bella and I confessed later that we had each privately thought of chucking. I would imagine that Simon had no such scruples. But in the event we came independently to the conclusion that it would have been a churlish return for what was both a favour and a dramatic improvement in our lot, so once again, shortly after eight o'clock, we crunched our car to a halt and made for the front door.

Simon was a changed man. The night before, his general braggadocio (unbeknownst to him, of course) had betrayed his social unease even to the unobservant. He had dropped names that had no kudos and spoken of social events that had either no currency value or with which he was clearly completely unfamiliar. In the end it was hard to resist a twinge of sympathy for his gaucheness despite the success he was having with his hostess. Like many actors, or civilians for that matter, he had been caught out by the need to demonstrate his right to belong in a world that he had long claimed as his own but seldom, if ever, penetrated. Tonight, however, he was free. He had that glow that distinguishes the insecure egomaniac when they find that their doubts were ill-founded and that they are *liked*. It was hard to avoid catching Bella's smiling eye as we made our way up to the family drawing room, with Simon trailing his hand along the gleaming banister and chattering amiabilities to the butler all the way, very much the Friend of the Family. Once there, we witnessed him greeting both Lord and, particularly, Lady Uckfield as Old Pals.

Of course, one of the basic truths of life is that, as a general rule, the world takes you at your own estimation. Just as the inexperienced hostess will tremble over her guest list, pondering endlessly whether or not she dare invite some grandee or media personality she hardly knows, only to discover in later years that nobody usually questions anyone's 'right' to send them an invitation. If they want to go, they will accept. If they don't, they won't. So, now, it would not have occurred to Lord Uckfield to ponder whether or not Simon Russell was his social equal. He appeared to consider himself so, and that, coupled to the fact that his role in Lord Uckfield's life consisted of eating dinners and telling funny stories, more than justified his amiability and relaxation in the peer's eyes. Just so are many social careers, particularly in London, constructed. Simon was no different to the art-dealers and opera-enthusiasts that are taken up by the various duchesses of our day, whose grinning images, sandwiched between media personalities and the wives of the heirs to great fortunes, are glimpsed in magazines. Of course, such people, like Simon, are generally unaware that beneath the superficial acceptance that their charm and easy manner can gain for them, their grand hosts do not seriously consider them to belong to their world. It is sad to watch the 'walker-favourite' of a great family arrive, after years of drawing-room service, at a public event – a wedding, say, or, worse, a memorial – only to find that they are placed in the back pew between the local MP and the central heating duct, while half-known and much disliked grandees are shown up to the front. Such is life. Or such, at least, are the values of this life. Something that Simon Russell was quite ignorant of, and Lady Uckfield knew very well indeed.

What interested me this evening, however, was not Lady Uckfield's response to Simon, which was predictably one of careful amusement, but Edith's. The sulks and rather affected hostility of the previous night had gone and been replaced by a mannered silence. She was looking more beautiful than she had been the evening before, in a black skirt and cream silk top, with some pearls at her throat and another string wound round her wrist in a chunky tangle. For want of a better word, she looked sexier than I had seen her since her marriage. She had not abandoned her cold *hauteur*, which I truly believe was already unconscious, but as we walked in, she looked up from the sofa with the kind of measured glance that I have learned from experience generally indicates that a woman means business.

Looking back, I am forced to conclude that Edith's plan to stay in the country in order to keep out of trouble was a poor one. Like some bored colonial wife in a hill station in India, the lack of sympathetic companions only really served to throw into advantageously high relief anyone who did make it to the outpost. I am not sure that if she and Charles had flung themselves into the whirl of parties, charities and all the other rubbish so eagerly awaiting them in London, that her virtue would have been in graver danger. I suspect it would have been quite the contrary. Society has the great merit of blunting the dullness of one's partner. The couple that never talk to each other never discover how little they have in common. Companionship, like retirement in the middle classes, can so often bring divorce in its wake. One thing I am sure of: in London, Edith would never have been attracted to Simon Russell. He was astonishingly good-looking as I have said, but in truth the trailer was better than the feature. He could talk and he was a really expert flirt, a joy to watch in action in fact, but when the chips were down and the doors were closed there was not much substance there. I do not mean to imply that I disliked him. On the contrary, I was extremely fond of him. And he could discuss mortgages or Europe or Madonna as well as anyone, but then couldn't Charles (at least the first two)? Of the *feu sacré*, that holy, charismatic flame that makes the world seem well lost for love, Simon had none at all. Or none that was discernible to me.

'Tell me, Mr Russell, what sort of acting do you like best?' This was Lady Uckfield. She was always careful to address strangers, especially those younger than herself as 'Mr' and 'Miss' or by their correct title. The main reason for this, indeed the reason for her whole vocabulary, was to underpin her image of herself as a miraculous survival of the

Edwardian age in modern England. She liked to think that in her behaviour and manner people had a chance to see how things were done in the days when they were done *properly*. How matters would have been managed by Lady Desborough or the Countess of Dudley or the Marchioness of Salisbury or any of the other forgotten *fin de siècle* beauties who made their lives their art, which consequently perished with them. As part of this carefully studied performance, everything she touched was credited with uniqueness. She would speak of 'receipts' and 'luncheon' as she made a special point of her Irish ham ('dry and delicious and quite *unfindable* in England') or her French cherries ('I'm simply *stuffing* myself with them') or her yellow, American paper ('I find I just can't *write* without it'). The fun of this approach was that all her guests were blackmailed, on the principle of the Emperor's New Clothes, into agreeing that they could perceive an enormous difference in everything that was set before them, thus reinforcing the very prejudices that had made them lie. Actually, the food was always good and well-chosen so I was as craven as the rest in pretending to discern huge shades of taste between different types of asparagus or whatever the challenge of the day might be. And anyway, the more I came to know Lady Uckfield the more I came to admire the completeness of her self-image. She never took time off from being the ultra-charming but ultra-fastidious marchioness of the long Edwardian Summer. Never. I am sure that if she were going in for a potentially fatal operation, she would be fussing about the make of the surgeon's scissors.

Edith never understood the strength of her mother-in-law's chosen path. She thought her a fuss-pot and a pain in the neck. But Lady Uckfield had a self-discipline that would have kept Edith out of trouble. She did not know what it was to be bored – or rather, to admit to herself that she was bored. The fact she was married to a man who hadn't a quarter of her brain had never disturbed her conscious mind for half a second. Her road was chosen and she would make a success of it without pity or remorse. In our sloppy century, one must at least respect, if not revere, such moral resolution. And, after all, to borrow a phrase from Trollope, when all was said and done, 'her lines had fallen in pleasant places'.

The other reason that Lady Uckfield called Simon 'Mr Russell' of course, was to stop him calling her 'Googie'.

'Well, I like being employed,' he said in answer to her question. 'I don't know that there's much more to it than that.'

'Don't you want to be a great film star?' To an actor, this is an unfair question. They all want to be great film stars but it is something that, by universal unspoken agreement, they are not supposed to admit to.

Simon fell back on the stock reply. 'I think I just want to do good work.' He looked awkward as he said it although there was, to be fair, more truth in this than one might suppose. Or rather, it would be true to say he wanted to be admired for doing good work, which is not quite the same thing. But how else was he to answer her? Obviously, he wanted to be a great film star, just as Lady Uckfield had supposed. But while he knew this, he also knew not to reveal it.

'And will you always be an actor?' Here Lady Uckfield unconsciously exposed her own prejudices and put Simon even more securely in his place. It is a question often asked and yet I cannot for the life of me imagine people saying, 'And will you always be a doctor? Will you always be an accountant?' The reason is simple: try as they might they cannot see acting as a 'real' job. There is a distinction to be made here between the middle classes, who in some mysterious way are often affronted by the choice of acting as a career – as if one was choosing to live off immoral earnings – and the upper classes, who are usually only too delighted for one to be having a jolly time. But neither group can envisage actually staying with it. Perhaps because, despite quite a large number of posh actors in recent years, very few seem to make it through into the top strata of the profession. This may be because of prejudice, or lack of temperament, or simply because the road is too thorny for those with financial options, but the result is that while almost every aristocrat knows someone whose younger son or daughter has had a 'go at the stage' almost none of them know one who has succeeded. It can't be encouraging.

'Will you always be a marchioness?' said Edith from her place on the sofa, without raising her eyes.

Lady Uckfield glanced at her daughter-in-law for a moment. She quite understood the significance of Edith's weighing in on Simon's behalf. But she turned it back with a laugh. 'These days, my dear, who knows?' The smile became general and although I could not resist exchanging a quick look with Bella, we set about the business of being guests.

Simon, delighted to have acquired so attractive a champion, joined Edith on the sofa and was soon regaling her with Tales of the Film Set in his most engaging fashion.

Within minutes he was sparkling like the Regent Street Christmas lights. I watched Edith as she laughed and answered and flicked her hair about and laughed again, and watching her, I became aware that Charles, half talking to his mother across the room, was watching too. We both knew that we were looking at a more animated Edith than we had either of us seen in many moons and I knew that, above all things, I must be careful not to catch his eye or I would become complicit in a knowledge that would ultimately bring him great unhappiness. When he glanced towards me, I looked away and joined Bella, who was, needless to say, telling some *risqué* story about being stranded overnight in a garage to a fascinated Tigger.

Once into the dining room, the evening was undemanding and pleasant enough. The food was excellent as usual and I noticed that the servants had begun to assume towards me that slightly ingratiating manner that is their usual defence in the case of 'regulars'. Having ascertained that you will be back, all servants who view their position as a career will abandon the (no doubt great but inevitably temporary) pleasure of assuming a patronising air and snubbing you on behalf of their masters. Instead they adopt a kind of respectful chumminess that will ensure large tips and a good mention for them if they come up in conversation. This pat-a-cake is usually accepted. I have known many people who should know better to feel flattered at being made a fuss of by the staff of the grand. They believe this intimacy will bring them many opportunities in the future of demonstrating their familiarity with a Great House that may be denied to other guests. They will enjoy these moments a good deal. Properly handled, the relationship soon develops into a mutual, if slightly glutinous, admiration society. At any rate, on this occasion I disappointed myself by feeling quite warmed by deference as we made our way back to the car. Bella and I chatted on the way home, both of us relieved that the evening was over and yet pleased that it had been easier than we had anticipated. Reaching Brook Farm, we loitered outside as Simon went in and started to turn on the lights.

'So he's made another conquest after all,' said Bella.

I nodded. 'Thank goodness really,' I said. 'After last night, I thought I might find myself keeping the peace.'

'Oh, I don't think that's going to be your role at all,' said Bella with a half-smile.

I raised an admonishing finger. 'Don't make scandal. We're all getting on very well and this is a cushy job. Let us look no further than that.'

Bella laughed. 'Maybe. But you haven't noticed one thing.' I raised my eyebrows quizzically. 'He hasn't spoken a word since we left the party.'

She was right. I think I had noticed but had forced the knowledge out. For when someone as eager for approval, as hungry for status, as ready for the world to know of his adventures as Simon Russell, spends the evening basking in the intimate glow of a young and beautiful countess and feels no need to brag about it, then it is generally because the story has only just begun.

And so it proved.

TWELVE

~

I was perhaps not as observant as I might have been around this period as it so happened that some time before beginning the film at Broughton I had met the girl whom I was going to marry. She does not play much of a part in Edith's story and so I shall try to be as brief as possible. There was nothing particularly unusual in our meeting. It was at a cocktail party in Eaton Terrace given by a friend of my uncle's and, as it happened, her mother's that neither of us had especially wanted to attend. I was introduced to her quite soon after she arrived (with said mother) and more or less at once decided that this was my future wife. Her name was Adela FitzGerald, her father was an Irish baronet, one of the *earliest* creations as she was wont to point out crisply from time to time. She was tall, good-looking and business-like, and I saw at once that this was someone with whom I could feasibly be happy for the rest of my life. I was consequently very taken up for the next few months trying to persuade her of this truth, which seemed manifestly self-evident to me but was not, I must confess, so immediately apparent to her. Quite why one makes one's choice in these matters is a mystery to me as much now, happily married as I am, as then when I was chasing after someone I hardly knew. I had spent many years trying and failing to find the right partner and it seems rather illogical that I should have been satisfied on the instant but I was. Nor have I had any cause to regret my decision since.

I concealed Adela from my acquaintance for a while. When you are approaching forty everyone is apt to make a great fuss over any companion you are seen out with more than once – well-meaning friends kill many romances in the bud – and so I thought I would keep quiet until I knew if there was 'anything in it'. However, in the end, I felt there was and so I introduced her around. My society friends and to a much greater extent my family were relieved that I had chosen from my old world rather than my new. My theatrical friends – more generous if more casual of heart as a rule – were just relieved that I'd found somebody.

We were nearly at the end of the shoot when I suggested that Adela might like to come down to Sussex one Friday, watch a bit of the filming and stay two nights at the farmhouse. This was to be arranged, to Bella's delighted hilarity, quite properly, with me giving up my room and sleeping on the sofa. Adela accordingly drove down on the appointed night in her rather battered green Mini, was introduced to the other two over a merry and, thanks to Bella, delicious dinner and promised to join us on the set the following day when she had done a bit of shopping.

The next morning, before she had arrived, Edith came stalking me. We were filming in a rose garden, which was at the end of a short avenue leading away from one side of the house. The scene had originally been scheduled for the first week but had been endlessly delayed, I forget why, and so here we were, shooting it in mid-October. However, the luck of our (fearful) producers held and the day dawned as bright and hot as any in late June. I was almost irritated that their improvidence should have been so rewarded. It was a long sequence, involving Elizabeth Gunning (the fiercest American, Louanne) and Campbell (Simon) in a love duet, which was ultimately interrupted by Creevey (me). I was therefore sitting and reading, waiting my turn on the edge of the proceedings and I must say enjoying the location when Edith came into view.

'What's this I hear? You're a very dark horse.' I nodded that I was. 'Is it serious?' I observed that since I was already established as a dark horse it wasn't very likely that she'd know anything about it if it wasn't. 'Is she an actress?'

'Certainly not.'

'There's no need to sound so indignant. Why shouldn't she be?'

'Well, she isn't. She works in Christie's.'

Edith pulled a face. 'Not one of those earl's nieces at the front desk who sound so superior and then never know the answer to anything you ask them?'

'Exactly. Except she's not an earl's niece, she's a baronet's daughter.'

'What's her name?'

'Adela FitzGerald.'

'Well, you do disappoint me.' She threw herself down on a bank near to my folding chair. There were other empty chairs near so I felt no guilt.

'I can't think why.'

'You, my artist friend, to sink to a suitable match.'

'I'm not sure I'm prepared to listen to that from you. Anyway, surely the point is whether the suitability is an incidental detail or the primary motive.'

Edith blushed faintly and was silent. The first assistant signalled to us to be quiet and the cameras started to roll on Simon and the deadly Louanne. She pouted her way into the best position before the lens. We had all more or less reconciled ourselves to Jane Darnell, who was playing Lady Coventry. She was inept but there was no malice in her and she didn't appear to think much more of her chances of impersonating an eighteenth-century Irish beauty than we did. She was only really interested in collecting horse-brasses to take back to her Laurel Canyon home. Louanne Peters was an entirely different matter. Not only was she convinced that she was possessed of a seriously remarkable talent but her egotism nearly ranked as mental illness. She would talk of her successes and her looks, her lovers and her earning capacity by the hour, and always without asking a single question of her unwilling listeners. At first one was inclined to think that it must be some sort of complicated joke and that she was waiting for us all to call her on it, to burst out laughing, to hold up our hands and shout, 'Enough! We give in!' Only it wasn't and she wasn't. Simon loathed her, which didn't help their rather underwritten love scenes.

The shot finished, releasing Simon and Louanne, just as Adela came striding down the avenue towards us. In her corduroy knee breeches and fisherman's sweater, her long hair held back with a briskly tied silk scarf, she was the very antithesis of Louanne's synthetic charms and, for a moment, she showed Edith's carefully painted face in a slightly unfavourable light. She was so ... healthy. But then again, of course, I was in love with her.

Edith stood up in greeting. 'Adela, how lovely to meet you at last. I'm Edith Broughton.'

'But I'm thrilled to meet you too!'

The girls exchanged their guarded greetings. That they were guarded was for two principal reasons, neither of which meant that there was the smallest romantic rivalry between them. Edith was not then and never had been in the least interested in me in that way. No, on her side it was the annoyance of having to surrender a confidant who has done good service and who will never be quite so useful married as he has been single. If you marry late there are many who feel this, even if those that love you attempt to control it. Added to which, just as happily married friends drive us all mad by their insistence that the married state is the only possible one, so do one's unhappily married acquaintance see it as their mission to turn all and sundry back from the church door. This stance is often used, half jokingly, as a means of insulting their partner in public. 'Get married! What on earth do you want to do that for?' one hears jocularly at a dinner party, and from further down the table comes a sour look from a lip-biting spouse. Ominously, this was a position that Edith, quite unconsciously I'm sure, was nudging into.

On Adela's side the guardedness was more subtle. She knew of course exactly who Edith was and, until meeting me, had been inclined to take the other point of view about the new Lady Broughton – that Charles, whom she had met a few times on the circuit, had been 'caught.' I had brought her at least to the point of suspending her judgement but in Edith's tone of greeting Adela had detected, with some justification, the faintest note of graciousness. Edith the Aristocrat welcoming this nice little actor's girlfriend. These things are hard to gauge correctly but it is true that Edith had developed a rather grand manner by this time so she may have been tempted into this dangerous area. Understandably, Adela, while previously prepared by me not to snub Edith, was damned if she was going to be patronised by her.

To make matters worse, just at this moment Charles arrived to see what was going on. He recognised Adela and I think in revenge (although she would have denied it) she lost no time in leading him into a conversation about several people that they both knew but Edith did not. In short she used Edith's dreaded Name Exchange against her. I suppose I should have felt indignant for one or the other of them but these things have a way of sorting themselves out without help from outsiders and anyway I could see that Adela had a point. I don't think I expected, even then, that she and Edith would ever be particularly close. Adela was too near what Edith wished to be (certainly so far as her past went) and while Adela was not a snob as a general rule, she was not above putting the likes of Edith in their place. I used to call it her

'Vicereine Mode.' All in all I could see that the best I might hope for was a kind of mutual tolerance. On this particular morning, before things could get sticky, Charles offered to show Adela the stables and with a nod towards me they set off. Edith watched them go.

'That's who should have married Charles.'

'Well, she's going to marry me.'

'No, I mean that's the kind of girl who would have made him happy. Giving out prizes, running the WVS. Can't you see it?'

'If that had been the kind of girl he wanted to marry, he would have married one. Lord knows there were plenty to choose from.'

'That doesn't sound very complimentary to your beloved.'

'You are talking of her obvious characteristics, which are, as you rightly observe, those of her time and her class. Her unusual qualities, of which you know nothing, are at the root of why she has chosen to marry an impoverished actor with a basement flat and not a rich earl.'

'Well, we'll have to watch our Ps and Qs around her.'

I wasn't having that. 'Don't make us into two teams, my dear. If you do, I warn you I'm on hers not yours.'

'Ouch.'

'Anyway, who says Charles should have married anyone but you?' Edith said nothing but lay back and stared at the sky.

'You two look very intense.' Simon appeared, stripped of his embroidered coat, more romantic than ever in his flapping linen sleeves. He threw himself down on the bank next to Edith with a gay disregard of his costume. I could see his dresser sucking his teeth in the background but Simon was playing Byron to Edith's Caroline Lamb and he was not going to let a detail like grass stains deflect him. 'Where's Adela? Wasn't she here?'

'She's gone off to see the stables with Charles,' I said.

'To catch up on old times,' added Edith dryly.

Simon laughed. 'Lawks,' he said. 'We'd better be on our best behaviour when those two get together.'

'Don't start that,' said Edith. 'I've just been ticked off.'

Simon gave a comic guilty look in my direction but actually I was rather interested that his social confidence had grown sound enough to attempt this kind of joke. I suppose I was faintly annoyed that Adela was being equated with Charles under some kind of 'dull nob' label by them both, but when I saw Edith smile and mutter to Simon under her breath I realised at once what a clever flirt he was. For by including me in his observation he had contrived to take the threat out of what was nevertheless a deliberate complicity, a shared joke with Edith, which excluded Charles. I saw then that Adela and I were quite irrelevant to his purposes.

It transpired that this weekend, Edith, in a spirit of revenge as well as generosity, and quite against Charles's will, had invited the very Bob and Annette who had been staying with the Chases during the Mallorcin honeymoon. She had done this partly to see Annette again (who had, of course, kept up a lively correspondence with her new and eminent pal), partly to annoy Charles, partly to annoy Googie, and mainly to annoy Eric Chase who was down at Broughton with Caroline. She thought it would infuriate him to have this pair introduced to his parents-in-law as 'friends of Eric' as if they were typical of his crowd. She was correct. It did.

Simon, Adela and I had been asked for dinner, Bella having taken off for a few days in London, so at eight that night we found ourselves joining this motley throng in the family drawing room. The mis-matched group promised a strangely disparate evening and in fact, Adela initially got the wrong end of the stick and spent the first hour assuming that Eric was something to do with the film and not the family. The more names he dropped the more she was confirmed in her opinion until finally he referred to 'my father-in-law, Tigger', in red-faced exasperation. Even then she looked over to me for a second opinion.

Lady Uckfield's responses on the other hand were calculatedly, and deliberately, disappointing to Edith. She made a great fuss of Bob and Annette all weekend and simultaneously managed to convey, with a sort of discreet gush, what a relief it was to her to find a kindred spirit in Adela, which was, I think, meant as a compliment to me.

It reassured her that, having taken an actor into her circle, he should turn out to be her sort after all. She found it fitting that her friends should marry people she had more or less heard of. As it happened she knew one of Adela's aunts quite well and had come out the same year as her mother, all of which was as it should be in her quaintly ordered world. Obviously, it was exactly this security blanket that Charles's choice of Edith had withheld and it was hard not to suspect a touch of spite towards her daughter-in-law in the liveliness with which Lady

Uckfield took up my intended. Adela, naturally, blossomed under the attention, still only half aware of the games being played around her. I found Edith in one of the windows, staring grumpily at the ill-assorted party. She nodded at my beloved. 'What did I tell you? She's perfect.'

'I know.' I followed her gaze and saw that it had shifted from the cosy scene on the sofa to a far corner where Caroline Chase was listening absorbedly to Simon, apparently, as always, in full flow. Between the groups Charles wandered rather disconsolately, offering refills. 'Poor old Charles. Who's got him at dinner?' The question was more impertinent than I had meant but I suppose I wasn't thinking. At any rate, instead of reprimanding me as she should have, Edith shrugged.

'Who knows? We've got the most ghastly evening ahead.' I looked enquiringly. 'Bob and Annette Watson are taking us all out.'

'That's very nice of them. Why on earth should they?'

Edith did not share my view of things. 'That's not all. They've booked us into Fairburn Hall. Googie's in fits. She's thrilled, of course. She's been dying to see what they've done with it since the de Marneys left and she's never dared admit it.'

Her lack of gratitude at the Watsons' invitation did not surprise me. The plan was, naturally, a frightful prospect to the Broughtons and their ilk. In England one of the saddest mistakes a social climber can make is excessive generosity. It's odd really for what could be more charming? To arrive with presents and treats, to gather up whole house-parties and take them out on the town – what could be nicer than this? And yet these courteous acts are as clear a signal to the Insiders that the would-be benefactor is a newcomer to their world as if they had worn a sign on their hat. Of all these solecisms, that of offering to take people 'out' in the country is perhaps the worst. The English upper-classes do not as a rule leave their houses in the country in the evening except to go to other people's houses. They might be tempted by a country house opera or even the occasional play with a picnic attached, but if they want to eat in a restaurant they do it in the week and in London. Nor do they ever go to 'country house hotels' unless it is on a pilgrimage of personal curiosity. They might visit one because 'I used to spend my summers here when it belonged to my Aunt Ursula', but they would never, on pain of death, book in for dinner or a weekend. One of the saddest aspects of these places is that the gentility promised in the brochures can never, by its very nature, be reflected in the guests.

The Watsons, anxious to ingratiate themselves with Lady Uckfield and to become Broughton 'regulars' had hit on the sure way to render themselves ridiculous to their hostess for ever, as well as providing her with a welcome new source of funny stories. For this privilege they would pay a great deal of money.

Fairburn Hall was a large and ugly house on the other side of Uckfield. It had belonged for several centuries to the ancient if low-achieving family of de Marney, who had finally managed a baronetcy by befriending, of all people, Lloyd George. The de Marney of a particularly unfortunate architectural period in the 1850s had encased a blameless Queen Anne manor house in a hideous, neo-gothic shell, studded with bas-reliefs of the family's triumphant, historical moments. These apparently were few and as a result rather nebulous and un-sourced scenes of 'Gerald de Marney welcoming Queen Eleanor to Fairburn', or 'Philip de Marney taking the colours at Edgehill' gave rise to great hilarity among the Broughtons. I need hardly say there was no love lost between the families and never had been. Technically the de Marneys were the older family and had consequently always tried to assume a lordly manner towards their neighbours. This was absurd of them as the Broughtons, whether the de Marneys liked it or not, were much richer and much grander as they had been for the previous three centuries. A couple of years before this, the current incumbent, Sir Robert de Marney, had given up the unequal struggle, sold Fairburn on a long lease to a large group of 'Leisure Hotels' and moved with his family into the dower house four miles away.

'Do you think we ought to be *veiled*?' whispered Lady Uckfield, as we climbed out of the cars. She turned to me. 'It was always the vilest house in the world. My mother-in-law used to swear they'd muddled up the plans with Lewes prison and got the wrong one.'

The entrance was through a wide semi-conservatory, with stone flags and odd, quasi-armorial grills at the window, like a rather grand bank. Through this one came into a cumbrous entrance hall. Thick, square Victorian columns stood everywhere, but the decision in the rebuilding not to raise the original ceiling height of the old house gave it the look of some central German under-vault, making one feel like a caryatid. The de Marney crest in loud colours was on every wall and an ornate family tree, framed in gilt, hung over the gas-log fire. Lady Uckfield stared at it. 'They've got the wrong branch,' she said happily.

An immensely important head waiter came towards us and mistaking Bob Watson's nervous enquiry about the reservation for the general tone of the party he attempted a very superior air as he ushered us into what he referred to as the 'withdrawing room'. He was soon disabused.

'What a horrid colour!' said Lady Uckfield, ignoring the chair he was indicating and plumping down onto a sofa instead. 'Too sad, as this was really the only room that was nice at all. It was the music room in the old days although they were tone deaf to a man!' She laughed pleasantly, as the crushed waiter tried to salvage his position by fawning over her for her choice of 'aperitif'.

'I think Lady Uckfield would like some champagne,' said Bob loudly, and one or two lacquered heads in the corners of the room looked round. He, in his turn, wanted to get some mileage out of bringing such a distinguished group to this, as he imagined, smart venue and I can't say I blamed him. Heaven knows he was going to pay dearly for it. His tone further flattened the attendant who was sufficiently familiar with the area to realise by now the extent of his initial *faux pas*. The party was becoming uncomfortable and Charles and Caroline exchanged a quick, edgy look. I found myself longing to defend Bob and his kindness of spirit, but I knew I would be fighting insuperable odds and, coward-like, I seized one of the huge, leather-bound menus when they arrived and hid behind it until the wine was brought with a great flurry of silver and glass and linen. At this moment, to everyone's amazement except possibly Caroline's, Eric leaned forward, plucked a bottle out of its silver-plated, ice-lined nest and spoke, not to Bob but to the waiter:

'Haven't you got any of the ninety-two?'

The waiter shook his head with murmured apologies. Just as Bob's timorousness had at first made us all worthless so far as he was concerned, now Lady Uckfield's presence made us all fine folk indeed.

Eric glowed at his deference. 'Then you shouldn't say it's ninety-two, should you?' He dropped the bottle back into its holder and sat back as the waiter poured.

Across the group Edith caught my eyes and rolled hers.

Bob was fumbling. He knew he faced a bill of something in the region of seven or eight hundred pounds and already the mixture of suppressed giggles and secret smiles was telling him that, mysteriously, his treat was making him not eminent but ridiculous. This was doubly irritating to him as his wife had tried to talk him out of it and had suggested, instead, asking the Broughtons and the Uckfields to dinner at the Ivy in London (which would, of course, have been perfectly acceptable to them).

Charles came to his aid. 'This is delicious,' he said firmly, sipping his wine and looking towards the rest of us.

'Absolutely lovely,' said Adela, and I nodded away.

Actually, it was quite nice but too cold. However, Simon, on this dangerous evening, had clearly decided to go for broke. Once and for all he was determined to shake off the concept that he was in any sense overawed by the present company.

'Would it be a great bore if I have a whisky?' he said.

'Good idea,' said Eric. 'Me, too.'

The careful cruelty of this was that Bob had already ordered three bottles opened, which the rest of us could not now possibly finish. He was foundering. His wine had been rejected, he had been insulted and yet somehow he had to go on as if everything was going swimmingly. 'Of course!' he smiled broadly. 'What about you, Edith?'

Edith sank back into the over-stuffed, chintz-covered chair and stared her pellucid stare. I could see her gaze trailing over Charles, who was giving her an admonishing look, imploring her to behave. Poor man. These were his wife's friends and yet it was he who was having to work to save the evening. Behind him, Simon stood beaming at her. 'I wouldn't mind some vodka,' she said. Simon half winked, and they both caught in their smiles before they spilled over into impropriety.

'Fine,' said Bob in a lacklustre voice. He looked around for more trouble but Caroline, with a deliberate gesture, reached across Eric to help herself to a large glass of champagne. The battle-lines were forming.

The food was predictably pretentious, with bonfires going at practically every table. Inadequate portions arranged like cocktail hats followed each other in blank, tasteless succession, fussed over by suspiciously French waiters. The maître d' would not, by this time, leave us alone and kept dashing up for a review of the current course until Simon finally suggested he might like to take a seat to save himself the bother. Of course we all laughed and of course he was never seen again. In truth the dinner itself was the least awful part of the evening because of Simon. He certainly was on very funny form that night. He could match Annette's stories without challenging her and the pair of them did keep things going. Even Lady Uckfield gave in to the prevailing mood and chuckled away as she toyed with her unsatisfactory and costly dishes.

Charles, on the other hand, was more or less in hell the entire time. He was not quick enough to get the point of most of the anecdotes, let alone tell his own. These were not his kind of people and unusually for him (for he seldom risked the possibility) he was outnumbered. Unlike his father he was not a flirt, unlike his mother he had very little sense of humour. Caroline tried to rescue him once or twice but she was in a dark mood of her own and in the end it was Adela who got him onto the business of improving the shoot at Feltham. He had apparently only restarted it three years before after a long gap and the topic released some of the pent-up flow within him, but even this had a limited success for when Simon was telling a story about some production he'd been in where the stage manager had filled the bath with boiling instead of cold water, he paused for the punch line and into the silence came Charles's voice: 'The great thing is to leave a wide enough headland of kale, which of course some of the farmers are reluctant to do ... '

Simon laughed. 'Well, obviously Charles is fascinated,' he said. He meant it pleasantly enough, I think, and all would probably have passed on if Edith had not spoken up at that moment: 'Oh, Charles for God's sake, shut up about your bloody shoot.'

I imagine she thought that in some way this would be a joke too and we would all smile but it came out wrong. Her voice was harsh and I suppose unloving in a way that, particularly in the presence of Charles's parents as we were, made a strange and embarrassing tremor at the table. I saw Annette catch Bob's eye as I felt Adela nudge my foot.

Charles looked up, hurt rather than angry, like a puppy who has been smacked for some other dog's pee. 'Am I being very boring?' he said.

There was a faint pause and then Eric, either misguidedly thinking to be amusing or, more probably in his case, just in order to be unkind, said, 'Yes, you are. Better have some more to drink.' He started to pour wine into Charles's glass but Charles shook his head.

'Actually, I don't know why but I'm terribly tired.' He turned his harassed eyes to Bob. 'Would you forgive me if I skipped the coffee and headed on home?'

Bob knew by now, long before he had reached for his plastic, that the evening had been the most crashing flop and so he shook his head merrily. 'Of course not! You go. We'll be fine.'

Charles smiled wanly and stood up. 'Well then, I think I will be off if I may. We've lots of cars, haven't we? Will you be all right, darling?'

Now it was perfectly plain to everyone present that Edith ought to have jumped to her feet, said that she, too, was tired and left with her husband. Normally this is exactly what she would have done but this evening some kind of devilry had got into her. Or maybe it was simple lust. At any rate, she neither moved nor spoke and it was Simon's voice that broke the silence:

'Don't worry about Edith. I'll bring her home.'

Charles looked at him and for a second they were what the Americans call 'eyeballing' each other. It might seem that Charles, rich and titled as he was, and really not that bad-looking in his 1930s-ish way, held all the aces, which of course in the long view he did, but Simon Russell, feeling successful and busy and as handsome as a man can be, bristled or rather shone with charismatic confidence that night. To all the onlookers at the table Charles paled before him and I at least felt a pang of real pity for this man who had everything. Obviously, looking back, I know that Simon had the confidence of a man in love whose love is returned and Charles conversely had the fear of a man facing ruin but even without that knowledge the figure of Russell, clad in his waisted blue velvet coat, eyes and hair aglow, looked like the embodiment of some unconquerable force in a mythological painting. I say this that one may perhaps be less hard and more forgiving of Edith. Having taken in the tableau for a moment, it was Lady Uckfield who spoke.

'That's very kind of you, Mr Russell. Are you sure?' She broke the mood further by rising and forcing the company to their feet. 'Am I leading the ladies out? Or do we all go through together, here?'

Even in this supreme moment of face-saving she could not resist pointing up the fact that she thought this place quite extraordinary and so, presumably, not governed by the normal rules of her existence. I have said before that I came to admire Lady Uckfield a good deal and this was one of the moments that underpinned my view of her. She had witnessed her son made a fool of, she had seen him dismissed by his wife, she was well aware of the danger in the air from Simon's offer and yet she would not have revealed any of these things for worlds. She would have cut out her tongue rather than give anyone the impression that she thought it a bad idea for Edith to travel home alone in the dark with Simon. And yet she would have given one hundred thousand pounds then and there to have Russell removed from her sight for ever. If Edith had only had her mother-in-law's control, there would have been no scandal of any kind, then or later.

Back in the horrible 'withdrawing room' Lady Uckfield beckoned to me to sit beside her. If she felt uneasy, she did not betray it with the slightest flicker. 'You must let me congratulate you on your choice.'

'You're pleased for me, then.'

'Well, as your friend I'm pleased but as a hostess I'm *furious*.' I smiled because she spoke the truth. She would forgive me the inconvenience of ceasing to be a single man but only because of the 'rightness' of the thing. 'When will you be married?' I explained that while I had every reason to believe I would be successful, it was not all quite settled yet. I imagined it would be five or six months. 'And what about children? Have you thought about that? I'm an old woman so I can ask.'

I shrugged. 'I don't know really. We both want them but I can't help feeling that the timing is rather up to the wife, isn't it? After all, my bit's rather easy.'

Lady Uckfield laughed. 'It certainly is. But don't wait too long. I hope Charles and Edith don't.' She looked me in the eye as she said this because of course we both knew that they had already waited too long. If Edith was now fretting over some golden head in the nursery or indeed if she was simply big with child, none of the threatened nightmare would be happening.

'I quite agree,' I said.

THIRTEEN

~

I had wondered, when Simon made his offer to escort Edith home, whether his plot would be foiled by finding that he had to take various others with them, but as soon as I emerged from the house with Adela I saw that this would not be the case: the whole back seat of his car was stuffed with a pair of chairs and what looked like an assortment of gardening tools. By my side I could feel Lady Uckfield taking in the same fact. My guess is that she had intended to join her daughter-in-law in the shabby Cortina, but, if so, it was not to be. I offered her and Lord Uckfield a place in Adela's Mini and, with a glance at Eric, who had brought some sort of Tonka Toy/Range Rover, they accepted. Lady Uckfield and I squeezed into the back seat, leaving Lord Uckfield and Adela in front. Eric gestured to them impatiently but in her sublime way Lady Uckfield affected not to notice. We drove off, leaving Bob and Annette to the tender mercies of Eric's red-faced driving.

'I hope he isn't stopped,' said Lord Uckfield.

Lady Uckfield made a slight *moue* with her mouth. 'Oh well,' she said.

We travelled in silence for a bit, all, I imagine, thinking of Simon and Edith whose car was nowhere in sight.

Lady Uckfield spoke again. 'Aren't those places too extraordinary? Who do you think goes to them?'

'Isn't it these whad'y'a call "yuppies"?' Lord Uckfield spoke in inverted commas, pleased to be so up to the minute.

'Well, it can't only be yuppies. Are there enough of them? There can't be that many round here. Americans too, I suppose. So sad, really.'

'Oh, I don't know,' said Adela. 'I'd rather see them as hotels than council offices or pulled down altogether.'

'I suppose so.' Lady Uckfield nodded doubtfully. In truth, she'd rather have seen them filled with the same well-mannered, rich people who'd lived in all these houses a hundred years ago. Even the ones whom, like the de Marneys, she disliked. For her there was no merit in the changes the twentieth century had wrought. Time had blurred her memory so that like the old recalling only the sunny days of childhood, she could think of nothing harsh or mean in the England of her beginnings. I found her views interesting. Even if her vision of the past was not quite as inaccurate or outlandish as Jeremy Paxman would have it, still Lady Uckfield's beliefs were rare by the closing years of the twentieth century. She had that absolute faith in the judgement of her own kind, seldom seen since 1914. No doubt it was common enough before then, which must have made Edwardian society such a philosophically relaxing place to be. If one were an aristocrat.

*   *   *

Simon made a show of fuss in getting out his car keys so that the other Broughton cars had all pulled away as he started the motor. He turned to look at Edith. She hugged her coat around her and leaned back against the window. They were two games players, with equal hands, and now at last they were alone with intent. 'With intent' because something in the nature of Edith's rudeness to Charles, something in the brashness of Simon's offer of a lift, had signalled to both of them that the fun was about to begin. Looking at Simon's roguish smile, the slightly crooked crease by the side of his mouth where his beard was beginning to push through, Edith felt a tremor of sexual excitement shiver through her body. She was startled by the immediacy of her own lust. She had been with men who had attracted her, she remembered enjoying making love with George and there had been a time, admittedly mostly before her marriage, when she had relished the thought of being alone with Charles, but she was sharply aware that this was something rather different. Looking into Simon's dark blue eyes, she realised she simply and absolutely wanted to be naked with him. She wanted to feel his hard, nude body against and inside hers. She felt hot and faintly uncomfortable. The terrifying, exhilarating thrill of her principles deserting her rippled through her stomach. 'Hadn't we better get going?' she said.

Simon was watching her carefully. Her blonde hair fell over her grey-blue eyes and she pushed it out of the way with a slightly petulant gesture. Her lips had not shut again after she spoke but stayed moist and parted with her white teeth just visible in the darkness. He too was excited but not in quite the same way as she. He had made love to a good many pretty women in his time and it was not the thought of the sexual delights to come that aroused him. It was the certain and confirmed knowledge of her attraction to him.

He was intensely aware of his own beauty. What is more he respected and enjoyed it as he sensed, quite rightly, that it was the core of his power. It was this simple truth that was at the epicentre of his flirtatious charm. From everyone, friend or foe, man or woman, he needed to eke out some response to his own physical desirability. Only then, in the warm glow of these aliens' admiration could he relax and be happy. The more threatening the situation, the more necessary it became to be wanted and wanted physically. He spent his life throwing out smouldering looks, laughing mysteriously, winking and twinkling at strangers solely in order to reassure himself that he was in control. Needless to say, he left behind a bewildered trail of wounded, who had responded for weeks or even months to clear signs of sexual and romantic interest only to find, once they were captive, that he had no more need of their love than if they had been trees in the field.

He did not trouble himself much over his search for constant reassurance. He simply expected his looks to break down all barriers, even if he did glimpse dimly that this is not the behaviour of a securely-based personality. In a way, this lack of faith in his other qualities meant that his vanity was closely entwined with a kind of modesty. He had no real respect for his own intellect, and socially, for all his bravado, he knew he could be clumsily inept. Given these reasons, it was probably inevitable that his bourgeois yearnings coupled to his compulsion to inflame desire should have led him to Edith. The irony being that she saw in him some kind of escape from the Broughton life, while he, conversely, saw her as the entrée to it. At this stage of the proceedings however these truths were concealed from them both. They were, in short, enraptured with each other.

Lust, that state commonly known as 'being in love', is a kind of madness. It is a distortion of reality so remarkable that it should, by rights, enable most of us to understand the other forms of lunacy with the sympathy of fellow-sufferers. And yet as we all know, it is a madness that, however ferocious, seldom, if ever, lasts. Nor, contrary to the popular teaching on the subject, does lust usually give way to a 'deeper and more meaningful love'. There are exceptions of course. Some spouses 'love' forever. But, as a rule, if the couple is truly well matched, it gives way to a warm and interdependent friendship enriched with physical attraction. Should they be ill-assorted it simply fades into boredom or, if they have the misfortune to be married in the interim, dull hatred. But, paradoxically, mad and suffering as one is in the heat of the flame, few of us are glad as we feel passion slip away. How many of us, re-meeting objects of desire who once burned a scar through seasons and even years, whose voices on the telephone could start up flights of butterflies, whose slightest expression could set off a peal of tremulous sexual bells in our vitals, search our inner selves in vain for the least attraction to the face before us? How many of us, having cried bitter, rancid tears over a failed love, are actually disappointed when we discover, seeing the adored one again, that all trace of their power over us is gone? How often one has resisted the freedom-giving knowledge that they have actually begun to irritate us as that seems like the worst kind of disloyalty to our own dreams. No, while most people have been at their unhappiest when in love, it is nevertheless the state the human being yearns for above all.

It was not that Edith really saw Simon as any solid part of her future life, entranced as she was. But she had long forgotten her early irritation with his flirtatious verbosity and now she loved to listen to his trials, to his hopes, to his dreams – as much as anything because she loved watching the way his mouth moved – and then, wonderful looking as he was, he made her feel so warm and so wanted. She liked physically to be near him, to let his arm brush her sleeve, his hand graze hers, but she thought no further than that. Or had not up to this moment. Unfortunately for her, he had come into her life at a time of wretched *ennui*. Before her marriage, yawning over her estate agent's telephone, she had dreamed of all the variety that her new life would bring her but she had not allowed for the fact that within months that new life would have acquired a sameness all its own. And so she was bored and, having expected nothing but excitement in the fulfilment of her social pretensions, she thought boredom more terrible than it is.

Slowly but inexorably she had allowed her residual affection for Charles to be driven out by his inability to interest her. Although, somewhere in her brain, Edith was aware that she need not have. If, like her mother-in-law before her, she had early on faced and dealt with the limitations of her husband then there could have been fondness between them. If she had ceased to look to him for her amusement, then she might have relied on him only for those things he could have given her: loyalty, security, even love in his unimaginative way. But, just as she had never really faced within herself that she had deliberately married a man she did not love for his position, so she could not now accept the responsibility for the fact that she was living with a man who was duller and stupider than she. It seemed to Edith to be Charles's fault that her life was so dreary, it was Charles's fault that they did not have a vivid round in London, it was Charles's fault that she dreaded their times together more than the hours she spent alone. Added to which she had already slid into that dangerous option, open only to those with high-profile, 'public' lives, of playing the part of the happy and gracious wife to an adoring crowd, which must always serve to throw the frigid inertia of her life at home into sharp relief. As popular as she was with the villagers, with her charities, with the estate workers, she had even begun to think that this happy and elegant woman she saw reflected in their eyes (and in the local press) was some kind of real truth and that it must be Charles's fault that he did not respond to her as her adoring, provincial fans did.

Not that she had any substantial taste for danger. She had accepted Simon's offer of a ride home as much to irritate her mother-in-law as anything else. She was, in fact, surprised if anything at the strength of her physical attraction to him when they found themselves, as they now did for the first time, alone and in the dark. But what took her even more unawares was an aerated sense of the raising of her spirits and with it that heady flavour of unexplored potential. This, she suddenly knew in a blinding flash of revelation, was the very thing she had most missed since her marriage. For months now there had seemed to be no open-endedness about her existence. All the decisions had been taken and must now be lived with. And yet here she was, looking at the corduroy of Simon's trousers stretched over the muscles of his thigh, and sensing a delicious awareness that there were still unplanned-for possibilities between her and death.

*　　*　　*

The Uckfields asked us in for a drink when we arrived at Broughton. I think they might have preferred us just to head for home but we accepted, partly out of politeness but also from that ghoulish sense that we all feel when we suspect an evening is not yet quite over. We were (or rather I was) still curious as to whether Charles really had gone to bed, how long it would take Simon and Edith to get home, how Lady Uckfield would behave – any number, in fact, of the different aspects of the case still to be revealed.

Charles was in the drawing room. He had hardly touched the whisky on the table beside his chair and was, I suspect, staring into mid-air until he heard our step. At any rate he seemed to be very puzzled by the women's magazine he had snatched up as we came in. He fetched Scotches for his father and me and some water for Adela (her customary, somewhat lacklustre late-night refreshment) and we all sat down. We had not been there long before the unmistakable sounds of Eric on the staircase told us that the Range Rover at least was back. The four of them came into the room.

'Where's Edith?' said Eric brightly, happy of course to see that she was not back and that therefore he might score some points off her.

'I hope they haven't broken down,' said Adela firmly.

'Oh dear. Might they have?' said Lady Uckfield.

Under silent instruction from Adela, I nodded. 'Simon's car is the most frightful wreck. I do hope not.'

Lady Uckfield recognised instantly that this was a life raft that she could rope to her decks in case of future need. She was not exactly grateful. For her to register gratitude she would have had first to admit to herself that there was anything wrong. But she was noticeably warm as she joined Adela on the sofa and started to question her about her aunt.

Eric had another try. 'They took forever before they even started the car,' he said. 'We were loaded up and out of the gates before I heard the engine.' But the initiative had slipped from him. The later the errant couple were, the more the family could hide behind fear of a breakdown or an accident. All other possible reasons for lateness had by this means been painlessly obviated.

As the conversation became more general and people flopped down into the various chairs and sofas around the room, Charles came up and asked me if I would join him in his office. I forget his excuse, some book or picture he had been meaning to show me, the usual sort of thing, but we both knew that he simply wanted to talk to me alone. I nodded and followed him out, uncomfortably aware of Chase's slightly quizzical smile, and we started down a corridor to the left. I wasn't looking forward to the interview as I had begun to feel responsible for the mayhem that even then I was only just starting to admit might be looming. I had after all been the one to introduce Simon to them. Had I not been in the film I am quite sure he would never have penetrated the charmed circle of the family.

Charles's office, its door sporting one of those 'private' notices that give one such pleasure to set aside, was a smallish corner room some distance away from the drawing and dining rooms used by the family. It was an extension of the main library, still on the principal floor, and so had handsome cornices and door cases and, by day, a fine view across the park from both of its tall windows. A pair of double doors would have connected it to the larger room if they were opened, which, as the library was one of the rooms on the public tour, they seldom if ever were. The fireplace was a delicate one of some kind of pinkish marble and the walls themselves had been covered with crimson damask that stretched from dado to ceiling. Against it stood high, glazed bookcases that looked as if they had been made for the room. A portrait of some female forebear, painted in a costume for a fancy-dress ball, hung over the chimneypiece, the gilded frame and the marble shelf below stuffed with a mass of invitations, snapshots, notes, postcards – the usual paper chaos with which the upper classes demonstrate their ease with their elegant surroundings.

'This is very nice,' I said. 'Where's Edith's sitting room? Is it next door?'

Charles shook his head. 'Upstairs,' he muttered. 'Quite near our bedroom.'

He stared at me mutely and rather than return his anguished glance, I started to peer at the spines of the books in the cases round the room. *Can You Forgive Her?* by Trollope caught my eye and gave me a disloyal inner smile. *He Knew He Was Right* by the same author sobered me up. I don't know that I had then any real understanding of Charles's capacity for jealousy, since I had no true knowledge of his capacity for emotion. The fact that someone is not particularly intelligent is no guide in these things. People may be stupid and extremely complicated just as they can be clever and incapable of deep feeling.

'What do you think?' I heard him say and for a moment I wondered if I was being asked my opinion of some unusual book but catching sight of Charles's face, I thought this was probably not the case. Just to be safe I answered with a question:

'What do you mean?'

'What are they up to?'

He was gruff and tweedy in his manner and I realised that we were embarking on what is called a 'man-to-man' talk. I shuddered at the prospect. Apart from anything else I am a firm believer in the 'least said soonest mended' school of marital harmony – a belief incidentally quite unshaken by marriage itself.

'Oh, Charles, come on,' I said warmly, implying that they couldn't possibly be 'up to' anything. I am not sure whether I was being dishonest in taking this tack. I rather think not. It seems naive but although, looking back, it is clear that Edith and Simon were drawn to each other from the second day, I don't know that their mutual attraction had really impinged itself on me much before that evening.

'You come on,' said Charles, more sharply than usual.

'Look,' I was very conciliatory, 'if you're asking me if I know anything, I don't. If you're asking if I think anything, I don't either. Much. I think they like each other, that's all. Is that so terrible? Haven't you ever wanted to flirt with anyone since you were married?'

'No,' said Charles, slumping into a Chippendale chair, and resting his elbows on a charming and untidy partner's desk. His let his head fall forward into his hands as he spoke and started to push his fingers through his hair. He was posing for a statue of misery. I felt wrong-footed in that I had judged badly to think that warm reassurance would do the trick and yet I didn't want to lead the way into a different level of intimacy, which Charles, whom after all I did not even then know well, might regard as an impertinence. I felt sorry for the fellow and wished to find a way to lighten rather than increase his load. My detached ruminations were interrupted by a sigh from the desk.

'She doesn't love me, you see.' He spoke to a pile of papers beneath his face but since the remark was presumably addressed to me, I tried to assess the correct level of response.

Of course, what made this doubly hard was that Charles's statement, bald as it was, was essentially true. There was no question in my mind but that Edith did not then love him. She did not desire him (which of course I only surmised at that time), she did not enjoy his company, she did not share his interests, she did not like most of his friends. I do not think, then or later, that she ever actually *dis*liked him but I could hardly say that in answer to Charles's cry of pain. I was silent, which I suppose was in itself a tacit agreement, and Charles looked up. I cannot say how moved I was by the terrible suffering in his simple, county face. His narrow eyes were reddening with tears, which had already begun to run down his large and bony nose. His hair, normally as sleek as a 1930s advertisement for unguent, was ruffled and untidy and sticking up in awkward little spikes. Great grief can be worn charmingly by a beauty and I have seen a lot of gracious dignity at funerals in my time but it is my experience that when grief is becoming it is also suspect. Real unhappiness is ugly and wounding and scarring to the soul. I blush to recall that I was surprised that Charles – nice, bluff Charles with his shooting and his hedgerows and his dogs – had a heart that could be broken. But he had and I was there to witness its breaking.

Before I could say anything there was a sound from the corridor outside. 'Charles?' It was Lady Uckfield. Rather than commit, even in a moment of emotional tension such as this, the social solecism of knocking at a sitting-room door (an action that, with white-gloved butlers, always plays so prominent a part in inaccurate television period drama) she contrived to wrestle with the door knob as if it would have been easier to get into the Ark of the Covenant. At any rate, having given us both enough time to dress had we so needed let alone dry our tears, she opened the door and came into the room. 'Ah, Charles,' she smiled easily into her son's face, ignoring the Fall of Rome that was written there, 'Edith's back. They got stuck getting out of the town. Too boring.' She nodded towards me. 'Your friend's gone straight on up to the farm.' Charles nodded his thanks in a kind of daze and started back towards the drawing room. I would have followed but Lady Uckfield, with an almost imperceptible pressure on my arm, held me back.

'We'd better be off, too.' I said. 'Where's Bob? I must thank him for dinner.'

'He's gone to bed,' she replied. 'Your nice Adela said thank you.' We were silent. She stood by the fireplace, idly fingering the pasteboard squares that summoned her child to various festivities. There was only one light on in the farthest corner of the room, a glass and ormolu desk lamp, which threw longish shadows about her and in the half-light grooved her face cruelly. For once she looked her years. The glamorous veil of her manner was momentarily lifted and a tired, worried woman in late middle-age was revealed to the naked eye.

'Well, this is a pretty kettle of fish,' she said, not looking up from the invitation to a wedding on which I could see a tick and 'Acc' in Edith's loose scrawl.

'Oh, I don't know,' I replied. My position was an awkward one for, after all, I was in that house as a friend of Edith. It behoved me to be loyal to her and yet I did think she had behaved foolishly. I was not, if you like, 'on her side' while finding it unsuitable that I should be on anyone else's.

'Well, I do.' She paused while I looked up in answer to her acid tone. 'It's worse than you think. Eric was by his car when they arrived. He saw them kissing.'

I was for a moment what a cockney friend of mine would call gobsmacked. I had thought we had been fringing around slight improprieties brought on by Edith's tedium. I had expected a little chat about Edith 'bucking up'. Of course, I suspected at once that Eric was not 'by his car' when they drove up but was quite consciously concealed somewhere near the entrance that he might not miss this Heaven-sent chance to nail Edith, whom, by this stage, he absolutely detested. Much more than I had realised. At any rate, whatever the truth of his motive, he had not lied about what he had seen. For old times' sake I tried to dig Edith out of the hole she had buried herself in. 'Oh, surely, she was just kissing him goodnight.'

'She was kissing him passionately. His hand was inside her shirt and hers was out of sight beneath the dashboard.' Lady Uckfield spoke with the dead-pan delivery of a policeman giving evidence in the County Court. I stared at her in silence. My first instinct was to apologise for being there at all and run for it. Certainly I could think of nothing more to say. Lady Uckfield continued. 'It is the greatest pity that it should have been Eric who saw them. He is quite incapable of keeping anything to himself and anyway I have a suspicion he is not overly fond of Edith. He has already told Caroline who told me. She will try to keep him quiet but I imagine she will fail.' What interested me most about all this was Lady Uckfield's manner. I had grown used to her passionate, half-whispered intimacy when she shared with you the day's headlines or your place at dinner. Now she really did have a secret to impart and all her girlish urgency was gone. She might have been an officer in the WVS addressing a group of recruits. 'I suppose we may hope that things have not progressed any further but I'm not sure what difference that makes anyway.'

'Will you tell Charles?'

She looked up startled. 'Of course not. Do you think I'm mad?' She relaxed again. Her shock at being thought unworldly was past. She dropped the card and strolled over to the window. 'He'll find out, though.'

'How?' I asked, meaning to imply that I too would be silent.

She smiled sadly. 'Probably because Edith will tell him. At any rate, someone will.' There was nothing I could profitably add to this since she was unquestionably right. Edith in her boredom was just ripe for succumbing to that fatal desire to 'bring things to a head' that so many married couples these days seem to indulge in. In sharp contrast to their great-grandparents who expended all their energy in trying to stop things coming to a head at any cost. My silence felt clumsy but I didn't in truth know exactly why Lady Uckfield was telling me any of this. For all her pseudo-intimacy she never usually imparted anything even faintly private, let alone potentially scandalous. She must have caught this question from my manner for she answered it without being asked: 'I want you to do something for me.'

'Of course.'

'I want you to tell the boy Simon to leave her alone.'

'Well . . .' Woe betide the man who accepts this kind of commission readily. Whatever opinion I might have of Simon's character or morals, I was hardly in a position to act the wise uncle with him.

Lady Uckfield drove full tilt at my hesitation. Her voice resumed more of its normal glib, light tone as the words gushed forth. 'She's bored. That's all there is to it. She's bored and she ought to get up to London more. She ought to see more of her friends. Or have a baby. Or get a job. That's what she needs. As for this boy . . .' She shrugged. 'He's handsome, he's charming and, above all, he's *here*. One does these things when one is settling into a new life. They mean nothing. The nuisance is that Eric saw her. He will almost certainly tell and it's our job to make sure no one can corroborate his story.'

I began to see things by her light. Of course, it was all a silly nonsense that was only horrid because it could hurt Charles if he found out. Yes, it was a pity that Eric had seen them. That was the pity. Her charming, even voice beat back the threat of anarchy and storm that had seemed to envelop us for a moment and returned us to the shore. 'I'll do my best,' I said.

'Of course you will, and the film's nearly over anyway. Too sad to be losing you,' she added hastily, remembering herself, 'but all the same . . .'

I nodded and she started towards the door. Her work was done. She had acted to contain the damage and that had necessitated taking me into her confidence. But I was already her ally. Things might have been worse.

'Lady Uckfield,' I said. She stopped and turned, her hand still resting on the gleaming door knob. 'Don't be too hard on Edith.'

'Of course not,' she laughed. 'You may not believe it but I was young once too, you know.' Then she was gone and I knew beyond a shadow of a doubt that she hated her daughter-in-law as fiercely as she would have hated any woman who had made her only son cry.

FOURTEEN

~

'What on earth was going on?' said Adela as soon as we drove away from the front of the house.

'What do you mean?'

'Well, first of all you two slope off and everyone looks haunted. Then Eric vanishes. Brief calm and then suddenly we're into farce with people running in and out of doors with stricken faces. I, meanwhile, am sitting there throughout with Lord Uckfield who's trying to explain something about trout farming. What happened to you? I thought I was going to have to ring and ask for a bed.' I told her everything of course and we drove on in silence for a while. Adela broke it. 'What can you possibly say to Simon? Unhand this lady? Won't he hit you on the nose?'

'I shouldn't think so. He doesn't look the type.'

'Well?'

I didn't really have an answer for her as I also could not quite envisage how to play this most embarrassing of scenes. And by what right was I even to open my mouth on the subject?

Adela gave me my motive. 'I suppose you'll just have to do your best for poor old Edith. It'll be a shame if she buggers it up after all that effort. And for such a nothing.'

We arrived at the farmhouse to find Simon sitting at the kitchen table nursing a glass of wine. His mood and the mere fact that he had not gone to bed seemed to suggest the desire for an unburdening talk although he could not have guessed that I already knew what he had to unburden. This was a worrying sign. We had already discovered, Bella and I, that Simon liked to talk of his romances, despite an almost constant stream of doting references to his children and their mother languishing at home. I did not then realise that for him the fame abroad was quite as pleasurable as the deed itself and this is a most dangerous characteristic in a married lover of married women. Adela went straight up to her room and I took Simon's proffered drink with a heavy heart. We sat in silence for a moment or two. At last he could curb his impatience no longer. 'Good evening?' he said.

I nodded in a half-hearted fashion. 'Quite. I thought the dinner was pretty filthy. Poor old Bob. He blenched visibly at the bill.' There was another silence. I suppose neither of us was clear about how to get on to the subject that was uppermost in both our minds. This time I tried the opener. 'You didn't come in.'

Simon shook his head. 'There was a bit of an awkwardness with that frightful brother-in-law when we got back. I thought I'd better just hop it.'

So that was it. No wonder Simon wanted to talk about it. Eric had made his presence known. The chances of his keeping his secret were statistically reduced to zero. Eric had made a scene. This, in my experience, generally happens when people want to make a scene. 'I heard about that,' I said.

Simon looked up. 'Oh? Who from? Not from Edith?'

I shook my head. 'From Charles's mother.'

I could see that this was a bit of a facer – as well it might be – but at the same time, while the flushed embarrassment of discovery was spreading over Simon's features, it brought in its wake, in the shy smile that he threw at me, a certain ominous delight in being the central figure in what I soon perceived he saw as a romantic drama. My heart sank even further at the realisation that with his actor's perverse pleasure in crisis, Simon would soon be all set to enjoy this chance of notoriety. 'Does Charles know?'

'Not when I left. Should he? Is there anything to know?'

Simon was not to be had so easily. He laughed gently and shrugged as he helped himself to another tot. I looked as paternal as I could. 'Don't start making a mess, Simon.' But still he only smiled and winked at me with that infuriating sexual confidence of the never-refused who think moral laws are designed for lesser mortals. My only recourse seemed to be some sort of appeal to his better nature. 'Edith is an old friend of mine.'

'I know.'

'And I don't want to see her made unhappy.'

'She's unhappy now.'

There was some truth in this, though much less than either he or Edith knew. 'She's not half as unhappy as she's going to be if you start making some silly little scandal for no better reason than that she's here and you're bored.' Again he smiled and shrugged. Of course I was on a hiding to nothing as few things could have given Simon more pleasure than to be begged to avert the arc-light of his fatal charm from some tender victim. Here was I, pleading with the Great Lord to have pity on a poor damsel. He was thrilled. I tried a new and faintly dishonourable tack. 'What about your wife?'

'What about her?'

'Won't she be upset?'

This, to my delight, did at last make him slightly uncomfortable – or at least irritated. 'Who's going to tell her? You won't.' This was obviously true as far as it went and for a moment I did wonder if I wasn't over-reacting when I heard a knock on the glass behind me. I turned and to my complete amazement I saw Edith, in an Hermès scarf loosely knotted on her chin, rapping at the window and begging, like Cathy Earnshaw, to be let in from the night. Simon, however, was no Heathcliff and it was I, not he, who jumped up to open the back door.

'What the hell are you doing here?' I said, but she pushed past me and sauntered over to the Aga to warm her hands.

'Don't you scold me as well. I've had enough for one night I can assure you.'

'Does Charles know?'

'Of course. Eric told him.'

'But does he know you're here? And why are you here, for God's sake? Don't make everything worse than it is.'

All this time Simon had neither moved nor spoken. Now, very deliberately he rose from his chair, put down his glass, walked over to Edith and slowly, for my benefit I assume, enfolded her in his arms and bent his head to kiss her with the slow, moist, hungry motion of a modern film star in close-up. He looked as if he were eating her tongue. For a moment I watched their two blond heads rocking against each other and behind them, like the ghosts in Richard III's tent, I saw Charles and his mother and the wretched Mrs Lavery whose dreams were being incinerated in a farmhouse kitchen in Sussex as I stood there. And behind them, the more distant figures of the Cumnors, and old Lady Tenby and her daughters, and all those others who would be enthralled and secretly (or not so secretly) delighted at the ruin that was being encompassed by these two silly people.

'Well?' said Adela, whom I had promised I would report to before turning in. She rolled over in bed, blinking herself into concentration.

'Hopeless,' I said.

'Wouldn't he listen?'

'He's loving it, I'm afraid. Anyway, I didn't say that much. I was just getting started when Edith turned up. She's down there now.'

Adela was quiet for a second. 'Oh,' she said. And then: 'So it is hopeless. Poor Charles.' And she rolled back into her pillow, pulling the covers up around her face.

Some time after this I proposed and was accepted. It was rather a tense period for me, I must confess, as I was inspected by an endless series of my intended's disapproving relations, most of whom were seriously unnerved by the thought of their beloved Adela relying on a stage career in future. 'Well, all I can say is *good luck* with that artistic temperament,' was the advice she received from a particularly unpleasant aunt. After a couple of months of this sort of thing, I was anxious to end the waiting. We decided to be married in April and, since it is a notoriously unpredictable month, to have a London ceremony. As Adela remarked, 'Country weddings can be such muddy affairs.' It was a 'Society Event', I suppose, though not quite on the scale of the Broughtons, but even so, anyone who has ever played a central part in a large wedding, let alone a large London wedding with all the paraphernalia it involves, will understand that I had very little time to worry about Edith and her *ménage* in the months that led up to it. I had asked the Uckfields and the Broughtons and, to my mother-in-law's delight, they had all four accepted. I was comforted by this, in the thick of the chaos of my nuptials, as I assumed it meant that the trouble had passed and the nonsense of an autumn night had been forgotten. Then, about two weeks before the wedding itself, I had a telephone call from Edith. 'Have you invited Simon?' she said.

I understood at once that she was anxious lest there might be an awkwardness and I was able to reassure her. 'No, I haven't. You're all right.' I laughed mildly, so that that hideous evening might be turned the sooner into a shared joke between us.

'Could you?' she said.

The smile left my face, the straw my clutch. 'No, I could not,' I said tersely.

'Why not?'

'You know very well why not.'

There was a pause at the other end of the line. 'Can I ask you a favour?' I didn't answer this as I dreaded to hear it. I was not spared. 'Could we possibly borrow your flat while you're away?'

'No.'

Edith's voice was cold and definite. 'No. Well, I'm sorry to have bothered you.'

'Edith, darling,' I said. This is the kind of thing that always happens just when one is entirely engrossed in some other large event. The night before crucial exams is invariably the moment that the parents of one's friends choose to die or go to prison. 'Of course you can't see Simon here. How could I possibly do that to Charles? Or to Simon's wretched wife for that matter? Don't be insane, darling, please. I beg you.'

But she was not to be won. With some perfunctory formula words she slid away and the line went dead.

I told Adela and she was not surprised. 'He thinks she can get him into things. That she can open doors. He's Johnny-on-the-make.'

'I don't know how interested he is in all that.'

'He's interested. He wants to be at the Head Table, that one. You'll see.'

'Well, I don't know how much poor old Edith can fix it for him.'

Adela smiled, a trifle coldly I thought. 'She can't. She'll be lucky to get a table in the St James's Club when all this is finished. Stupid fool.'

It was Adela who nudged me to look towards the door when, as we were standing to receive the line of our guests, the footman announced in ringing tones: 'The Marquess and Marchioness of Uckfield and the Earl Broughton,' rolling the words lovingly around his tongue like delicious sweets. The three of them entered.

'Where's Edith?' I said.

Charles shrugged faintly and we let it go. I was, in truth, rather touched that the Uckfields had made the effort to come. As a general rule, such people are long on friendship on their own terms but short on doing anything on yours. I don't actually think Lord Uckfield had any idea why he had been forced to dress up and sacrifice a perfectly good afternoon when he might have been watching racing on the box, but Lady Uckfield, I believe, liked me by this time and also, I suspect, wished to establish a beachhead on Edith's only pre-marriage friend that had made the transition into her new life. They were ushered on through into the reception and we turned back to the unending line of old nannies and relations from the shires.

It is not possible to speak to anyone properly at your own wedding – certainly not at a smart wedding where it is out of the question that the company should do anything as middle class or sensible as sit down to eat. The bride and groom are passed round, like one of those endless trays of nibbling things, for a few words here or there, justifying those overnight journeys down from Scotland or those flights from Paris and New York. Still, Charles did manage to seize me for a moment. 'Can we have lunch when you get back?' he said. I nodded and smiled but avoided discussing the matter since the beginning of one marriage seems a poor place to ruminate over the probable end of another. I must confess I was flattered that by this time Charles obviously thought of me as his friend as well as Edith's, flattered but also vindicated for I certainly was on Charles's side, if sides there must be. Of course, I knew well enough that I was not one of Charles's close pals, but I had the merit of being able to discuss his wife with some real experience of her, which most of his friends, since they had never met her before the engagement, could not.

Adela and I spent a delightful fortnight in Venice and when we got back to the flat we found, along with further piles of wedding presents from Peter Jones and the General Trading Company, a letter from Charles suggesting that I meet him at his club the following Thursday. I accepted. Charles's club was inevitably White's and I accordingly found myself outside its familiar Adamesque entrance at one o'clock on the appointed day.

Of the three smart clubs whose charming eighteenth-century facades dominate St James's, White's is, I would guess most people are agreed, the smartest. It boasts few sleek City *arrivistes* even among its younger members, perhaps because there is still enough of the *gratin* left to supply its needs, perhaps because the air is too thin for lesser mortals to breathe and after one or two visits they decide to try for something a little less rich. Having said that, I have always enjoyed White's. I would no more wish to be a member than I would apply to sponsor a polo team but one of the virtues of the English upper-class (and it is only fair to give some credit, alert as I am to their vices) is that when they are gathered together in familiar, congenial surroundings, they are a most relaxed and pleasant bunch. They've all known each other since they could first breathe and, when there is no one near to criticize them for it, they revel in this familiarity of the extended family. At their best, alone together and in a 'safe house', they are polite and unafraid, a charming combination.

I gave my name and asked for Charles at the mahogany booth in the entrance hall but 'his Lordship' had not yet arrived and I was invited to sit and wait for him. Not here the nodding through of strangers into the inner sanctums. But I had hardly had time to read the latest bulletins from the tickertape machine (alas now gone) before Charles clapped me on the shoulder. 'My dear fellow, forgive me. I got stuck.' We went on through the staircase hall to the little bar, where Charles ordered dry sherry for us both. He was looking a good deal more like his old self, I was happy to see, smartly dressed and neatly coiffed. His crinkly, blond hair in smooth Marcel waves, a tie of some educational or military significance at his throat. 'So, how are you? Busy, I hope.'

I wasn't frightfully, as it happens, but there was a chance of one or two things coming up so I hadn't yet reached the desperate stage that is the occupational hazard of Equity membership. I muttered away about Adela, the flat, Venice and so on but of course Charles was aching to get started. 'How are things with you?' I asked.

As if in answer he put down his drink. 'Let's go up and get a table,' he muttered, and we started up the staircase.

The dining room of the club is a grand, undisappointing chamber with a high gilded ceiling and long windows overlooking St James's. Against its damask-covered walls hang full-length portraits of erstwhile grandee members, the whole emanating that characteristic of aristocratic solidity that Charles correctly, if subconsciously, believed the mainstay both of his personality and his way of life. We gave our orders as we came in and found ourselves a table for two on the wall away from the windows.

'I think Edith's left me.' The statement was so bald that for a moment I suspected I'd misheard.

'What do you mean "you think"?' I didn't quite see how one could be mistaken about such things.

He cleared his throat. 'Well, perhaps I should say she thinks she's left me.' He raised his eyebrows. I suppose the only way that he felt he could have this conversation at all was by distancing the whole business. As if we were exchanging a piece of gossip about someone else. 'She telephoned this morning. She's rented a flat in Ebury Street. Apparently the idea is for them to set up there together.'

I think the phrase is 'the universe reeled'. My first response, rather unworthily, was that I couldn't believe Edith would be this stupid before the scandal had forced her hand. 'What did she say?'

'Just that they're in love. She's been very unhappy. Nobody's fault, blah, blah, blah ... You know. What you'd expect.'

At that moment my potted shrimps arrived, closely followed by Charles's avocado. I tried to use the silence to collect my thoughts but for the life of me I couldn't think of anything sensible to say. I chose badly. 'Who else knows?'

'You sound like my mother.'

At the mention of her name I yearned for Lady Uckfield to take the helm and steer everyone out of this ghastly mess. Not for her, be she never so young, a rented flat in Ebury Street shared with a married actor. 'Does your mother know?'

'She doesn't know all the details. Edith telephoned me a few days ago. When I sent round the note to you. I've been rather incommunicado since then. I don't see that there's much to be gained in facing the storm if the storm itself can be avoided.'

In my mind's eye I could see the articles in the very pages that had taken Edith up as Charles's intended and covered the wedding in such loving, glutinous detail barely two years before. I know, only too well, the high moral tone those raddled alcoholic journalists love to take when they choose to discuss the low lives of the *haut monde*. And Edith had made herself their creature, had willingly allowed herself to become a columnist's toy, something I knew would give them every licence to tear her in pieces now.

'Can it be avoided?' I asked.

'I don't know. That's where I need your help.'

Naturally my heart sank at the sound of these words. All of this was happening too close to me. I yearned to get back into the outer circle of this family's world. How little Americans know when they disparage acquaintanceship in favour of real, true friendship. It is in acquaintanceship, bringing with it as it does delicious dinners, comfortable weekends, gossip shared in picturesque surroundings, but no real intimacy, no responsibility, that the greatest charm of social intercourse lies. I am an observer. It troubles me to be forced into the role of participant.

'You'd take her back then?'

Charles looked almost puzzled by the question. 'What do you mean? She's my wife.'

It is hard to explain quite why I found these words so moving but I did. It sounds odd to write it in our tawdry era but at that moment I was aware I was in the presence of a good man, a man whose word could be trusted, a man whose morality was more than fashion. What could Edith possibly have found in the embrace of her tinsel lover that was worth more than this solid, unquestioning commitment? He looked almost embarrassed by his noble declaration.

'I just want you to talk to her.'

'Well, I assumed you didn't want me to kidnap her.' I put down my glass. 'But what can I say? I think she's quite mad.' Charles smiled. 'But I don't imagine that my telling her that will make much odds if she doesn't listen to you or her mother.'

Poor Mrs Lavery! This news would bring hara-kiri in its wake.

'I know that but . . .' Charles paused. 'I mean, you know the world that this Simon chap operates in. I don't mean to be, well, rude, but is it the sort of world that Edith would like? Has she thought about all that?'

Now this was quite a complicated question, certainly more complicated than Charles was aware. Nobody knows who is going to like the stage world. Adela took to it like a duck to water and never had a moment's difficulty synthesising it with her other, more traditional, social group. She found she liked the feast-or-famine, crisis-ridden, siege mentality of the whole thing. To others, my mother-in-law for instance, the people of the stage seem simply awful, a sleazy crowd of oiks, all plastered in make-up, falling in and out of other people's beds, and getting drunk in restaurants. There is a good deal of truth in this picture, too. Charles was of the latter school. It quite amused him to know an actor socially but it was no accident that the only one he did know had grown up in fairly traditional circumstances. If he came to us for a drink it was fun for him to see people he recognised from various television series but he had no desire to befriend them. This was one of his main difficulties throughout the whole affair. He found it impossible to understand how Edith, having known his world from the inside, a world that if nothing else is elegant and rooted in charming settings, could have deliberately renounced it for an environment as alluring to him as Cardboard City.

Of course, the danger of the stage world, even for those initially drawn to its glitter, is that there is always a risk that one may grow out of it. It is the choice of high colour over more muted shades in terms of one's daily drama and for many there comes a time when the sobbing in the dressing room, the anti-director cabals, the midnight telephone calls of reassurance, simply become an adolescent bore. Some actors slake this sense of growing emptiness by the discovery of a 'cause' and try to put their need for daily trouble and strife to some use. Nothing is easier than to raise a crowd of furiously indignant actors who will happily protest at almost anything. But causes are a taste not shared by all, certainly not much by the pragmatic. Besides, there is a risk, not always avoided by some quite famous stage names, of attaching oneself to so many noble struggles against injustice that the weight of one's contribution finally becomes rather flimsy. All in all, the most effective antidote to the palling pleasures of stage gossip is simply to become very successful. Then the money and the status that fame brings are pleasant enough in themselves and lead to a rather broader life willy nilly. Which thought brought me back to the question of Edith's adjustment to her new existence. I attempted to answer honestly.

'I think it would depend on how well Simon does.'

Charles shook his head impatiently. 'I'm not saying she'd mind moving in with Jude Law but how successful is this fellow? I've never heard of him. Edith's used to living high on the hog, you know.'

I knew. 'It's difficult to say. He's started picking up some good parts. He might easily get the lead in a series and then he'd be up and running.'

'But he might not.'

This was certainly true. People in the outside world talk of actors being 'successful', which roughly means stars that they have heard of, or 'unsuccessful', which means the bottom 60 per cent who never really make a decent living. You do not need to be a mathematician to work out that there is a large group in between these two, doing quite well, earning reasonable amounts, known within the business, any one of whom can be picked for a new television show and have their fortunes transformed, as the papers like to put it, 'overnight'. This is the trap of the stage life. It is easy to give up something if you are failing, almost impossible to do so if you are almost succeeding. Simon Russell was definitely in this category.

I bought some time as our main course arrived. 'The trouble is, Charles, what argument could I employ that would make any difference? As I have just told you, I think she's quite crazy but she's a grown woman. To give up what you've offered her in order to go and live with an actor of moderate talent and even more moderate means is beyond comprehension to me. But she already knows all this and so I don't know what I could add to it that would be helpful.'

'I suppose she loves him. I suppose it's sex.' He bit the word out of the air and two men on the next table glanced briefly in our direction.

'It might be sex,' I said. 'But I'm not at all sure that she loves him.'

Charles frowned disapprovingly. 'I can't quite follow you there,' he said, and turned his attention to the bones of his lamb chops, which he began to scrape fiercely, apparently anxious to retrieve every last morsel of edible matter.

It was clear Charles was not prepared to admit that his wife could differentiate between these elements, that she might be able to indulge her body without involving her heart. I loved him for it.

We didn't say much more. All I knew was that by the time I was back in Piccadilly strolling down the Ritz arcade towards Green Park Underground station I had agreed to telephone Edith and attempt to 'reason' with her.

FIFTEEN

~

As it happened Edith sounded quite eager to meet, 'so long as you don't start to lecture me.' I shouldn't have been surprised. Freud has some special word for this 'compulsion to reveal' that undermines us all. She longed to discuss everything with someone who knew all the characters involved and given that she would expect some sympathy from her listener, I was probably in a category of one. We decided on a cheap and cheerful little restaurant in Milner Street, alas long gone now, a victim of the developers, that we had occasionally used during her estate agency days. When I arrived I found her already seated in a separate booth in the corner. She wore a scarf tied tightly and pulled forward over her brow. It was all quite exciting.

'I suppose Charles has put you up to this?' she said. I nodded since I supposed he had. 'How is he?'

'How do you think?'

'Poor darling.'

'Indeed.'

She wrinkled her nose crossly. 'Now you're not to make me feel like a beast.'

'But I think you are a beast.' We were interrupted, perhaps just in time, by the arrival of the waitress. Of course it was easy to see that Edith was enjoying the whole adventure tremendously. 'How's Simon?' I said.

'Oh, terribly well. He's having lunch with his new agent. Apparently she thinks he's the natural successor to Simon McCorkindale.'

'And that's good, is it?'

'Very good,' she said crisply with an admonishing glance. 'At any rate, it's much better than his last agent who always seemed to think he was lucky to get a job.'

'Is he working now?'

'He's about to do a play in Bromley. A revival of *Rebecca*. Apparently they're hoping it might come into the West End.'

'Edith, it'll be a cold day in hell when a revival of *Rebecca* comes into London from Bromley.'

'Well, that's what they've told him.'

'They say such things for two reasons. One is to tempt you into being in it, and two, so that you have something slightly less pathetic to tell your friends when they ask you what you're doing. This is my world, remember.'

She nodded slightly. 'I imagine that's why Charles has chosen you to talk to me. You're to take the gilt off the gingerbread and show me the dingy lowlife that lies beneath. He's given up trying to remind me of the glories of Broughton although I dare say I've got all that to look forward to when Googie gets in on the act.' She shivered in mock dread.

I felt rather slighted. 'I don't see why I shouldn't remind you of the glories of Broughton,' I said. She shrugged. Suddenly I was irritated by her air of insouciance. I knew, better than most, the effort that had gone into netting Charles and I was damned if I was going to witness Edith playing the part of a jaded aristocrat coming to the end of an arranged marriage. 'Come off it,' I said, driving back the waitress who was approaching with our first courses. 'You loved it. You loved every minute of it. All those cringing shop assistants and sucking-up hairdressers. All that "yes, milady, no, milady". You'll miss it, you know.'

She shook her head. 'No, I won't. You know better than anyone that I didn't grow up with it.'

'It's precisely because you didn't grow up with it that you'll miss it so severely.' I sighed. 'You're in for a terrific setting down, I'm afraid.'

'You don't sound afraid,' she said. 'You sound thrilled.' She took a sip of her Perrier as the plates were laid before us. 'And if Simon becomes a star? What then? Aren't more people interested in meeting a star than some boring old lord?'

It was then that I perceived that Edith, in the full flush of something akin to love, had made two tremendous miscalculations. Firstly, in weighing up the relative merits of aristocracy and stardom she had assumed that the benefits that would accrue to her, as partner, would be roughly equivalent. In fact, nothing could be further from the truth.

The wife of an earl is, after all, a genuine countess. When people meet her it is not solely because they see her as a route to her husband. Better still, if the family she has married into still possesses its estates, as the Broughtons did, then the landed peer offers his wife a mini-kingdom where she may reign as queen. On the other hand, the wife of a star is . . . his wife. Nothing more. If she is cultivated by people it is usually only so that they may ingratiate themselves with her husband. He has no land where she may reign. His kingdom is the studio or the stage where she has no place and where in fact, on her rare visits, she is in the way, an unprofessional among working people. She is excluded from the shared jokes between her husband and his workmates, she holds no interest even for his agent except as a method of controlling him. At dinner her opinions only irritate the other professionals present. Finally and worst of all, while a divorced peeress faces the world and the search for a new husband with a dented but legal title, the divorced wife of a star has returned absolutely to square one. As many Hollywood wives have had to learn before now.

Edith's second miscalculation was simpler. The comparison was false. Charles was a lord. Simon was not a star. Nor was he, in my opinion, very likely to become one. I felt myself becoming caustic. 'What makes you think so well of Simon's prospects?'

'You're very acid this morning. Anyway,' she looked at me with a real expression of appeal and I felt myself softening a little, 'the simple fact is I love him. I don't know whether he's worth it, perhaps he isn't, but I do. And there we are. You wouldn't want me to deny the first genuine feeling I've ever had, would you?'

Part of me wanted to scream yes into her stupid ear but I could see that was not what the moment called for. Poor Edith. She was probably right when she said this passion for Simon was the first real emotion she had ever felt. That was precisely why she knew so little of what she was going through. She never guessed that after a year, however lovely the sex might be, it would no longer obscure from her the life they were leading together. Besides, I knew the strength of the ambition that lurked below Edith's placid surface. Modern psychology constantly harps on the dangers of suppressing one's true sexual nature. It seems to me that it is quite as dangerous to give one's sexual nature free rein and suppress one's worldly aims. Edith was, *au fond*, the ambitious child of an ambitious mother. Quite unconsciously, she had begun to defend her defection by assuming Simon's eventual stardom and wealth. In her mind's eye she already saw herself at a premiere in white fox (or whatever the glamour equivalent is in these ecological days), blowing a kiss to the waiting crowds and sweeping into a stretch limo with a motorcycle escort.

'Darling Edith,' I tried a softer tone, 'I'm not here to lecture you on your morals. I just want to be sure you understand that the likelihood of Simon being able to give you anything approximate to the life you have tasted since your marriage is more or less nil.'

'Well, hurrah for that,' said Edith.

We were done. For the rest of lunch we gossiped about various topics. Moving into the stage world she had of course crossed paths with a few people I knew so we had a new field for our malice. As we were leaving she asked after Adela. I said she was well. 'And madly disapproving, I suppose?'

'Well, she'd hardly be madly approving. Who is?'

'She should have married Charles. She'd have stuck to him through thick and thin.'

'Am I supposed to think badly of her for that?'

She smiled and ruffled my hair. 'You've earned your living in chaos and married into the system. I've been imprisoned in the system. Can you blame me if I yearn for a bit of chaos?'

We parted amicably enough. I telephoned Charles who was grateful and sounded more resigned, I thought. At any rate about a week later it hit the papers so the chance of sorting everything quietly was gone. Adela laid Nigel Dempster's column before my breakfast eyes and I studied the laughing, bosomy picture of Edith that had been selected. There was a more sombre one of Charles and a perfectly terrible 'cad' shot of Simon, which was presumably a still from some television show. It was clear from the illustrations and the headline – 'the Countess and the Showboy' that Dempster had already chosen his side. In fairness to him, both pragmatism and decency seemed (for once) to favour the same team and I couldn't see Edith picking up many supporters.

The story itself was a moderately accurate account of the meeting at Broughton with a dignified quote from Simon's wife that did her credit.

'Really!' Adela was always curiously unforgiving about this sort of mess. 'Stupid fools!'

I don't know why she was so offended when people appeared to let their hearts rule their heads. After all, she had chosen to marry me, which her mother, for one, had thought a choice reckless to the point of lunacy.

'Why are you so cross?' I said. 'I think it's all jolly sad.'

'Sad for Charles and for that wretched woman with her children. Not sad for them. They're just wreckers.'

Once Dempster had opened the floodgates, Edith was predictably savaged by those very journalists who had taken such pains to ingratiate themselves with her as a bride only months earlier. The timing didn't help. It was during the period of disenchantment with John Major's government, when New Labour was performing the Dance of the Seven Veils before an increasingly bewitched electorate, and this tale of high corruption suited the public mood exactly. So there were critical columns from Lynda Lee-Potter on the right and snide disparagement from *Private Eye* on the left. Edith the self-made success story had been replaced by Edith the Social Climber to end all, her greedy, grasping ways apparently a reflection of the heartless society Mrs Thatcher had created. Like the Hamilton scandal or the Spencer divorce, it was soon clear that the actual events and personalities had ceased to have much significance and instead it was simply what the papers decided they stood for that counted. Predictably, it was a nightmare for the Uckfields, who were completely of that school where a respectable woman's name only appears in print three times: hatch, match and despatch – that is to say, when she is born, when she marries and when she dies. Finding their daughter-in-law criticised in column headlines was like being stripped naked and whipped in a public square and if it was ghastly for them it was really horrible for Charles. Slightly illogically, since the press was already limbering up for the Blairocracy that was then in training, they decided that Charles, despite being a worthless aristocrat, was the innocent party (probably because there was no other way of telling the story) but even so, to see his wife's adultery gloated over in newsprint and magazines was a kind of martyrdom for him. The more they telephoned Broughton, urging him to tell 'his side', the more invaded and violated Charles felt. The truth was his horror of scandal was not an affectation but a deeply-held belief and here he was in the middle of one. He was being punished and he hadn't done anything wrong. This at least was Charles's view of the whole hideous episode and I do not think it was unjust.

After this circus had been played out for some weeks, it transpired that I had accepted an invitation for both of us to a supper party at the home of an actress I knew who had recently played Simon's mother in a television thriller. I thought there was every likelihood that the lovers might be there.

Adela was very cool when I told her. 'Well, I'm not going to flounce out of the room or cut her dead if that's what you're worried about.'

'I'm not worried. I'm just telling you they might have been invited. I think it's desirable to avoid publicly taking sides.'

'You need have no fear on that score,' she said witheringly. 'However,' she added, giving an unusually searching look in the glass and picking up her lipstick in real earnest, 'I'm not going to kiss her and wish her every happiness either.'

As it happened, I was right and Edith and Simon were on the guest list for that evening. Edith told me later she hadn't really wanted to go as they had been out every night since the scandal broke but Simon was insistent. He suffered from that common illusion among disappointed actors that it is good to be 'seen' at things. The truth is that it is good to be employed. Whether one is seen at parties is immaterial. However, he had acquired a newsworthy mistress and he probably wanted to get some mileage out of her. If I'm honest and at this distance, I suspect Simon was sorry it had not all been managed without her leaving Charles. That said, since the breach had happened, he would have wanted to profit from the publicity.

Simon Russell was one of those actors whose initial progress had seemed to point inexorably toward a stardom that, somehow, the years had never quite delivered. In the early days he had been given the lead in a series opposite a popular female star but the show had failed. Then he had landed a good part in a Hollywood sequel, which had died at the box office. And gradually the spotlight had shifted and slid away to those newer, younger, blonder men who seemed to arrive in such limitless supply. He was good – or good enough – and, as I have said, wonderful looking, especially when well photographed, and it could all still have happened for him but, by the point of our story, there was no time to lose. And now, most unexpectedly, his private life had put him into print. Edith had made him a topic.

As for his wife and children, I think it would be wrong to say he didn't worry about them. He did. As much as he was able. She, Deirdre, had done her best for him and he really loved the kids, but I suppose it had all become a bit dreary over the last few years and so terribly the same. Besides, it was obvious when you saw them together (which we did a couple of times during the early days of the filming at Broughton) that Deirdre had ceased to think of him as a romantic figure and had begun to treat him more and more as a kind of overgrown, recalcitrant boy. He wanted worship and what he got was someone telling him to eat his greens. Of course, I wasn't sure how much unmixed adoration he would be able to count on from Edith. Or for how long.

*　　*　　*

'Darling, please . . . we *must* go . . .' It was quite unconscious but Simon had fallen into the habit of dealing with Edith in a wheedling tone, a cross between a lounge lizard and a travelling salesman. 'I hate to be naff but you have to get used to the idea that I earn my living. I'm not Charles swanning around giving orders at the Home Farm. I have to be out there. I have to remind people that I exist.'

She sat before the little dressing table in their dreary bedroom, frowning with concentration as she studied her reflection. It did seem rather naff really. Edith was hating her black celebrity. Every time some 'friend' rang her with the news that yet another journalist had taken a swipe at her ('I thought I ought to tell you, darling, before you read it unawares,' the voice would gloat), her heart would sink anew. She wanted fame in a way but fame that brought status and conferred glamour, not this awful washing of dirty linen. She even caught herself feeling sorry for her parents-in-law when she thought of the papers that were probably being edited by Charles or the servants before the Uckfields could set eyes on them. Poor Charles . . . how was he coping with it all, poor dear? And these frightful parties that Simon kept wanting to take her to. Could it be so necessary to keep chatting up these weird representatives from another planet? She had been too long a Broughton to be able to throw off (easily anyway) the notion that Simon's crowd was a sort of joke – useful to enliven a party but not quite right for every day.

'Why?' she said.

He watched her painting her face with care and artistry. He knew what she was thinking but he didn't much care. If she wanted to go back among her old world rather than spend all their time in his, well, that was fine so far as he was concerned. In fact, he was becoming the teeniest bit impatient to get started on some of her gang. She had introduced him to a few Fulham Sloanes, but that wasn't what he had in mind as her contribution at all. Where she dreamed of shepherding him past the Press into his trailer on the Universal lot, he saw himself in tweeds, a gun on his arm, a welcome guest at other houses in the Broughton mould where he would flirt with other great ladies and be taken up by other great families. All of this his alliance with Edith would bring about. He did not grasp, perhaps because she did not yet either, that the great world was preparing to shut its doors on little Edith. From now on she would be condemned to the company of a few divorced wives of younger sons, eking out their alimony selling ugly jewellery or writing gossip columns for unread giveaway magazines.

She put down her mascara. 'Who is this woman tonight, anyway?'

'Fiona Grey.'

'Never heard of her. Have I met her?'

'No, I don't think so but you do know her. She was the girl in the film about the confidence trickster. When he fell off the train. On television last week. Michael Redgrave was the policeman.'

'Never heard of him, either.' Simon winced. 'She must be a thousand.'

'She's about seventy.' Actually Simon was very flattered to have been invited by Miss Grey. For this was the other side of his schizophrenic ambition. While part of him wanted Edith to get him into the world of the 'nobs', the rest of him, in almost direct contradiction, longed to be taken seriously as an actor, by the kind of actors that other actors take seriously, and just such a one was Fiona Grey. She had played Juliet opposite Gielgud in her youth and Lady Teazle opposite Olivier. Now, when she appeared on television it was usually some sort of an event – a series directed by Peter Hall or written by Melvyn Bragg – and she was invariably mentioned lovingly in English stars' autobiographies.

Theatre folk are much given to making claims for the classlessness of their world but the truth is that there is a rigidly structured class system within the business. It is only classless in the sense that this system is based on different values to that of the outside world. Birth may mean nothing but success is all. And not just success but the right kind of success. Simon Russell was acutely aware that, even when he had tasted his little helping of fame, he had never come close to doing work that was 'rated' by his fellow members of Equity and, secretly, it pained him.

When actors tell television interviewers that they don't mind what the critics say so long as the public enjoys what they do they are lying. Few actors care anything for the public's opinion when set against the verdict of the critics and their peers. To be valued and given status behind the proscenium arch is their goal. If it can be accompanied by public adulation, fame and money – so much the better. At the core of the business is a clique whose pre-eminence in 'correct' work is unassailable, and Simon had ever longed to be included in it. The stars and directors, the writers and designers who count among this number patronise all but the most tumultuous public stardom. Their names may be linked to many causes, their interview manner and (certainly) their clothes may seem like a rejection of distinction, but the fact remains they form an elite whose exclusivity rivals that of the *noblesse d'épée* at the court of Versailles. Simon ached to be a member of this golden group who always get good reviews from *Time Out* and are never off the list at BAFTA.

His dreams were not realistic. On this particular evening, for example, he'd only been invited because he was in the papers. Despite their high-sounding principles, these players share one characteristic with their Hollywood brethren: they love to be with famous people. If they lunch with Labour politicians, they like them to be front bench Labour politicians, if they march in a cause, they like to march next to Ian McKellen or Anita Roddick, not some obscure enthusiast from Harlow. But if Miss Grey had taken Simon up because he was In The News, she was incurious about his talent.

*   *   *

The party was in a house in Hampstead, which seemed to Edith to have taken about a year to get to and which, from the street anyway, did not appear to be worth the effort. Inside, every trace of the labourer, whose domestic arrangements it was designed to house in the 1890s, had been swept away in a sea of gleaming wooden floors and concealed lighting. There were knots of earnest discussion in the large living room, which opened off the hall, but the loudest noise was, inevitably, coming from the kitchen downstairs. Adela and I were standing by the stove, surrounded by bowls of pulses and pasta interlarded with strange creatures from the deep, when they came in. I felt Adela nudge me with her elbow as she went on talking animatedly to the unemployed designer we had got stuck with.

Our hostess advanced to Simon and kissed him, staring at Edith throughout. 'Now first you must have a drink and then you must let me introduce you. Do you know David Samson?' She indicated a famous comedy star who had planted himself at her elbow almost as soon as the couple had appeared. Edith smiled and took his hand only to find that hers had been raised to his hoary lips.

'Lady Broughton.' His fruity and familiar tones rolled the name round his tongue, savouring its flavour. He spoke loudly enough for bystanders to turn in curiosity and connect Simon and Edith with the stories they had read or vaguely heard of. There was a faint buzz of awareness. Edith received Samson's adulation coldly, I thought, with a murmured, 'Edith. Please.' Samson was not to be put off. He drew her arm through his and prepared to wheel her about the room. He turned to an inquisitive group nearby, booming out, 'Do you know the Countess of Broughton?'

Edith, needless to say, was in hell.

I would have rescued her earlier but Adela restrained me. I wonder if she didn't take a malicious pleasure in seeing Edith exhibited like a captive in a Roman Triumph. Adela had never endangered her footing in the old camp when she ventured into this new one and I suppose it was hard for her not to feel a tremor of victory. Simon came up to us, beaming. There are some who shudder at the thought of being an 'item' in the news. There are, conversely, others who cannot live without it. Simon was on the latter team. As the half-curious eyes followed him about the room, he was in his element. We broke away, leaving Adela to work over a rather grim-faced casting director on my behalf.

'How are you getting on?' I asked.

'Fine,' said Simon. 'Great.'

'So what happens next?'

'What do you mean?'

'Well, divorce, marriage, statements to the press?'

Simon raised his hands and eyebrows. 'Woah!' he cried with a spangled laugh. 'You sound like my mother.' It is easy to forget that even people like Simon have mothers. Some decent widow of a civil servant sitting in a flat in Leatherhead wondering what on earth was going on. He made me rather cross.

'You do know that you've got in very deep here? You do see that a lot of people are very upset about all this?'

He stroked my cheek. 'Oh well,' he said.

Of course, Adela enjoyed the whole evening hugely. Quite as much as Edith detested it, paraded round the rooms, as she was, like a sacred cow. Adela watched her struggling for small talk with these people who were so remarkably like ordinary people – the very people, in fact, that Edith had spent her twenties trying to escape from forever. The irony of all this was that, for all her hatred of the world of the Name Exchange, Edith had grown used to the comforting snugness of its limited membership. Suddenly she was back in open country where nobody seemed to know anyone she'd ever met. She felt something akin to panic. What did one talk about to people with whom one had no interest and no acquaintance in common? After her time in Broughtonland, she had forgotten.

'Well, I hope she's enjoying herself.' Adela snuggled down into her coat as we started the long trek south.

'Do you?'

'Well, really! What has she done? And to leave without producing a child! So when the door shuts it's shut for ever. What a fool!'

I was still capable of being shocked by my wife's intense worldliness that lived so happily alongside her great, and I knew quite genuine, kindness.

'Isn't it better that there aren't any children?'

'Better for whom? Better for Charles and Googie. Not for her. To produce the heir is the only effective second act for a first wife. Think of Consuelo Vanderbilt's triumph when she returned to hated Blenheim as the mother of the new duke. There'll be none of that for little Edith.' She sighed wearily. 'As for him!'

'I thought you rather liked him.'

'He's pleasant enough in his silly, blond way but hardly the craft to be entrusted with the cargo of life's happiness. What is she thinking of?'

*   *   *

Similar thoughts were flickering somewhere at the back of Edith's brain at just that moment as they too sped back towards what she regarded as

172

Civilisation. She was conscious of a kind of dull disappointment deep in her vitals. She had just been to another 'show business party' and as the phrase echoed through her brain she remembered the image it used to conjure up: vivid actresses, over made-up beauties in sequinned *haute couture*, intense, Jewish writers lecturing groups in the corners of the room, singers helping out a drunken pianist and, all the time, glassy laughter slashing the air ... In fact, when she thought about it, she realised that the whole scene had been taken, more or less unchewed, from *All About Eve*. It seemed to have so little to do with this pack of suburbanites, eating health food and talking about their holidays in Greece.

Nor did she care for their fascination with her as the envoy of a different, and obviously disapproved of, world. She was not indifferent to the glamour of the stage but she had started to see that the quality of glamour as such was no longer rated by the fashionable thespians themselves. To make matters worse, she felt that she had entered this strange arena not as a star (which privately she had counted on) but as a freak.

'What a ghastly bunch! Who were those people?'

Simon never answered these questions, which were in truth more or less rhetorical. They both knew that what Edith was pointing out was that she found theatre folk 'common', though she would never quite say it. Simon, partly because he was not interested in whether they were common or not because it wasn't relevant, and partly because he suspected (deep in his heart) that by her standards he was pretty common himself, never rose to this one. 'I had a good time,' he said.

'You didn't have some frightful man with a voice like a bowl of fruit salad slobbering over your hand all evening. Are all your parties going to be like that?'

'Are all your parties going to consist of six Sloane Rangers and someone who lost money in Lloyd's? Because, if so, I'll take the fruit salad. Any day of the week.'

They drove home in silence.

SIXTEEN

~

It happened that I was in the Fulham Road late one afternoon running various errands and Adela had asked me to look in on Colefax and Fowler to collect some braid she had ordered a few weeks before. Normally I would have refused the commission since at that time (unlike today) all the assistants there seemed to have taken a degree in Higher Rudeness, but she insisted and in fact I was dealt with by a pleasant enough woman. Even though, as Adela had expected, the order had still not arrived, she did seem quite sorry about it.

At any rate, I was just receiving my token apology together with the standard assurances that it would be in next week when I glanced back towards the street and there, leafing idly through the racks of samples, was Edith's mother. I had last seen Mrs Lavery almost exactly two years before, around the time of the festivities of the wedding. It moved me now to think of that victorious figure, trembling with satisfied ambition in the Red Saloon at Broughton, as I looked at this lost and broken soul. She stared glassily at the huge flapping areas of pattern as they waved past her face but she saw nothing. Nothing, that is, except the ruin of all her dreams, which clearly played endlessly like a cursed tableau in her brain.

'Hello, Mrs Lavery,' I said.

She turned to me, gathered the knowledge of who I was from some distant mental shelf and nodded a greeting. 'Hello,' she answered in a hollow, frigid tone.

I learned later that she blamed me for introducing Simon to the Broughton family. With some justice, I suppose. It is customary nowadays for people to shrug off guilt in this sort of thing by saying 'it would have happened anyway' but I am not at all convinced by this argument. Most of our lives are not the fulfilling of some inexorable design laid down at birth but rather the sum total of a series of random events. If Edith had never met Simon – or not met him until after she'd had a child – I think it quite unlikely that the whole thing would have happened. However, she had met him. And it did happen. And, when all is said and done, I had introduced them.

'Have you seen anything of Edith lately?' I said. The sense of her daughter's Banquo-like presence in the room, of her daughter's story, was making us both uncomfortable. It seemed easier to normalise the situation by talking about it.

'Not very much, no.' She shook her head. 'But she . . .' she hesitated, '*they* are coming to dinner tonight. I dare say I shall catch up then.'

I nodded. 'Well, give her my love.'

But Mrs Lavery was not quite prepared to let me go. 'You know him, I gather. This new fellow.'

'Simon? Yes, I know him. Not very well but we were in a film together. Down at Broughton. That's how they met.'

'Yes.' She stared at the floor for a moment. 'And is he nice?'

I was rather touched at this. Mrs Lavery was trying to force herself to be a Good Mother and to concentrate on the timeless values in assessing her daughter's new beau when we both knew that if Simon had been the nicest man in Europe he could never have repaid what had been lost with Charles. 'Very nice,' I said. 'In his way.'

'I don't suppose you've seen much of Charles? Since all the – business happened?'

'I have, in fact. I had lunch with him the other day.'

Mrs Lavery was surprised. I suppose in her romantic imaginings of her son-in-law's world she had erected much fiercer divisions than in fact exist. Also my admission gave the impression that I might not have encouraged Edith in her folly. She softened noticeably. By this time she had convinced herself, of course, that her affection for Charles was genuine and based entirely on his qualities as a man. It wasn't but I don't know that it was any the less felt for that. 'How is he? I'd love to see him but . . .' She trailed off miserably.

'Oh, you know. I'm sure he'd love to see you,' I lied. 'He's still pretty cast down.'

'Well, he would be.' She sighed wearily and without hope. 'I'd better get going. They're coming at eight and I haven't done a thing.'

And she left the shop, her shoulders stooping as she pulled at the heavy door. When I had last seen her she had resembled a character from some frothy Coward comedy. Now she looked like Mother Courage.

*   *   *

Simon was oddly nervous as they turned right off the King's Road down the Vale towards Elm Park Gardens. He'd been fiddling with his tie every time they stopped at a light and as they drew closer, he started picking at his nails. Edith could feel herself tensing with irritation. She couldn't decide if he was apprehensive because he thought her parents were much grander than they in fact were – or if he was nervous of his role as a Wrecker of Marital Bliss. Either way she just wished he'd relax, as the evening promised to be quite sticky enough as it was.

'What is the matter with you?'

Simon just smiled and shook his head. He himself was not exactly clear as to why he had such butterflies although it was true he did think that the Laverys were smarter than they were. He had a very unclear idea of the nuances of London Society and, since he had no knowledge of the Inner Circle whatever, he was unaware of the extent to which Edith had been an outsider at the time of her marriage. Since he still thought of his new mistress as fearfully smart he imagined her background was correspondingly impressive. But that was not actually the source of his unease on this particular evening. Probably it was the more ordinary complaint that this formalisation of their relationship, this presentation to the parents, seemed to set some sort of seal of finality on what had originally been nothing more than a flirtation. He had not really, even now, faced that he was heading into the realms of 'divorce' and 'division of property' and 'maintenance' and 'custody' and all sorts of other depressing words and phrases and yet that is what suddenly seemed to loom ahead. He supposed that in some perhaps roundabout way Mr Lavery was going to ask him about his 'intentions' and it struck him that he didn't really have any intentions – not absolutely fixed ones anyway. But then he glanced across at Edith and she did look very lovely when he thought about it and he was aware of how much prettier her profile was than Deirdre's, who had always looked just a little gormless from sideways on and he thought that after all he could do worse. And thus mollified and heartened he got out of the car.

Mrs Lavery had confided in her husband about her meeting in

176

Colefax. The words of the conversation had gone round and round her head until she had tried to spin them into a skein of hope. Even as she cooked for her daughter's lover she shouted through to the drawing room, 'What do you think he meant by "cast down" exactly?'

Kenneth Lavery was almost as unhappy as his wife over the turn events had taken but for more honourable motives. He hated to see his beloved 'Princess' involved in a public scandal. He hated to witness his wife's despair. And he was not insensible to the fact that his daughter had thrown away a position of power from which she might have achieved fine things and run instead to a place barely within decent society. He had been proud of his daughter as a Great Lady and he was saddened by her fall. Having said that, he was a good deal more philosophical about the nature of Edith's folly than his wife. Unlike her he had never deluded himself that Edith's marriage was going to make all that much of a difference in his own life.

'I think he meant what he said. Charles is cast down. Of course he's cast down. His wife has just gone off with another man. What would you expect him to be?'

Stella Lavery stuck her head round the door. 'I just meant that it sounds as if Charles still hasn't got used to the idea. I wondered if there was any point in perhaps getting in touch with him . . . ?' Her voice trailed away, as her husband started to shake his head slowly but firmly from side to side.

'My dear, it is not Charles who decided to end the marriage. It doesn't matter what he thinks. He is not to blame for this. Nor do I think it fair to start trying to stir him up. Maybe he is getting over her, maybe he isn't. Either way it will not help him to have his hopes revived by you. He is a nice man and our daughter has behaved badly to him. It is fitting for us to keep out of his way.' So saying he returned to the television.

His wife did not resent this treatment by her husband because in her heart she agreed with it. Try as she might to affect some sort of modern tolerance the fact remained that she was deeply, deeply ashamed of Edith's behaviour. As long as she could remember she had imagined herself perfectly suited for a Great Role in the public life of England. She would daydream as she watched those ladies-in-waiting hovering behind the Queen in Parliament, all dressed in their fifties Hartnell frocks, and she had thought how well she, Stella Lavery, would have acquitted herself as Duchess of Grafton or Countess of Airlie if fate had only called her. She would have served well, she knew, even if, like the little mermaid, every step had been taken on knives. And all this fantasy had been passed on to her daughter who had, miraculously, made it come true. But now, instead of hearing that Edith had been asked to chair the Red Cross or to join the household of one of the princesses, the telephone had rung to tell her that it was all over. That her dream was in ruins. And at the bottom of this pit of slime into which she had been hurled was the bitter gall of knowing that all over London people were tut-tutting and saying that after all Charles had married beneath him, that Edith was a little nobody who just couldn't 'handle it' and that he should have stuck to his own kind.

The doorbell went but before they could get to it Edith had let herself in and was calling to them through the flat. As the lovers entered the drawing room, she hurried to kiss her father. He gave her an affectionate squeeze and she knew he at least would be no trouble as she led him over to be introduced to Simon. One glance at the frozen statue of her mother framed in the doorway, however, told her all she needed to know about the evening to come.

Mrs Lavery advanced stiffly and extended a hand. But she could not smile and in a way it was almost a relief that, as soon as Kenneth had left them to fetch some drinks, she dispensed with Simon's inept attempts at small talk and launched straight into the heart of the matter. 'You will understand that this is all very difficult for us, Mr Russell.' She deliberately ignored his attempts to make her call him Simon and in this there was a certain similarity to the way her idol, Lady Uckfield, would have managed the meeting. The latter would have been much cosier, of course. 'We are both very fond of our son-in-law. So you will forgive us if we don't fall on your neck.'

Simon smiled, crinkling up his eyes in a way that was usually effective. 'Neck-falling is quite optional, I assure you,' he muttered gaily.

Mrs Lavery did not return his smile. It wasn't that she was immune to physical attraction. She could see well enough that Simon was one of the handsomest men she had ever encountered but in her eyes his beauty was the explanation of her daughter's ruin. Nothing less. At that moment she could cheerfully have taken a knife and cut the features from his face if it would have turned Edith back from her chosen course. 'My daughter was,' she paused, '*is* married to a fine man. Obviously you've thought about what you're doing but it's hard for us to see her break her vows without a pang.'

'It wouldn't have cost you much of a pang if I was leaving Simon for Charles,' said Edith.

Now this was completely true. So true in fact that it made Mr Lavery smile momentarily as he came back in with a tray of glasses, but Edith was forgetting that Mrs Lavery had cast herself in the part of Hecuba, the Noble Widow. In Stella's shattered mind she and Googie Uckfield were two high-born victims in a cosmic disaster (she talked *of* Lady Uckfield as Googie but not yet *to* her. Now, she thought tearfully, she would never have the chance). There was no room for irony in her suffering. She looked at her daughter with brimming eyes.

'How little you know me,' she said, and retreated majestically into the kitchen. Edith, her father and Simon stared at each other.

'Well, I suppose we all knew it was going to be a rough night,' said Mr Lavery, tucking into his whisky.

Later, sitting round the oval reproduction table in the flat's modest dining room, the four of them did contrive some quasi-normal conversation. Mr Lavery questioned Simon about acting and Simon questioned Mr Lavery about business and Mrs Lavery fetched the food and removed the plates and made elaborately courteous remarks all evening. She had that uniquely English talent of demonstrating, through her scrupulously polite manner, just how awful she thought the company. She could leave a roomful crushed and rejected and yet congratulate herself on behaving perfectly. It is of course of all forms of rudeness the most offensive as it leaves no room for rebuttal. Even at the height of hostility the Moral High Ground is never abandoned.

Edith watched the three familiar faces and tried to question herself as to what was really taking place. Was this the cementing of a new alliance that would shape her future life? Would these three people be her companions through twenty Christmases to come? Would Simon and her mother build their bridges and talk about the children and come to share private jokes? Handsome as Simon was and strong as her desire for him remained, she was struck this evening by the dreariness of them all.

She had lived the last two years in the front rank of English life and on reflection she was surprised to discover how normal it had become for her to do so – until, that is, she had removed herself from it. While she had been at Broughton she had been oppressed by the lack of event, by the emptiness of her daily round. Now that she had left it, however, hardly a day passed when at least one of her acquaintance from her life with Charles was not in the newspaper. And when she thought about it, having at the time complained ceaselessly that they never did anything, she remembered dinner after dinner where she had sat opposite some faintly famous face from the Cabinet or the opera or simply the gossip columns. Bored to sobs as she was by Googie and Tigger, she had become used to hearing political and Royal chat days or even weeks before it hit the headlines. She was accustomed to knowing the details of the private lives of the great before they became common knowledge – if indeed they ever did. She and Charles had not spent a great deal of time staying away but now her memory reminded her of three or four shooting parties during the winter and a couple of house parties in the summer. She knew Blenheim by this time and Houghton and Arundel and Scone. She had lost the sense of these places' historicity. They had become the homes of her circle. In this she was almost being honest – as honest certainly as those born to the class to which she had so briefly belonged. Edith had learned well all the tricks of aristocratic irrever-ence. She would stride like the best of them into a dazzling great hall by Vanbrugh, lined with full length van Dycks, and curse the M25 as she threw her handbag into a Hepplewhite chair. By this stage, she understood how to make that statement of solidarity. 'This wonderful room is ordinary to me,' their actions say, 'because it is my natural habitat. I belong here even if you do not.'

Now, it seemed to her, looking at Kenneth and Stella with their framed flower prints from Peter Jones, their pseudo-Regency furniture, their Jane Churchill print curtains, that her membership of that club where she could curl up in an armchair in the long library at Wilton and leaf through Vogue, hugging a vodka and tonic, had been revoked without reference to her. In a rare moment of clarity she understood that in choosing this actor, far from making a wild bohemian statement, she had in fact returned to her own country. That Simon was far more of a piece with Stella and her faraway baronet cousin or Kenneth and his business friends than Charles had ever been. This world, where, as a general rule, one laughed and cried alongside the obscure – this was her real world. The world in which she had grown up and where she would now again live. Charles and Broughton and the Name Exchange only touched her people tangentially. They were, whatever her mother might like to think, an entirely different tribe.

'Phew!' said Simon, as they pulled away from the curb and headed back towards the King's Road. Edith nodded. They had survived. That was the main thing. She had taken the first step in explaining to her mother that her dream-life was over. Simon winked at her. 'We're alive,' he said. For a moment they rode on in silence. 'Do you want to go straight home?'

'As opposed to?'

'Well, we could go on somewhere.'

'Where?'

Simon made a slight pout. 'What about Annabel's?'

Edith was rather surprised. 'Are you a member?'

He shook his head, a little petulantly, she thought. 'No, of course I'm not. But you can get us in.'

Edith wasn't at all sure that she could get them in. Charles was the member, after all, and although they had been together fairly frequently and they certainly knew her at the club she wasn't clear as to where that left her. Nor was she convinced that it was a good idea. There were bound to be people there from Charles's set. 'I don't know,' she said.

'Come on. Charles is in Sussex and you can't run away from being seen all the time. We've got our life, too, I suppose.'

This time, unlike her excursions with Charles, they parked in the square and walked to the entrance steps. Simon had only been once before and was grinning like a madman as they descended. Edith was less certain of herself and the moment they had entered the corridor hall she knew she had been right. This was a Mistake. The club servant in charge greeted her affably enough. 'Lady Broughton,' he paused to take in Simon, 'are you meeting someone? Can I tell them you're here?'

Edith felt herself blushing. 'Well, we're not actually. I just wondered if we could come in for a moment.'

Again the answer was scrupulously polite. 'I didn't know you were a member, milady.'

'Well, I'm not. I mean, Charles – Lord Broughton – is and I just thought . . .' She tailed off in the face of the regretful smile on the face of the attendant.

'I'm very sorry, milady . . .'

If fate had been kind that would have been it but at that precise moment the door pushed open and with a sinking heart Edith heard the shrill tones of Jane Cumnor. Turning, she smiled straight into the huge, sweating face of Henry as he lumbered in, puffing with the effort of clambering down the basement steps. For a fraction of a second Jane was silent as she took in Edith and, of course, Simon. Then her smile returned.

'Edith! How lovely!' She kissed her coldly on both cheeks. 'Aren't you going to introduce us?'

'Simon Russell. Lord and Lady Cumnor.' She didn't really know why she hadn't used their Christian names. Could it be that she felt the need to impress Simon? After the evening they had just spent?

Jane gave her a slightly old-fashioned look. 'Are you coming in?'

For a moment Edith was going to say that they were in fact leaving when Simon spoke. 'They won't let us. Apparently you have to be a full member.' He didn't really understand the enormity of his betrayal of Edith in this. He simply wanted to get inside the club and so far as he could see, here were two people who could manage it for them.

But Henry was not to be caught. Sensing what was coming he nodded briskly. 'Edith,' he said, and strode on past her down the corridor towards the bar.

Jane smiled wanly. 'What a bore for you,' she murmured. 'I'm not a member either. I, um, I suppose I could go after Henry if you want...' She tailed away to demonstrate how very much she did not wish to carry out her own suggestion and Edith let her go.

'No, no,' she said. 'It couldn't matter less. We're late anyway. I don't know why we looked in.' She kissed Jane perfunctorily with Simon twinkling away by her side, still hoping to be taken in and still missing what was going on. And then they were alone again. The attendant, ever impeccably polite, was anxious to bring about a satisfactory conclusion. 'I am sorry, Lady Broughton...'

Edith nodded. 'We're just off,' she said.

They were outside the door and at the bottom of the steps when a voice hailed them from above. 'Edith?' They looked up and there was the lanky figure of Tommy Wainwright descending towards them. 'Fancy meeting you.' He smiled affably enough and shook Simon's hand. His wife, Arabella, a cooler customer entirely than her husband, was silent. 'Are you going already?' said Tommy.

'Yes,' said Edith. But before she could stop him Simon was having another shot at completing his evening in the way he had planned.

'Edith thought she could get us in but she can't,' he said, thereby giving Arabella Wainwright a funny story and a parable of Edith's fall all in one phrase.

Tommy smiled. 'Then you must let me.'

'Really, it doesn't matter,' protested Edith.

'Come on,' said Simon.

Arabella murmured gently, 'If she doesn't want to . . .' It was quite clear that she was no more anxious than Jane Cumnor to be seen escorting Edith Broughton and her new lover into Annabel's but Tommy was made of stouter stuff. A few minutes later he had equipped them all with drinks and they were seated at the foot of a giant Buddha in the little red smoking room to one side of the bar. Simon saw Arabella as a challenge and they had hardly sat down before he was inviting her to dance. Perhaps because being seen dancing with an unknown was preferable to being spotted in Edith's company, she accepted and Tommy and Edith were left alone.

'How've you been?'

Edith shrugged. 'You know.'

'I do.' He smiled at her quite kindly. 'You mustn't let the newspaper nonsense get to you. I should know, in my job. Today's scandal really is tomorrow's budgie paper. People forget more or less everything.'

Edith nodded. She knew well enough that while this is a general truth, it is seldom a personal one. She had been touched by scandal and inasmuch as she would ever feature in the papers again once it was all over, there would always be a small paragraph referring to her separation from Charles until the end of her life. 'Have you seen Charles?' she said.

Tommy nodded. 'I saw him in White's last week. We had a drink together.'

'How is he?'

'Not very chipper but I suppose he'll manage.' Edith felt a sudden pang of nostalgia for Tommy and White's and even Jane Cumnor, whom she had nodded to across the bar but had not attempted to join. Six months ago she would have sat with Tommy and ranged over the up-to-date stories of their mutual acquaintance and whatever she might say about all that now, it would have made her feel rather cosy. But on this evening there didn't seem to be any point. It wasn't her world any more and they both knew it. As for Charles. Poor old Charles. What had he done to deserve this? He'd just been dull company. That's all. Nothing worse than that. And then Simon returned and, much to Arabella's relief, led Edith away to the dance floor.

She was silent in the car although she smiled at Simon to allay his fears that she might be angry about something when she really wasn't. As she put the key into the lock of the Ebury Street front door Simon allowed the arm that had enclosed her waist to slip down to her buttocks, which he caressed gently as they walked through the little hall and stopped outside the door to the flat. Edith could feel a tingling sensation start to warm her at the base of her stomach. Simon leaned forward and kissed the back of her neck, his tongue licking her softly between his parted lips. They were hardly inside the door before she was kissing him in a strong, fierce way, and running her hands over his body and down to his crotch. She felt his large, hard penis pushing against her. 'Darling,' he said with the anticipatory smile of a man who understands and enjoys his work.

They made love three times that night at Edith's insistence. Simon had never known her throw herself into it with quite such abandon before. She mounted him and pushed herself down, forcing as much of him into her as she could. Because it was suddenly quite clear to her that this was the decision she had made. When she came home with Charles the evening was over as they shut the door. When she went out with Simon the evening was something that had to be endured until they could be alone together again. Fate had given her the choice between her private and her public life. Neither man, it seemed, could provide her with both. Well, she thought as she lay back watching the dawn and listening to Simon snoring gently beside her, she had chosen private fulfilment over public splendour and she was glad of her choice. Glad, that is, in the night, when she lay naked and satisfied and far from the world.

It was in the morning that she had to make up her mind all over again.

PART THREE

~

Dolente-Energico

SEVENTEEN

~

I did not see Edith for some months after this. In the autumn I was given the part of a villain in one of those series that are optimistically described as 'family viewing' because no one can decide into which category they really fall. At any rate, it was shot on location in Hampshire and I was consequently a good deal out of London for some time. I took a cottage in Itchen Abbas and Adela joined me when she could. Some time in November we discovered she was pregnant and the thought that my life was about to take yet another quantum leap rather drove all other considerations from my mind. We purchased books by the dozen to learn more about our new condition and spent the evenings looking up why Adela kept tasting metal filings or feeling back pains. Actually this was pretty fruitless as the answer to more or less everything we asked was 'the cause of this is not yet known'. However, we were kept quite merrily occupied.

Of Edith, Simon and Charles we had little news. The papers had dropped them as there did not appear to be any signs of divorce and presumably they were all saving the second half of the story for when it came to court. Once I wrote to Charles because I had seen, in some obscure art magazine, that a Broughton portrait was up for sale and I thought he, or some relation, might be interested. Naturally I also imparted our news and I received, almost by return, quite a touching letter wishing us well. 'How right you are not to wait too long,' he wrote. 'Being married is all very well but it's having a child that makes a real family. I envy you that.' I do not necessarily agree with this view but I took it, correctly I think, as a comment on his own marital disappointments. He concluded by asking us to get in touch when we were back in circulation and I thought I would. I felt that by this time Charles and I had gone through enough together to qualify as friends even by English standards and the potential awkwardness of attempting to prosecute friendships with the Mighty no longer seemed to apply. I was interested that he had not mentioned Edith and indeed we had no news of her from any quarter. Gossip confirmed that she and Simon were still together and that, either because his notoriety had paid off or just conceivably because of his talent, he had landed a running part in some police series. I had made up my mind that I would also contact her when I returned to London, as I was determined not to be cast in the role of someone who drops their friends when their status diminishes, but in actual fact it was not I but my spouse who renewed our links.

We had not been back in London long when Adela received an invitation from a cousin to attend Hardy Amies's spring dress show. The relation in question, Louisa Shaw, was in the household of a junior member of the Royal Family and either for this reason or (more probably) because she was an occasional purchaser she had got onto the various lists to be invited to these glittering events, always with jolly good seats. She and Adela had been friends from childhood and consequently she allowed my wife to share her good fortune on a regular basis.

Unbeknownst to us as Adela and Louisa made their plans, it so happened that our old familiar, Annette Watson, was also a Hardy Amies customer. She had been, as I have said, something of a screen beauty of the Lesley-Ann Down vintage and she had always provided willing fodder to the photographers at bashes where there was a scarcity of celebrities but now she figured on the pages of the glossy magazines wearing *couture*, which naturally made her a welcome guest at these galas. Annette, in fact, was doing quite well by this stage, largely because, against all predictions, the dreary Bob had gone from well-off to extremely rich during the heady nineties. I seem to recall that his success was somehow connected to the 'dot.com' revolution although I cannot remember exactly what he did, if I ever knew. Anyway, whatever it was he obviously did it profitably. In the two or three years since the Watsons had been Eric's embarrassing guests in Mallorca they had consolidated their social position and, in London at any rate, they had gathered up quite a satisfactory address book. They had not penetrated Lady Uckfield's charmed circle on any level but they were on good terms with a couple of the more disreputable young marchionesses and the 'It' girls who were busy on the London scene at this time. Annette had even been pictured in *Hello* shopping with the Duchess of York. On the whole, she was satisfied.

A good part of that satisfaction was because she was now in a position to refuse the Chases' invitations, which had become more pressing of late. Caroline Chase, of course, cared little one way or the other, but Eric's shadowy dealings on the outer fringes of what he optimistically described as 'Business Skills and Public Relations' had been badly hit by the recession. These skills, it seems, were among the first economies in the newly hard-pressed companies that had bloomed so fast and were now looking as if they would wither as quickly. Eric felt that a helping hand from Bob Watson might make all the difference. Indeed it might have, I suppose, but perhaps because of that terrible dinner at Fairburn, the hand was withheld. The Chases, or Eric anyway, had ceased to be necessary to the social game-plan of the Watsons. Apart from anything else Eric was not expected to be around all that much longer. It was known that they were living on Caroline's money and questions were beginning to be asked among her circle as to how long this would go on. Particularly as there were no children to confuse the issue. To Caroline's set, there did not seem to be much logic in being married to someone who was common *and* poor. Although I reject these people's values in many areas, when dealing with someone as abrasive as Chase I must confess to understanding them.

It is pleasant to record that one friend who had not dropped Edith and automatically taken Charles's side in order to keep in with the Broughtons was this same Annette Watson. For Edith had paid a severe penalty for her chosen path. Actually I didn't much blame most of their crowd. They had been Charles's friends to begin with and Edith certainly had behaved badly. But this was not the real reason that they flocked to the Broughton banner. To a man they would have remained on Charles's team if he'd beaten Edith while keeping a string of chorus girls in the attic. However, I suppose one must concede that in this particular instance it was hard to argue with them. At any rate, Annette, partly because she knew she held few charms for Charles or his mother and partly because she really did like Edith, had stuck by her pal and one of the invitations she'd proffered was to accompany her to the Hardy Amies afternoon show and have some lunch beforehand.

* * *

Edith had never been to the first-floor restaurant of the Meridien in Piccadilly, which had recently been subjected to an exhaustive 'renovation'. The dining room was formed out of the old terrace, which had been glazed and palmed and marble-floored and generally made into a home from home for all those natives of Los Angeles who were now, hopefully, going to flock through the newly re-opened doors. Edith picked her way among the tables, following Annette's waving hand. She was smartly dressed in a snappy winter suit, complete with pearls and a brooch. She had surprised herself by being tempted to wear a hat. She didn't, but the costume, as it stood, was perhaps an expression of a part of her life that had been suppressed for a time beneath the T-shirts and sequins, apparently the only two options of Simon's crowd. Even he had commented on her outfit as he lay on a sofa happily reading the next day's scenes: 'Heavens, very smart! You look like your mother-in-law!' But she hadn't risen. Maybe, subconsciously, she'd felt complimented.

Annette kissed her and ordered glasses of champagne for them both. It was not long before they had moved from the customary greetings to the real business. 'So, when do you make your next move?'

'Move?' said Edith.

'Well. The divorce. Are you getting on with it?'

Edith shifted slightly uncomfortably. 'Not really. Not yet.'

'Why not?'

She shrugged. 'I suppose I – we – rather feel that we might as well wait out the two years and do it with a minimum of fuss. Otherwise it means such a palaver...'

'Two years!' Annette laughed. 'Oh, I don't think Charles is going to be happy waiting two years.'

'Why not?'

Annette stared at her. 'Darling, you must know the race is on.'

Edith was surprised to find that her stomach lurched. 'What do you mean?'

'My dear, as soon as the news was out he was absolutely pounced on. How could he not be? You haven't even had a child so there's nothing to hold them back.'

Edith felt herself growing irritated. How dare this woman know more about her husband than she did? 'I don't think he's seeing anyone particularly.'

'Then you think wrong.' Annette took a sip to punctuate her pause. 'You remember Clarissa Marlowe?'

Edith laughed and breathed easily again. The Honourable Clarissa Marlowe, great-granddaughter of a courtier who had been raised to a lowly barony in the 1920s, was a second cousin of Charles's through their mothers. She was a hearty, healthy brunette, good in the saddle and helpful at sticky dinner parties. She worked as an up-market receptionist in a dubious property company, thereby lending it some respectability, and she lived in a flat with her sister just off the Old Brompton Road. A classic member of the Alice Band Brigade and, Edith thought comfortably, not at all Charles's type.

'Don't be silly. She's his cousin. She's just chumming him.'

Annette raised her eyebrows. 'Well, she chummed him to the West Indies for a week just before Christmas and she spent the New Year at Broughton.'

There was no denying that this was a blow. In fact Edith was astonished at its severity. What had she thought? That Charles would stay single for ever? She had been gone for eight months now and he was only human. As she conjured up the image of Clarissa, Edith felt herself washed with a tide of rage towards this blameless, county girl. In truth she had always rather liked Clarissa, who put herself out to be useful and laughed at Edith's funny stories and had never been one of those relations who persisted in treating her as a tiresome foreigner. When she thought about it she supposed that his cousin had always had rather a soft spot for Charles. With a sinking heart she recognised Clarissa for what she was, the sort of girl men like Charles marry.

'Oh,' she said.

The waiter had arrived to hand them enormous, leather-bound menus in ungrammatical French. He retreated with a murmur of guttural Rs.

'Cheer up, darling,' said Annette with a piercing look. 'Tell me about Simon. Is he well?'

'Oh yes,' said Edith, bracing herself again. 'Very. He's got a series that goes on until June and then, with any luck, starts again in December.'

'How marvellous! What is it?'

'Oh, you know,' said Edith, trying to decide between liver and seared tuna. 'Some detective police thing. He's the nice side-kick who keeps missing the point.' She finally fixed on kidneys with a salad.

'Well done him,' said Annette. 'Who else is in it? Do you go on the set and everything?'

Edith appreciated Annette's efforts at enthusiasm. It was kind of her. 'Not really, no. Sometimes. So I can put a face to the stories. It puts him off a bit.'

The truth was that, try as she might, she had found that she just could not get really involved in Simon's work. There were parts of it she quite liked, first nights and a few (very few) of the parties and meeting people one knew from television. She was quite interested in reading scripts and then comparing them to the finished product but most of it, well ... At the beginning she had gone down to the location a few times but, honestly, it was *so* monotonous. They just seemed to say the same three lines to each other from a thousand angles until she ended up in the make-up room, gossiping to the girls. If she was really honest she couldn't understand why Simon made such a song and dance about it all. Most of it seemed to be pretty straightforward. You learned the lines, they trained the camera onto you and you said the lines. She was quite able to see that some people could do it and some couldn't, but fretting about it didn't seem to help. She never noticed that Simon was much better in the parts he had sweated over than in the ones that he did off the top of his head. One thing she had grasped since our lunch together in those early days – there wasn't really a place for her down on the set. After her initial forays she would roll up once or twice, or stay on location for a weekend, so that she could say hello to the other members of the cast and crew and leave it at that. It seemed to be the best way to play it.

'Give him my love,' said Annette. They locked eyes for a moment and to Edith's relief the waiter reappeared at this precise moment to take their orders. That done, they shifted their ground back to more general topics.

*   *   *

Louisa rang our basement bell promptly at a quarter to one. They had decided to lunch at home as they were going on to Fortnum's for tea after the show. Adela, at five months, had only recently stopped feeling sick and was sorely in need of a Treat. I was to give them a lift to Savile

Row on my way to a wig fitting in Old Burlington Street. I liked Adela's cousin. The daughter of an Anglo-Irish landowner, she had that slightly fey, unjudgemental quality of her tribe, so unlike their English counterparts, that made her easy company for anyone, despite her tweeds and sensible shoes. She was also a natural spinster for whom, I suspected, a lifetime of Royal service was going to have to do the work of husband and children. Of course, she was thrilled by the idea of the impending baby and I could see before Adela asked me that she was classic godmother material.

The traffic was not heavy and accordingly it was no later than a quarter to three when the two of them climbed the staircase of Hardy Amies's headquarters and entered the large, first-floor salon overlooking Savile Row itself, where the collection was to be displayed.

There is no real benefit in getting to these things early as all the seats are clearly and unarguably allocated but they had enough to gossip about to pass the time and so, once they had been ushered to two seats labelled, in a flowing hand; 'Lady Louisa Shaw & Friend', they were soon so engrossed in their own soap-opera that they were oblivious to the rest of the fast-filling room. They were seated well, at the foot of the catwalk on the short side of the room near the door from the staircase and therefore had a full view not only of the length of the catwalk but also of most of the rest of the seating. So Adela was quite surprised, on looking up as the lights were turned on to signify that the show was about to begin, to see Edith Broughton tucked into the far corner, in the back row, opposite the door where the models make their entrance. It seemed odd that Edith had not said hello, since she must have brushed past them to get to her seat and even now, while looking at Adela, she made no real sign of recognition. I am afraid that one could have read in this the treatment that Edith had had to endure over the previous months but at any rate Adela, for whom even the vestige of any kind of feud is anathema, immediately smiled and waved, and Edith, relieved perhaps, waved back.

The conversation was beginning to die away in anticipation when there was a slight confusion at the door. Adela turned in time to see one of the princesses enter the room, followed by Lady Uckfield. Smiling their apologies, they made their way to two seats reserved for them near the foot of the catwalk beyond my wife and Louisa, in the front row. They were in their places before Adela looked back to where Edith sat, her eyes fixed on her mother-in-law. The contrast between the state of the two women was not lost on Adela and it must have seemed vividly clear to Edith. She sat in the back row, with her over-made-up friend, about to look at clothes she could not seriously entertain a thought of buying. Two rows before her sat the woman she might herself have been, with a member of the Royal Family, envied by more or less every other woman present. The music started, a selection of Copacabana rock, which seemed a surprising choice given the age of the majority of the clients. Adela glanced down at her programme for the description of the first presentation. Three models appeared, the numbers of their dresses displayed on plastic discs in their elegant hands, and the show had begun.

It was a lively hour with the audience chatting relentlessly as each ensemble was paraded before them. 'Lovely for Spain', 'What an odd colour, I wonder if they do it in cream', 'Pretty dress, wrong model', and other similar phrases would ring out, quite audibly, as the girls sailed imperviously by. From time to time a little fun was added by a model dropping her number disc (I gather these have since been abandoned, perhaps for this reason) or one might stumble in a graceful spin but these were rare breaks in the super-smooth operation. Still, Adela was distracted. Every time she glanced over to where Edith sat, she could see that her gaze was not on the catwalk but on the back of her mother-in-law's head, still blithely unaware of Edith's presence, as she scribbled on her programme and exchanged whispers with her august companion.

The collection was presented and the company, notes jotted and images fixed, rose to go. A way was made for the Royal Highness to pass, with Lady Uckfield following on. With proper diffidence Adela did not draw attention to herself but it so happened that the princess recognised Louisa at the same moment that Lady Uckfield saw my wife. Accordingly she was presented, made her curtsey, and for a few moments the crowd fell deferentially back to leave them in a foursome. They were chatting quite amiably about which frocks they had preferred when Adela caught sight of Edith edging towards them through the thinning crush. These situations are hard. Though I say it myself, Adela is not one to shirk a difficult task, but what was the point of spoiling Lady Uckfield's afternoon or placing her in an invidious position as regards her companion? Her daughter-in-law was a figure of scandal and this was a public place stuffed with journalists. Judas-like, Adela opted for Damage Containment, and catching Lady Uckfield's eye nodded slightly in the direction of Edith's advancing figure. Lady Uckfield, demonstrating the skill that ran the Empire, became aware of her daughter-in-law's presence without so much as a flicker of recognition. Even Adela would have been hard put to it to deny that her immediate departure was simply fortuitous, had it not been for the conspiratorial squeeze of her arm by the older woman. In a moment princess and attendant were gone, leaving Adela to introduce Edith as she drew alongside a slightly bemused Louisa.

They talked for a while with Edith asking about me and Adela rather pointedly not asking about Simon and then they parted. Though not before Edith had observed brightly, 'My dear mother-in-law looks well.'

'Very well, I gather,' said Adela.

Edith laughed. 'How funny to think one has turned into an awkward relation! Oh well. She can't avoid me entirely. She might as well get used to the idea that I do still live in London, whether she likes it or not.'

'I don't think she was avoiding you. She just didn't see you,' said Adela, adding lamely, 'I never thought to say anything...'

'No,' said Edith. 'Why would you?'

And so they parted, Adela and Louisa to Fortnum's and then back to the flat to tell me every detail, Edith to Ebury Street and Simon, who was in a rage because one of his speeches had been cut from tomorrow's scene. He suspected his co-star, whom he was already beginning actively to dislike, and his brain was so full of this particular injustice that he had very little time for Edith's narrative. I doubt she told him much anyway. Only that she'd seen Googie but Googie hadn't seen her. In truth, beyond lesser horrors like the evening at Annabel's, this had been the starkest illustration so far of the extent of her fall and she could not yet talk about it without beginning to feel slightly ill.

I knew enough from Adela's account to understand that Edith must be going through a pretty rough time however happy she was with Simon and I resolved to telephone her and buy her a decent lunch. But before I got around to it, I was surprised to receive an invitation from Isabel Easton to go down to Sussex for the weekend. The envelope was in fact addressed to Adela. Isabel had apparently learned her lessons well and grasped that the upper classes only ever address an envelope to the female part of a couple. Why? Who knows? At any rate it was Adela who read it first and she who suggested we accept. Adela was only mildly fond of Isabel and she didn't like David much so I suspected at once that she had an ulterior motive.

'We might give Charles a ring when we're there,' she said, so I didn't have to wait long to know what it was.

I don't think I had stayed with the Eastons since that time, three years before, when we had all been summoned to Broughton to witness Edith's triumph. I had seen them in London so the gap was not obvious and, looking back, I'm not sure why I had got out of the habit of going there. Perhaps the fact that Edith and I had become friends over their heads had made an awkwardness between us. I'm not sure. At any rate I was quite glad to find myself and my wife, a couple of Friday nights later, back in their familiar, GTC drawing room of frilled tables and chintz sofas and over-stuffed cushions. We had unpacked and bathed and been given a pre-dinner drink, but not much more than this before the real reason for our invitation became clear.

'Are you going to go over to Broughton while you're here?' said David.

I looked at Adela. 'I don't know. I don't know if they're there. We thought we might give them a ring.'

'Good,' said David. 'Good.' He paused. 'Give our love to Charles when you speak to him, anyway.'

And there it was. I should have guessed. After all, what a situation they were in! For years they had been driven nearly mad by their inability to get onto any sort of terms with the local family. Then, miracle of miracles, their friend marries the heir. They start to inch their way into the County. They are just beginning to make a little headway with the Sir William Fartleys of this world when, bang, a scandal erupts. Suddenly Edith, their friend, the woman they first invited down to these parts (for one may be sure they had made no secret of the role they had played), runs off with an actor, disgraces the family, lets down poor, darling Charles. Exeunt David and Isabel Easton.

I think one would have to be very hard-hearted indeed not to feel some sympathy for them, poor things, even if their goal was a worthless one. It is easy to laugh at the pretensions of others – particularly when their ambitions are trivial – but most of us have a thorny path of it in some area of our lives, which is not worth the importance we give it. I suppose it is hard to live in a small society and to be obliged to accept that one is excluded from the first rank of that little group. This is what drives so many socially minded people back to the towns where the game is more fluid and up for grabs. On top of which the Eastons had come, at least in their own minds, so near the prize . . .

David continued. 'I'm afraid the simple truth is that our dear Edith has behaved most fearfully badly.'

We all, including Isabel, greeted this with a slight silence. Even Adela (who, I knew, most thoroughly agreed with this assessment) seemed reluctant to weigh in with David in Edith's absence. 'I don't know,' I said.

'Really!' David was quite indignant. 'I'm surprised to hear you defending her.'

'I'm not defending her exactly,' I said. 'I'm just saying that one doesn't "know". One never knows anything about other people's lives. Not really.'

This is a truism but it isn't completely true. One does know about other people's lives. And I, in fact, knew quite a lot about Edith's and Charles's lives but, even if I was guilty of a certain dishonesty, there was some truth in what I said. I am not convinced that one ever knows quite enough to come down with a full condemnation.

Isabel entered with her peace-making hat. 'I think all David means is that we felt so sorry for poor Charles. He didn't seem to deserve any of it. Not from where we were sitting anyway.'

We all agreed with this but it was nevertheless perfectly obvious that David hoped to be able to ditch Edith and by demonstrating his indignation to someone who would report it to the Broughton household, he believed he would earn points and end up back on their list. Or on their list, full stop, since he wrongly thought he had penetrated the citadel during Edith's reign. In this I think he was mistaken for two reasons. The first was that he was simply not Charles's cup of tea. The English upper classes are, as a rule, not amused by upper-middle-class facsimiles of themselves. This brand of *arriviste* has all the dreariness of the familiar with none of the cosiness of the intimate. On the whole, if they are to fraternise outside their set they choose artists or singers or people who will make them laugh. But the second reason was more personal to Charles. I had a feeling that he would not admire David for attempting to abandon Edith and her cause, however he, Charles, had been treated.

At any rate, following both David's urgings and Adela's original suggestion, I did indeed telephone Broughton that night. Jago, the butler, answered and told me that Charles was in London but when I was about to sign off there was the sound of an extension being lifted and Lady Uckfield came on the line.

'How are you?' she said. 'I ran into your pretty wife the other day.' I said I knew. 'Is there any chance of seeing you down here in the future? I do hope so.' She spoke with the intimate urgency, with that voice of a Girl With A Secret, that I had come to associate with, and enjoy about, her social manner.

'In actual fact we are here. Staying with the Eastons. I just rang to see if Charles was down.'

'Well, he should be back tomorrow night. What are you doing for dinner? I don't suppose you can get away?' She made the heartless request without the glimmer of a qualm. Did she know that David would give his life's blood to be included among her intimates? Probably.

'Not really,' I said.

Her tone became even more conspiratorial. 'Can't you talk?'

'Not really,' I said again, glancing over to where David stood by the fireplace watching me like a sparrow hawk.

'What about tea? Surely you can manage that?'

'I should think so,' I answered, still rather non-committally.

'And bring your nice wife.' She rang off.

David was bitterly disappointed that the call had not resulted in the general invitation that had been his unspoken plan. He suggested rather grumpily ringing back and asking the Uckfields to dinner instead but Isabel, always more reasonable, prevented him. 'I expect they want to have a bit of a chat about Edith and everything. Who can blame them?' In conclusion, deciding perhaps that since he had asked us down to re-establish relations with the Great House there wasn't much point in preventing us from doing so, he agreed that we should go for tea but carry with us an invitation for a drink on the Sunday morning.

EIGHTEEN

~

There were about six or seven people staying the weekend, which was par for the course with the Broughtons. I recognised Lady Tenby, who nodded at me quite pleasantly and a cousin of the family whom I had met with Charles and Edith in London a couple of times. I did not then know that there was any special significance in Clarissa Marlowe's presence but we did both notice that she was very proprietary in her manner, worrying about whether we were comfortable or had a sandwich or whatever and I suppose in retrospect that marked her out from an ordinary guest. The others, men in corduroys and sweaters, girls in skirts and walking shoes, barely looked up from their respective tasks, reading, gossiping, stroking the dogs, making toast at the glowing fire, as we came in.

The Uckfields, by contrast, could not have been more solicitous. They asked our news, chatted about the dress show, discussed some film they had seen me in, fetched crumpets, topped up tea-cups until it must have been as plain to the other occupants of the room as it was to us that we were about to figure in some Master Plan. The normal manner one has come to expect from hosts and fellow guests alike in an English country house is a state of moderately amiable lack of interest. The guests loaf about, reading magazines, going for walks, having baths, writing letters, without making any great social demands on each other. Only when eating – and even then only really at dinner – are they expected to 'perform'. This lack of effort, this business of people barely raising their heads from their books to acknowledge one's entry into a room, may seem rude to the foreigner (indeed it is rude), but I must confess it brings with it a certain relaxation. They make no effort to be polite to you and you therefore are not required to make any effort to be polite to them. In fact, when a great fuss is made of someone in a house party it is almost invariably because they have been recognised as an 'outsider' or at the very least someone with a terminal illness on whom extra energy must be expended. For everyone to jump to their feet and gush is therefore more or less an insult to the recipient.

Adela and I, however, did not read any kind of social 'set-down' in the lathering we were receiving. We simply understood that a favour was about to be asked. Consequently, when Lady Uckfield wondered if I would like to see her sitting room, which had just been decorated and which, apparently, we had discussed at some time in the past, I got to my feet at once. My wife was included in the invitation but something in Lady Uckfield's manner told her that what was wanted was me on my own and since we were both dying to know what was going on, she opted to stay with Lord Uckfield and have some more tea to precipitate the expected intimacy.

The sitting room in question was quite far from the rooms I knew and was situated in one of the wings, separated from the main block by a curving corridor from which the windows looked across the park. Once reached it was revealed as a charming and elegant nest, displaying Lady Uckfield's sure touch for *gemüchtlich*, fussy grandeur. It was quite a large room, with walls upholstered in rose damask and pretty chairs covered in delightful chintzes. Little japanned bureaux, painted bookcases and delicate inlaid tables stood about, all littered with the debris of the aristocratic rich, flowers, bits of Meissen, pretty lamps, miniatures, bowls of dried lavender, enamelled candlesticks, small paintings on carved stands, and, of course, on her main desk (a handsome, ormolu-mounted *bureau plat*, which sat sideways to the wall), a mass of papers and invitations and official requests. A day bed upholstered in buttoned moiré was placed at right angles to the little fire, which twinkled and crackled in the leaded and polished grate. Above the mantelshelf, where china figures and snuff-boxes jostled with chewed dog toys, a knitted rabbit and postcards from friends in Barbados and San Francisco, was a pastel by Greuze of an earlier Lady Broughton. It was, in other words, the definitive HQ of a Great Lady.

'How nicely you've done it,' I said.

But Lady Uckfield had forgotten on what excuse she had brought me here and just waved me to the armchair on the other side of the fire from the day bed as she sat down with a grave expression.

'Have you seen Edith lately?'

'Not lately, no. Not since Adela saw her at the dress show.'

'I see,' she said. She was silent for a moment. In truth I had never before seen her uncomfortable but that is certainly what she was at this moment.

'How's Charles?'

She answered with a shrug of the mouth. 'I want to ask you something. I know that Edith is still with what's-his-name. Does she intend to marry him?'

I was rather taken aback. 'I don't know. He isn't divorced yet – I'm not even sure he's started the whole process.'

She nodded to herself. 'Charles has told me she's planning to wait the two years and go for a non-contested separation.' She paused and I sort of nodded back. This was news to me but it didn't seem such a bad idea, if only because it would hardly be headlines by that time. 'The thing is, Tigger and I are not behind this plan . . .'

She hesitated, more awkward than I had ever seen her. 'We feel that the sooner Charles can draw a line under the whole thing and start his life afresh, the better for him. We hate the idea of everything dragging on and on and his never really feeling that anything's over.' She looked at me quizzically. 'You do see what we mean?'

'I suppose I do.'

'You may not know it but it has cut him up most dreadfully. He's not a great one for showing his feelings but he was in the most frightful state, I can tell you.'

I nodded. I had only to think of that scene in his study when he had cried in front of me to believe this implicitly. Charles was one of those men, much less rare than modern women's magazines would have us believe, who make their choice in marriage and then never question it. They do not ration the commitment they give their wives because it never occurs to them that they will have to regroup their emotions before death separates them – and even then they tend to assume that it will be the husband who will go first. I do not necessarily think that he would have been incapable of infidelity. On some farming convention in America, during some shooting party in Scotland, who knows what could happen? But I would say that he would have been incapable of instigating the end of his own marriage. Having chosen Edith, he had given her all the love of which he was capable and, as a natural sequitur, all the trust. Neither of these would have been very interesting in their quality but they would have been given in great quantity. Of that I am sure. No, I was not surprised to hear that he had been in 'a frightful state'.

Lady Uckfield had not finished. 'We are so desperately hoping he can rebuild his life and we really feel that he has a chance of that now.'

'Has he met someone else?'

She inclined her head to one side without answering and I knew he had. Or that they hoped he had. Minutes later I had worked out it was probably Clarissa.

'The point is if he was free he could plan in those terms. Now he can't. The past is pulling and pulling at him until I don't believe he can think straight.'

Now this was an intriguing choice of phrase. In what way was Charles not 'thinking straight'? She watched me, waiting for some acknowledgement.

'How can I help?' I said. I wanted to find out what Lady Uckfield had in store for me. I knew it would be something big because it is an absolute truth that for a woman of her type to discuss any aspect of the intimate life of her family with anyone other than a life-long, contemporary friend of similar rank (and that only rarely) was a kind of torture. Whether she liked me or not was irrelevant. This interview was agony for her.

'Can you talk to Edith? Can you ask her if she'll let Charles divorce her now? Of course, in the past that would have been an uncomfortable way round but do people think like that these days? I don't believe they do – and you must assure her that it would make no difference to the settlement. None at all.' She was gushing to cover her own embarrassment. And no wonder. This was a vulgar request if ever I heard one. Perhaps the only vulgar thing I ever knew to issue from her lips. My surprise must have shown on my face. 'You must think this a very tiresome commission.'

'I don't know that tiresome is the word I'd have chosen.' My tone was a little severe but Lady Uckfield was enough of a lady to know that she had transgressed her own code. She took the reprimand gracefully as one who deserved it.

'Of course, it's an awful thing to ask.'

'You do Edith an injustice,' I said. 'She wouldn't think about the money.' This was true. I do not think it ever occurred to Edith to take anything off Charles beyond a few thousand to give her a breathing space. It was enough that he had paid the rent in Ebury Street and left her able to cash cheques in this interim. What Lady Uckfield did not understand was that Edith was fully conscious of having behaved badly. People like the Uckfields can be slow, indeed unable, to realise that 'honour' is not a perquisite of their own class. They have heard so often about the materialism of the middle classes and the grace and self-sacrifice of their own kind that they have come to believe these two fictions equally.

She raised her eyebrows slightly. 'I suppose that might be true.'

'It is true,' I said. 'You do not like Edith and because you don't like her you underestimate her.'

At this she unbent slightly. She did not deny what I had said and when she answered me she spoke with a slight smile. 'You are right to defend her. You first came to this house as her friend – and you are right to defend her.'

'I will tell Edith what you've said but I really cannot do much more than that.'

'You see, we can't have Charles bringing a case and her contesting it or challenging it in any way. We must know that won't happen. You see that?'

'Of course I do.' Which I did. 'But I can't advise her. She wouldn't listen to me if I tried.'

'You'll tell me what she says?'

I nodded. Our interview was over. We stood and had almost left the room when Lady Uckfield clearly felt impelled to convince me further of the urgency of her request.

'You see, Charles is so dreadfully unhappy. It can't go on, can it? It's so terrible for us. Seeing him like this.'

In answer I put my arm round her shoulders and gave her a squeeze. It was considerably more intimate an action than anything I had attempted before. Perhaps it was a sign that we were somehow bonded by this awful mess of tears and waste. At any rate, she didn't object. Nor did she assume that faintly perceptible stiffness that her kind of English women use at such a moment to demonstrate that some unwarranted liberty has been taken.

We went back to the drawing room where Adela, in an effort to escape from Tigger's meticulously outlined plans for the South Wood, was attempting to teach one of the dogs to balance a biscuit on its nose.

She looked up when we came in and, since she was burning to hear what had happened (as I was to tell it), we made our excuses fairly soon after that. We still had the awful burden of David's invitation to impart but, since it was the price by which we had bought our tea, we knew it had to be done. Lady Uckfield followed us down to the Under Hall so it was easier than it might have been.

'David and Isabel,' I started. She looked quizzical so I clarified, 'Easton. Our hosts.' She nodded. This interchange alone would have been enough to have depressed David for months. 'They wondered if you'd like to bring your party over for a drink tomorrow morning?' It was done.

Lady Uckfield smiled briskly. 'But how *very* kind. I'm afraid we're too many for that. But do thank them.' Her customary urgent intimacy was back as she rejected an invitation I knew well enough would never be accepted. But she surprised me by continuing. 'Why don't you come back here instead – and bring them?'

This was kindness above and beyond the call of duty. Feeling guilty at the thought of David's delight had he but known, I shook my head. 'I think that's rather a bore for you, isn't it? Let's leave it for another time.'

But Lady Uckfield, to my further bewilderment, was insistent. 'No, please. Do come.' She smiled. 'Charles will be back. I know he'd love to see you.'

At the time, I didn't understand what she hoped to achieve by bringing us together with Charles. It seemed if anything a risk to her plans, for if I had confided her mission to her son, I am certain he would have been furious. But later I realised that she wanted me to see Charles in his misery for this would be her justification and might motivate me more than ever to carry out her wishes. It is possible too that she believed that by allowing us to bring our friends to Broughton we would be even more tightly strapped to the family carriage. 'Don't feel you have to,' said Adela, but we could protest no more and so, bidding her goodbye until the morrow, we set off to deliver our happy message to a delighted David and a less enthralled but pleasantly surprised Isabel.

Charles was waiting for us in the drawing room when we reappeared the next day or so it seemed. He bounded out of his chair, kissed Adela on both cheeks and almost wrung my hand. He wasn't able to say much more than how pleased he was to see us, as his mother approached to normalise the situation and lead us over to the drinks cupboard, cunningly inserted behind a dummy door that had originally been constructed to balance the door that led, through an ante-room, to the dining room. Tigger stood there in his role as Mine Host, dispensing Bloody Marys. He presented one to his wife. She wrinkled her nose fractionally. 'Not enough Tabasco, the wrong vodka – and you've forgotten the lime juice.' I was waiting for a bowl of fresh limes to be rung for when to my surprise Lord Uckfield took down a plastic bottle of lime juice cordial and sloshed a great measure into the jug. I was about to request one without this ingredient then thought better of it and took what I was given. Naturally enough, it was delicious.

'How do you think he's looking?' said my hostess.

She knew well enough that Charles looked perfectly terrible. His face was tired and lumpy. His skin, which normally shone with the kind of uncomplicated health redolent of grouse moors and hunting fields, looked sallow and almost dirty. His hair hung in unsorted tendrils down his neck.

'Not great,' I said.

She nodded. 'You do see why I felt I had to ask your help?'

She drifted away without referring again to our curious interview of the previous day. To be honest and in her defence I could see why, as a mother, she had been driven to pretty desperate measures. Clearly her son was dying by inches before her eyes. What puzzled me was this hinted-at, burgeoning romance that promised new life and happiness. He really did not look like one who has found his True Love, even though Clarissa was in his eye-line. There were some other pre-lunch drinkers and she was again playing the hostess, leading people here and there and introducing them but, so far as I could tell, without exciting any special interest in her cousin's heart.

The house-guests were as surly as they had been the previous day and I saw a couple of them being grudgingly yoked to David and Isabel. One, Viscount Bohun, who had been out for a walk the day before, I had met occasionally in London. His youngest sister had been a vague friend of mine at one time and I had always suspected him then of being mentally sub-normal – or at least as near sub-normal as one can be without actually risking clinical classification – so I had been quite surprised to read somewhere that he had married a pretty girl with a respectable job in publishing. Remembering this, I was curious to see the new Lady Bohun, she who had made this unholy contract. She was easy to spot. Her shining hair swept back flawlessly under a velvet band, her nose tilted in the air, she was being as grand and as difficult with a foundering David as it is possible to be without actually resorting to insults. The poor man struggled on, hopefully dropping names and references, all of which were courteously spurned, until I could almost see the sweat popping out on his brow. I can only hope that such petty victories were worth the terrible sacrifice of her life that she had made. Bohun himself had caught the wretched Adela and was telling her some interminable story, which he kept punctuating with a shrill and unprovoked laugh. I could see her checking the exits.

Charles approached and touched me on the elbow. 'So how are you? How was your filming?'

'OK. How about you?'

He gestured towards a window seat where, untroubled by the others, we might perch and be a little alone. He stared out over the gardens for a moment in silence. 'Oh, I'm fine.' He smiled rather wryly. 'Well, quite fine.'

He didn't look it but I nodded. 'I'm glad.'

'Mummy said you were over here yesterday.'

'We came for tea.'

'I expect they wanted to talk to you about, you know, the mess.'

'A bit.'

'What did they say?' I wasn't really prepared to betray Lady Uckfield to her son. Apart from anything else, although I thought her request had been intrusive and improper, I did not question the honesty of her motives. Her child looked like hell. Of course she wanted to bring things to an end, what mother wouldn't? I couldn't blame her for that so I shrugged. Charles continued. 'They're very keen to hurry everything on. They want me to "put it all behind me"'.

'And shouldn't you?'

He stared back out of the window. It was early May and the flowers that were springing into life all over the lovingly tended terraces should have looked fresh and gay but there had been a cloudburst that morning and instead they all seemed rather soggy and careworn. Beyond the ha-ha, the trees in the park were in leaf but still light, their first foliage so much more subtle in its colours than the thick lushness of high summer.

'They packed me off to Jamaica in November with Clarissa and some friends of hers.'

'Was it fun?' I found Clarissa who was busying herself with refills. Charles followed my glance.

'Poor old Clarissa. Yes. Quite fun. I like Jamaica. Well, Ocho Rios anyway. Have you ever been?' I shook my head. 'My dear old mother's trying to make a match for me. She doesn't want to take her chances on the open market a second time.' He laughed.

'I suppose she just wants you to be happy,' I said.

He looked at me. 'It isn't quite that. You see, she does want me to be happy but this time she wants me to be happy in a way she understands. She fears the unknown. Edith was the unknown. She thinks she's working for my happiness but more than that she is anxious to prevent a repetition. There are to be no more strangers at Broughton. Edith and Eric have been quite enough.'

'Well, I can see her point so far as Eric's concerned,' I said, and we both laughed.

I looked back at Clarissa who was beginning to cast slightly nervous looks in our direction as if she sensed that our conversation would bode her no good. I felt sorry for her. She was a nice girl and she would have made a success of all this – far more of a success probably than the wretched Edith ever could. Why shouldn't she have a go at making Charles happy? But even as I entertained such thoughts, I knew the whole thing was a figment of Lady Uckfield's imagination and destined to remain so.

'Have you seen Edith lately?' he asked.

I was struck again by the common error, into which I have often fallen, certainly with Charles, of assuming that stupid people are spared deep feeling. Not that Charles was exactly stupid. He was simply incapable of original thought. But I knew now that he was more than capable of great love. It is endlessly fascinating to speculate on the reasons for love's choices. I liked Edith and I had since I met her. I enjoyed her beauty and her low-key self-mockery and her naturally cool manner, but I could not pretend to understand how she had become so great a love object for this Young Man Who Had Everything. Her greatest merit as company, after all, was her sense of irony, which Charles was not capable of appreciating or even understanding. In my way I was as puzzled as Lady Uckfield as to why he had not chosen someone of his own sort who would have known the ropes and the other members of his world, who would have chaired her charities and ridden her horses and bossed the village around without a qualm, certainly with none of the suppressed sense of self-ridicule that underlay so much of Edith's role-playing. At all events, there it was. Charles had fallen in love with Edith Lavery and he loved her with a disinterested heart. The blow she had dealt to his self-esteem and indeed to his life had obviously been critical but it was quite clear from the look he turned to me that he loved her still.

'Adela saw her the other day at something.'

'How was she?'

'Well, I think.' This was a thorny path, if you like. I did not want to say she had looked rather down in case it stirred up hopes in his breast that were doomed to disappointment, nor did I care to say she was bursting with happiness as that would be needlessly painful. It would also be, from what I could gather from Adela, untrue.

'Will you be seeing her soon?'

'I thought I might give her lunch.'

'Tell her – tell her I'll do whatever she wants. You know. I'll fit in.' I nodded. 'And give her my love,' he said.

Predictably David had not enjoyed his sojourn in Valhalla. As so often in such cases, the realisation of the dream brings resentment in its wake. Perhaps because, in their imaginings, David and his like see themselves as inner members of the Charmed Circle, chums of half the peerage, swapping stories about childhood friends and making plans to share a villa in Tuscany. Inevitably, the reality of these attempts at intermingling tends to make them bitter and irritated as they find themselves snubbed as aliens by those very people they have spent their adult life admiring and emulating.

'I must say,' he muttered as he climbed into the back seat of my car, 'I found those Bohuns pretty hard going. Do you know them?'

'I used to know him a bit.'

'Really? I don't know what I thought of him.'

I smiled. 'He's a half-wit. What's she like?'

'Quite difficult, I'd say.'

Isabel nodded. 'Diana Bohun has made a hard bargain and her only compensation is the envy of strangers. I wonder how long she'll bear it.

No doubt in five years we'll read that she's run off with the local doctor.'

Adela shook her head. 'No, we won't. I knew her when she came out. She'd stay with Hitler if he brought her a title and a house.'

Isabel raised her eyebrows. 'I think I'd rather have Hitler.'

I was interested in this exchange because, even as they ridiculed the pitiful hypocrisy of Diana Bohun, I was well aware that Adela and David and even Isabel, whatever they might say, fundamentally approved of her pact with the devil. Perhaps none of them would have been prepared to marry someone who actually repulsed them, but nevertheless those girls in their acquaintance who had done so (and I could name at least seven in my own address book) were not despicable figures to them unless they reneged on their bargain. To the members of this world this was Edith's real crime. Not marrying Charles without loving him, but leaving him for love of someone else. To them, her folly was in abandoning the false values she had endorsed with her marriage and in attempting to return to the timeless virtues. Her decision was unworldly, it was not *mondaine*. Americans may affect to admire this in their fiction if not in their lives but their British counterparts, at least among the upper-middle and upper classes do not. In the States, the Abdication story, for example, is portrayed as The World Well Lost For Love while the English, of a certain type anyway, see it only as childish, irresponsible and absurd.

And it was by these standards that Edith had been judged and found wanting.

NINETEEN

～

Here was a hard task. On the one hand I had a commission from Lady Uckfield, which I had sworn to carry out, to ask Edith to allow herself to be divorced at once, on the other, I had been made fully aware during our time at Broughton that Charles was still in love with his wife.

'So what are you going to say?' said Adela on the day when I had arranged to meet Edith for lunch. Naturally I had told my wife all. I don't know that I had been sworn to secrecy but even if I had been I never feel it includes one's spouse except in the most exceptional cases. Nothing can be more irritating than attempting to live intimately with a Keeper of Secrets.

'What Lady Uckfield wants me to say, I suppose.'

'Don't tell me you're going to promote the cause of that wretched Marlowe girl?'

I shook my head. 'No, I'll keep off that. I'll tell her they want it to be over, that's all.'

Adela pondered. 'Tell her Lady Uckfield wants it to be over. That'll be nearer the mark.' Considering her prejudice, I thought this was commendably just.

I had arranged to meet Edith at the Caprice. At lunchtime particularly it seems to combine a sense of clean, business-like lines with a whiff of glamour, which I thought would be an appropriate and undepressing setting for our proposed conversation. I arrived to find that I had been allotted the table at the far end of the restaurant away from the bar. This was by chance but it could not have been more suitable. I ordered a glass of champagne to cheer myself up and waited for my guest.

Edith was glad of my choice of venue. Simon was working a lot these days and earning quite respectable sums but what with his mortgage and his wife and the general financial backlog that any actor has to pay off when things start to roll again, he was not one for much West End entertaining unless it was at someone else's expense. Edith could have managed it as she had been given no real guidelines as to how much she could spend but she was reluctant to use Charles's money for inessentials. She had been known to interpret this term fairly widely but somehow to take Simon out for treats on her husband's money didn't seem quite cricket. And then the bore was she had no money of her own – something that had come to seem quite strange to her, so far had she travelled from the world of her girlhood. At all events she was always glad to have an excuse to dress up and go out.

We kissed and chatted and ordered, knowing as we did so that there was a conversation of some substance to come, but by mutual consent we waited until our first courses, bang bang chicken for me and some hot *hors d'oeuvres* for Edith, were on the table. The waiter filled our glasses and retreated and we knew that we had a little while to ourselves.

'We saw David and Isabel last weekend,' I opened. 'We stayed with them in fact.'

'How are they?'

'All right. David's quite busy though I never really know what with.' I paused. 'We all went over to Broughton for a drink.'

Edith took a bite of something in thin batter. 'David must have enjoyed that.'

'He didn't much. He was stuck with Diana Bohun. He kept trying to impress her, which I don't think was very successful.'

'I should say not. She cut me dead the other day in Peter Jones.' She continued to eat and drink with some gusto but she would not give me the slightest help with my task. With an inward sigh I soldiered on.

'Lady Uckfield was there.'

'So I imagined. How is dear old "Googie"?' She was of course being ironic although not uncomfortably bitter. The tiresome nickname had once again gone into inverted commas as it had been in the first weeks of her marriage. And there was the recognition of a barrier there, a deep divide, which now separated the existences of her former mother-in-law and herself.

'Very well. I think. Of course, she wanted to talk about you.'

'There's no "of course" about it. As a matter of fact, I'm rather surprised. Googie is not one for discussing the family troubles. You should feel very flattered.'

'I think she felt that I might be of some use.'

Edith nodded. The penny was dropping and she began to understand that this talk might be leading to deeper waters than she had come prepared for. 'Ah,' she said.

'She told me you were planning to wait the two years.' Edith looked at me in a non-committal way. 'It's not what they want. They want Charles to divorce you now. Straight away. She needs to know what you would think about that.'

I had said it and there was some relief. The words were out. Edith stopped eating and laid her fork down gently on the plate. Very deliberately she sipped her wine as if she were savouring each separate droplet. I suppose the point was it had come. The End of Her Marriage. I am not sure to what extent she had truly accepted that this was where her romance with Simon had brought her until this moment. Though I must say her voice was quite calm when she spoke. 'You mean they want Charles to divorce me for adultery. Citing Simon.'

I nodded. 'I suppose so. I don't think it really works like that these days but I would guess that's the general idea. We didn't actually talk details. If he were to divorce you now it would have to be for a reason, or has that finished? I'm not too sure.'

'I can't say it seems very gentlemanly.'

'It wasn't very ladylike going off with a married actor.'

She nodded and resumed her eating. 'So what do you want from me? What am I to say?'

'I think they feel they have to know that if the divorce does go ahead now you won't suddenly try to fight it. It won't interest you but it won't make any difference, you know, to the money.'

She looked at me rather sadly. 'I don't want any money. Not much anyway. Less than Charles would give me tomorrow if I asked him.'

'I know,' I said. 'I told Lady Uckfield that.'

'Anyway,' she added after a pause, 'it's not a generous offer. Nowadays there isn't a "guilty party". It never does make any difference financially. Didn't you realise that?' I shook my head. 'Well, I bet "Googie" does.' We continued eating in silence for a while. The waiter returned, took away our plates and came back with salmon fishcakes and a bowl of *pommes allumettes*. But the subject remained there on the table like a weeping centrepiece. It was Edith who introduced the character we were both thinking of. 'What does Charles say about all this? I assume he was there. Did you talk to him?'

'Yes, I talked to him.' While theoretically correct, my answer was a lie, for Charles had not been there when Lady Uckfield was sketching out her plans, which is what Edith had meant by her question. I very much doubted he would have allowed his mother to talk as she did had he been. I corrected myself, suddenly oppressed by my implied deception. 'Actually he wasn't there when I was talking to his mother but we went back the next day.'

'And?'

'He says he'll abide by your decision. Whatever you want to do.'

'That sounds more like him. Poor old Charles,' said Edith. 'How was he?'

I had dreaded this. If I could have said that he was looking fine and dandy I would have. I had come to feel, like Lady Uckfield, that it was time to call a halt to this unsuccessful experiment in miscegenation. The problem was he had not looked fine and dandy. 'OK,' I said. 'I don't think all of this has done him much good.'

'No.' She helped herself to some more chips. 'Was Clarissa down there?'

I nodded and Edith was silent. I was about to tell her to discount whatever she had heard, that it was a rumour inspired by Lady Uckfield's ambitions and nothing else, but I was silent. What was the point? She had to let Charles go and where was the good in slowing up her decision? For the rest of lunch we chatted about Simon and acting and Isabel and buying a flat, but as we were leaving Edith reopened the topic.

'Let me think about it.' She smiled slightly. 'Of course, we both know that I'll do what I'm asked but let me think about it. I'll telephone you.'

*   *   *

Edith Broughton did not go home – or rather she did not return to Ebury Street – at once. It was a crisp, sunny, spring day, when everything seems as clear as a cut-out, cold and bright as a jewel. She was warmly dressed and so, once past the Ritz, she turned left into the Green Park. She strolled down the path, past Wimborne House, past the restored, statue decorated splendour of Spencer House, past the Italianate magnificence of Bridgewater House until she stopped and looked up at Lancaster House, the golden pile, built and occupied for many years by the mighty Dukes of Sutherland. Their duchesses had dominated London Society, one after another, summoning the great and the good of the different eras to ascend the giant, gilded staircase in the grandest of all grand London halls to pay court to each other's wealth and power.

It struck Edith then that she would have enjoyed that older, simpler world when these houses had held sway over the capital. When the Guests and the Spencers and the Egertons and the Leveson-Gowers had lived their ordained lives under these teeming roofs instead of the charitable organisations and government departments and Greek shipping magnates who occupied them now. Forgetting for the moment that she, Edith Lavery, would have had the greatest difficulty in penetrating even the outermost fringe of this golden troupe in any period but our own, she saw herself in her crinoline, never questioning her own happiness and, consequently, being happy. And as she did so, she was struck by how similar her fantasies of the old, pre-Great War world were to those fantasies about her coming life as Lady Broughton, which she had entertained while lying in the bath just before her wedding. How simple things were to be, how the villagers and tenants were going to love her, how the family would bless the day she had come among them! She found herself smiling wistfully as the dream image of herself as the Great Social Force of Twenty-First Century Society receded before her inner gaze, swathed in mist, tearfully waving goodbye.

Pondering this, it seemed at first to her troubled brain that her mother had been wrong and the media had been right all along, that these dreams and ambitions were outmoded, that no one nowadays wants titles and rank and inherited power, that these are the days of the self-made man, of talent, of creativity. But then, looking about at the office workers and sweepers and job interviewees who loitered near her in the park, she was struck by the dishonesty of the media pundits of our time. Was there one here who would not change places with Charles if they could? Was it not possible that the small screen gurus praised meritocracy because it was the only class system that would accord them the highest rank? Even if unearned riches and position had no moral merit, even if they embodied the Dream That Dare Not Speak Its Name, it was still a dream that figured in plenty of people's fantasies. And she had casually discarded it.

Then she thought again with puzzled wonderment of her own supposed unhappiness with Charles. Why exactly had she been so unhappy? When she tried to think back to their time together, she kept remembering those pretty rooms at Broughton and the servants and the park and her work in the village. The only discomforts she could recall were things like packing the car and standing behind Charles at a shoot in the rain. Were these so terrible? And if she thought of Charles, himself, it was with a rather intimate affection. She remembered him swearing at fellow motorists or farting in his sleep and it provoked in her a kind of nostalgic warmth. There was no trace of relief at his passing. If only there had been. Instead she found herself worrying about his loneliness. It pained her to think he was suffering. And increasingly she asked herself what exactly was this personal fulfilment for which so much disruption had been necessary? Was it sexual? Was she admitting that she had done all this because of Simon's cock? Or was it simply to do with boredom? But if it was, how much less bored was she now, sitting in Ebury Street talking to girlfriends on the telephone or meeting them for lunch than she had been working with her committees in the library at Broughton?

She turned away from Lancaster House and walked slowly towards the Victory Arch with Buckingham Palace on her left. The Royal Standard announcing the monarch's presence in London hung limply against its staff. Tourists hovered at the railings, peering in with rapt attention, as if they hoped to catch a glimpse of some Royal Highness strolling down a corridor or coming out for a breather. And again, as she walked, Edith considered the mystery of unearned greatness. She thought how Tigger and Googie and Charles would all be invited to the next court ball, an event of unimaginable glamour to these Japanese travellers with their clicking cameras, to these northerners in their hideous anoraks, blobs of bright, synthetic colour against the cold grey, neo-Georgian facade. Any one of these would have made an invitation to the Palace into a life-long story, sodden with repetition and yet she had turned away from her role in this fairy tale in order to be – to be what precisely? Happy?

The fact was that of late Edith had come to wonder just how much she could be fulfilled by 'personal happiness', if that was what Simon was offering her. Perhaps because she had never succeeded in disentangling her ambitions of fulfilment from her mother's values, she had already begun to hanker for that sweet sense of self-importance that her life at Broughton had brought with it. She understood that these feelings did her no credit but her defence was a pragmatic one. How else was she to enjoy the good things in life if she did not marry them? And her faith in Simon's eventual triumph was waning. She knew more about show business now than she had when they met and she sensed that the series he was in, with a couple more to follow, was probably the best he could hope for. Whatever they might pretend together, they would not be holding hands tightly, stiff with anticipation, at the Oscar ceremony. What was her life to be then? A vicarage in the Home Counties and the occasional interview for an evening newspaper? Was she really expected to provide vocal and emotional support through twenty years of semi-failure to prove she was a real person? Some might say it is only personal achievement that should lead on to glory but what of those who have no talent or special gift with which to achieve? Are they so blameworthy to want to live among the blessed? Poor Edith was aware that she could neither weave nor spin but was she therefore forbidden to covet a life of splendour? Was this so shameful? She shook her head in irritation. At the far corner of her brain, these thoughts were beginning to tell her that despite the reckless choice she had made, her own assessment of the world and her place in it had not really changed in the least. She felt herself resenting anew the accusations she heard from her parents and friends when she first made her run for it, that she could not settle to her new life because beneath the skin of a rebel beat the heart of Mrs Lavery's little girl. And she resented them because she was beginning to be horribly afraid they might be true.

Walking towards Victory Arch, watching the afternoon light glint against the windows of Apsley House, whither she and Charles had been summoned for a party the previous summer, one of the first engagements she had been obliged to cancel because of the split, she recalled with amazement (and it really had begun to seem almost unbelievably strange) that she had jettisoned a high place in the world of the worldly for the position of partner to an obscure man in a generally despised profession. And not for the first time she sat down to think about the extraordinary events of the last year of her life in more detail.

Simon was at the flat when she got back. He was drinking tea and watching an old film. When he was working he was at peace and so inclined to relax and take it easy. It was only when he was out of a job that he would go haring about London keeping lunch dates with people he disliked and telephoning his agent every four hours.

Edith left her coat in the hall. 'Is there a cup for me?'

He waved his mug in the air. 'I just made it with a bag. The water's still hot if you want some.' He had taken his trainers off and they lay, pigeon-toed on the hearth rug. His coat had been thrown across an armchair and books and scripts were littered about the room. Edith stood at the door, taking in the whole scene like a spectator from another country. *The Way We Live Now*. This was the way she lived now, with sixties sofas covered in stained, oatmeal tweed, with large nondescript flower prints in coloured mounts on the walls, with a Perspex coffee table and a gas-log fire. This was the way she was living now. She was acutely aware that she had no desire to enter the room.

Simon, sensing some strangeness between them, stood and approached her in the doorway. He slid an arm around her waist and squeezed her, pushing his mouth onto hers. They had been in an Indian restaurant the night before and she could still taste the spices on his breath. He pressed himself against her and she could feel that he was already aroused. 'Good lunch?' he said.

She nodded. 'Googie sent him. He and Adela were down in Sussex last weekend. They went over to Broughton and of course Googie dragged him off to her lair. The meeting was her idea.'

'And?'

'They want to hurry the divorce.' She paused, sensing his recoil. 'Googie wants to involve you.'

'Jesus!' Simon didn't know what to think. Part of him revelled in it. Visions of more picture spreads on page three in the *Daily Mail* flickered through his brain but with them came trailing streamers of a distant panic. He felt as if he was hurtling down some tube, weightless and powerless, into the unknown. 'Is she serious?'

'I think so but you can calm down. They're wrong. I'm fairly sure no one has to be cited any more. The point is they want to get on with it.'

'What did you say?'

Edith studied the pretty boy before her. He had abandoned his customary flirtatious, winking manner and, although he didn't realise, he looked the better for it. A little seriousness added charm to his bright blue eyes and the careless locks of shining hair that fell forward to veil them. 'I said I had to think about it.'

'Can you stop them?'

'If I want to.'

'How?'

'I'll tell Charles not to go ahead with it.'

Simon laughed. 'And that would do it?'

Edith observed him coolly. How provincial he was! How little he understood men like Charles! She was almost haughty in her defence of her discarded husband to her preferred lover. 'Yes. That would do it.' Simon had stopped laughing but suddenly there seemed to be something irredeemably irritating about him. She couldn't be bothered to embark on the usual chats about how bad everyone was in any film they were watching, how jealous his fellow actors were, how stupid the cameraman. 'I'm going to have a bath,' she said, disengaging herself from his embrace.

Simon threw himself back into the sofa, fixing his gaze once more upon the screen. 'You're very sulky,' he said. 'I shall be charitable and blame the time of the month.'

She didn't answer but went instead down to the basement bathroom that opened off their dark, little bedroom. An attempt had been made with a looking glass and a wallpaper of enormous poppies to brighten the two rooms up but it only deepened their lightless gloom. She ran the bath, undressed and climbed in. She was aware that since she had entered the park she had been in a kind of strange, unworldly mental state. She felt intensely aware of every movement of her limbs, of every ripple of the water against her skin. She felt spacey, almost drunk – although she certainly drank very little at lunch. A vague sense of apprehension seemed to bloat her stomach and her very nerve ends prickled individually the length of her body. But then, at last, she realised what it was that was catching at the edge of her attention.

Simon had said no more than he knew. It was her time of the month. She was as regular as clockwork.

And she was five days late.

TWENTY

~

The morning following my lunch with Edith our doorbell rang at not much later than a quarter past eight.

'Christ!' said Adela. 'Who on earth's that?' We were in our tiny bedroom, which overlooked the area. As the front door was just out of sight to the right, it wasn't possible to sneak a preview of our visitor but, in any case, at that time in the morning, I just assumed it was the postman so I was not particularly careful with my toilet as I shouted that I was coming. When I unlocked the door in my underpants with my hair unbrushed, I discovered it was not the postman, who must after all be accustomed to such sights, but Edith Broughton who stood on the mat.

'Hello,' I said with something of a tone of wonder.

Edith pushed past me into the room. 'I have to talk to you.' She threw herself down onto the sofa that divided the living bit from the eating bit of the flat's solitary 'reception room'.

'Can I dress first?' I asked.

She nodded and I hurried back into the bedroom to inform the amazed Adela, busy struggling into her clothes, of the identity of our early morning caller.

She was ready first and when I rejoined them Edith already had a cup of coffee in her hand and a piece of toast before her. 'So?' I said. There didn't seem to be much point in pretending that this was a normal way of carrying on. Edith glanced at Adela who jumped up.

'I'd better be off, hadn't I? Not to worry. I've a mass of paperwork to do . . .'

Edith waved her back to her seat. 'Stay. There's no secret. Anyway,' she glanced around at our minuscule accommodation, 'I imagine you'd be within earshot wherever you went.' Adela settled herself and we both waited.

'I want to see Charles.' Her voice was quite flat as she spoke but of course we were both most interested by what she said. I did not really understand why she had felt the need to come round and communicate this to us at dawn but I was fascinated nevertheless. I was soon to understand what my part was to be. 'I want you to arrange it.'

Adela caught my eye and faintly shook her head. She had all the horror of her kind for getting involved in this kind of thing. Whatever the outcome, somehow one is always blameworthy. She also, as she told me later, had no wish to incur Lady Uckfield's enmity and she suspected that this would be an inevitable by-product of the proposed plan of action. One must remember of course that Adela, from first to last, was entirely on Lady Uckfield's side and never on Edith's.

'Why do you need me?' I said rather wanly.

'I rang Broughton last night. I asked for Charles but I got Googie. She said he wasn't there but I'm sure he was. I rang London and Feltham and they said he was at Broughton. I know he was. She doesn't want me to speak to him.'

All this would only confirm Adela's suspicions that in some vague way we were being asked to take on Lady Uckfield. 'I don't really see what *I* can do.'

'They'll let you speak to him. Say you want to ask him to lunch or something and then, when he comes on the line, tell him I want to meet him.'

'I don't think I can do that,' I said. 'I don't mind telephoning,' which was a lie, 'but if Lady Uckfield asks me what I'm going to say, I'll tell her. She can't imagine she can prevent you meeting for ever.'

'Not for ever, no. Just long enough.'

'I don't believe that,' I said. Although I did.

In truth, I was pretty sure that I too was on Lady Uckfield's side when it came down to it. The facts were simple enough. Edith had married Charles without loving him in order to gain a position. She had then made a complete failure of that same position, abandoned it, broken her faith with Charles, made a great scandal and caused him a good deal of pain. Lady Uckfield now wished to be rid of her once and for all and, frankly, could anyone wonder at it?

'Do you think Charles will want to see you?' asked Adela. 'Perhaps it was he who refused to come to the telephone.' Which was certainly a point worth considering.

'If he doesn't, I want to hear it from him.'

The three of us sat in silence for a while. Adela crunched her toast and turned to Nigel Dempster.

'Anything?' I said.

'Sarah Carter's sister's married some painter and the Langwells are getting a divorce, which we knew last October.'

'Will you do it?' said Edith.

Adela and I looked at each other but I refused the message in her eyes. Ultimately, much as I would have liked to, it would have been wrong of me to have abandoned Edith to her fate and espoused the cause of the Broughtons. Whatever I might privately think about the wrongs and rights of the matter, this would have been a dishonourable course. First, and before everything else, I had been Edith's friend, as even Lady Uckfield had acknowledged.

'I will,' I said. 'But I won't do it either at this time of the morning or with you listening. Go home and I'll telephone you.'

Edith nodded and, after finishing her coffee, left.

'Something's up,' said Adela.

I rang at half past ten and asked for Charles. Despite what Edith had said I was quite surprised when Lady Uckfield came on the line.

'Hello,' she said. 'How are you?'

'I was trying to track down Charles.'

She was very smooth and clearly four steps ahead of me. 'I'm afraid he's not here. Can I give him a message?'

I toyed with the idea of bluffing but she was obviously well aware of why I was ringing and it seemed a foolish corner to paint myself into. 'I'm on an errand, I'm afraid. And I'm not at all sure you'll approve.'

'Try me.' Her voice had gone from reserved to glacial.

'It's Edith. She wants to see Charles.'

'Why?'

'I don't know why.' This was true.

'What's the point?'

'I don't know that there is any point but I do know that you won't get a straight answer out of her concerning your proposals re the divorce unless she sees him.'

'You've asked her then?'

'I've asked her and she says she wants to think about it. Part of that thinking, I take it, has to go on in Charles's presence.'

There was a pause for a moment and I could hear down the line that eerie echo of other conversations, other, strange anonymous bits of lives being lived, a thousand miles away. 'Are you free this afternoon? Can you meet me for tea?'

'There's nothing I would enjoy more but in this instance I don't know that I'll be able to add anything to what I've already told you.'

'I'll be at the Ritz. At four.'

I was interested that she did not want me to come to their flat in Cadogan Square.

'Perhaps Tigger's coming up with her. Perhaps Charles is there,' said Adela and for a moment I was tempted to walk round and ring the bell. I thought better of it, having decided that it might behove me to hear what Lady Uckfield had to say first.

I did, however, telephone Edith.

'What are you going to say to her?'

'I don't know. That she is wasting her time trying to keep you two apart, I suppose. If that's what she's doing.'

'Of course it's what she's doing.'

'I mean without Charles's knowledge.' Edith was silent. 'At any rate, I'll call you this evening.' I rang off.

I asked tentatively whether or not Lady Uckfield had arrived but the manager was not one to let such an opportunity slip by. 'Gentleman for the Marchioness of Uckfield,' he observed loudly to a passing waiter, who escorted me courteously past the turning heads to where she waited. She was sitting trimly at a table in the Marble Hall to the right of the great, gilded fountain. She smiled and waved a little hand as I approached, and stood to greet me with her neat, bird-like movements. The man brought the tea with a lot of milady'ing, all of it gently and serenely acknowledged. She laughed gaily. 'Isn't this a treat?'

'It is for me,' I said.

Her manner became not exactly more serious but at any rate more direct. She was a little less breathlessly urgent and remembering that scene in her sitting room at Broughton I understood that she was going to impart some real, as opposed to faked, intimacy. 'I want to be quite honest because I think you may be able to help.'

'I'm simultaneously flattered and dubious,' I said.

'I don't want Charles to have to see Edith.'

'So I gathered.'

'It's not that I'm being unkind. Truly. It's just that I think he's in the most tremendous muddle and I don't want him any more confused.'

'Lady Uckfield,' I said, 'I know very well why you think it a bad idea. So do I. You believe the marriage was a mistake and you had rather not prolong it. I quite agree. The fact remains that, at this moment, Edith is Charles's wife and if she wants to see him and if he, as I suspect, also wants to see her, then hadn't we better get out of the way?'

A momentary flicker of irritation shadowed her face. 'Why do you think he wants to see her?'

'Because he's still in love with her.'

She said nothing for a moment but poked among the sandwiches to find an egg one, which she nibbled with exaggerated delight. 'Aren't these *good!*' she whispered covertly, as if we must prevent anyone else hearing at all costs. She looked at me with her darting, cat-like eyes. 'You think I've been unfair to Edith.'

I shook my head. 'No. I think you don't like her but I don't think you've been particularly unfair to her.'

She nodded in acknowledgement of this. 'I don't like her. Much. However, that's not the point.'

'What is the point?'

'The point is that she cannot make Charles happy. Whether I like her or not is neither here nor there. I detested my mother-in-law and yet I was fully aware of what a success she had made of Broughton and of Tigger's wretched father. It took me twenty years to bury her memory. Do you think it would matter to me if I simply didn't like her? I'm not a schoolgirl.'

'No.' I sipped my tea. This was flattering indeed. For some reason Lady Uckfield had decided to draw aside the curtain that habitually clothed all her private thoughts and actually talk to me. She had not finished.

'Let me tell you about my son. Charles is a good, kind, uncomplicated man. He's much nicer than I am, you know. But he is less . . .' She faltered, searching for a loyal adjective that would fit the need.

'Intelligent?' I ventured.

Since I had said it, she let it pass. 'He needs a wife who values not just him but who he is, what he does. What their life is. He is not one to be able to give weight to a different philosophy in his own home. He could not be married to a socialist opera singer and respect her for her different views. It is not in him.'

'I don't think it's in Edith either,' I said.

'Edith married an idea of a life that she had gleaned from novels and magazines. She thought it meant travel and fashion shows and meeting Mick Jagger. She saw herself throwing parties for Princess Michael in Mauritius . . .' She shrugged. I was quite impressed that she'd heard of Mick Jagger. 'I don't know if some people live like that. Maybe. What I do know is that will never be Charles's life. His whole existence is the farming calendar. For the next fifty years he will shoot and farm and farm and shoot and go abroad for three weeks in July. He will worry about the tenants and have fights with the vicar and try to get the government to contribute to rewiring the east wing. And his friends, with very few exceptions, will be other people reroofing their houses and farming and shooting and trying to get government grants and exemptions. That is his future.'

'And you're sure it could never be Edith's?'

'Aren't you?'

I could remember Edith sobbing with boredom on the shoot at Broughton and sulking through evening after evening of Tigger's stories and Googie's charm. But of course, what Lady Uckfield did not know and I suspected, was how bored and depressed Edith was with her new life. I thought of her at Fiona Grey's party being led around like a prize heifer. Lady Uckfield interpreted my silence as agreement and her manner warmed. 'It's not entirely her fault. Even I can see that. That terrible mother has stuffed her head with a lot of Barbara Cartland nonsense. What chance had she?'

'Poor old Mrs Lavery,' I said. Lady Uckfield shuddered with a tiny grimace. This was the woman Mrs Lavery had planned to share scrumptious lunches with and trips to the milliner.

'I'm not a snob,' started Lady Uckfield but this was really too much and I could not prevent at least one eyebrow rising. She attempted to rebuke me. 'I'm not! I know people can marry up and bring it off. I have lots of different sorts of friends. I do!' She was quite indignant. I suppose she believed she was telling the truth.

'Who?' I said.

She thought for a moment. 'Susan Curragh and Anne Melton. I like them both very much. I defy you to say that I don't.' She had named an immensely rich American heiress who was now the wife of a rather dull junior minister and the daughter of a clothing millionaire who had married an impoverished Irish earl thereby putting him on the social map. I knew neither woman but I trembled for Edith if Lady Uckfield thought them good examples of 'marrying up'. 'You don't believe me, I know, but I was brought up not to think in terms of "class".'

What interested me in this was that Lady Uckfield could have made that statement quite safely on a lie detector while the truth was, of course, that she had been brought up to think in terms of nothing else and she had largely (if not entirely) been true to her teaching. She continued. 'The important thing is not Edith's class, whatever that means, but that she simply doesn't enjoy the job. She and her frightful mother are "London Ladies". They want to lunch in Italian restaurants and go to charity balls and fly to the sun for the winter. Running a house like Broughton, or Feltham for that matter, is just slog once the gilt's worn off. It's paperwork and committees. It's arguing with English Heritage inspectors who all hate you for living there and want to make everything as difficult for you as they possibly can. It's pleading with government departments and economising on the heating. Those houses are fun to stay in. Even "London Ladies" like that. But they're hard, hard work to own. She could never take either pleasure or satisfaction in that life. I don't even blame her but she couldn't. And to be quite frank,' she paused, almost hesitating in case she was giving away too much ammunition, 'I'm not sure how much she likes Charles.'

I thought of that far away engagement dinner with Caroline Chase on my left. *It's frightfully dreary down here ... flower shows all summer, freezing pipes all winter.* I could hear the echo of her cold, hard voice. *I suppose Edith's ready for all that?* And how triumphant Edith had seemed. How she had swept the pool and gained the prize.

'If what you say is true then where's the danger of letting them meet?'

'Because I suspect that eight months with an out-of-work actor in Ebury Street has reminded her of why she found Charles attractive, or should I say an attractive proposition, in the first place. I think she may want him back.'

'And you're against that?' I felt a bit sorry for Simon to be described as an 'out-of-work actor' when he, poor soul, thought he was dazzling in his success. Still, it didn't seem the moment to cavil.

She spoke with statesmanlike clarity. 'I am against it with every fibre of my being.' I suppose in some part of me I was surprised at her honesty. I was used to the token revulsion for divorce that is one of the obligatory attitudes in Society. Although in truth they care little whether people are divorced or not, simply whom they are married to at the time. Even so, she was of the old school and I was fairly sure there was no such thing as a divorce in either her, or Tigger's, genealogy. She nodded. 'You're surprised I'd prefer the scandal to run its course. I admit it. I would rather have what little of this story is left than patch things up and risk a bigger smash in five years when Edith has either rediscovered how bored she is, or found someone as rich as Charles who bores her less. There may be children involved by that time and I prefer to see my grandchildren brought up at Broughton by both parents.'

'I do see,' I said. It was fruitless to deny that there was a good deal of logic in her reasoning.

'So can you help me?' She tucked busily into another sandwich and filled both our cups. She had been honest with me and I could not be less than honest with her.

'No, Lady Uckfield, I cannot help you.' She stopped pouring in her surprise. I suppose she felt that she had extended such an enormous privilege to me by revealing so much of her hand that I could not fail to be firmly attached to her interest. Seeing her disappointment, I clarified. 'It is not because I do not agree with you. As a matter of fact I do. It is because I do not believe any argument will turn Edith from her meeting. And I do not believe I have the smallest right to interfere.'

She nodded slightly, a sharp, jerky movement, which betrayed her terrible pain. 'I imagine you mean I have no right either.'

I shook my head. 'You're Charles's mother. You have the right to interfere. I am not sure you have any hope of success but you have the right to try.' I felt the interview had come to an end and I stood. As it was, I doubted that Lady Uckfield and I would be so easy in each other's company again. She'd abandoned too many of her customary defences to be able to forgive me quickly for witnessing her in this state. To make matters worse I could see that her eyes were beginning to moisten and before my horrified gaze a single tear, amazed to be released from a duct that must have held it prisoner for twenty years, started to make its tentative way down her carefully powdered cheek.

She stood and put her hand on my arm. 'Just don't help her.' Her voice was urgent, it is true, but not with that girlish, don't-tell-Father, pseudo-urgency that I had grown used to. This was a cry of desperation. 'Just don't encourage her. That's all I beg. For her sake as much as for his. They'll both be wretched.'

I nodded and gave what assurances I felt I could, thanked her for my tea and watched her pull herself together before my eyes so that, by the time I turned at the arch taking me towards the Arlington Street entrance, she could wave at me as composed as if she were in the Royal Box at Ascot. All I knew was that I could not have been less clear as to quite what I was going to say to Edith.

'You're right, of course. She doesn't want you to meet.'

'I told you.'

'Even so, I don't really see how she can prevent it.'

'She'll send him away again. To America. For horse sales or something. She'll fix it up with her friends. They're everywhere.'

'Sounds like Watergate.'

She gave a harsh little laugh. 'You think you're joking.'

'At any rate,' I said, 'he can't stay in America for ever. You'll just have to keep trying. I don't think he'll avoid you when you do run him to earth. Really I don't. You must just bide your time.'

'I haven't *got* time,' said Edith.

Something in the tone of her voice prevented my asking for clarification and, indeed, I confess that I deliberately put the remark out of my mind. I did not want to address it, I suppose, and I certainly did not want to share it with Adela, sensing perhaps that it could mean everything or nothing. If everything, why risk the release of that knowledge into the ether? If nothing, why not forget it?

We were silent a moment with Edith perhaps aware that she had said more than she'd intended. She may have been pondering how to contain the remark without referring to it again.

'What do you plan to do then?' I asked.

'I don't know,' she said.

TWENTY-ONE

~

She didn't know. It seemed crazy but she literally did not know how she could contact her own husband. It may surprise some people but for a time, Edith had assumed that either Sotheby's or Christie's would rescue her from this dilemma. The public is not aware of it but over the last decade the summer parties of those two great auction houses have become in many ways the high points of the London social calendar, a chance for the genuine *gratin*, as opposed to the ubiquitous Café Society, to meet and mingle before they disperse for the summer. Edith knew that Charles would attend both, as would Googie. Even Tigger was prepared to struggle up from the country in order to renew his acquaintance with most of his class. It was an annual, pleasurable duty cheerfully undertaken by a large proportion of the high aristocracy much as the opening day of the Summer Exhibition used to be. There Charles would be found and there Edith would buttonhole him. The only trouble was that the days went by and every morning the envelopes flopped down onto the mat but the requisite, white, pasteboard cards with their embossed, italic script were not among them. Whether to spare Charles from embarrassment or perhaps to shield Lady Uckfield from discomfort (nobody can have thought that Lord Uckfield would even notice Edith's presence), for whatever reason, the Countess Broughton's name had clearly been excised from the list. She was not invited to either gathering.

At last it became impossible for her not to accept that she had been passed over. It was time for an alternative plan. She sat hunched over her address book, leafing through the neatly pencilled names. This was a habit she had unconsciously adopted from her hated mother-in-law. It meant the entries could be more easily rubbed out when their owners moved or when their use was finished and done with. This morning she stared at page after page, trying to find one who would help. At last, *faute de mieux*, she dialled Tommy Wainwright's number. Arabella answered and Edith asked for Tommy, a request that was greeted with a cool silence at the other end before Arabella spoke.

'He's at the House, I'm afraid.'

'When will he be back?'

'The thing is, he's most frightfully busy at the moment. Can I help?'

No, thought Edith. You cannot and you would not. 'Not really,' she said lightly. 'I don't want to be a bother. Just say I telephoned.'

'Of course I will.' It was obvious from her flat tone of voice that Arabella intended to say nothing but, in the event, she felt discomfort at the thought of being discovered in a lie so she did pass on the message while predictably urging her husband to ignore it. Edith had already played out this scenario or something like it in her brain so it was quite a surprise that evening when she picked up the receiver to hear Tommy speaking.

'I want to see Charles and everyone's stopping me,' she said after the usual pleasantries.

'Why?'

'Because they're frightened of Googie, because they want to stay in with the family. I don't know why.'

There was a short silence. The request may not have been articulated but it had nevertheless been made. 'I don't want to land him in it.'

'Nor do I,' said Edith firmly. 'I just want to see him.'

Another silence. Then with something like a sigh, Tommy spoke. 'He's coming here for a drink on Wednesday at about seven. You could always drop in then.'

'I will never forget this.' Edith's voice was sonorous with significance and from it Tommy could easily gauge the treatment she had been receiving elsewhere from her erstwhile world.

'Don't get your hopes up too much,' he said. He was after all fully aware of the powers she was ranging herself against.

*   *   *

I was already in the Wainwright drawing room when Edith arrived. It wasn't a large party, roughly twenty or thirty souls who had nothing better to do. They had dutifully assembled in the cramped mews house near Queen Anne Street to start their evening with a few smoked salmon whirls from Marks & Spencer and some bottles of Majestic champagne. The gathering was already past its zenith and the guests had begun to peel away, heeding the call of dinner reservations and theatres and baby-sitters, when Edith came through the door. She was smiling with anticipation but I could see her face shrink with disappointment as she surveyed the room. I went up to her.

'Don't tell me Charles has gone. I got stuck in traffic and I left too late anyway.'

It was easy to see why. She had taken immense trouble with her appearance and I could not remember seeing her in better fettle, her lovely face flawless, her hair shining and an alluring evening outfit encasing her already desirable form.

'Stop worrying,' I murmured reassuringly. 'He hasn't arrived yet.'

'But he is coming?'

'I suppose so. Tommy said he was.'

'That's what he said to me but where is he?'

She bit her lip in annoyance as a couple of her former friends grudgingly decided to acknowledge her presence and draw her into conversation. Adela came up to me.

'What's she doing here?' she said. 'I thought this was the other camp.'

'Not really. I gather Tommy was trying to bring them together.'

'You amaze me. Two days ago, I ran into Arabella at Harvey Nicks and she was saying the break-up was the best thing that could have happened.'

'I don't doubt it but even married couples can on occasion disagree. Or don't you believe such a thing possible?'

'I believe it,' said Adela sourly, 'but I still don't see how Arabella could have allowed the invitation in the first place.'

The answer, of course, which I could not give then but I was able to supply later, was that Arabella had given no such agreement.

The party was on its last legs. A few of us had been invited to stay on for dinner and we were in that uncomfortable, if familiar, period when almost everyone who is not invited to remain has gone but there is always a couple who do not realise that they are delaying the launch of the next stage of the evening. Usually, the hostess weakens and says to the obdurate, 'Do stay for something to eat if you'd like to.' To the trained ear, this translates as, 'Please go. We are hungry and you are not invited.' The old hand on the cocktail party circuit will then look around, blush and scuttle away, muttering about having to be somewhere else. But there is always the risk that the stayer will be uninitiated in these rituals or stubborn or simply stupid – in which case they may accept the unmeant offer of hospitality. In this instance, Arabella Wainwright was clearly not prepared to take a chance on having to entertain Edith for the rest of the evening and so she said nothing. But still Edith would not leave. I strolled over to her.

'I suppose you're having dinner here?' she said.

'We are. And so I imagine is more or less everyone else in the room.'

She looked around. When she spoke her voice had a bleakness that almost brought tears to my eyes. 'I was all geared up. It didn't occur to me that he wouldn't come. His mother must have got wind of it and put him off somehow.'

'I don't see how. Tommy didn't tell me you were coming and I can't imagine he would have told anyone else.'

She didn't linger all that much longer. When Arabella brought a pile of plates out of the tiny kitchen and plonked them noisily onto the dining room table alongside an arrangement of sporting mats even Edith had to admit defeat.

'I must run,' she said to her detached and unbending hostess. 'Thank you. It's been lovely seeing you again.'

Arabella nodded silently, only too glad to be rid of her but Tommy took her to the door. 'I don't know what happened,' he said. 'I am sorry.'

Edith gave him a sad little smile. 'Oh well. Perhaps it's not meant to be.' Then she kissed him and left. But for all her pretended acceptance of fate, she continued to think someone had wrecked her chances. And she was right.

It was much later in the evening when, in a rare break with my personal tradition, I was helping to clear some plates away, that I overheard a short snatch of conversation coming from behind the kitchen door.

'What do you mean?' said an exasperated Tommy.

'Exactly what I say. I thought it was unfair to spring an ambush on him when we're supposed to be his friends.'

'If that was really what you thought then why didn't you tell Charles and let him make up his own mind?'

'I might ask you the same question.'

Tommy was clearly flustered. 'Because I'm not sure he knows his own mind.'

When Arabella spoke again, it was hard to discern the faintest traces of regret. 'Precisely. And that is why I told his mother.'

'Then you're a bitch.'

'Maybe. You can tell me I was wrong in six months time. Now take in the cream and don't spill it.'

Unable to pretend that I was arranging the dirty plates for much longer, I pushed the kitchen door open to find no sign of dispute within.

'How kind you are,' said Arabella, smoothly relieving me of my burden.

My wife was reluctant to be drawn into a moral position as we drove home. 'Just don't do anything of the sort to me,' she said, and I agreed. Not that I would criticise Tommy. Indeed I thought he had acted the part of a true friend but, rather feebly perhaps, it was not a position I was anxious to find myself in. I did not repeat what Arabella had said about the six-month interval probably because, even at that stage, I did not want to take it on board.

*   *   *

A few days later, Edith awoke to find herself vomiting into the lavatory bowl. She must have fumbled her way there in half-sleep and it was only the act of retching that finally brought her to her senses. When at last it seemed that even the very lining of her stomach must have been discharged into the pan, she stopped, gasped for air and sat back. Simon came to the door, with his hand over the portable telephone. He slept naked and normally the sight of his godly form cheered her into a sense of present good but this morning, his lightly muscled charms were wasted on her.

'Are you all right?' he asked superfluously.

'I think it must have been those prawns,' she said, knowing full well that he had chosen the soup.

'Poor you. Better out than in.' He smiled, holding up the receiver, and mimed, 'It's your mother,' with a comic grimace. Edith nodded and reached out her hand for the telephone. 'I'll make some coffee,' said Simon, and wandered off to the kitchen.

Edith wiped her mouth and settled her thoughts. 'Mummy? No, I was in the bathroom.'

'Was that you being sick?' said Mrs Lavery at the other end.

'Well, I don't know who else.'

'Are you all right?'

'Of course I'm all right. We went to a ghastly place in Earl's Court last night that's been opened by some failed actor Simon knows. I had shellfish. I must have been mad.'

'Only I thought you were looking rather green around the gills when I saw you.' Edith had accompanied her mother on a fruitless search for a hat the previous week. That was enough in itself to make most people fairly green but she said nothing. 'So you're not ill?'

'Certainly not.'

'You would tell me if there was . . . something, wouldn't you?'

Edith knew very well that she would hesitate to trust her mother with the time of day but there was no point in going into that now. 'Of course I would,' she said. There was a pause.

'And I suppose there's no news. About . . . everything . . .'

'No.'

'Oh, darling.' However irritated, Edith did feel sorry for her mother. She was forced to concede that Mrs Lavery, shallow as her values might be, was experiencing some perfectly genuine emotions. Particularly regret. 'You won't take any . . . step you might be sorry about, will you?'

'What step?'

'I mean . . . you won't burn your bridges until you're sure . . .'

Edith was used to her mother's seemingly limitless supply of clichés so she needed no translator to tell her what they were discussing. Oddly, despite the paucity of her mother's vocabulary, the question had succeeded in centring her thoughts on the matter. As she brought the conversation to an end and cleared the line, she knew the time had come for positive action.

It was a Saturday, a mild, pleasant day for them as a rule, involving newspapers, a lunch out somewhere, perhaps a cinema or possibly a dinner with some friends in a Wandsworth kitchen but as Edith dressed she knew that no such day lay ahead for her. She selected her outfit with considerable care, casual country clothes, well bred, unshowy, exactly the type of skirt and jersey that she had renounced with a religious fervour so short a time ago. Just as when she was choosing her clothes for the dress show, she was once more conscious that her two lives demanded two costumes. A duke's daughter might get away with wearing some streetwalker's outfit from Voyage at a dinner in Shropshire, indeed she would be praised for her aristocratic eccentricity but she, Edith, would never be given the same licence. Had she dared to wear London clothes in the country, to Charles's circle it would only have been a confirmation of her ill-breeding. When she entered the kitchen, Simon looked up in surprise. 'My word. You look as if you're auditioning for *Hay Fever*.'

'I feel such a fool. I promised to take my mother to a lunch party today and I completely forgot about it. That's why she rang. Can you forgive me?'

'Whose lunch party?'

'Just some country cousins.'

'You don't have any country cousins. Wasn't that the whole point?' In saying this, Simon showed one of his rare flashes of understanding. It was exactly the point.

'I do but I never talk about them. They're too boring to live.'

'Which means you don't want me to come.' Simon hated to be left out of anything. Or at least, if he was, it had to be his choice. He didn't mind being too busy to join in, in fact he quite enjoyed it, but the thought that people were not anxious for his company – even if it was for a journey to the post box – was anathema to him.

Edith smiled a wistful, wouldn't-that-be-nice smile. 'I wish. But she's been begging me for us to have some time on our own. I suppose she wants to talk about everything.' This was accompanied by a half-shrug that brooked no argument.

'Just be nice about me.'

She gave him a warm and supportive smile, knowing that in her heart she was plotting his fall, and set off downstairs to their bedroom to collect her coat. She did not want to tell Simon where she was going as that would have detonated a scene and she was by no means certain of the day's possible outcome. The last thing she wanted was for him to flounce back to his wife in a pet, leaving her to come home to an empty flat.

The truth was she had determined, in that morning moment of surveying her own floating sick, that she was not going to be put off for one day longer. She would drive that very morning to Broughton and beard the lion – or rather the lioness's cub – in his den. As she sped out down the A22, she couldn't really understand what had taken her so long to come to this decision. This was her husband and she was going to what was, after all, her marital home. No one could argue with that.

An unpleasant surprise was waiting for her, as she had forgotten that on a Saturday in summer the house would of course be open to the public. Somehow that had slipped through her calculations and she was now in the faintly ludicrous position of having to choose between parking her car in the courtyard and going in through the family's entrance or entering by the public door and travelling up into the body of the house surrounded by tourists and housewives from Brighton. She made the bold decision to go in by the latter route. She thought there would be plenty of time to block her path if she rang the family's doorbell and she was gambling on Charles being in his own study, which was next to the library. It would be the work of a moment to slip through the cordon and open the door and she correctly guessed that none of the guides would stop her. Indeed, she made a point of pausing to say hello to the pleasant woman in a stout, country suit who stood taking tickets. 'Hello, Mrs Curley, how are you? Can I creep in this way? Would you mind?' Edith had mastered this particular trick of her husband's people, that of asking as a favour something that cannot be refused. 'Oh, Mrs So-and-so, could you *bear* to wait up until we get home? Would that be a *terrible* bore for you?' Of course, the wretched woman being instructed in this way (as well as her employer) knows that this really means 'You are forbidden to go to bed until I have returned' but it is of course a more self-congratulatory way to deliver a command. It is all part of the aristocracy's consciously created image. They like to pride themselves on being 'marvellous with servants', which usually means making impossible demands in the friendliest voice imaginable.

Mrs Curley was clearly uncomfortable with the request but as Edith had predicted, there was nothing she could do about it. 'Of course, mi-lady,' she said with a cheerful nod, and dialled the family's private number the minute Edith had passed by.

*   *   *

Charles Broughton was indeed in his study or, as Lady Uckfield liked to call it, the Little Library, just as Edith suspected. He was answering letters in a vague sort of way, pretending to be, rather than actually being, busy. The house party was of his mother's choosing and, as always, those friends she had selected for him were not congenial to his wounded soul. Diana Bohun he found cold and too self-consciously grand to be of interest while her husband was very nearly mad. Clarissa was not among them. He had at least managed to persuade his mother that she was barking up the wrong tree there but . . . if not Clarissa then who?

He knew about Edith's appearance at Tommy Wainwright's. Indeed Tommy had told him the following day, perhaps not wanting to have someone else deliver the news. At first Charles had been extremely angry, not with Tommy but with his mother. On the evening in question she had suddenly made him take her to visit some ancient friend in hospital, a mission that was represented to him as crucial but was of course, as he could see now, the simplest ploy to keep him from the Wainwright party. But then, after he had calmed down a little, he wondered for the thousandth time what would have been achieved by their meeting. Whatever his friends might say about the strangeness of her actions, he did understand why Edith had left him. He was dull. He knew this was true because, alas for him, he was just clever enough to be aware of it. He knew he was no company for her once the joy of her advancement had worn off. Half the time, if he was honest, he didn't really know what his wife was talking about. When she questioned the policy of the Opposition or tried to evaluate the benefits and harm of intervening in the Middle East . . . Charles knew there were differing points of view on these subjects but he didn't see why he was called upon to have them. So long as he kept voting Conservative and saying how frightful he thought New Labour, wasn't that enough? It was all and more than most of his pals in White's expected of him. Well, clearly it wasn't enough for Edith. Now even he had begun to suspect that she might conceivably want him back – or at least that she wanted to talk about it – but had anything changed? Wouldn't she tire of him again within a matter of months, if not weeks? Wouldn't it better for her and for him if they knew when they were beaten? This in short was how he had begun to think of his marriage. A defeat certainly but a defeat that should now be faced up to and walked away from. Which was of course precisely what Lady Uckfield had intended. It is customary these days to suggest that all interference in the private lives of one's children invariably leads to disappointment but this is not true. Clever parents, who do not play their game too fast, can achieve their aims. And the Marchioness of Uckfield was cleverer than most.

He looked up as the door opened and the sedate figure of the Viscountess Bohun slid into the room. 'Charles?' she said with a despairing roll of her eyes. 'Thank God you're here.'

'Why? What is it?'

'I'm in the most frightful fix. Peter's gone for a walk and we haven't got the car with us. Anyway . . .' Charles waited patiently. 'The thing is . . .' Diana moistened her lip nervously. She was really quite a talented actress. 'I've made a sort of muddle of the dates and I've come without anything . . .'

Charles looked at her, puzzled. This made no sense at all, like a piece translated badly from a foreign tongue. 'I'm so sorry,' he said in answer to Diana's pseudo-blushes, 'I'm not sure I . . .'

Diana overcame her revulsion for this sort of tactic. Desperate times breed desperate measures and as her hostess had made clear, these were desperate times. 'I wasn't expecting it but . . . it's that time of the month and I've got to get to a chemist . . .'

'Oh, Lord.' Charles leaped to his feet in a frenzy of embarrassment. 'Of course. What can I do?'

Diana breathed more easily. She had reached her goal and wonderfully quickly. 'Could you bear to run me into Lewes, only everything in the country shuts at one and—'

'Certainly. Right away.'

'I've just got to tell your mother something.'

'Righto. I'll get the car. Be outside our entrance in five minutes. And don't worry.'

She rather loved him for telling her not to worry about an experience she had been going through once a month since she was twelve but she chose not to assuage his anxiety. With a weak smile, she watched him scuttle out of the room. In this choice of lie, Diana had judged correctly if she wanted instant action. As she calculated, Charles, like all men of his type, had the greatest possible distaste for any of the mechanics of womanhood. One hint of them and he neither needed nor wanted further explanation in order to make him act fast. As he thundered down the family staircase, she listened with the just pride of an efficient workman.

*   *   *

Edith had hardly reached the landing by the bronze of the slave before Lady Uckfield issued forth from a roped-off archway. 'Edith? Is that you? Why didn't you tell us you were coming?' Her mother-in-law slid her arm through hers and attempted to drag her towards the door into the family sitting room. Edith knew that the game was up, silently cursing herself for not pulling a scarf over her face and sliding in unnoticed, but even so she would not give in at once. She extricated herself from Googie's grip and started towards the library and Charles's study beyond.

'I thought I'd be a nuisance and I only want a quick word with Charles. It won't take a moment.' She was walking so fast that, to the delight of the public present, Lady Uckfield was forced to break into a sort of trot to keep up with her. They passed into the splendid library with its high mahogany and ormolu-mounted bookshelves. Above the chimneypiece, an early Broughton in a chestnut periwig gazed down, startled at the scene being played out below him. A few tourists had recognised one or other of them and since the marital split had been in half the newspapers in the country, they left off their bored examination of the thousands of gilded, leather spines and turned all their attention to the two women, thrilled by this unexpected entertainment opportunity.

'Are you staying for luncheon?' said Lady Uckfield, aware of being the cynosure of all eyes and anxious to normalise this very abnormal situation.

'Why? Would you like me to?' said Edith. She in contrast was thoroughly enjoying the exposure of her mother-in-law to the gaze of the common multitude.

'Of course,' said Lady Uckfield, grabbing and pulling at Edith's sleeve in a vain attempt to slow her progress across the gleaming floor.

'I don't think so,' said Edith. She was at the study door by now and her hand was almost on the knob when it opened to reveal the stately form of Lady Bohun. Imperceptibly, with a movement hardly visible to the naked eye, she nodded to her hostess. Edith saw it and at once knew she was too late. The bird had flown.

'Hello, Edith,' said Diana in her slowest and most mannered drawl. 'Will you excuse me? I'm just running into Lewes for something and I must get there before everything closes. Will you be here when we get back?'

'What do you think?' said Edith, and Diana had gone without further ado. Left alone with her daughter-in-law, Lady Uckfield drew her into the room and closed the door. 'Sit down for a moment,' she said, taking her own place behind Charles's desk and absent-mindedly tidying his scattered papers into neat piles.

'There's no need for this,' answered Edith. 'If Charles isn't here, I'll go.'

'Please sit down,' was the repeated request, and Edith did. 'I am sorry you see us as your enemies, my dear.'

'You may be sorry but you can hardly be surprised.'

Lady Uckfield gave her a hurt look. 'I wanted your marriage to work, you know. You have misjudged me if you think otherwise. I always wanted you to be happy.'

'You wanted us to make the best of a bad job.'

'But you didn't, did you?' said Lady Uckfield crisply, all trace of her customary gush and *vibrato* gone.

There was a measure of reason to this that took some of the wind out of Edith's sails as she was forced to admit. Was it rational of her to suggest that Lady Uckfield should have celebrated when she, Edith, came into their lives? Why should her mother-in-law want her back now that this unpleasant episode was almost over? Lady Uckfield was not finished. 'A year ago,' she said, 'you were sick of the sight of Charles. When he spoke you gritted your teeth, when he touched you, you shivered. I am his mother and I lived in the same house with you. Did you think I wouldn't notice these things?'

'It wasn't like that.'

'It was exactly like that. He bored you. He bored you to death. Worse than that, he irritated you to the point of distraction. He could not please you however hard he tried. Nothing he said or did was right. He set your nerves on edge by his very presence and yet now ... what am I to make of this sudden eagerness to see him? What has changed?'

Edith drew herself up and looked her opponent in the eye. She was determined somehow to try to gain the initiative. 'Has it occurred to you that I might have had some time for reflection? Or am I too stupid in your eyes to think of anything but money and social climbing?'

'My dear, I never thought you stupid.' Lady Uckfield held up her palm in protest. 'You must at least give me credit for that.' There was a noise on the gravel and the older woman walked over to the window but it was not, as she had feared, Charles coming back for something he'd forgotten. 'I have to ask myself why now, why suddenly, a meeting is so essential when in the first months away you exhibited no such wish. I am a mother and I have to say to myself, what could have changed that might make a reunion with my son so desirable now when it was so *un*desirable then?"'

'Perhaps I don't feel I've made a good choice. Is that hard to understand?'

'On the contrary. I find it easy to understand. Especially since I think you've made a very poor choice indeed. But...' She rested her fingertips against each other like an avuncular preacher making a point in a pulpit. 'Why *now*? Why such a change upon an instant?'

Edith stared at her. 'You can't stop me seeing him for ever,' she said.

Lady Uckfield nodded. 'No. I dare say I can't.'

'Well then.'

'I think I can stop you seeing him for a few months. Six perhaps, or even three. Let us see how we all feel then about this poor choice you have made.'

At that moment Edith realised that of course her mother-in-law, dear Googie with her mind as pure as snow, knew. They never talked about it, neither at that time nor in the ensuing years, but they were always aware from then on that, beyond a shadow of doubt, they both *knew*. Edith stood up. 'I'm going now.'

'Are you sure? Can I at least give you something to eat? Or what about a loo? You've come *such* a long way.' Once again the tone had settled back into its usual intimate pattern with the rhythm of shared midnight secrets in the dormitory.

At this moment, in some strange way, it was hard for Edith not to admire this woman, her sworn foe, who held onto the high ground in every argument against all-comers. It was hard but it was not impossible. 'You are a fucking cow,' she said. 'A fucking cow with a hide of leather and no heart.'

Lady Uckfield seemed to think over these words for a moment

before nodding. 'Probably there is some truth in your unflattering description,' she acknowledged. 'And it is perhaps for that reason, or something resembling it, expressed hopefully in more fragrant language, that I have made such a success of my opportunities and you have made such a failure of yours. Goodbye, my dear.'

~

You may ask yourself why Edith, outfoxed at every turn, did not travel the more modern route out of her dilemma and, released from embarrassment after a short stay in some discreet, rural nursing home, why she did not then wait the three or six months stipulated by Lady Uckfield and outface them all. I suspect that she hardly knew the reason herself but somehow she was determined not to go that way. She was not, so far as I am aware, particularly religious and, I would have thought, operated on the minimum of moral scruples generally but perhaps because she had seen a way in which she could spare a life, a life that depended on her and her alone, she could not now bring herself to sacrifice it. It was, I think, an essentially animal decision rather than a sentimental one – or else then every tigress in the jungle is sentimental. Women, I suspect, can understand better than most men why something that hardly existed notionally and legally did not yet exist at all should still have been able to command such loyalties.

In the end, help came from a most unlikely sector. She had told me the following morning about her brief sojourn at Broughton and I was naturally dreading the request that I should take a more proactive hand in the whole business when she surprised me by telling me that she was going to wait until Charles's next visit to Feltham. 'He goes every fortnight or so. I'll collar him there.'

'How will you know when he's visiting?'

'Caroline's going to tell me. She'll drive me down.'

This information was both relieving and astonishing. Relieving because of course it meant I could be dispensed with and astonishing because it would never have occurred to me that Caroline would work against her mother's interest. Even now I am not completely sure of her motives. The Chase marriage was looking rocky. It is possible that she did not want the issue of her own satisfactory divorce arrangements being swamped by the divorce of the heir. It may have been an act of rebellion against her mother whose values Caroline always thought (quite wrongly as it happens) she had rejected. It may have been simpler. She loved her brother and she must have hated seeing him unhappy. In the end, I suppose it was, as always, a mixture of all these elements.

'When did you get in touch with her?'

'She telephoned me this morning. She'd heard about my visit to Broughton. I suppose she feels sorry for me.'

'Well, I won't say I'm not surprised but I'm pleased for you. It's certainly a good deal more suitable that Charles's sister should help you than that I should. Will you let me know how you get on?'

'I will,' she said.

*   *   *

Despite her explanation, Edith herself was not really clear as to Caroline's motives. They had never been close since Edith's admission into the family. They were not enemies. Indeed, despite Eric's almost continual stream of snide comments directed at Edith, she and her sister-in-law had achieved a kind of guarded familiarity but 'friendship' would have been too strong a word for it and Caroline would never have been confused as to where her loyalties lay. For all her professed modernity, Caroline Chase, devoid of self-knowledge as she was, remained very much a chip off her mother's block. She might despise the taut-faced countesses and ministers' wives that made up Lady Uckfield's coterie but when it came down to it her own friends were generally these women's rebellious and oddly-dressed children.

At all events, whatever her motives, she was as good as her word. Two days later the telephone rang in the Ebury Street flat and when Edith picked it up Caroline was on the line. 'Charles is at Feltham now if you're serious. He went down last night and he's on his own there until tomorrow.'

Edith glanced over to where Simon was deep in the *Daily Mail*. He also had the *Independent* delivered every day but he never read it. She steadied herself for one of those faintly Chinese telephone conversations designed to conceal their subject from the witnesses present. 'That's kind of you,' she said.

'So do you want me to take you down?'

'If you can,' came the stilted reply.

'Can't you talk?'

'Not really.'

'I'll be at the top of lower Sloane Street by Coutts at ten o'clock.'

'Fine.' Edith replaced the receiver carefully. It was not, as she explained later, that she ever wavered in her desire to see Charles but, just as she kept silent about the Sussex visit, she was not a big one for bridge-burning. As it happened, Simon had hardly been aware of the telephone conversation at all. She smiled across at him. 'Aren't you working today?'

He looked up. 'In the afternoon. Why?'

'That was Caroline. Asking me to lunch.'

'You're keeping your options open, then.'

She didn't answer but he didn't care.

Once again, she chose her clothes with some deliberation. The easy option was to repeat herself and simply to don a country outfit from her Broughton days but that seemed somehow dishonourable after her humiliation at the hands of Lady Uckfield. It was also, as she now saw more clearly, obvious, which was worse. No, if Charles were to take her back it must be as herself and not because she could pass as Diana Bohun or any of the other cold-hearted bitches who enjoyed their loveless marriages at the heart of Charles's world. Eventually she selected a tight black skirt that showed her legs and a loose blue sweater interwoven with coloured ribbons. She brushed her hair and applied her make-up fairly heavily (that is, for Charles rather than for Caroline). She surveyed the results and was pleased. She looked pretty and bright and just Londony enough for it not to seem as if she was trying too hard.

'Very nice,' said Simon. 'Where are you off to now?'

'I thought I'd do some shopping. I've got to get a birthday present for my father.'

'I suppose I'm not included in the girls' lunch.'

'It's at Caroline's flat . . .' She shrugged sadly. 'Why not come with me now? If I can find something for Daddy, I'm going on to Harrods. See what they've got in for the summer.'

It may seem that there was a calculated risk in this cunning approach but there wasn't really. No man in his right mind would accept the job of trailing a woman through a series of departments when she isn't even looking for anything specific. Especially when there's no lunch at the end of it. He shook his head as she knew he must. 'Not really. If it's all right. I'll see you tonight.'

'What time will you be back?'

He shrugged. 'Seven. Eight.'

They kissed and Edith seized a coat and was gone. A minute later she was walking towards the antique shops at the Pimlico Road end of the street. She knew that Caroline would ask her what she was up to in the two hours on the road that lay ahead and she was trying to determine both what she would say and what was the truth – not that these two would necessarily correlate.

She knew by now, if only from Lady Uckfield's near-hysterical opposition, that there must be a chance she could get Charles back. For a while she had pretended to herself that she was still simply exploring the possibility but in her heart she had already gone a stage further than that. She was bound to acknowledge that she would not have been as anxious as she had been in her attempts to secure a meeting had this not been the case. The question remained, how much did she want him back? Did she want him at any cost? Would she try to exact concessions? Would their life return to precisely the same pattern? And then again, could she gain concessions anyway? Weren't all the cards in Charles's hand? Worst of all: suppose she was wrong and he *didn't* want her back? In these ruminations, she was conscious that she had pushed the *real* reason for her change of heart to the back of her mind but she reasoned that if she was successful then that was after all where it was going to stay and so why worry about it now? It seemed to present her with such a yawning chasm that there was no reason to negotiate it before she absolutely had to. To all intents and purposes, from the moment she had known that she was at last to be permitted to see Charles, her secret had ceased to be true.

She stopped outside the art gallery opposite the Poule Au Pot and glanced at some sketches in the window. As she stood there, a gleaming limousine drew to a halt and the chauffeur helped a woman of some indeterminate Middle Eastern aspect to alight from the vehicle and enter the shop. Looking at this heavily-rouged, sable-wrapped creature, diamond bracelets flashing in the sun, Edith suddenly thought of her mother-in-law. How well she knew that this would not be Lady Uckfield's way. She would arrive in a taxi with a minimum of fuss, in sensible clothes and excellent pearls, and rely on the recognition of the manager. And yet the fact remained that, should these women meet, this Levantine would be nervous of Lady Uckfield while Lady Uckfield would be politely indifferent to her.

Her clash in the Little Library at Broughton, far from lowering Lady Uckfield in Edith's eyes, had paradoxically resulted in a grudging respect for her code. She had always faintly despised those members of her, or Charles's, circle who had fawned over her mother-in-law, but over the last days she had come to re-examine her feelings. In the early stages of her marriage she had perhaps yearned for more of what this Eastern woman in her furs took for granted in her daily round, luxury, glamour, famous faces. All these things – at any rate an English version of them – the young Edith Lavery had wrongly perceived as being connected to the world of a 'Lady Broughton' and she had been taken aback when so much of her new life had proved mundane. She knew that Lady Uckfield thought she, Edith, had gleaned her ideas from novels and nineteenth-century biographies, she had even attempted to defend her own mother occasionally from the accusation of filling her head with bourgeois fantasy, but she realised there was justice in the charge. The reality of life with Charles had seemed so flat and changeless compared to those action-packed plots, the glittering, power-filled ballrooms, that dizzying Lady-Palmerston-like career that she had been anticipating.

And yet, that day at the dress show, when the crowd had broken before Lady Uckfield and her minor Royal Highness like the Red Sea before Moses, Edith had seen what she had thrown away, the key to every closed door in England and most of the rest of the world – at least among the superficial. A landed title might not secure an invitation to Camp David but, even in the twenty-first century, she need never be alone in Palm Beach. And Edith knew by now that the kind of people who *were* superficial, the snobs whose social life was based around collecting people to underpin their own status, outnumbered the rest by ten to one. This kind of power might not be worth much in the great scheme of things but it was something and what had she gained in exchange for it? Life at Broughton might be dull but what was life in Ebury Street? Which did she prefer, lack of noise or lack of muscle? She had walked out of the world of the worldly in a petulant pout of boredom and overnight she had transformed herself from a high court card in the Game of Society into a non-person that people were ashamed to be seen with.

With something akin to a shiver she resumed her walk. Then she thought of the two men. Her subconscious assumption, because she knew that she had married Charles for his name and his fortune, had always been that, stripped of these things, she would never have looked at him. In their two years together she had grown to resent him, absurd as that now seemed even to her, for luring her with his worldly possessions without having the personality to amuse her once she was caught. The truth was she had pursued him and yet, in her self-justifying and dishonest mind, by the time Simon had come along, Charles had assumed the moral status of a baited trap.

Now, strolling down Pimlico Road, admiring the antique window displays, she thought back to her ruminations in the Green Park and realised that separation had changed things. It was her unconscious habit these days to think of her husband more gently. Was he really so disagreeable as company? So much less attractive than Simon? After all, men far worse than Charles find wives all the time. Would the idea of Charles as a husband have seemed so bad in the old days before her marriage? If she had been introduced to Mr Charles Broughton as a schoolfriend's suitor would she have wanted to run out screaming into the night, dragging the doomed girl with her? Of course not. Certainly Simon was a good deal better looking, there could be no doubt of that, but over the months she had grown used to his looks and she had begun to be irritated by the perpetual twinkling that seemed to accompany his every social interchange. All those half-smiles and narrowed lids lavished on waitresses and air hostesses and girls at the check-out in Partridges, all that tossing back of the golden locks, had started to bore her.

More troubling than the comparison of appearance (Charles, after all, while no beauty, was perfectly respectable to look at) was the question of sex. She had to concede that Simon was much the better lover, an excellent lover indeed by any standards let alone poor Charles's, and this was harder to dismiss. She enjoyed going to bed with Simon. Very much. In fact, the thought of making love with him was still enough to tickle her innards, to make her slightly fidgety and uncomfortable, to make her want to cross and uncross her legs. Dear Charles could never be a competitor here with his fumbling, five-minute thrust and his 'thank you, darling', which nearly drove her mad

But for the first time she acknowledged, predictably perhaps, that after a year, making love to Simon had lost its novelty. The sex, though less frequent than at first, was still excellent, no question, but it could no longer blind her to the life for which she had left her gilded cage. After all, how much time does one actually spend in bed making love? Was it really worth the rest of the bargain? Did a pleasurable half an hour two or three times a week compensate for those endless, terrible parties, those awful people with their flat accents, sitting around the flat smoking, or those frightful drama school pals discussing 'hair-dos' and gardening tips and bucket-shop holidays? And anyway, wasn't Charles rather sweet in his way? Wasn't he more decent than Simon? Wasn't he truer as a person?

So Edith continued up Sloane Street belabouring herself with her false values, all the while attempting to convince herself with a litany of Charles's essential worth until, in a rare moment of honesty, like the sun breaking through the clouds, she saw the irony of this inner conversation. She, Edith, was using these arguments as if the opposition to them would overwhelm her should she give it a hearing. She was forcing herself to the next step when any impartial observer, and of this she was suddenly quite sure, would have freely volunteered that of course Charles was more decent than Simon. In fact, in any real way, it was perfectly obvious that Simon wasn't decent at all. Unlike Charles he had no honour, only pragmatism. He could not be true because there was no truth in him. His morality was a tawdry bundle of received, fashionable causes that he believed would make him attractive to casting directors. Edith was talking herself into thinking that in some ways she preferred Charles to Simon when to anyone who knew them both there could be no comparison. Charles, dull as he might be, was infinitely the better man. Simon was a mass of nothing.

She saw then that people would not think ill of her for coming round to this opinion – something she dreaded – but, on the contrary, they were amazed she had ever walked out on her husband for such a hollow gourd. Even so, and at this moment she felt it behoved her to be honest for once in her life, it was not for Charles's virtues that she wanted him back nor even because of her secret. It was for the sense of protected importance that she missed and that now, in her unadmitted crisis, she needed more than ever. The truth was that her months away had only finally confirmed her mother's prejudices. Edith had gone for a walk and found it was cold outside.

'I think I'm leaving Eric,' said Caroline, as they nosed at last on to the M11. Edith nodded, raised her eyebrows slightly and said nothing. 'No comment?' asked Caroline. She was a terrifying driver, as she had never mastered the art of conducting a conversation without facing the other person.

Edith glanced nervously at a lorry that passed within inches and shook her head. 'Not really. I don't know that I'm in a position to make a comment. Anyway,' she stared out of the window, 'I never grasped why you married him. Leaving him seems much easier to understand.'

Caroline laughed. 'I've forgotten why I married him. That's the problem.'

'What luck there are no children.'

'Is it?' Caroline's face had assumed a hard Mount Rushmore look, which gave her the appearance of an Indian chief in some fifties western when one was still allowed to be on the side of the cowboys. 'I think it's rather a bore. It means if I want any I'll have to go through the whole bloody business again.' There was some truth in this. 'I can't help feeling sometimes that, within limits, it doesn't seem to make much odds whom one marries. One's bound to get a bit sick of them in the end.'

'Then why leave Eric?'

'I said "within limits",' answered Caroline with some asperity, taking her eyes completely off the road and narrowly avoiding a large transporter. 'In my old age, I have to concede that Lady Uckfield may have been right.' One of the most chilling comments on the private family life of the Broughtons was that Caroline and Charles, when talking to each other, would refer to their mother as 'Lady Uckfield'. It was sort of a joke and sort of a comment. Either way there was something troubling in it. Caroline continued. 'She told me it was a mistake to marry a man who was vulgar and had no money, which of course I went on to do. But she added that if I had to break these primary rules then I should be sure to marry a man who was polite and kind, rudeness and cruelty being the only two qualities that absolutely poison life.'

Edith nodded. 'I agree with her,' she said. She was perhaps surprised at the wisdom of her mother-in-law's injunction. She shouldn't have been. Lady Uckfield was far too intelligent not to realise that true misery stifles all endeavour. It was just that she was much more sensible than Edith about what constitutes true misery.

'Eric was so rude. Not just to me but to everyone. A dinner party at our house was a kind of survival course. The guests had to arrive armed and see how many brickbats they could avoid before escaping into the night. Looking back, I can't imagine why anyone ever came twice.'

'Then why did you marry him?'

'Partly to annoy my mother,' said Caroline, as if that was absolutely understood. 'Then partly because he was so good-looking. And finally, I suppose, because he tremendously wanted to marry me.'

'And now you don't think he was genuine.'

'No, he was genuine all right. He was desperate to marry me. But it was because I was a marquess's daughter. I didn't see that. Or I didn't see it was *only* that.'

Edith said nothing. The conversation was moving into a dangerous area. She heard the distant sound of cracking ice under her halting steps. 'Right,' she murmured.

But Caroline had not finished with her. 'Rather as you wanted to marry Charles,' she said. When Edith made no comment, she continued, 'Not that I blame you. There's much more point to it that way round. At least marrying Charles made you a countess. Even now, I can't see what Eric thought he'd get out of it.'

They drove on for a bit in silence. Then Edith re-opened. 'If that's what you think why are you driving me up here?'

Caroline thought for a moment, wrinkling her brows, as if the idea had only just occurred to her. She was almost hesitant when she spoke. 'Because Charles is so unhappy.'

'Is he?' said Edith, thrilled.

'Yes.' Caroline lit a cigarette and for a moment Edith thought they were going into the central divider. 'I know Lady Uckfield thinks it'll blow over. She has a fantasy that he will forget you and marry the daughter of some peer who'll give him four children, two of whom will inherit estates from relations of their mother's.' Caroline laughed wryly. This was of course a wonderfully accurate *résumé* of Lady Uckfield's dreams.

'Are you quite sure she's wrong?'

'How little you know my brother,' said Caroline, and lapsed again into silence. Edith naturally longed to hear more of this wretched and unhappy man, whose life was a misery without her and to whom, by some strange miracle, she was already married. She gave Caroline a quizzical look and the latter relented. 'In the first place I do not think that my mother's idea of your perfect successor is Charles's. To put it bluntly, if that was what he was looking for he could have found it with very little difficulty. But that is no longer the point. Charles is a simple man. He is capable of feelings but they are uncomplicated, straightforward and deep. He can hardly communicate and he cannot flirt at all.' Edith thought with wonder of her other love, who could only communicate and flirt. Simon's problem was the opposite of Charles's. He could not feel. Caroline was still talking. 'Charles has made his choice. You. You are his wife. In his heart that's it. Finish. I am not saying that if you did divorce him he wouldn't eventually settle for someone else as brood-mare but in his heart he would have failed and his real wife would be out there walking around with someone else. And that, my dear, would be you.'

The rest of the drive was accomplished in silence. It was almost as if they were waiting for the next event in the plot before they could continue their discussion. And so they wound their way through the flat Norfolk landscape until at last they turned into a well-kept but somewhat overshadowed drive, which in its turn, when they had been released from the high walls of rhododendron, brought them to the wide, gravelled forecourt of the main house.

Feltham Place had passed into the Broughton family in 1811 when the then Lord Broughton had married Anne Wykham, only child of Sir Marmaduke Wykham, sixth baronet and the last of his line. The house was Jacobean, more a gentleman's than a nobleman's residence, picturesque rather than magnificent with roofs bristling with barley sugar chimneys and possibly for this reason it had never managed to catch at the family's imagination. Like many houses of its period it was in a dip (before the pumping innovations of the late seventeenth century allowed those splendid, landscaped views), although the flatness of the county gave a certain openness at the bottom of its valley. It might have functioned as the Broughtons' Dower House or as a seat for the heir, but there were other houses nearer Uckfield that had served these turns at least until the Second World War and recently, as we know, the heir had chosen to live with his parents.

In the past, Feltham had been let but it was taken back for the shooting in the 1890s and had been farmed in hand ever since, despite the family's allowing the sport to lapse after the war. Charles had revived the shoot over the last few years and he was proud of the fact that he could now safely let two and three-hundred-bird days, secure in the knowledge that there would be no great disappointments. He and his keeper had worked hard. The covers and hedgerows had been replanted, the feeding pens reorganised, indeed the whole appearance of the countryside had been more or less restored to the condition of a century before. But despite this, he was not tempted to bring his own shooting guests to Feltham. They were offered the splendours of Broughton while businessmen, people with mobile telephones and gleaming sports wear, took the shooting at Feltham by the day. At a (considerable) extra cost they could even stay overnight, which may have accounted for the somewhat boarding-house quality within.

The Wykham who'd built the place had been a favourite of King James I and in those days it had been much larger but the king's beau had been improvident and his heir (a nephew since, unsurprisingly, the builder had never married) demolished two-thirds of it. This meant that the brickwork and carving on the façade and throughout the house was of a much higher standard than one would normally associate with the scale of building. Inside, all the first-rate furniture and pictures had long since been swallowed up by Broughton and most of what remained dated from its rehabilitation as a shooting-lodge at the end of the last century. Lumpy, leather-covered Chesterfields provided the seating and the walls were covered with second-rate portraits and enormous, indifferently painted scenes of hunting, shooting and all the other methods of country killing. Still, the rooms themselves were pleasant and the staircase, more or less the sole survivor from the days of the Jacobean favourite, was magnificent.

Edith hardly knew the place. In Charles's mind it was the nearest thing to an 'office' in his weekly round. He ran it as a business and apart from an occasional appearance at a village show and an annual cocktail party for all those neighbours who might be tiresome about the shoot were they not courted every so often, he had no social profile in the county at all. Quite frequently he stayed with the Cumnors at their infinitely larger and more luxurious house four miles down the road, rather than put the ancient care-taking couple to the trouble of opening a bedroom.

Caroline drew up by the front door and the two women made their way into the wide and gloomy hall that took up two-thirds of the entrance front. It was decorated by a frieze of slightly bogus armorial tributes to the Wykhams and the Broughtons but otherwise boasted no colour at all apart from the brown of the panelling and the less attractive brown of the leather furniture. 'Charles!' Caroline called out. It was a chilly day and the interior of the house was noticeably colder than the air outside. Edith pulled her coat tightly around her. 'Charles!' shouted Caroline again, and she set off through a doorway that led first to the staircase and then into the former morning room that operated as Charles's office. Edith followed her. Desks and filing cabinets stood about the room, the chill slightly alleviated by a three-bar electric fire in the grate that looked as if its very existence breached the entire safety code. They were still standing there when another door, facing them, opened and there all at once stood a flummoxed Charles. To her amazement, even to her delight, Edith suddenly realised that she was shocked at his appearance. Gone was that sleek country gentleman who always looked as if he was on the way to make an advertisement for Burberry's. She was astonished to see that her fastidious husband was looking scruffy and unkempt. He was almost dirty. Caught out by her stare, he pushed his fingers through his hair. 'Hello,' he said, with a watery smile. 'Fancy seeing you here.'

At this point Caroline took her leave. 'I'm going in to Norwich,' she said. 'I'll be back in a couple of hours.' It was a relief really that she didn't even try to normalise the situation or start any we-were-just-driving-past nonsense.

Charles nodded. 'I see,' he said.

Left alone, Edith was oddly blank as to quite what she was going to say next. She sat on the edge of a chair near the fire like a housemaid at an interview and leaned forward to warm her hands. 'I hope you're not cross. I did so want to talk to you. Properly. And I began to feel that I was never going to be allowed to. I'm afraid I thought I'd just chance it.'

He shook his head. 'I'm not a bit cross. Not at all.' He hesitated. 'I – I'm sorry about the telephone calls and all the rest of it. It wasn't my mother not telling me, you know. Well, it wasn't only that. I expect you thought it was. It was just that I didn't really know what to say. It seemed better to leave it all to the professionals. Of course now you're here ...' He tailed off disconsolately.

Edith nodded. 'I had to know what you were thinking about everything. I understand your parents want you free straight away.'

'Oh that.' He looked sheepish. 'I don't mind. Honestly. Whatever suits you.' He stared at her in the unflattering light of an overhead bulb. 'How's Simon?'

'Fine. Very well. Loving his series.'

'Good. I'm glad.' He didn't sound it but he was trying to be courteous. Edith was struck anew by the decency and kindness of this man she had tossed aside. What had she been thinking of? Her own actions sometimes seemed to her so hard to understand. Like a foreign film. And yet these had been her choices. The conversation limped on.

'I don't think I ever came to Feltham at this time of year. I must have but I don't remember. It's rather lovely, isn't it?'

Charles smiled. 'Dear old Feltham,' he said.

'You ought to live here. Do it up. Get some of the stuff back.'

He half nodded. 'I think I'd be a bit lonely, stuck out here on my own. Don't you? Nice idea, though.'

'Oh, Charles.' In spite of the cynicism with which she had embarked on this mission Edith had become a victim of her own justifications. Like Deborah Kerr in *The King and I*, whistling her happy tune to make herself brave, Edith had succeeded in talking herself into believing that she was a romantic figure who had lost her love rather than a selfish girl who bitterly regretted her comforts. Her eyes began to moisten.

Oddly perhaps, it was only at this moment that Charles fully grasped she had definitely come to try to get him back. Up to this point he was still wondering if it might not just be for some financial or time-related scheme that she had made the journey. Despite his earlier suspicions, his non-existent vanity made him slow to reach the obvious conclusion and he thought she might want him to agree to something before his lawyers could talk him out of it. He was not offended by this but, if it should prove to be the case, he was anxious to conceal his wretchedness from her. Both out of consideration for her feelings and from a (perfectly justifiable) sense of pride. It now occurred to him, with a lurch in his stomach, that this was not what he was dealing with. She wanted to come back to him. He looked at her.

For all his simplicity, he was not an idiot. Thinking along the same lines as that night in his study at Broughton he knew that he was no more interesting than when she left him. He also suspected that the world of show business had not really appealed to her, not at any rate for 'every day'. Just as a year of sin had served to give Edith a clearer idea of what Simon consisted of, so two years of marriage and a year apart had made Edith comprehensible to Charles. He knew she was an *arriviste* and the child of an *arriviste*. He saw her vulgarities of spirit now as sharply as he saw her fine points, of which, despite Lady Uckfield's comments, he still believed there were many. He also knew that if he made a move towards her the thing was settled.

He stared at the hunched-up figure, trying to scoop warmth out of the electric bars. Her coat was a sort of camel colour and looked rather cheap. Was this sad little figure, this 'blonde piece' as his mother would say, to be the next Marchioness of Uckfield? To be painted by some indifferent chocolate box portraitist and hung alongside the Sargeants, Laszlos and Birleys of the preceding generations? Was it in her to make a go of it?

But as he watched her, the sense of how vulnerable she suddenly seemed to him, with her bright make-up and her chain store coat, trying to charm him and looking instead somehow pathetic, overwhelmed him with pity and, in the wake of pity, with love. Whatever her suitability, whatever the limitations of her feelings, whatever her motives, he knew that he, Charles Broughton, could not be responsible for her unhappiness. He was, in short, incapable of hurting her.

'Are you happy?' he said slowly, knowing as he did so that the words gave her permission to return to him and to his life.

At the sound of them Edith knew her pardon had come through. Despite the difficulties with Simon, with her mother-in-law, with the newspapers, with the sun, with the moon, she could now be Charles's wife again if she chose, which, not very surprisingly given all the circumstances, she did. For a second she felt almost sick with relief but then, since she did not wish to appear too desperate, she waited for a minute before she spoke, deliberately punctuating the moment with a pregnant pause. Once satisfied that her answer was anticipated by them both she carefully raised her tear-stained eyes to his.

'No,' she said.

EPILOGUE

~

Smorzando

It did not, so far as I remember, cause any great murmur when Edith was delivered of a daughter seven months or so after the reconciliation. Of course, there was a lot of talk, particularly from her mother, about their being taken by surprise as Edith was 'so frighteningly early'. In fact, Mrs Lavery rather over-egged her performance by insisting on sitting in the hospital throughout the night because of the 'risks of premature birth', which naturally gave rise to a few funny stories on the dinner circuit, but nobody minded. Versions of this sort of folderol are still rather touchingly employed in Society on such occasions. These things are rituals rather than untruths and cause no harm. The point was the baby was female, which took any future strain out of the situation. It meant everything could return to normal without a lingering after-taste.

Even Lady Uckfield, usually so careful, gave herself away in a rare unguarded moment when I telephoned to learn the news.

'Boy or girl?' I asked when she picked up the receiver.

'Girl,' said Lady Uckfield. 'Isn't it a *relief*?' Then, quickly but not quickly enough, she added, 'That they're both doing so well.'

'A great relief,' I answered, going along with this dishonesty. There was no point in blaming her for retaining the deepest prejudices of her kind. Now that the baby could not inherit the glories of Broughton, thanks to the arcane laws governing the peerage that even Mr Blair, for all his trumpeting of women's rights, has not seen fit to change, she would present no further danger and might be lived with in peace. Since all three 'parents' were fair there was not much chance of the baby having the wrong colouring and, at least to date, the girl does not seem particularly to favour Simon, always assuming of course that the infant is his – something of which one can, after all, never be entirely sure. Not at least without resorting to DNA testing, which no entrant in

258

Debrett's would ever risk for fear of what it might reveal. One foreign visitor at Broughton, ignorant of the excellent Edwardian maxim never to 'comment on a likeness in another's child' asked me if I did not think she took after Charles.

I may have imagined a momentary chill in the room but I nodded. 'I do,' I said. 'She's not like Edith at all.' Thereby earning an especially warm glance from my host. Amusingly enough, when I looked at the toddler properly, she did seem to resemble him a bit. But then again that may have been in expression rather than feature. It might seem strange but in later years Charles came to love the girl so much that his younger children would complain of his favouritism. Even less logically, she would eventually develop into the preferred grandchild of Lady Uckfield, which only goes to show that the old maxim is correct and there's nowt so queer as folk. At any rate, barely fourteen months later, Lady Broughton was once more brought to bed, this time of a boy. The new Viscount Nutley was welcomed with bonfires and bun fights in Sussex and Norfolk and, frankly, to be brutal and unmodernist about it, the exact paternity of little Lady Anne had ceased to matter much to anyone.

Caroline did divorce Eric. It was a quiet business without acrimony and with more style than I confess I thought Eric capable of. He was not single long. Within eighteen months he had married the daughter of an immensely rich Cheshire industrialist, Christine somebody or other. They were much better suited than he and Caroline had been. For one thing, she shared Eric's ambitions, which she pursued as relentlessly as if they had been her own and of course they soon were. I happened to meet them both at Ascot a few months after they married and I must say I liked her. She was full of energy and in many ways a good deal easier to rub along with than Caroline, even if she was already infected with Eric's nonsense. I remember her using the phrase 'our sort of people', meaning, I imagine, some sort of exclusive social group to which they belonged. It must have been a luxury for Eric who had spent his entire first marriage being reminded daily of an Inner Circle forever closed to him.

He growled at me by way of recognition but I was not offended. I had by this time forgiven Eric his earlier insults and anyway one of the freedoms of growing older is that one is no longer obliged to dislike someone simply because they dislike you. After all, he was entitled.

Lady Uckfield had made no secret of how little she relished his company and had, somewhat maliciously I suspect, used me at times to demonstrate this.

'I suppose you still see them all?' he said when his wife had stopped discussing her new Poggenpohl kitchen.

I nodded. 'We've got a baby now so a bit less than I did. But yes, I see them.'

'And is dear Edith happy in her work?' Of course, it was quite understandable that he should be irritated when he contemplated one who had survived the course that had brought him down.

'I think so.'

'I'll bet she is. And how is darling "Googie"?' He spat out the name just as I had once heard Edith do before her rehabilitation. Now, for her at least, the name had re-normalised. 'I wonder what my dear ex-mother-in-law thinks of all the recent developments.'

'Oh, I'd say she was pretty merry, one way and another,' I said, for all the world as if I thought he cared, and we nodded to each other and moved on.

As I strolled away to rejoin Adela for tea with Louisa in the Household Stand I pondered my answers and concluded that I had spoken no more than the truth. Of course, as everyone had predicted, the children had changed everything. One may be exhausted but there is little time to be bored with two children under four, particularly as Edith, to her mother-in-law's bemusement, had eschewed a proper Norland nanny and chosen instead to have a series of Portuguese and Australians. Charming girls, one and all (or nearly all), but not the type to take over the nursery as their province. I thought it a wise decision and so, I was pleased to note, did Charles.

But as to quite what Lady Uckfield really made of it all ... One would have to get up very early in the morning to know precisely what she thought about anything, earlier than I rise, certainly. We were not, as I had predicted, quite such friends after the reinstatement of Edith. Although I have not yet given up hope of regaining my former position of Court Favourite. Poor woman, she had allowed herself to dream a little during the interregnum and the imagined life she had woven for herself with dear Clarissa or one of her kind as junior chatelaine had filled her with happy prospects. Ironically her imaginings had not been all that unlike the despised Mrs Lavery's. Lady Uckfield, too, had seen herself as a special friend of her daughter-in-law's family. The two grandmothers would lunch together perhaps and take in an exhibition ... So it was hard to reconcile herself to the Return of Edith, not least because she had allowed herself the rare luxury of admitting what she really felt while Edith was away. Worse, she had confessed these secrets not only to herself and her husband, which was bad enough, but to me, a non-relation. In doing so she knew she had given me a weapon. From now on whenever she referred to 'our darling Edith' there was a risk that I might catch her eye if I so wished and in her heart expose her. I had no intention of doing this but the threat of it introduced a coldness between us nevertheless. I was and am sorry but there is nothing to be done about it. Meanwhile, Adela and I continue to stay at Broughton pretty regularly.

I remember once Lady Uckfield did let herself go a little. There had been a dinner party and the guests were spread out in knots over the drawing room and the Red Saloon next door. Edith was at the centre of an admiring group, for you will understand that a lot of people had a good deal of ground to make up having dropped her during her period of exile. One might have thought that those who had been loyal, Annette Watson for one, would have been rewarded with a shower of invitations but I don't believe they were. Perhaps this was predictable. Anyway, on this particular evening, surrounded as she was, Edith made some remark, I forget what, which was greeted with gales of sycophantic laughter. I was alone, having helped myself to some more coffee, so there was no one to overhear when Lady Uckfield drew level.

'Edith *Triumphans*,' she said. I nodded. But she would not let it go. 'To the victor the spoils.'

'And is Edith the victor?' I asked.

'Isn't she?'

'I don't know.' I shrugged. I imagine I was attempting to be philosophical and by an easy and familiar transition had become dishonest.

'Of course she is the victor,' said Lady Uckfield, quite truthfully. 'You have won.'

Now this was irritating. She was right about Edith, I do admit, but not about me. If anything I had always been a partisan of the Uckfields during the struggle for Charles's soul and she knew it. 'Don't blame me,' I said quite firmly. 'You asked me not to encourage her and I didn't. It was your own daughter who arranged it all, not me. The fact is Charles wanted her back. *Voilà tout.* He must know what's best for himself, I suppose.'

Lady Uckfield laughed. 'That, of course, is precisely what he does not know.' Her tone was a little bitter but more predominately sad. It was also, as I knew it must be, the tone of resignation. 'I told you I didn't believe they would be happy and I wait anxiously to be proved wrong. However,' she waved her little claws and the jewels in her rings flashed in the firelight, 'the thing is done. We must make the best of it. It is time to move on to the next square. Let us at least hope they will be no less happy than everybody else.' And she was gone.

Would they be less happy than everybody else? That was certainly the question. Although she had returned to him without treaty, Edith had nevertheless wrung some considerable concessions in the process. To start with she had grasped the folly of her earlier belief that it was safer to be bored in the country than entertained in London and she had persuaded Charles into a house in Fulham, which had been purchased for more or less what the little flat in Eaton Place had gone for. Now she allowed herself a day or two in London a week. She had also found some committees to sit on and had become involved, down in Sussex, in the actual day-to-day running of a hospice near Lewes. All in all, she had started to evolve the life she would be leading at sixty when she herself, never mind everyone else, would have forgotten that there had ever been a hiccough in her early married life. I thought, on reflection, that it all boded quite well.

We went down to Broughton two or three times a year as a rule. Adela and Edith were never much more than amiable with each other but Charles became very fond of my wife and so we were easy guests, I think. We enjoyed it as, apart from anything else, we had a baby in tow and the houses we could stay in without feeling that we had imported a miniature anarchist were few. Our son, Hugo, was about five months older than Anne and that ensured a measure of shared activity, accompanied by a good deal of merriment from both mothers. It is a truism but it is still true that the longer one knows people the less relevant it becomes whether or not one liked them initially. As I knew from my friendship with Isabel Easton, there is no substitute for shared history and it was clear that by the time ten years had passed, my wife and Lady Broughton would think of themselves as close friends without ever necessarily liking each other much more than they did to start with.

Needless to say, at an early stage after the great patch-up, Edith wished me to understand that she was not interested in pursuing long conversations about her choices, past or present. I quite agreed with her so she needn't have worried. I know only too well how tedious it is to have the recipient of earlier intimacies still hanging around when those intimacies have become irrelevant embarrassments. Anyway, so far as I was concerned, she had seen sense and I hadn't the slightest desire to shake her resolve.

She tested me a few times, waiting, when we happened to be alone, to see if I would bring up the subject of Simon or Charles or marriage or, worse, the baby, but I never did and I am happy to say she began to relax into our old intimacy.

In truth, even had she questioned me, I would have had little to report on the Simon front. I don't know how anxious his wife was to take him back when she had been given the surprising news that his Great Affair was over but, whatever her feelings, she had done it. I saw him once, some months later, at an audition and he told me he was planning to move to Los Angeles to 'try my luck'. I wasn't surprised since this is not an unusual reaction for a player after a disappointing career. As a rule the Hollywood pattern for English actors is simple. They are delighted to go, they are told there is a lot of work for them if they stick it out, they tell everyone how fabulous it is, they spend all their money – and then they come home. It seems to take from two to six years. However, there are always exceptions and I would not be surprised if Simon were one. He seemed to have all the qualities the natives of that city admire and none that they dislike.

Perhaps because he knew we would not be meeting for a while, he asked after Edith. I muttered that she was well and he nodded. 'I'm glad.'

'Good.'

He shook his head at me and raised his eyebrows. 'I don't know,' he said. 'Women!'

I nodded and gave him a sympathetic laugh so we parted friends. I suppose one might gauge the extent of his heartbreak from this subsequent reaction. I do not think Charles would have shaken his head to an acquaintance and said, 'Women!' like a character from a situation comedy had his wife chosen never to return. I think he would have curled up in the dark somewhere and never mentioned her name again, so I suppose we must all concede that Edith had ended up with the man who loved her most. Even so, there was no malice in Simon's eyes and I think one should remember this at least, that when all was said and done there really wasn't any harm in him. It is surely not so terrible a testimonial.

Nor did I ever betray to Edith the Eastons', or rather David's, anxiety to stay in with the family, if necessary at her expense. Gradually even that slightly uncomfortable connection was also resumed. All in all, things went back to normal surprisingly quickly. Even the papers only gave it a couple of squibs – in the *Standard*, I seem to remember, and in one of the tabloids – and then it was over.

Just once she did bring it up, perhaps because I never had. We were walking in the gardens on a Sunday in summer three or even four years after she had returned to the fold and we found ourselves down by the approach to the rose garden where they had set up our chairs for the filming, however long ago it was. The others were playing croquet and as we strolled along, the sound of balls being hit and people getting cross wafted gently over us. Suddenly I was struck by the image of Simon Russell, in his frilled shirt, stretched out on the ground in all his comeliness, as he gossiped that faraway day to a younger, sillier Edith. I said nothing of course and I was taken by surprise when she suddenly spoke into my imaginings.

'Do you ever see him now?' she said.

I shook my head. 'No. I don't think anyone does. He's gone off to California.'

'To make films?'

'Well, that's the idea. Or at least to make a television series.'

'And is he making one?'

'Not yet but you never know.'

'What about his wife?'

'She's gone with him.'

Edith nodded. We strolled on into the rose garden. Some heavily scented, dark red blooms, Papa Meilland maybe, filled the warm air with their sweet stench.

'Aren't you ever going to ask me if I'm happy?' said Edith with a provocative flick of her head.

'No.'

'Well, I'll tell you anyway.' She broke off a half-open bud and fed its stalk through the top buttonhole of my shirt. 'The fact is, I'm happy enough.'

I did not question her statement. I am glad she was and is happy enough. That is a good deal happier than a large proportion of my address book.

Reading Group Gold

SNOBS
by Julian Fellowes

Get to Know the Author
· A Note About the Author
· An Interview with Julian Fellowes

Get to Know the Aristocracy
· Julian Fellowes on Class

Keep on Reading
· Reading Group Questions

A Reading Group Gold Selection

For more reading group suggestions
visit www.readinggroupgold.com

 ST. MARTIN'S GRIFFIN

A Note About the Author

Julian Fellowes is an English writer, actor, and film director who was born in Egypt and educated at Ampleforth College, Yorkshire. He went on to Magdalene College, Cambridge University, and the Webber Douglas Academy of Dramatic Art. As an actor, he appeared in *Monarch of the Glen,* the *Aristocrats, Damage, Shadowlands,* and other films and TV series.

As a screenwriter, his first feature film was *Gosford Park,* directed by Robert Altman, which won awards for the best original screenplay from the Academy of Motion Picture Arts and Sciences, the National Film Critics Circle, the National Society of Film Critics, and the Writers Guild of America. He also wrote the book for the Cameron Mackintosh/Walt Disney stage musical of *Mary Poppins,* before creating *Downton Abbey,* which entered the *Guinness Book of Records* as the most critically acclaimed show on television of 2010. Julian won an Emmy Award for Outstanding Writing for a Miniseries, Movie or a Dramatic Special for *Downton Abbey,* which also received the Emmy for the Outstanding Miniseries or Movie, in addition to winning the Golden Globe in that category.

In 1990, Julian married Emma Joy Kitchener, a lady-in-waiting to Princess Michael of Kent, with whom he has a son named Peregrine. In 2011, he was made a life peer of the House of Lords, with the title Baron Fellowes of West Stafford. The Kitchener-Fellowes family divides their time between London and Dorset.

Julian
Fellowes

An Interview with Julian Fellowes

Q: **What inspired you to write _Snobs_?**

A: It occurred to me that I had in my life, through no great merit on my part, inhabited two essentially "secret" worlds, Society and Showbiz. Many people fantasize about these groups, leafing through magazines in a dentist's waiting room, imagining all sorts of sin and splendor when they stare at the photographs of them. But I have known these people, close up, and I suppose I felt that it might be interesting to pull the curtain aside and reveal them in their less grandiose truthfulness. Like all of us, I had a certain amount that I wanted to say about the world that had nurtured me and about whose frailties and strengths I had kept silent for so long. Because there are strengths, as the reader will discover. I have my criticisms, of course, but I have also tried to demonstrate the elements in the beliefs of these folk that, when all is said and done, I respect. Though I probably shouldn't say it, I do think it is a pretty truthful account of them, humorous too, I hope, but truthful. I imagine this is why, in the end, despite a certain bristling from an acquaintance when the book first came out, I seem to have been forgiven for it.

Q: **How would you describe _Snobs_?**

A: People talk as if the book is entirely about class. For me, it is about choice. Edith makes a choice and, in my eyes, she has to learn to take responsibility for it. Our lives, to a greater or lesser degree, are the product of the choices we make.

Modern society is inclined to suggest that we can somehow wriggle out of the consequences, but I don't agree. We make our choices and, on some level or other, we are stuck with them. I suppose I feel that one of the greatest journeys in life is learning to accept that.

Q: **What did you do before you became a novelist? What else do you do now?**

A: I am probably better known as a screenwriter than a novelist, or indeed as an actor, both of which careers I have pursued, and continue to pursue, with differing degrees of success. It was after I had written the script of the film, *Gosford Park,* that I was asked to have a go at prose and a long suppressed desire to be a novelist came to the surface in answer to the invitation. I think what drew me to it was the cleanliness of simply working with one editor to refine and shape my own voice. I would not, for once, have to deal with the ideas of a hundred movie executives and directors and stars, all of whom want and need to make their mark on any script they work with, but with my own ideas. Mine. As I started to work, I found I gradually ceased the defensive position common to all screenwriters and started to examine what it was that I really wanted to say.

Q: **Were any of the characters in *Snobs* based on you?**

A: Inevitably perhaps, most people assume that the nameless narrator is based on me and of course there is a good deal of me in him—although my wife is always anxious to make it clear that she is NOT Adela (no comment). The narrator is an actor but not a very successful one. He is "in Society," whatever that means, but not at an especially elevated level. All of which would be true of me, particularly when I was starting out. I was taken up by the demands of "The Season" as an "eligible" young man (though why I was considered eligible, I have no idea) and I had many experiences of people like the Uckfields and their kind. There was in fact one family who played a big part in my life in the late teens and early twenties who might be regarded as the progenitors of the Broughton Clan. I had begun by falling in love with one of the daughters and I took to staying with her parents whenever I could in order to further my cause. I got nowhere with her but I ended up more or less in love with the whole family. Actually, I thought no one had spotted this connection but, the other day, at the last Christie's summer party (that I talk about in the book), a voice behind me said rather dryly: "We're the Broughtons, aren't we?" I turned and there was the eldest daughter. She had not much changed despite the gap of years, standing there with a caustic smile, and so of course I had to admit that they were. It will remain our secret. But, anyway, it is not the narrator's similarity of experiences to my own that made me create and use him. Rather it was because it seemed a good idea to have a really accessible character who might introduce the readers to the Broughtons and their life, who was not, in himself, much out of the ordinary and certainly not daunting. They would, in short, have a friend, a tour guide, to accompany them into this peculiar world.

Q: Do you have a favorite character from *Snobs*?

A: Well, I do have a soft spot for Lady Uckfield. Of course, no character in a novel is a complete portrait; they're almost always a slight amalgamation. But she is the nearest to a complete portrait of a very old friend of mine. She knew nothing about it until one day, when we were in a house party together in Sussex, she asked me what I was up to and, after a pause, I heard Emma saying sharply, "Tell her!" so I did. I thought and hoped she might be amused but she was in fact absolutely furious with me and it has taken quite a while to claw my way back into her good graces. She said to me the other day, "A lifetime of avoiding the newspapers and now look!" I suppose it's her mixture of benevolent tyranny and a sense of humor and a certain kind of understanding of the way things work, which at the beginning of the novel you wouldn't credit her with, that appeals to me. And finally, the reason she dislikes Edith is not because she is middle class but because Edith does not make Charles happy. Personally, knowing the true model, I am certain that if Googie had felt within a year or two that the couple were well suited and loving and content, she would have backed off and become supportive. In the end, any mother will forgive sons- and daughters-in-law their faults if they make their children happy. In this, aristocrats are no different from the rest of the human race.

"Aristocrats are no different from the rest of the human race."

Q: Which authors do you see as the major influences upon your writing?

A: Incredibly flatteringly, I have been compared to all sorts of writers in various reviews, Wodehouse and Waugh among them, but I suppose I was most pleased to be likened to Anthony Trollope and Edith Wharton. I would certainly love to believe there was any connection. I find that I no longer really enjoy the passionate polarities of Dickens and his ilk, who, like the makers of early Westerns, are always so anxious to establish who wears the white hats and who the black. To Dickens, the evil are wicked to their very core while his good characters, those wise old men, those saintly virgins, are unblemished by the slightest stain. Well, I don't know about you but, in my experience, things aren't like that. The characters of Trollope and Wharton are flawed but seldom irredeemable, any more than they are pure and sinless as driven snow. They exist, for the most part, in the largely well-intentioned but often fallible, gray territory known as Real Life. I love the way these writers both invite us to sympathize with characters, like Lily Bart or Glencora Palliser, who are full of the weaknesses of the world but somehow retain a sort of decency in their soul. This is my kind of heroine.

Q: What is your life's motto?

A: My family's motto is: Post proelia praemia— "After the battles, the prizes." My mother used to say: "Well, we've had the battles. Where are the prizes?" But it'll do just fine for me.

Q: Your own background is not so different from some of the aristocrats you write about in *Snobs*. Is this book an indictment of the British upper class? Affectionate teasing? A little bit of both?

A: My background is not quite as lustrous as it has been painted by some of the media. I mean, in one newspaper I was given a childhood in a Scottish castle with nineteen servants (why nineteen?). But I grew up as part of a junior branch since my grandfather was a younger son. And so, although I do belong to one of those families and my name is in *Burke's Landed Gentry* and all that kind of thing, it's in a very minor capacity. I think that was what gave me a unique perspective as an observer.

"I think it's a cliché to make out that every-one with money and success and birth is unhappy."

When I was eighteen or nineteen, the London debutante season was still very much going on. You'll hardly credit this, but there was a chap called Peter Townend who really ran the season. In order to find escorts for the debs, he would go through *Burke's Peerage* and *Burke's Landed Gentry* and take the names out of young men who were the right age and invite them for a drink. If you passed this test, and were deemed "safe in taxis," you were put on a list and given to the mothers of these girls to be invited to the various balls and cocktail parties. So you spent a lot of time going and staying with complete strangers in the country to attend the dances of girls you hardly knew. I was on that list. I was what was then called a "Debs' Delight," but I was simply "making up numbers." I wasn't good looking, I wasn't a great heir, I didn't have a title. So I was there, but no one noticed me. I was the one who had the bedroom next to the nursery with a lumpy bed, and what my mother used to called "starvation corner" at the table. And I think it gave me a much better kind of viewpoint. There is a famous moment when someone went to the Comtesse Greffulhe, who is the original of Marcel Proust's Duchesse de Guermantes in his great novel, and they said to her, "What was it like having Proust at your parties? That must have been incredible!" And the Comtesse replied, "Que j'ai jamais su! (If only I'd known.)" And of course, although he was in that society (not that I'm comparing myself to Proust), and attending their gatherings and strolling among them, because nobody thought he was of the slightest importance, nobody adjusted their behavior for him.

As for whether my novel is an indictment of that world, I have come to a conclusion in my late middle-age: I'm not convinced anymore that there is a kind of life that makes you happier than any other. I mean, I know—of course—there are lives that are happier than other lives, but I think you're just as likely to come upon them among coal miners or middle-class businessmen or people living in the suburbs or the very rich and great aristocrats. I think it's a cliché to make out that everyone with money and success and birth is unhappy. I don't think they are, I think there are lots of them that are very happy. But it's also a cliché to suggest that these things make you happy. And I hope that in the novel (and in life too) I take a fairly unprejudiced view of all of them. I do poke fun at them and there are sort of

Reading Group Gold

Get to Know the Aristocracy

observations and customs and habits that are rather amusing to the rest of society, but I don't think you hate any of the characters at the end, not Lady Uckfield nor poor Mrs. Lavery (the greatest "snob" of all of them, I think) nor any of them, really. I just hope that I paint a picture of a group of people who, in the last analysis, are trying to do their best like all the rest of us are.

Q: It's striking that both *Gosford Park* and *Snobs* explore the world and manners of different classes. Do you think this is a particularly English preoccupation?

A: Class does interest me; I won't run away from that. I can never really decide whether class is a kind of honorable thing: that you are brought up with these traditions—whether you are working class or aristocratic or whatever—and it's your job to keep all this stuff going and make sure people don't forget. Or is it a sort of terrible practical joke that's being practiced on 98% of the world? Telling them that they're not good enough. That, from the moment they're born, there's this other group of people who know more than they will ever know and who have standards they can never aspire to and who are more cultured and elegant than they will ever be. In the end, I sort of fall in-between those two really. It is odd that you take a baby, and you place them in this group, and you bring them up in a certain way with a certain vocabulary and prejudices and manners, and after that, they are indelibly stamped from then on. But

"I just hope that I paint a picture of a group of people who, in the last analysis, are trying to do their best like all the rest of us are."

on the other hand, isn't some variant of this happening in every civilization on earth?

Obviously, it's more obvious in Europe than it is
in America. I mean, where I do think America has
achieved something that is very enviable is that
here you have a very strongly entrenched hereditary upper class. People think you don't, but you
do. Where else in the Western world could you
have two generations of the same family being
president? This would be quite impossible with
the role of prime minister in England as, to us, it
would smack uncomfortably of privilege. Added to
which, you have enormous inherited fortunes
here, enough to launch ten dukedoms. But at the
same time, you have self-made men and women
who have come up in one generation. And they
live together—the old money and the new—in a
very unjostling way that doesn't seem to create
any difficulty. They mingle freely and contentedly.
This, of course, was Napoleon's vision, his
dream—to create an aristocracy in France that
was a mixture of old families with old traditions,
keeping things going, and new blood and new
high achievers that would mix on equal terms. I
can't think of any country, other than America,
that has truly managed that.

Reading Group Questions

1. What is your opinion of Edith? In what ways do you feel her choices are justified or otherwise? Did she know—or should she have known—what marriage to Charles would entail?

2. Edith might be said to have made a "bargain" in life. She has chosen to provide herself with a position of importance and power rather than to marry for love. Is this kind of bargain immoral in our day and age—or is it her failure to stick to the deal that puts her at fault?

3. Both the narrator and Julian Fellowes have a certain soft spot for Lady Uckfield. How do you feel about Googie's approach to life, including the value she places on doing things "properly"?

4. The Uckfields and Charles accept that their largely unearned status carries with it certain public duties and responsibilities. How is hereditary obligation, in exchange for privilege, useful in a society? In what ways is it detrimental?

5. Contrast the actors' world to life at Broughton. What are the attractions and limitations of both?

6. Who are the biggest snobs in the book, and how does this affect your view of them?

7. The ending of *Snobs* could be called cynical. Edith is "happy enough," which is hardly a fairytale conclusion. Is she right to "settle" for a reasonable level of contentment without continuing to search for more or should she have set off again into the unknown? In other words, is it moral or immoral to be realistic? In fact, what

sort of future do you envision for Edith and Charles? How about for the other couples?

8. The narrator describes the English as "addicted to exclusivity. Leave three Englishmen in a room and they will invent a rule that prevents a fourth joining them." How does this manifest itself in American society? Would you say that Americans are also "addicted" to exclusivity, or is this a peculiarly English phenomenon?

9. F. Scott Fitzgerald said, "The rich are different from you and me." In what ways do the wealthy characters in *Snobs* seem different from— or similar to—other people you've met?

10. What do you think of the narrator's observation that "one of the basic truths of life is that, as a general rule, the world takes you at your own estimation"?

11. Julian Fellowes says in his interview that he sees *Snobs* as being more about choice than about class. How do you rate the relative importance of social standing and their own actions in the main characters' lives?

12. How do the characters' perceptions of the different lives being lived around them differ from the reality? Is Charles's view of the stage world accurate? Is Mrs. Lavery's idea of the aristocratic life accurate? How much misunderstanding is caused by inaccurate preconceptions of what other people are going through?

PAST IMPERFECT

To Emma and Peregrine
without whom nothing at all
would ever get written

Damian

ONE

London is a haunted city for me now and I am the ghost that haunts it. As I go about my business, every street or square or avenue seems to whisper of an earlier, different era in my history. The shortest trip round Chelsea or Kensington takes me by some door where once I was welcome but where today I am a stranger. I see myself issue forth, young again and dressed for some long forgotten frolic, tricked out in what looks like the national dress of a war-torn Balkan country. Those flapping flares, those frilly shirts with their footballers' collars – what were we thinking of? And as I watch, beside that wraith of a younger, slimmer me walk the shades of the departed, parents, aunts and grand-mothers, great-uncles and cousins, friends and girlfriends, gone now from this world entirely, or at least from what is left of my own life. They say one sign of growing old is that the past becomes more real than the present and already I can feel the fingers of those lost decades closing their grip round my imagination, making more recent memory seem somehow greyer and less bright.

Which makes it perfectly understandable that I should have been just a little intrigued, if taken aback, to find a letter from Damian Baxter lying among the bills and thank yous and requests for charitable assistance that pile up daily on my desk. I certainly could not have predicted it. We hadn't seen each other in almost forty years, nor had we communicated since our last meeting. It seems odd, I know, but we had spent our lives in different worlds and although England is a small country in many ways, it is still big enough for our paths never to have crossed in all that time. But there was another reason for my surprise and it was simpler.

I hated him.

A glance was enough to tell me whom it was from, though. The writing on the envelope was familiar but changed, like the face of a favourite child after the years have done their unforgiving work. Even so, before that morning, if I'd thought of him at all, I would not have believed there was anything on earth that would have induced Damian to write to me. Or I to him. I hasten to add that I wasn't offended by this unexpected delivery. Not in the least. It is always pleasant to hear from an old friend but at my age it is, if anything, more interesting to hear from an old enemy. An enemy, unlike a friend, can tell you things you do not already know of your own past. And if Damian wasn't exactly an enemy in any active sense, he was a former friend, which is of course much worse. We had parted with a quarrel, a moment of savage, unchecked rage, quite deliberately powered by the heat of burning bridges, and we had gone our separate ways, making no subsequent attempt to undo the damage.

It was an honest letter, that I will say. The English, as a rule, would rather not face a situation that might be rendered 'awkward' by the memory of earlier behaviour. Usually they will play down any disagreeable past episodes with a vague and dismissive reference: 'Do you remember that frightful dinner Jocelyn gave? How did we all survive it?' Or, if the episode really cannot be reduced and detoxified in this way, they pretend it never took place. 'It's been far too long since we met,' as an opener will often translate as 'it does not suit me to continue this feud any longer. It was ages ago. Are you prepared to call it a day?' If the recipient is willing, the answer will be couched in similar denial mode: 'Yes, let's meet. What have you been up to since you left Lazard's?' Nothing more than this will be required to signify that the nastiness is finished and normal relations may now be resumed.

But in this case Damian eschewed the common practice. Indeed, his honesty was positively Latin. 'I dare say, after everything that happened, you did not expect to hear from me again but I would take it as a great favour if you would pay me a visit,' he wrote in his spiky, and still rather angry, hand. 'I can't think why you should, after the last time we were together, but at the risk of self-dramatising, I have not long to live and it may mean something to do a favour for a dying man.' At least I could not accuse him of evasion. For a while I pretended to myself that I was thinking it over, trying to decide, but of course I knew at once that I would go, that my curiosity must be assuaged, that I would deliberately revisit the lost land of my youth. For, having had no contact with Damian since the summer of 1970, his return to my conscious mind inevitably brought sharp reminders of how much my world, like everyone else's world for that matter, has changed.

There's danger in it, obviously, but I no longer fight the sad realisation that the setting for my growing years seems sweeter to me than the one I now inhabit. Today's young, in righteous, understandable defence of their own time, generally reject our reminiscences about a golden age when the customer was always right, when AA men saluted the badge on your car and policemen touched their helmet in greeting. Thank heaven for the end of deference, they say, but deference is part of an ordered, certain world and, in retrospect at least, that can feel warming and even kind. I suppose what I miss above all things is the kindness of the England of half a century ago. But then again, is it the kindness I regret, or my own youth?

'I don't understand who this Damian Baxter *is* exactly? Why is he so significant?' said Bridget as, later that evening, we sat at home eating some rather overpriced and undercooked fish, purchased from my compliant, local Italian on the Old Brompton Road. 'I've never heard you talk about him.' At the time when Damian sent his letter, not all that long ago in fact, I was still living in a large, ground-floor flat in Wetherby Gardens, which was comfortable, convenient for this and that, and wonderfully placed for the takeaway culture that has overwhelmed us in the last few years. It was quite a smart address in its way and I certainly could never have afforded to buy it, but it had been relinquished to me by my parents years before, when they had finally abandoned London. My father tried to object, but my mother had rashly insisted that I needed 'somewhere to start,' and he'd surrendered. So I profited from their generosity and fully expected not only to start, but also to finish, there. In truth, I hadn't changed it much since my mother's day and it was still filled with her things. We were sitting at her small, round breakfast table in the window as we spoke, and I suppose the whole apartment could have seemed quite feminine, with its charming pieces of Regency furniture and a boy ancestor in curls over the chimneypiece, were my masculinity not reasserted by my obvious and total lack of interest in its arrangements.

At the time of the letter incident, Bridget FitzGerald was my current
. . . I was going to say 'girlfriend' but I am not sure one has 'girlfriends'
when one is over fifty. On the other hand, if one is too old for a
'girlfriend,' one is too young for a 'companion,' so what is the correct
description? Modern parlance has stolen so many words and put them
to misuse that frequently, when one looks for a suitable term, the
cupboard is bare. 'Partner,' as everyone not in the media knows, is both
tired and fraught with danger. I recently introduced a fellow director
in a small company I own as my·partner and it was some time before I
understood the looks I was getting from various people there who
thought they knew me. But 'other half' sounds like a line from a
situation comedy about a golf club secretary, and we haven't quite got
to the point of 'This is my mistress,' although I dare say it's not far off.
Anyway, Bridget and I were going about together. We were a slightly
unlikely pair. I, a not-very-celebrated novelist, she, a sharp Irish busi-
nesswoman specialising in property, who had missed the boat romantically and ended up with me.

My mother would not have approved, but my mother was dead and
so, in theory, out of the equation, although I am not convinced we are
ever beyond the influence of our parents' disapproval, be they dead or
alive. Of course, there was a chance she might have been mellowed by
the afterlife, but I rather doubt it. Maybe I should have listened to her
posthumous promptings, since I can't pretend that Bridget and I had
much in common. That said, she was clever and good-looking, which
was more than I deserved, and I was lonely, I suppose, and tired of
people ringing to see if I wanted to come over for Sunday lunch.
Anyway, whatever the reason, we had found each other and, while we
did not technically live together, since she kept on her own flat, we'd
jogged along for a couple of years quite peaceably. It wasn't exactly love,
but it was something.

What amused me with reference to Damian's letter was Bridget's
proprietorial tone when referring to a past of which, almost by definition, she could know little or nothing. The phrase 'I've never heard
you talk about him,' can only mean that, were this fellow significant,
you would have talked about him. Or, worse, you *should* have talked
about him. This is all part of the popular fantasy that when you are
involved with someone it is your right to know all about them, down

to the last detail, which of course can never be. 'We have no secrets,' say cheerful, young faces in films, when, as we all know, our whole lives are filled with secrets, frequently kept from ourselves. Clearly, in this instance Bridget was troubled that if Damian were important to me and yet I had never mentioned him, how much else of significance had been kept concealed? In my defence I can only say that her past, too, like mine, like everyone's in fact, was a locked box. Occasionally we allow people a peep, but generally only at the top level. The darker streams of our memories we negotiate alone.

'He was a friend of mine at Cambridge,' I said. 'We met in my second year, around the time when I was doing the Season at the end of the Sixties. I introduced him to some of the girls. They took him up, and we ran about together in London for a while.'

'Being *debs' delights*.' She spoke the phrase with a mixture of comedy and derision.

'I am glad my early life never fails to bring a smile to your lips.'

'So what happened?'

'Nothing happened. We drifted apart after we left, but there's no story. We just went in different directions.' In saying this I was, of course, lying.

She looked at me, hearing a little more than I had intended. 'If you do go, I assume you'll want to go alone.'

'Yes. I'll go alone.' I offered no further explanation but, to be fair to her, she didn't ask for one.

I used to think that Damian Baxter was my invention, although such a notion only demonstrates my own inexperience. As anyone knows, the most brilliant magician in the world cannot produce a rabbit out of a hat unless there is already a rabbit *in* the hat, albeit well concealed, and Damian would never have enjoyed the success that I took credit for unless he had been genuinely possessed of those qualities that made his triumph possible and even inevitable. Nevertheless, I do not believe he would have made it into the social limelight as a young man, in those days anyway, without some help. And I was the one who gave it. It was perhaps for this reason that I resented his betrayal quite so bitterly. I put a good face on it, or I tried to, but it still stung. Trilby had turned traitor to Svengali, Galatea had destroyed Pygmalion's dreams.

7

'Any time on any day will be convenient,' the letter said. 'I do not go out now or entertain, so I am completely at your disposal. You will find me quite near Guildford. If you drive, it may take ninety minutes but the train is quicker. Let me know and I will either arrange directions or someone can meet you, whichever you prefer.' In the end, after my fake prevarication, I wrote back suggesting dinner on such and such a day, and named the train I would catch. He confirmed this with an invitation for the night. As a rule I prefer, like Jorrocks, to 'sleeps where I dines,' so I accepted and the plan was settled. Accordingly, I passed through the barrier at Guildford station on a pleasant summer evening in June.

I looked about vaguely for some Eastern European holding a card with my name mis-spelled in felt tip pen but instead of this, I found myself approached by a uniformed chauffeur – or rather someone who looked like an actor playing a chauffeur in an episode of *Hercule Poirot* – who replaced his peaked cap after introducing himself in low and humble tones, and led the way outside to a new Bentley, parked illegally in the space reserved for the disabled. I say 'illegally,' even though there was a badge clearly displayed in the window, because I assume these are not distributed so that friends may be met off trains without their getting wet or having to walk too far with their luggage. But then again, everyone deserves the odd perk.

I did know that Damian had done well, though how or why I knew I cannot now remember, for we shared no pals and moved in completely different circles. I must have seen his name on a *Sunday Times* list or maybe in an article on a financial page. But I don't think, before that evening, I understood quite *how* well he had done. We sped through the Surrey lanes and it was soon clear, from the trimmed hedging and the pointed walls, from the lawns like billiard tables and the glistening, weeded gravel, that we had entered the Kingdom of the Rich. Here there were no crumbling gate piers, no empty stables and lodges with leaking roofs. This was not a question of tradition and former glory. I was witnessing not the memory but the living presence of money.

I do have some experience of it. As a moderately successful writer, one rubs up against what Nanny would call 'all sorts,' but I can't pretend this was ever really my crowd. Most of the so-called rich I know are possessed of surviving, not newborn, fortunes, the rich who used to be a good deal richer. But the houses I was passing belonged to the Now Rich, which is different, and for me there is something invigorating in their sense of immediate power. It is peculiar, but even today there is a snobbery in Britain when it comes to new money. The traditional Right might be expected to turn up their noses at it I suppose, but paradoxically, it is often the intellectual Left who advertise their disapproval of the self-made. I do not pretend to understand how this is compatible with a belief in equality of opportunity. Perhaps they do not try to synthesise them, but just live by contradictory impulses, which I suppose we all do to some degree. But if I may have been guilty of such unimaginative thinking in my youth, it is gone from me now. These days I unashamedly admire men and women who have made their pile, just as I admire anyone who looks at the future mapped out for them at birth and is not afraid to tear it up and draw a better one. The self-made have more chance than most of finding a life that truly suits. I salute them for it and I salute their bejewelled world. Of course, on a personal level it was extremely annoying that Damian Baxter should be a part of it.

The house he had chosen as a setting for his splendour was not a fallen nobleman's palace but rather one of those self-consciously moral, Arts and Crafts, rambling warrens that seem to belong in a Disney cartoon and are no more convincing as a symbol of Olde England than they were when Lutyens built them at the turn of the last century. Surrounding it were gardens, terraced, clipped and criss-crossed with trim and tended paths, but seemingly no land beyond that. Damian had not apparently decided to adopt the ancient model of imitation gentry. This was not a manor house, nestling in the warm embrace of farming acres. This was simply the home of a Great Success.

Having said that, while not traditional in an aristocratic sense, the whole thing had quite a 1930s feel, as if it were built with the ill-gotten gains of a First World War profiteer. The Agatha Christie element provided by the chauffeur was continued by the bowing butler at the door and even by a housemaid, glimpsed on my way to the pale oak staircase, in her black dress and frilly apron, although she seemed perhaps more frivolous, as if I had suddenly been transported to the set of a Gershwin musical. A sense of the odd unreality of the adventure was, if anything, confirmed when I was shown to my room without first having met my host. There is always a slight whodunnit shiver of danger in this arrangement. A dark-clad servant hovering in the door and muttering 'Please come down to the drawing room when you are ready, Sir,' seems more suited to the reading of a will than a social call. But the room itself was nice enough. It was lined with pale-blue damask, which had also been used to drape the high, four-poster bed. The furniture was stable, solid English stuff and a group of Chinoiserie paintings on glass, between the windows, was really charming, even if there was the unmistakable tinge of a country house hotel, rather than a real country house, about it all, confirmed by the bathroom, which was sensational, with a huge bath, a walk-in shower, shiny taps on tall pipes coming straight up out of the floor, and enormous towels, fluffy and brand new. As we know, this kind of detail is seldom found in private houses in the shires, even today. I tidied myself up and went downstairs.

The drawing room was predictably cavernous, with a vaulted ceiling and those over-springy carpets that have been too recently replaced. Not the shagpile of the minted club owner, nor the flat and ancient rugs of the posh, but smooth and sprung and *new*. Everything in the room had been purchased within living memory and apparently by a single purchaser. There was none of the ragbag of tastes that country houses are inclined to represent, where the contents of a dozen homes, the amalgamated product of forty amateur collectors over two or three centuries, are flung together into a single room. But it was good. In fact, it was excellent, the furniture largely from the early years of the eighteenth century, the pictures rather later, all fine, all shining clean and all in tip-top condition. After the similar experience of my bedroom, I wondered if Damian had employed a buyer, someone whose job was just to put his life together. Either way, there was no very tangible sense of him, or any other personality really, in the room. I wandered about, glancing at the paintings, unsure whether to stand or sit. In truth it felt forlorn, despite its splendour; the burning coals in the grate could not dispel the slightly clammy atmosphere, as if the room had been cleaned but not used for quite a while. And there were no flowers, which I always think a telltale sign; there was nothing living, in fact, giving a staleness to its perfection, a kind of lifeless sterility. I could not imagine that a woman had played much part in its creation, nor, God knows, that a child had played any part at all.

There was a sound at the door. 'My dear chap,' said a voice, still with the slight hesitance, the suspicion of a stammer, that I remembered so well. 'I hope I haven't kept you waiting.'

There is a moment in *Pride and Prejudice* when Elizabeth Bennet catches sight of her sister who has returned with the dastardly Wickham, rescued from disgrace by the efforts of Mr Darcy. 'Lydia was Lydia still,' she comments. Well, Damian Baxter was Damian still. That is, while the broad and handsome young man with the thick curls and the easy smile had vanished and been replaced by a hunched figure resembling no one so much as Doctor Manette, I could detect that distinctive, diffident stutter masking a deep and honed sense of superiority, and I recognised at once the old, patronising arrogance in the flourish with which he held out his bony hand. I smiled. 'How very nice to see you,' I said.

'Is it?' We stared at each other's faces, marvelling simultaneously at the extent, and at the lack, of change that we found there.

As I looked at him more closely I could see that when he had talked in his letter of being 'a dying man,' he had been speaking the literal truth. He was not just old before his time but ill, very ill, and seemingly past the point of no return. 'Well, it's interesting. I suppose I can say that.'

'Yes, you can say that.' He nodded to the butler who hovered near the door. 'I wonder if we might have some of that champagne?' It didn't surprise me that even forty years later he still liked to wrap his orders in diffident questions. I was a veteran witness of this trick. Like many who try it, Damian imagined, I think, that it suggested a charming lack of confidence, a faltering but honourable desire to get it right, which I knew for a fact he had not felt since some time around 1967 and I doubt he knew much of it then. The man addressed did not seem to feel any answer was required of him and I'm sure it wasn't. He just went to get the wine.

Dinner was a formal, muted affair in a dining room that unsuccessfully crossed William Morris and Liberty's with a dash of the Hollywood hills. High, mullioned windows, a heavy, carved, stone chimneypiece and more of the bouncy carpet added up to a curiously flat and unevocative result, as if a table and chairs had unaccountably been set up in an empty, but expensive, lawyer's office. But the food was delicious, if quite wasted on Damian, and we both got some fun out of the Margaux he'd selected. The silent butler, whom I now knew as Bassett, hardly left us for a minute and, inevitably, the conversation played out before him was desultory. I remember an aunt once telling me that when she looked back to the days before the war, she was astonished at some of the table talk she'd witnessed, where the presence of servants seemed to act as no restraining force at all. Political secrets, family gossip, personal indiscretions, all came bubbling forth before the listening footmen and must presumably have enlivened many an evening in the local pub, if not, as in our more greedy and salacious times, their published memoirs. But we have lost that generation's sublime confidence in their own way of life. Whether we like it or not – and I do like it really – time has made us conscious of the human spirit in those who serve us. For anyone born since the 1940s all walls have ears.

So we nattered on about this and that. He asked after my parents and I asked after his. In actual fact my father had been quite fond of him but my mother, whose jungle instincts were generally more reliable, sensed trouble from the start. She, at any rate, had died in the interim since we last met and so had both of his, so there wasn't much to be said. From there, we discussed various others of that mutual acquaintance of long ago, and by the time we were ready to move on we had covered an impressive list of career disappointments, divorces and premature death.

At last he stood, addressing Bassett as he did so. 'Do you think we could have our coffee in the library?' Again he asked softly, as a favour that might be denied. What would happen, I wonder, if someone so instructed should take the hesitant question at face value? 'No, Sir. I'm afraid I'm a bit busy at the moment. I'll try to bring some coffee later on.' I should like to see it once. But this butler knew what he was about and went to carry out the veiled command, while Damian led the way into the nicest of the rooms that I had seen. It looked as if an earlier owner, or possibly Damian himself, had purchased a complete library from a much older house, with dark, richly shining shelves and a screen of beautifully carved columns. There was a delicate chimneypiece of pinkish marble and in a polished steel basket a fire had been lit for our arrival. The combination of flickering flames and gleaming leather bindings, as well as some excellent pictures – a large seascape that looked like a Turner and the portrait of a young girl by Lawrence among them – gave a warmth notably lacking elsewhere in the house. I had been unjust. Obviously it was not lack of taste but lack of interest that had made the other rooms so dreary. This was where Damian actually lived. Before long we were equipped with drinks and cups of coffee, and alone.

'You've done very well,' I said. 'Congratulations.'

'Are you surprised?'

'Not terribly.'

He accepted this with a nod. 'If you mean I was always ambitious, I confess it.'

'I think I meant that you would never take no for an answer.'

He shook his head. 'I wouldn't say that,' he said. I wasn't completely sure what he meant by this but before I could delve he spoke again. 'I knew when I was beaten, even then. When I found myself in a situation where success was not a possible outcome, I accepted it and moved on. You must grant me that.'

This was nonsense. 'I won't grant you that,' I said. 'Or anything like it. It may be a virtue you achieved in later life. I cannot tell. But when I knew you your eyes were much larger than your stomach and you were a very poor loser, as I should know.'

Damian looked surprised for a moment. Perhaps he had spent so much of his life with people who were paid, in one way or another, to agree with him that he had forgotten not everyone was obliged to. He sipped his brandy and after a pause he nodded. 'Well, be that as it may, I am beaten now.' In answer to my unasked question he elaborated. 'I have inoperable cancer of the pancreas. There is nothing to be done. The doctor has given me about three months to live.'

'They often get these things wrong.'

'They occasionally get these things wrong. But not in my case. There may be a variant of a few weeks, but that's all.'

'Oh.' I nodded. It is hard to know how to respond suitably to this kind of declaration because people's needs can be so different. I doubted that Damian would want wailing and weeping or suggestions of alternative cures based on a macrobiotic diet, but you never know. I waited.

'I don't want you to feel I am raging at the injustice of it. My life has, in a way, come to a natural conclusion.'

'Meaning?'

'I have, as you point out, been very fortunate. I've lived well. I've travelled. And there's nothing left in my work that I still want to do, so that's something. Do you know what I've been up to?'

'Not really.'

'I built up a company in computer software. We were among the first to see the potential of the whole thing.'

'How clever of you.'

'You're right. It does sound dull, but I enjoyed it. Anyway, I've sold the business and I will not start another.'

'You don't know that.' I can't think why I said this, because of course he did know exactly that.

'I'm not complaining. I sold out to a nice, big American company and they gave me enough money to put Malawi back on its feet.'

'But that's not what you're going to do with it.'

'I don't think so, no.'

He hesitated. I was fairly sure we were approaching what they call the 'nub' of why I was here, but he didn't seem able to progress things. I thought I might as well have a shot at moving us along. 'What about your private life?' I ventured pleasantly.

He thought for a moment. 'I don't really have one. Nothing worthy of the name. The odd arrangement for my comfort, but nothing more than that for many years now. I'm not at all social.'

'You were when I knew you,' I said. I was still transfixed by the thought of the 'odd arrangement for my comfort.' Golly. I resolved to steer clear of any attempt at clarification.

There was no further need to keep things moving. Damian had got started. 'I did not like the world you took me into, as you know.' He looked at me challengingly but I had no comment to make so he continued, 'but, paradoxically, when I left it, I found I didn't care for the entertainments of my old world either. After a while I gave up "parties" altogether.'

'Did you marry?'

'Once. It didn't last very long.'

'I'm sorry.'

14

'Don't be. I only married because I'd got to that age when it starts to feel odd not to have married. I was thirty-six or -seven and curious eyebrows were beginning to be raised. Of course, I was a fool. If I'd waited another five years, my friends would have started to divorce and I wouldn't have been the only freak in the circus.'

'Was she anyone I knew?'

'Oh, no. I'd escaped from your crowd by then and I had no desire to return to it, I can assure you.'

'Any more than we had the smallest desire to see you,' I said. There was something relieving in this. A trace of our mutual dislike had surfaced and it felt more comfortable than the pseudo-friendship we had been playing at all evening. 'Besides, you don't know what my crowd is. You don't know anything about my life. It changed that night as much as yours. And there is more than one way of moving on from a London Season of forty years ago.'

He accepted this without querying it. 'Quite right. I apologise. But, truly, you would not have known Suzanne. When I met her she was running a fitness centre near Leatherhead.' Inwardly I agreed that it was unlikely my path had crossed with the ex-Mrs Baxter's so I was silent. He sighed wearily. 'She tried her best. I don't want to speak ill of her. But we had nothing at all to hold us together.' He paused. 'You never married in the end, did you?'

'No. I didn't. Not in the end.' The words came out more harshly than I intended but he did not seem to wonder at it. The subject was painful for me and uncomfortable for him. At least, it bloody well should have been. I decided to return to a safer place. 'What happened to your wife?'

'Oh, she married again. Rather a nice chap. He has a business selling sportsware, so I suppose they had more to build on than we did.'

'Were there any children?'

'Two boys and a girl. Though I don't know what happened to them.'

'I meant with you.'

He shook his head. 'No, there weren't.' This time his silence seemed very profound. After a moment he completed the thought. 'I can't have children,' he said. Despite the apparent finality of this statement there was something oddly unfinal in the tone of his voice, almost like that strange and unnecessary question mark that the young have imported from Australia, to finish every sentence. He continued, 'that is to say, I could not have children by the time that I married.'

He stopped, as if to allow me a moment to digest this peculiar sentence. What could he possibly mean? I assumed he had not been castrated shortly before proposing to the fitness centre manageress. Since he had introduced the topic, I didn't feel guilty in wanting to make a few enquiries, but in the event he answered before I had voiced them. 'We went to various doctors and they told me my sperm count was zero.'

Even in our disjointed, modern society, this is quite a taxing observation to counter with something meaningful. 'How disappointing,' I said.

'Yes. It was. Very *disappointing*.'

Obviously I'd chosen badly. 'Couldn't they do something about it?'

'Not really. They suggested reasons as to why it might have happened, but no one thought it could be reversed. So that was that.'

'You could have tried other ways. They're so clever now.' I couldn't bring myself to be more specific.

He shook his head. 'I'd never have brought up someone else's child. Suzanne had a go at persuading me but I couldn't allow it. I just didn't see the point. Once the child isn't yours, aren't you just playing with dolls? Living dolls, maybe. But dolls.'

'A lot of people would disagree with you.'

He nodded. 'I know. Suzanne was one of them. She didn't see why she had to be barren when it wasn't her fault, which was reasonable enough. I suppose we knew we'd break up from the moment we left the surgery.' He stood to fetch himself another drink. He'd earned it.

'I see,' I said, to fill the silence, rather dreading what was coming.

Sure enough, when he spoke again his tone was more determined than ever. 'Two specialists believed it might have been the result of adult mumps.'

'I thought that was a myth, used to frighten nervous, young men.'

'It's very rare. But it can happen. It's a condition called orchitis, which affects the testicles. Usually it goes away and everything's fine, but sometimes, very occasionally, it doesn't. I didn't have mumps as a boy and I wasn't aware I'd ever caught it, but when I thought it over, I was struck down with a very sore throat a few days after I got back from Portugal, in July of nineteen seventy. I was in bed for a couple of weeks and my glands certainly swelled up, so maybe they were right.'

I shifted slightly in my chair and took another sip of my drink. My presence here was beginning to make a kind of uncomfortable sense. In a way I had invited Damian to Portugal, to join a group of friends. God knows, in the event it was more complicated than that but the excuse had been the party was short of men and our hostess had got me to ask him. With disastrous results, as it happens. So, was he now trying to blame me for being sterile? Had I been invited here to acknowledge my fault? That as much harm as he had done to me on that holiday, so had I done to him? 'I don't remember anyone being ill,' I said.

He did, apparently. 'That girlfriend of the guy who had the villa. The neurotic American with the pale hair. What was her name? Alice? Alix? She kept complaining about her throat, the whole time we were there.'

'You have wonderfully perfect recall.'

'I've had a lot of time to think.'

The image of that sun whitened villa in Estoril, banished from my conscious mind for nearly four decades, suddenly filled my mind. The hot, blond beach below the terrace, drunken dinners resonating with sex and subtext, climbing the hill to the haunted castle at Cintra, swimming in the whispering, blue waters, waiting in the great square before Lisbon Cathedral to walk past the body of Salazar . . . The whole experience sprang back into vivid, technicoloured life, one of those holidays that bridge the gap between adolescence and maturity, with all the attendant dangers of that journey, where you come home quite different from when you set out. A holiday, in fact, that changed my life. I nodded. 'Yes. Well, you would have done.'

'Of course, if that were the reason, then I could have had a child before.'

Despite his seriousness I couldn't match it. 'Even you wouldn't have had much time. We were only twenty-one. These days every girl on a housing estate may be pregnant by the time she's thirteen, but it was different then.' I smiled reassuringly, but he wasn't watching. Instead, he was busy opening a drawer in a handsome *bureau plat* beneath the Lawrence. He took out an envelope and gave it to me. It wasn't new. I could just make out the postmark. It looked like 'Chelsea. 23rd December 1990.'

'Please read it.'

I unfolded the paper gingerly. The letter was entirely typed, with neither opening greeting nor final signature written by hand. 'Dear Shit,' it began. How charming. I looked up with raised eyebrows.

'Go on.'

Dear Shit, It is almost Christmas. It is also late and I am drunk and so I have found the nerve to say that you have made my life a living lie for nineteen years. I stare at my living lie each day and all because of you. No one will ever know the truth and I will probably burn this rather than send it, but you ought to realise where your deceit and my weakness have led me. I do not quite curse you, I could not do that, but I don't forgive you, either, for the course my life has taken. I did not deserve it.

At the end, below the body of the text, the author had typed: 'A fool.'

I stared at it. 'Well, she did send it,' I said. 'I wonder if she meant to.'

'Perhaps someone else picked it up from the hall table and posted it, without her knowledge.'

This seemed highly likely to me. 'That would have given her a turn.'

'You are sure it is a "her"?'

I nodded. 'Aren't you? "My life has been a living lie." "Your deceit and my weakness." None of it sounds very butch to me. I rather like her signing it "a fool." It reminds me of the pop lyrics of our younger days. Anyway, I assume the base deceit to which she refers comes under the heading of romance. It doesn't sound like someone feeling let down over a bad investment. That would make the writer female, wouldn't it? Or has your life steered you along new and previously untried routes?'

'It would make her female.'

'There we are, then.' I smiled. 'I like the way she cannot curse you. It's quite Keatsian. Like a verse from 'Isabella, or The Pot of Basil': "She weeps alone for pleasures not to be."'

'What do you think it means?'

I wasn't clear how there could be any doubt. 'It's not very mysterious,' I said. But he waited, so I put it into words. 'It sounds as if you have made somebody pregnant.'

'Yes.'

'I assume the deceit she refers to must be some avowal of a forever kind of love, which you made in order to get her to remove her clothing.'

'You sound very harsh.'

'Do I? I don't mean to. Like all of us boys in those days, I tried it often enough myself. Her "weakness" implies you were, in this instance, successful.' But I thought over Damian's original question about the letter's meaning. Did it indicate that he thought things were not quite so straightforward? 'Why? Is there another interpretation? I suppose this woman could have been in love with you and her life since then has been a lie because she married someone else when she'd rather have been with you. Is that what you think it is?'

'No. Not really. If that's all she meant, would she be writing about it twenty years later?'

'Some people take longer than others to get over these things.'

'"I stare at my living lie each day." "No one will ever know." No one will ever know what?' He asked the question as if there could be no doubt as to the answer. Which I agreed with.

I nodded. 'As I said, you made her pregnant.'

He seemed almost reassured that there was no other possible meaning, as if he had been testing me. He nodded. 'And she had the baby.'

'Sounds like it. Though that in itself makes the whole affair something of a period piece. I wonder why she didn't get rid of it.'

At this, Damian gave his unique blend of haughty look and dismissive snort. How well I remembered it. 'I imagine abortion was against her principles. Some people do have principles.'

Now it was my turn to snort. 'I'm not prepared to take instruction from you on that score,' I said, which he let pass, as well he might. The whole thing was beginning to irritate me. Why were we making such a meal of it? 'Very well, then. She had the baby. And nobody knows that you are the father. End of story.' I stared at the envelope, so carefully preserved. 'At least, was it the end? Or was there some more? After this?'

He nodded. 'That's exactly what I thought at the time. That it was the start of some kind of . . . I don't know . . . extortion.'

'Extortion?'

'My lawyer's word. I went to see him. He took a copy and told me to wait for the next approach. He said that clearly she was building up to a demand for money and we should be ready with a plan. I was in the papers a bit in those days and I'd already had some luck. It seemed likely that she'd suddenly understood her baby's father was rich, and so now might be the moment for a killing. My offspring would have been about twenty then—'

'Nineteen,' I said. 'Her life was a living lie for nineteen years.'

He looked puzzled for a moment, then he nodded. 'Nineteen and just starting out. Cash would have come in very useful.' He looked at me. I didn't have anything to add since, like the lawyer, I thought this all made sense. 'I would have given her something.' He was quite defensive. 'I was perfectly prepared to.'

'But she didn't write again.'

'No.'

'Perhaps she died.'

'Perhaps. Although it seems rather melodramatic. Perhaps, as you say, the letter got posted by accident. Anyway, we heard nothing more and gradually the thing drifted away.'

'So why are we discussing it now?'

He did not answer me immediately. Instead, he stood up and crossed to the chimneypiece. A log had rolled forward on to the hearth and he took up the tools to rectify it, doing so with a kind of deadly intensity. 'The thing is,' he said at last, speaking into the flames but presumably addressing me, 'I want to find the child.'

There didn't seem to be any logic in this. If he'd wanted to 'do the right thing,' why hadn't he done it eighteen years before, when there might have been some point? 'Isn't it a bit late?' I asked. 'It wouldn't have been easy to play dad when she wrote the letter; but by now the "child" is a man or woman in their late thirties. They are what they are, and it's far too late to help shape them now.'

None of this seemed to carry any weight whatever. I'm not sure he even heard. 'I want to find them,' he repeated. 'I want you to find them.'

It would be foolish to pretend that I had not by this stage worked out that this was where we were headed. But it was not a task I relished. Nor was I in the least sure I would undertake it. 'Why me?'

'When I met you I had only slept with four girls.' He paused. I raised my eyebrows faintly. Any man of my generation will understand that this was impressive in itself. At nineteen, which is what we were when we first came across each other, I do not believe I had done much more than kiss on the dance floor. He hadn't finished. 'I knew all four until well into the early 1970s and it definitely wasn't one of them. Then you and I ran around for a while, and I kept myself fairly busy. A couple of years later, when that period had come to an end, we went to Portugal. And after that I was sterile. Besides, look at the writing, look at the paper, read the phrases. This woman is educated—'

'And histrionic. And drunk.'

'Which does not prevent her being posh.'

'I'll say.' I considered his theory some more. 'What about the years between the end of the Season and Portugal?'

He shook his head. 'A few, mainly scrubbers, and a couple left over from our times together. Not one who had a baby before that summer.' He sighed wearily. 'Anyway, nobody lives a lie who hasn't got something to lose. Something worth holding on to, something that would be endangered by the truth. She wrote to me in 1990 when the upper and upper middle classes occupied the last remaining bastion of legitimate birth. Anyone normal would have let the secret out of the bag long ago.' The effort of saying all this, plus the log work, had depleted what remained of his energy and he sank back into his chair with a groan.

I did not pity him. Quite the contrary. Suddenly the unreasonableness of his request struck me forcibly. 'But I'm not in your life. I am nothing to do with you. We are completely different people.' I wasn't insulting him. I simply could not see why any of this was my responsibility. 'We may have known each other once, but we don't now. We went to some dances together forty years ago. And quarrelled. There must be others who are far closer to you than I ever was. I can't be the only person who could take this on.'

'But you are. These women came from your people, not mine. I have no other friends who would know them, or even know *of* them. And in fact, if we are having this conversation, I have no other friends.'

This was too self-serving for my taste. 'Then you have no friends at all, because you certainly can't count me.' Naturally, once the words were out I rather regretted them. I did believe that he was dying and there was no point in punishing him now for things that could never be undone, whatever he or I might wish.

But he smiled. 'You're right. I have no friends. As you know better than most, it's not a relationship I could ever either understand or manage. If you will not do this for me I have no one else to ask. I cannot even hire a detective. The information I need would not be available to anyone but an insider.' I was about to suggest he undertake the search himself, but looking at his shaking, hollow frame, the words died on my lips. 'Will you do it?' he asked after a brief pause.

At this point, I was quite sure that I really didn't want to. Not just because of the prickly, time-wasting and awkward nature of the quest, but because the more I thought about it, the more I knew I didn't want to poke around in my own past, any more than his. The time he spoke of was over. For both of us. I had hardly kept up with anyone from those days, for reasons which involved him, as he knew, and what was there to gain by rootling around in it all? I decided to make a last attempt to appeal to his better nature. Even people like Damian Baxter must have a little. 'Damian, think. Do you really want to turn their life upside down? This man, this woman, they know who they are and they're living their life as best they can. Will it help to find they're someone different and unknown? To make them question, or even break with, their parents? Would you want that on your conscience?'

He looked at me quite steadily. 'My fortune, after death duties, will be far in excess of five hundred million pounds. My intention is to make my child sole heir. Are you prepared to take the responsibility for denying them their inheritance? Would you want *that* on *your* conscience?'

Naturally, it would have been *jejune* to pretend that this did not make all the difference in the world. 'How would I set about it?' I said.

He relaxed. 'I will present you with a list of the girls I slept with during those years, who had a child before April 1971.' This was again impressive. The list of girls I had slept with during the same period, with or without children, could have been contained on the blank side of a visiting card. It was also very precise and oddly businesslike. I had thought we were engaged in some sort of philosophical exchange but I saw now we were approaching what used to be called 'brass tacks.' He obviously sensed my surprise. 'My secretary has made a start. There didn't seem much point in your getting in touch if they hadn't had a baby.' Which was of course true. 'I believe the list is comprehensive.'

'What about the girls you slept with who did not bear children at that time?'

'Don't let's worry about them. No point in making work.' He smiled. 'We've done a lot of weeding. There were a couple of others I slept with who did have an early child but, in the words of the Empress Eugénie's mother when challenged over her Imperial daughter's paternity, *les dates ne correspondent pas*.' He laughed, easier now that he saw his plan would come to fruition. 'I want you to know that I have taken this seriously and there is a real possibility that it could be any one of the listed names.'

'So how do I go about it?'

'Just get in touch. With one exception, I've got the present addresses.'

'Why don't you ask them to have a DNA test?'

'That sort of woman would never agree.'

'You romanticise them in your dislike. I suspect they would. And their children certainly would when they found out why.'

'No.' He was suddenly quite firm again. I could see my comment had annoyed him. 'I don't want this to be a story. Only the true child must know I'm looking for them. When they have the money it will be their choice to reveal how or why they got it. Until then, this is for my private satisfaction, not public consumption. Test one who isn't my child and we will read the story in the *Daily Mail* the following week.' He shook his head. 'Maybe we should test them at the last, but only when you have elected which of the said progeny is probably mine.'

'But suppose one of the women had a baby without anyone knowing and put it up for adoption?'

'They haven't done that. At least, the mother of my baby hasn't.'

'How do you know?'

'Because then she wouldn't have stared at her lie every day.'

I had nothing further to say, at least until I'd thought about it all some more, which Damian seemed to understand and did not wish to challenge. He pulled himself unsteadily to his feet. 'I'm going to bed now. I haven't been up as late as this for months. You will find the list in an envelope in your room. If you wish, we can discuss it some more tomorrow morning before you go. At the risk of sounding vulgar, as you would say, you'll also find a credit card, which will cover any expenses you care to charge on it during your enquiries. I will not question whatever you choose to use it for.'

This last detail actively annoyed me as it was deliberately phrased in a manner designed to make me think him generous. But nothing about this commission was generous. It was a hideous imposition. 'I haven't agreed yet,' I said.

'I hope you will.' He was at the door when he stopped. 'Do you ever see her now?' he asked, confident that I would require no prompting as to the object of his enquiry. Which was correct.

'No. Not really.' I thought for a painful moment. 'Very occasionally, at a party or a wedding or something. But not really.'

'You aren't enemies?'

'Oh, no. We smile. And even talk. We're certainly not enemies. We're not anything.'

He hesitated, as if he were pondering whether to go down this path. 'You know I was mad.'

'Yes.'

'But I want you to understand that I know it, too. I went completely mad.' He paused, as if I might come in with some suitable response. But there wasn't one. 'Would it help if I said I was sorry?' he asked.

'Not terribly.'

He nodded, absorbing the information. We both knew there was nothing further to add. 'Stay down here as long as you like. Have some more whisky and look at the books. Some of them will interest you.'

But I wasn't quite finished. 'Why have you left it until now?' I said. 'Why didn't you make enquiries when you first got the letter?'

This did make him pause and ponder, as the light from the hall came through the now open door and deepened the lines of his ravaged face. Presumably he asked himself the same question a thousand times a day. 'I don't know. Not completely. Maybe I couldn't bear the thought of anyone feeling they had a claim against me. I didn't see how I could find and identify them without giving them some power. And I'd never really wanted a child. Which is probably why I wouldn't listen to my wife's pleadings. It wasn't one of my ambitions. I don't think I was ever naturally paternal.'

'Yet now you are prepared to give this unknown stranger enough money to build a small industrial town. Why? What's changed?'

Damian thought for a moment and a tiny sigh made his thin shoulders rise and fall. The jacket, which must once have fitted flawlessly, flapped loosely around his shrivelled frame. 'I'm dying and I have no beliefs,' he said simply. 'This is my only chance of immortality.'

Then he was gone and I was left to enjoy his library alone.

TWO

I have never been a good judge of character. My impressions at first meeting are almost invariably wrong. Although, human nature being what it is, many years had to pass before I could bring myself to admit it. When I was young I thought I had a marvellous instinct to tell good from bad, fine from shoddy, sacred from profane. Damian Baxter, by contrast, was an expert at assessment. He knew at once I was a patsy.

As it happens, we had both gone up to Cambridge in September 1967, but we were in different colleges and we moved in different crowds, so it was not until the beginning of the summer term of 1968, in early May I think, that our paths first crossed, at a party in the Fellows' Quadrangle of my college, where I was no doubt showing off. I was nineteen and in that heady stage of life for someone like me, at least for someone like me *then*, when you suddenly realise that the world is more complicated than you had supposed, that there is in fact a vast assortment of people and opportunities on offer, and you will not be obliged to continue forever in the narrow channel of boarding school and county, which was all that that my so-called 'privileged' upbringing had yielded thus far. I would not say that I was ever antisocial but nor would I claim much social success before that time. I had been rather overshadowed by handsome and witty cousins, and since I possessed neither looks nor a trace of charisma to offset this, there wasn't much I could do to make my presence felt.

My dear mother understood my predicament, which she was obliged to witness silently and painfully for years, but found there was little she could do to remedy it. Until, seeing the burgeoning confidence that admission to university had brought, she decided to take advantage of it to promote a spirit of adventure within me, providing introductions to London friends with suitably aged daughters. Surprisingly perhaps, I had followed her lead and begun to construct a new social group for myself, where I would have no more depressing comparisons to contend with and where I could, to an extent anyway, reinvent myself.

It would seem odd to today's young that I should have allowed myself to be so parentally steered, but things were different forty years ago. To start with, people were not then afraid of getting older. Our strange, patronising culture, where middle-aged television presenters dishonestly pretend to share the tastes and prejudices of their teenage audience in order to gain their trust, had not arrived. In short, in this as in so many areas, we did not think in the way that people think today. Of course, we were divided by political opinions and class and, to a lesser extent than now, religion, but the key difference, from today's viewpoint, is not between the Right and the Left, or the aristocratic and the ordinary, but between the generation of 1968 and the people of four decades later.

In my world, parents in the early Sixties still arranged their children's lives to an extraordinary extent, settling between themselves when parties would be given and at which houses during the school holidays, what subjects their offspring would study at school; what careers they should pursue after university; above all, what friends they would spend time with. It wasn't, on the whole, tyrannical but we did not much challenge our parents' veto when it was exercised. I remember a local baronet's heir, frequently drunk and invariably rude, and for these reasons beguiling to me and my sister and repulsive to our parents, who was actually forbidden entry to our house by my father, 'except where his absence would cause comment.' Can such a phrase really have been spoken within living memory? I know we laughed about this rule even then. But we did not break it. In short, we were a product of our backgrounds in a way that would be rare today. One hears people wonder about the collapse of parental authority. Was it deliberately engineered as the right-wing press would have us believe? Or did it just happen because it was right for the time, like the internal combustion engine or penicillin? Either way, it has vanished from whole chunks of our society, gone, like the snows of yesteryear.

At any rate, to resume, that spring there was a drinks party in the Fellows' Quadrangle to which I'd been invited for some reason. I cannot now say if it was an official function or a private bash, but anyway there we all were, feeling clever and chosen, and probably still enjoying the college's reputation for being 'rather smart.' How pitiful such mini-vanities seem, viewed from the tired vale of the middle years, but I don't believe there was much harm in us, really. We thought we were grown up, which we weren't, and posh, which we weren't very, and that people would be glad to know us. I say this although, after my painful youth, I still preserved that all too familiar blend of pride and terror, that is so characteristic of the late teens, when nose-in-air snobbery goes hand in hand with social paranoia. Presumably it was this contradictory mixture that made me so vulnerable to attack.

Oddly enough, I can recall the precise moment when Damian entered my life. It was fitting because I was talking to Serena when he appeared, so we both met him together, simultaneously, on the instant, a detail that seems much more curious on reflection than when I was living it. I don't know why she was there. She was never a college groupie. Perhaps she was staying with someone nearby and had been brought. At any rate I won't find the answer now. I didn't know Serena at all well then, not as I would later, but we'd met. This is a distinction lost on the modern world, where people who have shaken hands and nodded a greeting will tell you they 'know' each other. Sometimes they will go further and assert, without any more to go on, that so-and-so is 'a friend of mine.' If it should suit the other party they will endorse this fiction and, in that endorsement, sort of make it true. When it is not true. Forty years ago we were, I think, more aware of the degree of a relationship. Which was just as well with someone as far beyond my reach as Serena.

Lady Serena Gresham, as she was born, did not appear to suffer from the marbling of self-doubt that afflicted the rest of us and this made her stand out among us from the start. I could describe her as 'unusually confident,' but this would be misleading, as the phrase suggests some bright and brash self-marketeer, the very last description she would merit. It just never occurred to her to worry much about who or what she was. She never questioned whether people would like her, nor picked at the thing when they did. She was, one might say nowadays, at peace with herself and, in the teenage years, then as now, it made her special. Her gentle remoteness, a kind of floating, almost underwater quality, took possession of me from the first time I saw her and many years would pass before she did not pop into my defenceless brain at least once every half an hour. I know now that the main reason she seemed remote was because she wasn't interested in me, or in most of us for that matter, but then it was pure magic. I would say it was her dreamy unattainability, more than her beauty or birth or privileges, though these were mighty, that gave her the position she enjoyed. And I know I am not alone in thinking of 1968 as the Year of Serena. Even as early as the spring, I felt myself lucky to be talking to her.

As I have said, her privileges were great, if not unique, as a member of the select, surviving rump of the Old World. At that time, self-made fortunes were usually much smaller than they would be decades later and the very rich, at least those people who 'lived rich,' still tended mostly to be those who had been even richer thirty years before. It was an odd era for them, poor devils. So many families had gone to the wall in the post-war years. Friends they had dined and danced and hunted with before 1939 had tumbled down in the wreckage of their kind and it would not be long before most of the fallen had been engulfed by the upper middle class, never to regain their lost status. Even among those who had kept the faith, still in their houses, still shooting their own pheasants, there were many who gloomily subscribed to the philosophy of *après moi le déluge*, and regularly vans would chug away, out through the gates towards the London auction houses, bearing the treasures that had been centuries in the assembling, so the family could stay warm and have something decent to wear for one more winter.

But Serena was not afflicted by these pressures. She and the rest of the Greshams were part of the Chosen (very) Few and lived much as they had always lived. Perhaps there were only two footmen where once there had been six. Perhaps the chef had to manage on his own and I do not believe Serena or her sisters enjoyed the services of a lady's maid. But otherwise not much had altered since the early 1880s, apart from their hemlines and being allowed to dine in restaurants.

Her father was the ninth Earl of Claremont, a mellow, even charming, title and when I knew him, as I would do later, he was himself a mellow and charming man, never cross because he had never been crossed and so, like his daughter, very easy to be with. He too lived in a benign mist, although, unlike Serena, he was not a creature of myth, a lovely *naiad* eluding her swain. His vagueness was more akin to *Mr Pastry.* Either way, he never had much grasp of hard reality. Indeed, at times it felt as if the family's soothing title had generated a placid sense of unquestioning acceptance in the dynasty, for which I now think, looking back, they were to be envied. I did not at that time believe that loving came easily to any of them, certainly not 'being in love,' which would have involved far too much disruption, with its horrid, sticky threats of indigestion and broken sleep, but they did not hate or quarrel either.

Not that acceptance of their lot was very difficult. By dint of judicious investment and far-sighted marriage, the family had more than survived the rocky seas of the twentieth century thus far, with large estates in Yorkshire, a castle somewhere in Ireland, which I never saw, and a house on Millionaires' Row, the private road running parallel to Kensington Palace, which was then considered quite something. These days, eastern potentates and people who own football clubs seem to have snapped up those vast edifices and made them private again, but at that time they had mostly fallen into embassies, one by one, with scarcely a family left. Except, of course, for the Claremonts, who occupied number 37, a lovely 1830s stone wedding cake, a shade too near Notting Hill.

As if this were not enough, Serena was also very beautiful, with thick, russet hair and a complexion lifted straight from a Pre-Raphaelite painting. Her features added to her gift of serenity, of real grace, which is an unlikely word to use of a girl of eighteen, but in her case a truthful one. I do not know exactly what we talked about, either at that party in Cambridge or at the many gatherings and house parties where we would meet over the next two years, sometimes art, I think, or maybe history. She was never much of a gossip. This was not a tribute to her kindness so much as to her lack of interest in other people's lives. Nor would there have been talk of a career, although she is not to blame for that. Even in the late Sixties, serious professional ambition would have marked her out uncomfortably among her contemporaries. That said, I was never bored in her company, not least because I must have been in love with her even then, long before I would acknowledge the fact, but the hopelessness implicit in loving such a star would have been all too obvious to that bundle of insecurities I call my unconscious mind and I shied away from certain failure. As anyone would.

'Can I talk to you?' said a deep, pleasant voice, just as I was approaching the punchline of a story. We looked up to find we had been joined by Damian Baxter. And we were glad of it which, to me now, is the strangest detail of all. 'I don't know anyone here,' he added with a smile that would have melted Greenland. My impressions of Damian have been so overlaid by what came after that it is hard for me to dredge up my early feelings, but there's no doubt that he was wonderfully attractive in those days, to men, women and children alike. Apart from anything else, he was so handsome, in a healthy, open-air sort of way, very handsome really, with bright, almost unnervingly blue eyes and thick, dark, wavy hair, worn long and in curls, as we all wore it then. He was fit, too, and muscular but without being sporty, or, worse, *hearty*, at all. He was just redolent of both health and intelligence, an unusual combination in my experience, and he looked as if he slept ten hours every night and had never tasted alcohol. Neither of which would be borne out by the facts.

'Well, now you know us,' said Serena and held out her hand.

I need hardly say that of course he knew exactly who we were. Or rather, who she was. He gave himself away later that evening, when we ended up squashed into a corner table in a dubious and rather cramped restaurant off Magdalene Street. We had picked up a couple of other students when the drinks party disbanded but Serena was not with us. It would have been unusual if she had been. It was rare for her to drift into that kind of easily accessible arrangement. She usually had a good, if unspecified, reason for not joining in.

The waiter brought the obligatory, steaming plates of *boeuf bourgignon*, with its glutinous and shiny sauce, that seemed to be our staple fare. This is not a criticism of the eaterie in question, more an acknowledgement of how and what we ate then, but I must not be ungrateful. Mounds of glazed stew, with rough red wine, was a big leg up, considering what had been on offer ten years before. There is, and should be, worthwhile debate about the merits of the changes the last four decades have brought to our society, but there can be few who do not welcome the improvement of English food, at least until the raw

fish and general undercooking that arrived with the celebrity chefs of
the new century. There is no doubt about it that when I was a child
the food available to the general British public was simply pitiful,
consisting largely of tasteless school dinners, with vegetables that had
been boiling since the war. Occasionally, you might find something
better on offer in a private house, but even smart restaurants served
fussy, dainty platefuls, decorated with horrible rosettes of green mayonnaise and the like, that were more trouble in the eating than they
were ever worth. So when the bistros began to arrive, with their check
tablecloths and melting candles pushed into the necks of green wine
bottles, we were glad of them. A decade later they had become a joke,
but then they were our salvation.

'Have you ever been to Serena's house in Yorkshire?' Damian asked.
The other two looked puzzled, as well they might, since there had been
no mention of Yorkshire or of the Claremont dynasty at any part of
the conversation.

This should have set off a thousand flashing bells, but, like the fool
I was, I made nothing of it. I simply answered the question. 'Once, but
just for a charity thing a couple of years ago.'

'What's it like?'

I thought for a moment. I hadn't retained any very precise image. 'A
Georgian pile. Very grand. But pretty.'

'And big?'

'Oh, yes, big. Not Blenheim. But big.'

'I suppose you've always known each other?' Again, as I would come
to recognise, this was a clue, had I the sense to read it. From long before
that evening Damian had a fiercely romantic view of the golden group
from which he felt excluded, but which he was determined to enter.
Although, looking back, even in 1968 it was a slightly odd ambition,
especially for someone like Damian Baxter. Not that there weren't
plenty who shared it (and plenty who still do), but Damian was a
modern creature, motivated, ambitious, strong – and if I say it of him
it must be true. He was always going to find a place in the new society
that was coming. Why did he want to bother with the fading glories
of the blue bloods, those sad walking history books, when, for so many
of those families, as with the potato, the best was already in the ground?
Personally, I think he must have been cut dead at some gathering in

youth, in front of a girl he fancied perhaps, snubbed, ignored and insulted by a drunken toff, until he fell into the cliché'd but very real goal of: '*I'll show you! Just you wait!*' It has, after all, been the spur of many great careers since the Conquest. But if this was the case, I never knew the incident that triggered it. Only that by the time we met, he had developed a personal mythology about the British aristocracy. He saw all its members as bonded together from birth, a tiny, tight club, hostile to newcomers, loyal to the point of reckless dishonesty when defending their own. There was some truth in this, of course, a good deal of truth in terms of attitude, but we were no longer living under a Whig oligarchy of a few thousand families. By the 1960s the catchment area, certainly for what remained of London Society, was far wider than he seemed aware of and the variety of types within it was much greater. Anyway, people are people, whoever they may be, and no world is as neat as he would have it.

'No. I haven't known her long at all, not properly. I might have met her a few times over the years, at this and that, but we only really talked for the first time at a tea party in Eaton Square a month or two ago.'

He seemed amused. 'A tea party?' It did sound rather quaint.

The tea party had, in fact, been given by a girl called Miranda Houghton at her parents' flat on the north side of Eaton Square. Miranda was the god-daughter of my aunt or of some friend of my mother's, I forget which. Like Serena, I'd seen her from time to time but without either of us making much of an impact; still, it qualified me for her guest list when the whole business began. These parties were one of the early rituals of the Season, even if, when recording it, one feels like an obscure archivist preserving for posterity the lost traditions of the Inuits. The girls would be encouraged to invite other would-be debutantes to tea, usually at their parents' London homes, thereby forging useful friendships and associations for the larks to come. Their mothers would obtain lists of who else was doing the whole thing from the unofficial but widely recognised leader, Peter Townend, who would supply them free of charge and gladly, to those he considered worthy, in his gallant but doomed attempt to stave off the modern world for as long as might conceivably be possible. Later these same mothers would require of him other lists of supposedly eligible men and he would produce these too, although they were required more for drinks parties and dances than the teas, where men were few and normally, as in the case of me and Miranda, actually knew the hostess. Very little, if any, tea was provided or drunk at these gatherings and in my experience the atmosphere was always slightly strange, as each new arrival hesitantly picked their way across the floor. But all the same we went to them, me included. So I suppose we were committed to the coming experience from comparatively early on, whatever we might afterwards pretend.

I was sitting in the corner, talking about hunting to a rather dull girl with freckles, when Serena Gresham came in and I could tell at once, from the faintest *frisson* that went through the assembled company, that she had already earned a reputation as a star. This was all the better managed as no one could have been less presumptuous or more softly spoken than she. Happily for me, I was near the last remaining empty chair. I waved to her and, after taking a second to remember who I was, she crossed the room and joined me. It is interesting to me now that Serena should have conformed to all this. Twenty years later, when the Season had become the preserve of exhibitionists and the daughters of *parvenu* mothers on the make, she would not have dreamed of it. I suppose it is a tribute to the fact that even someone as seemingly untrammelled as Serena would still, in those dead days, do as she was told.

'How do you know Miranda?' I asked.

'I don't, really,' was her answer. 'We met when we were both staying with some cousins of mine in Rutland.' One of Serena's gifts was always to answer every question quickly and easily, without a trace of mystery, but without imparting any information.

I nodded. 'So, will you be doing the whole deb thing?'

I do not wish to exaggerate my own importance, but I'm not convinced that before this she had fully faced the extent of the undertaking. She thought for a moment, frowning. 'I don't know.' She seemed to be looking into some invisible crystal ball, hovering in mid-air. 'We'll have to see,' she added and, in doing so, gave me a sense of her half-membership of the human race that was at the heart of her charm, a kind of emotional platform ticket that would allow her to withdraw at any moment from the experience on hand. I was entranced by her.

I outlined a little of this to Damian as we ate. He was fascinated by every detail, like an anthropologist who has long proclaimed a theory as an article of faith, but only recently begun to discover any real evidence of its truth. I suspect that Serena was the first completely genuine aristocrat he had ever met and, perhaps to his relief, he found her to be entirely undisappointing. She was in truth exactly what people reading historical novels, bought from a railway bookshop before a long and boring journey, imagine aristocratic heroines to be, both in her serene beauty and in her cool, almost cold, detachment. Despite what they themselves might like to think, there are few aristocrats who conform very satisfactorily to the imagined prototype and it was Damian's good fortune, or bad, that he should have begun his social career with one who did so perfectly. It was clear that for him there was something wonderfully satisfactory in the encounter. Of course, had he been less fortunate in his introduction to that world he might have been luckier in the way things turned out.

'So how do you get on to the list for these tea parties?' he asked.

The thing was, I liked him. It feels odd to write those words and there have been times when I have quite forgotten it, but I did. He was fun and entertaining and good-looking, always a recommendation for anyone where I'm concerned, and he had that quality, now dignified with the New Age term of Positive Energy, but which then simply indicated someone who would never wear you out. Years later, a friend would describe her world to me as being peopled entirely by radiators and drains. If so, then Damian was King Radiator. He warmed the company he was in. He could make people want to help him, which alchemy he practised, most successfully, on me.

As it happened, in this instance I could not deliver what Damian was asking for, as he had really missed the tea parties. These little informal gatherings were very much a preliminary weeding process, when the girls would seek out their playmates for the coming year within the overall group, and by the time of our Cambridge dinner the gangs were formed and the cocktail parties had already begun, although, as I told him, the first I was due to attend was not in fact a deb party as such, but one of a series given by Peter Townend, the Season's Master of the Ceremonies, at his London flat. It may seem strange to a student of these rites to learn that for the last twenty or thirty years of their existence they were entirely managed by an unknown northerner of no birth and modest means, but the fact remains that they were. Naturally,

Damian had heard the name and almost immediately, with his hound-like scent for quarry, he asked if he might tag along, and I agreed. This was distinctly risky on my part as Townend was jealous of his powers and privileges, and to turn up casually with a hanger-on, was to risk devaluing the invitation, which he would certainly not take kindly. Nevertheless, I did it and so, a week or two later, when I parked my battered green mini without difficulty in Chelsea Manor Street, Damian Baxter was sitting beside me in the passenger seat.

I say Peter was jealous of his role and so he was, but he was entitled to be. From a modest background, with which he was perfectly content, and after a career in journalism and editing where his speciality was genealogy, he had one day discovered his personal vocation would be to keep the Season alive, when Her Majesty's decision to end Presentation in 1958 had seemed to condemn the whole institution to immediate execution. We know now that it was instead destined to die a lingering death, and maybe simple decapitation might have been preferable, but nobody knows the future and at that time it seemed that Peter, single-handedly, had won it an indefinite reprieve. The Monarch would play no further part in it, of course, which knocked the point and the stuffing out of it for many, but it would still have a purpose in bringing together the offspring of like-minded parents, and this was the responsibility he took on. He had no hope of reward. He did it solely for the honour of the thing, which in my book makes it praiseworthy, whatever one's opinion of the end product. Year by year he would comb the stud books, Peerage and Gentry, writing to the mothers of daughters, interviewing their sons, all to buy another few months for the whole business. Can this really have been only forty years ago? you may ask in amazement. The answer's yes.

Peter's own gatherings were not to select or encourage the girls. That had all been done some time before. No, they were basically to audition those young men who had come to his attention as possible escorts and dancing partners for the parties to come. Having been vetted, their names would either be underscored or crossed off the lists that were distributed to the anxious waiting mothers, who would assume that the cads and seducers, the alcoholics and the gamblers and those who were NSIT (not safe in taxis) would all have been excised from the names presented. They should have been, of course, but it was not entirely plain sailing, viz. the first two young men to greet us as we pushed into the narrow hall of the squashed and ill-furnished flat, at the top of a block built in the worst traditions of the late 1950s. These were the younger sons of the Duke of Trent, Lord Richard and Lord George Tremayne, who were both already drunk. A stranger might have thought that since neither was attractive or funny in the least, Peter would not deem them ideally suited to the year ahead. But this would be to ignore human nature and it was not really his fault that there were those he could not exclude. Certainly, the Tremayne brothers would enjoy a kind of popularity, somehow acquiring the reputation for being 'live wires,' which they were not. The fact is their father was a duke and, even if he could not have held down the job of a parking attendant in the real world, that was enough to guarantee their invitations.

We moved on into the crowded, main room, I hesitate to call it the drawing room, since it had many functions, but that was where we found Peter, his characteristic cowlick of hair falling over his crumpled, pug-like face. He pointed at Damian. 'Who he?' he said in a loud and overtly hostile voice.

'May I introduce Damian Baxter?' I said.

'I never invited him,' said Peter, quite unrelenting. 'What's he doing here?' Peter had, as I have said, made a decision not to pass himself off as a product of the system he so admired and in a moment like this I understood why. Since he had not posited himself as an elegant gentleman, he did not feel any need to be polite if it did not suit him. In short, he never disguised his feelings, and over the years I came both to like and to admire him for it. Of course, his words may read as if his anger was directed towards the unwelcome guest, when it was instead entirely meant for me. I was the one who had broken the rules. In the face of this attack I'm afraid I foundered. It seems odd, certainly to the man I am today, but I know I was suddenly anxious at the thought of all those treats, which I had planned for and which were in his gift, slipping away. It might have been less troublesome if they had.

'Don't blame him,' said Damian, seeing the problem and moving quickly in beside us. 'Blame me. I very much wanted to meet you, Mr Townend, and when I heard he was coming here I forced him to bring me. It's entirely my fault.'

Peter stared at him. 'That's my cue to say you're welcome, I suppose.'

His tone could not have been less hospitable but Damian, as ever, was unfazed. 'It's your cue to ask me to leave if you wish. And of course I will.' He paused, a trace of anxiety playing across his even features.

'Very smooth,' said Peter in his curious, ambiguous, almost petulant way. He nodded towards a bewildered Spaniard holding a tray. 'You can have a drink if you like.' I do not at all believe he was won over by Damian's charm, then or later. I would say he simply recognised a fellow player who might be possessed of great skill and was reluctant to make an enemy of him on their first encounter. As Damian moved away, Peter turned back to me. 'Who is he? And where did he pick you up?' This in itself was curiously phrased.

'Cambridge. I met him at a party in my college. As to who he is,' I hesitated. 'I don't know much about him, really.'

'Nor will you.'

I felt rather defensive. 'He's very nice.' I wasn't quite sure how or why I'd been cast as protector, but apparently I had. 'And I thought you might like him, too.'

Peter followed Damian with his eyes, as he took a drink and started to chat up a wretched overweight girl with a lantern jaw, who was hovering nervously on the edge of the proceedings. 'He's an operator,' he said and turned to greet some new arrivals.

If he was an operator, the operation bore fruit almost immediately. This would not have surprised me much further on in our acquaintance, as by then I would have known that Damian would never be so idle as to waste an opportunity. He was always a worker. His worst enemy would concede that. In fact, he just did. Damian had, after all, made it into Peter's sanctum without any guarantee of a return engagement. There was no time to be lost.

The awkward lantern-jawed girl, whom I now recognised gazing up at Damian as he showered her with charm, went by the name of Georgina Waddilove. She was the daughter of a city banker and an American heiress. Quite how Damian had selected her for his opening salvo I am not entirely sure. Perhaps it was just a warrior's sense of where the wall might most easily be breached and which girl was the most vulnerable to attack. Georgina was a melancholy character. To anyone who was interested, and there were not many, this could be traced to her mother who, with an imprecise knowledge of England and after a courtship conducted entirely during her husband's posting in New York after the war, had been under the illusion at the time of her wedding that she was marrying into a much higher caste than was in fact the case. When they did return to England, in late 1950, with two little boys and a baby daughter, she had arrived in her new country with confident expectations of stalking at Balmoral and foursome suppers at Chatsworth and Stratfieldsaye. What she discovered, however, was that her husband's friends and family came, almost exclusively, from the same prosperous, professional money-people that she had played tennis with in the Hamptons since her girlhood. Her husband, Norman (and perhaps the name should have given her a clue), had not consciously meant to deceive her but, like many Englishmen of his type, particularly when abroad, he had fallen into the habit of suggesting that he came from a smarter background than he did and, far away in New York, this was only too easy. After spending nine years there he came almost to believe his own fiction. He would talk so freely of Princess Margaret or the Westminsters or Lady Pamela Berry, that he would probably have been as surprised as his listeners to discover that everything he knew of these people he had gleaned from the pages of the *Daily Express*.

The net result of this disappointment was not, however, divorce. Anne Waddilove had her children to think about and divorce in the 1950s still exacted a high social price. Norman had made quite a lot of money, so instead she resolved to use it to correct for her offspring the deficiencies and disappointments of her own existence. For the boys this meant good schools, shooting and proper universities, but from early on she was determined to launch her daughter with a dizzying season that would result in a dazzling marriage. Grandchildren would then follow, who would do her Royal stalking by proxy. So did Mrs Waddilove plan the future of the wretched Georgina, condemned to live her mother's life and not her own from more or less the moment the child could walk. Which may explain the parent's blindness to a simple truth, so clear to the rest of the world, that Georgina was hopelessly unsuited to the role expected of her. Good-looking and poised as Anne Waddilove was, she had not anticipated that nature would play a joke on her in giving her a daughter who was as plain as a pikestaff, fat as a barrel and *gauche* to boot. To make matters worse, Georgina's shy nervousness invariably gave a (false) first impression of stupidity, nor was she at all, by choice, gregarious. Since she wasn't in line for a major inheritance – the presence of two boys in a family generally knocks that on the head – the match Mrs Waddilove had dreamed of seemed what can only be described as highly unlikely by the time Georgina had completed her first few weeks as a debutante.

I have to say that when I got to know her I liked Georgina Waddilove and, while I cannot pretend to a romantic interest in her at any point, I was always happy to sit next to her at dinner. She was knowledgeable about films, one of my interests, so we had plenty to talk about. But there was no escaping the fact that she did not appear destined for success in the harsh and competitive arena her mother had chosen. There was something almost grotesque in watching her lumpen frame wandering, sad and alone, through ballroom after ballroom, decked out in the girlish fashions of the day, her hair sewn with flowers, her frock made of lace, when all the time she resembled nothing so much as a talking chimp in an advertisement for PG Tips tea. I'm sorry to say that she became, if anything, a comic figure among our crowd and, older as I am now and less impervious to others' suffering, I very much regret this. It must have caused her great pain, which she concealed, and the concealment can only have made it sharper.

Was it an instinct for this that took Damian straight to her side, when shining beauties of high rank stood about Peter's drawing room, laughing and chatting and sipping their drinks? Was it as a fox might scent a wounded bird that Damian surveyed the crowd, locating the ugliest, most awkward girl there, and made for her like a missile? If so, his tactic was completely successful and a few days later he dropped by my rooms to show that the morning's post had brought his first stiffy, a thick white card bearing the proud, engraved name of 'Mrs Norman Waddilove, At Home,' who was inviting him to attend a cocktail party 'for Georgina,' on the seventh of June, by the Dodgem Track at Battersea Fun Fair. 'How can she be "at home" by the Dodgems?' he said.

Battersea Park has altered its position in London in the decades since the war. It has not moved physically, of course, but it is an entirely different place today from the scene of so many childhood memories of half a century ago. Built by the Victorians as a pleasure ground for the local *bourgeoisie*, with sculpted rocks and fountains and gentle paths by swan-stocked lakes, the park had cheerfully run to seed by the 1950s and had become instead important to a whole generation of children as the site of London's only permanent fun fair. Erected in 1951, as part of that icon of lost innocence, the Festival of Britain, the fair flourished into the Sixties, when newer forms of entertainment began to steal its thunder. A tragic accident on the Big Dipper in 1972 hastened the inevitable and two years later came closure. The dear, old fun fair, grey and grubby and downright dangerous as it had become, was swept away without a trace, like the hanging gardens of Nineveh.

It is more beautiful today, its ponds and waterfalls and glades restored, than when I first walked there, clutching the hand of an aunt or a nanny and begging to be allowed one more ride before we went home, but it is not more beautiful to me. Nor am I alone in this rose-tinted memory and, in fact, nostalgia was already beginning to envelop the place by 1968 as we, the children who had felt sick from too much candy floss when the fair was at its height, were now in our late teens and early twenties, and for this reason it was a clever choice by Mrs Waddilove as a venue for her party. Georgina, as I have said, was not popular and she might easily have had to endure the humiliation of a sparsely attended gathering had it been held in one of the Park Lane hotels or in the coffee room of her father's club, when half the guest list might easily have chucked. The casualness of the young, as they abandon their social commitments for something more recent and more enticing, was horrible to adults then. These days parents are inclined to shrug and roll their eyes at their children's unreliability, but not to take it very seriously. I don't suggest the phenomenon is new, chucking, dodging, gatecrashing and the rest, but in 1968 nobody saw the funny side. However, on this occasion Battersea Fun Fair appealed and everyone turned up.

I was quite late arriving, as it happens, so the hubbub of chatter was what guided me through the fair and past the stalls, until I came to a temporary white-painted wicket fence, where two officials guarded the entrance and a large card on a blackboard stand announced that the Dodgems were 'closed for a private party.' This ensured some glares from would-be customers, which Georgina's guests affected to ignore, but these disgruntled few did not spoil things. Whatever they may pretend, the privileged classes, then and now, enjoy a bit of envy.

Some of the girls were already in the cars, shrieking and laughing and spilling their wine, as their boyfriends-for-the-night posed and preened, banging and whacking into the cars of others. Nowadays there would be signs requesting that glasses should not be taken on to the track, or there would only have been plastic cups anyway, but I do not recall anyone concerning themselves with such things as slippery surfaces or broken glass. There must have been plenty of both. A marquee with an open side had been erected to accommodate the other guests who were already well away. I looked round for Georgina, hoping to find her at the centre of a grateful crowd, but as usual she was standing alone and silent near the champagne table, so I saw the chance to fetch a drink and simultaneously greet my hostess, killing two birds with one stone.

'Hello,' I said. 'This all seems to be satisfactorily rowdy.'

She smiled wanly. 'Are you going to have a go?'

'Oh, I think so.' I smiled gamely. 'What about you?' But she did not seem to hear my question, her eyes fixed on the track itself, and I could now make out a car with the distinctive figure of Damian crouched over the controls. His co-pilot appeared, from a distance anyway, to be rather an unlikely one. Her face was almost concealed by a curtain of curls, but I could see how calm she was, and unattached. She did not shout like the others, but merely sat there, like some stately princess forced to endure the indignity of a peasant's ferry in order to get to the other side.

Georgina turned. 'What's your dinner in aid of?'

I was nonplussed. 'What dinner?'

'Tonight. Damian said he couldn't come to the Ritz with us because he'd pledged himself to you.'

I realised at once the significance of this, that poor Georgina had already fulfilled her function in Damian's life by getting him started and could now be dispensed with. The doomed girl had yielded to his flattery and friendly charm, and opened the door for him into this world, but now, having gained entry, he had no compunction in leaving her to her own devices. So Georgina's dream of having this new and glamorous companion sitting next to her at the dull, staid dinner that would have been arranged by her mother for a favoured few was to be shattered. As to the fib that had got him out of it, I blush to say I covered for him. In my defence, this was not really by choice but entirely in obedience to natural impulse. When any woman talks of a man's excuse to another man, he is somehow bound to support the fiction as part of a kind of race loyalty. 'Robert says you're having lunch with him next week' forces any male to respond with something along the lines of 'I'm looking forward to having a good catch-up,' even if it's the first he's heard of the plan. Often, afterwards, a man may chastise the friend or acquaintance who has brought this about. 'How dare you put me on a spot like that?' Even so, it is against male nature to speak the truth. The alternative would be to say, 'I have never heard of this lunch. Robert must have a mistress.' But no man can utter these words, even when he is entirely on the side of the woman being lied to. I smiled at Georgina. 'Well, it's just a dinner for a few of us. It's not at all crucial, if you really need him.'

She shook her head. 'No, no. I don't want to mess things up. Daddy was annoyed when I asked him, anyway. That's why I didn't invite you,' she added lamely. 'He thinks we're too many as it is.' Too many duds, I thought, and not enough possibilities. But then, Damian would not qualify in this group. Mrs Waddilove was not in the market for an adventurer.

'Who's coming?'

'I wish you were,' she muttered obediently. 'But as I say, it's not a big party.' I nodded. Having paid lip service to form, she listed half a dozen names. 'Princess Dagmar. And the Tremayne brothers, I think, but there may be a problem.' I bet there will be, I thought. 'Andrew Summersby and his sister.' She ticked off these people in her head, although the list carried her mother's fingerprints, not her own. 'That's about it.'

I glanced over to where the lumpen, red-faced Viscount Summersby stood glumly nursing his drink. He had apparently abandoned any efforts at conversation with his neighbours. Their state was no doubt the more blessed. Meanwhile, in front of him, his sister, Annabella, was shrieking and shouting as she tore round the track, a pale and lean companion trembling beside her. Her tight cocktail frock, raided from her mother's post-war wardrobe, seemed to be bursting at the seams as she wrenched the wheel this way and that. Annabella Warren was not a beauty any more than her brother but, of the two and if forced to choose, I preferred her. Neither was an enticing prospect for an evening's entertainment, but at least she had a bit of go. Georgina, following my gaze, seemed silently to agree. 'Well, good luck with it,' I said.

The dodgem cars had stopped and the drivers and passengers were being forced from their vehicles by the waiting crowd of guests surrounding the track, anxious for their turn. They had a distinctive look, those girls of long ago, racing across the metal, bolted floor to squeeze into the dirty and dented cars awaiting them, part 1950s Dior, part 1960s Carnaby Street, acknowledging the modern world but not yet quite capitulating to it. In the forty years that followed, that decade has been hijacked by the voice of the Liberal Tyranny. Theirs is the Woodstock version of the period – 'if you can remember the Sixties, you weren't really there,' run the smug and self-regarding phrases – and they have no conscience in holding up the values of the pop revolution as the whole truth, but they are either deceiving or deceived. What was genuinely unusual about the era for those of us who were around at the time was not a bunch of guitar players smoking dope and wearing embarrassing hats with feathers, and leather singlets lined with sheepskin. What marked it apart from the other periods I have lived through was that, like Janus, it faced both ways.

One part of the culture was indeed about pop and drugs and happenings, and Marianne Faithfull and Mars Bars and free love, but the other, if anything far larger, section of the community was still looking back to the 1950s, back towards a traditional England, where behaviour was laid down according to the practice of, if not many centuries, at least the century immediately before, where everything from clothes to sexual morality was rigidly determined and, if we did not always obey the rules, we knew what they were. It was, after all, less than ten years previously that this code had reigned supreme. The girls who wouldn't kiss on a first date, the boys who were not dressed without a tie, those mothers who only left the house in hat and gloves, those fathers wearing bowlers on their way to the city. These were all as much a part of the sixties as the side of it so constantly revived by television retrospectives. The difference being that they were customs on the way out, while the new, deconstructed culture was on the way in. It would, of course, prove to be the winner and as with anything it is the winner who writes history.

A great fashion then was for adding false hair, in ringlets and falls, to dramatise a hairstyle. They were intended to look real but only with the reality of a costume in a play, that could be discarded the following day with no loss of face. So a girl might appear on Monday night with curls to her shoulders and at Tuesday lunch with an Eton crop. The idea was really to use hair like a series of hats. In this one disguise, perhaps alone among their habits and unlike the wig wearers of today, there was no intention to deceive. The vogue was further enhanced by the practice of depositing these 'pieces' at the hairdresser's a day or two in advance, where they would be rollered and treated and even sewn with flowers or beads, before the whole elaborate coiffure would be pinned to the owner's head in the afternoon before a party. The style reached its apogee when the dances began, but even in the early stages, during the first cocktail parties, it seemed a parable of the unreality we were all participating in, as the debs would alter their appearance almost completely, twice or three times a week. Partygoers would see a stranger approach, only to discover, as they drew near, the face of an old friend peeping out. So it was, on this particular evening, that I suddenly recognised the sedate highness in transit, riding in the seat next to Damian, was none other than Serena Gresham, who climbed out of the car, as cool as a cucumber, and walked over to where I was standing. 'Hello,' she said.

'Hello. How are you getting on?'

'I'm shaken to pieces. I feel like a cocktail ready to be poured.'

'I was going to ask if you wanted another go, with me.'

'Not likely,' said Serena. 'What I do want is another drink.' She looked around and had secured a new glass of champagne before the offer to help her was even out of my mouth.

Leaving her surrounded by would-be gallants, I wandered over to the Dodgem track, where the cars were already fully occupied. Then I heard my name called and I looked round to see Lucy Dalton waving at me. I walked over. 'What is it?' I said.

'For Christ's sake get in.' Lucy patted the battered, leather seat beside her. 'Philip Rawnsley-Price is coming this way and my bottom will be quite bruised enough without that.' Behind me I could hear the man shouting for us to clear the track. 'Get in!' she hissed. So I did. It wasn't a complete reprieve. Before we could set off, Philip, ignoring the shouts of the operator, had strolled across between the now moving cars – in those days, you understand, 'Health and safety,' as a phrase, had yet to be invented.

'If you're avoiding me, you can give up now,' he said to Lucy with a leer that I assume was supposed to be sexy. 'We're destined to be together.' Before she could think of a suitable wisecrack, there was a harsh and sudden jolt. We had been hit broadside by one of the Tremayne brothers with his cackling companion beside him and, with dislocated backs, we were flung into the tangled maelstrom. Philip laughed and moved lazily back to the edge.

Lucy Dalton will figure at some length in these pages and deserves an introduction, although she was not essentially, I think, a complicated character. Like Serena, she was the recipient, unearned, of most of this world's blessings but at a (slightly) more modest level, which had divorced her a little less from the ordinary human experience. It is always hard for outsiders to perceive the differences in status and possession within an envied, privileged group, but these distinctions exist, whichever ivory tower one is dealing with. Champion footballers, all richer than Midas, know well who, within their crowd, merits envy and who should be pitied. Film stars can easily distinguish among themselves the careers that are going nowhere and the ones that have years more to run. Of course, to most of the public the very suggestion that this millionaire is less to be envied than that one seems pretentious and isolationist, but the gradations are meaningful to the members of these clubs and, if one is to attempt to understand what makes any world tick, they have a part to play in that. So it was with us. The Season in the 1960s, even if the concept was already embattled, still involved a narrower group than it would do today, if anyone were foolish enough to attempt its revival. Looking back, we were a halfway house between the genuinely exclusive group of the pre-war years and the anything-goes world of the 1980s and after. There were certainly girls included who would not have made the grade in the days of Presentation, but they were still made to feel it and the inner crowd was mostly drawn from the more traditional recruiting grounds. Within this set, then, the different levels of good fortune were clear to see and to appreciate.

Lucy Dalton was the younger daughter of a baronet, Sir Marmaduke Dalton, whose ancestor had received his title in the early nineteenth century, as a reward for pretty routine service to the Crown. The family was still possessed of a substantial estate in Suffolk but the house itself was let in the 1930s and had been a girls' prep school since the war. I would say the Daltons themselves were fairly happy in the dower house, from which, above the trees, they could just about glimpse the scene of their former splendour, albeit surrounded by prefabricated class-rooms and pitches for the playing of lacrosse. In other words, it wasn't ideal.

As a citizen of the modern world, I am now, in late middle age, fully aware that Lucy's upbringing was privileged to an extreme degree. But most humans only compare themselves with people in similar circumstances to their own and I would ask the reader's tolerance when I say that, given the times, to our gang her origins did not seem so remarkable. Her family, with its minor title, in their pleasant dower house, lived much as we all lived, in our rectories and manors and farmhouses, and the important distinction, or so it seemed to us, was between those who lived normally and those who lived as our people had lived before the war. These survivors were our battle pennants, our emblems of a better day, our acknowledged social leaders. With their footmen and their stately drawing rooms, they seemed in magic contrast to our own lives, with our working fathers and our mothers who had learned to cook ... a bit. *We* were the normal ones, *they* were the rich ones, and it was many years before I questioned this. In my defence, it's a rare individual who grasps that their own way of life is extravagant or sybaritic. It is always those much richer than oneself who deserve these sobriquets, and I would say that Lucy never thought of herself as much more than reasonably lucky.

At any rate, to me she was a cheerful soul, pretty but not beautiful, funny but not fascinating. We'd met when we found ourselves in the same party for a charity ball the year before and so, when the Season started and we discovered we were both to be part of it, we naturally gravitated towards each other as one is drawn to any friendly, familiar face in a new and faintly challenging environment. To be honest, I believe I might have been rather keen on her if I had been more careful at the start, but as it was I missed my chance if there was one, by allowing us to become friends – almost invariably the antidote to any real thoughts of romance.

'Who is this fellow you've wished on us all?' she said, steering wildly to avoid another merry prang from Lord Richard.

'I don't know that I've wished him on anybody.'

'Oh, but you have. I saw four girls writing down his address before he'd been here twenty minutes. I assume he's not sponsored by Mr Townend?'

'Hardly. I took him along to one of Peter's things last week and I thought for a moment we were going to be thrown out.'

'Why did you "take him along?" Why have you become his promoter?'

'I don't think I knew that I had.'

She looked at me with a rather pitying smile.

Probably it was a half-subconscious desire to bury my lie to Georgina by making it true that prompted me to organise a group for dinner as the party began to thin out, and later that evening about eight of us were climbing down the treacherous basement stairs of Haddy's, then a popular spot on a corner of the Old Brompton Road, where one could dine after a fashion as well as dance the night away, and all for about thirty shillings a head. We often used to spend whole evenings there, eating, talking, dancing, although it is hard to imagine what the modern equivalent of this sort of place might be, since to manage all three in a single location seems impossible now, given the ferocious, really savage, volume that music is played at today anywhere one might be expected to dance. I suppose it must have begun to get louder in the discotheques after I had ceased to go to them, but I was not aware of the new fashion until perfectly normal people in their forties and fifties adopted it and started to give parties that must rank among the worst in history. Often I hear the notion of the nightclub, where you sat and chatted while the music played, spoken of as belonging to the generation before mine, men and women in evening clothes sitting around the Mirabelle in the 1930s and '40s, dancing to Snake Hips Johnson and his orchestra while they sipped White Ladies, but like so many truisms this is not true. The opportunity to eat, talk and dance was available to us and I enjoyed it.

Haddy's did not really qualify as a nightclub. It was more for people who couldn't afford to go to proper nightclubs. These places, Haddy's, Angelique's, the Garrison, forgotten names now but full every night then, provided a simple service, but as with all successful innovations they filled a need. The dinner would belong to the recently arrived style of *paysanne* cooking, but this predictable repast would be combined with the comparatively new invention of dancing, publicly, not to a band but to records, presided over by some sort of disc jockey, a job description then only in its infancy. The wine was rarely more than plonk, certainly when we young ones were paying, but the bonus was that the owners did not expect to sell the table much more than once throughout the evening. Having eaten, we sat drinking and banging on about what preoccupied our adolescent troubled minds into the small hours, night after night, without, as far as I remember, the smallest problem with the management. They cannot really have been businessmen, I'm afraid. No wonder their establishments did not stand the test of time.

That particular evening, for some strange reason, Serena Gresham had joined us among the rest, tagging along when I told her where we were going. I was surprised because usually she would listen politely to the plan, make a little *moue* of regret with her mouth and wish aloud she could have come. But this time she thought for a moment and said 'all right. Why not?' It may not seem a very enthusiastic response, but at the sound of her words songbirds rose in flight in my heart. Lucy was there, trying and failing to escape Philip, her nemesis, who had proposed himself after her car had left. Damian came, of course, and a new girl, whom I had not met before that evening, a ravishing, Hollywood-style blonde with little to say for herself, Joanna Langley. I say I did not know her, but I had heard of her as being very rich, one of the richest girls of the year, if part of the new post-Presentation crop. Her father had founded a sales catalogue for casual clothing or something similar, and while the money ensured that no one was rude to her face, things were not quite so pleasant behind her back. Personally, I liked her from the start. She was sitting on my left.

'Are you enjoying it?' she asked as I sloshed some wine into her glass.

49

I wasn't sure if she meant the dinner or the Season, but I assumed the latter. 'I think so. I haven't done much yet, but it seems a nice crowd.'

'Are you?' This came from Damian, further down the table. I could see he was already training his headlamp glare on to Joanna. Like me, he clearly knew who she was.

She was a little startled, but she nodded. 'So far. What about you?'

He laughed. 'Oh, I'm not part of it. Ask him.' He indicated me with a jocular flick of his chin.

'You're here, aren't you?' I replied rather crisply. 'What other quali- fication do you think we have?' Which was dishonest, but I didn't worry much, as I knew nothing would dampen his ardour.

'Don't let him mislead you.' Damian had brought his gaze back to Joanna. 'I'm a perfectly ordinary boy from a perfectly ordinary home. I thought it would be fun to see it for myself, but I'm not part of this world at all.' It was carefully measured, like everything he said, and I can understand now what it was intended to achieve. It meant that every girl at that table would at once feel protective of him and none of them, or their friends, would ever be allowed to accuse him of pretending to be something he was not. His apparent modesty would give him permission to take and take, but never to feel any responsibility to a world he had declared he did not belong to and to which he owed nothing. Above all, it washed over their defences. From then on they were not afraid of being used by such a man. How could they be when he said himself he had no ambition? We had not even ordered before he was writing down his address for Joanna and two of the other girls present.

I note I have stated that Damian was 'of course' with us. Why was it so understood that he would be? At this early stage of his London career? Perhaps because I had begun to reckon his gifts. I looked down the table to where he sat, with Serena on one side and Lucy on the other, making them both listen and laugh but never overplaying his hand with either, and I understood then that he was one of those rare beings who can fit seamlessly into a new group until, before much time has passed, they seem to be an integral, a founder, member of it. He joked and ribbed, but frowned a little, too. He took them seriously and nodded with concern, like someone who knew them well, but not too well. In all the time I knew him, he never made the classic *parvenu* mistake of lapsing into over-familiarity. Not long ago I was talking to a man before a shoot. We had got on well at dinner the night before and he, supposing, I imagine, that we were now friends, began to poke me jocularly in the stomach as he joshed me about my weight. He smiled as he said it and looked into my eyes, but what he saw there cannot have encouraged him as I had decided, on that instant, I would never seek his company again. Damian made no such error. His approach was relaxed and easy but never egregious or impertinent. In short, it was carefully thought out and well delivered, and that evening gave me one of my first opportunities to witness the skill with which he would land his quarry.

The dinner was finished, the girls' uneaten stew had been carried away, the lights had been lowered a few degrees and couples around the room were beginning to take to the floor. Nobody from our group had ventured forth yet, but we were nearly there and, during a slight lull in the conversation, I heard Damian turn to Serena. 'Do you want to dance?' he suggested, almost in the tone of a shared joke, a funny secret only fully understood by the two of them. It was beautifully done. They were playing some record we all liked, was it *Flowers in the Rain*? I forget now. At any rate, after a fractional pause she nodded and they stood. But next came the wonder. As they passed by my end of the table I heard him remark quite casually: 'I feel such a fool. I know you're called Serena and I remember where we first met, but I never got your surname. If I leave it much longer it'll be too late to ask.' Like a conman or a courtier he waited, just for a second, to see if his ploy would work. Did he breathe more easily when she gave no indication that she knew what he was up to?

Instead, she smiled. 'Gresham,' she whispered gently and they stepped on to the floor. I watched this in amazement and is it any wonder? Not only did Damian know her name long before that night, and where her family lived, and almost certainly the acreage. I would guess he could have listed the dates of every Earl of Claremont since the title was created and probably the maiden names of every Countess. I caught his eye across the room. He knew I had heard the exchange and I knew he knew. But he made no acknowledgement of the fact that I could have shown him up and spoiled his game. This is the kind of high-risk strategy in a career of social mountaineering that must surely almost merit admiration.

Lucy was watching me watching him, a small smile on her lips. 'What's so funny?' I said.

'I have a feeling that until tonight you thought you were Damian's patron, when we must both suspect you will be lucky to find yourself his chronicler by the time the Season is done.' She watched the couple on the floor and grew more serious. 'If you want to stake your claim in that department, I shouldn't leave it too long.'

I shook my head. 'He's not her type. Nor am I, no doubt. But he isn't.'

'You say that because you idolise her and consider him inferior in every way. But these are the views of a lover. She won't think that herself.'

Now I studied them. The music had become slow and smoochy, and they were swaying from side to side in that stepless dance we all did then. I shook my head again. 'You're wrong. He has nothing that she wants.'

'On the contrary, he has exactly what she wants. She won't be looking for birth or money. She's always had plenty of both. I doubt she's very susceptible to looks. But Damian ...' as she spoke, her eyes focused again on the dark head, taller than most of the men dancing near him. 'He's got the one quality she lacks. That we all lack, if it comes to that.'

'Which is?'

'He belongs to the present century. He will understand the rules of the Game as it will be played in the future, not as it used to be played in the days before the war. That could be very reassuring.' At this precise moment Philip leant over her with an optimistic offer but Lucy turned him down, nodding at me. 'He's already asked me and I've said yes.' She got to her feet and I escorted her obediently to the floor.

Lucy

THREE

The list, which I found lying on the pillow when I went up to my bed, was not long. But it still included some surprises. There were five names and all of them, it seems, had slept with Damian before he had been sterilised *en vacances* under the hot Portuguese sun. They had also all given birth to a child within the dictated time span. Lucy Dalton was there, I was a little sad to see. I had hoped for better from her, since she had been one of the first to see through Damian's disguise. Joanna Langley's inclusion surprised me less. I had been aware of a romance between them at the time and they seemed to me well matched. I'd wondered then why nothing came of it. No doubt I was about to find out. I was not expecting HRH Princess Dagmar of Moravia to figure among the notches on Damian's bedpost, nor the red-faced, loud, man-eater of the day, Candida Finch, whom I wouldn't have thought his type at all. Heavens. There was no denying that he got about a bit. Terry Vitkov, on the other hand, was a routine entry on many lists of that year's conquests, including mine. An American adventuress from the Middle West, she had less money than she liked to suggest and only came to London after exhausting the social possibilities of Cincinnati. Her sexual mores, which would prefigure the next decade rather than, like most of the girls, harking back to a time before our own, ensured that she would be made welcome. At any rate by the boys.

Each name was neatly typed. Next to it was the woman's current, married surname and, where clarification was needed, the name of the husband. After that came the name, sex and birth date of the child in question with a brief note of any other children in the family. Finally, there was a column of addresses, in some cases two or even three, with telephone numbers and e-mail contacts, although somehow I didn't imagine much of this was going to be accomplished via the Internet. A covering note at the top, 'as far as we have been able to ascertain, the details are as follows,' meant that I could not be wholly confident about the information and some of the entries were much fuller than others, but most of it looked pretty accurate to me. I no longer ran into any of them, but the little that I did know tallied with the contents of the sheet. Behind the paper, held to it with a small clip, was an envelope. This turned out to contain, as promised, a platinum credit card made out in my name.

I breakfasted alone, with what seemed like every newspaper in the known world neatly arranged at the other end of the long table. The butler asked if he might pack, or was there some reason for him to delay this? There wasn't. He bowed, thrilled with my permission to be of use, but before he left the room to carry out his task he spoke: 'Mr Baxter wonders if you might have time to look in on him before you leave for the station.' I can recognise an order when I hear one.

Damian's bedroom was in a different part of the house from the one I had occupied. A wide gallery from the top of the staircase led towards a pair of double doors, standing half open. I heard my name called as I lifted my hand to knock and found myself in a light, high chamber, lined with panelling painted in a soft *gris Trianon*. Perhaps I had been expecting some dark, magician's lair but no, this was clearly the other place, along with the library, where Damian actually lived. A large Georgian mahogany four-poster stood against a tapestry-hung wall, facing a carved rococo chimneypiece, which was in turn surmounted by one of the many Romneys of the lovely Lady Hamilton. Three tall windows looked out across the gardens to what I saw now was a kind of mini-park, with a tidy and impressive display of, I am sure, rare trees. There were inlaid chairs dotted about, and a desk, and little tables piled with books and precious things, and a rather beautiful day bed, of the type that is called a *duchesse brisée*, with a folded rug at the end, waiting to make its master comfortable. The whole effect was charming and delicate and curiously feminine, the room of a finer spirit than I would have credited him with.

Damian was in the bed. I did not see him immediately as the shadow of the canopy blurred him for a moment, hunched and crunched up

56

as he was against the pillows, surrounded by letters and another mass of newspapers. I could not help but feel it would be a black day for the local newsagents when Damian shuffled off his mortal coil. 'You found the list,' he said.

'I did.'

'Were you surprised?'

'I knew about Joanna. At least I suspected it.'

'Our main thing was over long before. But I slept with her one last time the night she got back from Lisbon. She came round to my flat. I suppose she wanted to see if I was all right.'

'I'm not surprised.'

'We went on from there.'

'But hadn't you already got the mumps?'

'I didn't develop a sore throat until a few days afterwards and, anyway, apparently you store a certain amount of whatsit, which isn't affected.'

'A little too much information.'

'As you can imagine, I am by this point the world's greatest living expert.' He gave a wry chuckle. He was wonderfully unbowed by the whole thing. 'What about the rest of them?'

'Well, even I slept with Terry and I'm not exactly surprised by Candida, though I wouldn't have thought she was your type. But I didn't suspect the other two.'

'I suppose you're disappointed in your old pal, Lucy.'

'Only because I thought she disliked you as much as I did.' This made him laugh for the first time that morning. But the effort was painful and we had to wait for a second while he recovered.

'She was only attracted to people she disliked. All the others she turned into friends. Including you.' This was probably true in its way, so I didn't interrupt him. 'Do you see any of them now?'

It was strange to hear him talk so breezily, when I considered how it had all ended. 'Not really. One bumps into people. You know how it is. They all married, then?' It seemed odd, suddenly, that I didn't know.

'Yes, for better or, in some cases, very much for worse. Candida's a widow. Her husband was killed in 9/11. But I'm told they were happy before that.'

Moments like this, when friends from a different era of your life are suddenly forcefully connected to the modern world, can be quite shocking. 'I'm sorry. Was he American?'

'English. But he worked for some bank that had its New York office on one of the top floors. It was his bad luck that he was summoned to a meeting there on that day.'

'God, how awful. Any children?'

'Two with him. But he couldn't be the father of the baby I'm interested in. The boy was eight when they married.'

'I remember she was a single mother. Very courageous.'

'For a peer's niece in 1971? You bet. But she *was* courageous. She was a bit rough but she was punchy. That's why I liked her.' He paused, a slight smile pulling at the corners of his mouth. 'Were there any names missing that you expected to find?'

We stared at each other. 'Not when the list isn't complete.'

'What do you mean?'

'It's only the girls who gave birth within the time limit.'

Damian nodded. 'Of course. That's right. No, in any other sense it's not complete.' But he didn't elaborate and I so didn't want him to. 'You got the card?'

'Yes. Though I don't think I'll need it.'

'Please don't be English and silly.' He sighed. 'You have no money. I have so much that if I spent a million pounds a day for the rest of my life I wouldn't dent it. Use the card. Have some fun. Do what you like with it. Take it as your payment. Or my thanks. Or my apology, if you must. But use it.'

'I don't have "no" money,' I said. 'I just don't have as much money as you.' He did not trouble to confirm this and I did not protest further, so I must have been convinced.

'Do you have any preference as to where I should begin?' I asked.

He shook his head. 'None in the least. Start where you will.' He paused to take a breath. 'But please don't delay more than you have to.' His speech was coarser and more rasping than it had been the previous evening. Was this usual in the mornings? I wondered. Or is he getting worse? 'Of course, I don't want to hurry you,' he added. What made this poignant, even to me, was his striving to achieve a kind of light courtesy, like something out of a Rattigan comedy. 'Anyone for tennis?'

he might have said in just such a tone. Or, 'Who needs a lift to London?' It was brave. I don't deny that.

'I imagine it must take some time,' I said.

'Of course. But no more time, please, than it has to take.'

'Suppose I can't find any evidence either way?'

'Eliminate the ones it cannot be. Then we'll worry about who's left.'

There was logic in this and I nodded. 'I still don't know why I'm doing it.'

'Because if you refuse, you'll feel guilty when I die.'

'Guilty for the child, maybe. Not about you.' I wouldn't describe myself as a harsh person in the normal way of things, and I do not completely understand why I was so harsh with him on that morning. The crimes I held against him were old crimes by then, forgotten, or if not forgotten then irrelevant, even to me. That said, he seemed to understand.

My words had died away in the silence between us, when he looked at me quite steadily. 'I have never had a friend in all my life I cared for more than I cared for you,' he said.

'Then why did you do it?' He misjudged me if he thought these nice, saccharine sentiments would somehow cancel out the memory of his behaviour on the worst evening of my, and I would hope anyone's, life.

'I'm not entirely sure.' He seemed to lose himself in thought for a while, concentrating his gaze on the view beyond the windows. 'I think I have suffered since I was a child from a kind of claustrophobia of the heart.' He smiled. 'The truth is I was always uncomfortable with any kind of love. Most of all when I was the recipient.'

Which is how we left it.

It may sound as if I had been obsessed with all these people, and mainly with Damian, since I had walked off the last dance floor over forty years before, but I had not. Like anyone else, I'd spent the time between dealing with the bewildering illogicality of my life and it had been many years since I had taken the time to consider the way I was, the way we all were. The world we lived in then was a different planet, with different hopes and very different expectations and, like other planets, it had simply drifted away in its own orbit. I glimpsed a few of the girls, now lined and greying matrons, from time to time, at a wedding or a charity function, and we smiled and talked of their children and why they'd left Fulham, and whether Shropshire had proved a success, but we did not tear at the changes in the world around us. I had abandoned that world completely in the years immediately after Portugal and, even after it was all forgotten, I never really went back in. Now, when I thought about it, there were some characters from that time I regretted. Lucy Dalton, for example, had been a great ally of mine. Indeed, it was she who sealed my commitment to the Season. I didn't like her husband, it is true, and I suppose that's why we drifted apart, but now that seemed a feeble reason to lose a friend and I decided on the spot to begin my investigations with her. The sheet told me she had moved to Kent, not far from Tunbridge Wells, so it would not be difficult to call her and ask myself for lunch, on the pretext of being 'in the area.'

I say my commitment had been 'sealed' by Lucy for the simple reason that it was at her invitation I attended Queen Charlotte's Ball, then the official launch of the dances and the central ceremony of the whole business. Not to be there meant one was not quite a full player but I had made no plans to go since I had not originally aimed at full membership. In fact, the ball wasn't far off when, to my surprise, I received a card from Lady Dalton asking me to join their party. I rang her daughter before I answered. 'We were taking my cousin, Hugo Grex, but he's chucked,' said Lucy without any prevarication. 'Don't worry if you can't come, but say now so we can find someone else. Almost everyone who wants to is already going.' It was not the most flattering invitation known to man but I was quite curious and I had begun to feel that, when it came to the Season proper, if I was going to do it I might as well *do it*.

'No. I'd like to come. Thank you.'

'Write to Mummy or she'll think you're odd. Then she'll tell you where to be and when. You know it's white tie?'

'Absolutely.'

'See you then if not before.' She had rung off.

Perhaps because I had not originally intended to be at the ball it came as something of a revelation later that day, to discover that Damian Baxter was already going. In those days students at Magdalene, and in many other colleges no doubt, were not provided with anything so simple as a bedsit. Instead, every student had a sitting room as well as a bedroom, which required a certain spread in the accommodation. That year my rooms were to be found in an old converted cottage, which had been swallowed by the new 1950s quadrangle built round it on the other side of Magdalene Street from the college itself. They were rather charming apartments and I still remember them with affection, but they were in separate parts of the building, so it was a surprise to walk back into the sitting room, having gone to my bedroom for a book, to find Damian standing by the chimneypiece, warming his legs in front of the gurgling gas fire. 'I gather you're going to Queen Charlotte's with the Daltons,' he said. 'I don't suppose there's any chance you could put me up? I really don't want to struggle back here after that one.'

'How do you know?'

'Lucy told me. I said I was in the Waddilove party, so she told me she was going to ring you. I'm rather jealous.' Now, there was a good deal of information in this statement. More, possibly, than he knew. But then again, perhaps not. Clearly, he had been determined to go to the ball and knowing and I am sure nursing the captive Georgina's crush on him, he had seen that as a route. But what he was also telling me was that he had been Lucy's first choice as a replacement when her cousin had dropped out. I was only the fallback, and he wanted me to know it.

'You never said you were going.'

'You never asked.' He pulled a slight grimace. 'Georgina Waddilove. Yikes.' We shared a smile, which was shamefully disloyal on my part. 'Where are you hiring your white tie?'

'I've got my own,' I said. 'Inherited from a cousin. I think it still fits. Or it did when I went to a hunt ball last Christmas.'

He nodded a little grumpily. 'Of course you've got your own. I wasn't thinking.' The mood had altered slightly. He sipped the sour white wine I had provided him with. 'I don't know why I'm going, really.'

'Why *are* you going?' I was genuinely curious.

He thought for a moment. 'Because I can,' he said.

The history of costume is, as we know, a fascinating subject in itself and I find it interesting that I will almost certainly live to see the death of one outfit, at least, that was significant enough in its heyday, namely White Tie. From early in the nineteenth century, thanks to Mr Brummell, until the middle of the twentieth, it was the male costume of choice for any Society evening, the club colours of the British aristocracy. When, in the late 1920s, the Duke of Rutland was asked by his brother-in-law if he *ever* wore a dinner jacket he thought for a moment. 'When I dine alone with the Duchess in her bedroom,' he replied.

Of course, it was a surprise to some that it survived the war, since six years of dinner jackets and uniforms might have killed it off, but Christian Dior's revival of an almost Edwardian style of dress, with his bustles and corsets and paddings and linings, had launched a fashion for sumptuous evening clothes that made the short, dull dinner jacket seem quite inadequate as a pair. Then, in the summer of 1950, the Countess of Leicester gave a ball for her daughter, Lady Anne Coke, at Holkham, which was attended by the King and Queen. The following morning yielded two discoveries. The first was a waiter who had fallen into the fountain and drowned, the second that white tie for men was definitely back. Of course, what Dior and so many others failed to understand was that white tie was not just a costume, it was also a way of life, and it was a way of life that was already dead. White tie belonged to the ancient bargain between the aristocrat and those less fortunate that they would spend much of their day in discomfort in order to promote a convincing and reassuring image of power. After all, splendour and glamour had been inextricably linked to power for centuries, until the comparatively recent appearance of Government by the Drab. Before the first war, among the upper classes, five or six changes a day, for walking, shooting, breakfast, lunch, tea and dinner, were *de rigueur* at any house party and three at least were necessary for a day in London. They observed these tiresome rituals of dress for the simple reason that they knew once they stopped looking like a ruling class they would soon cease to *be* a ruling class. Our politicians have only just learned what the toffs have known for a thousand years: Appearance is all.

Why, then, did it die so suddenly? Because they stopped believing in themselves. It was not just the loss of the valet that was to prove fatal to the costume; it was a loss of nerve that gripped the Establishment in 1945, and would continue to undermine their confidence until, by the end of the Seventies, for all but a few their role in our National life, and with it the point of their white tie, was gone. My generation saw the last of it. When I was eighteen, all hunt balls were still white tie, as well as all the May balls at Cambridge and the Commem Balls at Oxford. A few coming-out parties still tried for it and one event where it was worn without dispute was Queen Charlotte's Ball. Now, when, apart from a state banquet at Buckingham Palace or Windsor, or something rich and rare at one of the Inns of Court, it has almost vanished, it seems strange to think that forty years ago we still got enough use out of our tails for it to be worth owning them.

Queen Charlotte's Ball was not a private party. It was a large-scale charitable event and, as such, did not conform to the normal rules. To start with, it was what was then called a dinner-dance, meaning that we were to eat there and so we would assemble much earlier than usual. Dinner-dances, in those pre-breathaliser days were thought by some to be rather common, I forget now why, perhaps because they had an air of a night out 'at the club' in some Imperial outpost, but on this particular evening there was a ceremony to be got through that was considered sufficient to justify it. The plan was to gather at the Daltons' London flat in Queensgate, to make sure that the group was all present and correct, and then to move on to Grosvenor House almost immediately.

I rang the bell at the Daltons' front door, the buzzer (for we already had those) admitted me and I knew their flat was on the ground floor, so there was no long climb ahead. The front door must once have been the door into the dining room, when the newly built house had been home to a prosperous late-Victorian family, but by the 1960s that dining room had been carved up into an entrance hall and a medium-sized drawing room. A few good things, as is the wont of such families, had been spared for the flat, in case we might mistake their rank, and what looked like a Lazlo of Lucy's grandmother, painted as a girl of nineteen, stared down glassily from above the chimneypiece, which, owing to the division of the room, was awkwardly off centre. The oddness of proportion was enhanced by the fashion, then prevalent, for blocking grates with large flat sheets of hardboard, often, as in this case, with an electric fire placed in front. I cannot think of any vogue in my entire life more guaranteed to kill a room stone dead than this blanking of the fireplace, but we all did it. Like the hideous enclosing of banisters on a staircase, which one found in almost every house divided into flats, it was supposed to make the space look modern and streamlined. It failed.

'There you are.' Lucy kissed me briskly. 'Are you dreading it?' There were four other girls in the room and, counting Lucy, all five were dressed entirely in white, a survival of the custom of wearing white for a girl's first presentation at Court before the war. It had not, of course, been continued in the last period of Royal Presentation, which had taken the form of garden parties, and the girls would then wear pretty, summer dresses and wide-brimmed hats, but with the end of that and the installation of Queen Charlotte's as the official start of the Season, the white rule had been revived. They wore long, white gloves, too, but instead of the Prince of Wales feathers that decorate the heads of both mothers and daughters in all those pre-war photographs by Van Dyck or Lenare, this year, at least, white flowers were worn in the hair, tiaras not being considered proper for unmarried girls. Lady Dalton, I was pleased to see, sported rather a good one, which flashed its fire round the room as she walked towards me, smiling pleasantly.

'You are kind to come,' she said, holding out her own gloved hand.

'You're very kind to ask me.'

'Lord knows what we'd have done if you'd said no,' added a bluff, soldier type, whom I took, correctly, to be Sir Marmaduke. 'Flag down a bus and just collar someone, I suppose.' One often suspects that a late invitation signifies that a certain scraping of the barrel has gone on. But it is a little depressing to be told it.

'Pay no attention,' said his wife firmly and led me away to where the other young stood. The party was more of an age mixture than usual as most of the mothers and fathers of the girls, if not the boys, were to be with us for the evening, so I met a couple of pleasant enough bankers and their wives, together with a rather pretty, Italian woman, Mrs Wakefield, married to Lady Dalton's cousin, who'd come up from Shropshire to begin the launch of her youngest daughter, Carla. We moved on to the girls themselves. Among them was a plain and russet-faced character, Candida Finch, whom I'd already met. To be honest, I had found her a bit uphill, but we were programmed in those days to make conversation with anybody nearby and so I fell into the small talk demanded of me without much hardship, naming mutual acquaintances, reminding her that we had both been at this drinks party and that one, although we had never spoken more than a few words to each other before now. She nodded and answered, civilly enough but, as always with her, too loudly, too aggressively and, every now and then, with a sudden, stentorian laugh that made you jump out of your skin. Of course, now I can see that she was very angry at what had happened to her life, but one can be so blind and so heartless in youth. I looked at the grown ups sipping their cocktails at the other end of the room.

'Is your mother here?'

She shook her head. 'My mother's dead. She died when I was a child.' This was, of course, rather more than I had bargained for and her voice, as she said it, was raw. I muttered vaguely about being sorry and how I must have muddled her with someone else as I thought I'd seen a photograph of them together in a magazine. This time she spoke with considerably more authority. 'You mean my *step*mother. No. She is not here. *Thank God.*' There was no mistaking the tone and the expletive at the end was presumably intended to bring me, and anyone standing near us, up to date with the way things were between them. I wonder sometimes why people can be so anxious to share their unsatisfactory domestic situation with strangers. It must be because it is often the only arena where they have the power to say what they think of the people concerned and there is some satisfaction in that. Anyway, I grasped the situation. It was not, after all, a very unusual one.

As I later learned, Candida's was a sad story. Her mother had been the sister of Serena Gresham's mother, Lady Claremont, making the girls first cousins, but Mrs Finch had died in her thirties, I don't think I ever knew what of, and her widowed husband, already rather looked down on in the family, had proceeded, once his tears were dry, to make what was referred to as an 'unfortunate' marriage to a former estate agent from Godalming, saddling Candida with an unhelpful step-mother, whom incidentally she detested, and the Claremonts with a nearly-sister-in-law from hell. To make matters worse, when the girl was in her early teens, the father, Mr Finch, had also died, of a heart attack this time, leaving Candida entirely in the clutches of his widow, to whom he had left every penny of what remained of his fortune, as well as custody of his daughter. At this point her aunt, Lady Claremont, had stepped in and tried to take the reins. But Mrs Finch from Godalming was no pushover. She was deaf to any advice on schooling and it was only with the greatest difficulty that her permission had been gained for Candida to do the Season, for which, so one gathered, Lady Claremont was footing the bill. Obviously, all this placed the girl in an invidious position, which one might have sympathised with more, had it not been reflected in her loud and awkward manner. Nor was she helped by her appearance, with her dark, unruly, frizzy hair somehow compounding the complexion of a navvy. She had freckles, too, and a nose straight out of Pinocchio. All in all, Candida Finch had been dealt a tough hand.

'Right. Time to leave, everyone.' Lady Dalton clapped her hands firmly. 'How are we going? Who's got a car?' Some of the fathers drained their double martinis and held up their hands.

One detail of the different world I once inhabited that is not often referred to, but which affected every minute of almost every day, was the traffic. That is to say, there wasn't any. Or none to compare with today's. The cars one encounters now midmorning on a normal weekday in London would only have been seen at six o'clock on a Friday night in late December, as people were leaving town for Christmas. The whole business of parking being impossible simply hadn't started. The time you allowed for a journey was the time it would take. London, or the London most of us occupied, was still small and it was rare that one left more than ten minutes before any appointment. In terms of the general stress of being alive, I cannot tell you what a difference it made.

Another contrast with today concerned the area we lived in. To start with, in London, the upper middle, and upper classes had not yet strayed from their traditional nesting grounds of Belgravia, Mayfair and Kensington – or Chelsea, if they were a bit wild. I remember my mother driving me past a very pretty Georgian terrace on the Fulham Road, before one gets to the football ground. I admired the houses and she nodded. 'They're charming,' she said. 'It's such a pity no one could ever live here.' And if Fulham was outside the pale, Clapham, or worse, Wandsworth, had no hold in their lives or on their mental map whatever, other than as the place where their daily lived, or where one might get glass cut or rugs mended or find a cheaper saleroom. This would soon change when my own generation started to marry and the gentrification of the south bank of the Thames would begin. But in the late Sixties it had not quite happened yet. I remember distinctly driving with my parents to have dinner with some impoverished friends of theirs, who, *faute de mieux*, had bought a house in Battersea, just at the dawn of the new era. As my mother carefully read the scribbled directions to my father at the wheel and the location of our destination became ever clearer, she looked up from the paper. 'Have they lost their minds?' she said.

One must remember that, until the middle Sixties at any rate, there was fairly cheap housing to be found in any part of the city, so there was no pressing need to move out. One might not occupy a palace but that didn't mean one couldn't stick around. We lived at one time on the corner of Hereford Square and, behind the west side, if you can believe it, lay a small field where someone kept a pony. In the corner of this was a cottage, probably originally part of some stabling arrangement, and in my mid-Fifties childhood it was lived in by a not-very-successful actor and his potter-wife. They were delightful and we saw a lot of them but they must have been as poor as church mice. Still, there they were, living in a cottage on the corner of a fashionable square. The next time I entered that building was thirty years later. It had been rented by a Hollywood star who was shooting a movie at Pinewood. Recently it retailed for seven million. The result of the property boom was not just the dispersal of people from their home territory, but the end of the 'mix' in London's population. Struggling painters and penniless writers no longer live in the mews cottages in Knightsbridge or behind Wilton Crescent, where they would once rub shoulders with countesses and millionaires in the local shops and post office. Teachers and poets and professors and explorers and seamstresses and political subversives have all been driven away. They have been replaced by bankers. And we are the poorer for it.

The Great Room at Grosvenor House was an appropriate setting for the formal opening race of the Season. It twinkled with that now distinctive, self-important, 1960s, sub-deco glamour, so memorably christened 'Euro-Splendour' by Stephen Poliakoff. One came through the hall of the hotel on to a kind of gallery, where a wide, aluminiumbalustered staircase within the room itself led down towards the gleaming floor below. At the sight of it I was suddenly glad that I had come. It was early June, and a warm night, too warm for the boys' comfort, really, as our tails in those days were made from woollen cloth, but there is something about a party on a warm summer night that always seems to promise much. Usually more than it delivers.

Some years later, before the end of it all, the Season would have to take account of the exam year and cater for career girls sitting their A levels and the like, but not then. For such a consideration to have been raised by anyone in 1968 would have been regarded as quirky, eccentric and very middle class. Looking back, I realise there was hardly a parent there who thought their daughters' future would be anything more than an extended repeat of their own present. How can they have been so secure in their expectations? Didn't it occur to them that more change might be on its way? After all, their generation had lived through enough of it to push the world off its axis.

I stood for a moment against the balustrade. There was something very seductive about looking down from above on a ballroom apparently filled with flower-decked swans. At that moment, whatever the rights and wrongs of the ritual, I confess I was happy to be part of it, as Lucy and I descended together, smiling and nodding in the way one does. From across the room, Serena gave me a slight wave, which was gratifying. 'Whose table is she on?' I asked.

Lucy followed my gaze. She did not need to be told whom we were discussing. 'Her mother's. She's the one in blue. The couple talking at the end look like the Marlboroughs and I'm pretty sure the fat one next to Lord Claremont is a princess of Denmark. I seem to remember she's one of Serena's godmothers.' I decided not to push in.

Lucy stopped. 'There's your friend, making hay while the sun shines.' A few yards ahead of us Damian was joking merrily with Joanna Langley.

I wasn't going to let her get away with that. 'Your friend, too, I gather,' I said sharply, which earned me an apologetic glance.

Watching the gossiping couple, somewhat sourly, was the tragic figure of Georgina Waddilove. Pitiful Georgina. The style that was so becoming to almost all the others did not show her to much advantage and she resembled nothing more than an enormous, white *blancmange*.

The flowers sewn on to a mountain of artificial ringlets battened to her head looked like scraps of torn paper caught in a tree. I walked up to where Damian was standing. 'Have you brought your stuff here?'

Damian nodded. 'It's all in the cloakroom.' He smiled at Joanna. 'He's putting me up for the night.'

'Don't your parents have a place in London?' By such questions Joanna would occasionally give herself away. At least she would signify that she was not a founder member of this set-up. I am confident, even at this distance, that there was no malice in her, far from it, but she had not learned to spare someone's feelings by avoiding any subject that might prove delicate. This was partly because, despite her great expectations, she was not really interested in money. If the reason Damian's parents did not have a London home was because they could not afford one, she would not have thought any the less of them for that. Which is to say she was possessed of a larger generosity of spirit than most of us. Damian, as usual, was unfazed.

'No, they haven't,' he said, without further qualification. I had not yet noticed it in him, but he never gave out any information about himself unless asked a direct question. Even then it was carefully rationed.

'I think we'd better sit down.' Georgina had clearly had just about enough of Damian's being cornered by Miss Langley, as she would have put it.

I smiled at the object of her irritation. 'Are you in this party?'

'With *my* mother? Of course not.' Joanna shook her head, laughing, and I found myself watching the movement of her lips. To me, her beauty had a mesmerising perfection, as if one were standing close to a celluloid icon projected on to an invisible screen. 'You don't think she would have missed out on the chance of hosting a dinner of her own?' She nodded at a point further up the room and I could see an eager, bustling, little woman, wearing a good deal of jewellery, who was staring anxiously in our direction. 'Better go.' She sauntered away.

'I suppose you're going, too,' said Damian, 'Think of me.' The last was added in an annoying half-whisper, just audible enough for Georgina to have caught it, although I am not sure that she did.

'You didn't have to be in this group. You could have had my seat if you hadn't taken the first offer.' I made no attempt to prevent Lucy hearing this, nor had I intended to, so Damian was able to direct his answer at her.

'To quote Madame Greffulhe: "*Que j'ai jamais su.*"' Lucy laughed. But by now people really were starting to sit down, and so we set out on the journey back to her mother's table.

'Who's Madame What-Not?' I asked.

'Marcel Proust used to go to her parties, when he was young. Years later, they asked her what it was like having such a genius in her salon, and she replied: "*Que j'ai jamais su!*"'

'If only I'd known.'

'Precisely.'

I was silent, wondering how Damian knew these things. How did he know Lucy knew them? I learned later it was one of his gifts. Like a squirrel, he would seek out and store any unlikely tidbit, in this case the startling news that Lucy Dalton read Proust, and he would save it for a time when it could be used to create an instant, magic bond that would exclude the others present, making him and whoever his target might be into a cosy club of two. I have seen the trick employed by others, but seldom to such effect. He never misjudged the moment. Lucy smiled. 'Please don't tell me you're surprised.'

'I am a bit.' I looked around at the chattering, giggling throng, pulling their chairs up to the tables with their shining, white cloths. 'I doubt that most of this lot read Proust.'

'If they did, they wouldn't tell you. The men here will exaggerate what they know. The women will conceal it.' I hope these words would not be true now, but I'm afraid they were true then.

She enjoyed my wrong-footed silence, until I was the one to break it. 'I thought you didn't like him,' I said, which seemed a non sequitur, but wasn't.

She shrugged. 'I don't much. Who told you I'd asked him first?'

'He did. Why? Was it a secret?'

'No.' She looked at me. 'I'm sorry. I should have invited you before him. I must have assumed you'd already be going.'

I nodded genially. 'That's all right. Don't apologise. Why shouldn't you ask him first? He's much better looking than I am.' Which annoyed her as I intended that it should, but the opportunity for rebuttal was gone. We were back with their party and Lady Dalton was pointing us to our allotted chairs. I had been placed between Carla Wakefield and Candida.

During the first course I talked to Carla about whom we both knew and where we'd both studied, about our plans for the summer and the sports we enjoyed, until the half-eaten salmon was taken away and the inevitable chicken was brought in and I turned to my other neighbour. I could see at once that more of the same would not quite answer.

'You're very good at this, aren't you?' she said and, while it was not exactly voiced in a hostile manner, it wasn't all that friendly, either.

'Thank you,' I replied. She had not, of course, meant it as a compliment, but by taking it as one I hadn't left her any room for manoeuvre. She glowered at her plate. I tried a more honest approach. 'If you don't enjoy it, why are you doing it?' I asked.

She stared at me. 'Because my aunt arranged the whole thing before I was given a choice. Because she is the only relative I have who cares whether I live or die. Most of all, because I don't know what else to do.' As usual, when discussing her family arrangements she spoke with a kind of ill-repressed fury. 'My stepmother has had charge of me since I was fourteen, and as a result of her bizarre requirements when it comes to female instruction, I am uneducated, untrained and completely unequipped for any productive work. Now I am supposed to "make a life for myself," whatever that means. My cousin Serena tells me that things would improve if I knew more people in London. I do not dispute this – only these are not the sort of people I want to know more of.' With a dismissive snort she indicated the body of the room.

It did seem very hard to have lost both parents by the time she was eighteen, even if Oscar Wilde would have thought it careless. 'Where were you at school?'

'Cullingford Grange.'

I had vaguely heard of it. 'Isn't that in Hertfordshire?'

Candida nodded. 'It's the kind of place where they worry if you're reading too much, instead of being out in the nice fresh air.' She rolled her eyes at the strangeness of her stepmother's choices. 'I could recite the rules of hockey in my sleep, but unfortunately nothing was taught about literature, mathematics, history, art, politics or life.' I believed her because her account was only too familiar.

I think, I pray, I come from the last generation of the privileged to pay no attention to the education of their daughters. Even in 1968 there were women's colleges at Cambridge and Oxford, but they were, as a rule, filled with the daughters of the *bourgeois* intelligentsia. Posh girls were an oddity and indeed almost the only one I can remember from my own year left after one term to marry a man with a castle in Kent. There were exceptions, but these generally came from families who were known to cherish an eccentric tradition of educating their women, rather than from the run-of-the-mill squireachy. For the rest, parents would scrimp and save to send the boys to Eton or Winchester or Harrow, while their sisters were put into the charge of some alcoholic, Belgian countess, whose main instruction was not to bother the parents.

After leaving, a girl might spend a year at a finishing school where she could polish her languages and her skiing, then another year would pass in coming out, after which she would get a job arranging flowers in the boardroom or cooking lunches for directors or working for her father, until she had discovered Mr Right who, with any luck, would be the heir to Lord Right. And that would be that. Hopefully, the Hon. John Right would be right for Mummy and Daddy, too, since they, like their own parents, would expect to approve the choice. Our mothers may not have been pushed into their marriages in the Thirties and Forties, but they had certainly been kept out of any marriages their parents disapproved of. We all had stories of aunts and great-aunts who had been sent to study painting in Florence, or to live with a grandmother in Scotland, or to improve their French at some mountainous chateau in the Swiss Alps, to break them of a bad love habit and, lest those Barbara Cartland addicts think differently, usually it worked.

I do not mean to imply that all who followed this path were wretched. Lots of them were as happy as clams. They spent the early years of marriage in some part of London their mothers found unlikely, then, if they'd chosen well, they might move into the big house on their father-in-law's estate ('Fizzy and I were just *rattling around* and we thought it was time to let the kids have a go'). For some the father proved stubborn and wouldn't move out, and for most there wasn't a house to inherit, so the young couple would generally buy a cottage or a farmhouse or, if things were going *really* well in the City, a Queen Anne manor house in Gloucestershire or Oxfordshire or Suffolk. After that, he would shoot and complain about politics, they'd both ski and worry about the children, and she would work for charity, entertain and, if things were going *less* well in the City, sell artificial jewellery to her captive friends. Until the children grew up and it was time first to downsize and then to die. All of which, lest we forget and before we feel too sorry for them, was a lot better than scratching for a living in the dirt of the plains of Uzbekistan.

But where did it leave someone like Candida Finch? She was obviously clever but her appearance and her manner would not help to offset her lack of qualifications to say the least. Nor would I have thought there was any certainty of a husband coming up on the next lift. And there wouldn't be much money. What were her options? 'Do you know what you'd like to do?' I asked.

Again, she rolled her eyes in exasperation. 'What *can* I do?'

'I asked what would you *like* to do.'

This was enough to soften her a little. It was, after all, a genuine enquiry. 'I think I might have liked to work in publishing, but I have no degree. And before you suggest I take one now, we both know that won't happen. It's too late and I've missed it. I thought I might squeeze a few quid out of a godparent and push into a vanity publishing firm, but they'd have to accept they'd lose every penny, and all to buy me the right to talk about publishing at dinner parties. Which is the most I'd achieve.'

'Be careful you're not determined to fail in order to annoy your stepmother. It doesn't sound to me as if she'll care much either way.' I nearly didn't say this, since our very brief acquaintance did not at all justify it, but she laughed.

'Well, that's true anyway.' Her voice was warmer than it had been. 'You know, you really *are* quite good at this.'

When dinner was over, by some pre-arranged signal the white-clad debutantes slipped away, leaving the tables occupied only by the parents, the young men and the odd non-deb girl, glum and in colour. It was time for the ceremony that we had come for and while I would not pretend to the ecstasy of anticipation that gripped the mothers throughout the room, the rest of us were quite curious. First, an enormous cake, literally six or seven feet high, was wheeled out on to the centre of the dance floor. Next the Patroness of the Ball arose from her chair with sober grandeur and walked across to stand next to it. I seem to remember that this was always Lady Howard de Walden, but maybe I'm wrong, maybe it alternated with the Duchess of Somewhere. Either way, she was a heavyweight in the scales by which these things are weighed. I don't actually think the whole thing would have worked if she were not. As it was, her rigid upright posture and the confident dignity of a crowned monarch, which a lot of those women seemed to possess quite naturally then in contrast to so many of their daughters, gave the exercise a certain credibility even before it had begun. The band struck up and we looked towards the head of the staircase, where the Girls of the Year stood lined up in couples, side by side, poised, waiting. Then, slowly, they began to descend at a measured pace, as solemnly as if they were serving at a Pope's funeral.

Down they came, the lights playing on the white flowers among their gleaming curls, on their long white gloves, on the white lace and silk of their dresses, on their shining, haughty, hopeful faces. Once they had reached the bottom, each pair advanced to where the Patroness stood, dropped into a deep Court curtsey, and moved on. They were not all presented to absolute advantage. Georgina looked like Godzilla in a shroud as she lumbered down towards terra firma. But for most of them there was something almost ethereal in their uniformity. Sixty versions of the Angel of Mons coming down to ease the pain of those beneath.

It may, of course, be with the wisdom of hindsight, but I am fairly sure it was at that precise moment that I first became aware that what we were witnessing did not have long to live. That there would not be many more generations taking part in this performance or, indeed, anything like it. That our parents' dream of somehow rescuing enough of the old, pre-war world for their children to live in, was a chimera, that I was, in short, witnessing the start of the finish. Funnily enough, and you probably will not believe me, it was an impressive sight. Like all disciplined, synchronised movement, the procession was commanding in its execution, as on and on they came, pair after matched pair, gliding down, curtseying low, moving on. All before a giant cake. Yet it was not ridiculous. It probably sounds ridiculous in the telling. Absurd. Even laughable. I can only say that I was there and it was not.

The display was done. The girls were blooded, their status as this year's debutantes confirmed and it was time for the dancing to begin. To counter their former solemnity, the band now played a tune at the top of the hit parade of the day, *Simple Simon Says*, one of those rather exhausting songs, which is full of uninvited instructions for the listener, 'Put your hands on your head, shake them all about,' and so on, but, although almost definitively naff, it was quite a good icebreaker. Lucy was already dancing with one of the other men in the party, so I made the offer to Candida and we walked together on to the floor. 'Who's that man you were talking to, before dinner?' she asked. I did not need to follow her eye-line to know the answer.

'Damian Baxter,' I said. 'He's up at Cambridge with me.'

'You must introduce us.' It was at this moment that I first encountered a particularly terrifying part of Candida's repertoire. Whenever she spotted someone she thought attractive there would ensue a kind of manic, as she thought flirtatious, ritual rather like a Maori dance of welcome, where she would roll her eyes and snicker and rock back and forth with a kind of shouted laugh more suited to a thirsty bricklayer than a young girl coming out. In fairness, I suppose it must have achieved her immediate ends reasonably often, since there could be no doubt as to what was on offer and we were not spoiled for choice in those days, but I do not think, as a routine, it was ever very conducive to long-term commitment, and in fact earned Candida a reputation, by the end of the Season, of being something of a bicycle. I was never treated to this display head on, as she was not at all interested in me, but even for a witness from the stalls it was pretty unnerving.

Following her hungry glance, I looked back to where Damian was standing at the centre of a small but admiring crowd. Serena Gresham was there, laughing, with Carla Wakefield and a couple of girls I did not recognise. Georgina was hanging back in her usual position of resentful witness to the fun of others. I saw now that Andrew Summersby was one of the party and Mrs Waddilove was busily, but ineffectually, trying to draw him into conversation; or, more to the point, she was trying to involve him in a conversation with her own daughter. But neither would play due, I would imagine, to a complete lack of interest on both sides. A friend of mine from Atlanta always called this kind of social interchange 'Pumping Mud.' They were watched from the other side of the table by an older woman, presumably another of Mrs Waddilove's guests, but I did not recognise her. She was an odd specimen, even in that company. Her face was that of a snobbish, Dutch doll, while the weird combination of her unlikely near-black hair, more Benidorm than good old British, with a pair of piercing pale-blue eyes flecked with shades of green and amber, made her look more than slightly mad, half Lizzie Borden, half stoat. She stood very still as she listened to the conversation limping along, but her stillness held a kind of inner threat of danger, a beast of prey, motionless but waiting to spring. 'Who's that standing opposite Mrs Waddilove and Andrew Summersby?'

Candida tore her eyes away from feasting on Damian and glanced across. 'Lady Belton. Andrew's mother.' I nodded. I might have guessed since I could now see that his sister, Annabella Warren, was among the girls in the Waddilove group. I looked back at *Madame Mère*, as she stood surveying the troops. I had heard of Lady Belton but I had not seen her before that night. One glance was enough to endorse the truth of her reputation.

The Countess of Belton was not generally liked, probably because she was not at all likeable. She was stupid, snobbish to the point of dementia and inexplicably arrogant. Admittedly, she was not vain, nor was she extravagant, but she took this to such a degree that it ceased to be a virtue. In fact, that night she was dressed in what looked like the window display of a Sue Ryder shop in West Hartlepool. Later I would come to know and loathe her, but despite all this, in a funny way I cannot quite explain at this distance, she did have something. Perhaps her absolute refusal to bend to her own times gave her a sort of moral conviction. Certainly she stands out vividly in my memory among the mothers of that year, although I had not then met her beleaguered husband, who always seemed to find an excuse to stay away, and I had only chatted, and not much more, to Lord Summersby, the dull and lumpen eldest son and heir. But even without all this information I saw at once that Georgina's mother was too obvious and her ambition was not realistic.

Watching her flash her smiles between them all and attempt to ensnare her daughter's interest, Candida spoke my thoughts. 'Dream on, Mrs Waddilove.'

She was right. This was a hopeless fantasy. It was quite clear to the most casual observer that Lady Belton's prejudices would never favour a match with the likes of the Waddiloves, however happy she was to dine and drink through that night at their expense. She wouldn't have dreamed of it, even if the girl had been pretty. That is unless a sum of money had been involved that was roughly equivalent to the combined African National Debt. As for the boy, I already suspected he was incapable of independent thought, in which I would be proved right. But anyway, the sad truth is that Georgina was not the type to inspire reckless love.

We danced on. Like the well-mannered chap I was then, I partnered my hostess, Lady Dalton, a custom universally observed in those days but almost abandoned now. To me, there was always something faintly comic in the practice, as one steered these middle-aged women around the floor, she wishing it were a foxtrot, you longing for it to end, one's hand resting lightly on the stiffened stays that were usually detectable beneath the fabric of the evening gown, but, funny as I found it, I am not glad the tradition of dancing with one's friends' parents has gone. It made a kind of bridge between the generations in our increasingly fragmented society and I suspect we can use all the bridges that are going. 'Do you know what you're planning to do when you leave university?' she said genially, as we stumbled around in our unsyncopated way.

I shook my head. 'Not really. Not yet.'

'There isn't a preordained pattern to be followed?'

Again I answered in the negative. 'There's no estate to come, or family business to swallow me up.'

'What does your father do?' At the time, in the late 1960s, this question would have bordered on impertinence, since the smart English had not yet abandoned their pretence that one's professional activity was of minor, and then only personal, interest. But of course Lady Dalton was engaging in research.

'He's a diplomat. But the Foreign Office isn't looking for my type any more, even if I wanted to follow him.' Which was more or less true. Had I been an exceptional candidate it might have been different, but for the more regular intake the Foreign Office, always a kingdom of its own in Britain, had decided at some point in the sixties that the day of the gentleman ambassador was over, that henceforth the role must be downgraded socially in order, I imagine, to be taken more seriously by the post-war intelligentsia. Either that, or it was a way of shifting their political loyalties. Forty years later, the results of the policy have been mixed, especially since it has not been adopted by the rest of mainland Europe. The British ambassador these days is generally regarded as rather an oddball in the world's capitals, both by the international brigade and by the Society of whichever city they find themselves in. One would have thought this might have diminished our backstairs influence. But perhaps that was what they were after.

Lady Dalton nodded. 'It's going to be so *very* interesting, seeing which directions you all go in.' With that the music ended and I walked her back to the table. She was a nice woman and we were friendly for as long as our paths were to cross, but from that moment she had entirely lost interest in me.

Some time around one in the morning the band leader approached the microphone, instructing us to take our partners for the gallop, and by this sign we knew the evening was nearly done. As always, surveying the modern generation, it seems perfectly incredible that we, who were after all simultaneously participating in the swinging sixties, still ended a good many parties with this period romp, but we did. Unlike the Scottish reels that were also part of most of the parties, the gallop was only ever the last dance of the event and it was really just an excuse to show how drunk you were. You seized some luckless girl and raced back and forth across the floor, bumping around, vaguely in time to some loud, rum-ti-tum music, falling over, shouting and generally demonstrating that you were a very good sport. Needless to say there was a rather desperate quality to it, even a sort of lonely sadness, as one watched those shrieking girls up from the country, their ringlets collapsing, their dresses frequently torn, their make-up vanishing beneath a sheen of red jowls and sweat. At any rate for good or ill we, the merrymakers of 1968, danced it and with that, Queen Charlotte's Ball was over for another year.

My parents' flat was to be found on the ground floor of a tall house in Wetherby Gardens, a street that runs between South Kensington and Earl's Court. In those days this was roughly like passing from heaven into hell and it was an important detail to my mother that the flat was considerably nearer the former than the latter. Now, naturally, either end would command a price beyond rubies. Again, much like the Daltons' London home, the former dining room of the Victorian family for whom it was built had been carved into drawing room, hall and, in our case, kitchen. What had presumably been some sort of library had become a small, dark and rather poky place to eat in, and what must have been a charming morning room, overlooking the small garden attached to the flat and, beyond it, the very large communal garden shared by the block, had been split into two bedrooms, with some unsatisfactory jiggling of the paper wall to get one half of a double door and a reasonable proportion of window into each. Like so many of their generation, my parents were curiously accepting about their accommodation. When, later, in the Seventies and Eighties, we all started pulling down walls and moving bathrooms and converting attics, they watched in semi-horrified wonder, my father, particularly, believing that if God had wanted that shelf in a different place He would have arranged it and who was he to interfere with Providence? It's odd, really, when one thinks how their eighteenth- and nineteenth-century ancestors thought nothing of pulling down ancient family houses to build something more voguish in their place. Maybe it had something to do with rationing or making do during the war.

I was already in bed and asleep when I was summoned back to the surface by the repeated ringing of the doorbell. For a while this took the form of a church bell being rung, for some strange reason, by William Ewart Gladstone, but then I woke up and the ringing continued.

Damian was hugely apologetic. 'I'm so sorry. I should have asked for a key. Then I thought you'd probably be going on with the rest of us.'

'Where?'

He shrugged nonchalantly. 'Round and about. We looked into the Garrison for a drink and then we went to get a sandwich and a cup of coffee from that hut on the other side of Chelsea Bridge.' As it happens, we would do this quite often as the year wore on, boys and girls in evening dress, queuing at dawn behind the bikers for a bacon butty from the little wooden kiosk in the shadow of the great power station. They were nice people, those motorcycle men, and friendly as a rule, amused rather than affronted by our pampered appearance. I wish them well.

'Was that the end of it?'

Damian smiled. 'Not quite. We wound up at the Claremonts' house.'

'On Millionaire's Row.'

'Next to Kensington Palace.'

I nodded. 'That's the one,' I said. How cool and ordered he looked. He could have been about to go out, rather than coming in after what could only be described as a *long* night. 'You have been busy. How did you manage that?'

He shrugged again. 'Serena suggested it and I didn't see why not.'

'Did you wake up her parents?'

'Not the mother. Her dad came down and asked us not to make too much noise.' He looked round the drawing room vaguely.

'Would you like a drink?'

'Just one, maybe. If you'll join me.'

I poured out two glasses of whisky and water. 'Do you want any ice?'

'Not for me.' He was learning fast.

'What happened to Georgina? Was she with you?'

He could barely suppress a laugh. 'No, thank the Lord. We didn't even have to lie. They were dropping off Lady Belton and Andrew at their flat, and Mrs Waddilove wouldn't let Georgina escape.'

There was something slightly unsatisfactory in this. 'Poor Georgina. I'm afraid she's a bit in love with you.'

This time he did laugh. 'There are many who must carry that burden.' It seemed to me, in that moment, that to have this kind of self-confidence at the age we then were must be a kind of Paradise. He mistook the envy in my eyes for a trace of disapproval and hurried to reassure me. 'Come on. I chummed her to Queen Charlotte's. I'll always be friendly when we meet. You can't expect me to marry her because she was the first to ask me to her party.'

Which, of course, I could not and would not. 'Just be nice to her,' I said. Then I took him down the passage and showed him into what was usually my own, cramped bedroom. But my parents were in the country and I had chosen to sleep in theirs. 'Was it what you expected?' I asked, as we were about to close our respective doors. 'Or did you disapprove?'

'I don't know what I expected.' Damian thought for a moment. 'And I'm in no position to disapprove of anything.' He paused. 'One thing

I do notice and even perhaps envy.' I waited. 'You all belong to something, even if it's hard to define quite what. Contrary to myth, you don't necessarily all know each other and you certainly don't all like each other. But you do have some sort of group identity, which I don't share.'

'Perhaps you will.'

He shook his head. 'No, I won't. But I don't think I'd want to. Not for much longer, anyway. I have a suspicion that before we're finished I'll be the one who belongs to something. And you won't.'

Which, of course, is exactly what happened.

FOUR

I cannot tell you with any real exactitude whether it made me laugh or cry when I heard, late in 1970, that Lucy Dalton was going to marry Philip Rawnsley-Price. I do remember it came as something of a shock. It was not only his awkward and unsubtle courtship, of her and every other girl who would stop to listen, that made him so unsatisfactory a character. He was born unsatisfactory. He had one of those flat faces, like a carnival mask that had been dropped in the road and run over by a heavy lorry. His skin was sallow, verging on olive, but this did not, as it might have, give him an exotic quality. Rather, he resembled an ailing Mediterranean lift attendant, with round, moist eyes resting in a pool of wrinkles, two fried eggs in fat. After what seemed a very short engagement I was invited to the wedding and I went, but it was a restrained and slightly bewildering affair. Lady Dalton was not her usual, cheery self, as she kissed and handed us down the line, and while all the usual forms were observed – the ancient village church, the marquee on the lawn, the plates of unappetising nibbles, the rather good champagne – none of it seemed to be celebrated with much *brio*. Even the speeches were pretty formulaic, the only memorable bit being when Lucy's aged uncle forgot what he was doing and addressed us as 'fellow members,' though quite what he thought we were fellow members *of* was never revealed.

Obviously, all of the above became comprehensible when Lucy was delivered of a baby girl early the following year. I saw the couple for a bit after that, kitchen suppers with other girls like her and boys like me, but long before the *Sloane Ranger Handbook* had given that tribe a name and an identity. In my day they were just the girls in pearls and we were the chinless wonders. But I never thought much of Philip, even after the dancing was done and we had all begun to grow up a little. He was one of those who manage to combine almost total failure with breathtaking arrogance and in the end life gently separated us. Besides, they had enthusiastically embraced the Sixties (which, as we know, largely took place during the Seventies) and like many others had to find ways of dealing with the disappointment that set in once it had become clear that the Age of Aquarius was not going to happen after all. They moved out of London while Philip went through a series of jobs or, as he would put it, careers, the last of which, I now learned, was some sort of farm shop that he and Lucy had opened in Kent. By that stage catering, 'hospitality,' sportswear and, I think, a variation of property development had all played their part, so it was hard to feel optimistic in the long term and I was curious to learn if the number on the list still worked, when I rang her for the first time in, I should imagine, at least thirty years. But Lucy answered and, after our initial joshing, I explained that I was going to be in her neighbourhood the following week and I thought it would be fun to look in and catch up. There was a slight silence at the proposal. Then she spoke again. 'Of course. How lovely. What day were you thinking of?'

'Up to you. I'll fit my other stuff round whenever you're free.' Which was unfair of me, but I suspected that if I had been specific it would have been the one day she couldn't manage. This way there was no alternative but to give in gracefully.

'Don't expect much to eat. I'm no better in the kitchen than when we last met.'

'I just want to see where you live.'

'I'm flattered.' She didn't sound very flattered but even so, the Thursday after that, I found myself bowling through the Kent lanes on my way to Peckham Bush.

I followed the directions, through the centre and out the other side, until eventually I turned into a gap between two high hedges and drove down a bumpy track into a former farmyard. Large signs pointed me to a brightly lit shop and showed me to a car park with a surfeit of empty spaces, but the old, red-tiled farmhouse lay a little beyond this commercial centre, so I stopped outside that instead. I wasn't out of the car before Lucy emerged. 'Well, hello,' she said. We had not seen each other, as I have explained, for many years, and it is only by such long gaps that we can chart the cruelty of time as well as, in this case, disappointment.

Things were not always so for her. In what I now see was the restrained manner of the days of our youth, she had been a modest darling of the media in her way, an early 'It Girl,' a precursor of the celebrity culture that was soon to overwhelm us. The point was that, unlike most of the girls, she had embraced the trendy Swinging Sixties to quite a degree, if not so fiercely as to frighten the mothers. She wore miniskirts that were slightly shorter and eyeliner that was slightly blacker, and she would give quotes to make journalists laugh. She would praise 'those darling train robbers' or declare Che Guevara the world's sexiest martyr. Once she was asked for her happiest moment and she replied it was when P. J. Proby split his jeans which made a headline in the *Evening Standard*. It was soft rebellion, drawing-room subversion, an endorsement of every value that would destroy her kind, but done with a cheeky grin. It played well and raised her profile and, during the Season, there had been model shoots and photographs on those feature pages in the *Tatler*, that read today like a message from the Land that Time Forgot: 'This Year's Debs,' 'Fashions to Watch,' 'The Young Trend Setters,' and so on. Lord Lichfield asked to take her picture and was accepted, and I distinctly recall some now forgotten television 'personality' (a concept so new as to be barely dry) inviting her on to his show. She declined, of course, at the insistence of her mother, but even the request had given her a certain cachet.

Of all this fun and bubble there remained not a trace in the sad, tired face before me. She still wore her shoulder-length hair loose, but the bounce had gone, and it was lank, thin and greying. Her clothes, which had once been racy, were now just old: old jeans, old shirt, old scuffed shoes. They covered her nakedness and that was all. Even her make-up was no more than a tired acknowledgement that she was female. She nodded towards the house. 'Come in.'

After this beginning it was almost a relief to see that time had not converted her to domesticity. In fact, it looked as if a terrorist bomb had just exploded in the hall, blowing every possession of the family into a new and illogical place. There is a kind of messy house that cannot quite be explained by the laziness of the occupants; where a sort of anger, a protest against the values of the world, seems to be involved in its brand of farrago, and I would pay Lucy the compliment of thinking this was one of them. The whole place seemed to have been decorated in the very worst years of the 1970s, with bold, depressing designs in brown and orange, framed posters of over-praised films and a good deal of cane and Indian weave. The kitchen was predictably pine-slatted with terracotta, tiled surfaces, the grouting blackened with filth. Its walls were lined with lots of shelves supporting a jumble of non-matching mugs, pictures of the children, ornaments won at long-ago fairs, pages of magazines torn out for some lost reason. And dirt. Lucy looked around, seeing it all with fresh eyes, as one does when a stranger arrives. 'Jesus. I'm afraid we're in rather a pickle. Let me give you a drink and we'll get out of here.' She fished about in the large refrigerator, found a huge, half-empty bottle of Pinot Grigio and, grabbing two cloudy, furry-looking glasses from beneath the sink, led the way into what must have been the parlour of the farmer's wife who lived here once, so tidily, before the world turned upside down.

If anything, the drab, disintegrating chaos was even more dispiriting than in the other rooms I had passed through, with tired, crocheted rugs strewn over the lumpy, disconnected chairs and sofas, and a bookshelf made from planks of wood and bricks. Quite a nice portrait of a young woman in the 1890s hung skew-whiff above the chimneypiece, making an improbable status statement from another time and another place. Two invitations and a bill were jammed into its chipped frame. Lucy followed my eyes. 'My mother gave me that. She thought it might help make the room more normal.' She leant forward and straightened it.

'Who is it?'

'My great-grandmother, I think. I'm not sure.' For a second I thought of that earlier Lady Dalton, coming in from riding, dressing for luncheon, deadheading the roses. What would she make of her role in this dustbin?

'Where's Philip?'

'In the shop, I'm afraid. He really can't leave it. I'm going to give you some lunch, then we'll walk over together.' She sipped her wine.

'How's the shop going?' I grinned brightly. In fact, I could feel myself consciously trying to inject a perky quality into my speech, though whether I was attempting to cheer her up, or myself, I could not tell you.

'Oh, all right,' she smiled vaguely. 'I think.' Obviously yet another of Philip's ventures was about to bite the dust. 'The thing is, a shop ties one down so much. Before we started I thought it would be friends coming in all the time for a chat, and having cups of tea and baking cakes and things, but it isn't. One just stands there, hour after hour, talking to complete strangers who never know what they want. And by the time you pay for everything, you know, the stock and the people who help and so on, there's only about threepence left.' She pronounced 'threepence' in the old way: 'Thruppence.' For a moment, I felt quite nostalgic.

'What will you do if you pack it in?'

She shrugged. 'I'm not sure. Philip's got some idea about renting paintings to people.'

'What paintings? To which people?'

'I know,' she acknowledged my query disloyally. 'I don't understand it, either. He thinks there might be quite a lot of money in it, but I can't see how. Are you OK with pasta?'

I followed her back into the germ-rich kitchen and watched her take small bowls filled with leftover, dark, half-eaten things out of the fridge. She set about shuffling plates and banging saucepans together as she organised our feed. 'How's your mother?' I asked.

Lucy nodded ruminatively, as if somehow this question had already been the subject of a long consideration. 'Fine. Good.' She looked across at me. 'You know they sold Hurstwood?'

'No, I didn't. I'm sorry.'

She shook her head firmly from left to right. 'Don't be.' She wasn't having any of that. 'Best thing that could have happened.' Having rapped this out as severely as a Tsarist ukase to get the point of no regret across, she allowed herself to relax and elaborate. 'It was about four years ago and of course it was terribly boo-hoo when it was going on, but there was no alternative. Not when Daddy did the sums. And the bonus is that they're completely free now, for the first time in their lives. Johnny was never very interested in taking over, so it really is . . .' She hesitated, trying to find a word she had not already employed that would support her argument effectively. She failed. 'It's fine.'

86

This phenomenon, where the losers in a revolution try to demonstrate their support for, and approval of, the changes that have destroyed them, always fascinates me. I suppose it is an offshoot of the Stockholm Syndrome, where kidnap victims start to defend their captors. Certainly, we've seen and heard a lot of it over the past few decades, especially among those toffs who are determined to show they are not being left behind. 'We mustn't cling on to the past,' they say cheerily, 'we have to move with the times.' When the only movement possible for them, once all their values have been denigrated and destroyed, is down and out. 'Where are they living?' I asked.

'Quite near Cheyne Walk. They've got a flat in one of those blocks.'

'And Johnny and Diana? What happened to them?' I had got to know Lucy's brother and sister as the Season went on, not all that well, but enough to smile and kiss when we met.

'Johnny's got a restaurant. In Fulham. At least, he *had* a restaurant in Fulham. When I last spoke to him it sounded as if it was all going a bit off *piste*. But he'll be OK. He's always full of ideas.'

'Is he married?'

'Divorced. Two boys, but they live with his ex quite near Colchester, which is a bit trying. Mummy made a terrific effort at the beginning. But you know what it's like, it meant hours on the train for the kids and all they ever wanted to do when they got to her was go home. So she's slightly given up at the moment, but she says it'll be much easier when they've grown up a bit.' Lucy brought over the unappetising plates of yellow-grey pasta, smeared with what looked like the guts of a rabbit, and laid mine reverently before me. The world-weary bottle of Pinot Grigio was back in play.

'What was his wife like?' I lifted my fork without enthusiasm.

'Gerda? Rather dull, to be honest, but not horrible or anything. She wasn't someone you'd know. She's Swedish. They met at Glastonbury. I quite liked her, actually, and the whole split was very civilised. They just didn't have anything in common. She's married to a neurosurgeon now, which seems to be much more the ticket.'

'What about Diana?' I always thought Lucy's elder sister was the more beautiful of the two. She looked like a young Deborah Kerr and, unlike her more frenetic sibling, she had a sort of serenity unusual in someone of her age. We all thought of her as quite a catch and, to her mother's unfeigned delight, she'd been heavily involved with the heir to a borders earldom when I knew them, though I had heard since that this hadn't, in the end, come off. I noticed the question had penetrated Lucy's armour slightly and I understood before I was told that all was not well here either. Time, it seemed, had been unkind to all the Daltons. 'I'm afraid Diana's *not* too good just now. She's divorced as well, but hers was pretty grim.'

'I know she didn't marry Peter Berwick.'

'No. More's the pity, though I never thought I'd say it. He was always so stuck up and tedious when they were going out, but now, glimpsed across the chasm of the years, he seems like Paradise Lost. Her husband was American. You wouldn't know him either. Nor would I, if I didn't have to. They met in Los Angeles and he keeps promising to go back there, but he hasn't so far. Worse luck.'

I had a sudden, vivid memory of Diana Dalton laughing at a joke I had told her. We were next to each other in the dining room at Hurstwood, before going on to a ball somewhere nearby. She was drinking at the time and did a massive nose trick, right into the lap of the Lord Lieutenant, seated blamelessly on her other side. 'Did she have any children?'

'Two. But of course they're grown up now. One's in Australia and the other's working on a kibbutz near Tel Aviv. It's annoying because since she's been in the Priory the whole thing has landed on me and Mummy.'

One more sentence and I would have cried. Poor Lady Dalton. Poor Sir Marmaduke. What had they done to merit this annihilation by the furies? When I last saw them they were model representatives of the class that had run the Empire. They managed their estates, played their part in the county, frightened the village and generally did their duty. And I knew too well they had dreamed of a future for their children that would have consisted of much the same. Certainly their reveries bore no resemblance to what had actually come to pass. I thought of Lady Dalton at Queen Charlotte's, gently probing me about my prospects. What splendid marriages she had planned for her two daughters, pretty and funny and well-born as they were. Would it have damaged the universe if just one of her wishes had come true? Instead, in forty years the entire Dalton edifice, centuries in the building, had come crashing down into the street. Their money was gone, and what little was left would soon be gobbled up by a feckless son and a reckless son-in-law. That's if the Priory fees didn't drain the pot dry before then. And the crimes that merited this punishment? The parents had not understood how to manage the changes the years would bring, and the children, all three of them, had believed the siren song of the Sixties, and invested everything in the brave new world they were so mendaciously promised.

There was a noise at the door. 'Mum. Have you got it?' I looked up. A young woman of about twenty was standing there. She was tall and would have been quite good looking, had she not been encased in an angry mist, irritated and impatient, as if we were needlessly keeping her waiting. Not for the first time I was struck by the phenomenon, another by-product of the social revolution of the last four decades, whereby parents these days frequently belong to an entirely different social class from their children. Obviously, this was Lucy's daughter, but she spoke with a south London accent, harsh and unlovely in its delivery, and her plaited hair and rough clothes would have told a stranger of long, hard struggles on an under-supported housing estate, not weekends with her grandfather, the baronet. Having known Lucy at roughly the same age, I can testify that they could have come from different galaxies for all they shared. Why don't parents mind this? Or don't they notice it? Isn't the desire to bring up your young with the habits and customs of your own tribe one of the most fundamental imperatives in the animal kingdom? Nor is this restricted to any one part of our society. Everywhere in modern Britain parents are raising cuckoos, aliens from a foreign place.

The newcomer paid no attention to me. She was obviously solely concerned in obtaining an answer to her query. 'Did you get it, Mum?' The words hung sharply in the air.

Lucy nodded. 'I've got it. But they only had it in blue.'

'Oh, no.' I write 'Oh, no,' but, in truth, it was much nearer 'ow now.' She sounded like Eliza Doolittle before Higgins has taken her on. 'I wanted the pink one. I told you I wanted the pink one [i.e. Oi wan'ed ve pink wun].'

Lucy's even, patient tone never wavered throughout. 'They didn't have any left in pink, so I thought blue was better than nothing.'

'Well, you were wrong.' The girl flounced off, sighing and stamping her way upstairs.

Lucy looked at me. 'Do you have children?'

I shook my head. 'I never married.'

She laughed. 'Not quite the same thing these days.'

'Well, I haven't.'

'They drive you completely mad. But of course one couldn't do without them.'

I felt I could do without the recent exhibit pretty easily. 'How many have you got?'

'Three. Margaret's the oldest. She's thirty-seven and a farmer's wife. Then there's Richard, who's thirty and trying to get into the music business. And that one. Kitty. Our surprise.'

Needless to say, the eldest was the object of my special interest. 'And Margaret's marriage has turned out well?'

Lucy nodded. 'I think so. Her husband's not very exciting, to be honest, but nobody's perfect and he is quite ... steady. That seems to be what she wants.' Thank heaven for small mercies, I thought. 'They've got four children and she still runs her own business. I can't imagine how she manages, but she has sixty times as much energy as any of the rest of us.' An image of Damian hovered over the table.

'They're quite spaced out, then. The children.'

'Yes. Mad, really. Just when one thinks the days of bottle warmers and carting cots round the country are over they begin again. For twenty years, whenever we loaded the car for a weekend away, we looked like refugees trying to get out of Prague ahead of the Russians.' She laughed at the memory. 'Of course, I never meant to start quite so early, but when Margaret —' She broke off, her laugh tapering to a nervous little giggle.

'When Margaret what?'

Lucy gave me a shy glance. 'People don't mind these days so much, but she was already on the way when we got married.'

'I hate to shock you, but most of us had worked out that few healthy babies are born at five months.'

She acknowledged this with a nod. 'Of course. It's just one didn't talk about it then. It all got lost in the wash.' She thought for a moment, then looked up at me. 'Do you ever see anyone from those days? I mean, what brought on this sudden interest?'

I shrugged as nonchalantly as I could manage. 'I don't know. I looked at the map and saw I was passing your front door.'

'But whom do you keep up with?'

I shook my head. 'I'm in a different crowd now. I'm a writer. I get asked to publishers' parties and PEN quiz nights and the Bad Sex Awards. My days of making small talk with countesses from Shropshire are done.'

'Aren't everyone's?'

'I still shoot occasionally. When I'm asked. That's when some red-faced major comes staggering across the room and says "Weren't we at school together?" or "Didn't you come to my sister's dance?" I never get over it. I'm always shocked into silence that I could belong to the same generation as this boring, bibulous old fart.' She did not answer, sensing my evasion. 'I do run into some familiar faces occasionally. I saw Serena at a charity thing not long ago.'

This seemed to confirm an unraised issue. 'Yes, I thought you might have stayed in touch with Serena.'

'But I haven't. Not really.' She raised an eyebrow quizzically and so, to move things on, I volunteered: 'As a matter of fact I saw Damian Baxter quite recently. Do you remember him?'

The last question was redundant. She had changed colour. 'Of course I remember him. I was there, remember.'

I nodded. 'Of course you were.'

'Anyway, even without that nobody forgets the Heartbreaker of the Year.' This time her laugh had a slightly bitter twinge. 'I gather he's terribly rich now.'

'Terribly rich and terribly ill.'

Which sobered her up. 'I'm sorry. Is he going to be all right?'

'I don't think so.'

'Oh.' This information appeared to put her bitterness back into its cage, and she became more philosophical. 'It used to make me laugh to think how our mothers steered us away from him. Had they but known at the time, he was almost the only man we ever danced with who could have kept the show on the road. Did he marry?'

'Yes, but not for long and no one you'd know.'

She absorbed this. 'I was terribly keen on him.'

I found myself becoming rather irritated by my own apparent ignorance. 'You wouldn't have known it,' I said.

'That was only because you were starting to hate him by that stage. I'd never have dared tell you. Are you disappointed in me?'

'A bit. You always pretended to dislike him as much as I did. Even before. Even when he and I were friends.'

She passed easily over my contradiction. 'Well ...' Her voice had now progressed through philosophical to wistful. 'It was a long time ago.' Then, as if ashamed of her momentary retreat, she rallied. 'I'd have married him if he'd proposed.'

'What would your mother have said about that?'

'I wouldn't have cared what she said. In fact, at one point I thought I was going to have to force him.' This was accompanied by a little, indignant puff. I looked at her, waiting for an explanation. She smirked. 'When I started Margaret I wasn't *completely* sure whose she was.' Naturally, this almost made me cry out. Could I have scored a goal with the very first kick? It was with some difficulty that I kept quiet and let her finish her story. 'I wasn't really going out with Damian at that stage, but then there was a moment, one afternoon in Estoril.' She gave an embarrassed giggle. 'You were all on the terrace and I sneaked off, and ...' I suppose I must have looked disapproving in some way as she gave a little, comic snort. 'It was the Sixties ! Did we use the term "Wild Child"? Had it been invented by then? I can't remember. Anyway, I suppose I was one. It's funny, because Margaret is *much* the straightest of my children. The only one who's straight at all, really.'

This was a familiar situation to me. 'Our parents used to talk about the problem child in any family,' I said. 'Now, it seems to be more the norm to have one child who isn't a problem. If you're lucky.'

Lucy laughed. 'Well, that's Margaret in this house. It's odd, when you think of it, because we had quite a scare with her when she was little.'

'What sort of scare?'

'Heart. Which seems so cruel for a child, doesn't it? She developed something called familial hypercholesterolaemia.'

'Blimey.'

'I know. It was about a month before I even learned to say it.'

'It trips off your tongue now.'

'You know how it is. At the start you can't pronounce it and by the end you're qualified to open a clinic.' She vanished momentarily into that never quite forgotten, terrible episode in her life. 'Funny. I can almost laugh about it, but it was unbelievably ghastly at the time. It means you're making far too much cholesterol, which eventually gives you a heart attack and kills you. Of course, nowadays no sentence is complete without that word but then it was foreign and frightening. And apparently it had always been more or less a hundred per cent fatal. The first doctor who diagnosed it in Margaret, at some hospital in Stoke, thought it still was. So you can imagine what we went through.'

'What were you doing in Stoke?'

'I can't remember now. Oh, I think Philip had an idea of reviving a china factory. It didn't last long.' I'd had another glimpse of the tangled odyssey that was Philip's non-career. 'Anyway, my mother turned up and scooped us off to a specialist in Harley Street and the news improved.'

'So it was treatable by the time Margaret had it?'

She nodded, reliving her relief. 'Completely, thank God. But only just. Literally, it had all changed something like four years before. It took us ages to get over the shock. We were both in the grip of terror for months. I remember getting up one night and finding Philip bending over her cot and crying. We never talk about it now, but whenever I get cross with him I secretly think of that moment and forgive him.' She hesitated, contradicted inwardly by the Spirit of Honesty. 'Or I try to,' she added. I nodded. I could easily see why. The Philip who wept for his innocent child in a darkened nursery sounded not only much nicer but a thousand times more interesting than the ballroom show-off I had known. Lucy was still talking. 'What we couldn't understand was that we kept being told it was completely hereditary, but neither of us had any knowledge of its occurring in our families. We questioned our parents and so on, but there was no clue. Still, as I say, Mummy found us a wonderful doctor and once we'd nailed it properly it came right.' She paused. I would guess she didn't venture into this territory very often. 'I always think that Margaret's passion for normal, ordinary life was probably fostered by that early threat of losing it. Don't you agree?'

Obviously, this entire speech went straight to the heart of the case that had brought me to Kent, but before I could say another word I was aware of a presence in the door. 'Hello, stranger.' The battered, bloated figure of a man who bore only the slightest resemblance to the boy I had known as Philip Rawnsley-Price was standing there. In our salad days Philip had resembled a young and much better-looking, cheeky-chappy actor called Barry Evans, famous then for a film, *Round the Mulberry Bush*, in which he represented those of us who wanted to be trendy but didn't quite know how, a large group at any time, which ensured his popularity. Sadly, his stardom didn't last and the former actor was found dead in the company of an empty whisky bottle at the age of fifty-two, having spent the previous three years driving a taxi in Leicester. I seem to recall there was some pressure on the police to investigate the circumstances of Evans's death, involving, as they did, cut telephone wires and other peculiar details, which naturally gave his relatives concern, but the police could not be bothered. A decision that might, I imagine, have been different had the unfortunate Mr Evans died at the peak of his fame.

Looking at Philip, framed in the doorway, it was hard not to feel at that moment, that the fate which had engulfed him was almost as bad. He wore ancient, stained cords, scuffed loafers and an open-necked check shirt with a worn, frayed collar. Old clothes were obviously a family uniform. Like me, he had put on weight and his hair was thinning. Unlike me, he had developed the mottled red face of a drinker. More than anything it was the sagging, tired look about those poached-egg eyes, so characteristic of the born privileged who fail, that gave him away. He held out his hand with what he imagined to be a roguish grin. 'Good to see you, old chap. What brings you to this part of the forest?' He took hold of my fingers and gave them the ruthless, wince-making squeeze that such men use in a vain attempt to persuade you they are still in charge. Lucy, having waxed so lyrical about him, now seemed put out to be interrupted.

'What are you doing here? We were coming over as soon as we'd finished lunch. Who's in the shop?'

'Gwen.'

'*On her own?*' Her voice was sharp and admonitory. And it was directed to include me. It was obviously her deliberate intention to show me that her husband was an incompetent fool. One minute earlier we had been swept up in the moving pathos of the tear-drenched daddy, but now it was apparently necessary for Lucy to point out that things had not gone wrong in their lives because of *her*. On the face of it this behaviour was of course illogical and contradictory, but among these people it is not uncommon. Their marriage had clearly reached that stage where she, and probably he, could be generous and gallant about the other when they were apart, but the actual physical presence of their partner would set their teeth on edge. This emotional conundrum often occurs in a culture where divorce is still seen as essentially giving in. Even today, the upper and upper middle classes find personal unhappiness, at any rate the admission of it, tedious and ill-bred, and they must always talk in public, or to close friends for that matter, as if everything to do with their family situation were going tremendously well. Maintaining the legend is the preferred option for most of them, as long as nobody is in the room whose presence undermines the performance. They generally adhere to this, right up to the moment of blow-up. It can be quite odd for members of this social group, as their circle will often contain many couples who appear to be perfectly content, until a call out of the blue, or a scribbled line in a Christmas card, will suddenly announce the divorce.

Philip nodded in answer to her harsh interrogation. 'She can manage. Nobody's been in for more than an hour.' There was a kind of resigned hopelessness in this simple account of the state of his business. In the area of his professional activity Philip had lost the energy required by pretence. He could just about stand behind the counter, but to talk up his drudgery would have been too exhausting. He picked a spoon off the counter and started to feed himself out of the pasta pot. 'Lucy tells me you're a writer now? What have you written that I might have read?'

Naturally, this was a defensive attempt to diminish me and my activities, but I do not believe it was malicious. He suspected, rightly, that I was judging him, so he was showing that he reserved the right to judge me. Anyone of my kind and my generation who has chosen to make their living in the Arts will be familiar with this treatment. In our youth the careers we had decided on were considered completely mad, by our parents and by our friends, but as long as we were struggling our more sober contemporaries were happy to encourage and sympathise and even to feed us. The trouble came when we arty folk achieved any kind of success. Then the idea that we should be making money or, worse, making more money than our adult and sensible acquaintance, was akin to impertinence. They had chosen the boring route in order to be secure. To have achieved security but to have enjoyed jokes and larks along the way was nothing short of irresponsible and deserved to be punished. I smiled. 'Nothing, I should think. Since if you had read anything by me I have no doubt you would have made the connection.'

He raised his eyebrows at Lucy, comically signifying, presumably, that I was a touchy artist who must be humoured. 'Lucy's read some of your stuff. I gather she thinks very highly of it.'

I did not point out that this remark meant his earlier question had been entirely redundant. 'I'm glad.' My words fell into a silence and we sat for a moment. There was an inertia in the room and we all three felt it. This often happens when old friends get together after an interval of many years. Prior to the meeting they imagine that something explosive and fun will come out of it, but then they are usually faced by a lacklustre group, in late middle age, who have nothing much in common any more. For better or worse, the Rawnsley-Prices had negotiated their journey, I had travelled mine and now we were just three people in a very dirty kitchen who didn't know each other. Besides, I needed further information before my pilgrimage could be considered complete and I wasn't going to get it while Philip was with us. It was time to break up the group. 'Can I see the shop?' I said. There was a pause, with a sense of the unspoken in the air. I assume this was simply Philip's male need to present himself as my equal in terms of worldly success which, modest as mine has been, might prove hard when I had actually seen the business. Or maybe it was Lucy's sudden realisation that for the same reason I was not going to take away from our day spent together the idea that everything was going swimmingly. It is an unspoken ambition for most of us that our contemporaries should see us as successful, but in Lucy's case she was about to be denied it.

After a pause, Philip nodded. 'Of course.'

It will come as no surprise that the farm shop was a hopeless place. Fittingly, I suppose, it was housed in a former cattle shed, which had been converted quickly and with insufficient money. There was a cheery, if forced, optimism in the inevitable pine counters and shelves. Above them, brightly coloured cards in *faux*, red, giant handwriting proclaimed the scintillating array of produce on offer: '*Fresh* vegetables!' they shouted. '*Home made* Jams and Jellies!' But in that yawning, unpeopled space they took on a dismal, pathetic quality, like someone eating alone in a paper hat. The floor was cheap and the ceiling had not been properly finished and, as I could have predicted, the whole place was full of items no one in their right mind would ever want to buy. Not just tinned pâté made from wild boar or goose wings, but gadgets to prevent wine losing its flavour in the fridge and woolly things to wear inside your boots while fishing. Christmas stocking presents to be bought and given by someone who knows nothing about it. The meat counter looked particularly unattractive, even to a carnivore like me, and seemed actively to repel further investigation. A single customer was paying for a cauliflower. Other than that the place was deserted. We looked around in silence. 'The trouble is all these shopping malls –' Philip drawled the word in a bad, American accent, trying to convert his pain into a joke. 'They're building them every-where. It's impossible to match the prices without going broke.' I hesitated to mention that they seemed to be going broke anyway. 'We keep being told that everyone's environmentally conscious nowadays, that they care about where their food comes from, but . . .' He sighed. What might have been intended as an ironic shrug just turned into a sad sag of his shoulders. I freely confess I felt tremendously sorry for him in that moment. Whether or not I used to dislike him, I had after all known him for a very long time and I did not wish him ill.

It is a fact that in the brutal periods of history, what changes is not the cutting edge of every new market, or the ambition that drives a new factory owner or a new hostess, or a new conquest from the performing stage, or a new triumph in a political drawing room. All that is constant. It is the level of coasting that goes on behind the bright and harsh façade that is different. In a gentle era – and my youth was passed in a fairly gentle era – people of little ability could drift by in every class, at every level of society. Jobs were found for them. Homes were arranged. Someone's uncle sorted it out. Someone's mother put in a word. But when things get tough, when, as now, the prizes are bigger but the going is rougher, the weaklings are elbowed aside until they fall back and slip over the cliff. Unskilled workers or stupid landowners alike, they are crushed by a system they cannot master and find themselves ejected on to the roadside. Just such a one was Philip Rawnsley-Price. Subconsciously, he thought his *braggadocio* would carry him through, that he had the charm and the connections to make it work, however he might choose to live his life. Alas, his connections were the wrong connections and his charm was non-existent, and now he was in his late fifties there was no one left alive who cared much whether he swam or sank.

I had never taken to Philip when we were young, but I pitied him now. He had been defeated by our 'interesting times' and he would not rise again. A hand-to-mouth existence lay ahead, of inheriting a cottage from a cousin and trying to rent it out, of hoping he would be remembered when the last aunt bit the dust, of wondering if his children might manage a little something for him on a regular basis. That was what he had to look forward to and it was anyone's guess whether Lucy would hang around to share it. It rather depended on what alternatives presented themselves. All this we both knew as we shook hands awkwardly outside. 'Come back and see us again,' he said, knowing that I never would.

'I will,' I lied.

'Don't leave it so long the next time.' And he was gone, back to his vacant counters and his empty till.

Lucy followed me to the car. I stopped. 'Did you ever get to the bottom of Margaret's condition?' She looked at me, puzzled, for a moment. 'You said it was hereditary but there was no trace of it on either your side or Philip's.'

'That was the thing. Of course I had the most nerve-racking suspicions. I kept thinking I ought to be poring through Damian's medical records . . .'

'But you didn't.'

'No. I was about to confess and suggest it, with a sinking heart as you can imagine, when we found out that Philip's aunt, his mother's eldest sister, had died of it, the very same thing, in childhood. And his mother never knew. Nor did either of her siblings. You can imagine how it was in those days.' She gave a little grimace. 'They were all just told that our Father in heaven had taken their sister because he loved her. Basta.'

'How did you find out?'

'Total luck. My ma-in-law was talking to *her* mother, who must have been about a million by then, and for some strange reason she told her all about Margaret. We'd never explained to Granny what was wrong, because we didn't want to worry her. At any rate this time she finally learned the truth, and right away she started weeping like a fire hydrant and it all came pouring out.'

'Poor woman.'

'Yes. Poor old thing. Of course she blamed herself and it more or less finished her off. We all told her that it wasn't her fault, that it wasn't a killer any more and so on, but I don't think it made much difference.' She smiled sadly. 'So the mystery was solved. The tragic thing was that the aunt could so easily have been saved with the right drugs but it happened in the twenties, when it was a question of hot drinks and cold compresses and having your tonsils out on the kitchen table. Anyway, as I say, Margaret's been fine ever since.'

'Were you at all sorry?'

This time she was genuinely bewildered. 'About what?'

'That she was definitely Philip's and not Damian's.' This was unkind of me, since it would hardly help her to dwell on heaven, trapped, as she was, in an outer circle of hell.

But Lucy only smiled and, just for a second, the minxish child-woman she had once been, looked out from behind her wrinkles. 'I'm not sure. Not at the time, because the whole drama had been explained and that was *such* a relief. Later, maybe. A little. But please don't give me away.'

We'd kissed and I was back in the car, when she tapped on the window. 'If you see him . . .'

I waited. 'Yes?'

'Tell him I remember him. Wish him luck for the future.'

'That's the point. I don't think he's got a future. Not a very long one, anyway.'

This made her silent and, to my amazement, I thought for a second

99

she was going to cry. At last she spoke again, with a softer and more gentle voice than I had heard from her since my arrival. Or indeed, ever. 'All the more so, then. Give him my best love. And say that I wish him nothing but good things. Nothing but good, good things.' She stepped back from the vehicle and I nodded. Her simple encomium spoke more for Damian's treatment of her than I would have credited him with.

The interview was over. I put my foot on the accelerator and started on the road back to London.

Dagmar

FIVE

Her Royal Highness Princess Dagmar of Moravia, despite her name, was a mousy, timid, little character. She had an apologetic, poignant manner, as if she were aware of always being disappointing, which I am sorry to say was usually true where we were concerned, because we all wanted to like her more than we did. You will probably not believe me, or put it down to excessive snobbery on my part, but the tiny Princess and her enormous mother, the Grand Duchess, were immensely impressive to us all in those dim and distant days. Nobody could believe more firmly than I in the miracle of constitutional monarchy, but the years of constant exposure in every branch of the media has inevitably resulted in a certain devaluation of Royal blood, as the public came to realise that for the most part these men and women, often pleasant, sometimes intelligent, occasionally physically attractive, are no more remarkable than any other person one might stand behind at the grocer's or the bank. Only Her Majesty, by never being interviewed, by never revealing an opinion, has retained a genuine mystery. Of course, we the public love to conjecture what her response to something might be. 'She must hate this,' we say. Or 'How pleased she will be about that.' But we do not know and it is our own ignorance that fascinates us.

If you can imagine it, forty years ago, we had that fascination for virtually anyone with genuine Royal blood in their veins. I don't just mean snobs. Everyone. Because we knew nothing, we wondered about everything and the glamour Royals brought into a social gathering is quite unparalleled today. No film star at the peak of her success can confer anything like the excitement of finding Princess Margaret among the dancers in a ballroom in the Fifties or Sixties. Or at a cocktail party, to walk in and discover a ducal cousin of the Queen chatting in the corner was to know that *this* was the place to be tonight. In my own youth, in 1961 to be exact, my school once bussed all the boys, plus thirty musical instruments, for a bumpy hour across Yorkshire so that we could solemnly stand on the grass verge at the side of the road and cheer the cars carrying the wedding party of the Duke of Kent from York Minster to the bride's home at Hovingham. Six hundred boys, however many buses, a brass band specially rehearsed, all in order to watch some cars that did not stop nor even, as I remember, slow down. Perhaps the bride and groom did a little, at least my image of the young Duchess is in focus, but not the others. The band played, we waved and feverishly shouted our hip-hip-hoorays, the cavalcade shot past, blurred faces in Molyneux and Hartnell, and then they were gone. The whole thing took five minutes from start to finish, if that. Then we climbed back into the buses and returned to school.

So it was that even a member of a minor, deposed Royal house seemed to confer a favour on every invitation they accepted in those dead days, and Dagmar was no exception. Her dynasty, the Grand Ducal House of Moravia, was not in fact very ancient. It had been one of those invented families, installed by the Great Powers in different Balkan states as the Turkish Empire gradually disintegrated throughout the second half of the nineteenth century. During those years, German and Danish, and in some cases local, princes were pushed on to thrones in Romania and Bulgaria, in Montenegro and Serbia, in Albania and Greece. Just such a one was the mountainous and modest state of Moravia, which bordered on almost all of the above. The Turkish governor having finally retreated in early 1882, a minor princeling of the House of Ludinghausen-Anhalt-Zerbst was selected, largely on the basis of his being a godson of the then Prince of Wales. Whether or not his selection reflected the British Prince's close friendship with the boy's mother at the time of his birth I could not say, although Lord Salisbury was asked by Marlborough House, as a personal favour, to suggest Prince Ernst for the post, thereby signalling our government's approval. Since the territory was not much larger than the estate of an English duke, and considerably less profitable, it was not thought that a kingly crown would be appropriate and at the Settlement of Klasko, in April 1883, the area was solemnly proclaimed a grand duchy.

It must be said that the wife of the new Grand Duke was not enthusiastic. Until then, she had been having quite a jolly time between their home in Vienna and a sporting estate in the Black Forest, and after two years she was still writing to a friend that she thought she lacked an important requirement for the job, namely the smallest desire to remain in Moravia, but the couple persevered with some success. Their new country's good fortune was to be located at a sensitive crossroads of many of the trade routes. This ensured invitations to every Royal fête around the world, as well as cheering offers for their daughters' hands in marriage, and before very long a Russian grand duchess, an Austrian archduchess and a princess of Borbon-Anjou had all begun life in the airless, cramped nurseries of the hideously uncomfortable palace in the capital of Olomouc, a building not much larger than the dean's residence in the close at Salisbury and a lot less manageable to run.

Surprisingly, perhaps, Grand Ducal Moravia made it as far as the Jazz Age, but the forces of Stalin, coupled with a swelling resistance to the monarchist solution, proved the undoing of the dynasty. By 1947 it was over and the ex-reigning Moravian family had taken up residence in a five-storey house in Trevor Square, a pleasant enough location and very convenient for Harrods.

But even easy shopping could not revive the spirits of the defeated Grand Duke and in a matter of months he had given up the unequal struggle. It was at this point that his son, having assumed the grand ducal title, the last of his family to do so, and released perhaps by the demise of his august papa, made a spirited decision that would vastly diminish his chances of regaining the throne of his forebears and vastly increase his chances of living well in the interim. With the dignified, if pained, acceptance of his widowed mother, a princess of a cadet branch of the Hohenzollerns, he contracted to marry the only daughter of a businessman from Leeds, one Harold Swindley, who had made a fortune in self-catering, package holidays. In the following three years, two children had arrived to bless this most sensible of unions, the new, so-called Crown Prince Feodor and his sister, the Princess Dagmar.

But for us, and even more for our parents, the Fall of the House of Moravia was still pretty recent and even the elevation of Miss Marion Swindley could not dim the lustre of a genuine crown. Only twenty years had passed since their deposition when Dagmar arrived at our parties. Besides, the Communist regime that replaced them was not popular, the family was still on the guest list at Buckingham Palace and there was talk at the time of a restoration coming in Spain. In short, forty years ago the Royalist cause didn't seem hopeless by any means.

The new Grand Duchess had delivered. The Swindley money may not have been particularly fragrant but, for the first years of the marriage at least, there was quite a lot of it. And she learned her part pretty well until, like every fervent convert, she was soon *plus Catholique que le Pape*. Admittedly, she was not by any standards a beauty but, as the Dowager Grand Duchess was once heard to sigh when watching her daughter-in-law stump across a drawing room looking like a Marine in training, 'Oh, well. One can't have *everything*,' and nobody could say she was not impressive. Her size alone guaranteed that. Nor was she a fool, having inherited more from her (discreetly invisible) father than she might care to admit in terms of solid, common sense.

For all the bowing and ma'am'ing that still went on in those days, the Grand Duchess understood that no throne awaited her timid daughter in the post-war world. She also knew that she had not anticipated the drain on her capital made by a husband who wished to live *en prince* but did not intend to do a day's work, nor earn a single penny. She was, at heart, a sound northern lass and well aware that no fortune can hope to survive when the expenses are limitless and the income nil, and she was anxious to see the girl settled as well as might be, before the gilt had quite gone off the gingerbread. So she decided that, even though British princesses by that stage never 'came out' in any normal way and only occasionally appeared at the parties of special friends, nevertheless Dagmar would participate fully in the whole year-long business. The girl would thereby build a position for herself in British Society and, with any luck, land one of its prizes. The Grand Duchess also accepted – unlike many, if not most, Royals – that she would have to put her hand in her pocket to achieve this. By 1968, when the Grand Duke had been spending like a sailor for a quarter of a century, this could not have been as easy as it was once, but she had bitten off the mouthful and she fully intended to chew it. I am happy to say I was on the list to be invited.

The inspiration for the party was the Duchess of Richmond's Ball, that famous 1815 gathering, given in Brussels on the very eve of Water-loo, and it was held at the Dorchester in Park Lane. Today, one thinks of the hotel as the haunt of film stars and merchants from the East, but in those days it played quite a major part in what was still referred to as 'Society.' On the night in question we came in, I think, by the ballroom entrance at the side, situated on Park Lane itself, and the theme of the evening was quite clear the moment one stepped inside, into that long, rather low, hall. Liveried footmen stood to attention, all modern signs, 'Exit' and the like, had been hidden behind greenery and there were candles everywhere. None of these last details would be legal today, of course, but nobody cared then. In truth, the party seemed to have taken over most of the ground floor of the hotel. It can't have, really, can it? But that's what it felt like on the night. Of course, we didn't arrive much before eleven, having eaten our dinners elsewhere, and the champagne that greeted us, held out by the white-wigged flunkeys, was not by any means the first drink of the evening. One has to remember that in the late 1960s, while nobody suggested that it was a good idea to drive a car when plastered, it was still long before such considerations had begun to shape our social life. 'Which of you is drinking tonight?' would have bewildered the couple arriving at a dinner, since the answer would invariably have been 'both.' For this reason no hostess scrupled to ask various friends to provide dinners for her guests before a ball.

Later in the Season, when more dances were given in the country, this would entail putting them up for the night, and essentially meant throwing a house party for strangers, who would drunkenly rattle around the countryside in their cars at all hours. But in London the thing was more easily managed. Sometimes you were flattered to receive an invitation to join the dinner provided by the parents of the deb of the evening, but this didn't happen (to me, anyway) all that often and usually a pleasant little postcard would drop through the letter box, saying that the writer believed you were going to the dance being given for So-and-So and she would be 'terribly pleased if you would dine here first.' At the end of which dinner, fairly far gone or at least merry, we would cheerfully climb into our vehicles and head off for the location of the party proper. This system had obvious advantages. The bonus for the young was that the dances went on forever, because they didn't really get going much before eleven. While the benefit for the old was plain economy. The parents of the girl in question usually had to hire the place, at least in London, and even in the country marquees would be expected unless the house was vast. Then there was the music, as well as a pretty good breakfast at the end of the event, but by adopting this system the hosts were spared the additional burden of dinner and wines for three or four hundred young and hungry people. No wonder the custom cheered the fathers up no end.

Having taken in the thoroughness of the arrangements, I made my way into the ballroom and here the illusion was impressive. At that time it was customary for a limited number of the older generation to be invited to these gatherings. They would be drawn from the god-parents of the debutante, as well as from the relatives and close friends of her parents, and as a rule they would fringe the proceedings, chatting in some other drawing room, watching the children dancing, occasionally venturing on to the floor to demonstrate an adapted foxtrot or quickstep, before retiring fairly early for the night. They were not expected to participate as full guests since, as we all know, the sight of dancing parents is torture for the young and always was. All this was especially true of costume parties, which are rather a bore for anyone out of their thirties, and the adults would simply arrive in evening dress, occasionally with some gay little gesture, worn as a brooch or a hair ornament. None of which applied to this particular event. I do not know if it was respect for the Grand Duchess or terror (probably the latter), but every single attendee, old and young, was in costume. As a particularly witty detail, or possibly after an instruction from on high, several of the mothers and fathers had deliberately chosen outfits of a slightly earlier date than those worn by their offspring. Men in wigs and ruffles, women in high-piled, powdered hair and beauty spots, from the 1780s or '90s, gave us all the sense that we were indeed back in the Regency and this was the older generation of the day, frowning and disapproving of modern youth. It always amuses me that this particular era, redolent as it is of Versailles and Queen Marie-Antoinette, is such a favourite costume theme with toffs. They seem to have forgotten that it did not as a whole turn out well for the privileged classes, so many of whom would leave their heads, and no doubt wigs, in the basket below the guillotine.

'What have you come as?' Lucy was dressed in a Jane Austen, white frock, high-waisted and pure, with a ribbon round her throat and her artificial ringlets sewn with tiny, white silk roses. She looked artful rather than innocent, but charming nonetheless.

'I'm a hussar,' I replied slightly indignantly, 'I should have thought it was obvious.'

'The trousers are wrong.'

'Thank you for that.' The trousers *were* wrong, as it happens, but the rest of the outfit was perfect, bright scarlet, heavily braided, with a fur-edged jacket slung between my left shoulder and my right armpit. I thought I looked fabulous. 'They're only wrong for 1815. They would be right by 1850. Anyway, it was the best I could manage. It was too late to find anything in London, so I had to raid the costume store of Windsor Rep.'

'It looks like it.' She stopped and stared round the room, which was beginning to fill up. 'Where was your dinner?'

'Chester Row. The Harington-Stanleys.'

'Any good?'

'Well, the food was like a shooting lunch that had been brought up to London in a rusty cake tin, but it was quite fun apart from that. What about you?'

She grimaced. 'Mrs Vitkov. With a group to meet her daughter, Terry. At that new French place in Lower Sloane Street.'

'The Gavroche?'

'That's it.'

'Lucky you.'

She gave me what used to be called an old-fashioned look. 'Have you met Terry Vitkov?'

'Not yet.'

'Don't.'

'Where are they from? The Balkans?'

'Cincinnati. And believe me, Miss Terry is a piece of work.' She stopped and nodded with a tight smile. 'Careful. That's her.' I turned to look. I could see at once that we needn't have worried and that Terry Vitkov was quite happy to be the subject of our discussion. She looked as if she were more than used to being the centre of attention. She was a good-looking girl. Indeed, she would have been very good-looking if it were not for a certain prominence of nose and chin, faintly suggesting a Man-in-the-Moon profile, which, combined with the intensity of her piercing and heavily made up eyes, gave her the air of a prisoner on the run, desperately searching the room for either an enemy or an escape route. Tonight she appeared to be dressed as a Regency courtesan, rather than a great-lady-from-times-gone-by, like every other woman there. Indeed, she was more or the less the only person in the ballroom, who would patently *not* have figured on the guest list of the real Duchess of Richmond. She walked up to us and we were introduced.

'Lucy's been telling me all the dos and don'ts for getting on in London.' She spoke with a breathy urgency, the voice of one determined to make every human interchange register. I could see at once that despite her flashing frequent smiles, designed no doubt to suggest a spirit of girlish, flirtatious fun and displaying thereby a set of admirably white, if rather large, teeth, Terry Vitkov took herself tremendously seriously.

'I don't think I've covered them all, have I?' said Lucy laconically.

Our companion was already training her searching gaze on the other guests. 'Which one is Viscount Summersby?' she asked.

Lucy checked the ballroom. 'Over there. With the blonde girl in green, next to the big looking glass.'

Terry sought him out. Her shoulders sagged. 'Why do they always have to look like the man from Pest Control?' She sighed. 'Who's that one?' A tall and handsome young man flashed her a smile as he passed.

'Don't bother. No money. No prospects.' Lucy clearly understood her companion's priorities. 'Of course, he's clever and he's headed for the City. He may make something of himself.'

But Terry shook her head. 'That takes twenty years and by the time they've got there they're ready to trade you in for a younger model. No. I want some money from the outset.'

I nodded, sagely. 'But not Lord Summersby.'

She smiled. 'Not until I know I can't get something better.' What made this amusing, of course, was that she meant it.

We had been moving slowly in a rather sloppy presentation line and by now had nearly reached our hosts, who stood, all four together, posed against a rich curtain erected as a kind of screen for the purpose.

The Grand Duke cut a melancholy figure. He was a slight and pasty-looking creature anyway, especially when placed at the side of his massive spouse and, in truth, I do not believe I ever heard him say an interesting sentence. He wore his elaborate costume, which I took to be that of the Duke of Richmond, with an air of surprise, as if he had been put into it while under sedation. Perhaps he was. His son, dressed as an officer of the guard, stared straight ahead stiffly. He could have been posing for an early daguerreotype, when you had to keep your head still for four or five minutes until it was done. His bland, mottled face exuded an air of bored and generalised geniality.

The daughter, Dagmar, technically of course the Star of the Night, looked frightened and if anything a little drab. She was a tiny creature, literally no more than five feet tall and, while one is always being told that Queen Victoria was four foot eleven and managed to run an Empire, still for most of us it is very, very small and means you spend your whole life looking up. Standing there in the shadow of her mother, to paraphrase Noël Coward, she looked like the Grand Duchess's lunch. Dagmar wasn't what you would call plain, even if her sallow mini-face was hard to define or at least to categorise. She wasn't exactly pretty either, but her large eyes were arresting and she had a soft, moist, trembling mouth, usually half open and quivering and seeming to suggest she was always on the verge of tears, which, in a way, touched your heart. But she never appeared to have any idea of how to present herself. Her hair, for instance, was very dark and straight and, with imagination, it might have been effective. But it just hung there, as if it had been washed in a hurry and left to dry. I really did think something might have been made of her on the night of her own ball, but as usual nobody had tried. The dress was from the correct period but it was dull, and only faintly enlivened with a thin blue sash beneath her modest bosom. To be honest, she looked as if she had taken five minutes to get ready for a game of tennis, and so fragile that one good, strong puff of wind would carry her out of the window and down Park Lane in an instant.

Which could not be said of her mother. I cannot be sure, to this day, whether the Grand Duchess was intending to impersonate the original Duchess of Richmond. It would seem logical, given the wording of the invitation, but the costume she had chosen was more suitable for a great empress, Catherine the Great maybe, or Maria Teresa, or any other absolute female monarch. Acres of chiffon blew softly this way and that, while a river, a torrent, of purple velvet, embroidered in thick, gold thread, cascaded from her more than ample shoulders to the floor and lay there in massive hillocks and dunes, its ermine trim forming a kind of plinth to set off the huge, majestic figure above. Her bosom, like a rock shelf beneath the sea, was ablaze with diamonds and a sparkling crown-like tiara rose from her lightly sweating brow. I suppose the display was all that remained of the Moravian crown jewels, either that or they had been rented from the Barnum Brothers for the night. This was a scene-stealing one-woman show and none of the others got a look in, least of all the wretched Dagmar who, knowing her mother, must have expected something of the sort. At any rate, while the crowds spun, buzzing, round her mama, she didn't seem unduly put out, unlike the Grand Duke and the Crown Prince who both looked as if they were aching to go home. We were announced.

'Good evening, Ma'am.' I bowed and she accepted my obeisance gracefully. I moved on to her husband. 'Your Royal Highness.' I bowed again. He nodded vacantly, his mind probably on some long-ago Court reception in dark and dusty Olomouc. Leaving him to dream alone, I passed into the body of the room. Looking back, I think that evening was when I first understood what I have now come to recognise all around me, viz. that when it comes to aristocrats, or even royalty, most of the members of those worlds (who have not moved away from the whole performance entirely, that is) fall into separate, apparently similar but in fact quite disparate, groups. The first, made familiar by a million lampoons, have a clear understanding that the world of their youth and their ancestors has changed and will not be coming back, but they continue to mourn it. The cooks and the valets, the maids and the footmen who made life so sweet will never again push through the green baize door, busy with the tasks of the day. The smiling grooms who brought the horses round to the front at ten, the chauffeurs washing their gleaming vehicles, standing in deference when one strolled into the stable yard, the gardeners ducking out of sight at the sound of a house party's approach, all that army dedicated to their pleasure have left for other climes. These people usually know, too, albeit half subconsciously, that the deference they still receive within their social circle is somehow thin and even false, compared to the real respect accorded to their parents and grandparents, when high birth had solid accountable value. They know these things, but they do not know what to do about them, other than to weep and live out their lives with as much comfort as they can muster.

Into this category one could squarely place the last Grand Duke of Moravia. There was something in his aimless and depressive grace that told of his awareness of the truth. 'Don't blame me,' he seemed to be saying. 'I understand this is absurd. I know you have no reason to bow and scrape before me, that the game is over, that the band has played, but I have to go through the forms, don't you know? I have to look as if I take it seriously or I would be letting other people down.' This was the text permanently hovering in the air above him. Of course, the same group boasts a nastier version. 'It may be over,' they flash from their pitiless eyes, 'but it isn't quite over for *me*!' and they toss their heads and prey on their rich, social-climbing acolytes and sell the last of their mother's jewels, that the show may struggle on for a few more years at least.

But the other category in this group is different from these and, as a type, is largely undetected by the general public. These men and women also have the status that pertains to them from the old system and they enjoy it. They like the rank and the history that supports them. They are glad to be seen as part of the inner circle of aristocratic Britain. They make sure that one member at least of the Royal Family is present at every major bash they throw. They dress, at least the men dress, to please the diehards. They shoot, they fish, they know their historic dates and other people's genealogy. But all the time they are pretending. Far from being bewildered as to the workings of the new and harsher century, they understand precisely how it turns. They know the value of their property, just as they knew it would regain it. They fully grasp the intricacies of the markets, how and what to buy, what and when to sell, how to achieve the right planning permissions, how to manipulate the payments from the EU farming policy, in short, how to make the estate, and their position, pay.

They decided long ago that they did not want to belong to some fading club, endlessly nostalgic for better days that will never come again. They wanted to retake a position of influence and even power and if it was not, after the 1960s, to be overtly political power then so be it, they would find another route. They are fakes, really. Despite their lineage, despite their houses and their jewels and their wardrobes and their dogs, despite their mouthing the traditional prejudices of their class, they no longer think like most of their own kind. They belong to today and tomorrow, far more than to yesterday. They have brains and values as tough as any hedge fund manager's. But then again, they would argue that they are only being true to their own race, truer than the defeatists, because the primal job of any aristocrat is to stay on top. Bourbon or Bonaparte, king or president, the real aristocrat understands who is in power and who should be bowed to, next.

Of course, forty years ago much of this was hidden from us. The old world had taken a swingeing blow during and after the war from which it was deemed unlikely to recover. Everyone lamented the end in unison and it was only much later that we began to realise we were not all in the same boat as we had thought, and that some families had not, after all, trodden the same downward path, whatever they may have said at the time. In many cases it was my own generation, debutantes then, with brothers at university or just starting out in the city, who began secretly to reject the notion of going down with the ship and started looking about for ways to get back to dry land. These would prove the survivors, and this group was the one to which the Grand Duchess of Moravia, in contrast to her fatalistic spouse, was drawn, even before it was truly formed. She wanted to create a beachhead within the new world, from which to re-launch the family. I liked her for it.

The music was starting now, a group had taken up their positions on the modest stage and were performing cover versions of the current top ten. They were not, I think, a very famous group, but at least they had been on television, which seemed considerably more exciting then than it does now, and couples were drifting on to the floor at the end of the long chamber. The ancient parents, sitting in their costumes on sofas against the wall, were less helpful to this part of the evening and several of them, sensing it, rose and moved towards the doorway leading to the sitting-out rooms and the bar. Lucy and I walked forward. As we did so there was a slight murmur of jostling admiration and I caught a glimpse of Joanna Langley surrounded by her customary group of admirers. She was brilliantly dressed as Napoleon's sister, Princess

Pauline Borghese. Her costume, unlike mine or most of the others, was new, copied, presumably for the occasion, from a portrait by David. Of course, the Princess would have been an unlikely guest at a ball given by her brother's arch enemies and anyway, Joanna's modern, celluloid beauty made her unconvincing as a period piece, but she was a joy to look at all the same.

The group shifted a little and I was surprised to see the familiar figure of Damian Baxter standing next to her. As I watched, he leaned in and whispered into her ear. She laughed, nodding a hello to me as she did so and thereby drawing me to Damian's attention. I walked over. 'You never said you were coming to this,' I said.

'I wasn't sure I would, until this afternoon. Then I suddenly thought "what the hell," got on a train and here I am.'

'You never said you'd been invited.'

He fixed me with a look, the corners of his mouth twitching. 'I wasn't.'

I stared at him. Did I feel a slight trace of Baron Frankenstein's terror, when his monster first moved of its own volition? 'You mean you've gatecrashed,' I said. He smiled covertly by way of an answer.

Lucy had been listening to this. 'How did you get your costume at such short notice?' And what a costume. In contrast to mine, with its wrong trousers and slightly rubbed sleeves, Damian looked as if the outfit had been made for him by a master tailor. He was not an officer, as most of the men in the room had chosen to be, but a dandy, Beau Brummell or Byron or someone similar, with a tightly fitting tailcoat hugging his torso, and buckskin breeches and high, polished boots to show off his legs. A dazzling cravat of white silk was wound round his neck and tucked into the brocade waistcoat beneath. Lucy nodded at me. 'He had to go out to Windsor Rep and that was what they came up with.'

Damian looked at me. 'Poor you. Never mind.' Any notion I'd cherished of looking rather good withered and died, as Damian chattered on in his light, unconcerned way. 'I got a friend to sort one out at the Arts Theatre, in case I wanted to come. She managed to get it ready in time and that's what decided me.' I'll bet she did, I thought. Some wretched girl, pricking her fingers to the bone, standing over the washing machine at midnight, burning her hand on the iron. I'll bet she did. And what would be her reward? Not to be loved by Damian. Of that I was quite sure.

Today, pushing into such a function would be a good deal harder than it was forty years ago. The endless security consciousness of the present generation, to say nothing of their self-importance, ensures guards and lists and ticking and 'please bring this invitation with you' to every gathering more exclusive than a sale at Tesco. But it was different then. There was a general supposition that people who hadn't been invited to something did not, as a rule, try to attend it. In other words, what the gatecrasher of those days relied on, what he or she required, was only nerve, nothing more, which, naturally, Damian had in plentiful supply. But I had less than he and I did not want to be seen chatting to someone who might be thrown out at any moment. I despise myself now when I think of it, but I took Lucy's arm and steered her on to the floor.

'You can't keep a good man down,' said Lucy cheerily. But I wasn't inclined to see the funny side. Drowning in my youthful egotism, I could only fear that Damian's appearance might in some way damage me.

He, needless to say, was enjoying himself enormously. I could see at once that, like a child who will be naughty until it is smacked or a gambler who must play until he loses, Damian had to promote his uninvited appearance until somehow the law enforcers registered it. He danced first with Joanna, as if to announce his arrival. He was the best-looking man in the room and she was the best-looking woman in Europe, so they made quite a pair. Other couples turned to watch them and admire, parents glanced over and asked each other about the glorious duo. A little while later, the ball now well and truly under way, the band announced an eightsome reel. It may seem curious to a modern reader that we should have danced a Scottish reel in the middle of a perfectly normal party, not at some Caledonian festival or even a Burns Night in Kircaldy, but we did. In fact, we danced it at most of the parties that year and, with the steps demanding a less cluttered and less crowded floor, it was a sure way to be noticed, so it came as no surprise to see Damian walking forward to take his place in one of the sets with Terry Vitkov on his arm. She gleamed and beamed, this way and that, clearly enjoying her newly found status as troublemaker, as she leaned proudly on the arm of the rebel. I wondered later whether it was at this particular party that Damian's own position began to shift from social observer (or climber, depending on your generosity of vision) to subversive. From admiring student to hostile agent. Am I jumping the gun and did it remain in the balance that night? Or had he already decided he hated us all?

Watching them take their places, waiting for the chord that would start us off, it struck me then that he and Terry were rather a good pair. Both outsiders in their different ways, both with everything to gain from the future and nothing to lose with the vanishing past. I assumed she had money – she did, but less than I thought at the time – just as I assumed that Damian would make money – again, I was right. He did. And much more than I thought at the time. Might they not combine and conquer the world? They were both adventurers. Why should they not join forces?

I was partnering a rather dull girl from somewhere near Newbury and now we set off, marching round in our hand-held circles. Glancing across, I was momentarily impressed by the skills Damian had already acquired in this, so recently foreign, territory. He knew the steps and performed them well; he took his turn in the centre of the ring without a trace of self-consciousness, holding himself erect, executing the different parts of the reel with a degree of grace and dignity I could not have claimed for myself. He chatted to the girls around him and to the other men, part of their crowd now, part of their world, after only a few cocktail parties and dances. We had almost forgotten that we did not know him.

After that the pop group resumed, but Damian showed no sign of flagging. He danced with plenty of the girls, Lucy Dalton and a raucous, ruddy-faced Candida Finch among them. He was about to dance with Georgina Waddilove, who would certainly have betrayed her country to make him stay by her side, but in that instant, just as the music started he seemed to get a stitch and beg her, instead, to join him in a drink. I lost sight of him as they drifted away together into the room serving as a bar. It is hard, looking back, to state with any accuracy my precise feelings at that stage towards this cuckoo I had brought into the nest. As I have said, I'd begun to suspect he had an agenda more complicated than I had first understood, but I still admired his *chutzpah*, and never more so than when he returned to the ballroom that evening. Somehow, while he was away, a happy conjunction had allowed him to achieve what he came for. To my amazement and the admiration of all those present who knew he was there illegitimately, he reappeared in the open doorway leading the hostess, at least the girl who but for her indomitable mother should have been the centre of the evening, Princess Dagmar herself, onto the dance floor. It was a slow number. The lights were lowered, the band strummed away and, in full view of her guests, Dagmar slipped her arms round the interloper and pressed her tiny face into his chest. Lightly caressing her lank hair as they smooched, Damian noticed me watching him from across the floor. He caught my eye. And winked.

The trouble, which I suppose we all knew would come in the end, happened at the breakfast and in a way it was a miracle it was delayed until then. The custom, at every private dance, was to provide breakfast towards the finish, starting usually at about half past one or so. These repasts varied in quality and were sometimes, frankly, not worth waiting for but the Grand Duchess had clearly invoked the old proverb of 'in for a penny, in for a pound' and laid on the best the hotel was capable of, which was very good indeed. We waited in a group, rather than a queue, ready to help ourselves to eggs and bacon and sausages and mushrooms, all laid out before us in silver chafing dishes.

Damian was standing a little ahead of me. He appeared to have resigned his charge of Dagmar, who was nowhere to be seen, but moved on to the equally great, or greater, prize of Serena, who was as animated as I had ever seen her, laughing and chatting, and leaning her head close to his. I remember I was surprised at the time to register how well they appeared to know each other. She had come as Caroline Lamb dressed as a page, taken from the famous portrait by Thomas Phillips and, of course, the trim tailoring of her velvet coat, displaying, as it did, her wonderful legs in stockings and knee breeches, made all the other girls present look stuffy and dowdy by comparison. Damian, at her side, was a convincing Byron and perhaps that had been the original idea behind his costume. In fact, they could almost have planned it, they made so well-matched a pair. Serena was not as beautiful as Joanna Langley – no woman was – but she had a fineness of feature that offset it. In short, they looked wonderful together and once again Damian found himself the cynosure of all eyes. 'Excuse me, Sir, but do you have an invitation?' The voice, loud and with a trace of a Midlands accent, transcended the chatter and hung like a seagull in the air above us.

The question had come so entirely out of the blue that it succeeded in silencing everyone present. I saw one girl stop dead, half a fried egg hanging from a spoon until it slipped and fell back on to the plate beneath. A suited man, presumably a manager or something similar, was standing next to Damian. He was standing too close, impertinently close. So close that he was obviously using his closeness to express that he belonged there, in this room, in this hotel, but that in his opinion Damian Baxter did not. Of course, the truth was more complicated. Most of those present knew that Damian did not have an invitation, but he had been present at the party for so long by that stage that for the majority this argument seemed to have become semantic. He had not created a disturbance, he had not got drunk, he had not been rude, all the things that people dread from gatecrashers had simply not happened. Besides, he knew many of the other guests. He had come as a friend and chosen the correct costume. He had danced and talked and even partnered the girl whose ball it was, for heaven's sake. What more did they want? The answer to this was, apparently, proof of an invitation. He blushed, something I do not believe I ever saw him do again. 'Look,' he said softly, laying a placatory hand gently on the man's grey, worsted sleeve.

'No, Sir. *You* look.' If anything the voice was getting louder and word had spread. Couples drifted into the breakfast room from the dancing next door to see what was going on. 'If you do not have an invitation I must ask you to leave.' Ill-advisedly, after shaking Damian's hand away, he tried to take hold of his elbow, but Damian was too quick for him and almost danced backwards to free himself. At this moment Serena, alone in that company decided to intervene. In my craven silence I admired her enormously.

'I am perfectly happy to vouch for Mr Baxter, if that would make any difference.' Judging by the man's expression it did not look at first as if it would. 'My name is Lady Serena Gresham, and you will find it on the guest list.' Now, what was peculiarly interesting about this was Serena's mention of her rank, something she would normally never have done; not if it meant having her tongue torn out. It is hard to understand for those who were not there, but the years of the 1960s were an odd, transitional period when it came to titles. I mean, of course, real titles, hereditary titles. Because at that precise moment of our history nobody quite knew what their future might be. An unspoken agreement between the parties not to create any more of them seemed to have been reached in about 1963 and the belief at that time, certainly outside aristocratic circles, was that the world was changing into a different place and that, among these changes soon, perhaps very soon, the status of a life peerage would far exceed that of an inherited one. In short, that the prominence of the ancient, great families would be vastly diminished in favour of the new people on their way up. But alongside this official doctrine (promoted by the media at the time and still touchingly upheld today by a few politicians and the more optimistic worthies of the Left), there was nevertheless a sneaking suspicion that despite confident pronouncements from the pundits on the subject, this would not prove quite true and that a historic name would continue to have muscle in modern Britain. It was not unlike Mr Blair's attempt to rebrand the country Cool Britannia. There was a period when everyone thought it might work, then a second chapter when the media would insist the experiment was working even though we all knew it wasn't and finally a universal acknowledgement, from Left and Right, that it had been a ridiculous and colossal failure.

But, at the time this contradictory attitude towards hereditary rank meant that as a weapon, titles had to be used circumspectly and that all public display was self-defeating. Just as anyone who shouts 'Do you know who I am?' at a hotel or airline employee immediately forfeits what little advantage they might possibly have gained from their position.

Forty years later all this has altered. After half a century, while a life peerage is a perfectly respectable honour, it is only really meaningful in a political context. In smart society it has failed to garner any real aura or kudos beyond that of a knighthood. Mrs Thatcher tried to acknowledge this with a few hereditary creations in the early 1980s, but she was not supported and after that the nobility remained shut, despite continuing to dominate the social pyramid unchallenged. In fact, when toffs *are* given life peerages they tend to wear them lightly as if anxious to show that they do not take their new rank seriously. 'We're just the day boys,' said one to me recently. Obviously, the old system should either be reopened or abolished, since the present situation should be judged untenable in any democratic society, but there is little sign of reform. Instead, today, up and down the land the descendants of some lucky mayor or banker in the Twenties, reign graciously over us, while the great of our own day, often with far more significant achievements than the forebears of the grandees present, give place and sit forever below the salt.

The point is that today Serena would never question the advantage of her position and using it in this context would almost certainly work. But in those days, forty years ago, it was an act of bravery for her to hold it up and risk a potshot. She was right to be diffident, since it was clear her intervention wouldn't do the trick. The man stared at her officiously. 'I'm very sorry, Your Ladyship,' he started, 'I'm afraid—'

'This is absolutely ridiculous!' Dagmar's shrill cry rang out across the room. One of her striking and even poignant qualities was the absolute Englishness of her voice, making her foreign name and rank feel even stranger. And it was not just English, but a sound from the England of sixty years before, the voice of a miniature duchess opening a charity bazaar in 1910. She strode towards the table, pushing the crowd apart as she came, like a Munchkin general. 'Of course Damian does not have to go!'

This complication really flummoxed the man. 'But Her Royal Highness asked most particularly—'

'Her Royal Highness doesn't know anything about it!'

'Oh, I think I *do*!' The vast bulk of the Grand Duchess was now added to the mix. The guests fell back as she swept majestically through the room, a re-enactment of Sherman marching through Georgia, scorching the earth on her journey, accompanied by, interestingly, Andrew Summersby, who hovered beside her like a small and ugly tug in the shadow of an ocean-going liner. 'I'm very sorry, Mr Baxter, I am sure you did not mean to offend in any way.' She paused for breath and I saw Damian try to cut in, presumably with a view to improving his chances, but she was not interested in a dialogue, only in a statement of policy. 'However, I feel there are rules in these things and they must be adhered to.' She smiled to sugar the pill. 'We can't risk Society crashing down about our ears. I hope you won't think too harshly of me.'

'No, indeed,' said Damian waggishly, still hoping to regain his balance.

'But Damian *was* invited!' The cry came from a hideously embarrassed Dagmar. Naturally it made an interesting contribution to the argument. The crowd's eyes swung towards her, like the audience of the tennis match in Hitchcock's *Strangers on a Train*. 'I invited him!' I am sure everyone present knew this was a lie, but it was a gallant and generous lie, and it sent her higher in the estimation of her guests, most of whom were not particularly fond of her before that night, despite their readiness to take full advantage of her hospitality. I say this so you may know that her intervention did achieve some good. As an argument against her mother's decision it was of course completely fatuous.

'Excuse me, my dear, but Mr Baxter was *not* invited. Not by you. And, more to the point, not by *me*.' The Grand Duchess's tone brooked no argument. She had not finished. 'This was something he made quite clear within earshot of Lord Summersby, who was good enough to bring it to my attention. I would go so far as to say that Mr Baxter was *boasting* of his lack of invitation.' The shade of the Grand Duchess's face was darkening and it was not a becoming alteration. Coupled with the primary colours of her costume, she was beginning to resemble a blow-up Santa Claus hovering between the buildings in Regent Street at Christmas; but, as always with her, there was a quality to be reckoned with. I especially enjoyed a slight flavour of Eastern Europe in her voice as her rage intensified, as if her duty towards her people – subjects in a country which, lest we forget, she had never even visited – had somehow infused her with a new and different past, washing away her healthy, early years in West Yorkshire and making her Moravian in spite of herself.

Her words had naturally revealed who was to blame for the incident, which I would like to describe as 'horrid,' but which had, of course, completely *made* the party for most of those present. The sneak responsible was none other than Andrew Summersby. I would guess that this public unveiling was not part of his original plan and he looked uncomfortable as the eyes of the company now turned upon him. He hesitated for a moment before making the decision, which I cannot blame him for, given his situation that, having been uncovered, he had better brazen it out.

Until this point he'd been hovering at the back of the proceedings, but now he strode forward. 'Come on,' he said, laying hold of Damian by the upper arm, rather like someone making a citizen's arrest, which I suppose he was doing, and attempting to guide him away.

In one swift move, and to the amazement of us all, Damian again got free, this time with a thousand times more fury than he had vented on the hotel employee when the man had tried something similar. 'Take your hand off me this instant,' he snarled. 'You stupid, ridiculous *oaf*!' Obviously, Andrew was not expecting anything of this sort when he had first decided to betray the uninvited guest, least of all from someone whom he judged to be far beneath him in God's scheme of things. Andrew unquestionably was an oaf, and a *very* stupid one, but few people would then have called him such to his face and he was quite unprepared for it. To be honest, I think he just wanted to have a go at Serena or one of the other girls who had been hovering around Damian all evening and he'd got jealous. I'm quite sure nobody was sorrier than he that the whole situation seemed to be spiralling out of control.

He was dressed, like some of the others, as a Death's Head hussar, with tight, in his case unbecoming, trousers, and a coat slung across his back, all of which may have fatally impeded his movement, but he couldn't back out now. He lunged forward, making a second attempt to grip the miscreant's arm. Once more, Damian was too quick for him, stepping back in a sort of pirouette, like Errol Flynn in a Warner Brothers romance, and before anyone could stop him he had swung the full force of his right fist into a punch that met Andrew's nose with a loud and sickening crunch. Several of the girls screamed, particularly the nearest, one Lydia Maybury, whose white, organza frock, charmingly cut on the bias and embroidered with lilies of the valley, was copiously sprayed with a mixture of gore and snot from Andrew's smashed proboscis. He himself looked so startled, so astonished by the unbelievable course events had taken, as if the sea itself had suddenly come rushing in through the ballroom windows, that he stood for a moment in a trance, staring through sightless eyes, stock still, blood spouting from his nostrils, before staggering backwards. Watching this, but paralysed with a kind of ecstatic horror, none of us thought to catch and save him, and instead he collapsed full length on to the breakfast buffet, pushing it over as he fell, showering himself and the bystanders with hot plates and sausages and jugs of orange juice and bacon and toast and burners and scrambled eggs and mustard and cutlery and all. The crash was like the Fall of Troy, echoing through the hotel passages, frightening the horses, wakening the dead. It was succeeded by complete and total silence. We all stood there, rabbits caught in the headlights, stunned, amazed, hypnotised, watching the bloody, breakfast-decorated body of the fallen Viscount. Even Dagmar was as still and as silent as a statue.

Then Damian, with one of those gestures that made me forgive him more, and for longer, than I should have done, took hold of the Grand Duchess's hand, hanging limply by her side as she stood witness to the ruin of a party that had cost a large percentage of her annual income. 'Please forgive me for making such a mess, Ma'am,' he raised her unresisting hand to his lips, holding it there for a second, with exquisite elegance, 'and thank you so much for what, until now, has been an enchanting evening.' So saying he released her fingers, bowed crisply from the neck like a lifelong courtier, and strode out of the chamber.

I need hardly add that once the story had gone round London, and with the sole exception of the ball given by Lady Belton for Andrew's sister, Annabella, before very long Damian had received invitations to every other major event of that Season. This was not because of any increased approval on the part of the mothers, all of whom were more terrified than ever that Damian Baxter would ensnare one of their sacred children.

It was at the absolute and unbending insistence of the girls themselves.

SIX

The Grand Duchess had been right to make her investment, even if things did not quite turn out as she had wished. In 1968 the family had just enough money and just enough status for Dagmar to have landed a big – or a biggish – fish. That she did not, I attributed at the time to her setting her sights too high and thereby missing whatever chance there might have been of something decent. As I would discover, I was not completely right in this analysis, but I suspect that even so, like many of rank or fortune, Dagmar had grown up with unrealistic expectations. To begin with she had no clear idea of how pallid she really was. She could always assemble (then, anyway) a crowd who would conceal her shyness from herself and she did not seem to appreciate that she would have to make more of the running if things were to go her way. All this the Grand Duchess knew and, in the nicest possible way, she tried to encourage her daughter to make what hay she could before the sun went in completely, but like most young women, Dagmar did not listen to her mother when her mother said things she did not want to hear.

Part of the problem lay in her curious inability to flirt. Faced by a man, she would alternate between nervous giggling or complete silence, her huge semi-tearful eyes wide open, fixed on her partner, while he would flounder in his desperate attempts to find some topic, any topic, that would elicit a vocal response. There wasn't one. Eventually this helplessness provoked a protective instinct in me, and while I never exactly fancied Dagmar, I began to dislike anyone who made fun of her or, as I once heard, imitated her sad, little laugh. Once, I had to take her away from Annabel's when her date excused himself to go to the loo, before apparently running up the steps back to street level and jumping into a taxi. She cried on the way home and of course I had to love her a little bit after that.

To correct a popular misconception, I must point out that by my time the London Season was no longer, as it had once been, much of a marriage market. The idea was more to launch your young into a suitable world where they would thenceforth live and in due course find friends, and after a few years a husband or wife. Few mothers wanted this achieved before their sons and daughters had reached their middle twenties at the earliest, but Dagmar's case was different, as the Grand Duchess knew. They were selling a product in what promised to be a falling market and there was no time to be lost. We all thought at one point she had a reasonable chance of Robert Strickland, the grandson and eventual heir to a 1910 barony, awarded to a Royal gynaecologist after a tricky but successful birth. Robert didn't have much money and there was neither land nor house, but there was something and he was a kind fellow, if hardly the life and soul of the party. He worked in a merchant bank and had the supreme merit, certainly where the Grand Duchess was concerned, of being slightly deaf. Unfortunately, just as he was coming to the boil Dagmar fluffed it, Robert interpreting her nervous giggle as a lack of interest in his hinted-at proposal, and it was not repeated. By the end of that summer he was happily engaged to the daughter of a Colonel in the Irish Guards. There would be no other opportunities at that level.

Even so, everyone was a little taken aback to read in the gossip columns in the late autumn of 1970 that she was engaged to William Holman, the only child of an aggressive *parvenu* from Virginia Water. When I knew him William was about to be 'something in the City,' an all-purpose phrase beloved of our mothers. He had been a hanger-on at some of the dances in our year, wearing and saying inappropriate, desperate things, according to our youthful, shallow, snobbish yard-sticks, and was not taken seriously by anyone. I suppose, looking back, he was quite clever and perhaps he did seem to be going somewhere. It just wasn't evident to us that it was somewhere very nice. I missed the wedding. I think I had double booked it with a weekend in Toulouse. But apparently it was perfectly all right, if a bit rushed. They were married in an Orthodox church in Bayswater and the reception was held at the Hyde Park Hotel. The groom's parents looked ecstatic and the bride's were at least resigned. In the last analysis Princess Dagmar of Moravia was married, and to a man who could pay the bill for dinner and manage something more than a basement flat. As the Grand Duchess might have remarked, and probably did in the privacy of her bathroom, it was better than nothing. She was also presumably aware that there were other factors at work, rendering the ceremony welcome. Six months later the Princess was delivered of a son, a healthy boy and not noticeably premature.

For obvious reasons I didn't see much of Dagmar after the Portuguese holiday, and once I'd missed her wedding we lost touch completely. I didn't like William and he couldn't see the point of me, so there was not much to build on. To be fair, he did do well, better than I had anticipated, eventually making chairman of some investment trust, and being rewarded with both millions and a knighthood from John Major. When I read about him in the papers, or glimpsed him across the room at some function, I was amused to note that he had become a convincing version of what he had hankered for all those years ago, with suits made by some award-worthy cutter behind the Burlington Arcade and all the loudly mouthed prejudices to match. Someone told me he hunted now and was even a good shot, which made me rather jealous. It never ceases to amaze me the way real money continues to ape the habits and pastimes of the old upper class, in a day when they could afford to call a different tune. This was not widely true during the Seventies, but once Mrs Thatcher was on the throne, secret longings for gentility resurfaced in many a breast. Before long, every City trader exchanged his red braces for a Barbour, and was shooting, fishing and stalking like a middle-European nobleman, while the clubs in St James's, once desperate for new applicants, had pleasure in re-establishing their waiting lists and toughening again the criteria for membership.

One sign of all this that the sociologists seem to have missed was that from the Eighties onwards, the upper middle and upper classes resumed a different daily costume from those beneath them in the ancient pecking order, which was definitely a return to the way things used to be. A unique phenomenon of the 1960s was that we all dressed in the new, outlandish modes, quite irrespective of background, perhaps the only time in the last thousand years when most of the nation's youth wore versions of the same costume, though it seems a pity we should choose as our badge of unity those terrible hipsters and kipper ties and velvet suits and bomber jackets and all the other horrors on display. Hideous as the fashions were, nobody was immune. The Queen's skirts leaped above her knee and, at the Prince of Wales's inauguration at Carnarvon Castle, Lord Snowdon appeared in what looked like the costume of a flightdeck steward on a Polish airline. But by the 1980s the toffs were tired of this unsuitable disguise. They wanted to look like themselves again, and gradually first Hackett's and later Oliver Brown and all those others who recognised this secret longing and aspired to supply it, appeared in the high street. Suddenly posh suits were once more of a recognisably different cloth and cut, while country clothes, tweeds and cords and all the rest of that tested uniform, pulled themselves from the dusty wardrobes where they had lain unloved since the 1950s. The toffs were visually different again, a tribe to be known once more by their markings, and it made them happy to be so.

That said, for those of us who witnessed what seemed then to be the end of everything, the 1970s had first to be negotiated before matters would start to improve. Much that was teetering came crashing down and there were dark days to be gone through. It seems strange to write it now, when all is changed, but to us, then, Communism was here to stay. In fact, most of us privately, if silently, believed that world Communism would eventually be the order of the day and we set about enjoying ourselves with no expectation of a long future for our way of life, dancing to the band on the increasingly steep deck of the *Titanic*. The Sixties had come and gone by that stage, with their promises of free love and hair-worn flowers, but these attractive notions did not, in the event, compose the legacy of that troubled era. The trail that was left was not of peace and rose buds, but of social breakdown, and certainly some people who lost their currency value in those bleak years, never regained it.

So it wasn't a complete surprise when I dialled Dagmar's number and asked for the Princess, to be told that 'Lady Holman' was in the drawing room. I had prepared what I intended to say. My excuse was a charity ball that I'd been given to chair for Eastern European refugees. Some years before I'd written a moderately successful novel set principally in post-war Romania, which had inevitably taken me into this territory, and I was quite interested by what was happening in that stormy land. At last a voice came on the line. 'Hello?' she said. 'Is it really you?' She was still the diffident Dagmar of old, but somehow she sounded even more meek. I explained about the cause. 'I'm supposed to come up with some ideas for the committee and I immediately thought of you.'

'Why?'

'Wouldn't a Balkan princess look rather relevant? So far, all I've got is two actors from a soap opera, a TV chef whom no one's heard of and a bunch of dowagers from Onslow Gardens.'

She hesitated. 'I don't really use that name now.' There was a sorrow in her voice, though whether it was a momentary stab of nostalgia or a general critique of her present existence I could not, of course, tell.

'Well, even if you're listed as Lady Holman, everyone will know who you are.' One says these things and I said this, although, as is often the case in such circumstances, I did not believe it to be true.

'Well . . .' She paused awkwardly. I had hoped that William's success in the City would have bolstered her confidence, but the reverse seemed to have happened.

'Can we discuss it? I'm going to be driving very near you next week. Could I possibly look in?'

'When?'

Once more, as with Lucy Dalton, I sensed a trapped animal searching for a route out, scanning the net for a possible tear, which I firmly closed off with my next speech. 'It entirely depends on you. I've got some stuff to do in Winchester but I can easily fit it round your diary. What day would suit best? It'd be such fun to see you again after all these years.'

She was enough of a lady to know when she was caught. 'Yes, it would. Of course it would. Why not come for some lunch next Friday?'

'Will William be with you?'

'Yes. He doesn't really like my entertaining when he's not here.' This sentence had escaped her mouth before she fully grasped its ugly, bullying significance. The words seemed to reverberate down the line between us. After a silent pause she attempted to round off its sharp edges: 'He gets so jealous when he finds he's missed seeing people he likes. I know he'd love to catch up with you.'

'Me, too,' I answered, because I had to. I was not quite clear how I would carry out my mission if William was too controlling to allow us a moment together, but there was nothing I could do about that. 'I'll be with you on Friday, just before one.'

Bellingham Court was a real house. It was about five miles from Winchester and not perhaps quite far enough from the motorway, but it was a genuine Elizabethan *schloss*, with high mullioned windows and corbelled ceilings and panelled great chambers and whispering passages, a thoroughly satisfactory ego-puffer of a place. As I turned in through the neatly painted gates, and drove down the long, tended and impeccable drive, it was easy to see it had been the subject of a recent, and massive, restoration programme. I parked in the wide forecourt, bordered by two broad, shallow parterres of water, edged in new and expensively carved stone, and before I had time to ring the bell the door was opened by a middle aged woman in sensible shoes, whom I took, correctly, to be the housekeeper. She led me inside.

The money here was not comparable to Damian's Croesus-like hoards. The Holmans were very rich, that was all, not super-duper-Bill-Gates-unbelievably rich. Just rich. But they were rich enough, by heaven. The hall was large, stone-flagged, and off-white, with a dark, carved screen at one end and some wonderful furniture. These items had been selected as contemporary with the house, which I later discovered was not the theme in the other downstairs rooms, the designer having decided that Tudor artefacts are easy to admire but hard to live with. The style had therefore been confined to the hall, with a few pieces in the library. There was in this a kind of premeditation, a sort of thought-out pattern that, just as in Damian's Surrey palace, was oddly undermining to any sense of country living. Proper country houses have a kind of randomness, objects and furniture are deliberately thrown together, survivals of many other houses, which have somehow all ended up there in a kind of *chic* higgledy-piggledy. Nor is this a skill unknown to many designers who, given ample time and money, can rustle up a house that looks as if the family have owned it since 1650, when in fact they moved in the summer of the previous year. But here, at Bellingham, this casual, comfortable elegance had not been achieved. In fact, there was a slightly disconcerting quality to the whole house that I cannot exactly describe, as if it had been prepared for an elaborate party to which I had not been invited. Had I been told it had been dressed for a photo shoot and I wasn't to touch anything, it would not have surprised me. The pictures were almost all large, full, or three-quarter- length portraits, over-cleaned and a little too shiny. They had a foreign feel to them and I squinted at some of the name plaques on the most important ones, as I passed. 'Frederick Francis, 1st Grand Duke of Mecklenburg-Shwerin, 1756–1837' said one, while another announced 'Count Felix Beningbauer gennant Lupitz, 1812–1871, and his son, Maximilian.'

'You see we are very pro-Europe in this house.' The voice startled me and I looked up to see a tiny figure standing at the far end of the hall, looking more like a boy scout on bob-a-job week than a princess in late middle age. Of course, I knew it was Dagmar because her stature meant it had to be, but I could not at first find her in the face I was presented with. Her hair was grey, though as flat and lank as it had always been, and at last I recognised her wobbling, tremulous, anxious lips, but not much else of her youthful appearance had survived. Her eyes were still huge, but sadder now and, despite our luxurious setting, it seemed to me that for her, life had been a bumpy ride. We kissed, a little gauchely, two strangers pecking at each other's cheeks, before she led me into the main drawing room, a fine, light chamber, but again with a synthetic air. It was the perfect mixture of Colefax chintz and antiques, Georgian this time, beautifully chosen as individual items but with no coherence as a whole. There was more of the splendid, European parade on the walls.

I indicated a couple of them. 'I don't remember you having all these in Trevor Square. Or were they in storage?' We knew, without saying, that they formed no part of the provenance of Squire William de Holman.

She shook her head. 'Neither.' Now, at last, she was beginning to come back to me. The moist half-open mouth had firmed up a bit, but she still had that odd, discordant, tearful note in her voice, a faint, sad scrape of the vocal cords grinding together, that reminded me of the girl she had once been. 'William has scouts in all the auction houses, and whenever there is a picture coming up with the faintest connection to me he bids for it.' She did not elaborate on quite what this told us about her husband. No more did I.

'Where is he?'

'Choosing some wine for lunch. He won't be long.'

She poured me a drink from a supply concealed in a large, carved, rococo cupboard in the corner which I saw, to my amusement, contained a small sink, and we talked. Dagmar was more aware of what I had been doing with my life than I anticipated and she must have noticed how flattered I was when she spoke of one particular novel that had barely broken the surface of the water. I thanked her. She gave a little smile. 'I like to keep up with the news of the people I knew then.'

'More than with the people themselves?'

She shrugged lightly. 'Friendships are based on shared experience. I don't know what we would all have in common now. William isn't very ... nostalgic for that time in his life. He prefers what happened later.' Which did not surprise me. If I were him, so would I. 'Do you see anyone from those days?' I told her I'd visited Lucy. 'Heavens, you are having a time of it. How is she?'

'All right. Her husband's got another business. I'm not sure how well it's doing.'

She nodded. 'Philip Rawnsley-Price. The one man we were all on the run from and Lucy Dalton ends up marrying him. How peculiar time is. I imagine he's quite different now?'

'Not different enough,' I said ungenerously and we laughed. 'I've seen Damian Baxter, too. Quite recently. Do you remember him?'

This time she let out a kind of giggling gasp that brought the old Dagmar I had known completely back into the room. 'Do I remember him?' she said. 'How could I forget him when our names have been linked ever since?' My mind running, as it was, on another track, this remark amazed me. Had I entirely missed a romance that everyone else knew about?

'Really?'

She did a double take. Clearly she was puzzled by my slowness. 'You remember my party? When he flattened Andrew Summersby? And added about two thousand pounds to the bill? Which was quite a lot of money then, I can tell you.' But she was not made angry at the recollection. Quite the reverse. I could see that.

'Of course I remember. I also remember your attempts to pretend he'd been invited. I rather loved you for that.'

She nodded. 'It was hopeless, of course.' She smiled like a naughty, little elf at the thought of her long-ago gallantry. 'My mother was still living in some fantasy kingdom in her own head. She thought if she allowed one young man, who had behaved perfectly all evening, to stay on without an invitation, somehow Rome would fall. Needless to say, her intransigence made us ridiculous.'

'You weren't ridiculous.'

She flushed with pleasure. 'No? I hope not.'

'How is your mother? I was always so terrified of her.'

'You wouldn't be now.'

'She's alive, then?'

'Yes. She's alive. We might see her if you've time for a walk after lunch.'

I nodded. 'I'd like that.' There was a lull and I could hear the sound of a bee trapped somewhere against a window, that familiar buzzing thump. Not for the first time I was struck by the strangeness of this kind of talk, with people you once knew well and now do not know at all. 'She must be pleased with the way things turned out for you.' In saying this I was perfectly sincere. The Grand Duchess had been so determined on a sensational marriage for her daughter that William Holman must have been a crushing disappointment, however necessary he was at the time. Little did either she, or we, know that he would deliver a way of life that would far outshine the promises of the eldest sons on offer in 1968.

She looked at me pensively. 'Yes and no,' she muttered.

Before I could comment further, William strode into the room, right hand extended towards me. He was better-looking than I remembered him, tall and thin, and his greying hair giving him a sort of blond, youthful appearance. 'How nice to see you,' he said and I noticed that, unusually after such a time, his voice was more changed than his face. It had become important, as if he were addressing the boardroom of a corporation, or a village hall full of grateful tenants. 'How are you?' We shook hands and exchanged the usual platitudes about Long Time No See, while Dagmar fetched him a drink. He looked down as he took it. 'Isn't there any lemon?'

'Apparently not.'

'Why not?' Given that I was more or less a stranger to him, despite our protestations of delight in each other's company, William's tone to his spouse was oddly and uncomfortably severe.

'They must have forgotten to buy any.' She spoke as if she were locked in a cell with a potentially violent felon and was trying to attract the attention of the guards.

'They? Who are "they"? You mean "you." *You* have forgotten to ask them to buy any.' He sighed wearily, saddened by the pathetic mediocrity of his wife's abilities. 'Oh well. Never mind.' He sipped the drink, wrinkled his nose with displeasure and turned back to me. 'So, what brings you here?'

I explained about the charity, since I was not, naturally, about to go into the true reason. He looked at me with that face of *faux* concern that people use when listening to hard luck stories in the street. 'Of course, this is a marvellous cause, as I said to Dagmar when I first heard about it, and I admire you terrifically for getting involved . . .'

'But?'

'But I don't think it's one for us.' He paused, expecting me to come in and say that of course I understood, but I waited, without comment, until he felt sufficiently wrong-footed to elucidate. 'I don't want Dagmar to be held captive by all that. Obviously, the position of her family was a very interesting one, but it's finished. She's Lady Holman now. There's no need for her to cash in on some bogus title from the past, when she has a perfectly good one in the modern world. This kind of thing, vital as it might be,' he gave a smile but it did not reach his eyes, 'seems to me to take her backwards, not forwards.'

I turned to Dagmar for a comment, but she was silent. 'I don't see her position as bogus,' I said. 'She's a member of a ruling house.'

'An ex-ruling house.'

'They were on the throne until three years before she was born.'

'Which was a long time ago.'

This seemed needlessly ungallant. 'There are plenty of people living in exile who look to her brother for leadership.'

'Oh, I see. You think we'll all attend Feodor's coronation? I hope he can get the time off work.' He laughed suddenly, with a kind of sneer in the sound, as he brought his face round to Dagmar's, that she might fully register his contempt. It was intolerable. 'I'm afraid I find all that stuff is just an excuse for a few snobs to bow and curtsey and gee up their dinner parties.' He shook his head slowly, as if he were making a reasonable point. 'They should pay more attention to what's going on around them today.' He sipped his drink to punctuate the finality of his argument. In other words there could be no further discussion on the subject.

I turned to Dagmar. 'Do you agree?'

She took a breath. 'Well—'

'Of course she agrees. Now, when's lunch?' I saw then that the real burden of William's song was that for years he had endured being treated as Dagmar's moment of madness, the shaming *mésalliance* that had overtaken the Moravian dynasty, and now he didn't have to put up with it any more. Things had changed. Today, he was the one with the money, he was the one with the power and weren't we going to know about it. Worse than this, having triumphed, he could no longer tolerate Dagmar having any sort of position of her own. She must have no value at all other than as his wife, no podium where she might shine independent of his glory. In short, he was a bully. I understood now why the Grand Duchess's approval had been equivocal.

Luncheon was a curious event, providing as it did an endless series of opportunities for Dagmar to be publicly humiliated. 'What on earth is this?' 'Is it supposed to taste burnt?' 'Why are we eating with nursery cutlery?' 'Those flowers deserve a decent burial.' 'Shouldn't there be a sauce with this or did you ask for it to be dry?' If I had been Dagmar, I would have stood up, broken a large plate over his head and left him forever. And that was before we got to the pudding. But I know only too well that this kind of wife-battering, for that is what we were dealing with, destroys the will to resist and, to my sorrow, she simply took it. She even gave credence to his complaints by apologising for shortcomings that were entirely fictional. 'I am sorry. It should be hotter than this,' she would say. Or, 'You're right. I should have asked them to seal it first.' The limit came when William took a bite of the little *crêpes Suzette* that had been brought in and spat it back onto his plate. 'Jesus!' he shouted at the top of his voice. 'What the hell is this made of? Soap?'

'I don't understand you.' I spoke carefully. 'It's delicious.'

'Not where I come from.' He gave a merry laugh, as if we were all enjoying a jolly joke.

'And where do you come from, exactly?' I said. 'I forget.' I stared at him and he held my gaze for a second. Behind his head the housekeeper glanced quickly at a maid who had been helping to serve to check if she'd registered this exchange. I could see them silently acknowledge that they both had. In fact, they were nearly smiling. However, whether or not it was entertaining for the staff to witness the tyrant brought low, it was snobbish and self-defeating of me to do it. William, red in the face with fury, was on the brink of ordering me out of the house, which would have rendered my journey completely pointless. Mercifully, he was never one to allow his anger to undo him. Years of tricky negotiations in the City had made him cleverer than that. And I would guess the thought of the story going round London, coming from someone who was perhaps better known than he (not richer, not more successful, just a little better known) was something he was not prepared to risk. Of course, my chief crime in his eyes wasn't that I had been rude to him and failed to take his part. It was that I seemed to find his wife more congenial and more interesting than he was, which was even worse than my reminding him of the long journey he had traversed since we first met. I knew he made a point of editing every visitor who entered the house, so presumably this kind of challenge seldom, if ever, happened. He was out of practice when it came to being contradicted.

With a deep and deliberately audible breath, he put down his napkin, painstakingly rumpled, and smiled. 'The awful thing is I have to run. Will you excuse me?' I saw, to my amusement, he was trying to be 'gracious.' It was not in his gift. 'I'm at home on Fridays, but it doesn't mean I don't have to work. If only it did. Dagmar will see you off. Won't you, my darling? It's been such a treat to catch up again.' I smiled and thanked him, as if I had not just been instructed to leave, and we both pretended everything was fine. Then he was gone. Dagmar and I stared at each other, her little, crumpled face and narrow shoulders suddenly making her look like a picture of some starving child in war-torn Berlin. Or Edith Piaf. Towards the end.

'Do you feel like a walk after that?' she said. 'I don't blame you if you want to get away. I won't be offended.'

'Hasn't he just told me to get off his land?'

She made a little pout. 'So?'

'Don't make him angry on my behalf.'

136

'He's always angry. What's the difference?'

The gardens at Bellingham had been tidied, replanted and restored to an approximation of their Edwardian appearance, with a large walled garden and separate 'rooms' containing statues surrounded by box hedges or roses in neat and tidy beds. It was all very nice, but the park was something more. Survivors of the original build, the giant oak trees, ancient and venerable, gave the whole place a sober beauty, a gravitas lacking in the quaint gardens or the newly refurbished interior. I looked around. 'You're very lucky.'

'Am I?'

'In this, anyway.'

She also stared about her, admiring the stately trees and the roll of the hills surrounding us. 'Yes,' she said. 'I am lucky in this.' We walked on for a bit. 'How was he?' she said suddenly, out of the blue. I did not immediately understand her. 'Damian. You told me you'd seen him recently.'

'Not very well, I'm afraid.'

She nodded. 'I heard that. I was hoping you'd tell me it wasn't true.'

'Well, it is.' Again, we were silent as we crested a shallow slope with a wonderful view across the park towards the house.

'Did you know I was mad about him?' she said.

I was becoming used to surprises. 'I knew you'd had a bit of a walk-out. But I didn't know it was the Real Thing.'

'Well, it was. For me, anyway.'

'Then you were very discreet.'

She chuckled sadly. 'There wasn't much to be discreet about.'

'He talked of you the other day,' I said.

At this, her colour altered before my gaze and she raised a hand to her cheek. 'Did he?' she whispered. 'Did he really?' It was very touching.

I could see we were at last approaching the discussion I had come for, but I wanted to progress it carefully. 'He just mentioned that you and he had been out together a few times, which I hadn't known before.'

Released by the knowledge that somehow she was still alive in Damian's imagination, her words came pouring out. 'I would have married him, you know.' I stopped. This was astonishing. We seemed to have gone from nought to a hundred miles an hour in less than two minutes. Damian had given the impression of a one- night stand, but, for Dagmar it was *Tristan and Isolde.* How often it seems a pair of lovers can be engaged in two entirely different relationships.

She caught my expression and nodded vigorously, as if I were going to contradict her. It was an extraordinary transformation and the first time I had ever seen her take the lead in anything approaching an argument. 'I'd have done it if he'd asked me. I would!'

I raised my arms in surrender. 'I believe you,' I said.

Which made her smile and relax again, knowing by my action I was friend not foe. 'My mother would have thrown herself out of an upper window, of course, but I was ready for her. And I wasn't as mad as all that. I knew he'd do well. That was what I loved about him. He was part of the world that was coming.' She glanced at me. 'Not the world we *thought* was coming, all that peace and love and flowers-in-your-hair. Not that. The *real* world that crept secretly towards us through the seventies and arrived with a bang in the eighties. The ambition, the rapacity, I knew that another rich oligarchy would be back in place before I died and I was sure Damian would belong to it.'

A strange feature of growing older is the discovery that everyone who was young alongside you was just as incapable of expressing their thoughts as you yourself were. Somehow, in youth, most of us think that we are misunderstood but everyone else is stupid. I realised, with some sorrow, that I could have been much, much friendlier with Dagmar than I had been, if I'd only realised what was going on inside her little head. 'So, what happened? You couldn't convince your mother?'

'That wasn't the reason. She would have given in if I'd screamed loudly enough. After all, in the end she let me marry William who had no background at all, just because she thought he might make money.'

'What was it, then?'

She sighed, still sorry. 'He didn't want it.' She frowned, anxious to qualify her statement. 'I mean he liked me a bit and he was quite amused by all the ... stuff. But he never fancied me. Not really.' Of course, the sad truth was that none of us had fancied her. Not, at any rate, what Nanny would describe as *in that way,* she was too much of a waif, too much the loveless, pitiful child, but at her words I was struck with a wave of pity for our younger selves, bursting with unrequited love, as all we plain ones had been. Aching to tell, somehow believing that if only the object of our passions could be brought to understand the force of our love, they would yield to it, yet knowing all the time that this is not so and they would not.

Dagmar hadn't finished. 'There was a moment when I thought I could have him. At one particular point I thought I could promise him everything he was doing the Season to get. Social ...' She hesitated. She had been so carried away that it had led her into territory that made her awkward. Her timid diffidence came flooding back. 'You know ... social whatever ... I thought he might want it enough to take me as part of the deal.' She looked across. 'I suppose that sounds very desperate.'

'It sounds very determined. I'm surprised it didn't work.' I was. Whether he found her attractive or not, I would have thought the Damian Baxter of those years would have leaped at the chance of a princess bride.

Now it was her turn to look at me pityingly. 'You never understood him. Even before that terrible dinner in Portugal. You thought he wanted everything you had. More than you had. Which he did, in a way. But at some moment during the year we spent together he realised he only wanted it on his own terms or not at all.'

'Perhaps that's what you admire in men. William certainly has it on his own terms.' Which could have been cruel but she did not take it as such.

Instead, she shook her head to mark the difference in her mind between the two men. 'William is a little man. He married me to be a big man. Then, when he had made his own money and bought a knighthood, and generally became, as he thought, big, he didn't want me to be big as well any more. He wanted me to be little, so he could be even bigger.' I cannot tell you how sad these words were, as I listened to her far-back, 1950s Valerie Hobson voice issuing from her minute frame. She looked so breakable. 'He thinks as long as he ridicules my birth and criticises my appearance, and yawns whenever I open my mouth, he can demonstrate that I am the one who needs him and not the other way round.'

'He still buys portraits of your ancestors.'

'He doesn't have much choice. If we waited for his to come up we'd have to live with bare walls.' It was nice to hear her being waspish.

'Why don't you leave him?' It is hard to explain quite why, but this was not as intrusive a question at the time as it seems on the page.

She thought for a moment. 'I don't entirely know. For a long time it was the children, but they're not children now. So I don't know.'

'How many are there?'

'Three. Simon's the eldest. He's thirty-seven, working in the City. Gone.'

'Married?'

'Not yet. I used to wonder if he might be gay. I wouldn't mind, but I don't think he is. I suspect it's more that he's been put off the institution by his parents' example. Then there's Clarissa, who's happily married to a successful and very nice paediatrician, I'm glad to say, even if William doesn't approve.'

'Why not?'

'He would have preferred a stupid peer to a clever doctor.' She sighed. 'And finally our youngest, Richard, who's only twenty-four and starting out in corporate entertainment.' She paused, reflecting on her own words. 'Don't the young have funny jobs now?'

'Not like our day.'

She looked at me. 'Well, you went into a funny job. None of us thought you'd make a living. Did you realise that?'

'I suspected it. Just as I always expected you to do something surprising.' I only said this to cheer her up, but in a way it may have been true. To me, she had been a bit of a wild card, so retiring, so minor key, with her giggles and her long silences, that I used sometimes to have a sense that there was a completely different person living inside this shy and weeny head, even if I never investigated it at the time. I half expected the day to come when she'd break loose. Somehow it didn't seem possible that she would just slide into that Sloane life of buying school uniforms and cooking for the freezer in some provincial Aga kitchen.

Obviously, Dagmar found the idea of herself as a career girl rather flattering. 'Really? Very few of us did anything very spectacular. Rebecca Dawnay composes film music now and didn't Carla Wakefield open a restaurant in Paris? Or am I muddling her with someone?' She was combing her brain, 'I know one of the London editors is a former deb, but I forget which one . . .' she sighed. 'Anyway, that's about it.

'Even so.' I had quite recovered from my initial bewilderment at her unfamiliar appearance. Now Dagmar looked like herself again and it brought the memories rushing back. 'Do you remember in Portugal, on the first night? When we took a picnic to that haunted castle on the hill and talked about life? You sounded like someone plotting a break-out. I expect you've forgotten.'

'No, I haven't forgotten.' She stopped walking, as if to punctuate her sentence. 'I think you're right and I was planning something of the kind. But I got pregnant.' We had all known this, of course, in the unspoken way such news was received in those distant days, so I didn't comment. 'William asked me to marry him and, whatever you think of him now, I was pretty relieved at the time I can tell you. Anyway, then Simon arrived and that was that.'

We were nearly back at the house by this time and I needed some answers. 'When did you give up on Damian?'

Her muscles tensed and her face took on the look of a nervous chipmunk. I realised the question, or at least the return to 1968, was not at all easy for her, but there was no way round it. I waited while she composed her reply. 'I gave up on him when he didn't propose to me and William did.' She hesitated. 'The truth is, though I hardly know how to say it,' she blushed again, but clearly she had decided that she was too far in to back out now, 'either of them could have been the baby's father. I was going out with William at the time, but Damian and I slept together on the night we arrived in Estoril. I remember it very well because it was the last time that I thought I just might get him. Then, later that same night, he told me it wasn't going to happen. Ever. That he was fond of me, but . . .' She shrugged and suddenly the lonely, heartbroken girl of forty years before was there, walking beside us in the park. 'After that, when my period was late, I knew that it was either William or the abortion clinic. It's odd to think of it, given how William behaves to me now, but I cannot describe my relief when he did pop the question.'

'I'm sure.' I was.

She gave a sudden shiver. 'I should have worn a jersey,' she said. And then, with a shy glance. 'I don't know why I told you all that.'

'Because I was interested,' I said. Actually, this is quite true. Especially in England. Very few Englishmen ever ask women anything about themselves. They choose instead to lecture their dinner neighbours on a new and better route to the M5, or to praise their own professional achievements. So if a man does express any curiosity about the woman sitting next to him, about her feelings, about the life she is leading, she will generally tell him anything he cares to know.

We were passing the stable block, which was a few hundred yards away from the main house. It was much later, perhaps mid-eighteenth century, and the wall of the yard ended in a rather handsome lodge, built for some trusty steward or perhaps a madly superior coachman. Before we'd gone a few more steps the front door opened and an old woman came out with a wave. She was wearing the tweeds and scarf of a standard County mother. 'Dagmar told me you were coming,' she called over the grass separating us. 'I wanted to come out and say hello.'

I stared at the wrinkled, bony creature walking towards me. Could this really be the majestic Grand Duchess of my youth? Or had her head been transplanted on to another's body? Where was the weight, in every sense? Where were the charisma and the fear she had inspired? Vanished entirely. She approached and I bowed. 'Ma'am,' I murmured, but she shook her head and pulled me towards her for a dry kiss on both my cheeks.

'Never mind all that,' she said gaily and slipped her arm through mine. This simple action in itself was a marker of how much had vanished from the world in the years since we last met. My sentimental side approved it as a friendly and relaxing alteration. But, all things considered, I suspect that more had been lost than gained for both of us. She looked across at her daughter. 'Is Simon here yet? He told me he was trying to be with you for lunch.'

'Obviously he couldn't get away. He won't be long.' Dagmar smiled at her mother, this cosy, easy pensioner who had stolen the identity of the warlord of my early years. 'We've been talking about Damian Baxter.'

'*Damian Baxter.*' The Grand Duchess rolled her eyes to heaven, then smiled at me. 'If you knew the rows we had over *that* young man.'

'So I gather.'

'And now he's richer than anyone living. So I suppose he's had the last laugh.' She paused. 'But anyway, whatever she's told you, it wasn't my fault that it didn't happen. Not in the end. You can't blame me.'

'Whose fault was it?'

'His. Damian's.' Her voice had the finality of the Lutine Bell. 'We all thought he was a climber, an adventurer, a man on the make. And so he was, in his own fashion.' She turned back to me to wave a pointed finger at my nose. 'And you brought him among us. How we mothers used to curse you for it.' She laughed merrily. 'But you see . . .' Suddenly her tone was becoming almost dreamy as she clambered back through the lost decades, searching for the right words. 'He wasn't after what we had. Not really. I didn't see that at the time. He wanted to experience it, to witness it, but only as a traveller from another land. He didn't want to live in the past where he had no position. He wanted to live in the future where he could be anything he wished. And he was quite right. It was where he belonged.' She looked back at her daughter, now walking behind us. 'Dagmar had nothing useful to give him that would make life easier there.' She lowered her voice. 'Maybe if he'd loved her it would have been different. But without love, there wasn't enough in it to tempt him.'

I was struck by Damian's journey in that year of years. At the start he had been thrilled by his first invitation from Fat Georgina. By the end he had turned down the hand of a perfectly genuine princess. Not many can say that. There was a noise of footsteps, and around a laurel-sheltered corner of the drive William came almost goose-stepping towards us in a gleaming new Barbour and spotless Hunter gumboots. He caught sight of me and frowned. By his reckoning I should have been safely back on the road by then. 'Here's William,' I said brightly. His mother-in-law looked at him with disdain and in silence. 'It must have been a relief that he stepped up to the mark when Dagmar needed him.' Obviously, I had spoken without thinking.

She turned a freezing fish eye upon me. 'I do not understand you,' she said coldly. It felt like the return of an old friend.

'I meant if Dagmar was anxious to marry.'

'She was not "anxious" to marry. She just felt that it was time.' Having settled this, the Grand Duchess relaxed and, after her brief outing, vanished back inside the chipper, little pensioner. 'William wanted what Dagmar could bring him. Damian did not. That's all there was to it.' She glanced in my direction. 'I know you didn't like him by the end.' I said nothing to contradict her. 'Dagmar told me about that business in Portugal.' Someone told everyone, I thought wryly. 'But it blinded you to what he was and what he could be. By the time Damian left our life, even I could see he was an unusual man.' I wonder now if she wasn't enjoying herself, discussing these events with someone who had been there when they were all taking place. Especially as I was an old friend, or at least I was a person she had known for a long time, which after a certain point is almost the same thing, and in all probability we would not meet again. I had provided her with an unexpected chance to make sense of those years and those distant decisions. I would guess they were not much talked of in the usual way of things and she wanted to make the best use of me. I cannot otherwise explain her next comment. 'William never had Damian's imagination,' she said. 'Nor his confidence in what the future would bring. Whatever his faults, Damian Baxter was a visionary in his way. William was just a tedious, vulgar social climber.'

'That doesn't mean he didn't love your daughter.' I saw no reason why we couldn't give him the benefit of some doubt.

But she shook her head. 'I don't think so. She made him feel important, that's all. That's why he resents her now. He can't bear the thought that he ever needed her to flatter his little ego.' I said nothing. Not because I disapproved of her disloyalty. If anything, I was honoured by the trust implicit in her indiscretion. But I had nothing I felt I could usefully add. She looked at me and laughed. 'I can't stand him, really. I don't think Dagmar can, but we never talk of it.'

'There's no point. Unless she's going to do something about him.'

She nodded. The rightness of this comment made her sad. In fact, the whole conversation had taken her into a strange, uncharted territory and I could see a light coating of glycerine beginning to make her eyes shine. 'The thing is, I don't know how we'd all manage. He'd find some way to give her nothing if they separate, some shyster lawyer would savage her claims and then what?' She sighed wearily, a hard worker in life's vineyard who deserved more rest than she was getting. There was the distant noise of an engine and her eyes looked up to find it. 'It's Simon, at last. Good.' The distraction had pulled her back from the cliff edge. She was probably already regretting what she had revealed.

A gleaming car of some foreign make was spinning down the drive towards us. As I watched it, I felt a sudden surge of longing. Let this man be Damian's son, I thought. Please. I cared about it in a way I had not cared with Lucy. In their scatterbrained way, the Rawnsley-Prices would shake out some sort of future, juggling Philip's demented schemes, surviving on luck and others' charity, but here, today, I felt as if I had been visiting old friends trapped in some hideous, third world prison for a crime they did not commit. Like all her kind, the old Grand Duchess was more frightened of poverty than it was worth. It would only be comparative poverty, genteel poverty, after all, but at a distance even that seemed unacceptable to her. I suppose she felt she had seen enough change and we must surely forgive her for that. This is always a delicate subject where the British upper classes and most Royalty are concerned, if they are facing poverty when they are used to living well. Most of them dread not only the coming discomfort but the loss of face that attends the loss of income, and they will submit to almost any humiliation rather than have to reduce their circumstance in public. Of course, there is another smaller group among them that doesn't give a damn either way. They are the lucky ones.

I thought again of the delivery from suffering that might be coming down the drive towards us. A quick DNA test and they would all be free of this horrible despot and their miserable existence. Dagmar and her mother and the other children would escape into a new land, where they would do just as they liked, and William would sit alone at his table, grumbling and fuming and insulting his servants to the end of his days. I wondered how we were going to get Simon to agree to a test. Would he worry about William's feelings? Did William have feelings? Dagmar had dropped back to stand by me. Her mother and her husband were a little way in front of us, waiting for the car as it drew nearer. 'It's been so lovely seeing you again,' I said. 'And your much-mellowed mama.' I wanted her to think of me as a friend. Because I was one.

She acknowledged my words with a quick smile, but then grew serious. Clearly, she'd deliberately manoeuvred a last moment with me out of earshot of the others. 'I hope you won't pay too much attention to what I was saying before. I can't think what came over me. It was just self-pity.'

'I won't mention it to anyone.'

'Thank you.' The crease of worry faded away. On the sweep before the house the shiny car had stopped and a man in his late thirties climbed out. He turned with a wave to face us.

And in that moment Dagmar's fate was sealed, as all my fantasies of playing Superman to this lost family came crashing down. But for their ages, he could have been William's identical twin. There wasn't a trace of his mother in him. Eyes, nose, mouth, hair, head, figure, manner, gait, they were like two peas in a pod. Dagmar saw me looking at him and smiled. 'As you can see, he was William's son after all.'

'Clearly.' We had reached my car by this stage and I opened the door.

'So everything worked out for the best,' she said.

'Of course it did. It often does, despite what they tell us on television,' I replied, climbing into the vehicle, taking her better, happier future with me. For a moment it seemed she was going to say something more, but then she thought better of it. So I said it for her. 'I'll give your love to Damian when I see him.'

She smiled. I had guessed right. 'Please do. My best love.' She looked round. 'Are you sure you won't stay and say hello to Simon?'

'Better not. I'm late and he'll be tired. I shall just enjoy you as a loving family group while I drive past.' Dagmar nodded, with a certain irony in her expression. I know she was glad to see the back of me that day and no wonder. I had committed the sin of reminding her of a happier time. Worse, I had made her admit to truths about her present life that she preferred to keep buried even from herself. I had my reasons, but it was cruel all the same.

At any rate, without further protest she stepped back, politely attending my departure, and a moment later I was on my way.

Serena

SEVEN

By the time I had got lost finding the motorway and caught in the evening traffic as I came into London, the whole excursion took longer than I'd planned and I did not arrive home much before eight. Bridget had let herself in some time earlier, and polished off half a bottle of Chablis in the interim. This made her rather sour as she banged around the kitchen making dinner. I cannot now think why I never questioned that she should always cook for me, when she spent her days in an office tussling with important decisions behind a desk, while I lolled around for most of the time, performing needless, invented tasks to fill the daylight hours as I waited for inspiration. In my defence, I don't remember her ever objecting to the arrangement. If it was my turn we went out. If it was her turn she cooked. Sometimes you just accept things.

'Your father rang,' she said. 'He wants you to call him back.'

'What about?'

'He didn't say, but he tried twice and the second time he sounded rather annoyed that you weren't here.'

There was a vague but completely unreasonable reprimand buried in this somewhere. 'I can't manage my day in case my father might ring.'

'Don't blame me.' She shrugged and went back into the kitchen. 'I'm just the messenger.' I was struck, not for the first time, by the tremendous mistake that about half the human race usually finds itself making when it comes to wobbly relationships. The division is not by sex or class or nationality or race or even age, since almost every type is found on both sides of the divide. The mistake is this: When they are in a partnership that is not going well, they attempt to inject a kind of drama into it by becoming moody and critical and permanently not-quite-satisfied. 'Why do you *always* do that?' they say. 'Now, are you listening because you *never* get this right?' Or, 'Don't tell me you've forgotten *again*!'

Not belonging to this team, I find it hard to penetrate their thinking. Do they imagine that by being demanding and edgy and cross, they will force you to work harder to make things better? If so, they are, of course, completely wrong. This kind of talk just gives one permission to go. The more dissatisfied they are, the more their gloom will become a self-fulfilling prophecy. In fact, the first time you hear that put-upon sigh, 'I suppose I'm expected to clean this up,' you know it is simply a matter of time. The irony being that the ones who are truly hard to leave are those who are always happy. To desert a happy lover, to make them unhappy when they were not unhappy before, is hard and mean, and involves guilt of a major kind. To leave a miserable whinger just seems logical.

Of course, this implies it is easy to get up the nerve to end an affair that is past its sell-by date. But for many it is not. They tell themselves they are being nice, or honourable, or adult, in struggling on, but what they are being is weak. I do not mean a bad marriage or when there are children involved. But when we're only talking childless cohabitation it is plain cowardice to settle for failure. The years spent after we have decided that we will not die and be buried next to *this* one, are just wasted, so why do we put it off? Is it misguided kindness or false optimism or because we've taken a villa for the whole of August with the Grimstons and we can't let them down? Or even: Where on earth would I put all this stuff? It doesn't matter. Once the inner voice has spoken and given the verdict, every day spent evading the end is unworthy of you. And when it came to Bridget FitzGerald, I was unworthy.

My father was quite grouchy when he picked up the receiver. 'Where have you been all day?' he said.

'I had to go to Hampshire for lunch.'

'Why, for God's sake?' As any adult child knows, when dealing with an aged parent there is no point in engaging with this stuff.

'You could have rung me on the mobile,' I suggested.

'It's illegal if you were driving.'

'I've got an ear thing.'

'Even so.' Again, silence is the only sensible option. At last, his anger spent, he returned to his topic. 'I want you to come down and see me. There are some things we ought to talk about.' In fact, he lived above London on the map, on the border of Gloucestershire and Shropshire, but my father was of that generation where London was the highest point in Britain. So he went 'up' to London and 'down' to everywhere else. I rather loved him for it. I suppose he went down to Inverness, but I don't remember trying him on this. I cannot ask him now for he has died since I lived through these events. I miss him every day.

Bridget came out of the kitchen, carrying a plate of food on to which she had already spooned a huge helping of some stew and various vegetables. 'I've served it up in the kitchen. I know you don't like me to, but we haven't got all day.'

I always find this kind of talk intensely irritating, draped as it is with self-importance. 'You are quite right,' I said coolly. 'I don't like having a plate piled up with things I have not chosen since I have been out of the nursery for some years. Nor do I see why we haven't got all day. What pressing engagement are we racing to meet?' Having delivered this twaddle, no less self-important than the speech that had provoked it, I sat down at the table.

But Bridget had not quite finished. 'I'm afraid it's very overcooked,' she sighed, as she laid the concoction before me.

It was clearly time to acknowledge that we were having a spat and with that remark she had finally used up the last stock of patience I had kept in reserve. 'I cannot think why, since I was here before eight,' I muttered, deliberately using a harsh and frigid tone to combat hers. 'At what hour were you planning to eat?' She bit her lip and said nothing.

Of course, as I knew well enough, this was a dishonourable dig. Before meeting me, Bridget had generally tucked into her evening feed at about half past six or seven, and she still found my insistence on dining at half past eight or nine not so much unreasonable as weird. This will be familiar to many who have ventured beyond their home pastures to find a mate. Even in this day and age, even after almost everyone, south of Watford anyway, says 'lunch' and when all sorts of foods from avocados to sushi have become ordinary fare, still the time for evening eating can provoke an absolute clash of cultures. To me, early eating can only be explained if food is considered essentially as fuel to strengthen one for the adventures yet to come. So, people will dine at six or six thirty in order to be fuelled by seven, in time to fill the next few hours with fun. This time may be spent in a club or in a pub or keeping fit or studying macramé or learning Mandarin or line dancing or simply watching television while sitting on a sofa. The evening is your oyster and, by eating early, you are free to enjoy every pleasure while it lasts.

The reason this is completely bewildering for the upper middle and upper classes is simply because for them the dinner *is* the pleasure. It is the apex, the core, the point. If the whole business of feeding is over by half past seven, what on earth is one to do until bed? These people don't go to self-help groups, or engage in amateur acting, nor do they study art or quilting, or drop into a bar. This is why any role in local government is so difficult for them. It takes place just when they prefer to be sitting at a table for a very different purpose. For those who cross the great social divide, there can be few habits harder to adjust to, whichever direction they have travelled. Certainly, Bridget had found it difficult and now, here I was, deliberately goading her, insulting her, putting her down. I was ashamed of myself. But not, it seems, sufficiently ashamed to regain my good humour. I stared at the plate. 'And I wish you wouldn't pile it up like that. It's so off-putting.' I whined as I unfolded my napkin. 'I feel like a tramp being fed before retiring to my cubicle in a Rowton House.'

'And I feel like the skivvy serving him,' said Bridget without the trace of a smile, and we let it rest there.

At the time of these events my father lived in a modest village called Abberley, on the Gloucestershire borders. He was eighty-six then and he'd chosen it as his retreat after my mother's fairly early death ten years before. There was no pressing reason for him to go there, since their marriage had largely been spent abroad and the first years of his retirement had been passed in Wiltshire, but I suppose he wanted a change and our family had been based for the latter half of the nineteenth century at Abberley Park, a rather over-christened large house of negligible architectural merit, situated behind a cobbled forecourt, at one end of the main street of the village. It meant little to me, as it had only been a third-rate hotel in my lifetime; still we would visit it occasionally for lunch or tea, and Pa would pretend a kind of nostalgia for the place. This, I suspect, was to encourage me to take an interest in my family's history, but I always found his Turgenev-style melancholy fairly unconvincing. The large, dreary hall and the largish dreary drawing and dining rooms on either side of it were all hideously decorated, and any trace of private life had long since vanished from the atmosphere. My father had no memories of the house anyway, since his grandfather had sold it, after the agricultural depression, in the early years of the twentieth century before he was even born. I suppose the staircase, in slightly crude nineteenth-century baroque, was pretty and the dark, panelled library may once have been nice, but its translation into a bar, complete with upside-down bottles on silver holders, had obliterated its fragile charm. However, the seller-grandfather, plus his wife and various other members of the two preceding generations of our clan, lay in the graveyard of the local church and were commemorated with plaques in the nave, and I imagine this gave my papa a sense of belonging, something neither he nor my mother had ever quite achieved in their previous home.

His life in Abberley was pleasant enough but a bit sad, of course, as all old men living on their own are sad, in a way that old women are not. He had a housekeeper called Mrs Snow, who was reasonably civil and would cook him lunch every day and depart after it was washed up and put away. She would leave his dinner in the fridge, in a terrifying array of dishes covered in cling film, with post-it notes carrying strict instructions: 'Boil for twenty minutes,' 'Put in a pre-heated oven at gas mark 5 for half an hour.' I could never see the point of this, since she wasn't a very good cook, to say the least of it, her repertoire consisting entirely of English nursery food from the 1950s, and he could have bought everything at the local Waitrose. It would have been quicker and easier to prepare, as well as much nicer to eat. But, looking back, I think he rather enjoyed the disciplined activity of unwrapping everything and obeying her iron will. It must have taken up quite a bit of the evening and that would have been a real bonus.

On the day that I went to see him Mrs Snow was preparing our lunch when I arrived, but he told me in dulcet tones, as he poured two glasses of very dry sherry, that she was going to leave us as soon as she had brought in the pudding. In other words she was not going to stay to wash up. 'We'll have the place to ourselves,' he muttered out of the side of his mouth as he led the way to a chair in his chilly and unsuccessful drawing room. Why is it that some people can live in a house for twenty years, yet the furniture still looks as if the removal van has just pulled out of the gates? In this, his last house he had copied a few rooms from earlier homes that my mother had decorated, but he never seemed to find a template for the little, irregularly shaped drawing room, so it just waited, with its magnolia walls and disparate collection of furniture, for an inspiration that never came.

'Good,' I answered, since that was what seemed to be called for.

He nodded briskly. 'I think it's better.' Years in the diplomatic had made him secretive as a rule, in addition to which he shared the usual prejudice of his kind that it was impossible to have any kind of conversation about money, outside the walls of a bank or a brokers', were it not serving one of two purposes. These comprised discussing your future son-in-law's net worth and prospects, and talking about your own will. Since my sister was long married, I gathered at once that the second was what we were in for and so it proved.

We had exchanged bits of family information in a desultory fashion through some unsalted, tasteless shepherd's pie and we were staring at an uninviting plum duff with custard, when Mrs Snow leant round the door in her coat and hat. 'I'll be off, then,' she said to my father. 'I've put coffee in the library, Sir David, so don't let it get cold.' In response to this, he twisted his face into something akin to a wink, signifying that as with all, lonely old people who employ one servant, the relationship was becoming dangerous, and he nodded his thanks. We heard the door bang and he started.

'I had rather a turn the other day and I went to see old Babbage. He's run a few tests and it seems I may be cracking up at last.'

'I thought you said Babbage ought to be struck off.'

'I never did.'

'You said he couldn't diagnose a gunshot wound.'

'Did I?' My father was slightly cheered by this. 'Perhaps I did. Anyway, it doesn't alter much. I'm going some time and it won't be long now.'

'What did he say?'

'Nothing to bother you with.'

'I have driven for two and a quarter hours. I deserve details.'

But he could not break the habits of a lifetime. 'It was all about blood being where it shouldn't be. Revolting stuff that I have no intention of discussing over pudding.' There wasn't much to come back with, so I waited while he got to the point. 'Anyway, I realised that you and I had never had a proper talk about everything.'

How strange death is. It seems to make such nonsense of the years that have gone before. Here was my father about to die, presumably of some form of cancer, and what had been the point of it all? What had it all been for? He'd worked pretty hard, in the way his generation did work, which was different from, and more sensible than ours, with their late starts and long lunches and getting home by half past six. Even so, he had done his best and travelled the world and stayed in horrible hotels, and sat through boring meetings and listened to heads of state lying, and experts making dire predictions that proved quite unfounded; he had studied worthless reports without number, and pretended to believe government spokesmen when they made ludicrous and mendacious claims for their inadequate ministers, and . . . for what? He had no money. Or not what my mother would have called 'real' money. This house, a few shares, one or two nice things left over from his forebears who had lived better than he did, a pension that would perish with him. My sister and I had been given good educations, which must have set them back, but Louise had largely thrown hers away by marrying a very ordinary stockbroker and bringing up three children, all of whom were dull to the point of genius, while I —

'I want you to know what I've arranged, in case you think I've made anything unnecessarily complicated. You're the executor, so you'll have to deal with it if I've made a nonsense.'

I nodded. My thoughts would not get back in their box. Poor old boy. It had been a good life, I suppose. At least that's what people would say when his funeral eventually came to pass. 'He had a good life.' But did he really? Was it a good life? Was it enough? He met my mother towards the end of the war, when she was working for someone in the Foreign Office. He had been seconded to assist with the settlement of Poland and other places where the British would make the wrong decisions, as a preparatory move to taking up his career again when the fighting stopped. They married in 1946, just before he was appointed second secretary to our embassy in Madrid, and, on the whole, they'd been quite happy. I honestly believe that. She liked travelling and the constant relocation of their home had pleased, rather than annoyed her. Once he made ambassador, I would go as far as to say she had a good time and, while he never got one of the really big ones, Paris or Washington or Brussels, still he did get Lisbon and Oslo, both of which they enjoyed, as well as Harare, which proved a lot more interesting than either had bargained for, and not in a good way. But when it was all over they'd come home to a farmhouse which they'd bought near Devizes, and that was it. He'd been knighted before his second-to-last posting and I was glad, as it helped them to feel they had made their mark, which of course they hadn't. It was also probably of mild use in getting them started socially in what was, for them, a brand-new part of England. But I never really understood the compulsion to make their home in the country when neither of them was the type to spend their lives walking dogs and working for local causes. Certainly, they were not at all sporty. My father had given up shooting twenty years before, after he spent four days on a grouse moor in the Borders without hitting a single bird, and my mother never cared much for anything that made her cold.

There is a tyranny that forces people of a certain class to insist they are only happy in the country and it is a cruel one. My parents were among its many victims. As everyone but they could see, their natural milieu was urban. They liked varied and informed conversation. They liked to mingle with different social groups. They liked their gossip from its source. They liked to talk politics and art and theatre and philosophy, and none of this, as we know, is much to be found beyond the city limits. Nor were they big local employers and, since their families had no historic connection with the part of Wiltshire they had chosen, they would never have more than a day pass to the County proper, so their egos were doomed to starvation rations as long as they remained there. In short, there was no real chance for them of happiness, or even entertainment, in that society, not as there would have been in Chelsea or Knightsbridge or Eaton Square but they made do, with introductions and dinners and charity functions and signing petitions about local planning and getting cross about the way the village pub was run and all the rest of it. And then my mother died, which was exactly what my father had never expected. But he showed courage as he packed up his life in Devizes and exchanged it for an equally meaningless one in Gloucestershire, and now here he was, after ten years of non-event, telling me about his own approaching death as we tucked into the disgusting splodge on our plates. I have never felt the ultimate absurdity of most lives more strongly than at that moment.

'It's all written down, so there shouldn't be any confusion,' my father said, producing from somewhere near the table a plastic folder filled with typed sheets. He handed it to me as he stood up. 'Let's go through.'

He led the way into the little library, which he used for most of his daily activities, and as usual I was touched by the sight of it. Unlike the characterless drawing room, the library was an exact reproduction, in miniature, of one my mother had designed for the Wiltshire farmhouse, with walls lined in red damask and fluted bookshelves in a soft dove grey. Even the cushions and lamps had been transferred intact after the move. A portrait of her, rather a good one, painted just after their marriage, in a snappy, 1940s suit, hung over the chimneypiece and my father would glance at it from time to time as he spoke, as if seeking her approval for his decisions, which I imagine was exactly what he was doing.

In front of the green corduroy sofa, a table held a tray made ready by the indefatigable Mrs Snow, with coffee equipment for two. He poured himself a cup, nodding at the folder. 'Funeral, memorial, it's all there. Prayers, hymns, who should do the address if you don't want to, everything.'

'I thought you hated hymns.'

'So I do, but I don't think a funeral is a good place for a "statement," do you?'

'It's your last chance to make one.' Which made him smile. 'I'll do the address,' I said.

'Thank you.' He chuckled gently to cover his emotions. 'I've left this house to Louise, since you got the flat.'

His words were perfectly logical and true but, irrationally, I felt a twinge of irritation. Does anyone ever feel content with the way things are arranged at these times? An only child, perhaps. Never a sibling. 'What about the stuff?'

'I thought you could split it. But I haven't really specified.'

'I wish you would.'

'What? Every teaspoon?'

'Every last teaspoon.' He looked sorrowful at this. He probably wanted to believe that his children got on well, which we did, quite, but we were not really close any more and I knew Louise's *über*-tiresome husband would push in and make her take anything decent if he weren't stopped now. 'Tom will say that they have children, and I don't, so they must have all the family things. Then there'll be a fight and Louise will cry and I'll shout and Tom will look wounded. That's unless you just write it down in black and white so there's no argument.'

'All right, I will.' He nodded gravely. 'In fact, I tell you what. I'll leave your mother's jewellery to her and you can have the rest of the contents. If you want to give her a stick or two you can. I suppose it'll all go back to her sprogs if you don't have any of your own.'

'I imagine so. It's not going to the cats' home, anyway.'

'I wish you had a family.'

This was a frequent observation and normally I would have fobbed it off with a joke or an exasperated sigh, depending on my state of mind; but given the topic we were discussing, a bit of honesty felt more appropriate. 'So do I, really,' I said.

'You still could, you know. Look at Charlie Chaplin.'

'I don't even need to go back that far.' Why does everyone over fifty still quote Charlie Chaplin in this context? Every day, there is some demented actor in the news, saying what fun it is to be a parent in his seventies, and how it makes every day bright and new. I sometimes wonder how long they can keep up this fantasy before they succumb to rage and clinical exhaustion.

'Of course . . .' He hesitated. 'I don't suppose . . . what's-her-name?'

'Bridget.'

'Bridget. I expect it's a bit late for her.'

Since Bridget was fifty-two, this was almost a compliment. I nodded. 'I expect so. But that doesn't necessarily . . .' It was my turn to tail away. We both knew what I was saying. My father cheered up considerably, which I have to say I found a bit annoying. I'd always known she wasn't his type, even if I'd pushed it to the back of my mind, but he'd been unfailingly polite to her and by that stage she was quite fond of him.

It felt unjust to realise that he had secretly been hoping throughout that eventually she would pass on by.

'Oh, I see. Well. You're a dark horse.' He poured himself another cup from the silver pot of lukewarm, brownish coffee'ish liquid left for our delectation. 'Do I know her?'

'There isn't anyone, in particular.' I gave a brisk shake of the head.

'What's the matter?'

I was unprepared for this, both the question and the tone, which was uncharacteristically warm. 'What do you mean?'

'You've been in a funny mood since you got here.' His comment was clearly directed at far more than my relations with Ms FitzGerald. I was taken aback because my father was not much given to introspection, either for himself or with regard to anyone else. When we were young, whenever a conversation at dinner threatened to get interesting he was inclined to cap it with the proto-English imprecation: 'now, don't let's get *psychological.*' I do not mean he didn't appreciate the importance of other people's inner life. He just didn't see that it was anything to do with him. Gossip bored him. He couldn't remember incidents or personalities well enough to savour the punchlines and he used to get quite impatient whenever anyone tried to intrigue him with some local scandal.

In truth, his stance drained my mother, since she was never allowed to discuss the private affairs and theoretical activities of their acquaintance, and this inevitably made their conversation very arid. 'What business is it of ours?' he would say, and she would nod and agree with him, and say of course and how right he was, and thereby be silenced. After I'd grown up, I used to defend her and quote Alexander Pope: 'The proper study of mankind is man' and so on. The fact remained he felt uncomfortable and ungenerous delving into the murky waters of others' personal histories and she gave up trying to change him, retaining these topics to enjoy with her friends and her children. It was all right, but I do give thanks that their later years were spent in the era of television, or the evenings would have been silent indeed. Still, here he was, showing an interest, asking for some sort of private explanation of my mood. It was so rare an event, that I couldn't waste time on prevarication.

'I have a feeling that I want to change my life.'

'What do you mean by that? Get rid of Bridget? Stop writing? Sell the flat? What?'

'Yes,' I said. We stared at each other. Then I thought again. 'Actually, I don't think I want to stop writing.'

'What's brought this on?'

I told him about Damian's request and how I had fared so far. He thought for a moment. 'I quite liked him at the time, until you had your falling-out.' He paused, but I had no comment to make. 'Even so, I'm rather surprised to find he left such a mark on all those lives.'

'Far be it from me to defend him after what he put me through, but he is the only member of that gang who went on to be one of the most successful men of his generation.'

'Yes, you're right. Of course that's right. I wasn't thinking.' My father spoke as one who feels himself justly corrected. 'So, what is it?'

'I'm not completely clear in my own head, but I believe I'm finding it depressing to be obliged to compare what we all thought was coming when we were young with what actually arrived.'

My father nodded. 'To quote Nanny, comparisons are odious.'

'They are also pointless, but that doesn't prevent one from making them.' For some reason, I felt it was important that he understood me. 'It's more than that. I'm not sure what we're all doing with our lives. Damian may have made his mark, but none of the rest of us has.'

'Not everyone can be a world-famous billionaire.'

'Nor should they be, but everyone needs to feel they're part of something worthwhile. That, in the last analysis, their life has some meaning in a larger context. The question is what am I part of? What have I done?'

But he couldn't take this very seriously. 'Don't you think people have been asking themselves that since Chaucer first sharpened his pencil?'

'I think there have been times when the majority felt they belonged to a culture that was working, that they had an identity within a worthwhile whole. "I am a Roman Citizen," "God Bless America," "The man who is born an Englishman has drawn a winning ticket in the lottery of life." All that. People have felt their own civilisation was valuable and that they were lucky to belong to it. I'm fairly sure I believed that too, or something like it, forty years ago.'

'You were young forty years ago.' He smiled. Clearly, he was not very worried by my soul-searching. 'So what are you asking? Do you want to sell the flat? If so, then that's what you must do.'

In a way I could have left then as, if I'm honest, I had really gone down there seeking his permission to do this very thing. I was taken unawares by his swift and open reaction to my complaints, as I had assumed it was all going to take much longer to get his agreement. Because I should be clear, this response on his part was very generous, more generous than an outsider can perhaps immediately appreciate. As I have said, my mother was the one who insisted on their giving me the London flat, thereby cutting down their capital by quite a chunk. He'd resisted it for a time, because he saw their standard of living would suffer, which it did, but he eventually surrendered to her pleading. Now, here I was, proposing to cash in my chips, to pocket the boodle, to take the money and run, and he wanted to make it clear that he did not mind in the least. Some months later I would learn that he'd already known he was much more ill than he had let on and that death could not be long distant, so I suppose he wanted us to be in step at the end, but to me that thought only makes his kindness more moving. 'That's so fantastically nice of you,' I said.

'Nonsense, nonsense.' He shook his head at the very notion. Now, what about some more coffee?'

Of course, his instinctive desire to downplay the moment was precisely what made it so poignant. Like too many of his type, my father had an absolute inability to express the love that motivated him, being always far too English to demonstrate his feelings. Even when we were little he hated kissing us goodnight and was visibly thrilled when the custom was allowed to lapse in our early teens. But there was nevertheless a silent unspoken affection in his words at this moment that makes my eyes fill now, months later, when I remember them. 'I don't want you to think it was wrong to give it to me when you did,' I said. 'It provided me with the perfect base, with a fantastic start. I was, and am, incredibly grateful.'

'I know. But because something was right for you then, doesn't mean it's right for you now. If you want to sell it you must sell it.'

'Thank you.'

'And the girl? Isn't it working?'

I couldn't help thinking, disloyally, that Bridget would be ecstatic to hear herself referred to as 'the girl,' however politically incorrect that might sound. She was very good-looking and had the kind of looks that would last, but she was no spring chicken, if not quite yet an old boiler. I wasn't sure how to answer him. 'It's not that, exactly. It works as well as it ever did.'

'But?'

'My problem is that during my searches I've been reminded of what it feels like to be in love. I think I'd forgotten.'

'Again, you are remembering what it feels like to be *young* and in love. Love at nearly sixty, whatever sentimental American films may try to tell you, ain't the same.'

'Maybe not. But I'm fairly sure it's more than I've got now.'

'Then of course you must move on.' He nodded slowly. 'Tell me, do you ever see Serena Gresham in your travels?'

The question came flying out of the blue and almost winded me. On this day my dear old father was full of surprises. Could he really remember Serena? Why would he know what I had felt about her? Unless he'd had some kind of personality transplant? We hadn't mentioned her name in thirty years at least and anyway I would never have given him credit for taking enough interest in my life to notice my romantic sufferings. 'No. At least, barely. Sometimes. At the odd thing in London. That's all.'

'She married, didn't she?'

'Yes.'

'And that was satisfactory?'

'I don't see enough of her to have an opinion. She's got two grown-up children and she's still with him.'

He considered my limp reply for a second. 'I'm not convinced you would have been happy, you know.'

This sort of thing is hard to take at any age from any parent, but it came so closely upon one of the kindest gestures he'd ever made that I didn't want to snap. 'I just wish I'd had the chance to find out' was all I said.

'You could never have been a writer. You'd have ended up in the City. To make the kind of money it would have taken to keep her.'

'Not necessarily.' At this he gave a little snort. As always with a father, the assumption of superior knowledge, particularly where it concerned people I had been close to and he barely knew, was infuriating. But again, after the earlier exchange I didn't want a fight. 'Plenty of people nowadays live completely differently from the way they were brought up. You do for a start.'

'Maybe. But my generation wasn't given the option and, believe me, old habits die hard. I should know.' He saw I was struggling not to join battle on Serena's behalf and relented. 'I don't mean I didn't like her, but I just never thought you were suited. For what it's worth.'

'Yes. Well.' I spoke and was silent.

An awkwardness had entered the proceedings. My father was suddenly uncomfortably aware that he had ventured into alien, possibly even hurtful, territory. He smiled jocularly to get things back to normal. 'Well, I hope I'm still around to meet the new girl, when she turns up.'

'So do I,' I said and I meant it. I'm very sorry that he won't be.

We spent the rest of the afternoon discussing his will, which I was now allowed to read. He had, as he said, left his home to my sister and the remainder of his capital was divided between my niece, my two nephews and myself. This wasn't quite fair, in my opinion, since for these purposes Louise and her children should have weighed as one person, but he telephoned his lawyer while I was there and dictated a codicil that gave me the entire contents of the house, so I didn't like to cavil. Then it was done. His requests for the church services seemed gentlemanly. In fact, it was all pretty modest, more of a decorous whimper than a bang.

We were in the kitchen, making a cup of tea prior to my departure, before my father mentioned the state of my life again. Mrs Snow had left the things laid out on the kitchen table, complete with cling-filmed biscuits. Obviously, she didn't believe him capable of instigating even the smallest domestic operation from scratch and she was probably right. 'I don't think Damian is behaving correctly in this,' he said after another silence, as he poured out two cups of builders' brew. 'You'll almost certainly end by disturbing the balance of a perfectly workable life. Some man or some woman will suddenly find themselves a thousand million times richer than their siblings, richer than every relation they have in the world. Their mother will face the task of explaining to her husband that the eldest child is a bastard. It's not going to be easy.'

'And if the money should mean that a life encumbered by poverty might suddenly take wing and achieve great things?'

'You sound like a novel from a railway bookstall.'

'You sound like an officer from Health and Safety.'

He bit into his digestive. Mrs Snow was not a risk taker, with biscuits or anything else. 'Nor do I think it fair for Damian to lay this burden on you. It's not as if he had much credit to call on.'

'No.' But I did not want to pretend that I didn't know why I had been asked. 'Unfortunately there really wasn't anyone else who could have undertaken it.'

'Maybe. But I don't believe he understood what he was exposing you to.'

This was an odd comment, which I had not anticipated. 'Why? What have I been "exposed to"?'

'You've been made to go back into your own past and to compare it with your present. You've been forced to remember what you wanted from life at nineteen, forty years ago, before you knew what life was. Indeed, you must face what you all wanted from life, those silly, over-made-up girls and the vain, self-important young men you ran around with then. Now, thanks to Damian, you must bear witness to what happened to them. To what happened to you. Eventually, in old age, almost everyone with any brains must come to terms with the disappointment of life, but this is very early for you to have to make that discovery. You've been rendered discontented when it's too late, or nearly too late, to fix, but soon enough for you to have many years ahead to live with that discontent. Damian ought to have spoiled his own life, not yours.'

'He doesn't have much of his own life left to spoil.'

'Even so.'

And of course he was right, really.

Is it serendipity? That explanation for those strange, coincidental happenings that seem, for a moment, to create a sense of planning in our arbitrary lives? Or is serendipity more to do with accidental knowledge of things? Of chance deductions that lead to greater understanding? Either way, I believe it was serendipity that took a hand in the next stage of my Damian-led journey.

We were staying for the weekend, Bridget and I, with a very tiresome architect and his very charming wife at a house he had purchased some years before in Yorkshire. It was an old house, a historical house, a 'great house' in a way and, oh boy, didn't he know it. The architect in question was called Tarquin Montagu. I did not believe that this was a name he, or more probably anyone, would have received at the baptismal font, and I certainly never discovered any link between him and the ducal house of Manchester, a connection that he liked to imply. He came into my life as the husband of a delightful novelist called Jennifer Bond who was also with my publisher. We'd been paired for a book tour one summer a few years before, forging a friendship in the process. I was not then clear about how he came by his money, since he was never associated with any vividly spectacular building, but he lived in a way that Vanbrugh would have envied and some years before our visit he had bought a splendid semi-ruin near Thirsk, called Malton Towers.

A George IV, Gothic confection, abandoned by its family after the war, Malton had followed the sad trail of such places in those years as first a school and then a training college, and after that a home for old people, and I am fairly sure at one point a finishing school specialising in *Nouvelle Cuisine*. Until finally it achieved a slight, if spurious, fame in the mid 1990s as a 'World Centre' for some later version of Transcendental Meditation, which attracted the members of one of the manufactured Boy Bands of the era. This last incarnation was run by a dubious character who claimed the authority and support of, I seem to remember, the Dalai Lama, but I may be wrong in that. At any rate the day dawned when a red-topped Sunday scandal sheet revealed that he was not, in fact, a philosopher in touch with the higher plane, as his earnest pupils had no doubt assumed, but instead an old fraud from Pinner who had previous form for shoplifting, car theft and making false claims on his insurance. His exposure resulted in a mass exodus of the faithful, shortly followed by that of their non-spiritual leader, and for the next eight years the wind had whistled through the dusty galleries and servants' attics and former drawing rooms of the decaying folly until, at what can only have been the eleventh hour, Tarquin showed up. I am quite sure that from the house's point of view it was a very good thing that he did. Whether it was quite so beneficial to

Jennifer's quality of life is rather more open to question.

The continuing craving on the part of the successful to reproduce the lifestyle and customs of the nineteenth-century aristocracy must be trying for our Labour masters. They would deny this, as they deny so many aspects of human nature, but I'm sure it is so. And the life these aspirants choose to ape is from a very specific period. Not for them the casual round of the eighteenth-century aristo, sleeping sitting upright, breakfasting at noon on sticky chocolate before a ride; who wore no uniforms for his sporting or social activities, who dined at five in the afternoon, drank three or four bottles of port a night and frequently, when travelling, shared a bed with his manservant, while his wife might hunker down with her maid. This is not an attractive model for the modern millionaire. Nor, certainly, would they copy the altogether more brutish customs of the sixteenth-century toff, whose personal hygiene, to say nothing of his politics, would make a strong man faint. No, their template was developed by the late Victorians, who had such a talent for mixing rank with comfort: Majesty and deference combined with warmth and draught-free bedrooms, splendour with thick carpets and interlined curtains, where the food is hot, but there are still footmen to serve it.

Sadly, to live like this requires much, much more money than most modern copiers ever imagine. They do the sums and there seems to be enough to bring the house up to date, tidy the garden, hire someone nice to help at table and they begin. Alas, these palaces were designed to preside over thousands of rent-producing acres, to be the window display of huge fortunes in trade and manufacturing, which might have been concealed from Society but, like the mole, were working busily all the while in the dark. Because these houses eat money. They gobble it up, as the rampaging giants of the Brothers Grimm eat children and every other good thing in their path.

When the genuinely, very rich buy these palaces I am sure they enjoy them and, even if they do not often stay long, still the houses are the better for their passing. The trouble comes when they are bought by the not-quite-rich-enough, who think they can just about manage. With these, as a rule, there is a pattern. They make their fortune, such as it is. They buy a castle to celebrate. They restore it and entertain like mad for eight to ten years and then they sell, exhausted by their own poverty and the constant effort to stay afloat. While the County, those families whose fortunes were never deconstructed, and whose houses and pretensions are built on solid rock, smile, occasionally with regret, and move on to the next candidates. Tarquin Montagu was about six years into the process.

Reviewing him now, having not seen him for a while, I feel more sympathy for him than I did. That is to say that I feel some sympathy, when before I felt none at all. At that time, when we were staying with him, he must have been worried that his whole self-ennobling adventure would implode, but it was part of his personality not to admit or ever discuss his fears. He would have seen that as weakness and loss of control. In fact, his main problem was his total inability to relax control under any circumstances. I would go as far as to say that his nature was the most controlling I have ever encountered. This made him not only impossible to entertain, or to be entertained by, but also lonely and desolate, for he could not admit to anyone, least of all his wife, that events were slipping out of his grasp. I had known him as a difficult and rather ill-tempered man, who always found any conversation not centred on him, hard to follow and harder still to contribute to. But I had not fully understood the extent of his mania before we arrived at his house, tired from the long drive, at tea time on that summer Friday. We were normal people. All we wanted was to be shown our room, to have a hot bath and generally to recover in order, like the model guests we were, to come downstairs refreshed, changed and ready to eat, or talk about, whatever our hosts might throw at us.

It was not to be. First, apparently, we had to sit and listen to a history of the house and when Jennifer suggested that we might be more in the mood for this lesson after we had rested, Tarquin replied that he did not judge us yet as 'ready' to see the rooms he had prepared. Naturally, my almost overpowering instinct was to tell him to piss off and drive straight back to London. But looking at Jennifer's tired and harassed face, I suspected this was an option taken by more than one guest before now, so in pity and to Bridget's relief, I allowed myself to be led into the library, to listen to the lecture like a good boy.

'The thing is,' said Tarquin, getting into his interminable stride, 'you have to understand that when Sir Richard decided to rebuild in eighteen twenty-four, he wanted both to be in the height of fashion, but at the same time not to lose the sense of historicity that his ancient blood demanded.' He took a deep breath and looked at us as if waiting for a response though what this might be I could not fathom.

'So that's why he chose Gothic?' I volunteered eventually, wondering if we were ever going to be offered sustenance. I had arrived wanting a cup of tea, but after twenty minutes of this I was ready for whisky, neat and in a pint pot.

Tarquin shook his head. 'No. Not exactly.' The smugness of his tone was enough to make one seize a chair and smash it over his head, like a cowboy in a Mack Sennett comedy. 'That was why he chose Sir Charles Barry as his architect. Barry was still young then. This was before the old Houses of Parliament burned down. He was known as a designer of churches and a restorer of ancient monuments, not a maker of country houses. To have a servant of God as the master of the works gave the whole project a gravitas that ensured respect from his neighbours.'

'Because he built it in Gothic,' I suggested. I wasn't going to give up easily and my boredom was making me angry. But I felt this was as challenging as I could be while still pretending to listen to Tarquin with respect. In other words I was a living lie.

'No!' he spoke, this time, with a harsh edge to the word. 'The style of the building is not the issue! The style is not important! I am talking of the spiritual background with which he approached the design.'

'In Gothic,' I murmured.

'Can I go to the loo? I'm bursting,' said Bridget and, as so often in the company of women, I wondered why I hadn't thought of that myself.

'Of course,' said Jennifer. 'I'll show you your room.' With a sharp glance at her husband she led the way out, stopping to allow us to take up our cases in the hall. During all of this Tarquin was so annoyed at having his dissertation interrupted that he remained, still and sulking, in the library, watching us in glowering silence as we made our way up the imperial, double staircase.

'God Almighty.' I fell backwards on to the bed, with a loud sigh, which I rather hoped the retreating Jennifer had caught as she crossed the landing. If she did, it cannot have been a novel experience. 'I don't think I can manage a weekend of this.' The bed itself was a large four-poster, at first sight grand and imposing, but in fact Edwardian export, cheap and clumsily carved, and clearly purchased by the Montagus for the overall effect, not for any intrinsic quality, presumably because they couldn't afford the real McCoy. I had already noticed that the whole house was like this, impressive at a glance but disappointing to any further study, like a lovely stage set to be admired from the stalls but not explored too closely. In fact, the whole thing *was* a stage set, on which Tarquin could play out his personal fantasies of high-born and literate grace. Oi vey.

That night, matters did not improve as we gathered to eat in the gloomy and under-furnished dining room, Bridget shivering beneath her gauzy shawl. A huge Jacobethan table dominated the centre of the room and as we came in I heard Tarquin remonstrate that the places had all been laid at one end, instead of the four of us being ranged around the vast board like the characters in an Addams Family film. That, or a BBC period drama where a combination of modern prejudice and complete ignorance frequently obliges their fictionalised upper classes to adopt inexplicable customs. 'If you're going to give us a sermon, I'd prefer to listen and not just watch your lips move,' said Jennifer, which brought the exchange to an end. We sat, Tarquin, needless to say, as our master at the head. He glanced at us, toying with a bottle of white wine on a coaster in front of him, a slight smile tweaking at the corners of his mouth. 'Give them some of that wine,' Jennifer murmured as she brought round plates of ethnic-looking broth.

'I'm not sure they deserve it,' said Tarquin, continuing to favour us with his twinkling, quirky gaze. 'For better or worse, I've chosen this. It's a fairly unusual Sauvignon, crisp but zingy at the same time, which I tend only to use on very special occasions. Is this one? I can't decide.'

'Oh, just give them some fucking wine,' said Jennifer, voicing accurately my own unspoken response. She sat down heavily on her husband's left, opposite Bridget, with me on her other side, and started to drink her soup. Tarquin did not answer her. Clearly, these rumblings of revolution had been getting more frequent of late. Like an unimaginative king, he was bewildered by the challenge to his authority and could not quite gauge the appropriate response. For a moment he sat in still and sober silence. Then he stood and poured the hallowed liquid into our glasses.

As he did so, I caught Jennifer's eye for a moment but she looked away, not quite ready to acknowledge, as one does in just such a glance, that she was trapped in a ghastly marriage to a crashing bore. I sympathised with her decision, not least because I didn't, for a moment, believe that I knew all the facts. There are many factors in a marriage or in any cohabiting arrangement, and just because someone gets too cross at dinner parties, or hates your best friend, or cannot tell an anecdote to save their life, these are not necessarily faults that outweigh the benefits of the union. That said, Marriage to a Controller is one of the hardest kinds of relationship for the outside witness to understand.

Genuine controllers are anti-life, killers of energy, living fire blankets that smother all endeavour. For a start, they are always unhappy on anyone's territory but their own. They cannot enjoy any party they are not giving. They cannot relax as guests in a public place, because that would involve gratitude and gratitude is, to them, a sign of weakness. But they are intolerable as hosts, especially in restaurants, where their manner to waiters and fellow diners alike poisons the atmosphere. They cannot admire anyone who is more successful than they are. They cannot enjoy the friends of their partner because these strangers may not agree to accept them for the superior being they are. But since they have no friends themselves, it means they must regard any human gathering with suspicion. They cannot praise, because praise affirms the worth of the person to whom it is given and the process of controlling is built on the suppression of any self-worth in whomever they are with. They cannot learn, because learning first demands an acknowledgement that the teacher knows more than they, which they cannot give on any subject. Above all, they are boring. Boring beyond imagining. Boring to the point of madness. Yet I have known women to espouse and move in with such men, clever, interesting women, good-looking, witty women, hard-working and successful women, who have allowed themselves to be taken in and dominated by these tedious, mediocre bullies. Why? Is it sexy to be controlled? Is it safe? What?

'Are there any plans for tomorrow?' Bridget, almost blue with cold by this stage, looked brightly across the table.

'That depends,' said Tarquin.

But Jennifer could not wait to learn what it depended on. 'Nothing until the evening, but then we thought we'd go to a charity fireworks thing at a house not very far from here. We've already got the tickets so we might as well. You take a picnic and there's some sort of concert. It could be fun, as long as it's not raining.'

'Are we to be limited by something so slight as the weather?' Tarquin adopted a dark and supposedly mysterious tone, by which I assume he was attempting to snatch back the conversation, but something in Jennifer's independent response had empowered us, and we carried on as if he had not spoken.

'That'd be lovely,' said Bridget and the matter was settled.

We got through the evening somehow, finishing up back in the library, an apartment that must once have been handsome indeed, with really superb late-Regency mahogany bookshelves, which had somehow survived the depredations of the post-war decades. I was quite surprised that the bogus high priest had not flogged them during his tenure or after his fall. Could the Sunday papers have been unjust? Of course, the original collection of books was long gone and Tarquin had been quite unable to replace it. He had made do with those huge sets, entitled *Stories from the Empire*, or something similar, bound in red artificial leatherette and machine-tooled, but there were lots of them and they did at least fill the space, creating once again a reasonable impression from a distance. 'Where is this house? Where we're going tomorrow?' asked Bridget, before Jennifer returned with a tray of coffee.

Tarquin raised his eyebrows, hesitating for the maximum effect. 'You'll find out.'

My sigh must have been audible.

EIGHT

I don't quite know why, but it was not until we were nearly there that I began to suspect our destination. We turned off the main road at a point I did not at first recognise. When I'd known it the road had not been a dual carriageway and there was no estate of modern housing, with its sickly yellowish street lighting, near the corner. But then, as we came into the village a bell did start to ring. The peripheries might have altered but the main street was much as it had always been, unspoiled and, if anything, improved. The pub was certainly much smarter, catering no doubt for the yuppie weekend trade and not just for the thirsty farm labourers who had crushed into the bar forty years before. We passed it by and, once out of the village, it was no more than five or ten minutes before I could see the familiar little Palladian lodge, and in a loosely stretched-out line of cars we turned through the gates into the drive and enjoyed the comfortable crunch of private gravel beneath the wheels.

But I said nothing. Not even to Bridget, who did not know the place or much about my life when I was a visitor here. My reason was simple: I could not see any profit in reviving the association, given the circumstances of my last meeting, not with Serena but with her parents. I could, after all, be fairly sure they had not forgotten that dinner, since few lives boast many such evenings. Thank Christ. And there was another, weaker motive for my silence, which was that they might have forgotten both the episode and me. My worst nightmare would have been for Tarquin to talk up my acquaintance with the family to gain some local mileage from it among the assembled throng, which he was more than capable of doing, and then for me not to be recognised by any of them. This may seem like vanity. It *was* vanity. But it was also a reluctance to let daylight in on my dreams. Even if my career with the Greshams had ended in disaster, I liked to think that I had been a feature of their lives in that distant era, when they had been so vital a feature in mine. And while logic told me this was unlikely, still I'd preserved the fantasy thus far and I wished to get back into the car at the end of the evening with my chimera intact. Anyway, they would not be there. I was quite sure of that when I thought more about it. They would be in London or on holiday or at any rate somewhere else when the locals and the lesser County invaded their demesne. 'Oh, look,' said Jennifer and there was the house, perched high on its terraces, lording it over the valley beneath, as we made our way down the winding drive. It was lit, rather gracefully, by spotlights concealed in the surrounding shrubs, an innovation since my time, and the shining beams seemed to give the cool grey stone façade a kind of ethereal beauty in the dusk.

'What a fabulous place,' said Bridget. 'What's it called?'

'Gresham Abbey,' said Tarquin, as if the words belonged to him and he was reluctant to allow them free range.

'Is it National Trust?'

'No. Still private. Lord and Lady Claremont.'

'Are they nice?'

He hesitated. 'Nice enough.' Which meant, of course, that he did not know them. 'They're quite old. They're not really out and about much.' As he said it, I found it strange to think of Lady Claremont as 'quite old.' She had been a frightening, powerful, if fundamentally benevolent figure in my youth, elegant, crisp, always competent, always charming, but with a rod of tungsten in her spine. She had not, of course, paid much attention to me as I hung about on the edge of her parties, obediently sitting where I was told, usually in the most junior spot at the table, obligingly talking to my neighbours during dinner, walking with their old relations in the gardens, buying things I did not want at the village fête, reading in the library.

I remember her coming in on me once, as I sat squinting at the page before me in the gathering gloom. She laughed and I looked up as she turned on all the lamps in the room with a single switch. 'You mustn't be too scared to put the lights on,' she said with a brisk smile and went on about her business, and I felt so humiliated that my back started to prickle with embarrassed sweat. Because I suppose I had been too scared to turn them on, or rather I was just hoping that someone else would come to turn them on for me and I wouldn't have to take responsibility for it. But as I say, she was never unkind. Nor was she cross to see me there again and again. Just uninterested.

As we approached the house, we were greeted by the customary cheery gardeners and groundsmen, each equipped with their torches, who waved and signalled and called instructions to each other, until we had been safely routed off the drive and into a large field, where row upon row of cars gave us an idea of the scale of the gathering. 'Will you look at this,' said Bridget, 'there can't be much else happening in Yorkshire tonight.'

'I think you'll find the music is of a very high standard,' said Tarquin in the voice of an ageing geography mistress, which momentarily stifled our good humour. We parked and started to lug the various bits of picnic apparatus out of the car. Tarquin had already taken responsibility for a frightful plastic 'wine carrier' and was legging it towards the gate that would lead us back to the festivities. By parking in the field, we had skirted the house, so the gate in the pretty, iron, sheep fencing led directly into one side of the gardens that stretched away from the back of the abbey in a falling series of terraces, leading down to the distant lake in the valley below. Clearly, taking in the crowd that was already here, Tarquin was determined to find a good spot and he was soon out of sight, leaving us to manage the rest. Bridget followed him with a collection of rugs and cushions, obliging Jennifer and me to carry the long, white cold box between us. We staggered along, nearly tripping on the tufts of cow grass, until we reached the gate.

'Can we stop for a moment?' said Jennifer. Actually, it was quite heavy and the rope handles were cutting into our sissy palms. We leant for a moment against the rail. In the distance we could hear the murmurs and laughter of the crowd, and some sort of canned music was coming out of hidden loudspeakers, Elgar or Mahler, or at any rate an inoffensive choice for those oh-so-British ears. Jennifer broke our silence. 'I think we've got until nine to eat and then the real music starts.' I nodded. 'You are kind to come,' she added in a tone of real gratitude. 'I know we kept saying we'd make a date, but I never thought we would and I do appreciate it.'

174

'Nonsense. We're loving being here.' But of course it wasn't nonsense and we weren't loving it. I was, as I have mentioned, very fond of Jennifer. There is something about a publicity tour that is so ghastly, and makes one feel so vulnerable, as your book or film or whatever it might be that you are flogging is paraded in front of the public gaze, like a Spartan baby exposed to the cruelties of Mount Tygetus, that a bond is formed with fellow sufferers which is hard to describe to anyone who has not been through it. Like survivors in a lifeboat, I suppose. Selling things is part of the modern world and if you have a product, you have to sell it, but by heaven it's no fun if it does not come naturally to you; and Jennifer, like me, came from a world that was uncomfortable with selling in any guise. Even buying should not be advertised, but professional, or worse, personal, selling can only ever be shameful. This prejudice manifests itself in lots of sharp, spiky comments. 'I saw you on the box with that man who can't pronounce his Rs. I never watch it normally but the au pair turned it on.' Or 'I heard you on the car wireless being grilled by some angry little northerner. Grim.' Or 'What on earth were you doing on afternoon television? Haven't you got any work to get on with?' And you listen, knowing that this same afternoon programme sells more books than any billboard or advertising campaign in Britain and in fact you're lucky, incredibly lucky, to have been invited on to it.

Of course you want so much to say that. Or at the very least to tell them to grow up or drop dead, or to open their eyes to the fact that the Fifties are over. But you don't. My late mother would have said 'they're just jealous, darling' and maybe they are, a bit, even when they don't know it. But I am jealous, too. Jealous that their living never requires them to make an ass of themselves at the end of the pier at a shilling a go, which is exactly what it feels like most of the time. In any life, in any career, only people who've made the same journey understand each other completely. Mothers want advice from other mothers, not from childless social workers, cancer sufferers need to hear from survivors of cancer, not from the doctors who cure it, even victims of a scandal will only really want to compare notes with some other politician or celebrity who has similarly gone down in flames. This was the bond that Jennifer and I shared. We were published authors of moderate and precarious success, and I valued her friendship. I wanted to please her and for some reason I knew it was important to her that we should come and stay in Yorkshire. I had assumed her urgency was a measure of her love but I suspect, now, that by this stage, it was because very few people would stay, certainly nobody would come twice who didn't need to borrow money, and that the weekends when she was alone with Tarquin were becoming intolerable.

'Is he always like this?' I asked. I felt that her honesty in thanking me for coming merited a bit of straight talking, although, as the words left my mouth I wondered if I hadn't overstepped the mark.

But she smiled. 'Not when he's asleep.' Her expression developed into an ironic laugh. 'I can't decide whether he was the same when we first married and I was so young and so insecure that I mistook his pomposity for knowledge and his patronising for instruction, or whether he's got worse.'

'I think he must have got a bit worse,' I said. 'I'm not sure Helen Keller would have married him if he'd been as he is now.'

She laughed again, but still her laugh was sad. 'I wish we'd had a child,' she said, but then caught my look. 'I know. Everyone thinks it would have solved everything and everyone is wrong.'

'Don't ask me. I'm the sad old bachelor who could never commit.'

'I just think, with him, it would have shored him up. Allowed him that bat squeak of immortality that children bring. Or even if he'd just succeeded at something convincingly. Because he never really has.'

'He lives very well for a failure.'

She shook her head. 'It's all inherited.'

This surprised me. 'Really? I hadn't got him down for a Trustafarian.'

She knew what I was saying and she wasn't offended. 'It's not old money. All that stuff about the Montagus is bollocks. It isn't even our real name. His father arrived from Hungary after the uprising of 1956. He started as a lorry driver, built up a transport business and sold out in the mid Nineties. Tarquin's his only child. He was a lovely man, actually. I doted on him, but Tarquin used to keep him hidden, so none of our friends were allowed to meet him. Now he wants you to think the money is the remains of an ancient fortune, amplified by his own recent success. It's neither. But I expect you knew that.'

I didn't confirm this, as it seemed superior and smug. 'It's rather a romantic fantasy, in a way,'

'It can't last for much longer.' She sighed wearily at the thought of impending collapse. 'The whole thing costs far more than either of us realised and there's very little coming in, now we've tied it all up in the house. I write my books so at least we can eat and go to the theatre, but I'm not sure how long that'll keep us above the waterline. He's a hopeless architect, you know. He gets taken on for particular jobs now and then, when a practice needs some extra help, but nobody ever asks him to stay.'

'Would you?'

This time she laughed out loud. 'Perhaps that's it. Perhaps he's a fabulous architect but anathema to have in the office.'

'So what are you going to do?'

Which made her stop laughing. 'I don't know. Everyone says I should leave him, most of all my mother, which would have astonished her and me if anyone had predicted such a thing twenty years ago, but the odd thing is, in a funny way I do still rather love him. You'll say I'm mad, but I watch him boring everyone to death and trying to control and impress and make people admire him, and I know he's so puzzled and frightened and bewildered inside. He can tell it isn't working, but he just doesn't understand why not. No one comes to stay any more.'

'Except us.'

'Except fools like you. And nobody wants to know us down here. I've seen them literally roll their eyes when we walk into a room. I somehow feel I can't leave him open to attack, when it's so obvious to everyone but him that he can't protect himself.'

As often as I am reminded that love, like everything else in this world, comes in many different shapes and sizes, I can still be amazed by some of the forms it takes. 'I don't think you're mad. It's your life,' I said.

'I know. And it isn't a dress rehearsal. But even if I don't add up to much in the end, the fact is I took him on, nobody forced me, and I have to see it through. I suppose that sounds like a quote from G. A. Henty.'

'It sounds like something only a very decent woman would say.'

She blushed and at that moment Bridget reappeared at the fence. 'Please come. If he doesn't stop talking about the wine we're going to drink I swear to God I'll break a bottle of it over his head.' So saying, she relieved Jennifer of her burdensome share of the cold box and guided us to our site on the top terrace where Tarquin had staked his claim. To a restful mixture of chattering crowd noise, music and Tarquin droning on, we unpacked our food and spread it forth luxuriously upon our waiting, cushioned rugs.

We had nearly finished eating when Tarquin suddenly broke off his current lecture. He had been telling us about the Ptolemaic dynasty of Egypt or some subject equally fascinating, and we had each retreated into a kind of glazed, mental cave of our own making, when his voice altered and took on a nervous edge: 'They're here.'

'Who?' Bridget was keen to support the introduction of any new topic, never mind what.

'The family. The Claremonts.'

As he said their name, I was amazed to find that, like a lyric in a wartime love song, my heart actually skipped a beat. Dear Lord, does there never come a time when we are too old for such foolishness? But when I looked there was no sign of Serena, only an elderly group, all in evening dress; presumably they had enjoyed a smarter, better dinner inside. They glanced benevolently at the crowds enjoying their policies in so pleasant and decorous a manner, and in their midst were two ancient pensioners who seemed to be impersonating the Earl and Countess of Claremont, darling Roo and Pel, as I had never known them well enough to call them, who had once been such a vivid part of my life. I looked at them now, these icons of my youth, confident that they could not see me. Was I avoiding them because the sight of me would make them start and stretch their eyes in horror, or because I could not bear to see that they did not recognise me and I was forgotten? Probably the latter. I was sneakily afraid that if someone had mentioned that one of the hundreds of picnickers was an acquaintance of theirs from four decades before and had thought of them many, many times in the interim, they would have been none the wiser. Not even had I been paraded before them in person.

This deflating suspicion was reinforced by the sad but apparent truth that my Lord Claremont had been more or less exchanged for another man. The handsome, corpulent, sexy, flirty hedonist, with his thick, wavy hair and his wavier smile, had completely vanished and been replaced by a bony, stooped individual. His nose, stripped of its flesh and unsupported by the plump cheeks on either side, had become prominent, hooked like the Duke of Wellington's to whom he was no doubt related in some wise, while his generous lips had been shaved down, as if by a razor, and he had almost no hair left. I would not say he appeared less distinguished. Not at all. This fellow looked like someone who read poetry and philosophy and pondered the great issues of life, while the Lord Claremont of my memories knew how to get a good table at the last minute and where you could find an excellent Château d'Yquem, but not much else. For a moment he glanced my way but of course registered nothing, which was not surprising since, while I knew him in those distant days, he did not know me. Not really. Certainly, he gave little sign of being aware of that awkward, plain young man whose only use was to make up a table for bridge. Even so, looking at this stick-like figure, with a Baron Munchausen outline, I missed the man he had been and it was hard not to feel a pang at the pitiless work of the passing years.

Lady Claremont was less altered. It seems odd to think of it, but I must have known her first when some of the bloom of youth was still upon her. Serena was the eldest child and her mother had married young so she cannot have been much more than forty-two or -three, when we met. It is always odd for the young grown old to realise how youthful the dominating creatures of their early years must in many cases have been. In those days her haughty, witty confidence was further empowered by her cold beauty and as a result, to me she had seemed formidable. It is true that her looks had largely, though not entirely, disappeared. But I could see, even from a distance, that she had replaced whatever she had lost with other qualities, some more sterling than the earlier version. She glanced our way and for a moment, forgetting everything that had kept me huddled out of her eyeline, I was tempted to signal my presence in some way, but the thought of her ignoring my wave and the fun it would give Tarquin when she did kept me still. Then came the broadcast announcement that told us the concert was about to begin. She looked at her husband, muttering some suggestion, I would assume about returning to their seats and a moment later, with a final, general acknowledgement, the group from the house climbed the stone steps towards the top terrace.

The concert was cheerful rather than profound, a Hungry Hundreds

medley of Puccini, Rossini and Verdi, with a bit of Chopin thrown in
to make you cry. The lead-up to the interval was the Drinking Song
from *Traviata*, which was adequately sung by quite a good tenor from
some northern company, and a fat soprano over from Italy, who was
supposed to be much better than him but wasn't. It was an appropriate
choice as the throats of the watching hoards were dry as dust by this
time, and you could hear the champagne corks starting to pop as the
couple trilled the final soaring note. Tarquin, naturally, had provided
some rare sustenance, Cristal, or the like, and was lecturing us on how
to savour it, when we were interrupted by a man in the neolivery of
the modern butler, striped trousers and a short black jacket. There was
no mistaking Tarquin as our leader and he went over to him, murmuring in his ear. Tarquin's surprise deepened to astonishment as he
pointed me out. 'That's him,' he said, and the man scuttled over
towards me.

'Her Ladyship wonders if you and your party would like to join the
family after the concert, Sir, to watch the fireworks from the terrace.'

I cannot deny I felt a warm sense of self-justification at his words, as
anyone must when they find what they had supposed was a one-way
relationship, is in fact reciprocal. I had been forgiven, or at any rate I
had not been forgotten. I turned to the others. 'Lady Claremont
has asked us up to the house for the fireworks.' Silence greeted this
extraordinary development. 'After the music's finished.'

Jennifer was the first to gather her wits. 'How tremendously kind.
We should love it. Please thank her.'

The man nodded with a slight inclination of his head, rather than a
bow, and pointed towards the steps. 'If you go up to the top there – '
He stopped, looking back at me. 'Of course, you'll know the way, Sir.'

'Yes.'

'They'll be in the Tapestry Drawing Room.'

'Thank you.' He hurried back to his normal duties. There was silence
as the other three stared at me.

'*You'll know the way, Sir?*' For once, Tarquin's determination never
to be impressed had deserted him.

'I used to come here when I was younger.'

Tarquin was silent. I knew him well enough by now to understand
that he was considering the facts with a view to reimposing his mastery

of the situation. So far, the solution had eluded him.

'Why didn't you say?' Jennifer's enquiry was, under the circumstances, a reasonable one.

'I didn't know where we were coming until we got here. We asked but Tarquin wouldn't tell us.' Jennifer threw a swift, admonitory glance at her pensive spouse. 'And I wasn't sure they'd be interested in seeing me again after such a long time. It's true that I used to stay here at one period of my misspent youth, but it was forty years ago.'

'Then she must have very sharp eyes, this "Lady Claremont" of yours.' Bridget spoke in derisive, inverted commas, as she always did when dealing with any part of my past that threatened her. I knew already, without being told, that of all the aspects of this uncomfortable weekend, the present episode would prove the *most* uncomfortable for her. But before we could discuss it further, the orchestra struck up and we were being sprayed with a deeply accessible version of 'Quando M'en Vo' from *La Bohème*, which may be played for laughs in context but is generally more lachrymose in concert and soon had all those MFHs and lifetime presidents of the village flower show committee reaching for their handkerchiefs.

I knew that in fact the Tapestry Drawing Room opened directly on to the gardens above us, but some trace of late-teen diffidence told me that to push in through the French windows with a crowd of strangers was overplaying my hand, so I devised the plan that at the end of the performance we would deposit our debris in the car, to obviate the need to collect it later, and make our way to the front of the house. The programme of events stated clearly that there was a fifty-minute break between concert and fireworks to allow the night to get properly dark, so I knew we had time. In that way we could come into the house via the front door, like normal people, and not be suspected of springing an ambush on our hosts.

I was glad of the decision when we got there, as quite a crowd was arriving and it was clear that the Claremonts had cunningly devised this plan to placate those locals who felt they had a right to be acknowledged by the family without the bore of giving them all dinner. The hall at Gresham was vast and high, stone-floored and with a screen of columns completing the square, behind which a graceful cantilevered staircase rose up to the next floor, its steps so shallow that a woman descending in a long skirt, which for our generation meant evening dress, seemed to float down as if her feet barely skimmed the steps beneath. It was a more awkward progress for men, who had to adjust quickly to the fact that each step taken only brought them about an inch nearer their destination, but for women the effect was like gliding, flying, and quite magical to watch, as I remembered so very well.

The portraits displayed here had been selected by Lady Claremont in a massive re-hang when she and her husband took over the house in 1967, just before my first visit, and which I could see at once had not been altered. They were chosen, as she freely confessed, unashamedly and entirely for their looks, and despite the anguished protests of Lord Claremonts' surviving aunts, those distinguished Victorian statesmen in undertakers' frock coats, those fearsome Georgian soldiers, all red faces and stubborn chins, those wily Tudor statesmen with their shifty eyes and avaricious mouths and generally the uglier members of the family, had been banished to anterooms and passages and bedrooms, except the ones by really famous painters, who had wound up either in the library or hung in fearsome double tiers against the crimson, damask walls of the great dining room. Both these chambers, Lady Claremont had explained to me at the time, were masculine rooms and so needed to be impressive but not pretty. Here, in the hall, charming children from every period were interlarded with handsome, nervous, young men in their Eton leaving portraits, trembling with anticipation at the welcoming life ahead, and lovely Gresham girls, painted on their betrothal to other lordly magnates or as part of some series of Court beauties for King Charles II or the Prince Regent, smiled down on their worshippers beneath. Their shining, gilded frames were set off by the apricot walls and the intricate plasterwork, picked out in varying shades of grey and white, while in the centre of the ceiling hung a huge chandelier, like a shower of glistening raindrops, frozen in their fall by a glance from the Snow Queen.

'How perfectly lovely,' said Jennifer, looking around, provoking a severe look from her husband, which I understood. Anything giving away that they were not regular visitors was to be suppressed. Jennifer grasped this too, of course, but had obviously made the interesting decision not to play along with his self-importance. Bridget, needless to say, was retreating into one of her silent-but-ironic moods, but I couldn't spare the time to administer to it. I was back at Gresham, which I never thought to be again, and I was determined to enjoy it.

The Tapestry Drawing Room was on the corner of the garden front, and the easiest way to reach it was through an oval anteroom at the back of the hall, where facing doors led left, to the dining room, and right, to our destination. It was a lovely place. The walls were lined in a kind of dusty blue moiré, with cream panelling edged in gilt up to the dado, and high panelled doorcases with over-door paintings set into them, taking the cream and gilt on up to the ceiling. Against the huge spaces of blue hung a set of Gobelin tapestries, celebrating a series of victories, achieved, I am pretty sure, by Marlborough. I forget precisely why they were here. Maybe an earlier Claremont had been in part responsible for the great duke's glory; in fact, now I am writing it I think that was why they were upped to an earldom in the 1710s. Beneath our feet was a ravishing Aubusson carpet, with its slight, distinctive wrinkling, and on it sat various magnificent pieces of furniture, most spectacularly a pedestal clock, seven foot high on its plinth, its inlaid case embellished with gilding, which had been presented to the third Earl by the Empress Catherine of Russia in return for some unspecified personal service, which no one had ever convincingly explained. The butler we had spoken to during the interval held a tray of glasses and a couple of maids were wandering about with more wine and bits of food. Lady Claremont, with that amazing eye for detail that had clearly not deserted her, had provided mini-savouries in the form of angels on horseback and tiny, pick-up bits of Welsh Rabbit or mushrooms on itsy bits of toast, all of which would be welcome, even after eating dinner.

'There you are. We couldn't believe our eyes when we saw you.' Lady Claremont kissed me swiftly and efficiently on one cheek, not for her the double-kiss import of the 1970s. 'You should have let us know you were coming.' I presented my party, who all shook hands. Jennifer alone thanked her for inviting us and Tarquin tried to start a conversation about the famous clock on which, needless to say, he had a great deal of information at his fingertips. But she had spent a life avoiding just such overtures, and soon gave a nod and a smile to indicate she had heard enough. Then she turned to her ancient neighbour, introducing me. 'Do you remember Mrs Davenport?' Since the woman did look a bit familiar I nodded as I shook her wizened hand. 'He was here all the time at the end of the Sixties,' Lady Claremont explained with a gay laugh. 'We used to feel terribly sorry for him.' She looked at me indulgently and I could sense my throat tightening at the prospect of what was coming next, but nothing could stop her as she looked about to gain the maximum audience. 'He was *so* in love with Serena!'

And she and the said Mrs Davenport laughed happily together at the memory of my roiling misery, which could still keep me awake at nights, and which I had thought private and brilliantly concealed from all but me. I smiled by way of response, to show I too thought it a terrific joke that I had wandered through these same charming rooms with my heart actually hurting in my chest. But her steady, even voice served to calm my remembered pain, as she chatted on about this and that, Serena and the other children, the lovely weather, the ghastly government, all standard stuff for a drinks party at a country house. I was interested that she had not mentioned the event we shared, that made an effective end to those dreams of long ago. Of course, it is a relatively modern American import, the notion that we must 'have these things out,' while the old, English traditions of letting sleeping dogs lie, and brushing things under the carpet, have been spurned. But who gains from this constant picking at the scabs of life? 'We have to talk,' says at least one character in almost every television drama these days, until one longs to scream at the screen, 'Why? Just let it go!' But I was not surprised Lady Claremont had avoided the culture of revisiting old wounds. In a way, her asking me up for a drink was her way of saying, 'It's all right. Like you, we've moved on. After so many years, surely we can have a chat again like normal people without even mentioning it.' And if she had made fun of my love pangs, still I appreciated her courtesy in this.

By the time I'd concluded my ruminations the tide of the party had separated us. Tarquin, having listened to the exchange with glee, could not decide whether to turn our hostess's ribbing into a way to belittle me and thereby derive some fun from my failed romance of long ago, or whether the mere fact that I had been to Gresham sufficiently often for Lady Claremont even to be aware that I was in love with her daughter and to welcome me now as an old friend entitled me to special handling. I left him to his indecisive review. Across the room, Jennifer had unearthed somebody they actually knew and seemed to be chatting quite merrily, and Bridget, as usual making a virtue of being out of her depth, was sulking, so I was essentially alone again in this, the haunting, painful setting of my earlier self.

Clutching my glass, nodding and smiling, I pushed back through the crush into the oval anteroom. We had passed through it quickly on our way in but, as I remembered so well, it was a lovely place, not huge but delicate and inviting, upholstered in a light and feminine chintz, and filled with light and feminine things. In this house it served as the boudoir and Lady Claremont's desk sat against one wall, a beautifully carved *bureau plat*, its surface littered with papers and letters and lists of things-to-do. I looked idly at a set of small Flemish paintings depicting the five senses, painted by David Teniers the younger some time in the 1650s. I had always admired them and I greeted them now like old friends. How delicate they were, how fine the detail, how strange that, since the paint first dried, not one, not two, but twenty generations had been born, had planned, had dreamed, had coped with disappointment and had died. I wandered over to the dining-room doors. They were closed but I turned the handle and pushed one open, startling a maid who was finishing laying the table. 'More than fourteen for breakfast?' I smiled to show that I came in peace.

She relaxed a little, answering in a rich, warm Yorkshire accent, 'We're nineteen tomorrow. And that's with two of the ladies staying in bed.'

'I remember the rule was always that fourteen or under ate breakfast in the small dining room. More than that and it was laid in here.'

I had succeeded in catching her attention. In fact, she was quite curious. She looked at me more closely. 'Did you used to stay here, then?'

'I did. At one time. It's reassuring to know that nothing's changed.' Actually, this was true. It *was* reassuring to find so much was still the same here, in this isolated appendix of my life, when almost everything had changed elsewhere. Although I later learned there was an element of illusion in this and that the estate, along with the country, had taken a downturn during the Seventies, successfully reversed from the mid-Eighties onwards in the hands of a new and gifted manager.

In fact, this happy story was true for many families I had known before their temporary fall. It should have been true for all of them, really, had not too many succumbed to that most dangerous of modern fashions among the born-rich, the desire to prove, to themselves and to everyone else, that their money is a reflection of their own brains and talent. The advantage of this is that it obviates the need to feel grateful to their forebears, or obliged to respect their successful, self-made acquaintance, who might otherwise demand some kind of moral superiority over those whose enviable position owes all to the efforts of others. The disadvantage, of course, is that it is not true. In denial of which, rich but silly aristocrats up and down the land will blithely launch into schemes they do not understand and investments that have no real worth, on the word of advisors without either judgement or merit, until their ignorance inevitably overturns them. I could name at least twenty men of my acquaintance who would be worth many millions more than they are if they had never left their bedrooms and come downstairs. And more than a few who began with everything and ended up with literally almost nothing. In this field I suspect that women, more pragmatic as a rule and less needy of self-worth when it comes to having a 'head for business,' have generally proved more sensible. Certainly, Lady Claremont would never have allowed her dearly loved spouse to get his hands on the wheel, or even near it, when it came to steering the Gresham inheritance.

'Mummy shouldn't have said that. I hope she hasn't driven you in here.' Her voice could always unnerve me. 'If you *were* even a bit in love with me I find it tremendously flattering.' That Serena should be so near to me was a joy, that she should have heard her mother's words was a nightmare, so it was with mixed emotions that I turned to find her looking at me through the door from the middle of the anteroom.

'At the time, I always rather hoped no one had guessed.'

'I didn't at the beginning.'

'Until Portugal.'

'Before. But never mind.' Unsurprisingly, she didn't want to be drawn into that one. 'Of course, Mummy told me afterwards that she knew when you first stayed here, but I suppose one's mother is bound to be more aware of these things.'

'Yours is.' We both smiled. 'It was kind of her not to bring up the whole Estoril thing, seeing it was the last time I saw them.'

'Was it really?'

'I might have glimpsed them across the room at a summer party at Christie's or something, but I haven't spoken to them properly between that night and this.'

She shrugged gently. 'Well, it was ages ago.' I wondered at her. As I have already mentioned, I had run into Serena occasionally over the years, so there was no four-decade gap to be leaped, but the sight of her was always an amazement. To start with, she seemed to have aged one year for every ten that the rest of us had gone through. In fact, she was hardly changed at all. A few fine lines at the sides of her eyes, a shallow crease by her mouth, her hair a slightly paler colour, nothing more. 'Are you all here for the weekend?'

'Most of us. Mummy made it a three-line whip. In case the whole thing went belly-up and we had to save the show. But the organisers were much better this year than last.'

'Is Mary with you? And Rupert?'

'Mary is. She was in the hall when I last saw her. Poor old Rupert's in Washington. He's been posted there for the last three years.'

'Washington? What an honour.'

'An honour and a bore. We're aching for him to get something in Paris or Dublin or anywhere he can get home from for the weekend.'

'What about Peniston? Have you brought him with you?' Serena had two children. The elder, Mary, whom I was doubtless about to see again after many years, was now married to the first secretary in the Washington embassy, Rupert Wintour, and was well on her way to being an ambassadress. When a child, she was ordinary in every way, and horribly like her father to look at, so I confess I suspected her husband's motives when I first heard about the marriage. His father, Sir Something Wintour, was an entrepreneur and his mother a former beautician, so the eldest child of an earl seemed like a suspiciously welcome choice, but once I had met him I felt I'd been unjust to Rupert. He was quite a bright spark. Serena's other child was the essential boy, Peniston, a little younger than his sister, whom I had seen occasionally in their house in Lansdowne Crescent, just as our friendship was petering out.

'Peniston's here but he arrived under his own steam, since he's married and has children of his own. These days I'm a grandmother three times over.'

'I need proof.'

She smiled pleasantly, used to compliments. 'Helena's come with William and the boys. You must say hello. And Anthony. I'm not sure where Venetia's got to. Mummy says she's in New York, but I got a card last week from Singapore. You know what she's like.' She rolled her eyes ceilingwards, with a tolerant laugh. There were three girls, starting with Serena herself and a brother who was, of course, heir to the kingdom. Helena, the second Gresham sister, had married an amiable landowning banking baronet in a neighbouring county, a union that had satisfied her mother, if it did not send her into ecstasies. However the youngest sister, Venetia, had defied the family by accepting the proposal of a pop impresario, an episode I remember only too well. The Claremonts had absolutely refused to countenance it at first. But to everyone's surprise, since she was not seen as particularly strong or rebellious, Venetia had stuck to her guns and in the end they caved in rather than endure the scandal of a wedding without their presence. As my own father used to say, 'Never provide material for a story.' Venetia was the winner in the end. Her husband made an immense fortune in the music industry and now she was richer than, or at least as rich as, any of them but the family exacted its revenge by continuing to patronise her, as if her life had been a trivial and wasteful mass of nothing, up to the present day.

Oddly, the male sibling, Anthony, was the one we all knew least. He came after Serena and before the others. He was still young, not much more than a boy, when Serena and I were running around together, but I can't say that even when he was grown up we were ever much the wiser where he was concerned. He was polite, of course, and pleasant to talk to at dinner or while having a drink before lunch, but he was always curiously opaque. He revealed nothing. The kind of person who, years later, might turn out to be a terrorist or a serial killer, without causing any great surprise. I liked him though, and I will say that he never demonstrated that supremely tedious habit that some people acquire, of loudly advertising to all and sundry the amount of information they are concealing. He hid everything about himself, but without pretence, mystery or conceit.

'So, how are you?' she said. 'Have you got another book out? I shouldn't have to ask. I feel rather feeble, not knowing.' There is a way of enquiring into an artistic career, which may sound or read as generous, but which in fact manages to reduce the value of it almost to nothing. The contempt is contained within its enthusiastic kindness, rather as a little girl's painting will be praised by someone who is hopeless with children. No one can do this better than the genuinely posh.

'There's one coming out next March.'

'You must let us know when it does.' Such people often say this sort of thing to their acquaintance in the media: 'Let me know when you're next on television,' 'Let us know when it's published,' 'Let us know when you're back on *Any Questions*.' As if one is likely to sit down and send off three thousand postcards when a personal appearance is scheduled. Obviously, they understand this will never happen. The message is really: 'We are not sufficiently interested in what you do to be aware of it if you don't make us aware. You understand that it does not impinge on our world, so you will please forgive us in future for missing whatever you are involved in.' Serena did not mean it unkindly, which is the case with many of them, but I cannot deny it is disheartening at times.

Her friendliness continued unabated. 'When did you know you'd be here tonight? You might have given us some warning. You could have come to dinner.' I explained the situation. Serena raised her eyebrows. 'Are they friends of yours? He's acquired the title of Bore of the County, but perhaps we're being unjust.'

'I wouldn't say that.'

She laughed. 'Well, it's nice to welcome you back. Has it changed?'

'Not really. Not as much as most of the rest of my life.'

'A trip down Memory Lane.'

'I'm living in Memory Lane at the moment.' Naturally, this demanded an explanation and I gave a partial one. I did not tell her the reason for why I was interviewing all these women from our joint past, only that Damian wanted to check up on what had happened to them and he'd asked me to do it, because he met them all through me in the first place.

'But why did you agree? Isn't it very time-wasting? And you

certainly don't owe him a favour.' She raised her eyebrows to punctuate this.

'I'm not completely sure why I'm doing it. I didn't intend to when he made the request, but then I saw that he was dying—' I broke off. She was visibly shocked and I rather regretted blurting it out as I had done.

'Dying?'

'I'm afraid so.'

She took stock, regaining command of herself. 'How odd. You don't think of someone like Damian Baxter as "dying."'

'Well, he is.'

'Oh.' By now she had quite recovered her equilibrium. 'Well, I'm sad. Surprised and sad.'

'I think he was always quite surprising.'

But Serena shook her head. 'I don't agree. He was exciting, but most of what he got up to was not surprising, it was inevitable. It wasn't at all surprising that he gatecrashed the Season so effectively. And it wasn't a bit surprising that he made more money than anyone else in recorded history. I knew all that would happen from the moment I met him. But dying thirty years before his time ...'

'How did you know?'

Serena thought for a moment. 'I think because he was always so angry. And in my experience people who are angry when young, either explode and vanish or do tremendously well. When I heard he'd gone into the City I knew he'd end up with zillions.'

I could not contain my curiosity, even if it felt like biting down on a loose tooth. 'Did you like him? When all was said and done?'

She looked at me. She knew the significance of the question, despite the years that we had travelled since it had the smallest relevance to either of our lives. On top of which she shared the usual reluctance of her tribe to give emotional information that might later be used in evidence against her. But at last she nodded. 'At one point,' she said. Then she seemed to gather up her carapace from the floor and wrap it firmly round herself once more. 'We really ought to join the others. I think it's about to start.' In answer to her words there was a sudden fizzing roar and through the uncurtained tall windows we could see a rocket darting across the night sky. With a loud bang, it exploded into a wide shower of golden sparks, accompanied by an appreciative 'ooh!' from the watching crowd.

'Is Andrew here?' In common courtesy I could avoid the question no longer. Even so, it felt lumpy, as if it had stuck to my lips.

She nodded. 'He's outside with the children. He always loves fireworks.' Behind her, the anteroom was suddenly filling up again, as some of the contents of the drawing room beyond spilled out to take advantage of another way outside. Serena started towards them. I fell into step beside her as we passed through the open French windows and in a moment we were enveloped in the sudden chill of the now dark, night air. Further along to the right, the rest of the house's guests were emerging from the doors of the Tapestry Drawing Room itself and the wide terrace was already becoming quite crowded. Another rocket, another bang, another twinkling shower, another ooh. 'Andrew, look who's here.'

It is still an offence to me that, of all people on earth, she should have married Andrew Summersby. How could my goddess have married this clottish beast of burden willingly? At least Shakespeare's Titania chose Bottom when she was on drugs. My Titania picked her Bottom when stone-cold sober and with her eyes wide open. Obviously, we all knew that Lady Claremont had propelled her daughter towards it, as in those days she did not question the accepted wisdom that a mother's job was to promote a suitable marriage, and a husband of equal rank and fortune trumped every trick. And obviously we all knew that Lady Belton was pushing from the other side until her shoulder must have been out of joint. But even so, it was hard to understand at the time, and harder still now, looking back. I wondered silently if Lady Claremont, with the different values and awarenesses of the modern world, would have promoted the match quite so furiously today. I rather thought not. But what good are such contemplations? If my grandmother had had wheels, she would have been a trolley car.

Andrew's stupid, bovine face, wider and flatter and redder and, if possible, even more repulsive than when I knew him, turned blankly towards me, with a solemn, self-inflating nod. 'Hello,' he said, without any question or courtesy to mark the gap since we last met.

Bridget had now found her way to us through the crowd and she chose this moment to curl her arm through mine in a deliberately possessive manner, advertising ownership, smiling smugly at Serena as she did so, all of which I found incredibly irritating but I did not show it. 'May I present Bridget FitzGerald?' I nodded towards my companions. 'Andrew and Serena Summers—' I corrected myself. This was wrong. Andrew's father was dead, which I knew. I just wasn't thinking. 'Sorry. Andrew and Serena Belton.' Serena smiled and shook Bridget's hand, but Andrew for some reason looked rather insulted and raised his glance back towards the fireworks. I thought at the time it was because I had got his name wrong, but I have a horrible suspicion, knowing his absolute lack of brain or imagination, that he had objected to being introduced to a stranger of lower rank as anything other than 'Lord Belton.' You may find this suggestion hard to believe, but I can assure you he was not alone among perfectly genuine toffs in this brand of foolishness, which takes the form of imitating the clothes and customs of their fathers from half a century ago and more. This is in the mistaken belief that it is an indicator of their good breeding, as opposed to absolute proof of their idiocy,

Serena continued blithely on, as if his rudeness were quite normal, which I suppose to her it was. 'This is my daughter, Mary. And my son, Peniston.' The introduction was for Bridget's benefit. I smiled and said hello, which greeting was returned by Mary pleasantly, as I willingly concede, and Peniston also held out his hand. They clearly knew who I was, which was pathetically gratifying. Serena smiled too, enjoying the presence of her children. 'When did you last see them?'

'In another lifetime, I'm afraid.' I smiled and shook the young man's hand in my turn. 'I won't mention the girl in sulks over having to wear some party dress she hated, or the boy in blue rompers, peddling his first tricycle round the kitchen.'

'That's a relief,' said Peniston.

'I remember that dress,' said Mary. 'Granny sent it and it was covered in the most hideous smocking, like an illustration from a Jack and Jill reader in the Fifties. I screamed the place down rather than wear it and I would do the same today.' We laughed, and I found myself revising my opinion of Mary, even if her resemblance to Andrew was very off-putting. Through all this, Bridget looked blank and Andrew once again assumed the expression of affront that I could already tell had become habitual. There was no obvious reason for this, although it might have been because the reference to his daughter's tantrums or his heir's rompers, or perhaps to his wife's kitchen, was some piece of iniquitous *lèse majesté* on my part. I neither knew nor cared.

But the young siblings eased the touchy moment by chatting away about mundane things and Andrew's gaucheness was soon forgotten. Presumably Peniston and his sister often had to perform this service to cover the tracks of their tiresome Papa. I was not, in truth, much disposed to like the new Viscount Summersby, as he now was, since his very name still made me shudder, but even I had to admit he seemed a nice fellow. I can't pretend he was exactly attractive, being overweight and shortish, and if his face was pleasant, it was not good-looking. But then again, my impression of him may be suspect. Most men, or women too for aught I know, have ambivalent feelings towards the children of those they once loved. Particularly if it was not their choice to end the relationship. In a way these boys and girls, symbols of some horrible misjudgement by the gods, should never have been born if things had gone right. Yet it's not their fault, is it? As one usually comes to see in the end. So it was for me, with Mary Wintour and Peniston Summersby. The news of their impending births had cut me like a knife from fore to aft, but of course, presented with this nice man, this agreeable woman, it was quite a different matter, and even I could see it wasn't fair to hate them because their father was a blockhead and their mother broke my heart. There wasn't much of Serena in either of them, to be honest, and even less as they had grown. As a little girl, Mary had been a miniature of Andrew, far more than her brother, but on that night he too looked more like his father, if he looked at all like either. Happily for them and for their prospects, neither seemed to resemble Andrew in charm.

Peniston smiled. 'Granny was frightfully excited when she spotted you. She's terribly proud to know a real novelist. She's read everything you've ever written.'

'I'm flattered.' I was. And astonished. Suddenly it was less extraordinary that I'd been found among the crowd.

'She just loves knowing a writer. Most of her friends have the greatest difficulty reading to the end of a restaurant bill.' A pretty woman in her early thirties had joined us. 'This is my wife, Anne.'

'What he says is quite true. Roo's thrilled you're here. She's got all your books, you know. I expect she's lining them up for you to sign.'

'She has only to ask.' Since Lady Claremont's interest in my work presumably implied an albeit slight interest in me, I was amused that in forty years she had never invited me to a single gathering either here at Gresham or in London, nor made the smallest attempt to re-establish contact. Why was that, if her fascination with my career was so great? At the time, my paranoia immediately attributed the cause to the Estoril evening, but I am fairly sure now that I was wrong. Occasionally one does come across this curious diffidence on the part of the posh and there is nothing sinister or deflating in it. I suppose it is the flip side of their tendency to patronise. They are still marking the absolute divide between their world and yours, but in this case it is demonstrated by a kind of modesty, a tacit recognition that their muscular, social powers may not always impress those who have other choices.

'You're missing everything.' Andrew's voice cut across our merriment, and we obediently turned our attention back to the fireworks. Fizz, bang, ooh. Fizz, bang, ooh. The display ended with what should have been a very impressive showing of the Gresham crest, a rearing lion holding a flag of some sort. In the event it didn't quite work, as most of the lion's head failed to ignite, rendering the image faintly macabre, but even so it delivered a reasonably big finish. And then it was over, and time for the guests, inside and out, those not staying the night anyway, to make their exit and not to take too long about it. I managed to find our hosts in the throng to thank them and say goodbye.

Lady Claremont was still smiling, with that glint in her eye. 'We must get you down here. If you could ever spare the time.'

'I'm down this weekend, so I must have some time to spare.'

'Of course you are. With those funny people who've got Malton Towers.' The phrase 'those funny people' told me everything I needed to know about Tarquin's chances of ever getting in with the County. 'One of Henry's great-grandmothers grew up at Malton. He used to stay there quite often before the war. But you thought it was ghastly, didn't you?' She looked at her aged husband.

He nodded. 'Coldest bloody house I ever entered. Cold food, cold baths, cold everything. I never had a wink of sleep in all the years I went there.' It was easy to see that his lordship had had about enough of this interminable evening and was more than ready for bed, but he hadn't quite finished. 'They're crackers to have taken it on. Ruined my cousins, ruined every organisation that came after them. And at least my relations had the land, much good did it do them. Your friends have just bought a bottomless pit.' Actually, to me this sounded not only like fairly accurate reporting but also curiously reassuring. It is easy to forget, watching the Tarquins fling every last penny they possess into supporting some pseudo-aristocratic, gimcrack fantasy, that there are still people for whom these are normal houses in which normal lives should be led. If they're uncomfortable then they're uncomfortable and that's that. Never mind the plasterwork or the Grinling Gibbons carving, or the ghost of Mary Stuart in the East Wing. There was a kind of no-nonsense quality to his dismissal of Malton Towers that seemed to earth my own experience of it, releasing me from reverence. At any rate Lord Claremont had said his piece and there didn't seem much point in getting him to elaborate, so I nodded and moved on.

I caught sight of Serena in the hall. She was with her family and talking to Helena, who was looking a good deal older than her older sister. But she was friendly when we met again, kissing me and wishing me well, as I grinned across her at the object of my ancient and unrequited passions. Looking back I cannot quite explain why the sight of Serena that evening, far from making me sad as it might so easily have done, had in fact given me a terrific lift. I felt marvellous, giddy, tight, high, whatever Seventies word is most appropriate, at being reminded of how much I once could love. Still loved, really. A whole set of muscles that had atrophied through lack of use sprang to life again within my bosom. Rather as you are empowered by discovering an ace has been dealt you when you pick up the cards from the baize. Even if you never get a chance to play it, you know that you are the better and stronger for having an ace in your hand.

'It's been so lovely to see you,' Serena said, sounding wonderfully as if she meant it.

'I have enjoyed it.' As I answered her I knew that my tone was strangely steady, almost cold, in fact, when I did not feel cold towards her in the least, very much the opposite. I cannot explain why, except to say that an Englishman of my generation will always protect himself against the risk of revealing his true feelings. It is his nature and he cannot fight it.

Again, she smiled her smile of the blessed. 'We're all fans, you know. We must try and get you down to Waverly.'

'I'd love it. In the meantime, good luck with everything.'

We touched cheeks and I turned away. Stepping out of the front door, I had not gone more than a few paces when I heard Andrew's indignant enquiry. 'Good luck with what? What did he mean by that?' I confess the temptation was too great and I sneaked back, staying out of sight from the front door.

'He didn't mean anything. Good luck. That's all.' Serena's patient and modulated tones dealt with him as one might soothe a frisky horse or dog. 'Good luck with life.'

'What an extraordinary thing to say.' He seemed to clear his throat to draw her attention to him. 'I'm rather surprised to find him so effulgent and you so welcoming, after everything that happened.'

'Oh, for heaven's sake.' They were alone now, or thought they were, and Serena's tone was less careful. 'Since the evening you speak of we've seen the fall of Communism, the Balkans in flames and the collapse of the British way of life. If we can survive all that, we can surely forget one drunken dinner that got out of hand, forty years ago—' But by then, Bridget was pulling at my sleeve with a funny look, and I had to come away and out of earshot. If Andrew had more to contribute on the subject after Serena's outburst it was lost to me. Not for the first time I wondered at how, among the upper classes particularly but perhaps in every section of society, extremely clever women live with very, very stupid men without the husbands' ever apparently becoming aware of the sacrifice their wives are making daily.

'That was the greatest treat,' said Jennifer, as we nudged our way out of the gates and back on to the main road. 'What luck we had you with us. Wasn't it, darling?'

I didn't expect an answer, as I realised that it was almost physically painful for Tarquin to acknowledge another's superior power at any time. Most of all in his own would-be kingdom. But Jennifer remained looking fixedly at him, driving through the side of her right eye, until he managed a sort of grudging response. 'Good show,' he muttered, or something along those lines. I couldn't really hear.

His envy and Bridget's misery combined to fill the car with a green mist of resentful, hurt rage, but Jennifer wouldn't give up. 'I thought they were so nice. And they're obviously very fond of you.'

'Well, he's *very* fond of them. Or some of them. Aren't you? *Darling?*' Bridget's contribution at moments like this was the vocal equivalent of throwing acid. Of course, as I was forced to realise, the downside of remembering what love *is* came in the form of a clear realisation of what it is *not* and whatever it was that I was sharing with Bridget was not love. I'd seen this coming. I had hinted as much to my dear old Daddy when I went to have lunch with him. But I don't think, before that evening at Gresham, I'd appreciated that the buffers were not only in sight but nearly upon us. In fairness, I cannot blame Bridget for feeling cheesed off. She was an intelligent, attractive woman, and she was obliged to accept that, once again, she had wasted several, long years on a dry well, on a bagless hunt, on a dead end. As I have mentioned, she'd made this mistake before, more than once, which I knew well, and until this very evening I'd always taken her line that the men in question were beasts and cads for not releasing her when they must have known it was going nowhere. Instead, they had, as I thought, strung her along until they had stolen her future and her children, who would never now know life. It was at this point, in that darkened car pushing through the Yorkshire lanes, that I suddenly realised that they had not been cads exactly, simply selfish, insensitive, unthinking fools. As I was. And from tomorrow morning I would be sharing their guilt, in the Sad Story of Bridget FitzGerald.

She didn't speak again until we were in our freezing, damp bedroom. She had started to undress in that angular, vengeful way that I knew so well, talking over her shoulder at me, or through the back of her furious head. 'The whole thing is so ridiculous.'

'What thing? There isn't a "thing".'

'Darn right, there isn't. She's not at all interested in you. Not in the least.' She spoke the words crisply with a vivid, sparky relish, as if Serena's lack of love for me was somehow all her own work, a real achievement to be proud of.

'No. I don't suppose she is.'

'Not in the least.' The repeat was heightened in volume and acerbity. 'Anyone can see that. She could hardly remember who you were.' This was, I thought, a punch below the belt but I decided not to argue. Instead, I settled for looking wounded. I was wasting my time. Bridget, in full flow by now, was unfazed by any perceived sense of injustice. 'She'd never leave him. You can't imagine that she would.'

'No.'

'And if she did? What makes you think she'd ever want to live with a sad, little depressive like you?'

'I don't.'

'Because she wouldn't, you know. You can't believe that would happen in a million light years.'

'Fine.'

'Give up all the privileges? All the profile? Go from Countess of Belton to Mrs *You*? Never.'

For a moment I was going to protest facetiously that she would have been more correctly styled as 'Lady Serena *You*' but thought better of it. I was rather interested by her suggestion that Serena and Andrew had a 'profile.' What did that mean? What is a 'profile' in this context? I suppose Bridget's rage had now taken on a life of its own and her editing faculties were impeded. 'I dare say it is unlikely,' I said.

'I'll say. That type never do.'

'She's a "type," is she? Well, that's encouraging. I must look out for some more of them.'

'Oh, fuck off.' I cannot complain at this since I deserved it.

But by the time I too had undressed and we were both shivering beneath our inadequate coverings in our ugly carved bed, she had calmed down. Up until now her anger had protected me against feeling guilt, but I was not to get off scot-free. Just before I turned out the light she lowered her book and looked over at me. 'What did I do wrong?' Her voice was quite gentle again and the soft Irish burr that I always found so beguiling gave it a poignancy that reminded me painfully how much I hate to hurt.

I shook my head and gave what I hoped was a warm smile, which in that temperature was quite a challenge. 'It's not your fault,' I answered her in what I felt was a suitably genuine tone. 'You've done nothing wrong. It isn't you, it's me.' As one mouths these oh so familiar sentiments, and this last, hackneyed sentence in particular, one likes to feel that one is expressing a noble and generous sentiment. That you are 'taking the blame' for the failure, 'shouldering the responsibility' and so on. In fact, of course, this is dishonest, as any serial love-rat, to lift a title from the tabloids, could tell you, and we are almost all love-rats at some stage. The phrases are a kind of lazy shorthand, designed to deflect the brickbats hurtling at your head and bring all discussion of the topic to a close as quickly as possible.

Bridget, quite rightly, felt she deserved more than this craven and mendacious reply. 'Please,' she said. 'I mean it.' And her tone was now pulling at my heart strings to an uncomfortable degree. 'Is there anything I could have done that would have made it better?'

I looked at her and decided on honesty. 'You could have been happier.'

She bridled. 'You could have made me happier.'

I nodded with almost military precision. 'Precisely,' I said. And with both of us feeling that her words had put us each inalienably in the right, I turned out the light and we pretended to sleep.

Joanna

NINE

It was the day after we returned from Yorkshire that I received another call from Damian. I say 'from Damian' but in fact Bassett's modest, unassuming voice greeted me down the receiver. 'Mr Baxter was wondering . . .' He paused nervously and I began to wonder what Damian could be wondering that would give me such offence, but the answer, when it came, was mild, 'if you might possibly be able to get down to see him at all soon.'

I felt I should confess my lack of progress straight away, not that it was very likely I was concealing a major find. 'I haven't much to report yet, I'm afraid,' I said.

But Bassett did not seem to be expecting anything different. 'Mr Baxter knows that, Sir. He assumed that he would have heard from you before now if there was anything to hear. But he would like to catch up with you all the same.'

Despite Bassett's dulcet tones, there was an absolute expectation of my agreeing to this suggestion that triggered an alarm bell in my vitals. I had the uncomfortable feeling that I had somehow put myself in Damian's power by agreeing to his request, that, in short, far from doing him a favour I had in fact been bought. I was not being paid, of course, but against my better judgement I had accepted the insulting credit card and in a way it made me an employee, which I should have spotted at the outset. I had broken my own rule, viz. that if one is bought, let it be for a high price. This is why no one should ever accept a charity lecture or brief local appearance where a fee is involved, at least in England. The sum is invariably tiny, but the organisers will most definitely feel, once they have pressed a few coins into your hand, that they own you body and soul. If you must do these things, and sometimes one must, then please do them for nothing. Do them out of the goodness of your heart. The money will make no difference to your life, but you will never have to endure the sense of being a purchased hireling, since you retain the whip hand of your generosity. Better yet, donate the fee you might have had to their cause, or to something equally worthy, and add a halo to your head for good measure. But in this instance somehow, by sleight of hand, Damian had tricked me and retained the moral high ground. I was no longer doing a good turn, I was carrying out a commission. It is quite a different matter.

Eventually the plan was settled. I had rather a heavy week coming up, so the decision was made that I would return to Surrey after lunch on the following Sunday. Accordingly, I took the train and was met once more at the station by the flawlessly uniformed chauffeur, but as we arrived at Planet Damian it came as a surprise to see what looked like a village fête going on in the gardens. The cars were parked in a field further down the road, and the booths and general activity were apparently cordoned off from the upper lawn, so the event did not really impinge on the actual house, but even so it was not very compatible with my cherished image of Mr Baxter, being altogether too philanthropic for his tastes. However, in answer to my question as I got out of the car, Bassett confirmed the situation. 'Yes. It's held over two days in the summer, Sir. It's in aid of the local Catholic church, St Teresa's. In Guildford.'

'Is Mr Baxter a Catholic?' The thought had never occurred to me. Not that I mind Catholics. It was just strange to think of Damian subscribing to any religion.

'I believe so, Sir.'

'And does he do this every year?'

'He does, Sir. Since he first came here.' I attempted to conceal my cynical amazement as I was shown directly to the library. When I walked into the room I realised at once why I had been sent for. Damian was dying. He had of course been dying before, when I was last there on the visit that started it all, but one may be dying without having death written all over one's face. This time it was not so much that he had a fatal illness. Rather, at first appearance, he looked as if he were already dead.

He lay back, stretched out, on his daybed, eyes shut. Were it not for the faintest movement of his emaciated chest I would have assumed I had come too late. I suppose I must have appeared shocked, as just at this moment he opened his eyes and let out a rasping, little laugh at my expression. 'Cheer up,' he snorted. 'I'm not quite as bad as I look.'

'That's a relief,' I said. 'Since you couldn't look worse.'

Naturally this bucked him up. He rang the bell by his chair and when the ever vigilant Bassett put his head round the door suggested, in that diffident way of his, that we might have some tea. 'Are you staying the night?' he asked when Bassett had gone off on his commission.

'I don't think so. I was planning to continue the search tomorrow, and I don't believe I should put it off.'

'No. For pity's sake don't put it off, whatever you do.' But he raised his eyebrows to make this reference to his coming demise, into a sort of joke. 'So, how have you been getting on?'

I told him about Lucy and Dagmar. 'They seem very fond of you.'

'Don't sound so surprised.'

Of course, that was the point. I was surprised. But I didn't feel I could word this acceptably so I didn't try. Instead, I repeated their separate messages of goodwill and felt glad I had delivered them faithfully. 'I don't think I was aware how well you knew them.'

'You weren't aware of a lot of things about me.' He waited, perhaps for me to contradict, but I was silent. 'Poor little Dagmar.' He gave a semi-comic sigh, inviting me to join in his contemplation of her hopelessness, but after my recent visit I would have felt disloyal so I resisted. He continued, undeterred. 'She should probably have been born in 1850, been married by proxy to some German grand duke, and just lived out her life observing the rituals. She would have done it very well and no doubt been much loved by all those loyal subjects who would never get near enough to find out how boring she was.'

'She's less boring now,' I said. 'Less boring, less diffident and less happy.'

He nodded, absorbing my report. 'I was surprised when she married him. I thought she'd go for dull and respectable, and end up in a farmhouse in Devon, with a lot of huge, Royal portraits looking out of place and filling the half-timbered walls from floor to ceiling. I never expected her to go for nasty and successful, and end up back in a palace and miserable.'

'Well, she's got the portraits, anyway.'

'Did she tell you she wanted to marry me?' He must have caught my expression on hearing this, as he read it very accurately. 'I'm past being ungallant. I'm nearly dead. At that point you truly can say what you like.' Which, on reflection, I feel is probably true.

'She did, actually.'

'Really?' I could see he was surprised.

'She said she longed for it, but you weren't interested. She said she had nothing to offer that you wanted or needed.'

'That sounds rather peevish.'

'Well, it wasn't. She was very touching.'

He nodded at this, somehow acknowledging Dagmar's generosity with a kinder tone than he had used before. 'I never said she wasn't a nice woman. I thought she was one of the nicest of all of you.' He considered for a minute. 'It was hard for ex-Royals.'

'I agree.'

'It was all right for the ones still on thrones,' he added, thinking more on the topic. 'After all the nonsense of the Sixties and Seventies was over, they were in an enviable position. But for the others it was hard.'

'I suppose you didn't want to take all that on. Not once you knew more about what it would entail.'

'There were lots of things I didn't want to take on, once I knew a bit more about them.' He looked at me. 'If it comes to that, I didn't want to take on your whole world, once I knew more about it.' He returned to the matter in hand. 'But you're quite sure she wasn't my pen pal?'

'I am.'

'And it wasn't Lucy either?' I explained further about the hereditary condition of the daughter. Thoughtfully, he absorbed the detail that ruled him out. 'So, how was she?'

'All right.' I tipped my head from side to side, in that gesture that is intended to signify so-so.

He was quite curious at this. 'You don't seem to be waxing lyrical. I always thought of you two as very thick.'

'Her life is more her own fault than Dagmar's.' The truth is I did feel more tepid about the Rawnsley-Prices. The phrase about people 'making their own bed' is not very meaningful, since we all to some extent make our own beds and have to lie on them. We have no choice. Even so, it does have some meaning. Unlike many people, Lucy had enjoyed real options when young and she seemed, to me anyway, to have chosen none of the more creative or interesting ones.

He spoke my thought. 'Lucy is another Sixties casualty.'

I felt it behoved me to stick up for my old friend a bit. 'She's not as bad as some. At least she's not one of those sad sixty-year-old television executives, wandering around in a leather jacket and talking about the Arctic Monkeys.'

'Maybe. But she assumed that her act as a madcap baronet's daughter, embracing the new values, with a zany, whacky sense of fun would run and run. She was mistaken.' He was right in this so I didn't defend her further. 'Besides, that particular routine is only convincing when the player is young. Zany and whacky at fifty-eight is just tragic.'

'She has our best wishes, though.'

'If you want. She'll survive.' He looked at me as I stared out of the window on to the gathering below.

'Your fête is very well attended, I must say.'

'I can see you're taken aback to find me doing something for charity.'

'I am a bit.'

'You're right. I am not very nice. Not really.' He spoke quite sharply, unwilling to lie, even by being silent. 'But I do approve of these people. I admire their ordinariness. When I was young I couldn't deal with anyone who lacked ambition. I couldn't see the point of a life that just accepted and had no wish to change. I was at ease with people who wanted to be millionaires and cabinet ministers and movie stars. I sympathised with any vaulting goal, no matter how ludicrous. But those with no desire beyond a decent life, a nice house, a pleasant holiday were quite alien to me. They made me uncomfortable.'

'But not now.'

He nodded, endorsing my comment. 'Now, I see the ability simply to embrace life and live it as noble. Not always to drive yourself like an ox through a ploughed field, which is what I used to admire. I suppose, hundreds of years ago, it was the same when people entered convents and monasteries to give their lives to God. I feel these men and women, in just getting on with it, are also in their way giving their lives to

God. Even though I don't believe in him.' He stopped to enjoy my amazement. 'I bet you never thought I'd say that.'

I agreed without hesitation. 'Or anything remotely like it.' He laughed and I continued, 'Presumably, this is all reflected in the benefiting Saint, young, innocent and surrounded with pastel-shaded flowers.'

'No. That's the other Saint Teresa. Our one is Teresa of Avila. She spent most of her life empathising with Christ's suffering and having visions of everyone drenched in blood. Then she started a new order and was locked up by the Pope, but she fought like a tigress and won through in the end.'

'You should have told me that straight away. I would have understood her appeal at once.'

This time he laughed out loud and we had to wait for his fit of coughing to subside. By then his mirth had been replaced by something gentler. 'I want you to understand that I have changed. It's important to me.' He was watching my face all the time for the effect of his words, which was quite disconcerting. 'At least, one says that. But one never knows if it is really change that one is experiencing, or simply qualities always present finally making their way to the surface. I do think I'm kinder than I was.'

'That wouldn't be difficult.'

'And less angry.' His words chimed with the dining room conversation in Yorkshire, and I must have somehow acknowledged this in my reception of his comments.

Which somehow he picked up. 'What?'

'Only that I ran into Serena Gresham, or Serena Belton as she is now, last weekend, and she said something similar. That you were very angry when she knew you, and that angry people tend either to explode or to achieve great things.'

'Or both.' We were interrupted by the arrival of a tray of tea, all laid out like a prop in a Hollywood film, with thin, cucumber sandwiches and a little silver dish of sliced lemon. But I could tell it was all for me. Damian was past eating or drinking anything for pleasure. When Bassett had gone he spoke again. 'You have been combing through the attics. How is she?'

'Pretty well. Andrew as awful as ever.'

'Was he there?' I nodded with a grimace, which Damian echoed. 'I always used to wonder how he would keep up through a family dinner in that house. All of them sparking away like firecrackers and Andrew sitting there like a lump of mud.'

'I think he keeps up by being unaware that he is not keeping up.'

'And her ladyship?'

'More or less unchanged. I'm sad to say jolly old Lord C. has been replaced by a carving, stolen from a tomb in the Capuchin Church in Vienna, but she's much the same as she was.' I told him about Lady Claremont's joke at my expense. It was a risky admission, given what came after my love had been revealed all those years ago, but I was in too deep by now to be careful.

He smiled. 'You should have married her.'

'Don't let's go down that route.' With all that had happened I was no longer surprised that my rage should be as near the surface as it was.

If I expected him to be chastened I was disappointed. 'I just meant that I bet Lady Claremont would have been better off with you than Andrew.' As usual, he made no reference to his own part in the whole business.

'Or you. Or anyone.'

'No. Not me,' he said flatly.

I couldn't break free of the subject quite yet. Once reopened, the wound felt as if it were freshly cut. 'Why did she marry him? What was she? Nineteen? And she wasn't even pregnant. The daughter came along ten months later and was the spitting image of Andrew, so there was nothing untoward. I just don't get it.'

He nodded. 'It was a different world then. We did things differently.'

'How involved were you? With Serena?' As I spoke, each word was like a lash, leaving a red stripe on my back.

He chuckled. 'What a wonderfully quaint expression. You sound like *Woman's Hour* thirty years ago. In what way "involved"?'

'You know in what way.'

He was silent for a moment. Then he shrugged. 'I was mad about her.'

Had I known this or not? It was so hard to decide, after everything that had happened. To hear him say it was still a kind of shock. Rather like the death of a great friend after a long terminal illness. I drank deeper of the poison. 'Who broke it off?'

I could see I was beginning to annoy him. Once again, we had used up our false friendliness and were getting back to our true feelings for one another. 'I didn't want to spend my life being patronised.' I could see he was back there for a moment, in the place that I had never left. 'I remember once,' he said after a moment, 'when I went to Gresham—'

'You used to go to Gresham?' I couldn't believe it. Where was I all this time? Sleeping in a box in the cellar? Why had I known none of this?

'You know I did. For the dance.' He was right. I did know it. 'She was giving me a lift. So I got myself to their flat. Where was it? Somewhere in Belgravia?'

'Chester Square. And it was a house, not a flat.'

He looked at me, understanding fully the significance of my exact recollection of the detail. 'Anyway, we'd loaded up the cases and then, as we set off, Serena said—' he paused, with a deep sigh, back in that smart little red two-seater that I once knew so well. 'She said, "Now this is going to have to be very carefully stage-managed" and she started to list what I was to do when I got there, how I was to behave, what I should and should not say to her mother when she greeted me, how I should manage her father's questions, what I should mention to her brother and her sisters. On and on she went, and as I listened I thought this isn't for me. I don't want to go somewhere where I'm a liability, where things have to be monitored so my hosts don't regret asking me, where I need to take a course before I can get out of the car, where I'm not a welcome member of the party.' He stopped, out of breath, and waited until he had caught up with himself.

'I can see that,' I said. Which I could.

He looked at me as if he suspected me of triumphing in his confession. 'I didn't face it at the time but, if I'm honest, I think that was when I knew it wouldn't work. Not in the long term.'

'Did you say anything to her?'

The question made him slightly uncomfortable. 'Not then.' He had recovered. 'Later.'

'But it was the end from that moment?' What did I want from him?

'I don't know. I can't remember. The point is I realised that if I ever did marry, I wanted it to be into a family that would hang bunting off the balconies, send up fireworks, take out ads in *The Times*, not roll their eyes in unforgiving silence at my unsuitability. You saw what that guy who married the youngest sister had to go through. He was an unperson by the time they'd finished with him.'

'Did Suzanne's family put out the flags?' This sounds rather unkind and I suppose it was, but I was so filled with jealousy that I felt I could have killed him. I'd say he got off pretty lightly.

His smile became rather wry. 'The trouble was you lot had spoiled me. I didn't like you or your world, and I didn't want what you had, but when I tried to go back to my old crowd I'd lost the taste for their tastes. I had become like mad old Lady Belton, too snobbish, too aware of unimportant differences and needing to be stage-managed, myself.'

'So we repelled you from our world and spoiled you for your own.'

'In a nutshell.'

'Serena must have got married almost straight away? When you and she were finished.'

'Not long afterwards.' He thought about this. 'I hope she's happy.'

I sipped my tea in a vague, and vain, attempt to soothe my troubled spirits. 'Not very, I would guess. But with her kind it's hard to tell.'

Once more he was watching me, with all the care of an anthropologist making a study of a rare and unpredictable beast. 'Are you enjoying it at all? This Proustian return? It's your past as much as mine.'

'Not much.'

'What does your . . .' He hesitated. 'I hate the word "partner." What does she make of it all?'

'Bridget? I don't think she's interested. It's not her scene.' This last was true, but the statement before it wasn't completely. Still, I couldn't be bothered to get into all that. 'It doesn't matter either way,' I continued. 'We've broken up.'

'Oh dear. I hope it's coincidental.'

'Not completely. But it was coming anyway.'

He nodded, insufficiently curious to pursue it. 'So, who's next?'

'Candida Finch or Joanna Langley. Joanna, probably.'

'Why?'

'I always had rather a crush on her.'

He smiled at my revelation. 'Obviously, something we shared.'

'Do you remember the famous Ascot appearance?'

'How could anyone forget it?'

'Were you with her then?' I asked breezily. 'I know you weren't in her party when you got there. Didn't you come with the Greshams?' Another crunch, hard down on that loose and aching tooth.

He frowned, concentrating. 'Technically. But I don't think I was "with" either of them at that stage. That all came later.'

I winced. 'I used to think you and Joanna made rather a good pair.'

He nodded. 'Because we were both common and on the make? And I wouldn't get in your way?'

'Because you were both modern and in touch with reality, which is more than you could say for most of us. The big learning curve we were all facing wasn't going to be necessary for you two.'

'That's generous.' He acknowledged my courtesy with a polite nod from the neck. 'But we weren't as synchronised as we must have looked from the outside. I was very ambitious, remember.'

'I certainly do.'

My tone was perhaps more revealing than I had intended and it made him flick his eyes up at me. 'And in those early months of the whole thing I still hadn't decided what I did, or didn't, want from all of you. Joanna wanted nothing. Except to escape from her mother and hide. She may not have known it, at least not consciously, not then. But it was in her and of course she found out the truth before very long.'

'As we all know.'

Damian laughed. 'As we all know.'

'And when she did, it was clear you weren't going in the same direction.'

He nodded in acceptance of this, although I could see, each time I interrupted, that it troubled him not to set his own pace. Actually, I fully understand how annoying this can be, those tiresome, unfunny men at dinners who heckle a speaker, destroying the jokes, but not replacing them with anything amusing of their own. Even so, I wasn't prepared to listen to Damian's cleaned-up and sanitised account of these events, without the odd comment. He continued, 'When you do see her and you've finished your snooping, I'm interested to learn what she feels about all that time now. I look forward to hearing when you've tracked her down.'

This was the question that was troubling me. Of all the women on the list she was the one with the least information. 'You haven't given me a lot to go on. To find her.'

Damian accepted this. 'Her name doesn't bring up much on the Internet. The Ascot story, of course, and some other early stuff, but nothing after the divorce.'

'Divorce?'

'In 1983.' I must have looked solemn for a moment. He shook his head, clucking his tongue as he did so. 'Please don't let's pretend it's a shock. The wonder is that they got fourteen years out of it.'

'I suppose so. What was the husband called again? I forget.'

'Kieran de Yong. You'll find there's plenty about him.'

'Kieran de Yong.' I hadn't thought of that name in so long, but it still had the power to make me smile.

Ditto Damian. 'I used to get a glimpse of him at the odd city *feste*, but he always studiously ignored me. And I haven't seen anything of Joanna, in print or person, since they split.' He spoke musingly. 'What do you think his real name was?'

'Not Kieran de Yong.'

He laughed. 'It might be Kieran. But I doubt it was de Yong.'

Now I too was trying to remember those headlines and that curious young man. 'What was he? A hairdresser? A modelling agent? A dress designer? Something that chimed with the *zeitgeist* of the day.'

'I think you'll be surprised. Most people get less from the future than they expected but some people get more. We've got an address for him. They should have given it to you.'

I nodded. 'If they've split up, will he know where to find her?'

'Of course he will. They've got a son.' He paused. 'Or I have. Anyway, even if he doesn't he may provide a lead. In any case I should start with him because we haven't come up with an alternative.'

I was leaving when I had to ask one last question. 'Are you really a Catholic?'

He laughed. I suppose the wording was rather funny. 'I'm not sure what you mean. I was born a Catholic. Didn't you know?'

I shook my head. 'So you "lapsed"?'

'I'm afraid so.'

His answer interested me. 'Why "afraid"? Would you like to believe?'

Damian glanced at me patronisingly, as if I were a child. 'Of course I would,' he said. 'I'm dying.'

The car was waiting patiently outside, but I knew there was a train every twenty minutes and so, with the immaculate chauffeur's permission, I allowed myself a little wander among the stalls of the fête below. I thought about Damian's unexpected words as I looked at these tables of old, unreadable books, at the piles of lamps from all the worst periods, at the cakes and jams, painstakingly made and all soon doubtless to be outlawed by the Health and Safety *Stasi*, at the dolls without their voice boxes and the jigsaws 'missing one piece,' and I, too, felt a kind of comfort and balm in the decency they represented. Naturally, it was very old-fashioned, and I am sure that if a New Labour minister could be offended by the Last Night of the Proms, she would be rendered suicidal by the sight of this comic, uniquely English event, but there was goodness here. These people had worked hard at what I would once have judged as such a little thing, yet their efforts were not wasted on me; in fact, they almost made me cry.

It is hard to be certain from this distance, but I think I'm right in saying that Ascot came after Queen Charlotte's Ball. I had anyway, as I have said, met Joanna Langley several times before the race meeting, but it was on that day that I suppose we became friends, which even now I like to think we were. It was then that I understood she was a creature of her own era, that she was not, like the rest of us, engaged in some kind of action replay of our parents' youth.

Ascot as a fashionable event is almost finished now. No doubt sensibly, Her Majesty's Representative has decided the meeting would better earn its keep as a day for racing enthusiasts and corporate entertaining. To this end the Household Stand (their sole remaining perk, poor dears, in exchange for all that unpaid smiling and standing) and various other, arcane sanctums were eliminated from the wonderful, new grandstand, and the famous Royal Enclosure is no longer workable in the altered layout. Once the Court felt unwelcome, many of its members found other things to do and after this retreat it followed as the night the day that first the smart set and next the social aspirants, those who do not live and breathe horses anyway, would start to drop away. Soon, most of them will abandon it, I would guess forever, since once British toffs are given permission to avoid a social obligation it is hard to make them take it up again. Some will say it was high time and the racing crowd will be glad that horses have once again become the business of the day. But whether or not we would agree with this now, in the 1960s we enjoyed it like billy-o.

For some reason, that year I had gone with the family of a girl called Minna Bunting. Her father held some position at Buckingham Palace which I cannot now recall, Keeper of the Privy Purse maybe, or at any rate one of those ancient-sounding titles that brought, among other privileges, a place in the Ascot car park reserved for the use of members of the Royal Household. This was, and is, located across the road from the main entrance to the course and has always been considered very smart, despite consisting of a large but unremarkable ashphalt yard, overlooked by the unfragrant main stables and boasting a single loo more properly reserved for the grooms. A sort of disintegrating Dutch barn provided a bit of shelter on one side and a couple of abandoned pony stalls offered some shade on the other. Otherwise it was lines of cars. But the whole arrangement was supervised every year by the nicest group of men you could hope to encounter, which always gave the place rather a lift, and I do know it was considered quite a feather in my cap to be having my picnic lunch there, even if there were moments when the aroma made swallowing hard.

I think Minna and I were fairly keen on each other, in a moderate way, for a brief while back then. I know we went out to dinner a few times and I could not now tell you why this ended. I am often struck by how hard it is to unravel your own motives when you look back on certain incidents or relationships in the dim and distant past. Why this girl failed but that one broke your heart. Why this man made you smile and that one made your spirits sink. They all seem to have been quite nice, friends and enemies and lovers alike, young and pleasant and, to be honest, all much of a muchness from the vantage point of hindsight. What was it about them as individuals that intrigued or bored me forty years ago?

We had finished our lunch and it was time to make our way over the road and on to the course, so we strolled together down the high, laurel-lined path to the entrance. The police were managing the traffic, as they did even then in those comparatively traffic-free days and we were obliged to pause. 'What on earth is going on?' said Minna.

She was right. On the other side of the road, by the main entrance, the gathering of what later came to be called *Paparazzi*, was going mad. As a rule there were far fewer of them then, not much more than a handful from the fashion magazines and the odd red top, but the public's taste for what celebrities were wearing was easily assuaged in 1968. On this day, however, you would have thought there was an item of international news being played out before us all. We crossed to the other pavement, passed through the gates and walked into the little courtyard where the disorganised could buy their badges on the day itself, and moved on to the gate into the Royal Enclosure. Something happening at the barrier was what was apparently fascinating the photographers most. Some were resorting to that trick, familiar now but novel in those days, of just holding their cameras above their heads and snapping away blindly, on the off chance that something worth printing might come out.

Armed with our badged lapels and a sense of entitlement, we pushed through the crowd and there was the cause of the riot. Joanna Langley, in an exquisite trouser suit of white lace, a pale hat trimmed with more lace and white flowers setting off her gleaming curls, white gloves on her hands, white bag by her side, was attempting to reason with the bluff ex-soldier in a bowler who sat guard. 'Sorry, Miss,' he said, without malice but without hesitation either, 'no trousers is the rule. And I can't change it. Even if I wanted to. Skirts only. That's what it says.'

'But this is almost a skirt,' replied Joanna.

'"Almost" isn't good enough, I'm afraid, Miss. Now if you'd like to stand aside.' He beckoned to us and we started forward.

'Hello,' I smiled at Joanna, as we drew near. I may not have known her well by that stage, but all our previous encounters had been friendly ones. 'You seem to be making news, today.'

She laughed. 'It's my mother's idea. She's put me up to it. I thought she was wrong, and they were bound to let me in. But it seems not.'

'Come on.' Minna pulled at my arm, anxious to dissociate herself from the media throng. As with all these people, then or now, this is not an affectation. They really hate it.

But I was too intrigued. I couldn't understand what Joanna was saying. If her mother was the one who thought she would be refused entry, how could she have put her up to it? 'Why did your mother want you to be stopped? Is she here?'

Joanna nodded towards a small group beyond the railings. I recognised the anxious, little woman from Queen Charlotte's Ball. She was wearing a tailored, fuchsia suit with a socking great brooch on her bosom. She seemed to be quivering with excitement watching her daughter, nudging her companions, sucking at her lower lip, but oddly she made no attempt to come nearer. 'What's she waiting for?' I asked.

Joanna sighed. 'What they're all waiting for. This.' Before my astonished gaze, she reached up under the tunic of her trouser suit and unfastened the waistband of her trousers. With a graceful movement she extracted first one long, shapely, stockinged leg and then the other, until she was standing there in a white micro-miniskirt, with the trousers making a pool of lace on the ground. Predictably, the frenzy of the photographers knew no bounds. They could have been witnessing the last appearance of Marilyn Monroe, the discovery of Hitler's child, the Second Coming, so excited were they by this *coup de théâtre*. 'I suppose I can come in now,' she said softly to the astonished, bowler-hatted gateman, who could not pretend to be uninterested.

'I suppose you can,' he said and nodded her through.

I was within earshot when Joanna was reunited with her family. 'Well, that was very silly,' she said as she rejoined them.

'Just wait. It'll be all over the evening papers tonight, never mind tomorrow morning.' Her mother spoke in short, sharp, chirrupy bursts, like a hungry bird in a hedgerow.

'I think it was a bloody embarrassment,' said a large man in a thick northern accent.

'That's because you don't know anything.' Mrs Langley always treated the man I came to know as her husband and Joanna's father with an odd and quite unusual mixture of deference and contempt. She needed to keep him in his place, but she also needed to keep him.

'I quite agree. Now, come and buy me some champagne.' Joanna slipped her arm through her father's. She always loved him best and she made no secret of it, but it somehow never empowered either of them to resist her mother's demands. It was an odd, uncomfortable set-up.

We watched them go. 'Do you want a drink?' I wondered.

Minna shook her head. 'Not yet. Not with them.'

It may have been because she heard these words, even if I hope not, but Joanna turned back once more and called, 'Come up to the box for some tea. Number five three one. Come about four and watch the next race.' I waved by way of answer and they were gone.

'We're meeting my father in White's at four,' said Minna.

'I'm sure we can do both if we want to.' We drifted up the steps into that long, faintly lavatorial tunnel at the base of the grandstand, built at such an unfortunate part of the Sixties and yet much missed now that it has been swept away despite its replacement being infinitely superior, and we set off on our way through to the back of the building and the Enclosure lawns. It was at precisely that moment I saw Damian loitering in the arch, looking at his race card, with his left arm casually draped round the waist of the girl standing next to him. He was dressed correctly, for my crowd, in a black morning coat and if his costume stood out it was only because it looked as if it had been made for him, not, as with most of us, like a misfit dragged from an upstairs wardrobe, from clothes discarded by forgotten uncles, which our mothers told us, without irony, would be perfectly all right once the sleeves were let down. I was amused to see that his silk hat was old and black, and wondered for a moment where he'd found it. In the great days of racing before the war, there were all sorts of rules about black and grey coats, and black and grey hats, being worn before the Derby or after the Oaks, or some such thing, but by the time I had begun to put in an appearance the matter had been simplified: If you were a toff you wore a black coat and a black hat, and if you were not you wore grey. The only real qualification to this that happened in my time was that after the early Eighties, again if you were posh or trying to be, you didn't take a hat to a wedding at all.

Actually, unlike many modern, sartorial adjustments, this was an improvement, as between the church and the reception there was hardly a moment to wear it and one always ending up leaving it in a pile behind a curtain, where it was liable to be taken in error, leaving you with an even worse one. The hat did, however, remain compulsory for race meetings and here there was a complication, because there came a point when they stopped making proper silk hats, I imagine for some politically correct, ecological reason, so the struggle was on to get hold of one before they either vanished completely or soared into the thousands to buy. As a result, you could tell the smart people as half the men were wearing hats that had clearly not been either made or bought for them, and were instead relics of dead fathers or grandfathers, or discards from uncles or cousins of their mothers, slightly bashed, slightly rubbed and either too big or too small. My own, courtesy of my dear old dad, balanced on the top of my head like a wobbly 1950s cocktail hat, but I made do.

'Goodness,' I said by way of greeting. 'Wherever I go, there you are.'

'Then you must go to all the right places.' He laughed, as his companion turned at the sound of my voice. It was Serena.

There are few markers of small-mindedness so clear as when people resent their friends becoming friendly with each other. But I am sorry to say that you see it often, a slight biting of the lip when they hear that this couple has met up with that couple and, despite their making the original introduction, they have not been invited. 'We're just *so* grateful to you for giving us the Coopers,' say the happy ones, and they are greeted with a cold smile and a murmured acknowledgement, but nothing more than this. Of course, some people pay no attention to the new amity that has been born over their own dinner table, others have the largeness of spirit to be pleased that their friends like each other, but there is a depressingly sizeable group that can never get over the feeling they have somehow been excluded, left out, ignored, that they are less loved because the love these men and women can give is going to each other and not, as it once did, to *them*. As the thinking world knows, this is an ignoble emotion, diminishing, sad, even pathetic, and should be avoided, certainly in public where it is as attractive as picking one's nose. And yet . . .

If it is bad enough with friends, it is much worse with lovers, or rather with would-be but never-were lovers. To witness someone you have adored unsuccessfully from afar actually fall in love with another of your so-called friends, so that you must watch this warm, well-suited, reciprocal, relationship bloom, in such sharp contrast to the withered, one-sided, bitter thing you cherished in the darkness of your secret thoughts, to stand by and watch all this is very hard. Particularly as you know you demean yourself by giving so much as a tiny clue as to your true feelings. But you lie in the bath or wait in a queue at the post office, and your inner being is hot with anger, boiling with hatred and destruction, even towards those whom, at one and the same time, you love with all your heart. So it was, I blush to admit, with me and Serena, or rather, with me and Damian since he was the author of all my woes.

That arm, so casually laid across the back of her pink Christian Dior suit, his hand lightly resting on the curve where her hip swelled softly down from her waist, that arm was a grotesque, violating betrayal. I'd touched her arm in greeting as people do; I had taken her hand, even brushed her cheek with mine, but all these privileges were available to anyone she had met more than twice. I had never touched her in any way that might imply intimacy. I had touched her as a friendly human being, but never as a man. I found myself wondering what the texture of her skirt must feel like. Was the slight roughness of the weave in the cotton imprinting itself on the edge of his palm and tantalising his fingertips with the almost undetectable movement of her body beneath? Could he feel its warmth? In my mind I could feel it and yet, unlike Damian, I could *not* feel it.

'Any ideas for the two thirty?' said Damian and I woke up.

'Don't ask me,' I said. 'I only ever bet on names that remind me of something else entirely.'

'Wildest Dreams,' said Serena, speaking into my hidden longings. 'Fletcher gave me a list and he was sure about Wildest Dreams. Then he says You'll Be Lucky for the Gold Cup.' Was there no horse running whose name did not encapsulate the hopelessness of my desires?

'Who's Fletcher?' asked Damian.

'Our groom at Gresham.' It was as if that simple sentence, carrying as it did in the few words it was made of the absolute divide between her life and his, flung him away from her side.

'Joanna Langley's waving at us.' He pulled his arm off Serena's flank, and started to walk across the grass towards the group centred on Joanna's miniskirted and lustrous form. I took his place, with Minna still loitering rather discontentedly on my other side.

'Did you see that nonsense at the gate?' Minna was squinting into the sun to get a clearer view of them.

'No, but I heard about it.' Serena smiled. 'It sounded quite funny but I don't really see the point.'

'She'll be all over the papers tomorrow,' I said.

I must have sounded like a complete idiot. 'I know that,' she said. 'But what does she want from it? What does she get out of it?'

'Fame?'

'But fame for doing what? Taking off her trousers? It might make her famous for being famous but what's the point of that?' Serena was bewildered by the choice that Joanna had made at the gate that morning, and as far as I recall, Minna and I just nodded and agreed with her. Perhaps it was what we both thought, or if it wasn't, it was what we all knew we were supposed to think.

The idea of being famous for being famous, a phrase we often used, was a risible and pejorative dismissal in those distant days, but the concept was, of course, a harbinger of our own time. The current fame mania is often mistakenly described as the Cult of Celebrity, but this at least is not new. There were always famous people and they were always interesting to the public. Nor, as again the argument goes today, were they all famous for doing wonderful things. There have always been well-known rakes and showgirls and criminals and worthless stowaways among the great, but as a rule they developed personalities that justified their stardom. What is genuinely new is the Cult of Non-Celebrity, the celebration as if they were famous of men and women who are perfectly ordinary. The oxymoron of the unknown celebrity really is a modern innovation. Maybe it was a sense of this coming fashion, this dawning interest in fame for fame's sake that would inevitably open the gates of Valhalla wider, that prompted the likes of Mrs Langley to exploit its possibilities. But there was a confusion at the core of her planning and that was in her intended audience. She was playing to the wrong gallery. The upper classes have never been attracted by fame. At least, they may sometimes enjoy famous visitors to their galaxy, but they do not see it as an appropriate attribute among their own kind. Even now, they don't need it to stand out in the crowd, and they do not, as a rule, see the point of it for any other reason. Maybe the modern heirs will occasionally employ these vulgar methods to promote their interests, but there still remains a moral obligation, even among this younger, savvier group, to pretend that publicity is invariably demeaning and worthless.

Joanna herself understood this fundamental truth, which her mother had not grasped. She saw that the more she became a darling of the press, the more she was invited on to *Top of the Pops*, or whatever it was in those days, the less welcome she would be in the world to which her mother was so wrong-headedly anxious for her to belong. I am afraid that poor, misguided Mrs Langley genuinely believed that her beautiful daughter was improving her chances of an eligible husband, and a place in Society, by these shenanigans when, in fact, she was diminishing them to the point of invisibility.

I learned this from a conversation I had with Joanna that same day, when I decided to take up her invitation and make my way to the Langleys' box. This decision came after a slight altercation with Minna, and in the end she went off alone to meet her father for tea while I retreated to the door in the wall, guarded like all the Enclosure entrances by those charming chaps in their obligatory bowler hats. My disagreement with Minna cannot have been sinister as I had dinner with them all later that evening, but perhaps it contributed to the end of our mini-romance. I have never been very good at people who cannot step out of their own setting even for a moment, whatever that setting might be.

Once through the door, I was suddenly propelled into the middle of the other Ascot and in some ways flung forward into the future, into our present day. Toughs in shiny suits, or with no jacket at all, jostled past with their women gaily, if sometimes surprisingly, adorned as I pushed on towards the covered escalator that would take me up to the floor where the boxes could be found in this different and even uglier stand. Here and there, dotted about in the crowd, there were fellow Enclosure members battling their way to and fro, and there was some joshing, wolf whistles and the like, to mark the difference in our costumes. This rapids-running element of journeying from the Enclosure to the boxes would in fact continue until the end of fashionable Ascot, but it grew a little less friendly as the years went on. Various politicians of every hue saw class warfare as so important a weapon in manipulating public opinion that they could not resist inflaming it. Even today, we are constantly encouraged to believe in a capitalist economy, but to despise and revile those who profit from it. It is an odd philosophical position, to say the least, a dysfunctional theory that has contributed to a largely dysfunctional society, but as I say, in the 1960s it was only just starting. Breaking down class barriers was still seen as a happy thing then, so the jokes at one's expense were, on the whole, good-natured.

The boxes at Ascot have always occupied a kind of limbo position when it comes to the whole event. There are boxes set aside for major trainers and owners, and of course I do not mean these. Their usefulness is logical and credible, but those people were always present at Ascot as part of the racing fraternity and never because of fashion. They will continue to be at the meetings, long after the *beau monde* has moved on. But for those who only went to Ascot for the fun and frolic, a day out with some horses in the background, the boxes were always faintly unconvincing. To start with it was not necessary to get an Enclosure badge to rent or visit one, and in the old days, when the authorities exerted some control over whom they admitted to the Enclosure, the boxes could become the haven of the socially not-quites, those divorced actresses and grinning, motor dealers who were snubbed by the Old Guard.

The second problem was that most of them were simply minute. You went through a door in a concrete gallery, to be admitted to an itsy-bitsy entrance hall, with a little kitchenette from a 1950s caravan on one side. This led into the space for dining and generally living it up, which was roughly the size of a hotel bathroom, and beyond was the balcony, where two people could just about stand side by side on two or three steps. All in all, the average box was about as capacious and gracious as a lift in Selfridges. But to the mighty ones who are socially insecure, a much larger group than many people realise, they offered a chance to enjoy the race meeting on their own terms, in a place which might be modest but where they were king, instead of spending the day detecting sneers and slights in the behaviour of the Enclosure crowd that surrounded them. I would guess this was the appeal for Joanna's father, and that Alfred Langley was prepared to accompany his wife and daughter, but only on the condition that he could have a box to hide in for most of the day.

Mrs Langley darted up to me, her eyes flicking round the empty room behind my back, checking that nobody more important needed attention. 'Joanna's on the balcony,' she said, 'with some friends.' Then, nervous that she had somehow given offence with this blameless statement, she continued, 'She told us you were coming.'

'I'm afraid Minna had to meet her father in White's, but she sends her love.'

Mrs Langley nodded. 'Sir Timothy Bunting,' she muttered, as if I were unaware of the name of my host.

'Yes,' I said.

She nodded again. There was something shifty about her that her smooth hair and tailored suit and really rather nice diamond brooch could not mask. She was jumpy, like Peter Lorre waiting to have his collar felt in a black-and-white thriller about the mob. As I got to know her better I found this sense of frightened uncertainty never left her. She couldn't relax, which I suspect was both part of what turned her daughter against her, but at the same time was the root of her power.

Joanna was leaning against the railing when I went out, attended by Lord George Tremayne and one or two other swains, all a little, but not very, drunk, and all holding empty or near-empty champagne flutes, that new glass that had only recently started to replace the gentle, bosom-shaped cup favoured in the previous decade. But then the Langleys were nothing if not up to the minute. That said, it was a lovely day and the sight of Joanna smiling up at me, her face framed with her own golden hair and the white brim of her lace hat, with the wide sweep of the lush green racetrack behind her, was very cheering. 'I came,' I said.

'So you did.' She walked up a step or two and kissed my cheek, then turned back to her companions. 'Push off, will you?' They protested, but she was quite definite. 'Go inside. Get some more to drink and bring me one in a minute.' She touched my sleeve. 'I've got something to tell him and it's private.' Naturally, none of this would have been sayable if she had lived even remotely within the rules of the crowd she was running with, but not for the last time I appreciated that the advantage of not being held captive by the need to observe correct form is that you can often get things done far more efficiently. In other words, they left.

I have already written about her beauty and it is probably true that I place physical beauty too high on my list of desirable attributes, but, in this case, it really was spectacular. No matter how closely one looked, Joanna's face was as near perfect as any I have ever seen not made of plastic, drawn on a page or enshrined on the silver screen. Smooth, evenly coloured skin, without a trace of a blemish; a mouth shaped with the soft curves of a petal, beneath widely placed deep-blue, almost purple, eyes, fringed with thick, long lashes; a statue's nose; and masses of gleaming born-blonde curls framing her cheeks and cascading to her shoulders. She was, as the song says, lovely to look at. 'What are you looking at?' Her voice, with its faint tinge of Essex, caught at my reveries, repeated the phrase and returned me to the present.

'At you,' I said.

She smiled. 'That's nice.' There was, in addition to everything else, something particularly charming in the contrast between her ethereal appearance and her absolute normality, her complete next-doorness which is hard to capture in words but was probably the core of the charm that delivered Charles II to Nell Gwynne, or enabled so many of the cockney Gaiety Girls to marry into the peerage in the 1890s. Her cheeriness was in some way the opposite of vanity, yet not self-consciously modest either. Just perfectly natural.

'What is this private thing you have to say to me? I couldn't be more fascinated.'

She blushed slightly, not an angry red, but with a soft, warm pink diffused evenly across her features, like someone caught unawares in the dawn light. 'It's not really private. That was just to make them shove off.' I smiled. 'But I was sorry you saw all that nonsense at the gate. I don't want you to think badly of me.' Again the direct simplicity of her appeal was both flattering and tremendously disarming.

'I couldn't think badly of you,' I replied, which was no more than the truth. 'And anyway, I am fairly sure the world will be reading about it tomorrow morning, so I will, if anything, feel rather bucked to have been an eyewitness.'

I'm afraid this had not made things better. 'My mum thinks it all helps. To be in the news. To have everyone going on about me. She thinks it makes me ...' She hesitated, searching for the right word, 'interesting.' Whatever word she had chosen this was clearly a question and a request for help, even if it was not phrased as such.

I attempted to look encouraging and not judgemental. 'To quote Oscar Wilde, the only one thing worse than being talked about is not being talked about.'

She gave a perfunctory laugh, more as a polite recognition that I had said something supposedly funny than because she found it amusing. Then, after a moment, she said, 'Yeah, I've heard that before, but you don't believe it, do you? None of you do.'

The trouble was this was true, really, but I didn't want to be a killjoy, certainly not to kill her joy. Still, she was asking my opinion so I strove to be as honest as I could be. 'It depends entirely what you want to come out of it. What are you striving for? What is your goal?'

She thought for a moment. 'That's the point. I don't know.'

'Then why are you doing the Season? What did you hope to gain when you began?'

'I don't know that either.' She spoke with all the hopelessness of a rabbit caught in a snare.

I understand that, theoretically, Joanna should have been freer than this. Her father was a self-made man, so she had not been brought up within the armed enclave, but in other ways her restrictions were even more severe. It was perhaps the last era when the aristocracy had the power to admit the new rich, or to refuse them entry. Later, when the posh way of life was back in fashion and the dream of joining it began again, the recent rich had far more muscle to push in whether the old world wanted them or not, but in the late Sixties the ex-Ruling Class still maintained considerable sway. I distinctly remember one friend of my mother's threatening a foolish youth, who had made a mess of her flat, uninvited. 'One more example of this kind of behaviour,' hissed the exasperated matron, 'and I will slam the door of every London drawing room in your face!' It was a meaningful threat because, then, it was a real one. In 1968 she could still have delivered. By 1988 those same doors were swinging free. Of course, today they are off their hinges.

To employ a phrase not actually in use for twenty years after this, I decided to cut to the chase. 'It is not complicated,' I said. 'If your mother and you are hoping for a grand marriage to come out of this year, you and she are going the wrong way about it. If you want to be famous and go on television or marry a film producer or a car manufacturer who is looking for a bit of glamour to invigorate his life, you're probably doing exactly the right thing.'

She looked at me. 'It's silly, really.' She sighed. 'You're right. My mum wants me to be Lady Snotty. That's what she dreams of night and day. That's why it's so sad that she thinks all this stuff is helping when I know, much better than she does, that it isn't.'

'Then make her listen. With a little backtracking, I'm sure you can still manage what she's after and it wouldn't be so reprehensible. As Lady Snotty, as you put it, with your other very considerable advantages you could do a great deal of good if you were so minded.' I know I sounded like a bogus prelate from *Hymns on Sunday*, but at the time I couldn't quite see what else to say. I even think I believed I was telling the truth.

Joanna shook her head. 'That isn't me. I'm not saying I disapprove of it but it's not me. Sitting on committees, cutting ribbons, hosting a bring-and-buy sale to get funds for the new X-ray machine at the local hospital. I mean—' she broke off, clearly afraid she had offended me. 'Don't get me wrong. I think all that's very good. But I just couldn't do it.'

'And your mother wants you to.'

She shook her head. 'Actually, I don't think she's got that far. She just wants me to have a big, posh wedding, with lots of pictures in the *Tatler*. She hasn't thought beyond that.'

'Then why don't you think beyond it for her? Maybe it isn't charity work for you, or standard charity work. Maybe you could get involved with a special school, or local government. All sorts of causes will want you once you have a bit of social muscle. What I'm trying to say is that I'm sure it's achievable.' I had a mental image of the Tremayne brother up in the box above us, happy to marry her, without condition, to get the loot. 'Maybe, if you think of the possibilities you might come round to the idea.' What interests me now, thinking back to this fruitless, pompous and patronising advice, is that it didn't occur to me to suggest that she pursue a career instead of this worthless and really rather immoral plan. Why not? There were working women then, and quite a lot of them. Perhaps it just didn't seem a likely outcome for anyone in my gang, or were we so far out to sea that we had lost sight of land? Whatever the reason, in this, as in so many things, I would turn out to be entirely wrong.

'You sound like Damian,' she said, taking me by surprise.

'Do I?'

'Yeah. He's always telling me to capitalise on my looks. To "go for it," when I don't know what I'm supposed to go for.'

'I wasn't aware that you knew him so well.' Was I fated to be a grudging camp follower, staggering along in Damian's trail?

'Well, I do.' She looked at me with a cool stare that told me everything. And as I returned her gaze I thought of Damian's hand, earlier that very day, resting lightly on Serena Gresham's pelvis, and I wondered what I had done wrong in an earlier life that I should be obliged to hear, in the span of a single afternoon, that Damian had wormed his way into the affections, if not the beds, of these women, both dream goddesses for me in their different ways; that, in short, my toy, my own invention, my action doll was apparently getting all the action. That months, or even weeks, after I had let him into the henhouse, this fox was ruling my roost. Joanna must have seen some of this in my troubled brow. 'Do you like him?' she asked.

I realised that this was a proper question and one that I had not addressed until now, and should have. But I chose to answer as if it were neither of these things. 'I'm the one who introduced him to all of you.'

'I know that, but you never sound now as if you like him.'

Was this the moment that I realised I didn't? If so, I did not face it for quite a while after. 'Of course I like him.'

'Because I don't think you've got much in common. He wants to get on, but he doesn't want to fit in, but not like you and not in the way you mean. You think he'll take advantage of the whole thing and keep in with these people, that he'll end up marrying Lady Penelope La-di-da and send his children to Eton, but you're wrong. He can't stand you all, really. He's ready to break out and say goodbye to the lot of you.' There was clearly something in the notion that excited her.

Was this news? I can't pretend I was surprised. 'Then perhaps you should break out together. You seem rather well suited.'

'Don't talk like that.'

'Like what?'

'All toffee-nosed and self-important. You sound like a berk.' Naturally, this silenced me for the next few minutes, while she continued, 'Anyway, Damian and I, we're not well-suited, not deep down. I thought we might be for a bit, but we're not.'

'You both seem to me to be very up to the minute.' For some reason I couldn't stop sounding like the stupid-berk-plonker she'd described. To quote my mother against myself, I was just jealous.

But the comment made her more thoughtful than indignant. 'He does want to be part of today's world,' she admitted, 'like I do. But he wants to dominate it. He wants to bully it, to take over, to push people like you around in it and be the big, bad cheese.'

'And you don't? Not even as a great lady, dispensing warmth and wisdom from the house at the end of the drive?'

Again, she shook her head. 'You keep going on about that, but it's not me. And I don't want to be on television either. Nor married to some big-business boss with a modern flat in Mayfair and a villa in the South of France.' The world she described so accurately in that single phrase was, of course, one she knew well and presumably also despised, along with County Society, the peerage and Damian's imaginative vision of himself as a City whizz-kid, which was impressively ahead of its time.

'There must be something that you do want,' I said.

Joanna laughed again, mirthlessly. 'Nothing I'll find pursuing this game.' She thought for a while. 'I don't mean to be rude' – always a precursor to rudeness of the most offensive sort – 'but you lot are all completely divorced from what's going on around you. Damian's right about that. You're just not part of the Sixties at all. The fashions. The music . . .' She paused, shaking her head slowly, dizzy with wonder at our irrelevance.

I felt a little indignant. 'We play the music.'

She sighed. 'Yes, you play the music and you dance to the Beatles and the Rolling Stones, but you're still in evening dress and you're still in some ballroom or marquee, with hot breakfast being served from two o'clock onwards by a line of footmen. That's not what they're singing about. That's not what's happening.'

'I don't suppose it is.'

'The world's changing. And I want to change with it.'

'Darling!' I knew Damian's voice well enough not to need to turn round.

'Talk of the devil,' said Joanna.

Which I completed: 'And there he is.'

Damian came lazily down the steps towards us and enfolded her in a hug when he drew level. 'Come and cheer us up. You've spent long enough with droopy-drawers. He'll start to think he's in with a chance and then there'll be no controlling him.' He winked at me, as if inviting me to share the joke, which had, of course, as we both knew been intended as an insult. Initially, at the start of the Season he had felt the need to defer to me a little, just to make sure that I was still on side, but the need for that was long gone. He was the master now.

'All right,' she said, 'I'll come. But only if you give me a certainty for the next race.' She smiled and started back up the steps towards the door of the box where her fan club hovered.

Damian smiled back at her, his arm still round her waist. 'There's only one certainty for you. And that is me.'

And with a shared laugh they were inside and lost to view.

I have often thought since of my conversation with Joanna on that bright summer's day in our privileged seats above the crowded racetrack. It was perhaps in some ways my closest encounter with the elephant trap of Sixties fantasy, that would swallow so many of my contemporaries in the following decade. Things were changing, it is true. The post-war depression had been shaken off and the economy was booming, and many old values were being rejected. But they would be back, most of them. Not perhaps white tie or taking houses in Frinton for the summer, but certainly those that governed ambition and rapacity and greed and the lust for power. There would be fifteen years or so of chaos, then most of the old rules would be resurrected. Until now, when there is a richer elite buying houses in Belgravia than at any time since the Edwardians. But these were not the changes that Joanna and her ilk expected.

They thought, they *knew*, a world was coming where money would be meaningless, where nationalism and wars and religion would vanish, where class and rank and every worthless distinction between people would drift away into the ether like untrapped steam, and love would be all. It was a belief, a philosophy, that coloured my generation so strongly that many still cannot find the strength to shake it off. It is easy to laugh at these infantile notions, mouthed with increasing desperation by ageing ministers and sagging singers as their pension age approaches. Indeed, I do laugh at them since these fools have apparently lived a whole life and learned nothing. But, even so, I don't mind saying I was touched that day, listening to this lovely, well-intentioned, clever, nice, young woman, sitting in the sun and putting all her bets on Optimism.

Predictably, every paper ran a picture of Joanna Langley removing her white lace trousers to gain entry to Ascot the following day and I seem to remember that either the *Mail* or the *Express* printed a whole series of them, like a literal strip cartoon. And we all joked about it and most of us took her even less seriously than we had before and Mrs Langley's aspirations were crushed still further underfoot. But of course it was soon immaterial. I never did find out whether Joanna tried to talk to her mother about her doubts. If so, it did not have much effect, as the invitation to her coming-out ball in the country, from 'Mrs Alfred Langley' arrived not long afterwards. It was printed on white card so stiff it might have been cut from seasoned oak, with lettering sufficiently embossed to stub a toe. I would guess most people accepted. With the ruthless reasoning of the English, we all expected that a lot of money would be spent on the evening's pleasures and so it would be worth attending, whatever we thought of the daughter. I personally, of course, liked her and I freely confess I was much looking forward to it, and seen from now, when such entertainments are rarer and, to my old and jaded palate, seem pretty indistinguishable, I can only imagine what delights Mrs Langley had ordered for our delectation. I am certain it would have been a night to remember with treats galore.

However, as things turned out we opened the newspaper on a sunny day in early July, to read the banner headline 'LOVE DASH HEIRESS!' and the article below explained that Joanna, only child of 'Travel King, Multi-Millionaire, Alfred Langley,' had eloped with her dress designer, Kieran de Yong. The couple had not yet married, an added, salacious delight for the journalists of the day, which would hardly merit a mention these days, but they were 'believed to be sharing Mr de Yong's flat in Mayfair.' After Joanna's comment at the races I could not prevent a slightly wistful wince at the final detail.

Two days later another card arrived from Mrs Langley. On it was printed the sober but straightforward information: 'The dance arranged for Miss Joanna Langley will not now take place.'

TEN

To my surprise, and contrary to my jokey and snobbish expectations, Kieran de Yong turned out to have been a busy boy since last we met. The printout filled me in on what he had been up to, during the intervening years and it was almost alarming. He had been twenty-eight when he ran off with 'Joanna, daughter of Alfred Langley, of Badgers' Wood, Godalming in Surrey,' making him nine or ten years older than most of us, and the following year he married her. After which, presumably putting some Langley gold to work, he'd built up a chain of dress shops by the late 1970s called Clean Cut, which I thought quite clever, and there were various photographs of him at 'red carpet' events during this period, clutching Joanna and wearing clothes that were terrible, even by the standards of that terrible time. What kind of blindness struck my generation? What allowed people to leave the safety of their homes wearing white, leather jackets with cowboy studs and fringe, or pale-blue, glistening suits, with black shirts and silver kipper ties? Or Russian peasant shirts or butchered army uniforms? I imagine they must have thought they looked like Elvis or Marlon Brando, when in fact they resembled a children's conjuror on speed.

But de Yong seemingly calmed down during the decades that followed. Later photographs, with assorted models and finally a striking second wife, showed him in clothes that went from first sleek and finally to good. He sold his chain for millions in the Eighties and turned his hand to property, the god of that era, with a huge stake in Docklands, which must have given him sleepless nights at one point before it proved the doubters wrong and came back sevenfold. Other buildings followed, a couple of famous, City landmarks, a resort in Spain, a new town in Cumbria. He had expanded into drug research and manufacture, and his company led the field in work on arthritis and some of the less bewitching forms of cancer, with profits channelled into education and addressing the problems of social mobility, or rather the lack of it, engendered by the fads of the academic establishment. I was impressed that this baby of the Sixties was sufficiently courageous to challenge a group still so completely enslaved by the Sixties message. In short, this was a brave, full life, and a terrifyingly worthy one. My only surprise was that I, and so presumably the general public, had heard so little of him.

I'd never known Kieran de Yong, really. The one occasion on which we met for any length of time was during that same Portuguese house party that still has a habit of revisiting my dreams, but even then we hardly spoke and after everyone was back at home, most of us never wanted to set eyes on any of the other guests ever again. At least I didn't, so it was the worst possible start for a friendship. But at the time I had anyway dismissed him as common and uneducated, dull and faintly embarrassing, with his nightmarish outfits and his sad attempts to be cool. Joanna made things worse by being furiously protective, and her aggression injected the atmosphere with awkwardness whenever they appeared. In my defence, you will agree that it is hard to listen closely to a man with dyed hair, even more so when it's dyed a strawberry blond. But now, staring at this impressive list, I felt thoroughly humbled. What had I done in my life that could even hold a candle to this account? What had my friends done, simply to be worthy of a mention in the same breath?

Of his private life there was little information. He had married Joanna in 1969, so in this case the disputed baby had been born firmly in wedlock and the impending birth had not been the cause of any questionable nuptials. The child was a boy, as I already knew, Malcolm Alfred, but there were no further details of him on the Wikipedia entry. The divorce had come in 1983 and, to be honest, I shared Damian's amazement that it had taken so long. The striking second wife was one Jeanne LeGrange, wed in 1997, whose name suggested a well-travelled, international life and apart from that, nothing. No more mention of divorces, nor more wives, no more children. My main point of interest was that according to Damian's account, Joanna had continued their affair well into her marriage. It seemed to confirm that she married de

Yong to escape her mama and not because of an unconquerable love, which did not surprise me, since I had never thought anything else.

Damian's list gave me a number for Kieran's business which, when I first read it, I assumed would take me more or less directly to him, but now I understood the scale of what we were dealing with I wasn't so sure. It seemed rather like telephoning Buckingham Palace and asking to speak to the Queen. But in the event I was put through to his office and eventually to his private secretary with very little fuss, and when I had reached her she was quite polite. I explained I was an old friend from many years before, and, employing a similar device to the one used with Dagmar, I explained that I wanted to come in and talk about a new charity I was involved with that I thought might interest him. She sighed, gently but audibly. I was probably the fiftieth applicant that day. 'Mr de Yong's charity work is handled by a different department,' she said. 'Would you like me to put you through to them?'

I decided to push my luck, since I had no viable alternative, but my confidence in a productive result was waning. 'Well, to be honest, I'd rather talk directly to Kieran, if he's got a spare moment.' I thought the slightly insolent use of his Christian name would make me sound more convincing, but I am not sure this was correct. She hesitated, then asked me to spell my surname once again, and I was put on hold and forced to listen to a rather bad recording of Stravinsky's *Rite of Spring*. This time I wasn't sure what I would do if he didn't want to see me. And in truth, I couldn't imagine why he would. If he had any memory of me at all it would only be the faintest reminder of a rather stuck-up, spotty youth who had snubbed him at every turn. That, and the dreadful evening when we last saw each other. Of course, one of the great pleasures of success, especially when many people have dismissed you and your chances, is to seek out those same ignorami and force them to retract their earlier opinions. To make them acknowledge, in their eyes if not with their tongues, that they were totally and completely wrong about you. That you, in short, have made them look like fools. I could only hope that the idea of my swallowing humble pie would be amusing.

Then, to my surprise, there was a click and Kieran was on the line. 'Good heavens,' he said. 'To what do I owe this unexpected pleasure?' The words may have been trite, but it was easy to tell from their delivery that he had mellowed. His East London accent had softened but not in a pretentious way, and his tone was, given the facts, unexpectedly warm.

'I'm surprised you remember me.'

'Nonsense. I've followed your career with interest. I've even read some of your books.'

I smiled with relief that my task was once more rendered do-able. 'Enough of this love talk,' I said and it was his turn to laugh. But when he asked me what it was about I fumbled as, naturally, I hadn't thought I would be talking so soon to the man in question and my story was not yet quite straight in my head.

Mercifully, he cut through my maunderings with an invitation. His lunches were taken for months to come, but he wondered if I might be free for dinner. 'Or is it difficult for you to get away in the evenings?'

'Not at all, I'm sad to say. What about you?'

'I'm the same.' So a dinner was indeed arranged, which, he suggested, might take place at the Savoy Grill since it was about to close for a couple of years of 'renovation.' This was unless I had an objection. Which I hadn't. Like him, I felt that a famous restaurant of our joint youths that was about to vanish forever seemed like a good, even witty, place to revisit the past. We had a date.

The old Savoy has left us now, that illogically impressive mixture of *Odéon* and *Belle Epoque*, which has been such a beacon in my life from childhood and growing up, when I would be taken for tea by ancient aunts past debbing days, with balls and cocktail parties in the River Room, and through the intervening years, smiling and cheering at weddings and birthdays and every kind of private celebration, right up to the present, when I have served my time at all those festival lunches and award-giving dinners, with their predictable menus and back-slapping, manufactured gaiety. Not long after my dinner with Kieran the new owner closed its doors and auctioned off the contents, and it would be a long, long time before the revelation of the reconceived hotel. And even if the team has recognised the special place the Savoy has occupied in London hearts for over a century, since Richard D'Oyly Carte first dreamed his dream, even if they have tried to serve its history as honourably as they could, still the stamping ground of Nellie Melba and Diana Cooper, of Alfred Hitchcock and the Duchess of Argyll, of

Marilyn Monroe and Paul McCartney, and all the rest of that glittering crew will have joined the palace of John of Gaunt that once stood on the site, and must henceforth trust to history books and memory.

I hadn't visited the Grill for a while and when I got there, it was to find it had already been much altered from the fashionable *rendezvous* of my adolescence that lasted well into my adulthood. In the early Sixties, I used to go regularly with a disreputable cousin of my father's who'd taken a shine to me, and who regarded the place as a sort of private club and would bring the most recent, luckless object of his fancy there for an orgy of oysters and dishonest vows. Naturally, he was a wonderfully dashing role model to an unattractive teenager with bad skin. On leaving the army in his forties, Cousin Patrick chose to live a short-term life, that is, to enjoy himself without putting down any roots or taking on any responsibilities. He was certainly very handsome and very charming, so this was more achievable than it might have been for some. My own mother adored him despite my father's disapproval, but in the end I suppose the latter's strictures about reaping what you sew were proved correct since our cousin's fun-filled years of avoiding commitment left him to face a stroke and early death alone, proving once again, as if we needed any more proof, that we generally end up with lives that are the product of our choices.

Even so, he was an inspiration to me, since he accepted no rules or boundaries and, having been brought up by my very straight and fairly strict pater, this seemed to me like an empowering paradise. I remember once being in a restaurant with him and, finding it difficult to attract the waiter's attention, Patrick reached round and picked up a stand, one of those whatnots that hold mats and menus and salts and peppers, and flung it the entire length of the room. It landed with a crash like a nuclear explosion that silenced the full, chattering space until you could have heard a pin drop, but instead of being reprimanded or ordered out on to the street, as I fully expected, the only tangible result was that the service improved enormously. There was probably a subversive lesson tucked in here somewhere, which my father would not have wanted me to learn.

As I walked in I thought of Patrick for a moment. I remembered him standing in that same doorway, checking the room with his lazy smile, to see if there were any pretty possibilities seated at other tables.

One of the strangest parts of growing older being that ever-increasing Team of the Dead, who stand behind your shoulder and take it in turns to jump in and out of your head. A picture, a shop, a street, a clock that someone gave you, an ornament that came from this dead aunt or a chair from that dead uncle, and suddenly for a second they're alive again, whispering into your ear. There is a religion somewhere in the world that believes we all die twice; once in the normal way and the second time when the last person who really knew us dies, so one's living memory is gone from the earth. I subscribe to that and I thought happily of my old cousin that day, if only to note that the place had changed since he was there. The murals had gone and with them much of the atmosphere, while the sleek panelling, pale and smooth, which had been installed in their place gave the sensation of sitting in a giant cigar thermidor. I suppose these things come under the heading of 'rebranding,' that twenty-first-century snake oil for every ailment. Kieran was already in his seat when I arrived. We waved at a distance, shook hands when I drew near and sat.

As everyone knows, the ageing process never fails to shock when it has not been witnessed on a daily basis. The Kieran I knew had been a fresh-faced oik, with fake hair and a fake tan, who bore almost no resemblance to the elderly, senior man of affairs sitting opposite me. But if his face was a great deal older, nevertheless, as he approached his seventieth year, it was also finer than it had been in his youth, less blotchy, less puffy and infinitely more secure. The too-red cheeks were gone and the glossy highlights, taking with them the true colour of his hair, whatever it may have been, but leaving him a rather distinguished grey, like a model in an advertisement for Grecian 2000. The hair itself had stayed, the lucky stiff, and his eyes were not, as I recalled, small and piggy but curiously kind for someone who had made such killings in the savage world of property.

'This is very nice of you,' I said, as he sent a waiter off in search of two glasses of champagne.

'It is my pleasure.' He studied his menu and I studied his face. He had acquired real stature, that is the only word I can think of to describe the change. He had acquired authority and the authority of the genuinely great. He was polite, relaxed and unstudied, but with that expectation of obedience that marks the powerful apart. The waiter returned with our drinks. 'So,' he said, when we were alone again, 'what's this about?' I murmured about my charity. It was not quite fictional as I felt that if he did wish to make a donation, there might as well be profit in it for someone, but I could see at once he wasn't really interested. 'I might as well cut you off now,' he interjected with a good-natured hand raised to stop the flow. 'I only give to about three things. I've had to ring-fence my interests as I find I get about a hundred applications a week these days. All of them perfectly worthy causes, of course, but I cannot cure every evil in the world. I'll give you a cheque if you like, but not for much and that will be your lot.'

I nodded. He was very compelling. I would have accepted this decision even if my request had been a truthful one. 'Thank you,' I said, but I was puzzled. His secretary had tried to tell me exactly this when I first rang and he could have finished the job without any rudeness when he came on the line. 'Then why are we here having dinner?' The words had not come out quite as I had envisaged and I hurried to qualify them. 'Of course, I'm terribly pleased that we are and it's the greatest treat to see you again, but I'm surprised you have the time.'

'I have time,' he said. 'I have a lot of time for things I want to do.' This was polite, but did not really answer my question, which he saw. 'I find that I spend most of my time these days thinking about the past, and about what happened to me and the life I have led, considering, in short, how I got to where I am.'

'So you always make a special case for people from that past?'

'I like to see them. Particularly if, like you, I have seen very little of them in the meantime.'

'To be honest, I'm amazed you remember me at all. I thought I was going to be greeted by a big, fat "*who?*"'

He gave a silent, little puff of laughter and I noticed, by contrast, how very sad his eyes were. 'I don't think any living human could forget that dinner.'

'No,' I said.

He raised his glass. His years at the top had taught him not to clink it against mine, as he would have done back then. 'To us. Are we much altered do you think?'

I nodded. 'Very, I'd say. I may only be a fatter, balder, sadder version of the young man that I was, but you seem to have changed into someone else completely.'

He laughed more heartily, as if pleased by the notion. 'Kieran de Yong, Designer to the Stars.'

'That's the man I knew.'

'God help you.'

'He wasn't so bad.'

'Drink or depression has made you kind. He was ghastly.'

I did not bother to contradict again since I agreed with him. I could see our waiter lingering nearby, waiting for a break in the conversation to step forward and take the order. Kieran gave him a slight nod and he leaned in, pencil and pad in hand. It is comforting to know that the skill of waiting well is not entirely dead even if these days you have to search, and certainly to pay, for it. I do not in any way dislike the tidal wave of Eastern Europeans whose appointed task is apparently to ask me what I want to eat. They seem cheerful and nice on the whole, and a pleasant contrast to the surly Englishman who always looks as if he is longing to spit in your soup. But I do wish someone would tell them not to barge in when the diner is halfway through a punchline.

The man had garnered all the necessary information and made off to put it into practice. 'What changed you?' I asked and he did not need to be reminded of the meaning of the question.

He thought for a moment. 'Education. Experience. Or are they the same thing? In those days I felt I'd come from nothing, which was obviously not true, as everyone comes from something. I also felt I knew nothing, which was truer but not completely true either, and consequently I felt I had to present myself as the man who knows everything, who is in touch with the universe, embodying the *zeitgeist*. I imagined that I looked like a giant controlling his destiny and not a saddo with a dye job.' He smiled at the memory and shook his head. 'Those jackets, alone. What was *that*?' I couldn't help laughing with him. 'And there you have the reason for why I hated all of you lot.' Which was an unexpected change of direction.

'What do you mean?'

'I felt you were so much more in charge than I was.'

'We weren't.'

'No, I can see that now. But your contempt for me, and everything about me, made me think you were.'

This made me sorrowful. Why do we spend so much of our lives making blameless people unhappy? 'I hope we weren't as bad as that. I hate the word contempt.'

He nodded. 'Of course, you're much nicer these days. I knew you would be. Anyone with any brains, gets nicer as they get older. But we were all angry then.'

'You seem to have harnessed your anger to great effect.'

'Someone once said to me that when young and clever men are angry, they either explode or achieve great things.'

The weird coincidence of the words made me sit up. 'How funny. A friend of mine said that about another chap I know, not long ago. Do you remember Serena Gresham?'

'I remember everyone at that dinner.' I raised my eyebrows to acknowledge that this must indeed be the case for all the guests who were present. But he hadn't finished. 'Actually, I remember her more than that. She was quite friendly with Joanna, even after she'd dropped out to run off with me. It was Serena who warned me not to explode.'

I was simultaneously impressed at Serena's generosity of vision in going on with Joanna and Kieran when most of the girls had dropped them and slightly disappointed, as one always is, at the realisation that what had seemed a *bon mot* fashioned expressly for one's own ears is in fact just a slogan for the speaker. 'When she said it to me she was talking about Damian Baxter, another member of the Portuguese Dinner Club.'

'The *founder* member.' He took another sip of his wine. 'In a way, Damian Baxter and I were the two graduates of that year's output from the University of Life.'

Of course they would know each other, these Masters of the Universe. Damian had told me Kieran avoided him and I was curious as to whether this was really true. 'I suppose you must run into each other from time to time, at gatherings of the Great and the Good,' I said.

'Not really.' And there was my answer.

'That evening will obviously be with us to the end.'

He smiled, with a slight shrug. 'Damian isn't a friend of mine, but not because of that.'

240

Naturally I wanted to know the reason but I felt it might have an uncomfortable bearing on what I intended to discover before we parted and it didn't seem quite the right time to open that can of worms. 'He's certainly kept his success less secret than you have.' In saying this I found that I already admired Kieran very much. There is always something good in knowing you admire someone without reservation. I enjoyed giving him his due. Particularly as it justified my disapproval of someone I had always disliked.

He shook his head. 'Damian hasn't courted fame. He simply let it happen. I have spent who knows how much money keeping my name out of everything. Which is the more vain and self-important response?'

'Why did it matter to you?'

He thought for a moment. 'A mixture. Part of me believed it was very grown up to avoid a public profile and part of me had had enough. I did quite a lot of first-nighting and glad-handing and the rest of it during my days as a pseudo-posh dressmaker. It was moderately necessary then, though not as necessary as I pretended. But for a property developer, fame gives you nothing that you need and plenty you don't want.' The waiter had arrived with a clutch of appropriate equipment and Kieran waited until the man had finished arming us for the delights to come. 'Fame has its uses. The jumping of queues on to aeroplanes and into hospitals. It gives you good tables in restaurants that were full before you rang. You get theatre seats and tickets for the opera, and even invitations from people you are genuinely interested to know. But money gives you all these things without the hassle. You're not besieged to open this and support that, because nobody knows who you are and it wouldn't help if you did. The newspapers don't comb your background and interview your school friends to see if you kissed someone behind the bicycle shed in 1963. I don't have to put up with any of that. I get requests for large donations and I give some. That's all that is expected of me.'

'Were you surprised when you made money? I mean, proper money?' This seems an odd question to ask of a slight acquaintance after a forty-year gap. I can only tell you it didn't feel odd at the time to either of us.

'Everyone who is very successful will tell you that the initial response is entirely schizoid. One part of you thinks: All this for *me*? There must be some mistake! And the other greets immense, good fortune with: What on earth took you so long?'

'I suppose self-belief is a key ingredient.'

He nodded. 'So they tell us. But it's never quite enough to prepare you for what's happening. I made a lot of money when I sold the shops, but even so, when I did the sums for the projected profit on the first development I thought I'd put in too many noughts. I couldn't believe it would generate so much. But it did. Then there was more and more and more and more. And everything changed.'

'You didn't.'

'Oh, but I did. In those early years I went completely crazy. I was a jackass, a micro-manager to a truly demented degree. My home, my clothes, my cars, everything had to be just *so*. Looking back, I think I must have been imitating some notion of how posh people behaved but I got it completely wrong. I kept complaining in restaurants, and insisting on different shades of towel and different kinds of water in hotels. I wouldn't go to the telephone when people I knew rang.' He paused, bewildered, trying to understand his own remembered lunacy.

'Why not?'

'I thought that important people didn't. It was crazy. Even the President of the United States goes to the telephone if he knows the person at the other end, but I wouldn't. I had armies of assistants, working from sheaves of messages, with endless lists doled out to all and sundry. And I cancelled; boy, did I cancel. Last-minute duck-out. That was me.'

'I've never really understood why people do that.' I haven't. And yet it is an increasingly common phenomenon among the would-be great.

He sucked at his lip. 'Nor me, really. I think I felt trapped the moment I'd agreed to do anything, because the coming event, whatever it was, wouldn't be under my control. Then, as it drew nearer I would begin to panic, and on the day I'd decide I couldn't possibly go, usually for some nonsensical and irrelevant reason, and all the people I paid to kiss my arse would tell me that my host or hostess would understand, so I'd chuck.'

'When did that end?'

'When I'd been dropped by everybody. I still thought I was a sought-after guest, until one day I realised I was only ever asked to celebrity stunts, but never to where anything interesting was happening. Politicians, performers, writers, even thinkers, I wasn't invited to meet them any more. I was just too unreliable.'

This admission fascinated me, since I have known so many film stars and television faces who've gradually removed themselves from society, or at least from the society of anyone remotely rewarding who is not a fan. As a rule they are quite unaware of it, and continue to think of themselves as pursued and desired when they are neither. 'My grandmother used to say that you should never be more difficult than you're worth.'

'She was right. I broke her rule and paid. I was *much* more difficult than I was worth.' His tone had gone through a kind of exasperation and was suddenly full of real pain. I looked at him. 'That was when Joanna left me. It was understandable. She'd married me as a protest against the rules of the Establishment and suddenly she was living with a man who thought it was important to have his shirts made with a quarter of an inch difference in the length of the two sleeves, who could only buy his ties in Rome or have his shoes mended by a particular cobbler in St James's. It was all so boring. Can you blame her?'

I thought it might be time to lighten the mood. 'From what I remember of your mother-in-law, I imagine she rather approved of the change in you. That and the money, of course.'

He looked at me, as the waiter brought the first course. 'Did you know Valerie Langley?'

'Not well. I knew her as Joanna's mother, not as "Valerie".'

'She has much to answer for.' His tone was not jocular. I tried to think of something to add to this, but he hadn't finished. 'Did you realise that she only took us out to Portugal to split us up? Can you imagine a mother doing that to her own daughter?'

I could, really, when the mother in question was Valerie Langley, but there wasn't much point in flinging petrol on to the flames, so I decided to move to different shores for a bit. 'I gather you married again after you and Joanna split up. Is your second wife still around?'

He almost jumped, as if my words had distracted him from something he was busy with. 'No. We're divorced. Years ago.'

'I'm sorry. It didn't say that in your biography.'

Again he looked at me as if I were forcing him to discuss a parking ticket that had been issued to somebody else in 1953. 'Don't be sorry. Jeanne was nothing.' Which was a chilling comment, but not just in its cruelty. Perhaps it said too much about his loneliness.

'How is Joanna?' He'd already mentioned her, so there didn't seem to be any reason why I shouldn't ask. 'Are you on good terms these days?'

The question seemed to take him by surprise and return him to the present. My words had told him something beyond their content. 'Why did you want to see me?' he asked.

Suddenly I felt as if I had been caught shoplifting, or worse, putting a school friend's torch into my pocket. 'I'm on an errand, really.'

'What errand? For whom?'

'Damian.' I hesitated, praying for inspiration. 'You know he's ill—'

'And like to die.'

It almost amused me he should quote *Richard III* in this context. 'Precisely. And he finds he's interested in hearing about how his friends from those days ...' I wasn't at all sure how to end this. 'How they turned out. Whether life worked for them. You know. Rather as you were saying about your own past and how you like to talk about it.' This last was a lame attempt to put them into the same boat.

'All his friends? Or just some of his friends?'

'Just some at this stage, and he asked me to help because he's really lost touch with them and we used to be quite close.'

Which wouldn't wash with Kieran and no wonder. 'I'm astonished that you, of all people, accepted the brief.'

Naturally, this was a perfectly reasonable comment. 'So am I, really. I didn't mean to do it when he first asked me, but then I went down to his home to see him, and I felt ...' I tailed off. What had I felt that overturned a lifetime of dislike?

Kieran answered for me. 'You felt you couldn't refuse. Because death was pulling at his sleeve and you had only thought of him as young before you got there.'

'That's the sort of thing.' It *was* the sort of thing, although that wasn't the whole reason. Underlying any pity for Damian I may, I admit, have felt I sensed a kind of larger, general sadness growing in me, a sorrow at the cruelty of time. At any rate, Kieran had succeeded in making me feel awkward and undignified with my nosy enquiries and my bogus charity.

'Which "some"?'

'Sorry?' The phrase sounded foreign. I couldn't understand him.

'Which "some" of Damian's friends?'

I listed the women. He listened as he ate his cod's roe, breaking the toast and pressing the pink squidge on to it with the kind of fastidious neatness that seems to tell of a man living alone. Not camp at all, nor fussy, but disciplined and *neat*, like a locker in an army barracks. He finished his plate before he spoke again. 'Has this got something to do with my son?'

Of course, the words were like a punch in the gut. I felt quite sick and for a second I thought I was actually going to *be* sick. But at least I decided to end the dishonesty at once, since it was clear I was as mysterious to Kieran as a sheet of laminated glass. I took a breath and answered, 'Yes.'

He absorbed this, seemingly turning it round and round his brain, looking at it from every angle, like a connoisseur unconvinced by the reputed excellence of a highly priced piece of old porcelain. Then he made a decision. 'I don't want to talk any more about it here. Do you have time to come back to my home for some coffee?' I nodded. 'Then that is what we shall do.' And before my eyes he threw off the intimate, self-deprecating persona he had demonstrated, and replaced it with a mask of smooth and easy sophistication, chatting away breezily about countries he liked to visit, how disappointing he found the government, whether the ecology movement had got out of hand, until we'd finished and paid and he led the way out of the hotel to a large Rolls-Royce with a chauffeur, who was standing by the open door.

Kieran nodded at the magnificent car. 'Sometimes the old ways are best,' he observed lightly and we got in.

We drove to one of those new and, it must be said, unlovely blocks that have recently been built by the side of Vauxhall Bridge. Never having entered any of them, I rather wondered at his choice of dwelling. I think I must have expected him to live in a ravishing manor house in Chelsea, built originally for a cheery gentleman farmer in the 1730s and now on the market for enough to refinance Madrid. But on stepping out of the lift at the top-floor landing, then into Kieran's flat – I always resist the word 'apartment,' but I suspect it would be a more accurate term – I understood at once. At the end of a long, wide hall the whole of one side of the building, about thirty feet deep and who knows how long, was a single, vast drawing room. There were tall windows in three walls, giving a view of London second only to the Millennium Wheel. I looked down at the curling, night-time Thames, with its busy, toy boats, twinkling with coloured lights, at the dinky cars whizzing along the ribbon-roads, at the tiny pedestrian dots, hurrying down the pavements under the lamp posts. It was like flying.

Nor was there less to wonder at inside. The whole place was filled with the loveliest things I have ever seen in a private dwelling. Normally in a family house, even a very grand one, the exquisite pieces are occasionally interlarded with a pair of chairs covered by Aunt Joan and something Daddy brought back from the Sudan. But there was none of that here. Two matching Savonnerie carpets covered the gleaming floor and on it sat furniture so beautiful that it looked as if it had all been removed from one of Europe's major palaces. The paintings were mainly landscapes rather than portraits and, while I usually find them a trifle dull, I could not say that about these spectacular jewels of the *genre*. These were landscapes by Canaletto and Claude Lorraine and Gainsborough and Constable and other names I can only guess at. There was one ravishing painting of *La Princesse de Monaco*, by Angelica Kauffmann, which caught my eye. Kieran saw where I was looking. 'I don't like portraits as a rule. I find them sentimental. But I bought that because it reminded me of Joanna.' He was right. It was very like her. Joanna wearing a wide, flower-trimmed hat and the looser casual fashions of the 1790s, which seemed so carefree until you remembered that the sitter was less than three years from her hideous death. The unfortunate princess had ridden in the last tumbrel of the Reign of Terror. The officers heard the rioting of the Thermidor *coup d'état* break out as they drove towards the guillotine but, unfortunately for their passengers, they decided to complete the grisly journey, reasoning that no one would blame them if the regime was overthrown, but if Robespierre survived in power, they would all die for sparing the victims. They were probably right.

The picture was above an elaborate chimneypiece, which I admired. He told me it was from the scattered trove of a great house that had been demolished in my time, releasing a flood of doorcases and fireplaces and balustrades and other plunder when it bit the dust during the hopeless years of the 1950s. The family are still there, happily ensconced, these days, in a charming converted orangery.

'Can you burn a fire in a building as new as this? Is it real?'

'Certainly. I wanted the penthouse, so I could construct a chimney. I hate a drawing room without a fire, don't you? They weren't too difficult about it.' He talked as if he'd installed an extra bathroom.

Not for the first time I wondered what it must be like to be astonishingly rich. Of course, we're all astonishingly rich when compared to the inhabitants of enormous parts of the globe and I do not mean to sound ungrateful. But what is it like when the only reason not to do something, or buy something, or eat something, or drink something is because you do not want to? 'It would be *so* boring!' one hears people say. But would it? It's not boring to have hot water every morning, or a delicious dinner every night, to sleep in good sheets or live in pretty rooms or collect a few nice pictures, so why would it be boring to be able to treble all these blessings at a touch? I am fairly sure that I would love it. 'Have you got a house in the country?' I asked.

'No.' He spoke with a slightly tolerant air, as if I should know better. 'Not now. I've done all that.' He chuckled. 'At one point I had an estate in Gloucestershire, another in Scotland, a flat in New York, a villa in Italy quite near Florence, and a London house in Cheyne Row. I'd arrive at each of them, fret about everything that had been done wrongly since I was last there and leave. I never seemed to stay in anywhere for more than three days at a stretch, so I never got beyond the complaining stage. Although I do quite miss the house in the Cotswolds.' A pink cloud of nostalgia hovered over him for a moment. 'The library was one of the prettiest rooms I've ever seen, never mind lived in. But no.' He shook his head to loosen these disturbing, self-indulgent images. 'I'm finished with all that. There's no point.'

This was an odd phrase, but I let it go. Kieran had ordered some coffee while we were in the car and now a discreet manservant brought it in. Once again, I was on the set of a Lonsdale comedy. I wonder now whether I fully realised what I would see of the modern world when I took Damian's shilling. Was it a shock that all this way of life, which we were told so firmly in the Sixties was most definitely dying, was instead alive and well, and not even very unusual any more? I consider myself able to move about pretty freely and I have spent a good deal of my time in enviable houses of one sort or another, but I was beginning to grasp that it wasn't, as it used to be, that there was the odd person still living in an Edwardian way, the occasional millionaire who invented electricity and we should all be grateful to him, dear. Nowadays there is a whole new class of rich people leading rich lives, as numerous as under the Georgians. The only difference is that now it goes on behind closed doors facilitating the dishonest representation of these things that the media go in for. As a result, the vast majority is largely unaware that there is a new and affluent group who live in this way but do not, unlike their predecessors a century ago, take much responsibility for those less blessed. This new breed feel no need to lead the public in public, but only from the shadows behind the Throne.

I poured myself a cup of coffee and sat in a tapestry-covered *bergère*, fashioned, I would guess, during the middle years of the eighteenth century. I felt we might as well get things started. 'So, how is Joanna?' I said, since that was where we had broken off.

Kieran looked at me quite steadily for a moment. Even he must have realised this was why we were here. 'Joanna is dead,' he replied.

'What?'

'And dead, I'm afraid, in a sad way. She was found in a public lavatory, not far from Swindon, with an empty hypodermic needle beside her. She had overdosed on heroin. When the police got there, they thought she'd been locked in the cubicle for about five days. They were alerted by the smell which, in that setting, as you can imagine, had to be pretty strong before it was noticed.' It was at this precise moment that I realised Kieran de Yong was a man cursed. This horrible, sordid, tragic image was always with him, of a woman I would guess he had loved much more than he believed he would at the start. It was a picture that hovered an inch or two behind his thoughts unless he was asleep, and then I am quite sure it visited his dreams. I saw that he had agreed to meet me because all he ever really wanted to talk about, or think about, was Joanna and I had known her. But when we did meet, he had found he couldn't begin the conversation without this account, and, whatever he may have originally planned, he couldn't give it in a crowded, noisy restaurant. Having acquitted this task, he almost relaxed.

Sometimes one hears or witnesses a thing so shocking that the brain cannot programme it for a second. I remember I was once in an earthquake in South America, and as I watched the ornaments and books jump and leap about, it took a second or two before my brain would tell me what was happening. This was just such a moment. Joanna Langley, enchanting, ravishing Joanna, was dead and in a way more suited to the forgotten, the abandoned and the lost; not to a darling of the gods.

'Christ.' For one tiny instant I thought I was going to burst into tears and when I looked over at Kieran it seemed that he might too, but then he recovered. At last he nodded slowly, as if my exclamation had been a comment. The fact is there are some deaths that have a gentle aspect, that bring a kind of comfort of their own to help the survivors bear their grief. This was not one of them. 'When did it happen?'

'October 1985. The fifteenth. We'd split up a couple of years before, as you probably know, and we didn't speak for a bit, except about Malcolm, because we were having . . .' he hesitated. What were they having? 'An argument. A disagreement.' He was gathering momentum. 'A fight. But then we got the judgement, which was at least a decision, and I felt we could move on, that we were both getting through it.' He gave a gesture of hopelessness with his hands.

'But you weren't.'

'Obviously not.'

'What was the disagreement about?' Again, on paper this seems intrusive, but we had, as they say now, 'bonded' during the evening, or I felt we had, and it didn't seem to be prying when I said it.

'Joanna was having a lot of problems. Well,' he ran his fingers through his enviable hair, 'you can tell that from the way she died. And I wanted to be Malcolm's principal carer. I don't mean I didn't want her to see him, or anything like that.' It was clear that guilt for his first wife's death coursed through his veins so hotly he could still feel it twenty-three years later. 'I just thought he would be better off living with me, rather than trailing round after his mother. I had more money than she did by then—'

'Jeepers.'

He shook his head. 'Alfred went down in a property crash a few years earlier, so there was nothing much left in that quarter. Their whole life had changed from when you knew them. They were really quite broke, living in a flat on the edge of Streatham.' I had a sudden, vivid vision of Mrs Langley, sparkling with gems and watching from the edge of a ballroom like a shifty ferret to spy any interest in her daughter from Viscount Summersby. I never liked her much but I was sorry all the same. At that time nobody would have imagined the future waiting for her. 'It wasn't only the money. Joanna was very disappointed in the way the world had turned out. She thought by then we'd all be living in some kind of spiritual Nepal, smoking dope and mouthing the lyrics from *Hair*. Not taking out pensions in Mrs Thatcher's Britain.'

'A lot of our generation thought that. Some of them are in government.'

But I couldn't staunch the flow. Kieran had to tell his story. As the television quiz show has it: He'd started, so he'd finish. 'And of course, looking at it from her point of view I was at the peak of my madness, screaming if there was a crease on my collar, sacking staff because the knives and forks weren't tidy enough in the kitchen drawer ... None of that side of it was her fault.' His effort to be fair to his late wife was more than commendable, it was heartbreaking. He sighed again. 'Anyway, we fought about the boy like a couple of cats. She said I'd poison his mind and make him a fascist. I said she'd poison his body and make him an addict. On and on we went, tearing at each other's throats. Until finally she dropped the bombshell. We were having breakfast one morning in that weird, angry way of two people who are still living together but know they won't be for long. We were sitting there in silence, until she looked up, preparing to speak. I knew some insult was on its way, so I deliberately made no enquiries. After a bit she got bored and just said it.'

'What?'

'That Malcolm wasn't my son.'

'How did she say it?'

'Like that. "Malcolm isn't your son."'

He stopped now to let the words sink in. So was this where my quest was to end? It felt strange to have reached my destination, and yet also satisfactory in a way that Joanna's death should be partially redeemed by the boy's father at last acknowledging his blood child. Even if there was an anticlimactic element in the thought of Damian's fortune going to the only family in England who wouldn't notice it.

Kieran hadn't finished. 'You mentioned the house party in Portugal.'

'Yes.' I knew Portugal would come into it.

'She said she'd met up with "the boy's father" there and that she'd slept with him when we were back in London. That night, in fact. As soon as we got home from the airport we had a row about why we'd gone at all and she walked out ...' He shrugged. 'It was obvious she was talking about Damian.' He must have caught and mistaken my response to this news, and hurried to undo any possible hurt. 'She was always very fond of you, but ...' How was he to phrase it?

I helped him out. 'She wasn't interested in me.'

We both knew she wasn't, so why should he argue? 'Not like that,' he said, accepting my own verdict. 'And Joanna couldn't have cared less about the Tremaynes. It had to be Damian.' He paused. However often he went over this territory, it obviously still hurt. 'So I sat there, with a piece of toast in one hand and a coffee cup in the other, while she blew my life out of the water. And I minded when she told me. I minded very much.'

'Of course you did.'

'It wasn't just the boy. She was unravelling our life. This was retro-active legislation. We'd only been married a year at the time she was talking about and I'd thought we were happy, then. I'd been against the damn holiday anyway, because I dreaded her being pulled back into a crowd that I didn't believe was any good for her.'

'But you went because her mother made you. And when you got back she slept with Damian.' At least I now understood his visceral dislike.

'That's about it. And by this stage of the battle she was glad to talk about it, because it was going to save her son from the vile Leona Helmsley world of mad indulgence that I was living in. She thought it would settle matters. That I would give up and back off, and Malcolm would go with her, and I would be left alone to count my money and weep.'

'But that didn't happen.'

'Of course not. My name was on the birth certificate for God's sake. I was married to her when he was conceived, never mind born. I loved him. He was my son.' He almost shouted this assertion, back in the grip of the row, but seeing my startled face he recovered, repeating the words in a gentler tone, which touched me as it would have touched anyone who heard him. 'I loved him. He was my son. I could have made my claim on that basis alone.' I sat up. I'd assumed he *had* made his claim on that basis alone, if he'd kept in contact with the boy. Which, from the way he was talking, he obviously had.

'But you didn't?'

He shook his head. 'I had a paternity test done. I wanted to know how tough the battle was going to be.' He looked at me again quite fiercely, and for a moment I rather sympathised with Joanna when I saw what she'd taken on. I suppose nobody can be as successful as Kieran had been without having some steel in them somewhere. 'When the results came back they showed Malcolm was mine after all.'

All my sense of matters being resolved deserted me on the instant. 'How did she take it?'

'How do you think?' He rolled his eyes at me. 'She wasn't thinking straight by then. She said she didn't believe me. It was exactly the kind of thing I would fix, blah, blah, blah. You can imagine.' I could. 'So we ran another test under her team's supervision and obviously the result was the same again, and by then she was coming apart at the seams . . .' He was standing, staring out of one of the windows, silhouetted against a dark-blue velvet sky studded with stars. He continued talking, facing on to the night, hardly aware I was there. 'As you might expect, she hadn't helped her case as a rational woman with all this screaming carry-on, so it wasn't a huge surprise when the judge gave me full custody, with visiting rights for her, which was much more than I'd asked for. We got the decision in September eighty-five.'

'And the following month she killed herself.'

'She killed herself, or she took an accidental overdose. Anyway,' he sighed, wearily, his remembered rage quite gone, 'she was dead. That's how it finished for Joanna. And it was all so unnecessary. Malcolm was fourteen by then. I couldn't have controlled his seeing her even if I'd wanted to, which I didn't, for more than a year or two at the most.'

Some decisions are so difficult to unravel; decisions made by countries and decisions of private individuals can be impossible to explain. Why did Napoleon invade Russia? Why didn't Charles I make peace when it was offered? And why did Joanna Langley run away and marry this man when he was an anxious and desperate grotesque, but leave him when he was at the beginning of his triumphs? Why did she try to pull their boy in half when he was old enough to make up his own mind about both his parents and their warring philosophies? Why did she spiral into death-dealing depression when she really had nothing to fear?

'I don't understand why we never heard about it. Why isn't it on the Internet?'

'Mainly because I have spent an enormous amount of time and money making sure that no one hears about it. I kept the reporting to a minimum at the time, I will not tell you how, and I have one man who spends his working life combing the Web to get rid of any stories that I dislike, including even a whisper of Joanna.'

'Why?'

'Because I owe it to her. I ruined her life. I won't let her be a tabloid item in death.'

I ruined her life. I was so struck by the unvarnished, stark, merciless guilt in this. He allowed himself no defence at all. 'How sad,' I said. And I meant it with all my heart. I was truly sad. Sad at the ruin that, in a few short minutes, I'd heard engulf the whole House of Langley. In my sorrowing mind, rich, nice Alfred and his scratchy, ambitious Valerie had been suddenly pulled from their golden pedestal, where they had been secure in my imaginings until now and dashed down, like Don Giovanni, back to the place below, from whence they came. While Joanna, my lifelong standard for how lovely a woman can be, lay desecrated and dead, her scabrous wrist pitted with needle marks, her dirty, tangled hair spread out on a urine-stained, concrete floor somewhere in the Midlands. 'How very sad.'

I looked at my watch. It was time to leave. I understood now that Kieran had embraced the chance to talk about the wife who had left him against his will, but who would never leave his head. He had simply wanted to talk about her with someone who'd known her and those opportunities must be getting rare, even for him. He noticed me checking the time. 'I'd like to show you something before you go,' he said, and leaving the magnificent Chamber of Privilege he led me down the passage, past half-open doors revealing delectable rooms for eating and reading and other delights, until we came to the last door in the row. He opened it and ushered me into what was postulated as a study of some sort, with a desk and a comfortable chair. I could sense that Kieran probably did his actual work in it, as opposed to leafing through papers with a scribbling secretary in the glamorous library along the passage. Certainly he spent a lot of time here, as much as he could I would say, but the reason was not because it was quiet or tidy. In fact, its role as a writing room was not its moral purpose. This was a shrine. All four walls were covered with framed photographs, one consisting entirely of pictures of Joanna, Joanna as I remembered her, young and definitively gorgeous; then Joanna a little older and a little older still, but never Joanna old. Joanna at thirty, looking more harassed and careworn and lined than she should have done; Joanna at thirty-three, pictured leaving the law courts during the divorce, a candid picture of her unhappiness, so generously taken by the snapper of some evening rag but presumably unprinted; Joanna at thirty-five, sitting with her son, laughing. Kieran was looking with me. 'That was taken by a friend of hers. Malcolm was there for lunch or something and this friend took it. It was the last picture of them together. It's the last picture of her. She had less than a week to go. You couldn't have told.'

'No, indeed.' I stared at the smiling mouth and the tired eyes. I found myself hoping it had been a really happy day, that last outing with her beloved child. I glanced around for newspaper pictures of the story. Even after all he'd said, I was surprised there weren't any. 'And there was no coverage at all? I still don't understand how you kept it out of the papers completely. Even the local ones?'

He looked uncomfortable. 'There were a few squibs, but not much.'

'I couldn't find anything on Google. There was really nothing about her at all, once you'd separated.'

Kieran knew why. 'She used my real name after the divorce. That was the name on everything in her bag when they found her. I managed to stop them making the connection.' He hesitated. 'You can read the coverage if you punch in Joanna Futtock.'

'Futtock?' I was so glad to know that I could still find something funny.

He looked rather sheepish. 'Why do you think I never gave up "de Yong"?'

'I did wonder. What was your mother's maiden name?'

'Cock.' He gave a despairing sigh. 'I ask you.'

'Some people have all the luck,' I said. Then we both did laugh.

I'd started to look round the other walls of this little star chamber. There were pictures of Joanna with Kieran, a young Kieran with his awful blond mop and an apparently endless supply of the ugliest clothes in the world. Then grown-up Kieran; Kieran successful; Kieran shaking hands with presidents and kings; even Kieran in better and better suits. And alongside Kieran, everywhere you looked, there were more and more pictures of the boy. Malcolm in the school photograph from pre-prep; Malcolm swimming; Malcolm on a bicycle; Malcolm on a horse; Malcolm the public schoolboy, with both parents, one on either side of the sulking child, resisting his role at some Speech Day celebration. Malcolm skiing; Malcolm at university; Malcolm graduating with a very serious face; Malcolm backpacking. 'What's he up to now?' I asked.

Kieran was silent for a second, then he spoke in as pleasant a manner as he could manage. 'He's dead, too.'

'What?' I did not know the boy at all and the father only slightly, but I felt as if I were being pistol-whipped.

'Nothing bad. Not like his mother.' This time I could see his eyes filling, even while he remained in admirable control of his voice. 'He was perfectly well, twenty-three, just starting at Warburg's and he couldn't shake off a bout of flu, so we thought he should be looked at.' He stopped to breathe, back in that terrible moment. 'I took him to hospital for some tests and he was dead seven weeks later.' He rubbed his nose swiftly with his left hand, trying unsuccessfully to push back the tears. He talked on, more to steady himself than to give me any information. 'And that was it, really. I didn't quite take in what had happened. Not at first. Not for a while. A few years afterwards I even married again.' He shook his head at life's absurdity. 'Of course, it was ridiculous and it didn't last long. I made a mistake, you see.' He looked back at me. 'I thought I could still go on living. Anyway,' he sighed, as if this at least was understood between us, 'after I'd got rid of Jeanne I sold the houses and everything else, and came here. I did bring a lot of stuff with me, as you can see. I hadn't signed off completely.'

'How do you spend your time?'

'Oh.' He thought for a second, as if this was rather a curious query and difficult to answer. 'I've still got quite a lot of things on the boil and I take a bit of interest in financing research, into cancer, mainly. I'd like to think that it might help to prevent it happening to someone else. And I do worry about education these days, or rather the lack of it. If I'd been born now, I'd have ended up pulling pints in a bar in Chelmsford. I mind about those kids who'll never have a chance, the way things are.' He seemed pleased to think about these issues and glad of his role in them. Which he deserved to be. 'Apart from that I read. I watch a lot of television and I enjoy it, which nobody admits to. You see,' he tried to smile but gave up, 'the thing is, when your only child is dead, you're dead.' He paused as if to mark the rightness of this sentence to himself. 'Your life is finished. You're not a parent any more. You're nothing. It's over. You're just waiting for your body to catch up with your soul.'

He stopped talking and we just stood there in that holy place of love. Kieran was weeping quite openly by this stage, with tears coursing down his cheeks, leaving a dark trail of water marks on his expensive lapels, and I freely confess that I was, too. We didn't say anything more and for a few minutes we didn't even move. It would have been a strange sight if anyone had interrupted us. Two rather overweight men in late middle age, standing motionless in their Savile Row suits, crying.

Terry

ELEVEN

Not very surprisingly, after an evening like that I decided I needed some air. Kieran offered to get his driver to take me home but I wanted to walk, just for a bit, and he didn't insist. So we shook hands in that funny English way, as if we hadn't been through an emotional trauma together, as though the whole thing hadn't really happened and the stains of our tears had some other, more banal and more acceptable explanation. We made the usual murmurings about meeting again, which one always says. Unusually, I rather hope it will happen, but I expect not. After that I set off down the Embankment.

It was a long walk home and quite cold, but it did not seem so. I strolled along, both reliving and then laying to rest my memories of Joanna. I was glad to have had a chance to revalue Kieran, even while I knew he was far beyond help, and I felt that I had been allowed to look into a soul that was worth looking into. Filled with these melancholy thoughts, I had just turned off Gloucester Road into Hereford Square when there was a scream, then laughter, then shouting, then the sound of someone being sick. I wish I could write that I was astonished to hear what sounded like a large Indian takeaway being splashily deposited on to the pavement, but these days it would require a Martian, and one only recently arrived from outer space, to be surprised at these charming goings-on. A group of young men and women in their early twenties, I would guess, were loitering on the corner of the square, perhaps recent refugees from the Hereford Arms on the other side of the road, perhaps not. One woman, in a short leather skirt and trainers, was throwing up and another, with suspiciously black hair, was tending to her. The rest just stood around, waiting for the next act in their evening's entertainment. Foolishly, I paused to study them. 'Got a problem?' said a man with a shaved head and a whole array of piercings down the edge of his right ear. I wondered the weight didn't throw him off balance.

'My problems seem nothing to yours,' I said and then rather regretted my clever-clogs answer as he took a menacing step towards me.

'Leave him, Ron. He's not worth it,' the girl with black hair and what looked like four different petticoats swaddling her bottom shouted over her shoulder. Happily he appeared to agree and turned away.

As he moved back, he shouted a crisp 'Fuck off' at me, but more as a kind of standard ritual, as one might say good morning in a village street. And so, before he could change his mind, I did.

It's not often that I walk at night, though more from laziness than fear, but when I do I am amazed at the changes that have come about in London during my adult lifetime, the main one being, of course, not the mugging and the general crime, nor even the dirt and uncollected rubbish that swirls and drifts in piles against the railings and the plane trees, waiting in vain for the men to come. It is the drunkenness that has transformed the streets, not just of London but of almost every town, into a lesser hell for lawful citizens. The kind of drunkenness that in years gone by used to be talked of in Siberia at the height of Stalin's iron rule as a reflection of the misery of the oppressed, or it was rumoured to be manifest up near the pole, where the long nights of winter drive strong men mad. Why did it happen here? When did it start? I used to think it was a class thing and somehow linked to the ills of social deprivation, but it isn't. Not long ago I attended a twenty-first party, held in one of St James's smartest clubs. The birthday boy was clever, charming, tipped for success and linked to half the peerage, and I watched as all the nice young girls and young men cheerfully tossed back the booze until they were staggering or vomiting or both. As I left, I heard a tray of glasses go west amid loud laughter, and a girl in a pretty *couture* dress of lilac chiffon pushed past me, hand on mouth, hoping to make it just in time. Outside, a fellow with traces of sick on his evening shirt was urinating against the car parked next to mine. I had escaped not a moment too soon.

Certainly some people drank too much in my day, as they always have, but drunkenness was rare and sad, and made men look like fools. Until as little as ten years ago being drunk was a mistake, a regrettable by-product of making merry, a miscalculation which, the next day, required an apology. Now it's the point. Does anyone out there understand why we let it happen? Because I don't. Of course I can see the charm of the 'café culture' we were said to be encouraging. But how long can a sane person contemplate failure without admitting it? At what point does optimism become delusion? The other day some fat-headed woman on the radio was lecturing her browbeaten interviewer, denying that there was anything wrong with binge-drinking, insisting that the true problem lay with the middle-aged, middle-class drunks, apparently swilling it down in their own houses. He, poor battered fellow, dared not argue that even if this were true, even if all the *bons bourgeois* were lying flat on the carpet, singing sea shanties every night of their lives, they would still not be a problem, because they would not be a problem to *anyone else*. Why do modern leaders not grasp that their job is to control antisocial behaviour but not private activity; to regulate our actions as regards others, but not where they only concern ourselves? At times it is hard not to feel that as a culture we are lost, in permanent denial and spinning in the void.

I turned the key and opened the door of the flat on to the darkness of living alone. I walked into the drawing room and switched on a scattering of lamps from the door. I was only beginning to get used to the notion that every time I returned to my home I would find it just as I'd left it. When Bridget went I will say she went most thoroughly. As I waved her off I suspected that she saw the separation as only temporary and that I would soon find telltale signs that she expected to be back, but I would say now that I wronged her, that in some way she had decided she was as glad to be rid of me as I to be rid of her. These things are peculiar. You agonise for months, or even years, on end. Should you finish it? Should you not? But having made the decision, you're as impatient as a child on Christmas Eve. It is with the greatest difficulty you refrain from packing for them, pushing them into a taxi and shooing them away that very night. You long for them to go, you ache for it, so you can begin the rest of your life. 'You'll miss me,' she said as she walked through the flat, checking for any last-minute items she'd forgotten.

'I know I will,' I said, as one must in such a case. There is an etiquette involved and this comes into the same category as 'It isn't you, it's me.'

Actually, I thought at the time that I would miss her. But I didn't much. Or far less than I expected. I can cook quite well when I put my mind to it and I'm lucky enough to have a woman who cleans a few times a week, so the main change was that I no longer had to spend the long, dark evenings with someone who was permanently disappointed in me. And that was nice. In fact, one of the great gifts of getting older is the discovery that the very thing you feared, 'being alone,' is actually much nicer than you thought. I should qualify this. To be old and ill alone, to die alone, is usually a sad thing, and at some point one may want to take steps to avoid this fate if possible. I suppose the prospect of a solitary death is even scarier for the childless, as they have no one they can reasonably expect to get involved with their disintegration, but even for them, and I am one of them, chunks on your own before you hove into sight of the Pearly Gates are simply lovely. You eat what you like, you watch what you like, you drink what you like, whoopee, and all without guilt or the need to hurry in case you'll be found out. If you feel social you go out, if you don't you stay in. If you want to talk you pick up the telephone, if not you don't, and all around is the blessed gift of silence, not the silence of resentment but of peace.

Of course, as a rule this only applies if one has recently come out of a relationship that was less than satisfactory. For the surviving widow or widower of a happy marriage things are obviously different. I will always remember my father, left on his own, remarking that while others might feel released by the death of their spouse to pursue an interest or a hobby or to get involved with some worthy activity that their marriage had prevented, he had personally gained nothing and lost everything, a very moving tribute, even if my mother deserved it more than he knew. But for the man or woman after a longed-for break-up things are quite different. There are missing bits, of course, the sex for one, but for a long time sex between Bridget and me had been more a question of feeling it was expected of one rather than demonstrating any real interest in the other on either of our parts. I won't deny that the thought of re-embarking on a career of 'dating' to fill the gap is a terrifying one to people in their fifties, but even so, freedom is a word that always shines.

The following morning, as I sat at my desk, I reviewed my non-existent progress in the search for the fortunate child, but I felt I must be approaching its conclusion. There were after all only two women left on the list to eliminate: Candida Finch and Terry Vitkov. After that, my task would presumably be done. When I had contemplated these possibilities, before this time, I had assumed that I would check out Candida first since she was in England. If she proved to be the one we were looking for I would not have to go to Los Angeles, which did seem rather a chore, so it was logical to try her next. But when I dialled her number, clearly printed for me on Damian's list, I was repeatedly treated, for almost the only time in this adventure, to the synthetic courtesies of an answering machine, made worse by my leaving message upon message, so far without tangible result. I wasn't comfortable any more with my bogus charity excuse, not since Kieran had somehow exposed it without meaning to, and instead of formulating another lie I decided just to make a simple request, stating my name, suggesting she had probably forgotten me but that we knew each other once and asking her to get in touch when she had a moment. I then left my numbers, put the receiver carefully back on to its cradle and hoped for the best. But the best was slow in coming and after three weeks of this, plus an unanswered postcard, I wasn't quite sure what to do next to serve my master. We did not, after all, have very long to play with.

'Go to Los Angeles,' said Damian down the line. 'Take a break, stay a few days. You can tick off Terry and do yourself some good. Do you have an agent out there?'

'Only as part of an arrangement with the London ones. I've never met him.'

'There you are, then. Give him a treat. Pick up some girls, take him out for the evening, give him the time of his life. I'm paying.'

Should I resent this attempt to sound generous? Or was he really being generous? 'My agent here says he's gay.'

'All the better. Flirt with him. Make him think he's the only man you've ever found attractive. Ask his advice and tell him how helpful it is when you receive it, then press an unfinished manuscript into his hands and give him a sense of ownership in what you're doing.' Comments like this made me painfully aware of how much more Damian knew about the world than I.

I had spoken to him of my evening with Kieran de Yong, not all of it, not the last bit, but enough for him to know that I had liked him

263

and that the dead boy had definitely not been Damian's child. He was silent at the other end for a minute or two. 'Poor Joanna,' he said.

'Yes.'

'She had every gift she needed for the era that was coming.'

'I agree.'

'If only she'd been a cynic. She died of optimism, in a way.'

'Like a lot of Sixties children.'

'I'm glad you liked him,' he said in an unusually generous tone. 'Of course, he can't stand me.'

'And we know why.' I hesitated, wondering whether I wanted to return to that troubling episode, yet conscious that every uncovered detail of this journey insisted on taking me there. 'Did we all know what you were up to? That time in Estoril? Are the accounts I'm getting truthful? Or are their memories playing tricks on them? Because it's starting to sound as if you slept with every woman in the world in the space of a few days.'

'I was young,' he replied and we both laughed.

I first met Terry, as I have said, at the ball given for Dagmar of Moravia. Lucy Dalton had disliked her on sight and so did some others, but I did not. I don't mean I was mad about her but, to invert Kieran's chilling phrase, she wasn't nothing. She was full of energy, full of what was once called pluck, and I did like her determination, and her mother's, to have first and foremost a very good time. Her father, of whom we would never see much, had made a killing with an advertising agency, first based in Cincinnati and later on Madison Avenue, at just the hour when the world was discovering quite what advertising could really do. Right through the 1950s, there had been a sense in many quarters that it was enough to say 'Use this! It's *Good*!' And that would do the trick, launching the product on a grateful public, until the moment, and it was in my teens, that the world of marketing would change forever and begin its remorseless campaign to take over civilisation. Jeff Vitkov spotted this coming era sooner than most. He was a simple, unpretentious soul, brilliant in his way but not, or so we thought, complicated in his wishes or his needs, the last man on earth to wish to climb the social ladder. Even after the move to New York he continued to regard Cincinnati as his home and he would possibly have left the family based there, flying back on the weekends, enjoying vacations in some modest but comfortable resort hotel, if his wife, Verena, had not made the unwelcome discovery that even the vertiginous improvement in their finances had not brought the social recognition she craved and, reasonably enough, felt entitled to. There is a fantasy one often hears voiced in England that America is classless, which, as any traveller will know, is arrant nonsense and never more so than in the provincial towns, whose social arrangements can be impressively resistant to the ambitious newcomer. Someone remarked, not all that long ago, that it would be easier to gain *entreé* to the King's chamber at Versailles than to break into the inner gang of Charleston, and much the same could be said in all the cities of the true, US *Gratin*.

This was always so. One of the main reasons for the great invasion by American heiresses in the 1880s and 1890s, the so-called Buccaneers, was that many of the daughters of those newly rich papas grew tired of having doors shut in their faces back home in Cleveland or St Louis or Detroit, and preferred instead to enjoy the deep and genuine warmth with which the well-born English have always welcomed money. It is hard to deny that the careers of girls like Virginia Bonynge, Viscountess Deerhurst, who began life as the daughter of a convicted murderer from the Middle West, would seem to confirm that things were much easier this side of the pond. Needless to say, this would often lead to sweet revenge, as the mothers of the Duchess of Manchester or the Countess of Rosslyn or Lady Randolph Churchill, or many, many others would sweep home in triumph to the place where they'd been snubbed, to rub their sisters' noses in it. I suspected at the time that this thinking, or something like it, was behind the plan, forming in Verena Vitkov's mind towards the end of 1967, to put her daughter through a London Season.

There were options open to mothers, in those days, to defray some of the expense if necessary. Things were already less abundant than they had been before the war, when there were three or four balls in London every night. Until the end of presentation there were half a dozen each week; by my time there were two or three; and fifteen years later it was down to less than ten in the whole Season. Even in '68, some girls gave only cocktail parties and no dance, others would throw both but share the ball, and there was no shame in this. Serena Gresham shared her coming-out ball with her cousin, Candida Finch, although this was of course because Lady Claremont was funding them both. But from the start, Terry Vitkov was anxious to cover every base and I have no doubt she was more than encouraged in this by her mother, the unsinkable Verena. In the event the drinks party, held early in the proceedings before they'd quite found their feet, was a standard affair at the Goring, but for the ball they were determined to make the evening memorable. This they undoubtedly achieved if not quite in the way they had intended, but that comes later and, to be fair, it was an original location. Mrs Jeffrey Vitkov, so ran the invitation, would be At Home, 'for Terry,' on such and such a night at Madame Tussaud's Waxworks in the Euston Road.

I do not know if you can still hire the waxworks for a private party. Not just a room, or a special chamber set aside for 'entertaining,' but the whole edifice and all it holds. I doubt it, or if you can, I imagine the price would be prohibitive to all save the super-rich, but forty years ago you could. There was less danger in it for them, of course, than there would be today. Apart from any other reason we were a more law-abiding lot. We took more care. Crime, as it might touch the middle and upper classes, was rare. People may groan when they hear that houses in the country were not locked, but they weren't. Not if one had just gone shopping. In central London we walked home alone at night without a qualm. Shoplifting was not considered cool by anyone. It was just stealing. I don't think mugging was sufficiently common even to qualify for a special name. And again, as I said, we were much less drunk. This did not mean, of course, that every party went without mishap.

I dined very well on the night of Terry's ball because my hosts for the dinner beforehand, had forgotten all about it. I turned up at the door of a rather smart house in Montpelier Square, joined on the step as I waited for the occupants to respond to my ring of the bell by Lucy Dalton and a man I hardly knew, who later became the head of Schroder's, or some such spangled operation, although you couldn't have told his future held such promise then. The three of us stood, shifting our weight from foot to foot, until the door was at last opened by Mrs Northbrook (for that was her name), who stood there in jeans and a jersey, with a gin and tonic in her other hand. At the sight of us the blood drained from her face and we were greeted with the telling words, 'Jesus Christ, it's not *tonight!*' The result of this was that Mr Northbrook was summoned with a scream and had to book a table for ten at an excellent place just across from Harrods, in that funny little triangle which I think used to have a grass bit in front of it, or have I made that up? As we waited, we all sat in their pretty, untidy and unready drawing room, swilling down some rather good Pouilly Fumé, which Laura Northbrook (we had moved on since the doorstep moment) had providentially found in the fridge before she joined her husband upstairs to struggle into their clothes. After such a welcome they could hardly stint with these frightful strangers wished upon them and the result was one of the best dinners I had eaten all year.

Our group was therefore in a jolly and convivial mood when we arrived at the famous entrance at about eleven that night. I suppose there must have been bouncers or someone similar to admit us, but, as I've already said, I have no solid memory of cards to be taken, or lists to be ticked off. The main party space had been arranged in what was then, and maybe is now, known as the Hall of Kings. The wax images of England's Royalty had been moved back into a circle round the dance floor, cleared at the centre, but the figures were still sufficiently spaced apart for us to be able to stroll among them and photographs would later appear in the press – though not in the *Tatler*, which had originally been the plan – of debs and their escorts apparently standing next to Henry VIII or Queen Caroline of Anspach. I was myself snapped with a girl I knew from my Hampshire years after my father's retirement from the diplomatic. It never, mercifully, appeared in print, but for some reason now forgotten I still have a copy of the picture. We look as if we're talking to a startled and offended Princess Margaret.

As we know, every waxwork ever made appears to be either under sedation, or recently arrested for criminal assault and in this respect almost uniquely, the last four decades have seen little change. Except perhaps in their subject matter. We certainly all knew far more history then, that is the whole nation did, not just the privileged, the educational establishment having not yet broken the link between teaching and the imparting of knowledge; so figures like Wellington and Disraeli and Gordon of Khartoum still had a resonance that spread far beyond the elite, the only group today who might have heard of them. Nor, when it came to waxworks, was there the modern, pusillanimous terror of causing offence and I can bear witness that the Chamber of Horrors in those days was really horrible. That night it had been set aside for a discothèque, and when Lucy and I went downstairs to explore it was quite clear the authorities were a long way from worrying about whether or not someone might get hit by a falling basket of nasturtiums or a stray conker.

There were stone pillars dividing the space and at the top of each, on a little ledge, was a severed head, disfigured with some hideous atrocity. Eyes hung out of sockets, flaps of skin revealed whitened bone, one even had an iron bar thrust right through it, causing the face to look very surprised, as well it might. A long glass case held miniature examples of every torture known to man, some quite new to me, and we walked slowly down it, wondering at human cruelty. Then there were the serial killers, although I don't believe that term was yet in use, but we certainly had them, if by some other title. George Smith, who drowned several unfortunate brides, presided over a bathtub which, we were told, was the actual one in which he had perpetrated his crimes, Dr Hawley Crippen was there and John Haig, who had met his chief victim in the Onslow Court Hotel, which I knew well since it was just down the street from where my grandmother used to live. Haig selected Mrs Durand-Deacon from among the diners in the restaurant and worked his way into her affections before he took her off to the country somewhere and plunged her into a vat of acid. Lucy and I stood, silenced by the sight of these drab and ordinary men who had caused such untold misery. Today these displays tend to have a comic, even camp, element to them which somehow protects one from the reality that what you are witnessing is true, that all these terrible things did happen, but then there was a counter-impetus, to make it as real as possible and the result was curiously haunting, even remembered now, after so long.

At last, in the very centre of the chamber we came upon a dingy curtain with an instruction not to pull it open without preparing well. I think it was forbidden to anyone under sixteen or something similarly enticing. It was the curtain that fascinated me. It was old, threadbare and dirty, like a curtain in a garden shed to hide the weedkillers from sight, and in a way this made it much more sinister than some self-advertising veil of scarlet satin. 'Shall we?' I said.

'You do it. I don't want to look.' Lucy turned away but did not, of course, move. People say things like this, not because they intend not to look but because they do not wish to take any responsibility for the horrors that will be revealed. It is a way of enjoying base pleasures while retaining their superiority.

I pulled back the curtain. The shock was immediate and stark. Even if it was not prompted by the young woman who was hanging from an iron hook that had penetrated her vitals and on which she was apparently writhing in vivid, screaming agony. This, I could handle. What almost made me cry out in pain was the sight of Damian holding Serena in a fierce embrace and quite obviously plunging his tongue so far into her mouth that she must have had trouble breathing. Although I cannot pretend that she looked, even to me, as if she were resisting his advances. Far from it. She clawed at his back, she ran her fingers through his hair, she squeezed her body against his, until she seemed to be attempting somehow to crush the pair of them into one single being. 'No wonder the curtain carried a warning,' said Lucy and they froze, then looked across at us. I desperately searched for a phrase that would contain my rage at Damian, my disappointment in Serena and my contempt for the new morality all at once. It was too ambitious. I might have been able to make up a combination word in German, but English has its limitations.

'You're busy,' I said. Which didn't exactly hit the mark I was aiming at.

They had broken apart by now and Serena was straightening herself up. Her body language told so clearly that she was longing to ask both of us, Lucy and me, not to say anything, but of course she felt the request would be demeaning. 'We won't say anything,' I said.

'I don't care if you do,' she replied with immense relief.

Damian, meanwhile, was carrying on with his usual *insouciance*. 'I'll see you later on.' He gave Serena a swift hug and wiped the lipstick off his mouth with a handkerchief, which he replaced in his pocket. Without a word to us he slipped through the curtain and was gone.

The sound of an O. C. Smith record, which was much in demand that summer, *Hickory Holler's Tramp*, suddenly filled the space, making an odd cultural contrast with all those severed heads and murderers and the luckless victim swinging on her hook, but the three of us still stood there. Until there was a noise and the unwelcome face of Andrew Summersby poked round the curtain. 'There you are,' he said, ignoring us, 'I've been looking everywhere.' He took in our grotesque, waxen companion. 'Ooh er.' He laughed. 'Someone's going to wake up with indigestion.' And he gave the figure a push, as if she were in a child's swing. The hideous thing moved slowly back and forth at the end of its rope.

'Let's dance,' said Lucy, and without another word to Serena we left her to the noble dullard, and made our way to a dark little dance floor in the shadow of a guillotine, on to which a French aristocrat in a jacket of cheap-looking wrinkled velveteen, was being strapped by two burly revolutionaries. From a draped alcove to one side the entire Royal Family of France looked on serenely.

'Are you all right?' To my bewilderment, Lucy appeared to be on the edge of tears. I couldn't imagine why.

She was irritated by the enquiry. 'Of course I am,' she said sharply, bobbing fiercely in time to the music for a bit. Then she looked up at me apologetically. 'Don't mind me,' she said. 'I had some bad news just as I was leaving home and it suddenly came back.' I looked suitably solicitous. 'An aunt of mine, my mother's sister. She's got cancer.' This was quite clever of her, I can see now. At the time I am writing of, the English had just about begun to move on from referring to cancer as 'a long illness bravely borne,' but there was still something dread in the word, still something, if not exactly shameful, at least to be avoided at all costs. In those days the diagnosis was generally considered a death sentence, and when one heard of people taking treatments one almost despised them for not being able to face the truth, although I suppose logic tells us some of them must have survived, mustn't they? Anyway, the point is it wasn't at all like today, when you really do have a reasonable shot, if not quite as reasonable in every case as non-medicos tend to assume. For Lucy to say the word at all was bound to distract me. Still, looking back, I admit I am slightly embarrassed that I completely believed her explanation.

'I am sorry,' I said. 'But there are all sorts of things they can do now.' One mouthed these clichés at the time, they were as routine as 'How do you do?' but one never thought they contained a grain of truth. She gave a routine nod and we danced on.

For some reason, an innocent one I am certain, Terry or more probably her mother had decided to cut a cake at the peak of the evening. This was not generally done. As I have observed, in those pre-don't-drink-and-drive days, we ate before we arrived and we did not generally eat again until the breakfast was served towards the end of the dance. There might occasionally be some sort of speech and a toast, although by no means always, at a mid point in the festivities, but this usually consisted of some old uncle just standing and saying what a marvellous girl so-and-so was, and we would all raise our glasses and that was that. There were dangers involved in this departure from the norm, but quite honestly, when there was no speech, which was usually the case, there were times when the proceedings fell a bit flat. We arrived, we drank, we danced, we went home and there had never been what my mother would refer to as 'A Moment' in the evening that really registered. The father of the deb in question would have the bitter knowledge that he had paid out thousands upon thousands for a night that no one would remember. On the other hand the danger of a speech and a toast is always that it may in some way feel rather naff. At least, when the occasion is not a wedding or something where speeches are generally expected. Anyway, on this particular evening, perhaps because neither Terry nor Verena was absolutely at ease with the rules, they decided to have cake and a toast, as if it had indeed been the wedding it was not.

I gather people wandering throughout the waxworks were summoned by a kind of tannoy, which would obviously have been installed in that building anyway for crowd control, but by then Lucy and I were back in the Hall of Kings, seated rather wearily at a table with Georgina Waddilove and Richard Tremayne, an unlikely couple if you like, overlooked by some of the duller members of the Hanoverian dynasty, one of whom was responsible for Richard's predecessor, the first Duke of Trent, in what I suspect must have been an uncharacteristic night of merriment. I have forgotten why Richard was with us, probably because he was tired and couldn't find anywhere else to sit. At all events Jeff Vitkov, who had come over from New York especially for the ball and was obviously determined to make his mark, took the microphone from the band singer and announced that he was going to propose a toast to his 'young and beautiful daughter, and her even younger and more beautiful mother.' This is the kind of thing that makes the English cringe, of course, and we were only just recovering when he added that we were all going to eat some genuine, American brownies, to mark the 'debut,' ugh, of a 'genuine, American girl.' Quite apart from the toe-curling sentimentality of all this, to most of us in those days 'Brownies' meant young Girl Guides, just as 'Cubs' meant young Boy Scouts, so there was a certain amount of hilarity released by the announcement that we were going to eat some, but we listened on as Jeff praised his daughter, Terry, who then seized the microphone for herself, paying tearful tribute to her wonderful 'Pop and Mom,' which made us freeze even more solidly in our chairs. Taking up a large knife, she sort of slid it through a mound of the brownies in question, and after that a mass of waitresses appeared, carrying decorated trays full of the little sticky brown cakes we now all know so well but didn't then. I hate chocolate and I remember so did Georgina, so, alone at our table, we didn't eat any, but they must have been good, because more or less everyone else did, and across the room I could see Damian absolutely piling in.

The events that followed a little while later seemed to start almost as a rumour, a sense of strangeness spreading through the gathering, before anyone was aware of the source. I recall that I was dancing with Minna Bunting, although our little walkout was over by that stage, and there was suddenly the sound of someone being violently sick. Which, then, was very startling. People on the dance floor began to look at each other, as there were more odd sounds, men and women started to scream with laughter, not ordinary amused laughter, but a shrill cackling like a witches' coven at work. In what seemed like no time at all we could hear shouting and singing and yelling and crying coming from every corner. I looked at my partner to share my puzzlement, but even she didn't look too clever. 'I feel incredibly ill,' she muttered and walked off the floor without another word. I hurried after her, but at the edge she suddenly clutched her head and ran off somewhere, presumably to a distant but welcoming cloakroom. Somehow the dancers themselves had maintained a kind of order, but once we had left them, the crowd filling the rest of the rooms and swirling around us felt slightly – or, before long, *very* – mad. One of the mothers rushed past me, with her bosom hanging out of her dress and I saw Annabella Warren, Andrew Summersby's sister, screaming and lying flat out, with her skirt hitched above her midriff, displaying some thoroughly unusual-looking underwear, possibly recycled by her nanny. Not far away a young man in the corner was in the process of pulling his shirt over his head. In the mêlée I had soon lost sight of Minna, but someone caught my arm.

'What the hell's going on?' Georgina was by my side, her impressive bulk providing me with something to shelter behind. A girl tripped and fell, spreadeagled at our feet, laughing.

'Come on, everybody! Clap your hands!' The voice, amplified by the microphone, was only too familiar. We turned and registered that the boy undressing was now revealed as none other than Master Baxter, who had shed the rest of his clothes, and was cavorting wildly round the stage in his underpants and looking in grave danger of losing even those.

By now the ballroom was bedlam. Some people must have escaped at the first signs of trouble, with that marvellous instinct that the British upper classes generally display in such a situation, but those who were not at the exits already were finding it increasingly hard to get to them. Suddenly I caught sight of Terry, in the midst of the demented crowd. Her hair had collapsed and a separate arrangement of ringlets had detached itself from her head and somehow got caught on a zip or hook fastener behind her neck, leaving a kind of mane to sweep down her back, making her look faintly feral as she attempted to claw her way through the ranks of her guests. I reached across a weeping man with his regurgitated dinner down his front and caught her wrist, pulling her through the crowd towards us. 'What is it? What's happening?'

'Somebody spiked the brownies. They were full of hash.'

'What?' Is it to be believed that the word was not immediately familiar to me? Or was it just the shock of discovery blocking my concentration?

'Hash. Marijuana. Dope.' Terry was altogether more at home with the topic, if angrier than Genghis Khan.

'Why? Who would do such a thing?'

'Someone who wanted to ruin my party and pretend to themselves it was a joke.' This was, I have no doubt, a completely accurate diagnosis. She was rich, she was good-looking, she was an outsider. That was more than enough to ensure enmity in several quarters, although this seemed an unusually unpleasant way of demonstrating it. Then again, the perpetrator may not have been aware of the level of mayhem that would ensue from their jolly prank. We were not all experts then.

'You seem OK.'

'I'm OK because I'm on a diet.' She said it snappily and it was almost funny, if we had not been in the middle of such desolation. At that moment a weeping Verena Vitkov claimed her daughter from the other side. Someone had trodden on her dress, and it had torn away from a seam at the waist, leaving not her legs but her roll-on exposed, which was of course much worse.

'Let's get out of here,' I said to Georgina and she nodded, but then two things happened. The first was that I could see Serena Gresham had climbed on to the stage with a dinner jacket, presumably Damian's, which she was trying to wrap round him despite his protests. She also had his trousers over her arm but obviously that task was a bridge too far and she didn't even attempt it. The second thing to catch at our attention was the sound of a police whistle, which echoed through the chamber like the shrill tolling of Doom. At once, what had already been chaos was transformed into a panicking stampede. It is easy now to think, almost calmly, of the notion of a drugs raid. In the forty years that have elapsed since these events, drugs themselves have ceased to seem extraordinary. Regrettable, I would hope, and something to be avoided for most of us even today, but no longer weird. In those days the vast majority of this crowd were strangers to the very notion. Whatever the impression that pop stars and Channel Four like to give of the Sixties, if their tales are true, which I often doubt, they were operating in a different world from my bunch. Obviously the bad boys among us were starting to experiment and by seven or eight years later a lot of us would have been introduced to the whole trendy culture of drugs and damn-it-all, but not by then. After all, most of what came to be called 'the Sixties' happened in the following decade. Yet here we were, debutantes and beaux, plus many of their mothers and fathers, in a full-scale drugs raid, which would provide, as we were only too aware, a perfectly wonderful story for the papers the following day. Out of family loyalty, if nothing else, all those nice, young sons and daughters of earls and viscounts, of high court judges and generals, of bankers and heads of corporations, had to get out of that room unseen and unapprehended, to stop their blameless daddies being soaked in the spray of public ridicule that was even then being loaded up, ready to flow. If the room had been on fire there couldn't have been a more urgent dash for the door.

I too would have headed in the same direction as the crowd, but Georgina held me back. 'It's hopeless,' she said. 'They'll be waiting for us on the pavement.'

'Where, then?'

'This way. There'll be a service exit for the group. And the maids must have been bringing the drinks up from somewhere.'

Together we pushed against the crowd. I glimpsed Candida Finch, green-faced and at the end of her tether, leaning against the opposite wall but she was too far away for me to help her. Some girls were dancing a sort of reel, accompanying themselves with alternating screams, in the middle of the floor between us. Then Candida was swept away and I didn't see her again. 'This is a nightmare.' Serena was nearly upon me when I realised who it was. She had an arm round Damian, who was still ranting and calling out to everyone to clap their hands. 'I'll clap *your* hands if you don't shut up,' she said, but it didn't seem to have much effect. Damian fell, and others surged over him, until I really began to wonder if he would be seriously injured. 'Help me get him up.' Serena was down among the lunging feet and I knew I had to do my best. Together we managed to hook our arms under his and literally drag him to the edge of the room.

'Why are you all right? Didn't you eat any either?'

Serena wrinkled her nose. 'I wasn't hungry.'

'Here we go!' The enterprising Georgina had found a service door at the back behind a curtain that a few people, but not many, were taking advantage of. Behind us, the whistles and general shouting had increased in volume, and it was clear that those who had tried to leave in a more orthodox manner were being subjected to hideous humiliations before they were allowed to do so.

'My God, the press is outside!' This from Lucy, who had started down the main stair, only to make this unwelcome discovery and beat a retreat whence she had come. 'If I get in the paper my father will kill me.' It's funny. We were so much more governed by these considerations than our equivalents are now.

Following our leader, Georgina, we came to a landing at the top of a stone, service staircase. Guests in various stages of dishevelment were hurrying down it. One girl broke her heel and fell the remainder of the second flight with a scream, but without pausing she scrambled up, tore the shoe off the other foot and plunged on. Unfortunately, Damian seemed to be getting worse. He had now ceased his requests for us to clap our hands and had decided instead simply to go to sleep. 'I'm perfectly all right,' he murmured, his chin sinking deeply into his chest. 'I just need a little shut-eye and then I'll be as right as rain.' Down went his chin even further, followed by his eyelids, and he began to snore.

'We'll have to leave him,' said Georgina. 'They won't kill him. He'll just have his name taken, and a warning or something of the kind, and that'll be the end of it.'

'I'm not leaving him,' said Serena. 'Who knows what they'll do? And what happens afterwards? If he has his name on a list at a drugs raid, he might never get a passport or a security rating or a job at an embassy or anything.' This string of words, flooding out as they did, created a rather marvellous contrast to the life we were leading at that precise moment, cowering on a dingy, back stairway, on the run from the police. It conjured up images of embassy gatherings at which Damian would shine, and foreign travel and important work in the City. I found myself wishing that Serena had voiced such fragrant worries about my destiny.

But Georgina was unconvinced. 'Don't be ridiculous,' she said. He's not newsworthy. That's the only thing we have to worry about. You're a headline. She's a headline. Even I'm worth a mention. He's not. Leave him here to sleep it off. Maybe they won't come up this far.'

'I'm not leaving him,' said Serena. 'You go without us if you want.'

I remembered her defence of Damian at Dagmar's ball, when she stood up for him alone and all the rest of us were silent. I decided I was not prepared for a repetition. 'I'll help,' I said. 'If we balance him between us we'll manage.' She looked at me. I could tell she was pretty grateful not to have been taken up on her suggestion of facing the Mongol hordes alone. So we did just as I said. Hoisting him up, and against a low chorus of Damian's mumbled protests about just needing a little shuteye, the group of us somehow got him to the bottom of the stair. We hurried past the ground floor, since we could hear the shouted protests of indignant adults being stopped and questioned, as well as screams and yells and singing coming from the young. Eventually we found ourselves in a basement, searching for a door or window that would open.

We were alone, a little club against the world, in a very murky passage, when a side door opened and a girl stuck her head out. 'There's a window here that seems to lead out to an alley,' she said and ducked back inside the room. I did not know her well. Her name was Charlotte Something and she ended up a countess, but I forget which one it was. Nevertheless, I shall always remember her with real gratitude. She had no obligation to come back and tell us of her useful find, instead of just climbing out and running for it. That kind of generosity, when there is nothing in it for the giver, is what always touches one most. Anyway, we followed her into what must have been a sort of cleaning cupboard because it was full of brushes and dusters and tins of polish, and sure enough there was an unbarred window, which had been forced open for what looked like the first time since the Armistice.

Here, as before, the problem was Damian, almost comatose by this point, and we wrestled with him for a bit until finally Georgina, who was stronger than any of us, bent down and threw her shoulder beneath him in a sort of fireman's lift and, with an exasperated sigh, flung him at the open space. Serena had already climbed out and was able to grab one arm and his head, and with her and Lucy pulling, while Georgina and I pushed, we did succeed in getting him through, although it was too much like assisting at the delivery of a baby elephant for my taste. There were men's voices in the passage outside, as Georgina squeezed out, and I would guess I was probably the last to make it to freedom by that route before it was sealed off by the enemy. We pulled down the window as quickly as we could, then raced to the end of the alley, Georgina and I dragging Damian between us. You will understand that to be pulling a largish young man, naked except for underpants and a dinner jacket, was unusual to say the least of it, and we could not consider ourselves out of danger until Serena, waving us into the shadows, had managed to stop an innocent taxi driver, who had no idea what he was letting himself in for.

'Where shall we take him?' she hissed over her shoulder and even I could see that this would be a large mouthful for the Claremonts to swallow on an empty stomach. I imagine he had originally planned to drive himself back to Cambridge, after a cup of coffee or two, as I blush to say we did in those days, but clearly that was now out of the question.

'My flat. Wetherby Gardens,' I said. My parents were there, but after nineteen years of me they were not entirely unequipped for this sort of escapade. Serena gave the address and, opening the door, she climbed in ready for Georgina and me to rush Damian across the pavement and into the welcoming darkness of the cab. We made it, clambering in with puffing and sighing, and Lucy hurried in behind us. It may sound as if the taxi was overloaded and so it was, but you must understand we thought nothing of that, neither passenger nor driver, and nor did the powers that be. They weren't concerned with micro-managing our lives, as they are today, and in this I think, indeed I know, that we were happier for it. Some changes have been improvements, on some the jury is still out, but when it comes to the constant, meddling intervention by the state, we were much, much better off then than we are now. Of course, there were times when we were at risk and the smug, would-be controllers will tut-tut at that, but to encourage the surrender of freedom in order to avoid danger is the hallmark of a tyranny and always a poor exchange.

'Should we put his trousers on?' Serena had somehow managed to keep the flapping items with her. We all looked down at Infant Damian curled up like an unborn child and the thought of the task defeated us.

'Let's not,' said Lucy firmly.

'What about your poor parents?' asked Georgina. 'Suppose they're still awake?'

Another glance confirmed the earlier decision. 'They're strong,' I said. 'They can take it.' With its distinctive rattle, the taxi started off, but as we came back out on to the Euston Road we could see that the police were still there with a host of cars and vans, and there was that now familiar, but then rare, accompaniment of the popping of cameras, blinding the poor wretches caught in their glare, all destined for unwelcome fame on the morrow.

My parents were philosophical, as they stood, blinking, in their dressing gowns, staring down at Damian slumped in a chair, still in his lively and distinctive costume, but now with his trousers deposited in a crumpled pool at his feet, like a ritual offering. 'He'll have to sleep on the floor in your room,' said my mother, without the possibility of any disagreement. 'I have a committee meeting in here at ten tomorrow morning, and there is *no* guarantee he'll be up and about by then.'

'No,' I said. And together we dragged Damian down the passage, depositing him on a folded eiderdown with some blankets on top.

'Where are the rest of his clothes?' asked my mother. I looked at her blankly. 'His shirt and so on.'

'At Madame Tussaud's, I suppose.'

'From where he had better not reclaim them.' Her voice was, I thought, unnecessarily severe. 'He could have got you all into a great deal of trouble.'

'That's rather unfair,' I said. 'It wasn't his fault.' But my mother paid no attention to my attempted defence. She was only displaying the behaviour that I have since discovered was absolutely endemic to her and to many like her. When they approve of someone in their children's lives, and when it is because of the social position of said individual, they will never admit it and will find endless excuses for no matter what bad behaviour. But when, instead, they *dis*approve, again for social rather than more meaningful reasons, rather than concede this, everything *else* about the unwanted friend must be condemned. This falls into the same category as when they give directions. If it is desirable that you should attend an event, it is 'easy-peasy, straight down the M4 and you're there,' but when they do not believe you should go, the same journey becomes 'quite endless. You trudge down the M4 forever and when you get off it there's an absolute maze of roads and villages to be negotiated. It's not worth it.' My mother was not a snob in any normal sense, she would have been shocked at the notion that she might be, but that didn't stop her being offended when she felt I had been 'latched on to' (her phrase), and this is what she felt about Damian. There was some truth in her analysis, of course.

Damian woke in the early hours of the following morning, I would guess at around three. I know this because he woke me, too, by whispering 'are you awake?' into my ear, until I was. He was completely sober. 'I'm starving,' he said. 'Is there anything to eat?'

'Couldn't it wait? You'll have breakfast in a minute.'

'I'm afraid it just can't. I can go and look for myself if you like.'

This seemed like a worse option, so I pulled myself to my feet, pulled on a dressing gown over my pyjamas, all of which garments date the incident, since, like almost every other male, I have abandoned traditional nightwear at some point during the subsequent decades, and I set off through the flat, with Damian following. With difficulty I persuaded him against a fry-up, and he settled for a bowl of cereal followed by some toast and tea. I joined him in the last, as we sat hunched over the tiny kitchen table. He started to laugh. 'What's so funny?'

'The whole evening. Lord only knows what they'll put in the papers.'

'Not us, which is the main thing. Poor Terry.' Nobody seemed to feel at all sorry for the ruin and waste inflicted on our hostess. I felt it was time someone did.

But Damian shook his head. 'Don't worry about her. She'll get a big story out of it. It'll probably be the defining moment of the Season before she's finished.'

'Perhaps it is.'

'Perhaps.' Looking back, that party did come to represent a moment for a lot of us, when the past, present and future fused together in some kind of crazy way. When the anti-authority, destabilising counterculture, which would win eventually (although not in the way we all then thought), swept in through the doors of our safe little, nearly-pre-1939 world and carried us off with it. Damian put another piece of plastic bread in the toaster. 'I don't know why I'm so hungry. Does hash make you hungry?'

'I'm not really the person to ask.'

He looked at me, hesitating and then deciding to speak. 'I'm afraid you got quite a shock when you pulled back that curtain.' I was silent, not exactly through indignation or a sense of being wronged. I just couldn't imagine what I could say that would convey the right message, because I didn't know what the right message might be. He nodded as if I'd spoken. 'I know you're keen on her.'

'Does she?' I couldn't help myself. Aren't we sad, sometimes? The odd thing was, and I remember this quite clearly, I wasn't sure what answer I wanted him to give.

Damian shrugged as he helped himself to butter. 'If I know, I dare say she does.'

'What about you?'

My question was oddly phrased and he looked up. 'What do you mean?'

Of course, the fact was I wanted to hit him. Right there, smack, in the middle of his face, with a great, heavy, wounding punch that would send him over backwards, with any luck cracking his head against the stove as he fell. I've often wondered what it must be like to live in a rougher world from the one I have always occupied, in a hit-now-ask-questions-later kind of society. One's always supposed to say how ghastly violence is, and of course it *is* ghastly, but there must be compensations. 'Are you serious about her?' I asked.

He laughed. 'Don't be so fucking pompous.'

'I just meant—'

'You meant you are so jealous your face hurts, and you're only assuming a poncy, pseudo-uncle pose so you can patronise me and put me down, and show me I'm a ridiculous interloper, out of my mind for daring to dream so far above my reach.' He put a bit more marmalade on to his toast and bit into it. Of course, I had to admit that every one of his words was documentary truth. If kicking him to death would have made Serena love me, I would have done it there and then. Biff, boff, bang. Instead, I opted for underhand fighting. 'I thought she was going out with Andrew Summersby now.' I was not without a trick or two of my own.

Damian looked up, sharply. 'Why do you think that?'

'He seemed very proprietorial when he came looking for her after you'd gone. Then they went off together.'

He gave a slightly annoyed grin. 'Andrew was at the dinner she had to go to and it is true that right now her parents think she's going out with him. Since Andrew seems to share this delusion, she couldn't be bothered to have it out with him tonight. No doubt, she soon will.'

I thought about this. It sounded to me as if Serena and Andrew were indeed an item, a thought that sickened me, and Damian was trying, for my benefit, to exaggerate his chances with her, when all he had managed was one kiss. We may have been more innocent then, but one kiss didn't mean much. 'Are you going to her dance?' I said.

'Can you ask? I'm staying at Gresham for it.'

I have never been a very confident person, although I do not really know why this is so. It is true that I was not good-looking when I was young, but I was quite clever and I seemed to get about. My parents loved me, I have no doubt of that, and I've always had a lot of friends. Nor were girlfriends an insuperable problem, if a few may have been on the lookout for something better. I even got on well with my sister before her marriage. Yet with all this, I was not confident and I had to admire Damian for that reason. No castle walls could apparently keep him out and I envied him for it. Even at that moment, when I wished him in chains, his feet encased in blocks of concrete, at the bottom of the sea. Even as I imagined his thick hair waving as the tides pushed it to and fro, fishes swimming across his staring, sightless eyes, in some way, *malgré moi*, I felt admiration. 'Has Lady Claremont invited you?'

'Not yet, but she will. Candida and Serena are sorting it out between them. Serena's going to tell her mother that Candida fancies me.' He looked at me as he said it. As an alibi this was perfectly sensible and Lady Claremont would believe it, since Candida fancied everything male that moved, but as well as this there was a meaning in his words which I could see he had not thought through properly before he spoke them. Their echo in the room annoyed him. Because his speech meant that if Lady Claremont had even a whiff of this man's interest in her daughter he would not be welcome in her house. 'It's OK,' he said in answer to my unspoken query. 'I understand that type. I know I can make her like me.' Obviously he did not understand Lady Claremont's type, nor that of her husband, nor that of any of their world, largely because those people were not then, and are not now, interested in being understood by the likes of Damian Baxter. As a matter of fact I think Lady Claremont might well have liked him under different circumstances. She might have enjoyed his humour and his self-belief, she might even have allowed him into their circle as one of those token Real World Members that such households go in for. But that is all.

TWELVE

I am not an Englishman who hates Los Angeles. I'm not like those actors and directors who insist that every day spent there is drudgery, that it's all so 'false' they cannot besmirch their souls for one more minute and that they shout with joy when the 'plane takes off from LAX. I suppose some of them may be telling the truth, but I would guess not many. More usually, they are just ashamed of their desire for the rewards that only Hollywood will bring, and they disparage the place and all its works in the hope that they will not lose caste among their soulful brethren back in Blighty. I had only been once before the trip in question, many years before, when I was seeking fame and fortune in a fairly disorientated way, but I have visited a few times recently and I always enjoy myself when I am there. It is a resolutely upbeat place and after a long unbroken stretch of British pessimism, it feels good sometimes to look on the sunny side of life. I know the natives take this to extremes. But still, there is something about the up, Up, UP!ness of it all that is a tonic to sad spirits and I am always pleased to be there.

In the forty years that separated my youthful friendship with Terry Vitkov and this, our re-encounter, she had enjoyed what is known as a chequered career. Even her time in London had not gone according to plan. She and her mother had done quite well, all things considered, but Terry had not ended up a viscountess presiding over twenty bedrooms in a house open to the public, which had unquestionably been the target, and they must have been disappointed. Looking back, I think the difficulty may have been that the Vitkovs as a group had made the common mistake of confusing a large salary with having money. A salary may enable you to live well while it's coming in, very well, but it does not alter the reality of your position and no one knows this better than the British upper class. Just as television fame, while it continues, feels like film stardom but seldom survives the cancellation of the series. Naturally, none of this would have mattered if a nice young man had fallen in love with Terry, but she was an abrasive personality, with her big features and her big teeth, loud in laughter, short on humour, and with a kind of unconcealed greed that was rather off-putting even to the worldly. In short she did not land her fish. There was a moment when she might have had an army major who was probably in line to get a baronetcy from an ageing uncle (although the latter was unmarried and these things are never certain), but the young officer took fright and fell back into the arms of a judge's daughter from Rutland. In some ways he might have been better off with Terry, as she would at least have filled the house with people who could talk, but how long would she have stood it, that life of rainy walks and discussing horses over plates of summer pudding, once the title had arrived? So, if the path the Major took was duller, it was also probably smoother for him in the long run.

I last saw her, I am fairly sure, around the time of the party in Estoril, but not because she was there. In fact, she was annoyed that she had failed to secure an invitation. If only I had been so lucky. She may already have been pregnant then, but if so, none of us knew it, only that she had a plain but eager American millionaire pursuing her, divorced but not too old, whom she subsequently married in time for the baby's birth. The millionaire's name was Greg Something and he had been working in Eastern Europe at the time. After leaving there they had returned together to sun-drenched California where he pursued a career with Merrill Lynch and we'd lost them. I never really knew him but I liked him and, judging by our few meetings, I would have said he was far better suited to her than any of her English beaux, and if I had given it a moment's thought, I would have hoped for many years of bliss before Abraham saw fit to part them. Unfortunately, or so the story goes, Terry, a decade further down the line, attempted to cash him in for a much richer banker from Connecticut, before the latter dumped her for a model and left her high and dry, her first husband having made his escape while the going was good and settled down in North Virginia with his second family.

So Terry and her daughter had stayed on in Los Angeles, where she pursued a career of some kind as a television presenter, dealing, or so I have been told, in something called the infomercial, where women chat about hair products and kitchen utensils and different types of luggage in a natural, unstudied way, as if it were remotely believable that they would do so were they not trying to sell you something.

I had rung from London, just to make sure she was still there, and she had been quite receptive to the idea we should catch up. I knew she was not one to be touched by charity, so I told her there was some interest in my latest book from a film studio and predictably that caught at her imagination. 'But that's wonderful!' she trilled. 'You must tell me all about it when we meet!' I had done a little homework and I suggested we might dine at a restaurant on the shore in Santa Monica the night after my arrival.

I knew her at once, when she came in and stood for a moment by the maître d's desk, as he pointed me out to her, and I waved. She started to make her way through the tables in that old no-nonsense way of hers. She was dressed as an American, East Coast, rich woman, which is a different costume from the jeans and chains favoured by workers in the Showbiz Industry, more Park Avenue than footballer's wife, which I found interesting. A neat, beige shirt-waister, a well-cut jacket over her shoulders, good, discreet jewellery. It was all less flashy and in better taste than I'd been expecting, but still unmistakably Terry. And yet, if I knew her, I also did not know her, this woman with the lacquered hair advancing towards me. I could see that the familiar chin was still too prominent, and the eyes and teeth too large, but other elements of her face had changed alarmingly. She appeared to have had her lips stuffed with some kind of plastic filler, in the way that American women often do now. As a practice it fascinates me, because I have yet to meet a man who doesn't profess to find it quite repulsive. I can only suppose that some of them must be lying or the surgeons wouldn't do such a roaring trade. Maybe American men like it more than European ones do.

Thankfully, if Terry's mouth had become bulbous and mildly unsettling, it was not yet actually disturbing. But it wasn't alone in betraying the telltale signs of tamper. Her forehead was so smooth she might have been dead, since no expression or mannerism seemed to make it move above the eyebrows, and the eyes themselves had become very fixed in their orbit. Of course, more or less all this stuff, carrying with it, as it must, horrible images of the pinning and stretching and sawing and sewing of bloody skin and bruised bone, has come about in my lifetime and I can't be alone in finding it an odd fashion to have developed alongside the supposed liberation of women. Cutting their faces about, presumably to please men, does not strike one as a convincing mark of equality. In fact, it feels uncomfortably insecure, a Western manifestation of female circumcision or facial disfigurement or some other dark and ancient method of asserting male ownership.

Plastic surgery is better now than forty years ago, when it was largely reserved for actresses and foreign ones at that. But even now, when the results can be spectacular, there is a high and ironic price to pay, because for most men it's a turnoff to end all. The knowledge that a woman has been sliced about diminishes to nothing one's desire to see her without her kit. Although here I admit that women pay less high a price than men. Women who have 'work done' lose their sexual power over men. Men who resort to it lose everything.

Terry had reached my table. 'My God! You look—' She hesitated. I think she had been planning to say '*exactly* the same!' but, having come nearer and actually seen me, it was obvious that my appearance had altered so completely that I should carry a passport to prove my identity to anyone who has not met me since the Sixties. '*Fantastic!*' she said instead, which did the work perfectly acceptably. I smiled. I had already got to my feet so I leaned over and kissed her on the cheek. 'Now, you *do* look fantastic,' I said and we sat, jovial and comfortable in our generous dishonesty.

A bland and pleasant-looking waiter stepped in briskly to tell us that his name was Gary and he very much hoped we were going to have an enjoyable evening, a hope I shared, even if I can never really see why it should matter much to the Garys of this world either way. He poured out two glasses of ice cubes, with a little water, and explained the specials, which all seemed to be frightening and hitherto unknown kinds of fish, and then, after promising to bring us some Chardonnay, he left us to our own devices. 'So, how is life in California?' This wasn't a very original opener, but I had by this stage of the Damian Mission, acquired the habit of going in gently, knowing that I would be investigating the paternity of their young before the night was out.

She gave a bright, generalised smile. 'Great!' she said, which was what I expected. I knew that with Californians this first act of any conversation is obligatory, where all decisions they have ever made are the right ones. Later, in some cases, the truth level may improve, but even for those rare individuals who long to unburden themselves of their pain they must still observe this ritual. Rather like having to eat the bread and butter before Nanny will give you cake.

'You never felt the need to go back to Cincinnati?'

She shook her head. 'It wasn't what I wanted. Not really. Greg's business was here.' She smiled and waved her hand towards the window. We could just hear the sounds of the sea under the restaurant hubbub. 'And there are no complaints about the weather.'

I nodded, mainly because one is always supposed to agree with this, but I can't be the only Englishman who finds those endlessly sunny days rather dull. I like our weather. I like the soft light of its grey days and the smell of the air after rain. Most of all I like the sudden changeability. 'If you're tired of the weather in England,' goes the old adage, 'just wait for five minutes.' I know it makes it hard to arrange outdoor events and no hostess with a brain would plan anything that was completely weather dependent, but even so . . . Anyway, I let it go.

Nice Gary had returned and poured out some wine, while we took a final glance at the menu. 'Is it possible to have the seafood salad but without the shrimp or the calamari?' Terry had begun the dismemberment of the official suggestions that is part of eating out with a West Coast resident. 'And what exactly is in the dressing?' Gary answered as best he could, but he did not achieve a sale. 'Is there chicken stock in the artichoke soup?' He thought not. But did he *know*? No, he wasn't completely sure. So he went to the kitchen and returned with the happy news that the stock was vegetarian friendly, but while he was away, Terry had moved on. 'Is there any flour in the tempura batter?' I looked at her. She smiled. 'I'm allergic to gluten.' It was something that obviously pleased her. Gary, of course, was used to this. He was probably a West Coast boy himself and had grown up in the certain knowledge that only people of low status order off the menu as it is printed. However, I think we were all coming to realise that Terry was approaching the moment when, even in Santa Monica, a decision might be required. 'I think I'll start with some asparagus, but no butter or dressing, just olive oil. Then scallops, but hold the mixed salad. I'll take hearts of lettuce, plain.' Gary managed to write all this down, relieved no doubt that his release was on the horizon. He turned to me. Too soon. 'Can I get some spinach?' Why do Americans say 'get' in this context? They are not presumably planning to go into the kitchen and fetch it themselves. 'Mashed but not creamed. Absolutely no cream.'

She turned to me, but I spoke first. 'You're allergic to dairy.'

She nodded happily. Meanwhile, Gary had noted every detail on his little pad. She still hadn't finished. 'Is the spinach cooked with salt?' With infinite and, I thought, admirable patience, Gary ventured that yes, the spinach was cooked with a little salt. Terry shook her head, as if it were hard to believe in this day and age, 'no salt when they cook it.' I could not imagine how, even under this provocation, Patient Gary kept his cool. He hoped that would be possible. 'It's possible,' said Terry. 'No salt.' By now I could see that even Gary, that laid-back boy from sunny California, was ready to sink his pencil deep into Terry's neck and stand by, watching, as the blood oozed out around its tip. But he nodded, not trusting himself to give a vocal response.

He turned to me and we exchanged eye contact, recognising our alliance in that strange way that one can befriend a total stranger who has been a co-witness to impossible behaviour. 'I'll have the artichoke soup, a steak, medium rare and a green salad.' He seemed almost bewildered that the process had been so speedy.

'That's it?'

'That's it.'

With the hint of a sigh, he was just moving away, when Terry spoke again. 'Is there mayonnaise in your coleslaw?'

Gary paused. When he spoke again his voice had acquired the super-softness of a doctor's when dealing with a potentially dangerous patient. 'Yes, madam,' he said. 'There is mayonnaise in our coleslaw.'

'Oh. Then forget it.' She dismissed him with a slight, insulting flick of her hand and picked up her glass for another drink.

In justice, having been a silent witness for so long, I felt the need to intervene. 'Terry.' She turned, surprised perhaps that I should have an opinion. 'There's always mayonnaise in coleslaw.'

Again that little shake of the head in wondering disbelief. 'Not in our house,' she said and Gary made his escape.

Obviously, what this little vignette had told me was that Terry's life in California was not *Great!* These bids to be different, this insistence on the power to change, to inflict absolute governance in the captive situation of a restaurant, are the recourse of those who feel no power to change anything elsewhere. Los Angeles is a town where status is all and status is only given to success. Dukes and millionaires and playboys by the dozen may arrive and be glad-handed for a time, but they are unwise if they choose to live there, because the town is, perhaps even creditably, committed to recognising only professional success, and nothing else, to be of lasting value. The burdensome obligation imposed on all its inhabitants is therefore to present themselves as successes, because otherwise they forfeit their right to respect in that environment. How's the family? Great! The new job? Best decision I ever made! The house? Terrific! All this, when the man in question is bankrupt, facing repossession, his children are on drugs and he is teetering on the brink of a divorce. There is no place in that town for the 'interesting failure,' or for anyone who is not determined on a life that will be shaped in an upward-heading curve.

'So, what happened to Greg? I heard you split up.'

This seemed to buck her up. 'They talk about me, then? Over there?'

'Oh, yes,' I said, although it had in fact been thirty years since anyone I knew had mentioned her name – before Damian, that is.

'I guess they still remember my party.'

They didn't, but even I could see they might have. 'Did you ever find out who did it?'

'Not until a long time later. Then someone said it was that guy who married Lucy Somebody. Your friend. He knew the girl who was making the brownies and he mixed it in when she wasn't looking. That was her story, anyway.'

Philip Rawnsley-Price. Much good did it do him.

She was back on track. 'Greg's OK. I don't really see him now.' She shrugged and poured another glass. We were nearly through the bottle and the first course hadn't arrived. I wondered if she'd like to change to red. She would. My old pal Gary arrived with some food and scuttled away to fetch more wine before Terry could question him about the contents of her plate. She moved some items around disdainfully with her fork. 'Jesus, I hope they don't use cornflour on these.'

'Why would they?'

'Sometimes they do. The next morning I look like a racoon.' How tiring it must be to live in an atmosphere of permanent danger. She started to eat with a certain amount of gusto, despite the risks. 'Greg's done pretty well, actually. He saw what was coming with the whole silicone thing and left Merrill Lynch to get into it. He understood the potential before most people did. Really. I should have stayed with him.' She laughed wryly with, I detected, a certain amount of real feeling.

'Why didn't you?' I was curious to know if she would tell me about the flighty millionaire who had tempted her from her vows.

'Oh, you know.' She gave me an inclusively immoral grin. 'I met a guy.'

'And what happened?'

Terry shrugged. 'It didn't work out.' She shook her hair back with a soft, mirthless laugh. 'Lordie, lordie, was I lucky to be rid of *him*!'

'Were you?'

The glance I received in answer to this told me that she was, in fact, very *un*lucky to have been rid of the man in question and that in all probability he represented the Big Plan which would never now reach fruition. 'Let's not talk about him.'

Of course, I probably shouldn't have probed this bit of her story. It was, after all, the failed part and therefore anti-Californian. I wondered how often she had regretted leaving Greg, now clearly as rich as Croesus. 'How's your daughter?'

'Susie?' She seemed quite interested that I had this information. 'You remember Susie?'

'Well, I remember you got married and had a baby straight away. And all much sooner than most of the rest of us.'

She was drunk enough by this time to grimace at the memory. 'Damn right she was born straight away. Boy, I took a gamble there and, I may tell you, I very nearly lost.' This was rather intriguing, so I said nothing and hoped for more. Which I got. 'Greg was a big mixture back then. His growing up was completely Troy Donahue and Sandra

Dee, going to the prom, dancing to the Beach Boys, you know the kind of thing.'

'I do.' In fact, the Americanism of my youth was powerfully evocative of a cleaner, more innocent world, when in Hollywood movies the whole world wanted to be American and the big issue, not only for Greg but for everyone, was who wore your pin. Yes, it was blinkered, but it was also charming in its fathomless self-belief.

Terry continued, 'His parents were religious, very Midwest, and that was their existence. But Greg was also a Sixties boy, talking the talk, walking the walk. Smoking the dope. You know how it was.' Of course I knew how it was. A whole generation waiting to see which side of the wall the world was going to jump. And half at least of them pretending that things were no longer important to them, when of course they were. 'Anyway, he kept saying he was too young to settle down and couldn't we just have fun . . .'

And couldn't you?'

Her eye narrowed for a moment. 'I needed a life. I needed to move on.' The alcohol was making her honest. 'I needed money.'

'Your father had money.'

'My father had a salary.' The distinction, as we know, was not lost on me. 'And I liked Greg. I thought we'd be happy. And I knew he'd never let his parents find out he had an illegitimate child.' She paused.

'That was the gamble.'

'As I said. We'd been living together for a few months, which was, if you remember, pretty wild at the time. Then Greg's bank posted him to Poland and he asked me to go with him. So I did. And he still couldn't make up his mind. So I got pregnant.'

'While you were there?'

'Sure. We married and she was born out there. In Warsaw.'

'How romantic.'

'It wasn't as romantic then as it might be now. Believe me.' I did.

'What did your parents think about it?'

'They were glad. They liked Greg.' She thought for a moment. 'They split up, you know.'

'No, I didn't know. I'm sorry.'

'It worked out. They're both fine. Mom got married again.'

'Give her my love.' She nodded. 'What happened to your father? Did he marry?'

She shook her head. 'Not yet. He's decided he's gay. Of course, he could still marry, I guess. These days. But he hasn't.'

'Is he happy?'

'I'm not sure. He hasn't got anyone . . . special. But then he hasn't got my mom yelling at him either.'

We both smiled at our joint recollection of the formidable Verena. But I was struck, for the millionth time, by the personal convolutions required by our new century. Would it have occurred to Jeff Vitkov, nice, boring, old Jeff, the brilliant entrepreneur and family man, to question his sexuality when he had got well into his fifties, in any other period but our own? If he had been born even twenty years earlier, he would just have taken up golf, seen a bit more of the chaps at the club and not given the matter another thought. Would he have been any worse off? I doubt it. Although this is not a topic that supports nostalgia. Even if I am not a fan of change for change's sake, nor indeed of most change if it comes to that, I am fairly sure that in the end we will all be better off for living in a world where any kind of sexuality is compatible with the twin notions of decency and commitment. But I suppose I just wish the whole subject could drop into the background again where it used to be, and not be compulsorily worn around society's neck day in, day out.

I didn't see I could contribute much on the subject of Jeff and his trials, so I just smiled. 'Anyway, you're all right. That's the main thing.'

'Yeah,' she also smiled, but hers stopped short of her eyes. 'Donnie's OK.' Donnie was obviously the new husband. I wasn't sure that 'OK' quite sold him with any strength of purpose, but I suppose they'd been together for a few years by then.

'Does he get on with Susie?' I was naturally much more interested in getting back to my quarry.

'Yuh.' She shrugged. 'I mean, Susie's a grown woman now. But yes, they get on, I guess.'

'I guess' ranked somewhere alongside 'OK' when it came to degrees of ecstatic joy. Try as I might, I couldn't read this as a household drenched in sunbeams. 'What does she do?'

'She's a producer.'

Of course, in Los Angeles this doesn't mean much more than 'she's a member of the human race.' Later, after this visit, when Damian's mission had resulted, perhaps ironically, in my opening up an American career for myself, I would be much more familiar with the ways of the city, but I was an innocent then. 'How exciting,' I said. 'What's she produced?' As I have observed, if I had known more I would not have asked this question.

Terry smiled even more brightly. 'She's got a lot of very interesting projects. She's working on something for Warner's right now.' She nodded as if this brought the subject to a close, which of course it did.

'Is she married?'

'Divorced. And fucked up with it.' The remark had slipped out, loudly, and now she regretted it. 'To be honest, we don't see a lot of each other. You know how it is. She's busy.' She shrugged. I can't imagine that she thought she was concealing her pain, but maybe she did.

'Of course.' I know I am sounding increasingly feeble in my report of this interchange, but Terry's volume was rising and I was becoming uncomfortably aware that the people on both sides of our table were pretending to talk and had in fact tuned into our conversation.

Gary the Wary now returned to our table, bringing huge, Californian, mounded platefuls, draining my appetite away, and Terry ordered another bottle. 'Do you see anyone now?' she muttered between sips. 'Anyone from the old crowd?' I was not convinced that Terry had ever really been in our old 'crowd,' if crowd there had been, but it seemed a good moment to bring up the subject of Damian, so I did. For once, Terry was genuinely interested in what I was saying. 'How is he?' I explained and I could see that even her flinty heart had been mildly touched. 'I'm sorry to hear that.' But then her mind flew away from sticky sentiment and back to its natural climes. 'He made a lot of money.'

'He did.'

'Would you have guessed he would? Then?'

I thought for a moment. 'I was always pretty sure he was going to do well.'

'Even though you hated him?'

So she had remembered quite a bit about the old days. 'I didn't hate him all the way through. Not at the beginning.' She acknowledged this. I thought we might as well get on with the matter on hand. 'You had a thing with him, didn't you?'

The question made her sit up with an amused snort at its impertinence, although I am not convinced one can be impertinent to someone like Terry. 'I had a "thing" with a lot of people,' she said. This was, of course, quite true, unusually true for the era we'd lived through, and came better from her than from me. She accompanied the sentence with a sideways glance, as well she might, since one of those no doubt fortunate people who had enjoyed a 'thing' with her was me. It had only been a one-night 'thing' but it happened. Sensing my moment of recall, Terry raised her glass in a toast. 'To good times,' she said with an unnerving, secret smile making me even more aware of that curious, semi-detached sensation, when you are talking to a person you once slept with, but the incident is so far away from your present life that it feels as if you are discussing completely different people. Still, as I say, it did happen.

I was staying at a house in Shropshire and the couple I had been billeted on were in the middle of a furious, poisonous row when I arrived. I'd been sent there for the ball of that same Minna Bunting with whom I had enjoyed my momentary and entirely virtuous walkout. Our time together was over and, since there was nothing to 'forget,' we had remained friends. Strange as it may seem, this was completely possible in those days. In 1968, to introduce someone as a 'my girlfriend' did not automatically translate as 'my mistress' in the way it does today. Indeed now, if she were *not* your mistress you would feel you were implying a lie. But not then. Anyway, I had received the usual postcard – 'We would be so pleased if you would stay with us for Minna's dance' – and I found myself parking outside a large, pleasant, stone rectory, which I think I remember was somewhere near Ludlow. The card had told me my hostess was a 'Mrs Peter Mainwaring' and she had signed herself 'Billie,' so I had all the information I needed as I climbed out of the car. That said, those names that are not generally pronounced as they are written can pose a problem. Would she be posh and call herself 'Mannering' or not posh and say it as it was spelled? I decided that, rather as it is better to be overdressed than under, I would go for

Mannering. As it transpired I needn't have worried, since she clearly couldn't have cared less what I called her. 'Yes?' she said, glaring at me, as she wrenched open the door. Her face was red with rage and the veins were standing out on her neck.

'I think I'm staying with you for the Buntings' dance,' I muttered.

For a moment I thought she was going to hit me. 'Oh, *for Christ's sake!*' she snarled and turned back into the hall. I confess that even now, older and wiser as I hope I am, I always find this kind of situation pretty trying, because one is hamstrung by being a stranger who cannot respond in kind. In those days, young as I was, I found it impossible. I remember wondering whether it would be more polite and, in truth, better all round, just to get straight back into the car and drive to a local hotel and arrive at the dance from there. Or would that make matters even worse? But Mrs Peter Mainwaring, aka Billie, had not finished with me. 'What are you waiting for? Come in!'

I picked up my suitcase and stumbled forward into a large and light hall. It was a brilliant, sunflower yellow, which seemed at variance with the cloudy scene being played out in it. The paintwork was white and a really lovely portrait of a mother and child by Reynolds hung against the back wall. A tall man, presumably Mr Peter Mainwaring, was standing halfway up the wide staircase. 'Who is it?' he shouted.

'It's another one of the Buntings' fucking guests. How many did you tell them? This isn't a fucking hotel!'

'Oh, shut up! And show him to his room.'

'You show him to his fucking room!' I was beginning to wonder if she had any other adjective at her command.

Throughout this unloving exchange, I may say, I stood there in the centre of the pretty hall quite still, motionless in fact, frozen with nervous terror, like a cigar store Indian. Then I had the bright idea that I should try to act as a soothing agent. 'I'm sure I can find my own way,' I said. This might be categorised as a mistake.

She turned on me like a ravening beast. 'Don't be so fucking stupid!' I could see that Billie's irritation at my arrival was now developing into an active dislike. 'How can you find your own way when you don't know the fucking house!'

At this point, and were I older and more confident, I would probably have told her to keep her anger to herself, basically, to employ her own language, to fuck off, and left. But part of youth is somehow to assume blame, to think that every problem must be in some way down to you, and I was no different. I'm sure most of the young of the late 1930s thought the Second World War was their fault. Anyway, as I stood there, blushing and stuttering while our hosts snarled at each other, by some heavenly miracle Terry Vitkov appeared on the landing above Peter Mainwaring and waved to me. I cannot think of a time when I was ever more pleased to see anybody. 'Terry!' I shouted, as if I had been in love with her since I was fourteen, and hurried up the stairs, past my angry hostess, past my host, to reach her. 'I'll show him where he's sleeping. It's next to mine. Right?' And before they could do much more than nod I had been rescued.

Terry and I became a unit of mutual support through the hours that followed. Apparently the husband, Peter, had bought a house, or a villa, somewhere in France without telling his wife, and Billie had heard the news for the first time about twenty minutes before Terry had got there. She'd come by train, I can't remember now why I didn't give her a lift. Maybe I was driving from somewhere else. The point was she arrived about an hour before me. In that time the fight had apparently escalated from quite a slow-burning start, until Billie was standing in the hall, screaming names that would be shocking even today and threatening a divorce that would cost him 'every fucking [naturally] penny he owned.' I never completely got to the bottom of quite why his crime was so terrible. I wonder now if there wasn't someone else involved. Either that, or Billie had made plans for the money that had been subverted by the very act of purchase.

My room was pleasant enough and much as I had come to expect during these sojourns with unknown hosts in the lesser houses of England: The pretty paper, with a faint, pseudo-Victorian pattern, the interlined curtains in not-quite-Colefax, and some flower prints framed in gilt with *eau de Nil* mounts. I had my own bathroom, which was by no means standard in those days; better still it did not boast too many earwigs and woodlice, and there was a perfectly decent bed. But no amount of comfort could offset the surreal quality of the shouting that continued below, amplified no doubt by the fact that they were once more alone and free to tear out each other's throats without interruption.

There were two more arrivals. The first was a boy called Sam Hoare, whom I recall better than I might normally have done because he was going to be an actor, a really extraordinary ambition at the time. In my social group, at least, wanting to go on the stage seemed not so much doomed to failure as requiring treatment. He was a tall, good-looking fellow and ended up, I think I'm right in saying, as quite a big wheel in television production, so in a way he was right to persevere, however annoying it was for his parents. The last guest, who was staying in the house and not just coming for dinner, was a nice girl called Carina Fox, whom I always liked without ever knowing especially well. We heard the dogs barking and some talk in the hall and, as Terry had done earlier with me, we sneaked along the gallery to the top of the staircase and rescued them. The Mainwarings transferred the pair into our custody without a backward look. Not for Peter and Billie any worry about whether their guests were tired after the journey and needed some tea. As we know, these incidents are very bonding. The four of us sat in my bedroom, comparing notes and wondering how we were going to get through the evening ahead, until in some way we felt we were all friends, and not at all the semi-strangers we might have been in more normal circumstances.

Dinner started moderately well. They had, after all, had some time to simmer down, and there were two outside, local couples, nearer our hosts in age, who had been invited to join the party, so, after an uneventful glass of champagne in the garden, the ten of us sat down at about a quarter to nine that night and at first made small talk as if none of the earlier episode had taken place. Indeed, I'm sure the newcomers, an army general with a nice wife and a nearby landowning couple, had no idea that their dear friends, Peter and Billie, had been playing out a touring version of *Who's Afraid of Virginia Woolf* until just before they broke up to have their baths. The dining room was quite handsome, with excellent china and glass on the table and again, surprisingly good pictures. I would guess that Peter came from a family that had lost its estates but held on to a lot of the kit, which was quite common then. Or now, really. But I'm not sure there was limitless money left and I imagine Billie had cooked the food. In ungrand, rectory-type houses, even where the owners belonged to what used to be called the Gentry, there wasn't nearly as much pulling in of temporary catering staff in the Sixties as there is today and most hostesses felt compelled, perhaps by some lingering war ethic, to do the work themselves. I have said before that the food was seldom much good and would often depend on ghastly magazine-printed receipts, as women then would cut these out and paste them into kitchen scrapbooks, printed especially for the purpose. The cooking done, it was quite normal to ask a couple of local women to come in and help serve it and wash up and so on, which was exactly what had been arranged on this particular night. We'd got through the first course easily enough, the obligatory salmon mousse that appeared in those days on almost every dinner table with taste-numbing regularity. It was followed by some sort of escalope in a glutinous sauce, covered in sprinklings of this and that, and with carrots cut into terrifying rosettes, which again we survived. But before the pudding made its appearance came the first rumblings of trouble. I was about halfway down the table, in my usual, junior position, when I saw the soldier's wife, Lady Gregson, turn to Sam Hoare who was sitting on her right, as the maid removed her empty plate. 'Wasn't that delicious?' she said, which could hardly be considered contentious.

Sam opened his mouth to agree, but before he could do so his host, on Lady Gregson's other side, cut in, 'It was more delicious than it was original, but that's not saying much.'

'*What?*' Billie Mainwaring's voice sliced through the atmosphere, silencing most of the rest of us, even those who didn't know what was going on.

Lady Gregson, who was a nice woman but not an exceptionally clever one, now took the measure of the situation and spoke before Peter could answer. 'We were just saying how much we enjoyed the last course.'

But Peter had been tucking into his excellent claret for quite a while by this time and clearly some sort of dam within him had at last given way. 'Yes,' he said. 'I always enjoy it. Every time you produce it. Which is more or less every time anyone is unlucky enough to dine in this house.' At which moment, with slightly unfortunate timing, one of the maids arrived at Lady Gregson's left, which placed her next to Peter's chair. She was holding a platter of what looked like white cheesecake. 'Oh God, darling.' He rolled his eyes. 'Not this again.'

'I *love* cheesecake.' Lady Gregson's tone was now becoming harder, as if she, sensing a whiff of rebellion, were determined to impose order on the gathering whether we liked it or not. She was the kind of woman who would have been very useful at Lucknow.

'What about the strawberries?' Peter was now staring straight at his wife.

'We're having cheesecake.' Billie's voice had all the animation of the Speaking Clock. 'I didn't think we'd want the strawberries.'

'But I bought them for tonight.'

'Very well.' There was a quality of tension in the air that reminded me of one of those films, so popular in that era, about the threat of nuclear war, a universal obsession of the time. The Big Scene was always centred on whether or not the President of Somewhere was going to press the button and start it. Having let the moment resonate, Billie spoke again: 'Mrs Carter, please fetch the strawberries.'

The poor woman didn't know what to make of this. She looked at her employer as if she couldn't be serious. 'But they're—'

Billie cut her off with a raised palm, nodding her head like a fatal signal from a Roman emperor. 'Just bring the strawberries, please, Mrs Carter.'

Of course, there are times when this sort of thing comes as a relief. As most of us know, there is nothing that will cheer a dreary dinner party more than a quarrel between a husband and wife. But this incident seemed to have acquired an intensity that made it slightly inappropriate as guest-pleasing fare. It was all too raw and real. At least we did not have long to wait for the next act. In the interim the rest of the company had taken the disputed cheesecake, but nobody had begun to eat. I saw Sam give a quick wink to Carina and, on my left, Terry's chair was beginning to shake with smothered giggles. Apart from these slight diversions we just sat there, divining that, in the words of the comic routine, we ain't seen nothing yet. Mrs Carter reentered the room and went to Lady Gregson's side with a bowl of strawberries, but as she began to help herself it was absolutely clear to everyone present that the fruit was completely frozen, like steel bullets, and had just been removed from the freezer. The wretched woman dug in the spoon and put them on to her plate, where they fell with a metallic noise like large ball bearings. Mrs Carter moved to Peter, who carefully spooned out a big, rattling helping. Clatter, clatter, clatter, they sounded as he heaped them on to his plate. On went Mrs Carter to the next guest and the next, no one was passed by, no one dared refuse, so the hard, little marbles fell noisily on to every plate in the room. Even mine, although I cannot now think why we didn't just refuse them, as one might refuse anything in the normal way of things. With a puzzled look Mrs Carter retired to the kitchen and then began the business of eating these granite chips. By this time you may be sure there was no conversation in the room, nor anything remotely approaching it. Just ten people trying to eat small round pieces of stone. At one stage the General seemed to get one lodged in his windpipe and threw his head up sharply, like a tethered beast, and no sooner were we past this hazard than the land-owner's wife, Mrs Towneley, bit down with a fearsome crack and reached for her mouth with a cry that she'd broken a tooth. Even this did not elicit a Governor's Pardon from our hosts. Still we crunched on, particularly Peter who bit and chewed and sucked and smiled, as if it were the most delicious confection imaginable. 'You seem to be enjoying them,' said Lady Gregson, whose destiny that night was to make everything worse, just when she sought to do the opposite.

'It's such a treat to eat something unusual,' said Peter. 'At any rate in this house.' He spoke loudly and clearly into the silent crunching room. Inevitably, all eyes turned to his wife.

For a moment I thought she wasn't going to respond. But she did. 'You fucking bastard,' said Billie, reverting to her standard vocabulary when enraged, although actually this time she spoke quite softly and the words were rather effective despite their lack of originality. Next, she stood and, leaning forward, picked up the bowl holding the remain-der of the icy inedibles. With a gesture like throwing a bucket of water on to a fire, she flung what was left of the frozen fruit at Peter, in the process spraying the rest of us, as well as the table and the floor, with sharp, bouncing, painful little missiles. She finished by lobbing the bowl at him which missed since he ducked and shattered against an attractive George IV wine cooler in the corner. In the pause that followed you could hear only breathing.

'Shall we get our coats?' said Lady Gregson brightly. 'How many cars are we taking to the dance?' In a commendable effort to bring matters to a conclusion she stood, pushed back her chair, stepped on a frozen strawberry and fell completely flat, cracking her head on the edge of the table as she went down, and with her evening frock riding up to show a rather grubby petticoat and a ladder in her right stocking, although that might have been a product of the moment. She lay totally motionless, stretched out on the floor, and for a second I wondered if she were dead. I suspect the others did too, since nobody moved or spoke, and for a time we were enveloped in a positively prehistoric silence. Then a low groan ameliorated this worry at least.

'I don't think we *all* need to drive, do you, darling?' said Peter, also standing, and the dinner party was at an end.

All of which goes to explain why I ended up in bed with Terry that night. We stayed together when we finally got to the dance, as it felt odd not to be with someone who had witnessed the previous events of the evening. Sam Hoare and Carina seemed to be similarly motivated and were soon dancing. In fact, they began a romance that was to take them through marriage, three children and a famously unpleasant divorce, when Sam ran off with the daughter of an Italian car manufacturer in 1985. At any rate, from our house party that only left Terry for me and I wasn't sorry. From then, somehow, as the night progressed it all seemed to become inevitable, in the way these things can and do. We jigged away while the music was brisk, but when the lights lowered at around one in the morning, and the DJ put on *Honey*, a sickeningly sentimental hit of the day, one of those ballads about dead loved ones, we moved into each other's arms without a question and began the slow, rhythmic clinch that passed for dancing in the last phase of these events.

In a way those mordant, melodic dirges were one of the hallmarks of the period, although the fashion for them has entirely faded long before now. It was an odd phenomenon, when you think of it, songs about husbands, wives, girlfriends, boyfriends, all being killed in car crashes and train smashes, by cancer and, above all, on motorbikes, the last scenario combining several pet crazes of the time. I suppose there must have been something in their facile, tear-soaked emotionalism that chimed with our largely false sense of trailblazing and 'release.' They ranged from the tuneful and robust *Tell Laura I Love Her* to those like *Terry* or *Teenangel* and, while we're on the subject, *Honey*, which were soppy beyond endurance, but the stand-out example, the exception that proved the rule, a song which, like the more recent *Dancing*

Queen, must have been performed in more bathrooms than any other hit of the day, was definitely *The Leader of the Pack* by the Shangri Las. There is a verse in it, which has always fascinated me: 'One day my Dad said "find someone new"/ I had to tell my Jimmie we're through/ He stood there and he asked me why/ All I could do was cry/ I'm sorry I hurt you, the Leader of the Pack.' No prize for guessing who's in charge here: Dad. This tough leather biker boy with his shining wheels, this girl in the grip of passion, both know better than to argue when Dad puts his foot down. 'Find someone new! *Now!*' 'OK, Dad. Whatever you say.' What would the lyric be changed to were it rerecorded today? 'I had to tell my Dad to get stuffed'? I cannot think of another vignette that tells of the collapse of our family structure and our discipline as a society more economically yet more vividly. No wonder so much of the world laughs at us.

At any rate on that evening the sad refrain did its work, and by the time Terry and I were helping ourselves to breakfast in the large marquee, rather imaginatively decorated with farming tools and sheaves of corn, we both knew where we were headed and I was glad of it. As most of us can remember, there is something sweet, during the early, hunting years particularly, in the knowledge that one's next amorous partner has been located and is willing.

I drove us back to the Mainwarings' house in my car, drunk as I was, with Terry nudging me to keep my mind on the business, and we let ourselves in through the unlocked front door as we had been directed. How would such arrangements work in these more fearful days? The answer, I suppose, is that they wouldn't. Then we climbed the stairs, attempting to make as little noise as possible. I do not think we even hesitated for form's sake as we approached our separate chambers. I am pretty sure that I just followed Terry into her bedroom without either explanation or permission, closed the door gently and began.

Of course, one of the problems of being male, which I suspect has never changed nor will it, is that young men tend to operate on an Exocet-type imperative to seek bed larks no matter what. This was perhaps especially true in those days, when a great many of our female contemporaries were having no such thing, with the result that the moment there was a possibility of scoring, the faintest breach in the wall of virtue, one simply went for it without pausing to consider whether this was something one really wanted to do. Unfortunately, that realisation, that questioning of purpose, sometimes came later. Usually, when you were already in bed and it was far too late to back out. My generation was not, including the men (whatever the ageing trendies like to imply), nearly as promiscuous as those who came after us, even before we reached the complete sexual mayhem of today. But it was beginning. The male in his early twenties who was still a virgin, a comparatively normal type for my father's generation, had become strange to us and the goal of achieving as many conquests as we could was fairly standard. And so from time to time, inevitably, any man would find himself in bed with a woman who might be termed unlikely.

Usually when this happened he would just bang on, and the dazed query, *What was I thinking of?* did not surface in the front of his brain until the following morning. But inevitably there were occasions when a Damascene moment would suddenly strike mid-action. The scales would fall from your eyes and the whole event would be rendered completely and indefensibly *insane* as you lay there, naked, with another, unwanted, body in your arms. So it was that night with me and Terry Vitkov. The truth was I was not in the least attracted to her; I didn't even like her all that much in the normal way of things, and without the Mainwarings' battles and the near hysteria of the evening we had lived through I would never have been in this position. If events had not created a sense of artificial closeness in our hearts I would have gone to sleep, happily alone. But now that I was in bed with her, now that I could smell the faintly acrid scent of her body and feel her wiry hair and spongy waist, and handle the rather pendulous breasts, I knew with an awful clarity that I wanted to be anywhere but there. I rolled back on to the pillow, heaving my body off hers as I did so.

'What's the matter?' said Terry in her now grating voice.

'Nothing,' I said.

'There'd better *not* be.'

Which, naturally, sealed my fate. I had a momentary vision of becoming a funny story, a fake who couldn't deliver, a joke to be sniggered over with the other girls as they wiggled their little fingers derisively, all of which I knew Terry was perfectly capable of delivering. 'Everything's fine,' I said. 'Come here.' And with as much resolution as I could muster on the instant I did my duty.

The dinner was not going particularly well. Gary had almost given up on us and Terry was, by this stage, airborne. We were staring at the menus for pudding and when Terry started to heckle over the ingredients of some sort of strudel it was clear from Gary's expression that we had reached the city limits. 'I'll just have a cup of coffee,' I said in a feeble attempt to push Terry forward to the next part of the evening. Inevitably, this gave her ideas.

'Come to my place for coffee. You wanna see where I live, don't you?' Her drawl was beginning to stretch out to positively Southern proportions. Inexplicably, really, since I knew she came from the Midwest. It reminded me of Dorothy Parker's description of her mother-in-law as the only woman who could get three syllables out of 'egg.'

'Shall I bring the check?' volunteered Gary eagerly, seizing at the chance of ridding himself of this potential troublemaker before the real storm broke. Not many minutes later we were standing in the car park.

Here we faced a dilemma. I had drunk little, knowing I would be driving back, but Terry had sunk the best part of three bottles. 'Let me drive you,' I suggested. 'You can send someone for your car in the morning.'

'Don't be so boring.' She laughed as if we were engaged on a teenage prank, as opposed to committing an offence that might very possibly include manslaughter. 'Follow me!' We then began one of the most hair-raising experiences of my entire life, shooting first up towards Beverly Hills, then skidding round the wide curves of the LA mountain roads, until we had somehow – don't ask me how – reached Mulholland Drive, that wide ridge, the spine that divides Los Angeles proper from the San Fernando Valley. There is a thriller, *A Portrait in Black*, a Lana Turner vehicle I think, which involves a woman who cannot drive being told nevertheless to get behind the wheel and follow her lover, i.e. the murderer, in a car. She weaves about and is almost undone when it starts to rain, since she has no idea how to work the windscreen wipers. From side to side she veers wildly, up, down, all over the place, weeping hysterical tears (or is that from *The Bad and the Beautiful*?). Anyway, this was more or less my experience the night Terry Vitkov took me home. Except that in my version I was following the crazy woman who was out of control of the vehicle, instead of her following me. I do not even now know how we arrived alive.

The house, when we got there, was perhaps a little more modest than I had been expecting, although it wasn't too bad. A large open hall, a bar that was pretending to be a library on the left and a big 'living room' that was glass on all three sides to make the most of the sensational view of the city below, a million lights of every colour, a giant's jewel box, twinkling below us. It felt as if we were coming in to land. But the rooms had a cheap and dingy feel, with dirty shagpile carpets and long sofas covered in oatmeal weave, going slightly on the arms. A couple of pretend antiques and a sketch in chalks of an artificially slimmed-down Terry by what looked like a pavement artist from outside the National Portrait Gallery completed the decoration. 'What'll you have?' she said, lurching towards the bar.

'Nothing for me. I'm fine.'

'Nobody's fine if they haven't got a drink.'

'Some whisky then, thank you. I'll do it.' This seemed more sensible if I were not to end up with a tumblerful. Terry poured herself some Bourbon, rummaging for ice in one of those ice-makers that loudly produce their chunky load at all hours of the day or night. 'Is Donnie here?'

'I don't think so.'

Again, her lack of enthusiasm made it hard to feel this was a union where their fingers were permanently on each other's pulse. I sipped my drink, wondering if I was glad to find we were alone, although whether I was fearful of a sexual advance or alcoholic poisoning I could not tell you. Either way it was time to start inching back to the story of Greg and the woman, Susie, which had to be done by Donnie's return. 'So, how long have you been married this time?'

'About four years.'

'How did you meet?'

'He's a producer. In television,' she added quickly, to differentiate this man as a working producer as opposed to simply a resident of LA. 'I make these programmes where we discuss what's on the market—'

'I know. Infomercials.' I smiled, thinking to show how up I was in the jargon of modern television.

Instead, she gave me a look as if I had slapped her across the table.

305

'I hate that word!' But the restaurant food wars had tired her out and she wasn't looking for another fight. Instead she just sipped her drink and then said in all seriousness, 'I prefer to think of myself as an ambassador for the buyer.' She spoke the words with great gravitas, so I can only suppose she expected me to take them at face value. After a suitable pause she continued, 'I went out with Donnie for a while, and then he proposed and I thought "what the hell".'

'Here's to you,' I said and raised my glass. 'I hope you're very happy.'

She sipped again, leaning back against the cushions. Predictably, her relaxation had brought down her guard and soon I learned that, as I had already surmised, she wasn't very happy. In fact, I would be hard put to it to testify that she was happy at all. Donnie, it seemed, was a lot older than her and since we were both at the upper end of our fifties, he can't have been much less than seventy. He also had less money than she'd been led to believe, 'which I find very hurtful,' and, worst of all, he had two daughters who wouldn't 'get off his back.'

'In what way?'

'They keep ringing him up, they keep wanting to see him. I know they're after his money when he goes.'

This was quite hard to respond to. There was nothing unreasonable in their desire to see their father and *of course* they expected his money when he went. It didn't make them unloving. 'At least they don't want it before he goes,' I volunteered.

She shook her head fiercely. 'You don't understand. I *need* that money. I've *earned* it.' She was extremely drunk by now, as she ought to have been, given how much Chardonnay, Merlot and Jack Daniel's had passed down her capacious throat that evening.

'Well, I'm sure he's planning to give you a fair share. Why don't you ask him?'

'He's planning to give me a life interest in half his money, which reverts to them on my death.'

What made this odd was that it was delivered as if she were describing a crime against nature, when it seemed eminently sensible, even generous, to me. I didn't dare go that far, reasoning that while I knew Terry, Donnie was a stranger to me so he could not feel justified in relying on my help. I settled for: 'That's not what you want?'

'*Damn right!*' She reached across me for the bottle and filled her glass. As she did so, she caught sight of a framed photograph among a group of them arranged on the shelves behind the bar. It was of an elderly, white-haired man with two young women, one on either side. They were all smiling. 'Those bitches,' said Terry with soft malignity and reaching out with the hand that was not holding the glass, smashed the picture forward, face down. It hit the wood with a loud smack, but I couldn't quite tell whether the glass had broken.

'And you've been married four years?' I asked tentatively, attempting to row for shallower water, but unable by the very nature of my task to leave her private life alone.

'Yuh.' More Jack Daniel's poured down her ever-open gullet.

'Then maybe he'll alter things when you've been together for longer.'

'Four years with Donnie is a lifetime, believe me.' What always fascinates me about people like Terry, and I have known a few, is their absolute control over the moral universe. You and I know that she had been approaching desperation while making her dreadful infomercials and wondering if her life would ever begin again. Then along comes this nice, lonely old man and she decides to marry him, in the hope of inheriting everything to which she had no right whatever, and the sooner the better. She then discovers that he intends to leave his fortune to his two daughters, whom he loves and who are obviously the very people he ought to leave it to. They are affectionate and close to Donnie, and apart from no doubt *loathing* their new stepmother they are, I'm sure, normal, sensible women. Yet Terry, and others like her, are able to take this kind of simple tale and turn and twist it until, with a glass splinter in their eye and through some kind of tainted logic, they recast the universe making themselves the ones who have the right to complain. They are the deserving put-upon victims of a cruel system. They are the ones to be pitied. I tell myself that they must know they are living a lie, yet they display no sign of it, and usually their friends and associates give in eventually, first by pretending to take their side and often, in the end, by actually believing they are in the right. My own value system had, however, survived the assault and in fact I wanted to write to Donnie with my support there and then.

My ruminations were interrupted when Terry's shrill voice brought me back to the present. 'Get this!' she shouted by way of introduction. Clearly, I was going to be treated to another example of Donnie's outrageous choices, with most of which I was sure I would agree. 'He's even planning to leave a sum to Susie. Outright.' She paused, to punctuate this unbelievable injustice. 'But not outright to me. For me, it's a "life interest".' She spat out the words, nodding almost triumphantly, as if at the end of a hilarious anecdote.

I was starting to like Donnie more and more. So much more than I liked his wife. 'She is his stepdaughter.'

'That's funny!' She rocked with artificial laughter.

'Where is Susie? Is she in Los Angeles?' With this question, as I should have seen, I had overplayed my hand. It was late and I was still faintly jet-lagged and perhaps, by this stage, a bit drunk and, anyway, I just wanted to get on. My words seemed to echo in the room, altering its atmosphere.

Terry was many things, but not stupid. 'Why are you here?' she said, and her voice suddenly sounded completely sober and absolutely reasonable.

You must understand that I was nearly at the end of my search. There were only Terry and Candida left, and so there had to be a fifty per cent chance that Susie was the Holy Grail Baby. In a way, I confess to hoping, for Damian's sake, that it would be Candida Finch's child, but there was no reason why it shouldn't be this one. I felt I might as well just ask the question, far away from home as we were. I had no intention of telling Terry about the list and after all, Damian wouldn't be especially newsworthy in this neck of the woods if Terry wanted to make a story about her infidelity to her first husband, which I doubted. 'You said you'd been with Greg for quite a while when you got pregnant.'

'Yes.'

'Damian remembers that he had an affair with you around that time.'

She smiled, not immediately making the connection. 'We didn't have an "affair," not then, not ever. Not what you'd call an affair.' She had relaxed again and was once more drawling her words. In some way I thought she was rather enjoying herself. 'We had a funny on-off thing for years. We never quite went out, we never quite broke off. If you're asking if I was unfaithful, I never felt it counted with Damian.'

'Anyway, the point is' – this was it – 'he wonders if Susie is really Greg's daughter.'

I had expected at least token indignation but, unpredictably, Terry threw her head back and roared with laughter. This time it was completely genuine. For a while she was quite unable to stop and she was still wiping her eyes before she could answer. 'No,' she said at last, shaking her head, 'she's not Greg's daughter.' I said nothing. 'You're right. I had been sleeping with Greg for a long time by then, for quite a long time since I decided to get pregnant. I was taking no precautions and I began to wonder if he could have children. If he was, you know, fertile.'

'So you revived things with Damian, to see if you could get pregnant that way.' I could easily see how this had happened. She wanted to bring Greg up to the mark and the whole paternity issue was much muddier in those days. It was a scheme that might easily have worked. Obviously, it did work. It just didn't quite fit with the original letter that had started all this, given that the whole thing had been planned by her. Damian could hardly be accused of seduction or 'deceit.' The charge would more properly be levelled the other way. Still, we could clarify that later.

'Yes. I guess that's exactly what I did.' She was defiant now, made brave and even brazen by the liquor. She tilted her face as if to challenge me.

'I'm not here to judge you. Only to find out the truth.'

'And what does Damian want to do about it?'

So, I had reached my goal. We had arrived. With this in mind I thought some modest helping of honesty would not now go amiss. 'He's dying, as I have told you. I believe he wants to make sure that his child is well provided for.' That seemed enough.

'Would Susie have to know?'

This was an interesting question. I would have thought that Susie would have wanted to know, but would it be a condition? Then again, was it up to her mother? Susie was in her late thirties, after all. 'That's something I'll have to check with Damian. There'll be a DNA test, but I dare say we can come up with some other perfectly believable reason for that if we have to, or it could be done without her knowledge.'

'I see.' From her tone I could tell at once that my words had changed things, but I couldn't quite understand why, since I was not aware I had made any very stringent conditions. She stood and walked towards the glass wall, taking what I could now see was the handle of one of the panels and sliding it back to let in the night air. For a moment she breathed deeply. 'Damian isn't Susie's father,' she said.

I hope I can convey how totally inexplicable this seemed. I had sat all evening and listened to a woman who was rapacious for money, other people's money, any money that she could lay her hands on; a woman disappointed by life and everything it had brought her; a woman trapped in an existence she hated and by a husband she cared nothing for, and now, here she was, on the brink of the luckiest break anyone living has ever heard of, the chance to make her daughter one of the richest women in Europe, and she was turning it down without the smallest argument. 'You can't know that,' I said. 'You say yourself she isn't Greg's. She must be someone's.'

She nodded. 'Yes. She must be someone's. But she isn't Greg's and she isn't Damian's.' She paused, wondering, I now realise, whether to go on. I am glad she did. 'And she isn't mine.'

For a moment I was too astonished to say an obligatory 'What?' or 'How can that be?' or even 'Oh.' I just looked at her.

She sighed, shivering suddenly in the draught, and moved back into the room towards the dingy sofa. 'You were quite right. About what I was trying to do. I wanted to be pregnant, because I knew Greg would marry me when I was. I'd been sleeping with Damian every now and then for a couple of years so I was sure he wouldn't mind. And he didn't. It was just after you all went on that crazy holiday in Portugal.'

'I thought he said it was before.'

'No. I called him and his flatmate said he was out there, so I left a message. He rang me the day he got back and I went round. It's funny. When we got together for the last time . . .' She had become wistful, a nicer person momentarily, in memory of her younger dreams, 'I thought we might go on with it. He seemed different when he got home, less . . . I don't know exactly, less unreachable, and for a day or two I thought that maybe it would be Damian and not Greg after all.'

'But it didn't happen?'

'No. He'd run into that beautiful girl out there, and he met up with her again when she was back in London.'

'Only once I think.'

'Really? I thought it was more than that. What was her name?'

'Joanna Langley.'

'That's it. What happened to her?'

'She died.'

'Oh.' She sighed, saddened by the inexorable process of life. 'The point is that when he got back, Damian was in a strange mood. I heard about what happened.' I nodded. 'I think the truth is he was sick of all of us. I lost touch with him after that.'

'So did we all.'

'Joanna Langley's dead. Wow. I used to be so jealous of her.' I could see that the news had made her stop in her tracks. For anyone, hearing of the death of a person you had thought alive and well is a little like killing them because suddenly they're dead in your brain instead of living. But with the Sixties generation it is more than this. They preached the value of youth so loudly and so long that they cannot believe an unkind God has let them grow old. Still less can they accept they too must die. As if their determination to adopt clothes and prejudices more suited to people thirty, forty, fifty years younger than themselves would act as an elixir to keep them forever from the clutches of the Grim Reaper. You see television interviews and articles in papers expressing shocked amazement whenever an old rocker pops his clogs. What did they think would happen?

At last, with a philosophical nod, Terry resumed her story. 'I slept with Damian two or three times before we finished. There were no hard feelings.' She paused to check that this squared with my information.

'I'm sure there weren't. But nothing happened?'

She shook her head. 'Nothing happened. Then Greg went to Poland and I followed him, and I slept with *him*, but still nothing happened and nothing happened, and finally I went to see a doctor while I was out there and guess what?'

'It wasn't him, it was you.'

She smiled, like a teacher pleased with my attention. 'It was me. All the time it was me. Some tubes were missing or something . . .' She raised her eyebrows, trying to control her delivery. 'You know the first thing that occurred to me? Why the hell had I wasted so much time worrying about getting pregnant? My late teens should have been a ball.'

'You didn't do badly,' I said.

Which made her laugh. 'Anyway, I knew that once Greg learned I could never have a child, once his mother heard about it, the whole thing would be over and it'd be back to square one. So I bought a baby.'

It seems strange now, but this sentence took me completely by surprise. Why? I cannot tell you. There was no such thing as surrogacy in those days, or if there was we knew nothing of it. She'd admitted she'd had a baby to get Greg to marry her and she'd told me she couldn't have children. What did I imagine she had done? Even so, I was flabbergasted. What I came up with was: 'How?'

She smiled. 'Are you planning it?' But she was far too deep in to telling the story to back out now. 'I was doing some social work then, with a group sponsored by the embassy. This was 1971, long before the end of Communism or anything else. There was no Solidarity. There was no hope. Poland was an occupied country and the people were desperate. It wasn't hard. I found a young mother who already had four children and she'd just discovered she was pregnant. I offered to take the baby, whatever it was, whether or not there was anything wrong with it.'

'Would you have?'

She thought for a moment. 'I hope so,' she said, which I liked her for.

'But how did you manage the whole thing?'

'It wasn't difficult. I found a doctor who could be bribed.' I must have looked shocked at this because she became quite incensed. 'Jesus, most of the time he was prescribing drugs to teenagers. Was this worse?'

'Of course not.'

'I didn't "show" until I was about five months "gone." I told Greg I didn't feel comfortable with sex, and with his puritan background he didn't either. Then I asked if he'd mind not being at the birth, as the thought made me uncomfortable. Boy, you should have seen the relief on his face. These days, if the father isn't there peering up your flue as the head appears, he's a bad person, but in 1971 it wasn't compulsory.'

'How did you manage the birth itself?'

'I had a stroke of luck when he was called to New York just before the baby came. The dates I'd given him were three weeks behind the true ones, to leave some room for manoeuvre. I did have a plan of checking into a different room. I think it would have worked but in the end I didn't need it. She went into labour and I took the mother to the nursing home where, thanks to the doctor, she just gave my name. The baby was delivered and the registration was perfectly routine. When Greg got back, I was waiting for him at home with little Susie. We cried a river. Everyone was happy.'

'And nobody ever found out?'

'Why would they? I told him I loved him, but I couldn't have sex until I got my figure back. He suspected nothing. Nobody was worse off. Including Susie. I mean that.' Clearly, she did mean it and I would say it was probably true, although one can never be quite sure about these things. Even if I do not endorse the present fashion for leaving babies with mothers who are clearly quite incapable of caring for them, rather than finding them decent homes. Terry was nearly finished. 'For a while I thought the doctor might blackmail me, but he didn't, so that was that. Maybe he was scared I'd blackmail him.'

'And there were never any tests that gave it away?'

'What tests? They're both blood group O, which was kind of a relief actually. But who runs a DNA test on their own daughter?'

'Did Greg have any more children?'

'None of his own. Two steps. He adores Susie and she adores him.' She sighed a little wearily. 'She much prefers him to me.'

I nodded. 'So he'll take care of her.' For some reason I was rather glad of this. Susie had missed a larger fortune which, in my fevered mind, she had possessed for maybe two or even three minutes. It was good to feel she would never know want.

'Oh yes. She's safer than I'll ever be.'

I had to ask. 'Would you have gone on with it if I hadn't mentioned the test?'

She thought for a moment. 'Probably. The temptation was too great. But of course there would have been some hurdle by the end of it, so I'm glad you did. Before I got too excited.'

It was once more the hour to depart and this time I knew for certain we would not meet again. Since, even if I were back in the town, I wouldn't look her up. But something in the story she had told had won me round a bit. I was reminded of the haunting words of Lady Caroline Lamb: 'With all that has been said about life's brevity, for most of us it is very, very long.' Terry's life had already been very long and very frustrating, with scant reward to show for it. That this had largely been her fault was no consolation, as I knew well. She had thrown away her only chance of a decent future with Greg and never replaced him with anything like an equal opportunity. Now she had lost even the child she'd invented to be with him. We kissed at the door. 'Please don't mention this to anyone.' She shook her head. I had something more to say. 'And please don't ever tell them.'

'Would I?'

'I don't know. If you got too drunk and too angry you might.'

She did not resent this, which was commendable, but she was confident in her denial. 'I have been drunk and angry many times since we last met and I haven't told them yet.' This, I am sure, was true. All of it.

'Good.' Now I really was going. But I had a last wish before we parted. 'Be kind to Donnie,' I said. 'He doesn't sound a bad chap.'

The evening had made me sentimental in my estimation of her. I should have been more clear-sighted. The truth was, with the sole exception of her feeling towards her not-daughter, the old Terry Vitkov was quite unchanged. 'He's a bastard,' she replied and shut the door.

Candida

THIRTEEN

Which only left Candida Finch.

I stayed on a few days in Los Angeles, in Beverly Hills to be precise, at the very comfortable Peninsular Hotel – a haven for the English, since it is the only one where you can actually walk out to the post office or get something to eat without having to stand and wait every time for a crisply suited 'valet' to fetch your car. I'd enjoyed meeting my agent who turned out to be charming, and if I did not quite follow Damian's instructions to the letter, still we got on very well and he sent me round the town to meet a few people while I was still out there. Since I was allowed the untold luxury of first class travel back to London, I felt quite relaxed and invigorated when I got home. How strange it is, the way enough sleep and the resulting physical energy can make one feel as if one's whole life is going well, while the lack of them has the opposite effect.

However, when I finally returned to the flat, if I was expecting to find a series of messages from Candida answering those I'd left before I went away, I was disappointed. There was nothing. Accordingly, I recorded yet another on her machine which was still not picking up, and settled down to a day or two of work on my latest novel, a tale of middle-class *angst* in a seaside town, which was approaching what I would hesitate to call its climax and which I had, understandably, recently neglected. It was on the morning of the following day, when I'd finally managed to get some way back into the rhythm of my troubled, marine triangle, that the telephone on my desk started to ring.

'You called Candida Finch yesterday,' said a female voice and, for a moment, quite illogically, I thought it must be Candida herself who was speaking. I can't think why, since it obviously wasn't.

'Yes, I wondered if I could see you, which I know sounds odd.'

'It does sound very odd, and I'm not Candida, I'm Serena.' A thousand bags of sherbet exploded in my vitals.

'Serena?' Of course it was Serena. It was her voice, for God's sake. What had I been thinking of? But why should Serena ring me? How could that have happened? I pondered the question without speaking, silently wondering, earpiece clamped to my ear.

'Hello?' Her voice had gone up in volume.

'Yes.'

'Oh, I thought you'd been cut off. It all went quiet.'

'No, I'm still here.'

'Good.'

I suddenly worried that I could hear in her voice a querying sound, as if she were afraid that the person she was speaking to was in fact a nutter and it might be dangerous to continue the conversation. I trembled lest she might act on this subconscious warning. All of which illustrates the fevered level of my imagination. 'How can I help?'

'I was talking to Candida this morning and she said she'd had a message to ring you, that you wanted to see her.'

'She's had more than one message from me, I'm afraid. I thought she must have emigrated.'

'She's been in Paris and she only got back last night.'

'It's rather wonderful that you're still in touch.' As the words left my mouth, I could hear their senselessness. Why did I say this? Why was it wonderful? Why shouldn't they be in touch? Was I mad?

'She's my cousin.'

Which I should have known. In fact, I must have known it. In fact, I *did* know it. Perfectly well. They gave a ball together, for God's sake. I was present at it. What kind of fool forgets something like that? What kind of stupid *moron*? 'Of course,' I said lightly. 'Of course you are. I should have remembered.' Where was this twaddle leading? To some International Idiots' Convention? Why couldn't I say anything that didn't sound illogical and inane?

'Anyway, I wondered if it was all part of Damian's search.'

My heart stopped. What had I said to her? Had I been so surprised by her presence at Gresham that I'd given it all away? Could I have?

What had I told her? My thoughts were flying about like a crowd of ravens with nowhere to settle. I couldn't seem to remember anything about that evening, yet I thought I'd remembered every moment. 'Search?' I said, feeling this was the best way to flush out information.

'You said Damian wanted you to look up some of his old friends. You told me when we met up that time in Yorkshire. I wondered if Candida was one of them, since she couldn't think of any other reason you'd want to see her again.'

'She's rather hard on herself. I can think of lots of reasons.'

'But was it? Is it?'

'As a matter of fact yes, it is. I thought I'd buy her lunch and get her news. That's all he wants, really.'

'Well, I've got a much better idea. She's coming down here next weekend, so I wondered if you could join her. Join us. We'd love it.'

My despair at my own stupidity was suddenly and totally replaced by a chorus of angels' wings. 'That's incredibly kind. Do you mean it?'

'Absolutely. Come on Friday, for dinner. And you can leave at some stage on Sunday afternoon.'

'As long as we've got that settled.'

She laughed. 'Andrew always needs to know he'll have the house back by dinner on Sunday.'

I'll bet he does, I thought, the mannerless toad. 'What about clothes?'

'He wears a smoking jacket but no tie on Saturday night. Apart from that we'll be in rags the whole time.'

'Well, if you're sure . . .'

'Completely sure. I'll e-mail you directions. We're very easy to find, but you might as well have them, if you'll give me your address.'

So I did. And it was settled. I wondered if I ought to ring Candida, but I never heard back from her, so presumably Serena had filled her in.

After this conversation I sat at the desk for several minutes, quite unable to resolve exactly what I was thinking. Naturally, as I have observed, the invitation had set off a peal of chiming, silver bells in my heart, ringing and singing with joy at the prospect of two whole days when I might look upon her face to my heart's content. But there is also the old proverb that it is better to travel hopefully than to arrive, and now that I was faced with a real prospect of having the Blessed

Serena back in my life, paradoxically, I wasn't completely convinced it was a good idea. Of course, all this was Damian's fault. It was Damian's fault she had left my life thirty-eight years before. At least I dated the beginning of the end from that dinner. Now it was Damian's fault she had come back. That she had been, would always be, the love of my life, was clearly established, to my satisfaction anyway, and, if I was honest with myself, it was her return to my conscious mind that had spelled curtains for poor Bridget, as I had more or less told my father. The reminder of what love is, of what it could be, made the thin facsimile that I had been living feel rather pointless.

But then Serena was content with the way her life was, and if she wasn't she would never leave her husband, of that I was quite sure, and if she did it wouldn't be for me, and if it would I had nothing comparable to offer her, and . . . so on. I was equally certain she was not the type for any extra-marital activity, and if even this too were wrong, I would certainly not be her chosen co-adulterer. I knew well enough that while maturity and some success had transformed me into a marriage possibility for various, lonely divorcees who were not quite clear as to how they would finance their latter years, still I was not the sort of man who tempts a girl to sin. I had neither the looks nor the chops.

No, the future that was on offer, or at least a possibility since nothing at all was yet on offer, would simply be as a friend, a walker, a companion. The literate ally that fashionable women married to fools or workaholics sometimes need to buy them lunch or carry their coat at the theatre, who might join a party at the villa in Amalfi and make the other guests laugh. Did I want this? I had done enough of it in the past, of course, and sung for my supper a thousand times and more, but did I want it with the added twist of pain? To sit and watch the woman I would have died for, as she chattered on about a weekend in Trouville or a play at the Almeida or her latest purchases? No. A man has his pride, I thought, my mind clearly still running on empty. I would go for the weekend. I had anyway to question Candida, or that was my excuse, but that would finish it. I was nearly at the end of the quest that had taken me through my old stamping ground of long ago. But once the search was done, Candida's child would get the money and Damian would die, and I would go home and write my books again, and say hello to Serena when I saw her at Christie's Summer Party. And it would be enough to know that she was well. Or so I vowed.

Waverly Park sounds a little more romantic than it is. The original seat of the Earls of Belton, Mellingburgh Castle, left the family when the senior line died out in an heiress during the 1890s and is now buried beneath the station car park in Milton Keynes, for much of which its walls supplied the hardcore. But the title had jumped sideways to a junior branch and they celebrated its arrival with marriage to a well-endowed American and the purchase of Waverly in Dorset, not far from the Jurassic coast. The estate had shrunk, after both wars and then again quite recently as when old Lord Belton died it turned out his provisions had been drawn up quite wrongly, making it impossible to prevent half the estate being divided between Andrew's siblings. I believe there was an expectation that they would gamely hand this back to their older brother, but as so often with these things, it didn't happen. To make matters worse, the sister, Annabella, had turned out a gambler and she sold her share within three years of getting it, leaving a gaping hole in the centre of the farms, and the other son, Eustace, married to an even worse bully than his mother, had divided his between four daughters, none of whom would stay long term. I was told later that the whole mess had occurred because Lady Belton insisted on using the son of a cousin as their lawyer, instead of someone who knew what they were doing. I cannot swear to the truth of this, but it sounds very likely. The net result was that Andrew was left with far too little land to support the house, a situation exacerbated by his almost chemical lack of brainpower, which ensured that no outside income would come to his aid. Serena may have had something to look forward to from her father, but families like the Greshams do not stay rich by enriching all the siblings and it would never have been much.

The house itself was a fairly large but unremarkable pile. There had been a dwelling there since the 1660s but all that remained of this period was the cantilevered staircase, the nicest thing to look at in the place. The entire building had been enveloped twice, well in the 1750s and badly in the 1900s, by the newly arrived and gleeful Beltons. A burst of optimism in the late 1940s on the part of Andrew's grandfather had swept away the service wing, relocated the kitchens to the site of a former morning room and converted the great hall to a library. The effect of this was to pull the entrance round the corner, away from the main portico, so the existing front door led one through a sort of tunnel towards the stairs, arriving at them from the back, at a slightly peculiar angle. It never works to fight a house's architecture and Waverly was no exception to the rule. The rooms had been tossed this way and that in the changeover, swapping their roles as they went, ending with dining rooms full of sofas and drawing rooms stuffed with tables and chairs. Huge fireplaces found themselves warming tiny studies, and dainty bedroom detailing adorned the walls of a semi-ballroom. None of which was improved by the timing of the work, during those post-war years when building materials were rationed, so almost everything had been contrived from plywood and painted plaster. Not all of it was bad. The loss of the hall was hopeless and dislocated the whole ground floor, but the library that replaced it was a great success, and the breakfast room was pretty, if too small. In truth, the house had a lost, bewildered feel, like a private home too quickly changed to a hotel, where the rooms have not been allowed a period of adjustment to get used to their new jobs. Naturally, Andrew thought it a palace and every visitor as lucky as a peasant from Nan Cheng allowed entry for a few, sacred moments to the glories of the Forbidden City.

The drive out of London on Friday afternoon was as murderous as ever, and it was after six when I finally arrived and staggered down the passage with my case. Serena emerged from a doorway and stood there in welcome, dressed in a shirt and skirt, casual and marvellous. 'Dump that there. You can go up later. Come and have some tea.' I followed her into what proved to be the library and a few faces turned to look at me. There were others besides Candida and what I perceived was an already grumpy Andrew, making a great show of being absorbed in *Country Life*.

One pair, the Jamiesons, I'd met a few times in London and the others, a sporty couple from Norfolk called Hugh and Melissa Purbrick whose life seemed to consist of farming and killing things and not much else, were some sort of connections of an old friend of my mother, so I didn't anticipate much trouble. 'Do you want tea? Or a drink to take upstairs?' said Serena, but I refused both and sat on the sofa next to Candida.

'I feel very guilty,' she said. 'I came back to my answering machine flashing like the Blackpool illuminations. I thought I must have won the Lottery. Either that, or somebody was dead. But they were all from you.' She had not aged well, certainly nothing like as well as Serena. Her hair was grey and her face was rough and lined and even redder than it used to be, although I would not speculate as to the cause. On the whole, unlike her cousin she looked her age, but her manner was very different from what it had been when I knew her and at first encounter considerably improved. She seemed much calmer, no, not calmer, calm. As the French say, she was *bien dans sa peau*, and as a result I found myself warming to her in a way that I never really had done when we were young.

'I'm afraid I was a bit eager. Sorry.'

She shook her head to free us from the need to apologise. 'I should switch it off when I go away. At least people would know I hadn't got the message instead of having to deduce it.'

'What were you doing in Paris?'

'Oh, just larking about. I've got a grand-daughter who's mad about art and I persuaded her parents to let me take her to see the Musée d'Orsay. Of course, once we were there we spent about three minutes in the museum and the rest of the time shopping.' She smiled, curious now to get to the bottom of it. 'So what's the big thing? Serena said that you were coming as an envoy of the mighty Damian.'

'In a way. No, I am.'

'You're looking up his friends from the old days.'

'I suppose so.'

'I'm rather flattered to be included. Whom have you seen?' I told her. 'Now I'm less flattered. What a peculiar list.' She pondered the names again. 'Weren't they all in Portugal that time?'

'All except Terry.'

She thought for a moment. 'Of course, that evening was another story.' She stretched her eyes silently at me, sharing the memory. 'Have we ever talked about it?'

'Not properly. We've hardly met since we got back.'

'No. I suppose that's right.' Again she thought over what I'd been telling her. 'Terry Vitkov ...' she grimaced. 'I'm quite surprised she was a pal of Damian's. I thought he had better taste.'

'Ouch.' I was amused by this as plenty of people from those days would probably have said something similar of her.

'Is she the same as ever?'

'She is the same, if you add the effects of forty years of disappointment.'

Candida absorbed this for a moment. 'Do you remember her dance?'

'No one who was there could forget it without medical intervention.'

She laughed. 'It was the first time I'd been in the papers since the announcement of my birth. My grandmother wouldn't speak to me for weeks.' I considered Candida's subsequent career of sexual profligacy, illegitimate motherhood and the more recent tragedy of 9/11, and pondered what the grandmother in question would have made of any of that. Presumably death had spared her. Candida was still at Madame Tussaud's. 'I know she did it. Whatever she said at the time.'

'She says not. She says it was Philip Rawnsley-Price.'

'He might have helped her. He was stupid enough. But she must have known. The choice of brownies for a start. We were all so innocent.'

'Quite innocent.' I didn't bother to defend Terry, although I didn't think the accusation true. I suppose I didn't care.

Candida was staring at the fire. By this time I knew the process of what I had to put these people through. I'd arrive and suddenly the woman of the week would be plunged back into a world of four decades ago, which she hadn't thought about in ages. 'Golly, we had some funny times that year. Do you remember Dagmar's dance?

'Who could forget?'

'When Damian gatecrashed and had a fight with—' She put her hand to her mouth. She'd suddenly remembered the identity of Damian's opponent. Our host shook out the pages of his magazine sharply.

'I remember it well,' I said. We shared the moment and tried not to look at the bump on the bridge of Andrew's nose.

Candida sighed. 'The main thing I recall is just how young we were. How little we knew of what was coming.'

'I think we were great,' I said. Which she took no exception to and smiled. 'What's your son doing now?'

'I have two sons and a daughter, in fact.' She flashed me a slightly defensive glance. 'But I know you mean Archie.' Perhaps sensing I meant her no ill, she relaxed. 'He's got his own property company. He's frightfully rich and successful.'

Not half as rich and successful as he's going to be, I thought. 'Is he married?'

'Absolutely. He's got a wife called Agnes and two kids, the shopaholic daughter, who's ten, and a son of six. Funnily enough, Agnes's mother is a girl you used to hang about with, Minna Bunting. She married a chap called Havelock, who was in the army. Do you remember her?'

'Very well.'

She pulled a slight face. 'That's the thing. I don't. I never really knew her at the time, but of course now we pretend we were terrific friends and we've almost convinced each other it's true.'

Was it comforting or smothering, this constant interlocking of the old patterns? Revolutions in morality might flare up, Socialism in all its indignant fury might come and go, but still the same faces, the same families, the same relationships, are endlessly repeated. 'I like the name Agnes,' I said.

'So do I. Quite,' she added, telling me more of what she thought of her daughter-in-law than she intended.

'Was it very hard with Archie?'

Candida was silent for a moment. She paid me the compliment of not pretending she didn't know what I was asking. 'It was easier in a way than it would have been for some. Both my parents were dead and so was my grandmother by then. Just. I hated my stepmother and couldn't have given a monkey's tiddly what she thought about anything. I was terribly broke, of course. My stepmother wouldn't give me a penny and by the end she didn't have much to give, but at least I didn't have to feel I was letting everyone down. Actually, Aunt Roo behaved very well, given that she thought I was out of my mind.'

'But?'

'Same as the earlier answer. My parents were dead and I hated my stepmother. I had no close family, no backup, beyond Aunt Roo and Serena, and they thought I'd gone mad. So did my friends, to be honest, but they were a little bit more circumspect about showing it.'

'I know you married in the end.'

'I did. A chap called Harry Stanforth. Did you ever come across him?'

'His name seems familiar, since I first heard it, so maybe I did, but if so I can't remember where. I was terribly sorry to hear what happened.'

'Yes.' She gave one of those twitchy smiles of bleak acceptance. 'It is difficult when nothing's ever found. I always used to feel for mothers of sons killed in foreign wars, who never got a body back to bury, and now I know just what it's like. I don't know why exactly, but you need a proper funeral with something there, something more than a photograph, which is what I had, in order to feel it really is the end.'

'The Americans call it "closure."'

'Well, I wouldn't, but I do know what they mean. You keep imagining that he's in a coma somewhere or struggling with amnesia, or he escaped and had a nervous breakdown in Waikiki. Of course, you tell yourself to accept it, not to believe anything different, but you can't help it. Every time the doorbell goes unexpectedly, or the telephone rings very late at night . . .' she smiled gently at her own foolishness. 'You do get over it in the end.'

'Awful.'

'But you mustn't think I'm a sad person. Please don't.' Candida's tone had changed and she was looking straight at my eyes. I could see that she was keen to convince me, and I think she was telling the truth. I suppose it was somehow a case of being loyal to his memory. 'I'm not at all sad. Really. I was sad before I met Harry, and trapped at the end of a cul-de-sac with a boy half my family felt uncomfortable with. I know you all thought me ridiculous in those days.'

'Not ridiculous.'

'Ridiculous. A loud, red-faced bed-hopper who was embarrassing to have around.' This was all true so I didn't contradict her, but as with almost all of the women I had visited I had that revelation of how much better we would have got on forty years before if we had only known each other's true natures. Candida shrugged off these memories with happier ones. 'Then Harry arrived one day and just saved me. He saved us. I don't know to this day what he saw in me, but we never had an unhappy hour.'

'He loved you.' Funnily enough I meant this. I could sort of begin to see what he had loved in her now, which came as something of a surprise.

She nodded, her eyes starting to glisten. 'I think he did. God knows why. And he took us both on. He adopted Archie, you know, completely legally, and then we had two more, and when he . . .' I could see that despite her strictures her eyes were filling, and so were mine. 'When he died it turned out he'd left some money equally to the three of them. Just split three ways. He made no distinction. And that meant so much to Archie. So *very* much. Did you know that all their mobiles worked, when they were trapped in the tower?'

I nodded. 'I read about that.'

'And what was so extraordinary, what was wonderful really, was that they didn't, most of them anyway, ring to yell for help. They rang the people who were nearest to them, their wives and husbands and children, to say how much they loved them. Harry did that. Of course I'd turned mine off – typical – and when I tried to call him back I couldn't get through, but he left a message saying how marrying me was the best thing he'd ever done. I saved it. I've got it now. He thanks me for marrying him. Can you imagine that? In the midst of all that fear and horror he thanked me for marrying him. So you see, I'm not sad at all in the greater scheme of things. I'm lucky.'

I looked at her coarse, ruddy face and her brimming eyes, and I knew she was absolutely right. 'So you are,' I said. I had arrived prepared to pity her, but in fact the time she'd spent since we last really talked had been infinitely more satisfactory than that same period in Terry's life or Lucy's or Dagmar's or, heaven knows, Joanna's. By anyone's reckoning Candida Stanforth, née Finch, was the luckiest of the five on Damian's list. In all the standard categories reckoned important among these people she had started at the back of the field and ended up way out in front. 'Did you ever get into publishing? You used to say you wanted to.'

She nodded. 'I did. But proper publishing. Not the vanity stuff I thought would be my only way in. Harry made me. He pulled a string and got me a job as a reader at a small outfit that specialised in women writers. But I stuck at it and they kept me on. Eventually I edited quite a few books.'

'But not any more?'

'Not at the moment. I felt I needed to take time off, when . . .' I nodded, anxious not to return her to that dreadful day. 'But I'm thinking of going back. Actually, I was rather good at it.' In this simple phrase I knew what her debt to Harry Stanforth was and why she still fought for people to appreciate her luck in finding him. This Candida had self-worth, of which there'd hardly been a trace when I had known her in her ugly, angry, unhappy youth. In those days her childhood was too recent for its ill effects to have been set aside. 'The fact is I had twenty-three years with a terrific, honourable, lovely, loving man.' It was a simple, moving tribute and I had no difficulty in liking Harry enormously on the strength of it. She leant towards me and lowered her voice to a whisper. 'I'd rather be in my shoes than Serena's.' And we laughed, which brought things to an end. Not long afterwards, we went upstairs to change.

I was sleeping in a panelled, corner room, painted off-white, with large windows on two sides, and far-reaching views across the well-wooded park. There was a pretty, canopied bed, upholstered in good, if old, chintz and some Audubon prints of birds around the walls. It was all reasonably attractive, if unoriginal, but the faded colours of the material and the bright shocking pink of the mounts on the pictures made the whole effect feel very 1970s, as if no money had been spent anywhere in its vicinity for thirty years at least. I had my own bathroom, with more of the same colour scheme and a hot tap that made distant, gurgling noises full of intent but the water, when it came, was less than tepid. I sponged myself down as best I could and pulled some clothes out of the case.

The posh English love to sound informal. 'Nobody's coming,' they say. 'It'll just be us.' Which it seldom is. 'You won't have to do a thing,' when of course you will. Most of all, when they say 'don't change' they don't mean it. They do mean you are not to put on a dinner jacket, but not that you are to stay in the same clothes. It's funny in a way, because all you are doing, for an 'informal' dinner in the country is putting on another version of exactly what you wore at tea, particularly the men. But the point is that when you come down it must *be* another version. The only thing to steer clear of for a weekend is the dark suit. Unless there is some charity function or a funeral or something which has its own rules, a gentleman will get no use out of a city suit in the country, where, increasingly, it seems that there are two costumes for the evening, grand or tatters with nothing in between.

The re-rise of grand is rather interesting in this context as well, or it is to me. Contrary to the expectations of only a few years ago, dinner jackets, having known a lean period, and even more, smoking jackets, are once more on the rise. Of these I am more fascinated by the smoking jacket, a garment whose rules have entirely altered in my own time. Not all that long ago it showed the depth of ignorance to wear one in any house where you weren't at least sleeping and preferably living. But now that's changed. More and more country dinners are enlivened by a myriad of velvet shades stretched tight across the broad backs of the chaps. Usually without ties, an unfortunate fad for the middle-aged, whose red, mottled necks do not show to advantage. But having fought the fashion for a time, protesting it was 'quite incorrect,' I rather like it now; putting men into colour, as it does, for the first time in two centuries. As for the rag rules, the one imperative, as I have said, is that they should be different rags when you come down the stairs from the rags that you went up in. To me, the business of pulling off a shirt and jersey and a pair of cords, in order to bathe and put on another shirt, another jersey and another pair of cords can be a bit comedic, but there we are. You can't fight Tammany Hall. Anyway, on this particular evening I did my stuff and I was ready to go down to the drawing room, when I caught sight of a framed photograph on a chest to the right of the carved and painted chimneypiece. It was Serena and Candida, standing side by side in what must have been the receiving line for their Coming Out dance at Gresham. I could make out the portraits in the hall behind them and in the picture Lady Claremont was just turning to one side, as if her attention had been caught by an arriving guest. Then I saw the figure of a young man a few paces back, behind the girls but with his face fixed eagerly on them as if he couldn't look away. Which I knew at once that he could not. For it was me.

As far as anything can be in this mortal setting, the ball at Gresham Abbey for Serena Gresham and Candida Finch was more or less perfection. For some reason it was held quite late, after the summer break, at a time of the year leading up to Christmas that used then to be labelled 'The Little Season.' We were fairly jaded by that stage, having been doing the rounds since the end of the spring and there was not much that a hostess could produce to surprise us, but Lady Claremont had decided, perhaps because she was aware of this, that she would not surprise, she would merely perfect. For some strange reason I kept all my invitations for quite a long time but I have lost them now, so I forget whether it was held in late October or early November. It was definitely a winter ball and we all knew it would be the last really big, private one before the charity balls took over and the whole rigmarole wound up, which in a way gave the evening a kind of built-in romance.

I had stayed at Gresham a few times by that stage and of course I had hoped to be included in the abbey house party, but the competition was predictably stiff and I was not. As it turned out, my host was a fairly dreary one but not insultingly so, a retired general, with his nice, typical army wife, who lived in a small manor house entirely decorated in that sort of non-taste that such people can go in for. Nothing was actually ugly or common, but nothing was charming or pretty either, except for the odd painting or piece of furniture they had inherited through no merit of their own. A couple of the ones who were staying qualified as friends, Minna Bunting and that same Sam Hoare who had featured as another witness to the Battle of the Mainwarings before Minna's dance, and the others were all quite familiar as well, since we had been performing this ritual together for six months by then. As usual, some local couples came for the dinner, a blameless concoction of salmon mousse (*comme toujours*), chicken à la king and crème brulée, a menu more suited perhaps to an aged invalid with no teeth than a bunch of ravenous teenagers, but we made the best of it and chatted away quite sociably. There was nothing wrong with any of this, but nor was there anything of much interest in it and it was certainly no distraction from the main purpose of the evening: To get to the dance. Sometimes the dinners and house parties could be so entertaining that one lingered and arrived at the dance a little too late to enjoy it. But there was certainly no chance of that on this occasion. After a polite interval had passed we drank up our coffee, slid away to the loo and clambered into the cars.

There was a kind of general excitement in the air when we entered the hall, though I did not then know why. Serena and Candida and the Claremonts were standing there receiving. 'I'm so glad you could come,' said Serena and kissed me, which nearly winded me, as usual. 'I wish you were staying here,' she added in a whisper, as a compliment rather than because she meant it. I had become a bit of a Gresham regular by the end of that year, having been billeted with them for a couple of northern dances and staying once on my own on the way down from Scotland, and I was in danger of succumbing to that awful smugness of trying to demonstrate that one is a welcome guest somewhere enviable, but I did not suspect at the time, what I know now, that the welcome I always received was a reflection of Serena's enjoyment of my being in love with her. I do not mean she was interested in me romantically, not in the least, only that she wanted me to go on being in love with her until it wasn't fun any more. The young are like that. I can now remember when the photograph was taken. I was still reeling in bliss from her comment and I was unable to make myself move out of the room where she stood, even though I knew I had to give place, so I stepped behind them, where I could linger a little longer; then a flash went off and I was caught forever, like a fly in amber. Lucy Dalton rescued me, taking my arm and walking me away. 'What's your house party like?'

'Dull but respectable.'

'Sounds like paradise compared to mine. There doesn't seem to be any running water. Literally. Nothing comes out of the taps except a dirty trickle of what looks like prune juice. Doesn't Serena look marvellous? But of course you're not the man to disagree with *that*. I hear the discothèque is *fabulous*. It was done by someone's boyfriend, but I forget who. Come on.' All this was delivered in one spurt without pause or breath, so I couldn't hope to come in with a comment.

The discothèque *was* fabulous. It occupied a large section of what must normally have been a basement servants' hall or even a section of the no doubt extensive wine cellars. A doorway under the main staircase was surrounded by synthetic flames and a sign read 'Welcome to Hell!' While on the other side of the door the entire space, including the walls of the staircase leading down, was covered in foil and flames made of tinsel and satin, blown with fans and lit by a spinning wheel, making them flicker and leap, so they really did feel quite real. At the bottom the hell theme embraced the entire area, with huge copies of the grimmer paintings by Hieronymus Bosch lining the walks with images of suffering, while the fire and flames played over the heads of the dancers. As a final detail the DJ and two of the waitresses had been put into scarlet devils' outfits, so they could attend to the guests while maintaining the illusion. The only discordant note came from the music, some of which seemed very out of place in Hades. When we came down the steps a popular ballad by the Turtles, *Elenore*, was playing. Somehow the lyrics, 'I really think you're groovy, let's go out to a movie,' didn't quite chime with the Tortures of the Damned.

We danced and gossiped and said hello to other people for a bit until, round about half past eleven or maybe midnight, a sudden rush for the staircase told us that something was happening we wouldn't want to miss.

Lucy and I struggled up to the hall in our turn and found we were carried along in the crush towards the State Dining Room, which had been designated the main ballroom of the evening. The space had been cleared of furniture and somehow, unlike most of the other houses I had penetrated, the stage erected at one end for the band and, more unusually, the lighting looked entirely professional. This put a spin on the proceedings from the start, even before we knew what was happening. I don't quite know why, but there was always something satisfactory in dancing inside a great house and not in a marquee with wobbly coconut matting and a portable dance floor, and Gresham Abbey was the very acme of a great house. Stern, full-lengths of earlier, male Greshams lined the walls of the enormous room, in armour and brocade and Victorian fustian, in lovelocks and perukes and periwigs, extending their white, stockinged legs to display the garters that encased them. Above the marble chimneypiece a vast, equestrian portrait of the first Earl of Claremont by Kneller dominated the chamber, a loud, impressive statement of self-congratulation, and the contrast between the rigid splendour of this symbol of high birth and high achievement and the crowd of teenage young writhing away below it was almost startling.

At this precise moment, the door opened that on ordinary days led to the servery and, further below, to the kitchens. Tonight it revealed a group of young men who came bouncing through on to the stage, and started to play and sing. With a kind of group sigh we suddenly all realised that this, incredibly, was Steve Winwood, lead singer of the group formed and named for the man who ran up on to the stage after him, Spencer Davis. This was the real live Spencer Davis. No sooner had this information penetrated our skulls, than they started to play their song of a couple of years previously, *Keep on Running*. It is hard to explain now what this felt like then. We are a jaded people, these days. We see film stars and singers and every other permutation of fame wherever we go, indeed sometimes, judging by the magazines, it seems that more people are famous than not. But this wasn't true in 1968 and to be in the same room as a real-live band playing and singing its own hit number, which most of us had bought anyway two years before and played ever since, was to be inside a fantasy. It was astonishing, mind-searing, completely impossible to take in. Even Lucy was silenced, if not for long. 'Can you believe it?' she said. I couldn't. We were so sweet, really.

It was then that I saw Damian. He was standing inside one of the window embrasures and so half in shadow, looking at the world-shaking sight but without any outward sign of excitement or even pleasure. He just stood there, listening, watching, but watching without interest. My own attention was taken back by the band and, to be honest, I forgot all about him until much later on, but I still have that image, a melancholic at the carnival, lodged in my brain. After that, I was back in the party, dancing and talking and drinking for hours, and finally, at about half past two, going off in search of breakfast, which I found in the conservatory. This was a huge glass-and-cast-iron affair, what was once called a winter garden, built for one of the countesses in the 1880s, and on this night it had been cleared and filled with little round tables and chairs, each one decorated with a pyramid of flowers. A long buffet stood against one end, and the exotic climbing flowers on the stone wall behind it formed a kind of living wallpaper. What made it even more unusual was that the whole space had been carpeted for the occasion in bright red, cut close round the stone fountain at its centre, and the route of access, normally a short walk along a terrace from one of the drawing rooms, had been covered in with a passage, fashioned in wood for that one night only, but as an absolute facsimile, in every way, of the room it connected to, with dado, panels and cornice, and the very handles on the windows made as exact reproductions of the originals. In short, there is a level, perhaps in all things, where the object or activity is of so exquisite a standard that it becomes an art form in itself, and for me that little, constructed passage achieved it.

Like everything else that evening, it was extraordinary.

I walked down the table, helping myself to the delights, then sauntered around, chatting with assorted clutches of guests. Joanna was there and I talked to her for a bit, and Dagmar, finally alighting at a table with Candida, which was in itself a bit unusual as normally by this stage of the evening she would be laughing like someone with terminal whooping cough and I would give her a wide berth, but on this evening, at her own dance which made it odd, she was curiously piano, so I sat down. I seemed to have shed Lucy by that time and I know I didn't fix myself up with a partner for the evening, as one usually did at these things, although I cannot tell you why. Certainly it did not in any way lessen my enjoyment. I think, looking back, that maybe it would have felt awkward and dishonest to have had to flirt and concentrate and pretend that some other girl was the centre of my attention for the evening when I was in Serena's house and at Serena's party. 'Have you seen anything of your friend Damian?' said Candida. Again, she seemed quite unlike her normal self and positively thoughtful, not an adjective she would generally attract at half past two in the morning.

I had to concentrate for a moment. The question had come out of nowhere. 'Not recently. I saw him in the dining room when we were listening to the band earlier. Why?'

'No reason.' She turned to one of the Tremayne boys who had arrived at the table with some pals and a plate of sausages.

I'd finished eating and Carla Wakefield wanted my seat, so I left the conservatory and wandered back through the emptying house. For no reason, I turned into the little oval anteroom, outside the dining room, where the music was still echoing through the rafters. There was a little group of paintings depicting the five senses that I found intriguing and I leaned in to see more of the detail, when an icy blast hit me and I stood to see that a door leading out to the terrace was open and Serena was coming in from the night. She was alone, and while she was, for me, as lovely as anyone can imagine a woman could be, she looked as if she were shivering with cold. 'What were you doing out there?' I said. 'You must be freezing.'

For a second she had to concentrate to work out both who I was and what I was saying, but having regained control of her brain, she nodded. 'It is a bit chilly,' she said.

'But what were you doing?'

She shrugged lightly. 'Just thinking,' she said.

'I don't suppose you want to dance,' I spoke cheerfully, but without any expectations.

I quite understand that, in this account of my relations with Serena Gresham I must seem pessimistic and negative to a tedious degree, but you have to understand that at this time in my life I was young and ugly. To be ugly when young is something that no one who has not experienced it should ever claim to understand. It is all very well to talk about superficial values and 'beauty of character,' and the rest of the guff that ugly teenagers have to listen to from their mothers, the 'marvellous thing about being different' and so on, but the plain truth is you are bankrupt in the only currency with value. You may have friends without number, but when it comes to romance you have nothing to bargain with, nothing to sell. You are not to be shown off and flaunted, you are the last resort when there's no one left worth dancing with. When you are kissed, you do not turn into a prince. You are just a kissed toad and usually the kisser regrets it in the morning. The best reputation you can acquire is that you never talk. If you are good company and you can hold your tongue, you will see some action, but woe betide the ugly suitor who grows overconfident and brags. Of course, things change. In time, at last, some people will start to see through your face to your other qualities and eventually, in the thirties and forties, other factors come into play. Success will mend your features and so will money, and this is not, actually, because the women concerned are necessarily mercenary. It is because you have begun to smell differently. Success makes you a different person. But you never forget those few, those very few, Grade A women who loved you when no one else did. In the words of a thriller, I know who you are and you will always have a place in my heart. But even the least of these did not come along before my middle twenties. When I was eighteen, ugly and in love, I knew I was in love alone.

'Yes. Let's dance,' said Serena, and I can still remember that strange mixture of butterflies and feeling sick that her answer gave me.

Spencer Davis had left by then. Presumably they were already racing down the motorway, or the equivalent in those days, having more than earned their wedge and made the evening legendary. God bless them all. I hope they know what happiness they gave us. It was three o'clock by this stage and nearly the end of the ball. A disc jockey had taken over again, but you could hear in his voice that he was winding down. He put on a slow record I rather liked, *A Single Girl*, which had been a hit a year or two earlier, and we moved closer. There is something so peculiar about dancing. You are entitled to slide your arm round the waist of a woman, to hold her closely, to feel her breasts against your chest through your shirt and the thin silk of an evening dress; her hair brushes against your cheek, her very scent excites you, yet there is no intimacy in it, no assumption of anything but politeness and sociability. Needless to say I was in paradise as we shifted our weight from foot to foot, and talked of the band and the party, and what a complete success the evening had been. But although she was obviously pleased to hear it, still Serena seemed thoughtful and not as elated as I had expected her to be. As she was entitled to feel. 'Have you seen Damian?' she said. 'He was looking for you.'

'Why?'

'I think he wants to ask you for a lift tomorrow.'

'I'm going rather early.'

'He knows. He has to get away first thing, too.' I was so absorbed in the wonder of dancing with her that I didn't register this much, although I remember it did occur to me that I should find any excuse to linger, were I lucky enough to be staying at Gresham.

'Have you enjoyed yourself?' I asked.

She thought for a moment. 'These things are such milestones,' she said, which was an odd answer really, even if it was true. These events *were* rites of passage to my generation and we did not much question their validity. It may seem strange in our aggressively anti-formal age but then we saw the point of ritual. The girls came out, the men came of age. The former happened when the girl was eighteen, the latter when the man was twenty-one. This was because the upper classes entirely ignored the government's altering the age of seniority to eighteen for many years, if indeed they recognise it now. These events were a marking of adulthood. After they had been observed you were a fully fledged member of the club, and your membership would continue to

336

be parsed by ceremony: Weddings and christenings, parties for our offspring, more weddings and finally funerals. These were the Big Moments by which we steered our course through life. That's gone now. There are seemingly no obligatory events. The only thing that really marks an aristocratic upbringing apart from a middle-class one today is that the upper classes still marry before giving birth. Or, when they don't, it is exceptional. Apart from that many of the traditions that once distinguished them as a tribe seem largely to have melted into the sand.

The song came to an end and Serena was claimed by her departing guests, while I wandered off through the house, reluctant, even now, to call it a day. I left the dancing and crossed the anteroom, where a girl in pink was asleep on a rather pretty sofa, before poking through the half-open door into the Tapestry Drawing Room which lay beyond. At first I thought it was empty. There were only a few lamps lit and the room was engulfed in gloom. The Empress Catherine's clock caught the eye as one lamp was so placed to make the glass on the face shine, but otherwise it was clearly a room that had done its work for the day. Then I saw that it was not in fact empty, but that one chair beneath a vast tapestry reaching to the cornice was occupied and the sitter was none other than Damian Baxter. 'Hello,' I said. 'Serena told me you wanted to ask me something.'

He looked up. 'Yes. I wondered whether you could give me a lift home tomorrow, if you're driving straight down. I know you're leaving early.'

I was interested by this, because I had never heard Damian speak of his home before. 'Where is home?' I said.

'Northampton. I imagine you'll drive straight past it. Unless you're not going back to London at all.'

'Of course I'll take you. I'll pick you up at about nine.'

That seemed to be the end of it. Mission accomplished. He stood. 'I think I'll go to bed,' he said. There was something curiously unembroidered about his manner, which I had come to see as endlessly calculated. But not tonight.

'What did you think of the party?'

'Amazing.'

'And did you have a good time?'

'So-so,' he said.

As promised, I arrived back at the abbey at approximately nine the following morning. The door was standing open so I just went in. As I had expected, the house party might still have been in their rooms, but the place was a whirl of activity. A great house on the day after a party is always rather evocative. Servants were wandering about, collecting missed glasses and things, and carrying furniture back to their proper places. The table was being assembled at one end of the dining room, while the huge carpet was unrolled in front of me, and when I asked after the house party's breakfast I was nodded through to the little dining room beyond it, a simple room, if not as little as all that, enlivened by some paintings of racehorses, with their riders in the Gresham colours. Lady Claremont had broken her usual rule and there were three tables, a bit jammed in, set for about twenty-four. Damian was alone, finishing off a piece of toast. He stood as I entered. 'My case is already in the hall.'

'Don't you want to say goodbye to anyone?'

'They're all asleep and I said goodbye last night.' So, without further ado, we loaded up his bag and left. He didn't say anything much as we drove along, beyond a few directions, until we were back on the A1 heading south. Then, at last, he did speak. 'I'm not going to do that again,' he said.

'We're none of us going to do much more of it. I think I've only got another two dances and a few charity things, then it's over.'

'I'm not even going to them. I've had enough. I should do some work, anyway, before I forget what it is I'm supposed to be studying.'

I looked at him. There was something resolute and glum about him, which was new. 'Did anything happen last night?' I asked.

'What do you mean?'

'You seem rather disenchanted.'

'If I am disenchanted, it has nothing to do with last night. It's the whole bloody, self-indulgent, boring thing. I've had enough of it.'

'Which of course is your privilege.'

After that, we drove more or less in silence until at last we reached Northampton. It is not a town I know, but Damian took me safely to a row of perfectly respectable semi-detached 1930s villas, all built of brick with tiles hung above the waistline, and each with a name on the gate. The one we stopped outside was called 'Sunnyside.' As we were unloading, the door opened and a middle-aged couple came out, the man in a rather loud jersey and worsted slacks, and the women in a grey skirt with a cardigan over her shoulders, held in place by a shiny chain. The man came forward to take the case. 'This is my father,' said Damian and he introduced me. I shook hands and said hello.

'Pleased to meet you,' said Mr Baxter.

'How do you do,' I said in return, deliberately blocking his cheerful welcome by not answering in kind, with what I foolishly imagined, in my youthful fatuity, to be good breeding.

'Won't you come in?' said Mrs Baxter. 'Would you like a coffee?' But I didn't go in and I didn't have any coffee. I regret it now, that refusal of their hospitality. My excuse was that I had an appointment in London at three o'clock and I wasn't sure I'd make it as it was. I told myself it was important, and perhaps it was, but I regret it now. And even if I couldn't bring myself to say it, I was pleased to meet them. They were nice, decent people; the mother went out of her way to be polite and the father was, I think, a clever man. I learned later that he was the manager of a shoe factory with a special interest in opera and it saddened me in a way that I had not met them before. That they had not been included in any of the year's frolics, not even at the university. Looking back, I realise it was a key moment for me, though I wasn't aware of it at the time, in that it was one of the first instances when I came to appreciate the insidious poison of snobbery, the tyranny of it, the meaningless values that made me reject their friendly overtures, that had made Damian hide these two, pleasant, intelligent people because he was ashamed of them.

On the morning in question, I realise now, Damian was making a kind of statement of apology, of non-shame, by bringing me here. He had hidden them behind a barrier because he did not want me to judge him, to look down on him, on the basis of his parents, with whom there was nothing wrong at all, and in this he was right. We would have looked down on him. I blush to write it and I liked them when I met them, but we would have done, without any moral justification whatever. He had wanted to move into a different world and he felt part of that would be shedding his background. He'd managed the transition, but on this particular morning I think he was ashamed of

339

his ambition, ashamed of rejecting his own past. The truth is we should all have been ashamed in having played along with it without question. At any rate, with avowals to meet again the following Monday at Cambridge we parted and I got back into my car.

We did meet again, of course, several times, but we did not meet alone for the rest of my time at university. Essentially my friendship with Damian Baxter ended on that day, the morning after Serena Gresham's dance, and I cannot pretend I was sorry, even if my feelings for him were less savage then than they would be when we did next find ourselves under the same roof. But that was a couple of years later, when we were out in the world, and quite a different story.

FOURTEEN

The weekend passed pleasantly enough. We ate, we talked, we slept, we walked. Sophie Jamieson turned out to share my interest in French history and the Purbricks were great friends of some cousins of mine who lived near them, so it all went very smoothly in the way of these things. I must say Andrew had not improved with the years. Having inherited the earldom and the savaged remnant that the family lawyer's depredations had left of the estate, it was as if the last vestiges of self-knowledge or self-doubt had been flung to the four winds. He was king, and a very angry king at that, raging at the gardeners and the cook and his wife about almost everything. Serena took it all in her stride but once, when I was on my way downstairs before dinner on Friday evening, I found him haranguing her in the hall about a frame that should have been mended or something. I caught her eye as I was on my way to the library door and she did not look away but raised her eyebrows slightly, which he would not have seen and which I took as more or less the greatest compliment an English toff can pay: to include you in their private, family dramas.

After lunch on Saturday, when we'd finished drinking our cups of coffee in the drawing room, Serena proposed a walk by the river and most of us stuck up our hands to join her. 'You'll need boots,' she said, but there were masses of spares for people who'd forgotten them, so we were soon equipped and on our way. The gardens at Waverly were pretty and predictable, the usual Victorian layout that had been calmed down by the restriction of only having two gardeners instead of twelve, and we walked through them, admiring vocally as we went, but they weren't the main pleasure ground event. Serena led us out of a gate and on down an avenue through a paddock and into a wood, until finally we came out on to a grassy bank, perfectly placed to allow us to walk along the edge of a wide river whose name I now forget. I admired the wonders of nature. 'It's totally artificial,' she said. 'They rerouted the riverbed in the 1850s and made the walks to go with the altered course.' I could only reflect on the brilliance of that generation in their understanding of how to live.

We were alone in a comfortable pair by then, as the others had lagged behind. I looked around at the view as Serena slid her arm through mine. On the other side of the water a huge willow leaned over, trailing its creeper-like branches on the surface, making ripples in the flow. Suddenly there was a flurry of movement and a heron appeared above the trees, wide wings beating back and forth, slowly and rhythmically, as it sailed across the sky. 'They're such thieves. Andrew says we should shoot them or the river will be quite empty.' But even as she spoke the words, her eyes followed the great, grey bird on its wondrous journey. 'It's such a privilege to live here,' she said after a minute or two.

I looked at her. 'I hope so.'

'It is.' She was staring me straight in the eye, so I think she was trying to be honest. 'He's quite a different person when we're alone.'

Naturally, this was very flattering, as the lack of names or qualifications implied a kind of shorthand between us which I was thrilled to think might exist, and even more thrilled by the idea that she recognised it, but in another way she was registering her guilt at signalling Andrew's preposterous behaviour in the hall the previous evening. Her statement is anyway the standard defence of all women who find themselves married to, or stuck with, men who all their friends think are awful. Often this comes as a revelation after quite a considerable period during which they thought people quite liked their mate, and it must be a disappointment to discover that the reverse is true, but I would guess this was not the case where Serena was concerned. Nobody had ever liked Andrew. Of course, it is an effective defence to claim hidden qualities for your other half, because by definition it is impossible to disprove. I suppose logic tells one that it must sometimes be true, but I found it hard to believe that Andrew Belton in private was sensitive, endearing and fun, not least because there is no cure for stupidity. Still, I prayed that it might be even partially the case. 'If you say so, I believe it,' I replied.

We walked on for a while before Serena spoke again. 'I wish you'd tell me what you're really doing for Damian.'

'I have told you.'

'You're not going to all this trouble just to get some funny stories from four decades ago. Candida tells me you've been over to Los Angeles to see the dreaded Terry K.'

I couldn't be bothered to be dishonest, since we were so near the end. 'I can't tell you now,' I said, 'because it isn't my secret. But I will tell you soon, if you're interested.'

'I am.' She pondered my answer for a bit. 'I never saw him again after that ghastly night.'

'No. Nor did most of the guests.'

'Yet I often think of him.'

She had brought it up and so I thought I would try to satisfy something that had been niggling me. 'When you planned that whole thing with Candida, turning up out of the blue, what were you hoping to achieve? I can remember you now, standing in that vast, sun-baked square, in those terrible black clothes you all had to borrow.'

She gave a snort of laughter. 'That was so crazy.'

'But what did you hope would come out of it?'

This was a big question and years before it would have been unaskable. But she did not reproach me, or even look cross to be put on the spot. 'Nothing, once my parents were on board. I should have given up the whole idea the moment they said they were coming. I don't know why I didn't.'

'But originally. When you first plotted it?'

She shook her head and her hair caught a glint of the sun. 'To be honest, I don't really know what I wanted to come out of it, given how I managed things later. I suppose I felt trapped. And angry. I was married and a mother and Christ knows what, all before I was twenty-one, and I felt I'd been lured into a cage and the door had slammed shut. Damian stood for everything that had been taken from me. But it was silly. We hadn't been honest with each other and that always makes for trouble. It would all have been different if we were young today, but how does that help?'

'Do you still feel trapped?'

343

She smiled. 'Isn't there a laboratory test where if animals are kept in a trap long enough, they come back when they're let out, because it's home?' We strolled on, listening to the birds. 'Does he ever talk about me?' Despite a Pavlovian irritation, this question interested me. More or less every woman I had seen on my quest had asked this and Serena wasn't even one of the contenders. It was pointless to deny that Damian clearly had qualities that I had been quite unaware of at the time.

'Of course we talk about you. You're the one thing we have in common.' I said it as a joke, although it was truer than I had previously known. I could not tell you how she took it, but she smiled and we walked on.

'Did you see the picture in your room?'

'I did.'

'Classic. I put it out for you. God, weren't we young?'

'Young and, in your case, lovely.'

She sighed. 'I can never understand why you and I didn't get off together at some point, during the whole thing.'

This made me stop in my tracks. 'Can't you? I can. You didn't fancy me.' There was no point in beating about the bush.

She looked a little miffed, perhaps because it sounded as if I were reproaching her, which I truly wasn't. 'You never pressed your case very hard,' she said at last. She was apparently attempting at least to share the blame for our non-romance.

'Because I knew that if I did, our friendship would become untenable and I would drop out of your life. It was fun for you to have me dying for love, as long as it never became embarrassing and I never put you on the spot. You could have had me any day you wished, with a crook of your finger, which you were fully aware of. But you never wanted me, except as a courtier worshipping at your shrine. And I was happy. If that was the best that was on offer, I was glad to oblige.'

She made a slight expression of horror at this perfectly honest account. 'Did you know all that, then?'

I shook my head. 'No. Except possibly instinctively. But I know it now.'

'Oh dear,' she said. 'You make me sound like such a bitch.'

But this wasn't right and I was anxious for her to know I didn't think it. 'Not at all. It worked well for a long time. I was your *parfit knight* and you were *la belle dame sans merci*. It's an arrangement that has been perfectly serviceable for hundreds of years, after all. It only went wrong because of Portugal and that wasn't your fault. It became embarrassing after that evening, so we dropped out of each other's lives, but it would only have happened sooner if I'd made a pass.'

She thought for a time, as we walked on again in silence. There was a rustle of movement in the undergrowth and the distinctive red of a fox's coat flashed through the browns and greens for a moment. As if recognising him, she spoke, 'Damian has much to answer for.'

'The interesting thing is I think he would agree with you.'

The others were closing in on us now and soon the conversation would become general again. But before they reached where we were standing Serena spoke softly. 'I hope you don't hate me.'

Her voice was gentle and, I think, sincere, and when I turned towards her, she was smiling. I don't think she meant it as a serious enquiry, but she was apologising for wounding me in those lost years, when heart pain could be so sharp and was so easily administered. I looked at her and for the millionth time wondered at every feature. A tiny crumb of something from lunch was clinging to the corner of her mouth and I imagined a life where I would have the right to lick it off. 'What do you think?' I said.

Dinner that night was the main event of the weekend and I dutifully bathed, putting on evening trousers, a shirt with no tie, reluctantly, and a smoking jacket. I went downstairs feeling rather cheery but, once in the drawing room, things got heavier with the inclusion among the guests for the evening of Andrew's mother, the now Dowager Countess, who lived not in the real dower house, a smart Georgian villa on the edge of the park, which was let to an American banker, but in a cottage in the village formerly reserved for the head keeper. She was standing stiffly by the chimneypiece when I came in. Lady Belton was a lot older, naturally, than when I had last seen her, but age had done little to soothe her incipient madness. She still stared out of those pale-blue, Dutch-doll eyes, and her hair was dyed to an approximation of the Italianate black it had once been. Nor had her sense of style made much of a leap forward. She wore a curious outfit, a kind of long, khaki nightgown with an uneven neckline. I'm not sure what effect she was aiming at, but it can't have been what she achieved. Her jewellery, I need hardly say, was excellent.

Serena introduced me, observing that her mother-in-law must remember me from the old days. Lady Belton ignored this. 'How do you do,' she said, extending her bony, knuckled hand. Is there anything more annoying than people saying how do you do when you have met them a thousand times? If there is, I would like to know what it might be. I had a recent instance where I was greeted as a stranger by a woman I'd known since childhood, who had grown famous in the interim. Every time I met her for literally years, she would lean forward gracefully and make no sign that we had ever seen each other before. Finally I resolved that if she tried it one more time I would let her have it. But something of my resolve must have shown in my face and all bullies are equipped with an antenna that tells them when the bullying must stop. She read my eyes and held out her hand. 'How lovely to see you again,' she said.

Serena had moved off to get me a drink, so I was left alone with the old besom. 'It's so nice to catch up with Andrew and Serena after all these years,' I said feebly by way of an opener.

'Do you know Lord Belton?' she replied, without a glimmer of a smile. Presumably this was to show me that I should have referred to him by his proper rank. There was a bowl of avocado dip quite near us on a side table, and just for a second I had an almost irresistible urge to pick it up and squish it into her face.

Instead, I opened my mouth to say 'Yes, I know them and I know you too, you silly, old bat.' But there's no point, is there? She would only have hidden behind my 'terrible rudeness' and never have recognised her own. I didn't draw her at dinner, hallelujah, and instead I watched pityingly as Hugh Purbrick battled through her silences, trying to engage her with talk of people she must have met but of whom she denied all knowledge, or on topics in which she made it clear she had no interest. In short, she gave him no quarter.

The young are often told, or were in the days when I was a child, that parvenus and other rank outsiders may on occasion be rude, but *real* ladies and gentlemen are never anything but perfectly polite. This is, of course, complete rubbish. The rude, like the polite, may be found at every level of society, but there is a particular kind of rudeness, when it rests on empty snobbery, on an assumption of superiority made by people who have nothing superior about them, who have nothing about them at all, in fact, that is unique to the upper classes and very hard to swallow. Old Lady Belton was a classic example, a walking mass of bogus values, a hollow gourd, a cause for revolution. I had disliked her when I was young, but now, after forty years to think about it, I saw her as worse than simply unpleasant and foolish. Rather, I recognised her as someone who would be almost evil if she weren't so stupid, as the very reason for her children's empty lives. There is much that makes me nostalgic for the England of my youth, much that I think has been lost to our detriment, but sometimes one must recognise where it was wrong and why it had to change. Where the upper classes are concerned, Lady Belton was that reason made flesh. She was an embodiment of all that was bad about the old system and of absolutely none of its virtues. I do not like to hate but I confess that, seeing her again, I almost hated her. I hated her for what she represented and because, ultimately, I blamed her for Andrew's worthlessness. If I were to be merciful where he is concerned, and I find it hard, I would acknowledge that with a mother like the one he had he never stood a chance. Between them, these two pointless people had wasted my Serena's life. Andrew was in fact Lady Belton's other neighbour at dinner that night, since she had been placed, in accordance with precedence, on his right. They did not exchange one word from soup to nuts. Neither could be judged a loser by it.

Afterwards, some of the party made up a table for bridge and a few of them sneaked off to watch a late film on television in some chaotic children's cubbyhole where Andrew had banished 'the foul machine,' so after the locals had gone home and the rest of the house party had taken themselves off to bed, I found myself with Candida in a corner of the library, hugging a glass of whisky, gossiping as the fire died. Serena had looked in and made us free with the tray of drinks but she was taken up with settling the others, and for me it was enough just to see her operating her existence, charting her course through the commitments that made her days real. And I was pleased to be left alone with Candida, since it meant that I was able to continue my investigations. I had told Candida about finding the picture in my room the night before, but now we were alone we fell to discussing that party of so long ago, how it went and how it ended. I reminded her that I had driven Damian home in rather a glump, and that it marked the finish of his career as a deb's delight. 'Poor Damian,' she said. 'I've never felt sorrier for anybody.'

This was an unexpected comment, since I had no idea what she was talking about. 'Why?'

My query was clearly as much of a surprise to her as her statement had been to me. 'Because of the whole drama,' she replied, as if this must be quite obvious.

'What drama?'

She gave me a quizzical look, as if I might be teasing and leading her on, but my gaze was as innocent as a newborn child's. 'How amazing,' she said. 'Did he really never tell you?'

Then I asked and I listened.

Candida knew Damian well, long before that night. She had flirted with him in her frightening way, she had danced with him, even, I suspected as she talked, slept with him and generally befriended him as the season had progressed. And she had managed to get him included in the Gresham house party, without drawing attention to Serena, and —

'But I don't understand. Why did you? I thought you fancied him yourself.' I remembered that other, different Candida rolling her eyes at Queen Charlotte's Ball and almost shuddered.

She shook her head. 'That was all finished long before. And by that time he and Serena were in love with each other.' Again she spoke as if I must surely have had some suspicion of these things at the very least, and it was precious of me to pretend that I did not. 'That is, I thought they were in love with each other. Serena was in love with him.'

'I don't believe it.' Of course, I didn't want to believe it and in truth I hadn't seen much evidence. They'd kissed. But if we were supposed to be in love with everyone we'd ever kissed . . .

She shrugged as if to say believe what you like, I am telling you the truth. 'She wanted to marry him, absurd as that sounds, and as you know, she was eighteen at the time and Damian was nineteen and still at university, so they needed her parents' consent.'

'Why? When did the law change?'

'At the beginning of 1970. It was still twenty-one in Sixty-eight.'

'But the Claremonts would never have given their consent if he'd been the Duke of Gloucester.'

'Yes, they would. They did. They pushed her into marrying Andrew the following year, and she was still only nineteen.' Which was true. 'Anyway, Serena had got it into her head that if they could only get to know Damian they would fall for him and in time give their permission, which obviously I can now see was a hopeless idea.'

'Worse than hopeless. Insane.'

My intervention was not soothing to her. 'Yes. Well, as I say, I know that now, but at the time I had convinced myself, or Serena had convinced me, that it might work. It wasn't that she wanted to plunge into obscurity with him. She was sure that Damian would do incredibly well in his career and history has, after all, proved her right a thousand times over.'

I nodded. This conversation was having an uncomfortable effect on me. I was feeling numb and strangely tingly, as if I were coming down with 'flu. I am not pretending I didn't know they were attracted to each other, they were both good-looking and on the circuit and, as I've admitted, I'd seen the kissing incident at Terry's ball. That was enough to make me jealous and angry and indignant, but this ... this was something entirely different. This was when I learned a lesson I will not now lose, although it has come too late to do much good. Namely, that just because you start people off, you do not control them there-after, nor do you have the right to pretend that you do. However Damian began that year under my aegis, however he met those people initially, he was living a life among them, in that world, by the end of it, that was as valid as my own. I had brought him out from under his stone, but at the finish he'd held the promise in his hands of what would have constituted my whole life's happiness. I was so jealous I wanted to kill almost anybody.

'Well, somehow her parents got wind of the whole plan. I thought later it might have been Andrew who had tipped off his mother, the dreaded Lady B. Wasn't she ghastly tonight?'

'Ghastly.'

'Well, she was desperate to catch Serena for Andrew and she might have deliberately put a spoke in the works, but we'll never know. On the day, Damian and Serena drove down together from London. I was coming from somewhere or other, but I got here at about five, after most of the house party, and they were all having tea in the drawing room. Of course, Aunt Roo was being very charming—'

'Why is she called Aunt Roo?'

She thought for a moment. 'I'm not completely sure. I think it's something to do with *Winnie the Pooh*. Remember the mother kangaroo was called Kanga and the baby was called Roo?' I nodded. 'It was some game they used to play at Barrymount, when they were growing up in Ireland. Her real name's Rosemary, but she was always Roo in the family.' Somehow Lady Claremont's nickname only reinforced the iron walls of the culture that Damian, in his youthful ignorance, took on all those years ago.

'Anyway, when I came in, Damian was trying very hard. Too hard. He smiled and chatted and giggled and flashed and flickered, and Aunt Roo laughed and asked him about Cambridge and so on, but I remember thinking Uncle Pel was very quiet – which he wasn't usually in those days – and I could tell by the look she gave me, that Serena knew it wasn't going as well as Damian obviously thought. The guests who were staying did that silent thing, of not quite laughing and not quite letting him in. My other aunt was there, and as Damian was rabbiting on, Aunt Sheila and Roo kept swapping quiet, sisterly glances, which seemed so unkind and disloyal. I can see that's not terribly logical for me to say, but I felt infuriated for Serena, for both of them really.' She paused, breathless with the memory. 'I suppose that was the moment when I realised it wasn't going to work.'

She stopped for a moment, as if this was the first time she had ever fully registered this salient point. 'So. We all went up to change and I was sitting at my dressing table, doing my best with my hair. I remember I'd forgotten to have it done, which seems a bit mad for your own dance, but at this precise moment there was a knock and Roo and Pel came into the room. They were already changed and Roo was covered in diamonds, and it should all have been rather merry and gay, but somehow it wasn't. Then Uncle Pel said, "How long has this been going on?" And we were all quite quiet, as if someone was supposed to ask what he was talking about, but of course we all knew what he was talking about, so there wasn't any point. Then I started a defence of Serena and Damian, of both of them, but even as I was talking I could hear that it all sounded so childish and ridiculous, as if I were suddenly seeing it through their eyes. I'd never been with Uncle Pel when he was so angry, in fact I'd never really seen him angry at all, but that night he was bulging with anger, blazing with it. "She wants to run off with this smarmy, little oik?" he said. "This greaser, with his oily hair and his dodgy vowels and his 'pleased to meet you' and his clothes from Marks and Spencer?" I've never forgotten that. "*His clothes from Marks and Spencer.*" And I looked at Roo and she said "Watson unpacked for him," and that was that. Then it was her turn. "Of course we want Serena to be happy," she said. "It's all we want. Truly." Which it obviously wasn't. "But you see, we want her to be happy in a way we understand, in a way that will last."'

'I said I thought that this would last, but even as I spoke the words I felt like some little, preppy, Sandra Dee figure asking to be allowed to stay out late.' Candida sighed. 'I'm afraid I wasn't much use.'

'Did Damian really say "pleased to meet you"?'

'Apparently. It just shows how nervous he must have been.'

'Poor chap. Was that it?'

She shook her head. 'By no means. Uncle Pel hadn't finished. He was absolutely fizzing and he sort of waved his finger at me, right under my nose, like a teacher in a situation comedy, as if I were the guilty one, which I now think he must have believed, since he knew I'd connived in getting Damian up there. "You tell Serena to get rid of this little social-climbing, money-grubbing shit," he said. "You tell her to dump him, if she doesn't want to leave it to me to manage. That kind of chap comes into this house by the servants' entrance, or not at all."'

I couldn't help interrupting. 'That sounds rather vulgar for the Lord Claremont I remember.'

Candida nodded. 'You're right. It wasn't him at all. I think he was just so angry that his mental, editing machine had switched itself off. In fairness to Roo, it was too much for her, too, and she slapped him down. She said, "Really, Pel, don't be so idiotic. You sound like a period drama on television. You'll be telling him to get off your land next." When she said that I smiled. I couldn't help myself, but Roo saw it as a breach in the wall and she turned to me in the most coaxing way. "We have nothing against this young man, Candida," she said, and she spoke very calmly, but in a way her calmness was more deadly to

Serena's hopes than Pel's fury, as I could tell it was not a mood that might blow away in the morning. "Honestly we don't. He is making an effort to be nice and he is perfectly welcome as a guest. But you must see it's out of the question. The whole thing is simply ludicrous and that's all there is to it." She paused, I assume to let me nod. Which I didn't, so she ploughed on. "Just find a way to tell Serena that we don't think it a good idea. It'll come much better from you. If we tackle her it'll blow up into a hideous production. She's a sensible girl. I'm sure she'll see the wisdom of what we're saying when she's had time to think.' I asked her if they wanted me to tell Serena that night, but she shook her head. "No. Don't spoil the party," she said. "Tell her tomorrow or the next day, before you leave. When you have a quiet moment." Then she waited for a response and I suppose, by being silent, in a way I'd agreed.'

'So did you?'

Again Candida shook her head. 'I didn't have to. That's the point. After we'd all stopped hissing at each other we could hear the sounds of the first batch of people arriving for dinner, and Pel and Roo went down to greet them. I was still sitting in front of the glass, feeling a bit bludgeoned to tell the truth, and I heard a voice. "That's me told." I looked over and Damian was standing there.'

'In your room?'

'Yes.' She nodded, scrunching up her eyes for a second at the memory. 'He was next door, which maybe I'd forgotten, if I even knew. There was a pair of interconnecting doors, those doors that were so useful to the Edwardians, with a space between them, a couple of feet wide, which formed a completely effective sound barrier, and neither Pel nor Roo had shouted, so I wasn't worried. The door was shut and since there was an armchair in front of it I must have assumed that it was locked, that they both were, but they weren't. I suppose he'd been standing in the space between the two doors and now he'd opened the one into my room and come through it. The whole thing was so terrible I can hardly frame the words to describe it. I remember it now, forty years later, as one of the most horrible moments of my entire life, which, believe me, is saying something. We just stared at each other, then eventually I muttered about their not understanding his feelings, and hoping that he wouldn't hate them and all that sort of thing. But

Damian shook his head with a brisk little chuckle, and said, "Hate them? Why should I hate them? They've found me out." And I didn't understand him at first, because I'd been so convinced by Serena that he really did love her. So I couldn't believe that he was telling me it wasn't true, that all the time he'd been out to catch her for her money and whatnot. I didn't want to believe him, but that's what he said. He told Serena later on that night, so I didn't have to. She and I talked about it, but only once. And I don't think they saw each other again – except for that one ghastly evening in Portugal, of course. They might have run into each other at some gathering over the years, I suppose, but I never heard her mention it, if they did. He wasn't at any more of the parties that year. He seemed to give us all up after the incident and I can't say I'm surprised.'

'Nor me. When did he tell her?'

'Right at the end. I'm sure he wouldn't have wanted to spoil the evening, but he couldn't have borne for her to hear it from anyone else and I think he'd already decided to leave first thing the next day. I seem to remember that he got her into the Tapestry Drawing Room just before it all folded, but I may have made that up.'

'And he told her it had all been his plan to advance himself and that he didn't love her?'

'I suppose so. I mean yes. Although, even now, I don't think it was ever the whole truth. He might have seen her as a ladder in some way, but I'm sure he was genuinely fond of her.'

'I doubt it was true at all. If said he loved her I'm sure he did.'

She looked at me, surprised. 'I thought you disliked him.'

'I hated him. I hate him now, really, if marginally less than before. That doesn't mean I think him a liar, which I don't, except under extreme provocation.'

She grimaced. 'As we know.'

But I didn't want to drift away to that other, cursed evening. I wanted to stay with the night of the ball. 'He was lying to you to save face. I wonder that you couldn't see that. She was never going to have much money anyway. If he was after that, he'd have gone for Joanna Langley.'

She blushed. 'You don't think he wanted a grand wife with a title?'

'He wouldn't have cared about it. Not then. Maybe at the beginning, but not by that stage. He turned down Dagmar of Moravia. He could have had a princess for a wife if he'd wanted.'

She thought about this. 'Well, I must have agreed with you at the time, or the whole Portuguese adventure would never have happened. I suppose the years have made me more cynical than I was.'

'Poor Serena. So she'd made her decision to defy her parents and marry her true love, and then, in one short evening, it was finished and there was nothing left for her to do but to go out on to the terrace for some fresh air and to come up with a new life scheme.'

'Did she? You know more about it than I do.'

'Yes, she did. And then she came in again and found me waiting in the anteroom, and we danced together just before I left.' I thought of Serena's blank eyes and her muttered 'these things are such milestones.' She might have said millstones. It would have been just as true.

'I see. Well, perhaps you're right about Damian. I hope so. But he's had his revenge in a way. He ended up a figure of far greater significance than any of the rest of us. I wonder if Pel and Roo ever think about that.'

'You did have a soft spot for him, then?'

'Damian? Oh, absolutely. I adored him. As I told you, we did have a bit of a thing, but it was earlier in the year than all this. Once Damian and Serena got together, I don't remember him being involved with anyone else in our crowd.'

'Until after.'

She blushed, slightly. 'Oh, yes. After. But you know how it is during the lonely years. Before life settles.'

'Can I ask an impertinent question?'

She smiled. 'I think after the talk we've just had I can hardly prevent it.'

'Who was Archie's father? Did I know him? Was he one of the gang from that era? Or was it someone you met when it was over?'

'It's hard to say.'

Which seemed a peculiar reply. 'Do you ever see him now?'

'I don't know.' I stared at her, looking, I imagine, fairly puzzled and she laughed. 'These days I'm an old, respectable banker's widow, but it was not always thus. You must know that everyone has some parts of their life that are hard to reconcile with their present.'

I nodded. 'I know it better than most.' And I certainly already knew it about her.

'The truth is I'm not quite sure who Archie's father was. I bounced around a fair bit at that time. I think my excuse was that I'd lost my way or I was trying to find myself, or some other Sixties cliché that allowed me to do as I pleased without feeling guilty, and I took full advantage of the philosophy. Then, one day I woke up pregnant. Every single entry in my address book wanted me to get rid of it, of course, friends and family alike, but I wouldn't and I am terribly grateful now.'

'But you never tried to find out?'

'I didn't see the point. What would I have gained? Someone poking their nose in where it wasn't wanted? Some emotional cripple who felt he had the right to lean on me because I'd carried his child? At one stage I thought it might be George Tremayne. I was pretty sure later that it wasn't, but imagine what it would have been like having him getting sloshed at the kitchen table.' I grimaced. 'So, no. I decided to battle through it alone.'

'How were you sure? That it wasn't George?'

She thought for a moment. 'I heard that he was having trouble getting his wife pregnant. That rather chubby girl whose father made cars. She'd got two children by a first husband, so it couldn't have been her.' She nodded, satisfied with her own conclusions. 'Anyway, having Archie put me back on the straight and narrow. It was a bumpy road for a bit, even if it was straight, and God knows it was narrow. But it led me to Harry.'

'So there was a happy ending.'

She smiled. 'That's so nice. To hear Harry described as my happy ending. These days everyone who says his name bursts into tears. But they're wrong and you're right. He *was* my happy ending. And now,' she stood, stretching herself, 'I really must go to bed or I'll die.'

I was deep in a dream involving Neil Kinnock and Joan Crawford and a woman who used to work for my mother as a cleaner called Mrs Pointer. We were all trying to have a picnic on Beachy Head, but the tartan rug kept blowing up and spilling everything, and for some reason we couldn't weight it down. Until we decided to lie on it to hold it steady, but how can that have worked and what did we do with the

355

food? Which didn't seem to matter much, as Joan was squeezing into my back and she slid an arm round my waist, letting her hand slide down as she did so, and ... I woke up. Except I hadn't woken up, because although it was fairly dark and I wasn't at a picnic any more, I could still feel Joan's body pressed into mine and a gentle hand enfolding my erect penis, and then a voice said 'are you awake?' very softly, and it didn't sound at all like Joan's. Not a bit. It wasn't even American. I thought about this for a moment, because the voice was familiar and I felt I should know it but I didn't recognise it until it spoke my name, and suddenly I knew beyond any doubt ... it was Serena's. It was Serena Belton's voice and she was here beside me, with her hand on my penis. And then I still couldn't believe I wasn't dreaming, because this, after all, was my lifelong dream, and I began to wonder whether I was in a dream within a dream, when you think you've woken up but you haven't. And I might have gone on thinking this for a bit longer if her lips had not nestled into the side of my cheek and I turned, and she was there.

In the flesh. In my arms. In my bed.

'Is this really happening?' I whispered, afraid that if I spoke too loudly the whole mirage would shimmer and disappear. It was very early dawn and the soft, dim, grey light had begun to creep in through the cracks in the curtains, lightening the room just enough for me to make her out, her shining, sacred head on the pillow next to mine.

'It is if you want it to.'

I smiled. 'Do you make a habit of stealing into men's rooms at night?'

'Only when they're in love with me,' she said.

I still could not accept this gift from heaven. 'But why? I know you don't love me. We had a long discussion about it this very afternoon.' Of all things, I didn't want to frighten her away, but I did want to understand.

'I love your love,' she said. 'I don't pretend to share it, and when we were young I doubt that I was much more than amused. But as the years went on and bad things happened, I always knew one man in the world at least loved me. And that was you. Seeing you again reminded me of it.'

'Is that why you got me down here?'

356

'You make me feel safe. When we met up in Yorkshire I felt glad to see you and that was why. I am safe in your love. I wish we saw more of you. I don't know why we drifted out of each other's lives.'

'I thought it was because of what Damian said.'

She shook her head. 'I knew it was nonsense. I knew it straight away but even more as time went on. He was in pain, that's all.'

'So was I by the end of that dinner.' For the first time in my life, I could envisage a day when I would find it funny.

She stroked my hair, or what was left of it. 'You should have stayed. You both should have stayed on afterwards and laughed.'

'I couldn't.' She did not argue, and together we let the bitter memory go and returned to the glorious present. Suddenly I felt the freedom to touch her surge through me, like a child who finally lets himself believe that it really *is* Christmas morning. I reached up and traced the outline of her lips with my finger.

She kissed it gently as I did so. 'You may not know it, but you have seen me through some dark times and this is your reward.' As she spoke she moved closer and brought her mouth to mine, and we began, as the phrase has it, to make love. And while many times in my life those words have not been an accurate description of the activity they refer to, on that occasion they were as true as the Gospel. What we were making in that bed on that blessed morn was love. Pure love. Nor was there the slightest diminution of passion because the woman in my arms was a matron in her fifties rather than the lissom girl I had hungered for so many years before. She was my Serena at last. I held her in my arms and, for this one time perhaps, I was hers. I had finally arrived at my yearned-for destination. And although I was so aroused by her presence that I thought I would explode at one more touch, still, when I entered her, the sensation that filled me with a hot glow like molten lava was not just sexual excitement but total happiness. It sounds sentimental, which I am not as a rule, but that moment of being inside Serena, of feeling myself held by her body, for the first and presumably the only time in my life, after waiting for forty years, was the single happiest moment I have ever known, the climax, the very peak of my existence, nor do I expect to equal it before the grave claims me.

I do not seek recognition as a skilful lover. I assume I am no better and no worse than most men, but if ever I knew what I was doing that was the day. I dare say I should have felt guilty, but I didn't. Her husband had the gift of her whole, adult life and he would never know the value of it. I did, and I felt that I deserved my hour without enraging too many of the gods. I am glad and relieved to relate that my tired, fat, flabby body rose to the challenge of the chance of paradise and never have I been so entirely engrossed in the present to the exclusion of all else. For those minutes I had no future and no past, only her. We made love three times before she slipped away, and when I stared at the gathered silk canopy above my head I knew I was a different man from the one who had lain down to sleep. I had made love to a woman I was absolutely and entirely in love with. The woman who held my heart had opened her body to the rest of me. There is no greater joy allowed us. Not on earth. And, in echo of Candida, I knew, because of that single episode, because of this one hour in a life of many years, because I had known real, unconditional bliss I could never again be a sad man. I thought it then, I think it now, and I am grateful. If Damian's search led me to this, then I was paid in full and far in excess of any mortal man's deserts.

Portugal and After

FIFTEEN

As it happened, the fateful invitation to Portugal came right out of the blue. One day the telephone rang in my parents' flat – where I was, on the principle of Hobson's choice, still living – and when I picked it up a familiar voice asked for me by name. 'Speaking,' I said.

'That was easy. I thought I was going to have to track you down through ten addresses. It's Candida. Candida Finch.'

'Hello.' I could not keep the surprise out of my voice entirely, since we had never been all that friendly.

'I know. Why am I ringing? Well, it's an invitation, really. Is there any chance I could tempt you to join a gang of us in Estoril for a couple of weeks at the end of July? An old friend of mine has got a job in Lisbon, in some bank or other, and they've given him this huge villa and no one to put in it. He says if we can all just get ourselves out there, we can stay as long as we like for nothing. So I thought it might be fun to mount a sort of reunion of the Class of Sixty-eight, before we've all forgotten what we look like. What do you say?' My surprise was not lessened by any of this, as I wasn't aware that I'd ever been a favourite of hers while the Season was going on, let alone why I should be chosen for a special reunion.

I had not seen Candida Finch much after the whole thing came to an end and by the time of the call almost two years had passed since the events I have been revisiting. It was in the early summer of 1970, when my days as a dancing partner were long behind me. I had left Cambridge that June, with a perfectly respectable if not overwhelming degree, and the perilous career of a writer beckoned. Or at least it did not beckon, because I soon realised that I was trying to push through a solid, brick wall. My father was not hostile to my plan, once he had got over his disappointment that I wasn't going to do anything sensible, but he declined to support me economically. 'If it isn't going to work, old boy,' he said genially, 'we'd better find out sooner rather than later,' which was, of course, in its way, a direct challenge. Eventually I got a job as a kind of super office boy in a publishing group for children's magazines, which would begin in the following September and for which I would be paid a handsome stipend that would have comfortably maintained a Yorkshire terrier. I did go on to do the job, for three years in fact, finally clambering up to some sort of junior editing post, and somehow I managed to make ends meet. My mother used to cheat, as mothers will; she would slip me notes and pay for clothes and pick up my bills for petrol and car repairs, but even she would not actually give me a regular allowance, as she would have felt disloyal to my father. Let us say that during this period of my time on earth I lived, I survived, but it was essentially a life without frills or extras. All of which harsh reality I knew would be my fate at the end of that summer and it made Candida's suggestion seem rather inviting.

'That's incredibly kind of you. Who else is coming?' Of course, I knew as I said this that I had to accept, because you can't ask who is coming to some event and then refuse. Inevitably it sounds as if you might have accepted if the guest list had been of a higher standard.

Candida knew this. 'I think we'll have fun. We've got Dagmar and Lucy and the Tremayne brothers.' I wasn't mad about the Tremaynes, but I didn't actually hate them, and I was actively fond of the other two, so the idea was growing on me. I knew there wasn't the smallest chance I would otherwise have a proper holiday that year before I started what I liked to call my 'career.' 'I've found a charter airline where they almost pay you, so the tickets will cost about sixpence. Can I definitely include you in?'

I am ashamed to say this settled it. I was confident I could get my dear mama to sub a cheap ticket, so all I would need was pocket money and a couple of clean shirts, and I would have ten days of luxury in the sun. I was pleased by the idea of seeing Lucy and Dagmar, and even Candida too, for that matter, all of whom I had not caught up with for a long while. 'Yes. I'm in,' I said.

'Good. I'll make the reservations and send you the bumph. There is one thing . . .' She tailed off for a brief pause, as if choosing her words, and then continued, 'We're a bit short of men. The trouble is so many of them have already started working and it's hard for them to get away at short notice. I have been slightly scraping the barrel.'

'As witness the inclusion of the Tremaynes.'

'Don't be unkind. George is all right.' This made me wonder briefly if Lord George was planning to take advantage of Candida in some way, but I couldn't think how.

'But if I come, won't we be three of each?'

Obviously, she hadn't done her maths and this momentarily threw her. 'Yes. I suppose we will ...' She hesitated. I could almost hear her sucking her teeth.

I decided to help. 'But you'd rather have extra in case someone drops out.'

'That's it. I hate it when the men are outnumbered.'

'What about Sam Hoare?'

'Working.'

'Philip Rawnsley-Price?'

'Ugh.' She laughed and began again. 'The fact is I was wondering if you might ask, you know, what's his name, Damian Baxter. Your pal from Cambridge who used to come to all the dances.' The studied casualness of this request told me it had been a long-term part of the scheme. I didn't answer at once and she came in again. 'Of course, if it's a nuisance—'

'No, no.' I had, after all, nothing specific against Damian then. He had been more successful than I with Serena and I resented it. But that was all I knew at the time. The worst I could have accused him of was enjoying a flirtation with her. More to the point, neither of us had got her in the end. To our, I assume, joint horror she had married Andrew Summersby in April of the previous year and in the following March, three months before this conversation, she had given birth to a daughter. In other words she had moved far, far away from us by now. 'All right, I'll try,' I said.

'You don't think he'll want to.'

'I don't know. He dropped out of the Season so completely that there might be a principle involved.'

'You haven't discussed it?'

'We haven't discussed anything. I hardly saw him after your dance.'

'But you didn't quarrel?'

'Oh, no. We just didn't see each other.'

'Well, you haven't seen me either and we haven't quarrelled.'

I didn't know why I was putting up such resistance. 'All right. You're on. I'll give it a go. I'm not sure if the numbers I've got still work for him but I'll do my best.'

'Excellent. Thanks.' She seemed a little brighter. 'OK. Let me know what he says and we will take steps accordingly.'

Things were more complicated in the years before mobiles. Whenever anyone moved you'd lost them, although one hoped only temporarily. Nor did we have answering machines, so if people were out they were out. Then again, we managed. However, when I looked in my old address book I found I still had Damian's parents' number and they were quite happy to provide me with the new number for his flat in London, which he'd apparently just moved into. 'I'm very impressed,' I said. And I was, actually.

'So are we,' I could hear that his mother was smiling as she spoke. 'He's on his way, is our Damian.'

I repeated this to Damian when I dialled the number and he picked up. 'I'm sharing a rented flat at the wrong end of Vauxhall, even supposing there's a right end. I am still some way from Businessman of the Year.'

'It all sounds quite advanced to me. Have you found a job already?'

'I fixed it before I left Cambridge.' He mentioned some dizzying, American bank. 'They were recruiting and ... they recruited me.' I was suitably awestruck. One thing I have learned in life: Those who get to the top tend to start at the top. 'I begin at the end of August,' he said.

'So do I, but I suspect in less style.' I explained about my lowly job as whipping boy in the magazine offices. We fell silent. I suspect that for both of us the exchange had only served to underline the extent to which we had lost touch while still at university. Damian had not only dropped out of the Season, but also out of my life, and I don't believe I had fully appreciated it before that moment.

I explained the reason for my call. 'I don't know.' He didn't sound keen.

'I told Candida I thought you might have had enough of us.'

'I always liked Candida.' I was quite surprised by this. I never took notice of their friendship at the time, but then, how much had I noticed? Although I couldn't help feeling that if Candida had known how she was remembered she would have rung him directly and not bothered with me. He spoke again. 'OK. Why not? After paying my deposit here and buying the clothes I need to work in I haven't a penny left, so there's no chance of any other holiday this year.'

'My position entirely.' I was a little surprised by his acceptance, maybe, but on the whole pleased. It seemed to offer an opportunity to take us past the slightly odd end to our friendship and to give us the chance to go our separate ways after the summer more peacefully.

'Did you go to the wedding?' he said.

I'd wondered how long it would take him to ask. 'Yes.'

'I didn't.'

'I know.'

'I was asked.' He needed me to hear that his absence had been his choice, not hers. 'Have you seen the baby?'

'Once. She's the image of Andrew.'

'Lucky girl.' He snorted derisively, trying to make a joke out of the sorrow we shared but did not admit. 'Right. Send me the arrangements when you've got them and I will see you in the sun.' The conversation was over.

The villa, when we arrived, was on the coast, wedged between Estoril and Cascais. I dare say it is much more built up now but then, thirty-eight years ago, there were only rocks below its terrace, leading directly to a wide and glorious, sandy beach and, beyond it, the sea. It couldn't really have been better. The house was built, along with two or three others stretching along the coast in those pre-planning days, during the 1950s and it consisted of a large, main room – one cannot call it a drawing room, full as it was of rattan furniture and the like – as well as a dining room/hall, which took up the whole of the entrance front, with a mass of kitchens behind. These we hardly penetrated, since they were full of busy, Portuguese women who always looked cross whenever we went in. The bedrooms were arranged on two floors, ground and first, in a long wing that stretched away from behind the main block at a right angle. Each room had its own bathroom and high French windows opening, upstairs on to a balcony with an outside staircase leading down, and on the ground floor directly on to a wide, balustraded terrace overlooking the sea.

Our host was a genial fellow, John Dalrymple, something of an egghead who would later play a role in Mrs Thatcher's government, but I never knew what, exactly. Given his straightness, his girlfriend was a little unlikely, a neurotic, American blonde with snuffles, complaining constantly of a sore throat. Her name was Alicky, which I assume was a shortening of Alexandra, although that was not confirmed. I remember her better than I might have, because she was the first person I knew to be in a permanent state about the poisons being put into our food by the government and how the whole world was about to implode. At the time we thought her a five-star whacko, but looking back, I suppose in a way she was ahead of her time. It was she who had decided that for reasons of security, although few people thought like that in those days, the girls would sleep upstairs and the boys down below, giving us the advantage of the French windows that opened on to the terrace and the wonderful view of the sea. My bedroom, at the far end of the wing, had that familiar, clean, sea-smelling feeling, with the pale tiled floor, the wicker furniture, the white covers and curtains, that always tells you this is a summer place. I sometimes wonder why attempts to reproduce this room back in England are invariably a failure. Probably because it does not work in the northern light.

I had flown in on the same 'plane as Candida, Dagmar and Lucy, but in the event, Damian had not travelled with us. He was already there and in his room, changing, when we arrived so we all set off to do the same. The Tremaynes had been staying in Paris and had driven across Spain in order to continue their holiday for nothing. They too were recovering in private, which meant that it was not until we all gathered on the terrace an hour or two later, the girls in their splendid, summer colours, me in my underwhelming, Englishman's 'summer casual wear,' which always makes us look as if we're aching to get back into a suit (which most of us are), that the party finally assembled, and it was a very nice way to begin. John had arranged for us all to be given glasses of champagne, while he explained the plan for the first evening, which was for the whole party to jump into cars and head for the Moorish ruins at Cintra, a little way along the coast, and have a picnic dinner there. It seemed a very appropriate, opening adventure.

Cintra is a magical place, or it was then. I have not seen it since. At some point in the nineteenth century a presumably unbalanced Bragança king had built a huge, turreted castle on the hilltop, more suited to Count Dracula than a constitutional monarchy, while a little way beyond, making the place even more special and strange and complementing the Disneyesque splendours of the Royal palace, there was a long extended ruin of a fortified, Moorish stronghold, running from hill to hill, which had been abandoned by the retreating hordes during the Middle Ages. On that summer night this pair of monuments to two forgotten empires made richly cinematic outlines against the sky, as the sun sank in the west.

What I had gathered since our arrival was that John Dalrymple was very bored in his posting, though whether this was the bank's fault or, more probably, because of his choice of romantic companion I could not say. Either way, he was only too delighted to have some people to entertain. He and Candida seemed to go back quite far, though as friends not lovers, and it was clear from this, our first 'moment' of the stay, that nothing was too much trouble. A table had been set up beneath the castle walls among some trees – Olives, perhaps? I picture them in my mind as twisted and scraggy, seemingly clinging to life in the dusty soil. Candle lanterns had been hung among the rather threadbare branches, and rugs and cushions strewn about, making the whole thing into the feast of some Arab emperor. We took our drinks and walked about among the outskirts of the ruins, where stray blocks and lumps of stone had rolled over the centuries. The Tremaynes were there, a little improved, I thought, from when I'd known them, poised as they were on the brink of City careers that had been conjured up out of nothing by some friends of their papa, and they were hovering attentively round Dagmar. Lucy was talking to Alicky and John.

A little way away, Damian walked arm in arm with Candida. When I glanced across at them, with a sinking heart I could see a trace of her terrifying, Gorgon-like, flirtatious manner beginning to surface. He made some no doubt blameless remark, which was greeted by her roar of a laugh, which made everyone look up to see her eyes rolling in her head in what I suspect she thought a beguiling and intriguing way. As usual, when it came to matters of this kind, her taste let her down.

Damian began to give telltale glances to anyone who'd pick them up, seeking an escape route. Even so, it seemed very peaceful, as if we were all in the right place at the right time. Which would prove quite ironic before we were finished. At that moment a bell was rung, announcing that we were to help ourselves to the first course, so we drifted up to the table, and, laden with plates, glasses and all the rest of the paraphernalia, we found our way over to the cushions. Lucy plonked down next to me. 'What are you up to now?' I asked. I hadn't heard much about many of the girls and nothing at all of her.

She made a slight mouth movement as she paused in her eating. 'I'm helping a friend with a gallery in Fulham.'

'What does it show?'

'Oh, you know. Stuff.' I wasn't convinced this was the language of complete commitment. 'Our next thing is to launch some Polish guy, whose pictures look to me as if he'd stuck a canvas at the end of a garage and thrown tins of paint at it, but Corinne says it's more complicated than that and they're all to do with his anger against Communism.' Lucy shrugged lightly. I noticed her clothes were more hippie'ish than when I saw her last, with an Indian shirt under a worn, embroidered waistcoat and different layers of shawls or stoles or something, leaking out over her jeans, until it was quite hard to know whether she was wearing trousers or a skirt. Both, I suppose. 'What about you?' I explained the dismal job awaiting me. 'I do think you're lucky. Knowing what you want to do.'

'I'm not sure my father would agree with you.'

'No, I mean it. I wish I knew what I want to do. I thought I might travel for a bit, but I don't know.' She stretched and yawned. 'Everything's such a palaver.'

'It depends what you want from life generally.'

'That's the thing. I'm not sure. Not some boring husband going in and out of the city, while I give dinners and drive to the country on Friday morning to open up the house.' She spoke, as people do when they make this sort of statement, as if her low opinion of the life she outlined was an absolute *donné* among right-thinking people, when the reality is that for women like Lucy to live a very different life from the one she had described is hard. They may do a hippie version of it, with bunches of herbs hanging down from the kitchen ceiling and unmade beds and artist friends turning up unannounced for the weekend, but the difference between this and the arrangements of their more formal sisters, who meet their guests off preordained trains, and make them dress for dinner and come to church, is pretty minimal when you get down to it. Apart from anything else, the guests of both types of parties are almost always closely related by blood. But Lucy hadn't finished. 'I just want to do something different, to live somehow differently and never to stop living differently. I suppose I'm a follower of Chairman Mao. I want to live in a state of permanent revolution.'

'That's not for me.' We had been joined by Dagmar, who settled down on a nearby, paisley cushion and dragged a rug over her knees, before she got down to her food. The night was beginning to hint that it would not stay warm forever. 'In fact, I don't agree with Lucy's definition of the fate to be avoided above all others. I wouldn't mind going to the country to open up the house on Friday. But I want to do something in the world myself, as well. Something useful. I don't just want to be a wife, I want to be a person.' In this one may gauge that the 1960s philosophies had begun to get into their rhythm in the last years of the decade and that they had done their work on the princess from the Balkans. She'd caught the classic disease of the era, that of needing permanently to occupy the moral high ground. As a philosophy it could be exhausting, and it would be for most of us, when every soap star and newsreader would have to prove that all they cared about was the good of others, but here, on that Portuguese night, I didn't see much harm in it.

'What?' I said with fake astonishment. 'A princess of the House of Ludinghausen-Anhalt-Zerbst with a proper job?'

She sighed. 'That's the point. My mother doesn't want me to work, but I've started doing things for various charities, which even she can't object to, and I'm hoping to build from there. And when Mr Right comes along, always assuming that he does, I know he won't fight my having an identity of my own because I won't marry him if he does. I don't want to be a silent wife.' She had been a pretty silent debutante, so I was quite touched listening to her. 'I want to feel . . . well, I'll say it again: Useful.' Then I noticed, to my amazement, that as she was outlining this scenario of modern certainties her eyes were following Damian. I saw that he had managed to unload Candida on to our hosts, John and Alicky, where she was trapped by her own good manners, while he helped himself to some more food at the table under the trees. He finished heaping his plate and turned, surveying the company, and at that moment both Dagmar and Lucy raised their hands and waved. He saw us and came over, making our group into a foursome.

'We're discussing our futures,' I said. 'Lucy wants to be a wild child and Dagmar a missionary. What about you?'

'I just want my life to be perfect,' he replied with complete sincerity.

'And what would make it perfect?' asked Dagmar, timidly.

Damian thought for a minute. 'Well. Let me see. First, money. So I mean to make plenty of that.'

'Very good.' This was a chorus from all of us and we meant it.

'Then a perfect woman, who loves me as I love her, and together we will make a perfect child, and we will live in high state and be the envy of everyone who sets eyes on us.'

'You don't want much,' I said.

'I want what is due to me.' I remember this sentence quite distinctly because, while there are many people who say such things in jest, there are very few who seem really to believe them. In this case time would bear out his pretensions.

'What constitutes a perfect woman?' This again from Dagmar.

Damian thought. 'Beauty and brains, of course.'

'And birth?' I was surprised to hear Lucy ask that.

He considered this. 'Birth, inasmuch as she will have style and grace and sophistication and knowledge of the world. But she will not be hemmed in by her birth. She will not be oppressed by it. She will not allow her parents or her dead ancestors to dictate what she says or does. She will be free and, if necessary, she will break with every human being she has ever loved before me and cleave to my side.'

'I never know what "cleave" means in that context,' I mused. But nobody was interested in my query.

The two girls, both of whom I could now see were vying for the vacant position in Damian's mind, at least as far as this conversation went, pondered his words. 'She certainly should, if she's got anything to her,' said Lucy, which gave her an immediate advantage.

'It's hard to throw off everything of value,' countered Dagmar, but then she faltered. 'I mean, if you think it has value.' Damian seemed to nod, as if giving her permission to continue. 'And it's hard to throw off people you love, people who may deserve your love. Would your perfect woman be true to herself if she broke away from her roots, entirely?'

'I am asking a lot,' he said thoughtfully. By considering his answer, Damian was treating Dagmar with respect and Lucy thereby lost the initiative. 'Nor am I defending my demands, which may be thoroughly unreasonable. But I am telling you what I would need to know she could do if it came to it.'

Then Dagmar said, 'I think she could if she had to, but I'm just pointing out it would be hard.'

'I never said it wouldn't.'

Obviously, I missed the significance of all this at the time because, as we all now know, I was almost completely ignorant of much of what had gone on over the Season two years before, but I have since learned that this interchange was the preamble to Dagmar's last night of fantasy that she could be Damian's dream woman. I hope she enjoyed it.

Over the next couple of days we drifted, getting up late, swimming, eating at long tables set out on the terrace under a line of umbrellas, and going for walks in the village – doing, in fact, what people like us do best: Taking advantage of other people's money. But then, the following Monday, 27th July to be precise, we awoke to hear the startling news that Antonio de Oliveira Salazar, ex-Prime Minister of Portugal, founder of the Estado Novo – which, with Spain, had been the last Fascist state of Western Europe – had died in the night at the age of eighty-one.

'This is incredible,' I said as the party began to gather for breakfast on the terrace, pulling fruit from great piles set out for our delight, pouring coffee, buttering toast. I had thought the announcement would have stilled the table. Not so.

'Why?' asked George Tremayne.

'Because the last of the dictators, who shaped the middle of the century, who fought the war, who changed the world, is dead. Hitler, Stalin, Mussolini, Primo de Rivera . . .'

'Franco's still alive,' said Richard Tremayne. 'So now he'll be the last of them to die.'

Which was, of course, a point. 'Nevertheless, it is extraordinary that we should be in Portugal, just outside Lisbon, when he went.' I was not going to give up easily. 'The newspapers say he's going to lie in state in Lisbon Cathedral for a few days. Obviously, we must all queue up and go.'

'To do what?' said George.

'To walk past his body. This is a historic moment.'

I turned to Damian for support, but he just helped himself to some more milk for his cornflakes.

I am not sure quite what it tells us about the battle of the sexes but in the event all the girls came and none of the other men. Naturally, they didn't have anything suitable to wear, and they borrowed black skirts and shawls and *mantillas* from the furious women in the kitchen, but they all came, including Alicky, despite her continuing complaints throughout the pilgrimage about her swelling and painful throat, of which we had heard more than enough by this point.

That said, the advantage of having Alicky with us was that she was able to be very stern with the driver, one of John's perks from the bank, who deposited us on the edge of the huge *piazza* in front of the cathedral, telling him exactly where he was to wait and, no, she couldn't give him an idea of how long we were going to be. In the lengthening shadows of the late afternoon we took up our positions in the endless line of shuffling, morose men and weeping women. Apart from anything else, I was impressed, or intrigued, or something, by the sorrow on display. I had been accustomed to think of Salazar as the last of the wicked old buffers who had plunged Europe into bloody turmoil, and here was a wide cross section of the Portuguese, from nobles to peasants (the last constituting the people who might have had the greatest right to complain against his rule), all openly sobbing at his departure. I suppose it's always hard to give up what you're used to.

'Candida?' The voice cut through me like a bacon slicer. I knew it as well as I knew my own without turning round, and I could not believe I was hearing it, in this ancient sea capital so far from home. 'Candida, what on earth are you doing here?' At this we all turned to greet Serena as she walked across the square, dragging a rather hot-looking Lady Claremont and the dreaded Lady Belton in her wake. In their party too the men were not interested in politics. Seeing all our faces, Serena let out a short scream. 'My God! What is this? I don't believe it! Why on earth are you all here?' We then embarked on an explanation and it turned out that, by an unbelievable coincidence, her own parents had taken one of the other villas in the development where ours lay, that they had invited Andrew's parents, that they'd arrived the day before and they would be staying for the coming week, and ... wasn't it *amazing*?

I need hardly tell you that, as it turned out, it was not amazing. It was not in the least amazing. It was not even a coincidence. The scheme, which I did not uncover for some time after this and then only because I ran into George Tremayne at a race meeting three or four summers later, had originated with Serena, who wanted to see Damian again. Even when I heard the truth from George I didn't understand quite why (although I do now), but it was anyway important to her. John had been asking Candida to bring out a group of friends for some time, that bit was true, and they decided that if Candida could get Damian into the group, Serena and Andrew would, by coincidence, take a villa nearby. Obviously, Damian would not come if Serena were to be in the party, nor would Andrew if Damian was, so the subterfuge was necessary, once you accepted the intention. Where the plan might be said to have gone awry was that Serena's parents, perhaps suspicious in some way, had announced they would bear the cost of the trip and join them. This Andrew would not allow Serena to refuse, since it was such a saving. The final button came when Lady Belton suggested that she and her benighted husband also come along, as she would 'welcome the chance to know the Claremonts better.' I never found out what would have happened if Damian had refused when I asked him. I imagine the whole thing would just have been cancelled. However, at the time, I suspected nothing. I thought the chance meeting was genuine chance, a heaven-sent miracle that Serena Gresham – correction, Serena *Summersby* – should be standing in a sun-drenched, southern square, also wearing ill-fitting, borrowed black and waiting to pay homage to a dead tyrant alongside me. I allowed myself to wonder at her properly. 'How are you?' I asked.

'Frazzled and worn out. Take my advice. Don't travel with your parents, your in-laws and your two-month-old baby, in the same party.'

'I'll remember that.' I looked at her. She was quite unchanged. That my golden girl was now a wife and mother seemed more or less impossible to believe. 'How are you getting on?'

She glanced swiftly across at Lady Belton, but the old trout was busily snubbing some tourist who'd attempted to strike up a conversation and enjoying it too much to notice us. 'All right.' Then, sensing that her answer had not sounded like the voice of love's young dream, she smiled. 'My life's terribly grown up now. You wouldn't believe it was me. I spend the whole time talking to plumbers and having things covered, and asking Andrew whether he's done the sales tax.'

'But you're happy?'

We did not need to exchange a glance to know that, with this question, I was pushing my luck. 'Of course I am,' she said.

'Where is Andrew?'

She shrugged. 'Back at the villa. He says he's not interested in history.'

'This isn't history, it's history in the making.'

'What can I tell you? He's not interested.'

To the fury of the people behind us, we stuffed Serena, her mother and her mother-in-law into our group, and together we all staggered up the cathedral steps. From there we passed into the cool, shadowed interior of the great church, where the sounds of crying were more audible and, as they echoed through the aisles and cloisters, curiously haunting. Grief is always grief, whether or not the deceased deserves it. At last we walked past the coffin. The head was covered in some sort of scarf, but the hands, waxy and still, were pressed together as if in prayer, raised and resting on the chest of the corpse. 'I wonder how they do that,' said Serena. 'Do you think they've got a special thing?'

I stared at the body. It was dressed, as are all dictators in death apparently, in a rather nasty, lightweight suit that looked as if it had come from Burton Tailoring. 'What I can never get over,' I whispered, 'is the way the moment people are dead, they look as if they've been dead for a thousand years. As if they were never alive.'

Serena nodded. 'It's enough to make you believe in God,' she said.

Once outside again the plan was made. The Claremonts, the Beltons and the Summersbys would go home now to change, and they would all join us for dinner in a couple of hours back at the villa. Full of this pleasant scenario, we climbed into the waiting vehicles.

I now think I must share a little of the blame for what happened later

374

as, for some reason which in retrospect seems completely inexplicable, I never mentioned to Damian that we had run into Serena. In my defence, I knew very little, if anything, of what I have since learned had gone on between them. I knew they'd kissed once and I genuinely thought that was about it, but even so it does seem odd. I did not consciously conceal it, because when we got back Damian was nowhere to be seen. He had not, we heard from Lucy, slept well the previous night and he'd retired to catch up so as to be on form for dinner. 'Don't let's wake him,' said Dagmar firmly and we didn't. Clearly, I should have gone to his room, propped his eyes open and told him what I knew, but I was not aware of the urgency and I suppose I imagined I would catch him before the others arrived. Then, a little later, Lucy volunteered to go and tell him, and before we could discuss it she'd vanished, leaving Dagmar biting her lip. At the time I did suspect Lucy's ultimate purpose in going to Damian's bedroom, but not that she would make no mention of the meeting at the cathedral, the dinner that was planned for that evening, or Serena. Which proved to be the case.

There was one more surprise in store, on this most surprising of all days – before the Big Surprise later that is – which John greeted us with when we got back. 'There was a call from a friend of yours,' he said as we walked out on to the terrace. Naturally I, and presumably the rest, thought this would be from Serena, making some change to the evening's schedule. John disabused us: 'Joanna de Yong? Is that the name?'

Candida was astonished. 'Joanna de Yong?' she said. 'Where was she ringing from?'

'She's here. She's staying with her husband and her parents quite nearby. They arrived today.' He was smiling as if he were bringing us glad tidings, but the response was not what he'd anticipated.

We all looked at each other in silence. Wasn't this too mad? Was Estoril the only holiday destination of choice? It was developing into a Russian play. I do vividly remember the oddness of all this, which later got buried beneath the horror. Dagmar commented at the time that it seemed as if we had arranged a modest reunion, and Fate had decided to get in on the act and bring everyone of significance from that period on to the stage at once. In other words she was as innocent as I was about what was taking place behind the scenes. At last Lucy spoke. 'What did she want?' She was always less a fan of Joanna than some, as I remembered well.

John was clearly a little undermined by the response to his news. 'Only to see you all. I've invited her and her husband over for dinner. I hope that's all right. She asked who was staying and she seemed to know every name, so I thought you'd be pleased.' He stopped, hesitant, afraid he'd made a boo-boo.

'Of course we're pleased,' said Candida. But she wasn't very, and now I know why. The planned, and morally dubious, dinner for Serena to re-meet Damian already had to absorb Serena's parents and in-laws, which was less than ideal. Now it was beginning to expand into a state banquet.

'She's bringing her parents,' said John.

Which put the tin lid on it. 'Jesus,' said Lucy and she spoke for most of the company.

Naturally, as you will have surmised, the de Yong arrival had nothing to do with chance either, and I learned about this strange turn of events much sooner than I did the other. I was still changing when there was a knock on the door and without waiting for permission from me Joanna came in. Without a hello, in fact without a word, she lay down on the bed with a loud sigh. 'I don't know what we're all doing here,' she said.

'Having a lovely time?' I had not seen her since the end of 1968's festivities but she was still a miracle to look at.

'You wish.' She stared up at me, rolling her eyes, as I waited for her to explain herself. 'My mother fixed the whole thing without any reference to me, you know.'

'Obviously, I don't know. What are you talking about?'

'I'd rung Serena—'

'Do you keep up with her?'

She caught my surprise and smiled. 'Not everyone's dropped me.'

'I'm sure not.'

She received this with a quizzical expression, suited to humouring the slow witted. 'Anyway, she told me she was going to Portugal with her parents. And that Candida would be here at the same time with some friends, including you and Damian.'

'Really?' This didn't quite square with the scene we had just enacted in Lisbon outside the cathedral, but before I had time to investigate it Joanna ran on. The silly thing is I recall her remark now, clearly, but I forgot it at the time, so I still failed to add two and two and get to four.

'For some unexplained and foolish reason I relayed all this to my mother and, lo and behold, a week ago she informed me that she'd planned a surprise for me and she'd taken a villa in Estoril. Obviously, I told her it was quite impossible.'

'But?'

'But she blubbed and blubbed, and sighed and fell about, and asked why I hated her, and hadn't she tried to help me since the marriage, and now they'd paid a fortune for the villa because they'd jumped the queue and all the rest of it, and I gave in.' She was holding a bottle of Coca-Cola, the old, rather pretty, glass type, and she took a long, lazy swig.

'I'm glad you did. It's nice to see you.'

She shrugged. 'She thinks I'm bored with Kieran. She thinks she can wean me off him with all of you as bait. You're here to remind me of the fun I'm missing. That's why she's brought us. She even asked if I would be glad to see Damian again.' She threw back her head and laughed out loud. 'Damian. Two years ago she wanted to commit suicide when she thought I was serious about him.'

And still I didn't put the information together: Serena knew Damian was coming all along. What was the matter with me? 'Poor Kieran,' I said. I had in fact met Kieran de Yong by that stage, as some weeks after the sensational elopement there was a cocktail party at the Dorchester for the newly-weds in an attempt by Valerie Langley to normalise the situation. I admit I didn't quite get the point of him then. But I was young and anyway I don't remember thinking any the worse of Joanna for her choice. There is, after all, no accounting for taste. 'How is marriage?'

'It's OK,' she said. But then, after a pause, 'It does go on a bit.' Which sounded uncomfortably eloquent. I said nothing.

'Have you seen Damian yet?'

She shook her head. 'He's still in his room. We were far too early. My mother's impatience wouldn't let us wait. This is the world she always wanted for me and she thinks Kieran is the reason I've dropped out of it. According to her I'm drowning. Socially. She wants to pull me back to the shore. She wants a divorce as soon as it can be arranged.'

'You can't be serious.' It's hard to explain how outlandish this seemed in 1970. Even ten years later it would have been perfectly believable.

'Oh, but I am. She thinks if I dump Kieran now, everyone will forget about him. We've had no kids, despite going at it like rabbits.' She paused to register that I was a little shocked. It's odd to think one could be by such references when they came from a woman, but lots of us were. Having registered my blushes with a blush of her own, she continued, 'The point is, if she can prise me free now, there'll be no baggage that can't be safely hidden inside the identity of my second husband, whoever he may be.'

'And she'd be happy with Damian?'

'After Kieran, she'd be happy with a passing Chinese laundryman.'

I smiled. Although, to be honest, in a way I was rather impressed with Valerie Langley's commitment. I knew that in similar circumstances my own parents would just have shrugged and sighed, and occasionally allowed only *very* old friends to commiserate, but it would never have occurred to either of them actually to *do* anything about it. It wasn't that I approved of the plan. Joanna had, after all, taken her vows and in those days that meant rather more than it does in these. But still, it certainly didn't make me dislike her parents. 'What does your father feel about it?'

'He quite likes Kieran, but he wasn't consulted.'

'And Kieran is here?'

She nodded. 'And he knows exactly what she's trying to do.'

'Yikes.' Of course, we hadn't touched on the nub of the matter. 'Are you going to allow yourself to give him up?'

She thought about my question, but I don't think there was any real doubt in her mind. 'No,' she said. 'I wouldn't give her the satisfaction.'

Kieran de Yong was the first person I spotted when I finally emerged to join the thrash. It would have been hard to miss him. His hair was dyed a particularly virulent shade of pinkish blond and he was wearing tight jeans under a kind of military jacket, which looked as if it had once graced an officer in the Guards, but the cuffs were now turned back to reveal a pink satin lining. His densely patterned shirt was wide open at the neck, to reveal two or three thick chains. The overall effect was not so much hideous as pathetic and, given what I had just heard, I felt very sorry for him. 'Do you know Portugal at all?' I asked, trying to make it sound as if I were interested in the answer.

He shook his head. 'No.'

Lucy had joined us and she tried next: 'Where are you and Joanna living now?'

'Pimlico.'

We were both rather flummoxed, since obviously we could not simply stand and ask him questions, receiving one-word answers, until the end of the evening. But then he said something that indicated he was a little less dense than we had all assumed: 'I know what this is all about. She thinks I don't, but I do. And I'm not leaving.'

Naturally, Lucy hadn't a clue as to the meaning of this, but I did and I rather handed it to him for agreeing to come at all. It was the decision of a brave man. I couldn't very well comment without getting myself into a mess, but I smiled and filled his glass and attempted to establish that I was not an enemy.

There was still no sign of Damian. I registered that his windows remained tightly shut, just as I heard a flurry of arriving cars, followed by voices and doors opening and shutting, and out on to the terrace issued the whole Claremont/Belton party. Serena had brought the baby girl and there was a certain amount of fussing attendant on her arrival. I suggested they put the cot in my room, since it opened directly on to the terrace where we would be eating, and this was generally reckoned a good idea. It saddened me to see that the infant, Mary, was still the living image of Andrew. Not only did this seem like thoroughly bad luck for her, but it also gave rise to painful images in my semi-conscious mind.

To mark his distance from all this 'women's business,' Lord Claremont hailed me in his vague and cheerful way. I think he was relieved to find a familiar face and also to have escaped from the exclusive company of his daughter's in-laws, since I could tell at once they weren't at all his type, however he may have urged the marriage. He started to walk towards me, but the temptations of Joanna and Lucy soon drew him in that direction for a little flirtation over his *Sangria*, or whatever the Portuguese equivalent is called. The Beltons clung together, staring out to sea, she too difficult and he too tired to talk to anyone else. Lady

Claremont walked across. 'How are you?' She smiled. I told her. 'So you're forging off into an artistic life. How exciting.'

'My parents don't approve either.'

This made her laugh. 'It's not that. I rather like the idea. It just seems so terribly unpredictable. But if you don't mind a few years starving in a garret, I'm sure it's the right thing to do. One must always try to follow one's heart.'

'I quite agree. And there are worse things than starving in a garret.' By chance, as I said this my eyes were resting on Serena, who was talking to Candida by the balustrade. Now this was purely because I couldn't find anywhere more satisfactory to rest my eyes than on her, but I could see at once that Lady Claremont had taken my comment as a criticism of Serena's life choices, for which she no doubt felt extra responsible, as well she might. Her face hardened a little as she looked back at me and her smile became fractionally taut.

'You must go down and see Serena and Andrew. They've got the *most* marvellous set-up, a simply lovely farmhouse on the edge of the estate. Serena is all geared up to decorate it, which she loves, and the village is within walking distance. It's ideal. Do you know Dorset?'

'Not really. I used to go to Lulworth when I was a child.'

'It's *such* a beautiful place, really enchanting, and still almost a secret from the outside world. She's too lucky for any words.'

'I'm glad,' I said. It was somehow important for me that Lady Claremont should know I didn't want to make trouble. 'I'm very fond of Serena.'

She laughed again, more easily, relieved to have passed the sticky corner. 'Oh, my dear boy,' she said, 'we all know *that*.'

It was then that I heard the doors open behind me and I looked round to find Damian standing there, the darkened room behind him throwing him into a kind of high relief. He was completely motionless, but I did not need to be told where his gaze had fastened. Some of the others had registered him too. Not least Lord Claremont, whose brow visibly darkened. If he'd had any suspicions as to what this was all about, his worst ones were in this instant confirmed. He shot a glance at his wife and I noticed her give a tiny, almost indiscernible shake of her head. Damian's silent stillness was becoming a little embarrassing, so I walked over. 'Isn't it extraordinary?' I said. 'Serena's parents have taken more or less the next-door villa. We all ran into each other this afternoon outside the cathedral. Wasn't it weird? You should have come.'

'Obviously,' said Damian, remaining completely stationary.

I pointed out Joanna and briskly explained the second not-coincidence. He smiled. 'Oh, brave new world, that has such wonders in it,' he said. But still he did not step forward into the party, or indeed alter his position at all. During this, Serena had been watching, waiting, I can only suppose, for him to make the first move, but if so, she was obviously going to be disappointed, so she decided it was time for her officially to register his presence. I admired her manner in doing it. A lifetime of emotional concealment can sometimes have its uses. She walked up briskly with a wide smile. 'Damian,' she said, 'what a treat. How are you?' Andrew had followed her across the terrace, and now stood, almost threateningly, as he locked eyes with the man who had after all knocked him down in front of us all at Dagmar's ball. She, Dagmar, perhaps recalling the same incident with shame, left her own conversation and drew near. 'You remember Andrew,' said Serena, as if this whole thing might be happening on any street in any city.

'Yes,' said Damian. 'I remember him.'

'And I remember you,' said Andrew.

I think the idea crossed several minds in that second that we might be about to witness a rematch, but Candida, sensing danger, came over, clapping her hands. 'Let's all have a walk before dinner. There's a path down through the rocks, directly onto the beach. Don't you agree?' And before Serena could mention it: 'Your mother-in-law says she'll stay here and watch out for the baby.' Behind her Lady Belton had parked herself in a chair, with the expression of one of the accused at Nuremberg hearing his sentence read out.

In a way it did seem a solution and nobody raised any objection, so we broke away in groups and followed Candida, who had collared her uncle, Lord Claremont, as her personal guide. He didn't put up much resistance and set off by her side, after refilling his drink and carrying it with him. We all pottered down on to the sand and I must say it was a marvellous sight, the wide, blue sea, shining and glinting in that pellucid, evening light. We loitered, listening to the waves for a while, but when we set off for our walk down the beach I realised with a faintly sinking heart – although why? When she was a married woman, and so no concern of mine – that Serena and Damian had slipped to the back of the group. With her marvellous instinct for avoiding trouble Lady Claremont had also taken this in and made a beeline for her son-in-law, sliding her arm through his, and involving him in some apparently intense flow of talk, heaven knows what about – what would one talk about when trying to interest Andrew Summersby? – as she dragged him down the beach with her. But I could see her husband watching his daughter and Damian at the end of the trailing line, and it was not hard to tell that the sight was becoming more and more disturbing to him.

Joanna had joined me, and now she whispered: 'Do you think we're going to see some fireworks?'

'I bloody well hope not.'

'My mother's furious. She thought I'd have Damian all to myself, but it's quite clear he couldn't care less whether I live or die. Not when Serena's around.' Of course, at the time I thought she was exaggerating. That's how slow I was.

At this stage Andrew drifted away from his mother-in-law. He cast an angry look at the pair who were now quite a long way behind us on the sand, but Lucy came to his aid. I think that by this stage we were all, by unspoken agreement, working together trying to avoid a collision. Andrew had left Lady Claremont walking on her own and I could hear Pel Claremont as he drew alongside his wife. 'Do you see who that is?'

'Of course I do.'

'Did you know he was here?'

'Obviously not.'

'What's he talking to her about?'

'How should I know?'

'By Christ, if he's trying something . . .'

'If you say one single word you will only make things worse. I want your promise. You will say nothing contentious, not one word, before you close your eyes on your pillow.'

Lady Claremont hissed the phrase 'not one word' like a giant, angry snake and it was easy to tell she meant business, but whether she got the answer she required I couldn't say, since I had to crane forward to catch the last of these muttered exchanges and her husband's reply was lost beneath the sounds of the surf. Not knowing most of the facts, I couldn't understand their hostility to Damian. I turned back to Joanna, on my left. 'Did you hear any of that? If so, what's it about?'

But she shook her head. 'I wasn't listening,' she said.

I noticed we had been joined by Dagmar on the other side. 'What about you?' I asked, but she'd also missed it. In fact, she seemed rather quiet that night and uncharacteristically thoughtful. I looked at her, raising my eyebrows to signify a question, but she shook her head and gave a sad smile. 'Nothing. I'm just pondering the rest of my life.'

'Heavens.'

She waited until Joanna had dropped back to walk with George Tremayne. 'You started it, last night,' she said. 'You and Damian.' With her moist mouth twitching she was at her most poignant. 'All I want is a nice man who loves me. It sounds so tragic but that's it. I don't care how I live, really, as long as it's not in a complete hutch. I just want a nice man who loves me and treats me with respect.'

'He'll turn up,' I said. How baselessly optimistic one is when young, although I did not then guess how completely her request for even a tolerable future would be denied.

Dagmar nodded, sighing softly. I did not understand why this melancholy had gripped her, but of course now I know. The previous night, after their final tryst, Damian had told her she would never have him, she would never have the one above all others whom she loved and wanted. Any of us who have lived through a similar dismissal will feel for her. At last she gave a wistful smile. 'Maybe. Que sera sera.'

'Well, no doubt everything will work out for the best.'

'But I do doubt it,' she said.

At last Candida, sensing or praying that the danger had passed, turned us around, and slowly we made our way back to the villa. The light was failing, now, and the maids had arranged lit candles down the table and turned on the lamps that threw their beams against the house, so we seemed to be climbing up the path through the rocks, towards a fairy palace made of jewels.

We started peaceably enough. The first course was a sort of Portuguese version of *Insalata Tricolore* with olives added for good measure. I forget what the proper name was but it was delicious and we ate of it

383

freely, which was just as well since it was destined to get us all through until the following morning. The trouble began when the main course arrived, some sort of fish stew, which looked and smelled delicious although I never got to swallow any, brought by the angry women in the kitchen. They did not hold it for us, but instead put three large, white, china bowls, filled with the steaming mixture, onto the table at intervals, leaving it to us to help ourselves and others. Meanwhile, and perhaps inevitably, Lord Claremont had been tucking into the drink since he arrived. In fairness to him, and again I did not know it then, he was simply livid to have found Damian at this house where, as he saw it, he and his wife had been lured by artifice. Once there, and presented with this bounder, which was bad enough, he found himself sitting next to a very common woman whom he did not know and who kept trying to engage him in a conversation about things and people of whom he had never heard. On the other hand, Valerie Langley was only too thrilled by her *placement*, since one of her main goals in coming out of England had been to catch the Claremont family for herself and for her daughter, and was quite unaware that it was not working well.

To get things straight, to trace the source of the explosion, one must bear in mind that Pel Claremont thought Damian Baxter a liar and a cad, who'd attempted to seduce Serena into a marriage that would have ruined her life, all in an attempt to promote his own slimy and ill-bred interests. This was not my reading of the matter at all, but it was his and he did not understand why he had to sit at dinner with the author of his misfortunes. The plain truth is that neither Serena nor Candida had thought this through. The whole thing was as doomed as their original plan that exposure to Damian, at Gresham, would bring her parents round. Clearly, once the Claremonts had invited themselves on this expedition, Candida should have cancelled, or at the very least made a totally different plan as to how Serena and Damian would meet, because, given my new and greater understanding of the situation I now think Serena was incapable of turning down the chance to see him when it was offered. Unfortunately.

Damian was silent as we returned from the walk, and he had been fairly monosyllabic all evening since then. I saw Serena make an attempt to sit next to him, but he deliberately placed himself in a different, empty, chair, where the seats on either side were already taken by Candida and Lady Claremont, who may have been a little surprised when he chose her as his neighbour, but who contained it. After that, Damian talked to Candida exclusively and of course it would have been to everyone's benefit if he had continued to do so, but Lady Claremont lived by certain rules and one of them was that at dinner, when the course changed and the next one was brought, it was time to turn to your other neighbour. Accordingly, she resigned George Tremayne to the claims of Dagmar and turned to Damian on her other side. 'So, what are you doing now?' she asked pleasantly. 'Have you made any plans for the future?'

Damian stared at her for a moment, long enough for most of us to register his deliberate insolence. 'Do you really want to know?' he said. Now, as I am happy to testify, this was very unfair. At the time it was completely bewildering to the rest of the party as we could not imagine what on earth Lady Claremont had done to deserve it, but even if I now accept that she had been an accomplice in wrecking his life, I still don't think it was fair. In this context she was just trying to get through dinner. Just trying to allow Candida or John or Alicky to feel that the evening was a success. What's wrong with that?

With something like a deep breath she nodded. 'Yes, I do,' she said, as steadily as she could manage. 'I'm very interested to know what lies ahead for all Serena's old friends.' Honestly, I would swear she meant this in a friendly way. She did not want Damian to marry her daughter it is true, but I don't believe she wished him ill beyond that. This may not have been true of her husband, but it was true of her. For a second Damian looked slightly ashamed. He seemed to gather himself and he opened his mouth to speak, presumably to talk about the bank or something.

But before he could utter a word, Lord Claremont cut in. 'Well,' he said as he reached for a bottle of red that required him to stretch right across the table, 'we *are* interested in a way. But only really to be sure that if you do have any plans they won't involve us.' The effect of this was electric. In an instant every conversation was dead. Lady Claremont slowly shut her eyes and held them closed against the tidal wave that she probably guessed was coming. John and Alicky were just puzzled as to why their guests had suddenly chosen to be so rude to each other.

The Langleys looked shocked, as did the younger group including me, while Lady Belton assumed her usual expression of indignant disdain. In the silence, Lord Belton took a huge slug of wine.

'They won't,' said Damian easily. 'What makes you think I'd make a mistake of that magnitude twice.'

'Stop this!' Suddenly Serena was as angry as I had ever seen her. 'Stop this right now!' Her eyes were blazing, but of course it was too late.

Lord Claremont quietened her with a sharp gesture of his hand, then looked his opponent in the eye and took another sip. Next, slowly and with some style, he lowered his glass and smiled before he spoke. In truth, his languor was not enough to conceal that he was very drunk. 'Now, you look here, you little shit—' This actually made half the people at the table jump, like mice they all jigged up and down in a row. Lady Claremont gave a sort of low groan, which sounded like 'Oh, no,' but might have just been a sound of mourning, as she leaned forward with one hand raised, and Valerie Langley let out a kind of wailing 'What?' to no one in particular.

But, by now, Damian was standing. 'No,' he said. '*You* look here, you pompous, ridiculous, boring, idiotic, unfunny, pretentious, ludicrous *joke*.' There were seven adjectives employed in this sentence and I was fascinated by them, because I cannot imagine that seven words could do more to change a life. When Damian had first got to his feet, he was part of a minor incident, which a few apologies and a 'have a drink, old boy' would soon have fixed. By the time he'd finished his speech, less than a minute later, he was out of this world for good and there was no possibility of return. The gates of the drawing rooms of 1970s England had clanged shut against him and the air was thick with the smoke of burning bridges.

Lord Claremont himself appeared stunned, as if he had been hit by a car and was not quite sure as to the extent of his wounds. 'How dare you—' he started to say.

But Damian was having none of it. We were way past that stage, by now. 'How dare I? *How dare I?* Who *on earth* do you think you are? What insanity gives you the right to talk to me in that manner, you *stupid old man*?' Now this was a curious moment, because to most of us present these words could easily have been said in their entirety except for the final insult by Lord Claremont to Damian, so the reversal of their direction created an odd sensation. We may be absolutely sure that never in Lord Claremont's fifty-eight years had he been addressed in anything even approaching this manner. Like all rich aristocrats the world over, he had no real understanding of his own abilities, because he had been praised for gifts he did not possess since childhood and it is hardly to be wondered at if he did not question the conclusions that every suck-up had fed him for half a century. He wasn't clever enough to know they had been talking bunkum and that he had nothing to offer in any normal market. It was a shock, a horrid shock, for him suddenly to feel that, rather than a universal figure of dignity and poise and admiration, he was in fact a fool.

At this point, most ill-advisedly, Lady Belton decided the time had come to intervene. 'You disgraceful boy.' She spoke loudly, addressing the company as well as Damian to make her point, but unfortunately in an imperious, fluting manner more suited to a farce than a real argument. I imagine she thought it lent her majesty, when in reality she sounded like Marie Dressler in *Dinner at Eight*. 'Stop it this minute,' she trilled, 'and apologise to Lord Claremont!'

Damian spun round and in the blink of an eye, to our universal horror, he suddenly snatched up a knife from the breadboard on the table. It was a large, wide kitchen knife that might be used in a butcher's and certainly lethal. The whole episode was now turning into a full-blown nightmare, which none of us felt able to control. Please don't misunderstand me. I was perfectly sure at the time that he would not use it to harm anyone, that wasn't in him. We weren't in any danger. But he knew how to play with it, flicking it about to punctuate his movements and speech, to make the moment tingle. In this he judged correctly. If we were still before, we were paralysed now.

Slowly and sedately Damian stalked Lady Belton down the table. Seeing him approach, she gripped the side arms of her chair and forced herself hard against its back. For this one and only time I felt a bit sorry for her. 'You pathetic, old harridan, you scarecrow, you freak, what possible business is it of yours?' He waited for an answer, as if this were a reasonable question. She looked at the blade and said nothing. 'You insane piece of wrinkled baggage with your demented snobbery and your ugly dresses and your even uglier pseudo-morality.' He was level with her by now and he stopped, leaning in slightly as if to get a better look at this sad object of his curiosity. 'What is it about you? Wait a minute. It's coming back to me.' He touched his bottom lip with the tip of the knife as if tussling with a knotty problem. 'Wasn't your father a bit dodgy? Or was it your mother?' Again, he stopped as if she might answer and confirm his diagnosis one way or the other. Instead, she stared at him, a bright glimmer of fear twitching beneath her hauteur. I must concede that this was a brilliant stroke, a real rapier thrust, that would have gone right up under the ribs. The truth was Lady Belton's mother had not been *tellement grande chose*, but she thought no one knew. Like many people in her position, she believed that because nobody ever gave her their true opinion, they literally had no knowledge of the things she wished concealed. But we did know it. We all knew it, that her mother had married up and then been left with a baby girl when she was abandoned by her noble spouse, who took off for green fields and pastures new, and never came, or looked, back. Doubtless this went some way to explaining Lady Belton's unhinged snobbishness. 'Don't worry,' said Damian. 'Nobody would know you're a mongrel. Just a laughable and imbecilic bully.' She listened to him, but still she said nothing. She seemed to be breathing heavily, as if after a long run; her cheeks were palpitating and appeared to be more red and blotchy than when he started. I wondered if she might be about to have a stroke.

I could not let it continue. However inflated Lord Claremont might be, however insane Lady Belton, this just wasn't cricket. I stood. 'Come on, Damian, that's enough,' I said. I could feel a slight sigh of relief among the group, as if I had marked the limits and we would now return to sanity. It was not to be.

Damian turned. Facing him, I at last understood that his anger had made him mad. Temporarily mad maybe, but mad. It cannot be much different for a traveller to find himself in a forest glade and suddenly to spy a wolf walking slowly towards him. I saw his grip on the handle of his weapon and I was frightened. I admit it. I was afraid. 'What? Is it your turn to tell me off?' he sneered. 'You sad, little, grubbing nonentity. You piece of dirt. You filth. You coward.'

'Damian, for pity's sake, he's your *friend*—' This came from Dagmar. I was touched that out of all of them she alone should try to defend me in the face of this onslaught. Perhaps Serena might have, but one glance told me she was in her own private hell.

Damian looked first at Dagmar, then at all of them. 'What? You think he's my friend? You think he's your friend? He's not your friend.' He shook his head, continuing to walk up and down the table like an armed panther. I could see two of the maids hovering in the shadows, watching, but no one at the table moved. They had seen the treatment of Lady Belton and they had no wish to be next before the guns. 'He despises you. Do you think he finds you funny?' He directed this at Lord Claremont. 'Or stylish?' He waited in vain for a response from Lady Claremont. 'Or interesting in any way?' That was aimed at the whole table. 'He thinks you're stupid and dull, but he likes your life. He likes your houses. He likes your titles. He likes the pitiful sense of self-importance he derives from knowing that people know he knows you.' He hit all the 'knows' in this with equal strength, so it sounded more like a song than a sentence. 'He likes to creep around after you and kiss your arses and brag about you when he gets home. But don't ever think that he likes you.'

Through all this Serena had sat completely still, her head bowed, and I could see now that she was crying. A steady stream of tears ran down from both eyes, leaving dark marks of mascara across her cheeks as it travelled south. 'And you think he's in love with you, don't you?' He was standing by her now and she did look up, but she did not answer. 'Your little swain, who sticks by you through thick and thin, and you laugh at him—' She had made the beginnings of a protest at this, but he silenced her with a raised palm, 'You laugh at him, you've laughed at him with me, but you tolerate him because he loves you and you think that's sweet.' Serena now looked across at me. I think she was shaking her head to distance herself from what he was saying, but I had gone into another place, a numb place, a hollow, lonely place, where I tried but failed to hide. 'He doesn't love you. He loves what you are, he loves what he can boast about, your name, your money.' He paused to take a breath, to be fresh again for the final strike. 'You should hear what he says about you, all of you, when we're alone. He's just a regular little toady, a Johnny-on-the-make, creeping and crawling like a bumboy round you, to worm and lick and slide his way into your lives.'

Lord Claremont probably spoke for the rest of them, when he let out a loud and disgusted 'Good God!' Damian had chosen well the right mud to throw at me if he wanted it to stick.

He hadn't finished with Serena. 'You idiot. You fool.' He spoke with an undiluted contempt that made the company shudder. 'You could have escaped. You could have lived a life. And instead, you chose to spend your days with this ... *oaf*!' He clipped Andrew's shoulder as he passed. 'This *twerp*! This *blob*! And for what? To live in a big house, and have people you don't like pull their forelocks and grovel.' Dagmar was crying out loud by now and Damian stopped when he got to her. Oddly, when he spoke next his voice was momentarily quite kind. 'You're not a bad sort. You deserve better than anything that will come to you.' But by then he had moved on and now he was standing almost next to Joanna, who was watching him with the fascination of a rabbit faced by a stoat. 'You might have escaped, without your vixen bitch of a mother. Keep trying.' What made all this so surreal was that everyone was here, all the objects of his attack were sitting in front of him. Mrs Langley let out a yelp, but her husband held her arm to keep her silent.

Damian was starting to run down and you could tell it, because Richard Tremayne rose from his chair and even Andrew looked ready to move. His grip was loosening. 'I hate you all. I loathe your false values. I wish you ill in everything you say or do. And yet, even now, I pity you.' The others, sensing from this that the tirade was coming to an end, began fractionally to relax. Maybe he saw this, or maybe he had always planned it, but the fact is that Damian was not quite finished. 'I'm going now but I must give you a moment to remember me by.' He smiled.

'I think we've already had it,' Candida re-entered the fray.

'No. Something more colourful,' he said, and in one sharp, aston-ishing movement he threw down the knife and grabbed the first bowl of fish stew, smashing it over the end of the table where the steaming mass of boiling sea life was sprayed over Lady Claremont and Lucy and Kieran and Richard Tremayne. At this there was anguish and cries of anger and pain as the burning liquid covered them, but there was no real physical reaction beyond shock, and before anyone could move, Damian had snatched up the middle bowl. Crash! Down it went, this time catching Candida, Lord Claremont, Dagmar, George and Joanna. But as he lunged for the third and final bowl the others snapped awake and made a dive for it themselves. Alfred Langley stood with both hands on the rim. Unfortunately for him, Damian had the strength of a tiger and with one wrench it was out of his hands. Seizing it, Damian raised it high above his head, like a pagan priest with an offering for a savage and unforgiving deity, and for a moment everything and everyone was motionless. Then he brought it down hard against an edge, ensuring that the mass of the bowl's contents covered Lady Belton, who received her anointing with a sickening scream. There was a thick tomato sauce involved in whatever the receipt had been and by now the table looked like the end of the battle of Borodino, with everyone at it covered in a sticky, smelly, steaming mess of fishy gore. The shards of china had shot about, too, and Lucy was nursing a cut on her forehead, while George was bleeding quite heavily from his right cheek. It's a miracle that nobody was blinded. 'I'll say goodnight, then,' said Damian, and without another word he walked across the terrace, through the open doors into his bedroom and closed them behind him. Once and forever, he was out of their lives.

After he'd gone we sat, all of us, not moving, in total shock. Like victims who have survived an air crash but are not yet sure of it. Then Serena and Dagmar started to cry quite loudly, and Lady Belton, who resembled nothing so much as a red-nosed clown in the *Cirque du Soleil*, with tendrils of lobster and crab stuck in her hair, began to scream out orders to her dazed and equally fish-festooned husband. 'Take me away from here! At once! Take me away!'

At this point Valerie Langley cried out that we should call the police, but Alfred did not need the quick, startled looks from the others to know this would never happen. They were not going to finish the evening by providing the press with the best gossip story they had printed in years. With silent understanding and a nod, Alfred steered his wife away from the very idea.

To say the party broke up soon after that would be a significant and major understatement. The party shattered, splintered, exploded, fell into ruins, with the Claremonts and the Langleys running to their different cars as if a gunman were on the loose and training his weapon from a window. Those of us who remained sat, stinking of fish, waiting to see what would happen next. George Tremayne poured himself a drink and brought one over to me, which I thought was decent of him, even if it confirmed the horrid sense that they were all pitying me, pitying and despising me, which they obviously were. They may have varied in the degree to which they believed Damian's words, but they all believed some of them and I understood what the consequence must be. Others back at home would hear the story, endlessly embellished, and I would thenceforth be tarred in London as a creeping toady, a social climbing greaser, a speck of smarmy, contemptible dirt. I felt my reward for taking up Damian and forcing him upon them had finally arrived. I was finished in the world of my growing-up years. I was an outcast. I was a pariah.

Candida approached, perhaps to offer sympathy, but before she could speak, I took her to one side. 'I'll leave tomorrow.' I spoke in a low voice, because I didn't want to become a *cause célèbre*, and, worst of all, have others feel obliged to take my side. 'First thing.'

'Don't be silly.'

'No. I must. I introduced him to everyone. He's my fault. I can't stay. Not after that.' I was grateful for her attempt at support, but it was true. I couldn't stay among these people for a minute longer than I had to. Andrew Summersby came alongside and Candida appealed to him to persuade me not to go. He shook his head. 'I should think it's the only course open to him,' he said in his most ferociously pompous manner. It was lucky the maids had removed the knife.

Candida did not argue any more that night. 'Well, sleep on it,' she said. 'See how you feel in the morning. We all know he was talking rubbish.' I smiled and kissed her, and slipped away to my room.

Knowing Candida better now, I think it's possible she had genuinely dismissed the charges against me but I did not believe it then. And later that night, when I was bathed and smelling a bit less like a welk stall in Bermondsey Market, I asked myself was Damian truly talking rubbish? In some ways I think he was. Most of all in what he said about Serena. Certainly every word was deliberately chosen to damage me irretrievably among those people. To finish me with them. As he was going to vanish from their sight, so, he vowed, would I. It was a cruel attack, and I am sure the best part of it for him was that it would ruin and diminish me in front of her. He wanted to make my love seem a petty and paltry affectation, a device to get invited to dinner, instead of the engine that turned my life.

Even so, it was not quite all rubbish. The funny thing was that there were times when I had envied Damian. I envied his power among these men and women. I had known many of them all my life but within a matter of weeks of their meeting him he had more power over them than I had ever achieved. He was handsome, of course, and charismatic and I was neither, but finally it wasn't that. Newcomer as he was, he did not allow them to dictate the rules of the game, but I . . . maybe I did. Had I not given more leeway to the jokes of Lord Claremont and his ilk than I would have done to those of a social inferior? Did I not pretend, by never arguing, that the fatuities I'd listened to after dinner in a series of great and splendid dining rooms were interesting comments? I had sat up late with fools and laughed and nodded and flattered their fathomless self-importance without revealing a trace of my real feelings. Would I have bothered with Dagmar were she not a princess? Did I not maintain civilities with someone like Andrew, a man I despised and would have actively disliked even if Serena had never been born? Would I have given him the little respect that I did if there weren't a faint impulse within me to bow down before his position? I'm not sure. Were my mother alive and able to read this, she would say it was all nonsense, that I was brought up to be polite and why should I be criticised for that. One part of me thinks she would be right, but another . . .

At all events the evening finished me in that world for many years. Damian was gone from their sight, but so, to a large extent, was I. With a few, a very few, exceptions, I dropped out of their round, at first because of embarrassment, but later in disgust with my own self. Even Serena seemed to back away from me or so I thought. For a time I would still drop by occasionally, once or twice in a year, to see her or to see the children or, I suppose, because I could not stay away but I felt that the shadow of that evening was always with us, that something had died, and at last I accepted it and severed all connection.

Of course, today I am older and kinder and, looking back, I judge that I treated myself harshly. I do not think Serena was responsible for my exile. Nor do I blame any of the others because I think I did it to punish myself and I was wrong. The truth is that Damian spoke that night out of anger and a desire for revenge, although I am still not quite sure why I was the target for such heavy, apparently unprovoked blows. It may simply be that he blamed me for pulling him into the unholy mess in the first place. If so, with the wisdom of hindsight, I'm inclined to think he had a point.

SIXTEEN

I rang Damian when I got back from Waverly and told him everything I'd learned. And I voiced a thought I hated to find in my brain. 'This is a silly question, but you're sure it's not Serena?'

'I'm sure.'

'Because I know now there's so much more to your story than I'd seen.'

'I'm glad, but no, it's not. I wish it were in a way, but it can't be.' I could hear that he really was pleased to hear that I'd come some way towards understanding what that year had been for him. 'I last slept with Serena in the autumn of 1968. She married in the spring of 1969 and there was no baby in between. I only saw her one more time after her dance, and that was for the evening in Portugal when she wasn't staying in the villa and she had her dreary husband, silly parents, horrible in-laws and a baby girl in tow. Besides, even if I'd muddled all the dates it would have to be that child, Mary, who I hear is still the spitting image of her ghastly daddy Andrew.' All of which was true. The missing mother was not Serena Belton.

'Then it's Candida. It must be.'

'Did you talk to her about me?'

'A bit. She mentioned that you'd gone out together, but it was quite early on in the Season.'

'Yes. But we never fell out. We were always friends and we picked up again when it was finished, just once or twice, for old times' sake. I know you weren't all that keen on Candida, but I liked her.'

I was very interested by this. With all these women he seemed to have been so much more aware of them, so much more clear-sighted as to their true natures, than I had been. 'She did imply there was a little hanky-panky when the year was over. Is that when the baby might have begun?'

'No, it wasn't then. That was finished a long time before the holiday.' There was a short silence at the other end of the line. 'She came to me, after that dinner, when everyone was asleep. I woke in the night and she was with me, naked in my bed, and we made love. Then, when I woke up in the morning she was gone.'

'Did you see her the next day, before you took off?'

'Nobody had surfaced when I went. I just called a taxi and disappeared. But she left a note in my room, for me to find, so we parted on good terms.'

'Did you meet up afterwards? In London?'

'I never saw any of them again. Including you.'

'No.' I too had gone to the airport at dawn, but somehow we managed to avoid each other. On my part consciously. And no, like all of us I had not seen Damian from that day until my summons.

He interrupted my thoughts. 'That is, I did see Joanna. Just once, but we know it wasn't her.'

'And Terry.'

He was puzzled for a second, and then he nodded and smiled. 'You're right. I'd remembered it as being before we left. But you're right. It was when we got back. Poor old Terry.'

'What did the note say? From Candida?'

'"I still love you" and she signed it with that funny scrawl of hers. I was very touched. I don't think I have ever been unhappier than I was that night.'

'Which goes for everyone who was there.'

'I used to pray that I would never be so unhappy again. Since I have minutes left, I can presumably be confident of achieving that at least.' He chuckled softly at the hideous memory. At least, I say he chuckled, but the sound was more like the rattling of old and disused pipes in a condemned building. 'I lay on my bed, listening to you talking outside and everyone leaving, and I wished I were dead. For a while I thought they were going to send for the police.'

'That lot? No chance. They do not care to make column inches. That's one thing that hasn't changed.' We were nearly at our destination. There seemed to be nothing left to do but tie up the loose ends. 'Shall

I go and tell her about her son's good fortune?'

'Why not? Then come down here. I want to hear what she says.'

Candida was quite content to get my call this time and equally content to let me invade her for a cup of coffee that very morning. She lived in the same old Fulham-type house that so many of her tribe have come to occupy since I was young. Harry had obviously made a decent living and she had fixed the place up very attractively. She greeted me with her usual, if to me newfound, calm, good manners, and took me into a pretty, chintzy drawing room, carrying a tray of coffee things. On the table behind a sofa was a large, framed photograph of, I assume, the late Harry Stanforth. He had a bluff, chunky, smiling face, rather an ordinary one really, but that is the great and timeless miracle of love. I saluted him silently, as Candida poured cups for the pair of us. Then she looked at me. 'Well?' she said.

I explained about Damian's search and my part in it. 'I didn't want to do it but even I could see he didn't really have a viable alternative.'

She sipped her coffee. 'I knew it was something. Though I'm not sure I guessed it was that. So, how do I come into it?' Then she just sat, patiently waiting for me to continue. I couldn't understand why she wasn't making the connection.

'We think it's you. We think Archie is Damian's son.'

For a moment she said nothing but just looked puzzled. Then she gave a little snort of laughter. 'How? I'm not an elephant.' It was my turn to look puzzled. 'I last slept with Damian almost two years before Archie was born.'

'But, when we talked, you implied that you had a fling with him after the end of your affair.'

'And so I did. In the summer of 1969. I felt rather sorry for him, the way things had finished with Serena, and when she sent out the invitations to her marriage I looked him up to see how he was coping. We met a few times after that. But then I lost touch with him. That's why I used you to get him to Portugal a year later. I wasn't completely sure he'd want to hear from me again, although I don't now think I need have worried.'

'But you slept with him on that night.'

'What night?'

'When Damian went mad and covered us all with fish stew. Surely you remember?'

'Are you nuts? Of course I remember. Who could forget? But I didn't sleep with him.'

'He woke up in the middle of the night and you were there next to him, in his bed.'

'And this isn't an extract from a novel bought under the counter?'

'You left a note in his room saying you loved him.'

This did bring her up sharp, as she concentrated. She nodded briskly. 'I did do that. I thought he must be feeling so ghastly after what he'd put us through and I scribbled a note saying . . . I forget now. "I forgive you," or something like that—'

'"I still love you".'

'Was it? Anyway, that sort of thing, and I pushed it under his door before I went to bed.'

'Are you sure you didn't sleep with him?'

I could see she was on the edge of becoming indignant. 'Well, I know I've been a bit of a slapper in my time, but I think I'd have remembered if I'd gone to bed with Damian Baxter on that ghastly evening. I cannot believe I would have forgotten any detail about that particular night.'

'No.' I stared at my cup. Was I back at square one? It didn't seem possible.

My words were still running round her brain. 'He woke up and found a woman in his bed, making love to him?' I nodded and she threw back her head, laughing. 'Trust Damian. Just when life couldn't get any lower, he finds himself in the middle of a scene from a James Bond film.' Her mirth had subsided into chuckles.

'But it wasn't you.'

'I can assure I would remember if I made a habit of that sort of thing.'

And then I knew.

Lady Belton was upstairs, apparently, but she would be delighted to see me if I wouldn't mind waiting in the Morning Room since, rather illogically to my mind, this was apparently where her ladyship always had tea. I would be delighted.

The Morning Room was one of the prettier rooms at Waverly, cosy rather than grand, but with some of their best pictures and a really beautiful, ladies' desk by John Linnell, which I would say was currently used by Serena, since it was covered in papers and letters and invitations waiting to be answered. The nice woman from the village who had let me in was settling the tea things as Serena arrived. 'Thank you so much, Mrs Burnish.' She had already acquired that slightly heartless charm that is assumed by the well-bred to ensure good service, rather than because of any touching of their heart strings. In fact, I could see in her poise and her clothes and even in her smile, that Serena was well on the way to being what is still sometimes called a great lady. 'How lovely to see you again so soon,' she said and kissed me on both cheeks. The fact that the last time we'd met we had made love, and not just love but the most passionate love of my entire life, was somehow, in a way that I cannot exactly define, boxed up and removed to a safe distance by her manner and tone. She was warm and friendly, but I knew then it would never be repeated.

'I can't believe you don't know why I'm here.'

She had poured herself some tea and now she sat, carefully smoothing the folds of her skirt as she did so. She took a sip, then looked at me and gave rather a shy smile. 'I bet I do. Candida rang to tell me what you'd said.' Unusually, she seemed rather embarrassed, an emotion I would not naturally attribute to her. 'I don't want you to think I always go around sliding into the beds of sleeping men.'

'You told me yourself it was only with men who are in love with you.'

She nodded. 'Thank you for remembering that.'

'I remember everything,' I said.

She started to talk again. It was obviously a relief finally to let it out. 'I wasn't sure at first, because I felt, if he were interested, he would have done something when I sent that idiotic letter. But he did nothing. Nothing at all and I know, because in those days, twenty years ago, I was still in touch with quite a few of the girls who might have written it. What's changed?'

'He's dying.'

Which brought her down to earth. 'Yes. Of course.' She looked at the ceiling for a moment. 'I want to explain. About that night in Estoril. I've felt guilty for so many years, particularly over you.'

'Why me?'

'Because you were the one who got it in the neck. All you'd done was ask him to a few parties, and suddenly you were labelled a crawling, social-climbing toady and Christ knows what. It must have been awful.'

'It wasn't great.'

'More to the point, it wasn't true. Most of all what he said about your feelings for me. I know that. I knew it then.' Serena gave me a slightly secret smile, the one open acknowledgement of what we had enjoyed together, and I was rather glad of it. It wasn't much but it was better than nothing. 'How much have you heard about what went on at my ball?'

'Most of it, I think. But only now.'

'Damian told me he'd used me, he wasn't in love with me, I was better off without him, all of it. And I just stood there because I couldn't believe the words he was saying. The music was still playing and some girl was laughing in the anteroom just beyond the door, and I remember thinking how can you be laughing when I'm in here having my life shattered? I loved him with every fibre of my being, you see. I wanted to run away with him, to be with him, to love him to the end of my days and if it meant breaking with everyone I would have done it. But when he started to talk I just froze. I suppose I was in shock, as they say now, but I don't think we had "shock" in those days. I think you were just supposed to go for a walk and get on with it. Anyway, he stopped and he waited for me to speak. And after a bit I looked at him and said, "Well, if you really think it's for the best." And when I was silent he nodded and he gave a funny little bow. I've thought of that so often. I can picture it now. A little bow, like a waiter or some assistant at the embassy who's been sent to make sure you change trains properly, to escort you from the *Gare du Nord* to the *Gare d'Austerlitz* or something. Then he left. And I went out on to the terrace, and after a bit I came in again and danced with you.'

'And I was so glad of it.'

But this time she wanted to tell me the whole story. 'After that I didn't really care what happened to me. I suppose I must have had a sort of nervous breakdown, but again, in those days people like us didn't have nervous breakdowns. That was the sort of thing actresses did, and men who'd embezzled their customers' money. I think people like us were just a bit under the weather, or getting out of the rat race or taking a break. Mummy and Daddy were pushing me and pushing me at Andrew, and he was keen.' She stopped, catching my expression. 'No, he was keen. I know you don't like him, but he isn't as bad as you think.' I made a sort of accepting expression to cover myself. 'And I didn't know what else to do. We weren't trained for anything, then.'

'I know.'

'It seemed a way out. I knew Damian didn't want me, and since I thought of him morning, noon and night, I didn't see what else to do. Anyway, the point is ...' She shrugged, helplessly. 'That's what happened. That is what happened to me.' She stopped and sighed. Then, suddenly she shivered and, looking up, caught my eye. 'Somebody walked over my grave.' What a strange and haunting saying that is. We sat for a moment in silence until Serena said brightly, 'Do you want some more tea?'

'Please.' I held out my cup.

There was more. 'So I got married and I was pregnant fairly soon and you know, all of that stuff is quite exciting when it's going on, and there's lots to do and lots to buy and lots of people making a fuss of you, and I sort of forgot how unhappy I was for a while, and then, when Mary was born, Candida came to see me and we started to talk. And she said something like it wouldn't have worked with Damian, not when my parents were so against him, or words to that effect, and I hadn't known they were against him. I mean, I could guess they weren't *for* him, I knew that from the dinner, but I didn't think they'd had a chance to be against him in any thought-out way, because he'd confessed his base motives and dumped me before they'd got to know him. And then I heard what had gone on. Do you know about that?' I nodded.

Serena was getting angrier. I could see it. Even though all her training was to keep such emotions under wraps, still she could not prevent a trace of her rage from seeping out. She put down her cup and stood, fiddling nervously with the ornaments and invitations that littered the mantelshelf. 'The more I thought about it, the more furious I felt at what had been done to me. Because now I understood why I'd been bundled up with Andrew. And eventually I decided I had to see Damian again. I had to.' She was almost panting. I would doubt she had gone over this ground in any detail for quite a time. 'You know the next bit.'

'I do.'

'Of course, once my parents had pushed in, let alone my ma-in-law, I should have cancelled, but I was so desperate just to set eyes on him, just to touch his hand, just to smell him that I didn't. In retrospect, I suppose they must have been afraid something of the sort was going on.'

'It certainly sounds like it.'

'But after I heard you were bringing him it was more than I could do to back out. I knew I should but I couldn't make myself. So that evening we arrived at your villa and we set off for the walk down the beach. And I asked him about what he'd said and he admitted it had all been a lie. None of it was true. He was in love with me, he said. He would always love me. And I told him that if he'd only told me the truth and not lied at the dance, I would have come away with him that night. I would have packed and left and married him the minute I was twenty-one, and we would have been together for the rest of our lives. He said that he thought he'd done the right thing, the honourable thing.'

'He had.'

She turned on me, her eyes flashing with fury. 'Had he? Then fuck your honour! Fuck his stupid honour! I don't care what his motives were. He lied to me and he ruined our lives!'

'That was the "deceit" you mentioned in the letter, I thought it was something else.'

She frowned for a moment, trying to make sense of this. 'Oh, you mean promising love to get me into bed?'

'Yes.'

'Well, he was the opposite. He feigned indifference. That was the lie.'

'Why didn't you leave Andrew? When you knew?'

Serena's anger appeared to be settling. 'That was my weakness,' she said sadly. 'That was the weakness I wrote about.' She returned to her chair and sat again. 'Damian asked me that. He said if I felt as I did it was the only thing we could do. He begged me to. But it was a different time. You know what they say: The past is a foreign country; they do things differently there. I had a baby. I had family coming out of my ears. The scandal would have been huge, even in 1970, and while my parents were responsible in a way—'

'In a way?'

She nodded. 'All right. They were responsible, but they thought they were acting in my best interests.' She caught my expression. 'Well, they thought their best interests were my best interests.' She paused. 'And I was tired of being pushed and pulled, this way and that, but …' She almost groaned and I could feel her breath as it left her body. 'Of course, if it happened today I would have gone with him. I should have gone. I should have done it, but my nerve failed me when it came to it. Damian was half the reason for the waste of our lives. But I was the other half.'

'And later that night?'

Now she almost smiled at the memory. 'We were back at the house we'd rented, which wasn't very far, and of course everyone was absolutely reeling. They helped themselves to huge drinks, even Lady B., and staggered into the many bathrooms to de-fish themselves, and so did I. And after that we all collapsed. But when Andrew went off to bed I said I wasn't tired. I wanted to stay up. I waited until I knew he'd be asleep, then I walked back.'

'You walked?'

'I know. One wouldn't do it now, would one? Or perhaps you would, if you were young and in love and desperate. Perhaps some things never change. I knew which Damian's room was, lord knows, as we'd all seen him flounce into it. I'm not sure exactly what I'd have done if the door had been locked. These days it would be locked, wouldn't it?'

'You'd have woken him up.'

'Yes. I suppose so. But it wasn't, so I slid in, climbed into bed and made love to him in the pitch dark for what I knew would be the last time. He was sort of awake after a bit, but not very, even then. I didn't mind. I was saying goodbye to the life I should have had. It was a private moment, really.'

'But why was it the last time? Even if you weren't prepared to divorce, you could have gone on with the affair.'

She shook her head. 'No. I couldn't have been his mistress, making up lunch dates with girlfriends and pretending to miss the train. That wasn't for us. That wasn't who we were. We should have formed a union that bestrode the world and frightened anyone who stood in our way. We weren't a backstreets number, with telephones being put down when the hubby answers. Absolutely not. Once I'd decided not to leave Andrew, from that second it was over.'

'I hope Andrew has some inkling of what he owes you.'

'No, but if he did it would wreck everything for him, so it would be rather self-defeating. Anyway, that night I got up and dressed and left, and I never saw Damian again. Finis.'

'How did you know that Peniston was his? Presumably Andrew put in an appearance occasionally.'

'Rather an unfortunate turn of phrase.' Then she smiled, tenderly this time, as she thought of her son, the lovechild. 'I knew because when he was born he was so like Damian. It was mainly gone before he was two. Isn't there some theory that newborn babies resemble their fathers, so they'll be looked after and provided for? His nose, his eyes . . . I used to thank God that no one noticed, although I did see my mother giving him an odd look right at the beginning. But I always knew.'

'Why did you write the letter? Why didn't you just go and see him?'

'I don't know. I was feeling sorry for myself. Andrew was being more tiresome than usual, so I'd come up to London to finish off the Christmas shopping on my own and I was drunk. I don't why I wrote it at all. I wouldn't have posted it if I'd waited until the next day, but someone picked the letters off the hall table before I got up and that was it.'

I laughed. 'Exactly what Damian thought had happened.'

Now she was serious. 'So what's next?'

'I tell Damian. He changes his will. Your son is very, very rich. The House of Belton rises in splendour.'

'Eventually.'

'I can assure you Peniston won't have long to wait.' I remembered one detail, which I supposed we should observe. 'We'll probably have to run some sort of DNA test. Would you mind?'

Without a word she went to her desk, opened a drawer and took out an envelope which she handed to me. On the outside of it was written: 'Peniston's hair. Aged three.' 'Will this do?' she asked. 'Or do you need a newer piece?'

'I'm sure it will be fine.'

'Don't use it all.' But I could see something else was on her mind. 'Does Peniston have to know? Is that one of the conditions?'

'Don't you want him to know?'

She looked around the room. Over the chimneypiece was a portrait of a Victorian, female forebear of Andrew's, 'The Third Countess of

Belton' by Franz Xavier Winterhalter, painted with chestnut ringlets and a good deal of bosom. Serena sighed. 'If he knows, he has to choose between living a lie or spoiling his father's life by cutting himself off from the Beltons' history and feeling a fool in front of everyone he's grown up with.'

'A rich fool.'

'A rich fool. But a fool.' She took a breath. 'No. I don't want him to know. I would like him to know that Damian was a wonderful man, I will happily say that we were in love. I want to. But I think that's enough.'

'I'll tell Damian.'

Serena had one more request. 'I'd like to tell him myself. Can I? Would he allow that?'

I looked at this woman, still healthy, still lovely, still in the middle of life, and I thought of that scarcely breathing corpse. 'I doubt it,' I said. 'You could always write him a letter. You've done it before.' We both smiled at this, but I could see that her eyes were starting to fill with tears. 'I'm not sure he's up to seeing anyone. Particularly anyone who hasn't seen him since he was . . .' I tailed off. I couldn't quite find the right word.

'Beautiful,' she said, as the first droplet began its journey down her cheek.

I nodded. 'That's it. Since he was beautiful.'

I spoke to Bassett as I left, giving him the facts of the case and, on his advice, I drove straight from Dorset to Surrey. By the time I got there, two and a half hours later, there was already a lawyer in attendance who told me that a new will favouring the Viscount Summersby had been drawn up and signed. I was glad, even if it felt peculiar for a moment to take such pleasure in a name that I had hated for so long. Damian had asked for me to be shown up as soon as I arrived, and when I entered his bedroom I realised that we were racing against the clock. Damian lay in his bed, with a fearsome array of tubes and bottles, and leaking things on stands, all of which seemed to be connected to some portion of his emaciated, shrivelled carcase. Two nurses hovered around him, but at the sight of me he waved them away and they left us alone.

'It's done. I've signed it,' said Damian.

'The lawyer told me. You didn't want to wait for the results of the test?'

I pulled out the lock of hair, taking it from its envelope and handing it to him. But he shook his head. 'No time. And it'll be positive.' I could see the hair itself was much more important to him. He pulled two or three strands from the twisted gold wire holding it together and gestured for me to take them.

'Give them to Bassett. Now. That's all they need.' I rang and the butler came and collected the precious filaments. When I turned back towards the bed I could see Damian holding the rest of the child's curl as, very slowly, he brought it to his lips. 'So we made it,' he said.

'We made it.'

'Not a moment too soon.' His thin lips drew back in a kind of laugh, but it was painful to witness. 'Tell me the story.'

And I did. He made no comment except when it came to the account of his interview with Serena at the ball. I told him I thought his behaviour had been honourable, but he shook his head. 'You are supposed to think it was honourable,' he said. 'But it was proud. I wanted them to want me. And when I drove down there with her I thought I could make them want me. But they didn't, and I wasn't prepared to be the family's *mésalliance*. That was just pride. I spoiled our lives through pride.'

'She thinks she spoiled your lives through fear on the beach at Estoril.'

For some reason this almost cheered him. 'She's wrong. But I'm glad, even now, to think she feels it as I do. That's selfish, of course. If I loved her less selfishly I would want her to forget me, but I can't.'

'She doesn't want the boy to know. That is, she wants to tell him about you, but not that you're his father.' He nodded, but without complaint. I could see he was prepared to abide by this. 'She asked to come and see you, to explain.' This produced something like alarm in the rheumy eyes on the pillow, but I shook my head at once to comfort him. 'I told her no, but she sent you a note.' I sat on a chair placed for visitors near the head of the bed and took the thick, cream envelope from my inside pocket. He nodded for me to open it. Beneath the embossed address in deep blue, Waverly Park, she had written in that thick, italic writing that I remembered well, 'I have loved you since I last saw you. I will love you to the end of my life.' It was signed with one word only: 'Serena.' I held it for him and he read it, again and again, his eyes flicking back and forth across the paper.

'You must tell her you were in time for me to see it and that I feel the

405

same,' he muttered. 'Just the same.' And then, 'Will you stay? They can sort out what you need.' I can hardly believe that I hesitated, my head full of those ridiculous, irrelevant things that fall off the shelves into the centre of your brain at the most unsuitable moments, a dinner party I'd said I'd go to, lunch the next day with some friends over from Munich. What gets into one at these times? Before I could answer he reached for my hand, which was resting on the surface of the counterpane, 'Please. I promise I shan't detain you any more than this one time.'

I nodded at once, ashamed it had taken me so long to speak. 'Of course I'll stay,' I said.

And I did stay. I was given dinner, together with the lawyer, a Mr Slade, who invited me to call him Alastair, and we made stiff conversation about global warming in the fourteenth century and the Curious Case of Gordon Brown, as we sat playing with our food in the splendour of the lifeless dining room below, until I was shown back into the bedroom I had occupied on that first visit, in what seemed like another era and was in fact only a couple of months before, where Bassett had found me things to shave with, and brush my teeth with, and wear in bed. 'I'll collect your shirt and the rest of your laundry and have them back with you for the morning, Sir,' he said. In truth, Damian had spent his last years in Fairyland, but a lonely Fairyland. That I did know.

It was Bassett who shook me awake in the early hours of the morning. 'Can you come, Sir? He's on his way.' I looked into his face and I saw that his eyes were full of tears, and it struck me that when a man is dying, if his butler cries then some at least of his life must have been well done. I snatched up the brand-new dressing gown provided, and hurried along through the passages to the chamber of death. It seemed quite full when I got there, with both nurses and a doctor and Alastair Slade on hand, who had clearly been ordered to attend in case of any last-minute alterations, but he was not needed. The atmosphere was stuffy and anxious, and I thought of Louis XVI plunging his fist through a pane of glass to give his wife some air at her *accouchement*. They all turned to look when I appeared, then fell back so automatically, clearing the way to the bed, that I assumed this had been yet another preordained plan in this most ordered of departures.

Damian was only just alive, but when he saw me his lips began to move, so I knelt down and leaned over him, holding my ear as near to his mouth as I could. And I did hear him quite clearly. 'Please tell her I feel the same,' he said. Then it was over.

The test was positive, as he and I had known it would be, so there was no doubt that justice would be done when Damian's affairs were settled. Alastair gave me a copy of the will before we left and invited me to read it through, in case there were any immediate queries he could satisfy, but it was all pretty straightforward, if overwhelming in its sheer magnitude. As I knew, Damian had no surviving close relations and so there was never any chance of a challenge to his some would say eccentric dispositions, and the document was clear enough. I discovered I had been allotted the onerous task of executor. This had been made slightly more bearable in two ways, the first being that I was sole holder of the office, so every other manager, banker, committee member, financial advisor of Damian's vast empire had to defer to me. The second sweetener of the unwieldy pill was that Damian had left me a large amount of money 'in gratitude for his kind execution of a tedious task,' which I had not looked for, but for which I was, and am, extremely grateful. I have no hesitation in saying that the bequest altered my life enormously for the better.

He had also set aside what seemed to me a huge sum to be disposed of by me between, and I quote, 'the others on the list, as he shall see fit. He will understand this designation. I make no recommendations as to how this should be done, since he is the philanthropist, not I.' I was shamelessly partisan in the distribution, giving Dagmar the lion's share which, I am happy to relate, resulted in her leaving William almost at once. I could not forget that she alone had been treated kindly by Damian during his terrible tirade, and I decided this must mean that her happiness was in some way important to him. I gave a sizeable lump to Candida, which she was very grateful for, and another to Lucy, which Philip lost within three years on ill-judged business ventures. Terry, surprisingly perhaps, invested her share well and now enjoys the proceeds. I did not give money to Kieran, since he didn't need it, but I saw him as the legitimate heir to Joanna's goodwill, so I purchased the Turner seascape, which I had admired in the library on my first visit, out of the estate and gave it to him. He was pleased, I think. The only other bequest for which I was personally responsible, but which, as executor I was fully entitled to make, was a substantial sum to Peniston's sister, Mary. This was partly because I felt a twinge of guilt, knowing that she, in truth and unlike Peniston, had the blood of the Beltons running in her veins and partly to substantiate the anodyne notion, helped by the lesser legacies to the other women, that Damian had decided to split his money between those he had loved and their offspring. There was so much money that none of the above made more than the faintest dent in the whole, and the gifts helped the legend that Serena was happy, indeed eager, to foster and promote. Naturally, I needed the promise of silence from Candida and Terry, the only other two who knew, but Candida was Serena's cousin and was never a risk. I was more concerned at having been indiscreet with Terry and I did think of somehow tying the money to a gagging clause but there was a risk this could prove insulting and counter-productive so I decided to rely on what remained of her decency. Thus far, at least, I have not been disappointed.

The funeral was small and simple, and Damian's body was laid to rest in the graveyard, fittingly, of the Church of St Teresa of Avila, which had benefited so much from his benevolence during his lifetime. A few months after that, we had a grander and well-attended memorial at St George's, Hanover Square. The will was public knowledge by this time, and had provided a good deal of conversation in London drawing rooms and at London dinner tables, so there were many faces from the past among the crowded pews, I hope not entirely because the luncheon afterwards, for all the attendees, was to be held at Claridge's. Serena was very helpful with the arrangements and at her suggestion Peniston read a piece. It was that one about death being 'nothing at all,' which I always find rather irritating, but apparently it had been specified. He spoke about his mother's admiration and love for Damian, which I thought rather courageous and good, and I must admit I was also impressed that Andrew turned up and maintained throughout both service and reception a grave, pompous solemnity, which I assume was the nearest he could come to any manifestation of sorrow. Given the circumstances, even the little he was allowed to know, he could hardly be expected to feel much of the latter. Of course, the enormous inheritance had propelled his dynasty overnight to a place among the top twenty families in England, so it behoved him not to look ungrateful, but still, good manners may never be counted on under any circumstances and I was glad of them from him.

Lucy was there, in a peculiar approximation of mourning dress, with a black, silk evening coat and a huge, plastic, purple flower pinned to its collar. Candida arrived with Dagmar, both of them looking elegant and genuinely upset, which warmed my heart, so far had I come in my estimation of the deceased. And even Kieran turned up, though it might have been to confirm that Damian really was dead. Terry did not make the journey from California. That would have been a lot to ask, but she sent a bunch of those fashionable and hideous flowers, beloved of urban florists, that look as if they feed on flies. One woman rather interested me. She was tall and large, but rather *chic* in her way, wearing a beautifully cut suit and one of the best diamond brooches I have ever seen. She looked at me and smiled and nodded, so clearly I knew her, and in case she came over to say hello I sought the assistance of Serena as to who she might be. Serena was rather surprised by the question. 'Surely you remember Georgina Waddilove,' she said.

'Fat Georgina?' I couldn't keep the astonishment out of my face. 'What happened?'

'You have been out of the great world.' She smiled. 'She married the Marquess of Coningsby.'

I had been out of the great world indeed. 'When?'

'About fifteen years ago. I can't believe you never heard, although they are in Ireland a lot of the time. It was her first and his second, but the miracle was that he only had girls before and Georgina whacked out two boys, the first when she was forty-three, and the second a year later. So she's the mother of the heir *and* the spare.'

'And is he nice?'

'Lovely. Exactly like John Thaw to look at and *so* grateful to Georgina for rescuing him. Number One took off with a friend of his, and he was very cast down when they met, but now he's as happy as a sandboy.'

Actually, this was a really joyful moment for me. I looked at the smiling and almost quite attractive Marchioness of Coningsby, and I knew that gloom is not universal, even in this misery-memoir age. For some people things do come right. 'How wonderful,' I said. 'I hope her mother was alive to attend the wedding.'

'She was. But if she hadn't been, I expect she'd have risen from the tomb to get there.' Serena laughed and so did I, before the other guests at the party claimed her.

So Damian's quest was done and I was not unhappy at the outcome, nor, in the end, about what I'd learned on my travels through my lost youth. I had thought that the secret love story of 1968, had been my own hidden and one-sided worship, which had ended in my exile, but I had discovered instead that Serena Gresham and my betrayer had been the lovers of choice for any true romantic. Even so, I cling to my belief that in rediscovering and recognising the workings of my own heart, and in having finally made love, albeit once, to the object of my passions, I had endorsed my life, in retrospect and for the future, to the end of my days. Whatever may yet come to me, something or nothing it remains to be seen, I have known what the poets write about and I am duly grateful.

I was standing in the hall of the hotel, with its wonderfully vivid, black-and-white marble floor, when Peniston Summersby touched me on the arm. Together we walked out on to the pavement, into the still bright, autumn day, as we discussed what had to be done next, since an estate like Damian's is bound to be a work in progress for many years, but then he hesitated and I knew he wanted to say something to show me that he was aware of his good fortune. 'It's a wonderful opportunity. I mean to try to be worthy of it,' he came up with at last.

'I'm sure you will be.'

'And I want to go on with the things that mattered to him. Then there's cancer research, of course, and. I thought we might look at setting up some new scholarships in his name.'

'To be honest, I don't think he'd really care much about perpetuating his name, but I agree with you. Let's do it.'

It was time to part, but I could see he hadn't quite finished. Poor fellow, he looked rather awkward, and in the last analysis there is something a bit odd about being left a kingdom worth more than the National Debt because some bloke was in love with your mother forty years ago, which is all he would ever hear about it. 'Mummy says he was a marvellous man. She wishes I'd known him.'

I considered this for a moment. 'I think he was a brave man,' which I truly do. 'He was unafraid of the rules that frighten people. He made up his own and one must always admire that. I suppose he was an original. It's something so many of us strive for and so few of us achieve.'

With that we shook hands and I walked away down Brook Street.

1. Julian Fellowes has said that his inspiration for writing *Past Imperfect* was the "odd sensation of being part of something that everyone had forgotten about," meaning the debutante seasons of 1960s London. Is there a time in your past that was important to you at the time but seems to have been forgotten? Do you tend to look at the past as perfect or imperfect?

2. What do you think of Serena, whom the narrator describes early on as "a creature of myth, a lovely naiad eluding her swain"?

3. The narrator notes that "the primal job of an aristocrat is to stay on top. Bourbon or Bonaparte, king or president, the real aristocrat understands who is in power and who should be bowed to, next." Who do you think are the "real aristocrats" in *Past Imperfect*?

4. How do the characters' perceptions of their society differ from the reality, and how does this disparity play into their fateful holiday and their lives thereafter?

5. Lucy's final moments with the narrator are quite telling, "'Give him my best love. And say that I wish him nothing but good things. Nothing but good, good things.' She stepped back from the vehicle and I nodded. Her simple encomium spoke more for Damian's treatment of her than I would have credited him with." Discuss each of the women—Lucy, Dagmar, and the rest—who might have been the mother of Damian's child, and how each changes the narrator's view of Damian.

6. Discuss the character of Damian Baxter. The narrator asks at the start, "Why did he want to bother with the fading glories of the blue bloods, those sad walking history books?" Now, having finished the story, how would you answer this question?

7. At the end, the narrator's father says: "You've been made to go back into your own past and to compare it with your present. You've been forced to remember what you wanted from life at nineteen, forty years ago, before you knew what life was. Indeed you must face what you all wanted from life, all those silly, over-made-up girls and the vain self-important young men you ran around with then. Now, thanks to Damian, you must bear witness to what happened to them. To what happened to you." Do you trust that the narrator has borne honest witness to his past?

For more reading group suggestions, visit
www.readinggroupgold.com.

A
Reading
Group
Guide

St. Martin's
Griffin

About the Author

Julian Fellowes is the Emmy Award–winning writer and creator of *Downton Abbey* and the winner of the 2002 Academy Award for Best Original Screenplay for *Gosford Park*. He lives in London and Dorset, England.